999 Years After Armageddon

The End of the Millennium

Ray Ruppert

999 Years After Armageddon

The End of the Millennium

Tex Ware
Everett, WA

ISBN-13: 978-1-935500-46-9

ISBN-10: 1935500465

To: Terri Ruppert, my wife, lover and best friend. Also my terrific editor.

Chapter 1

Robert's pulse pounded as he scrolled through the transcript of the ancient book he'd found in the University of Midrib's archived databases. For quite some time he had suspected that history had been altered to shed a favorable light on The Sovereign Yehowshuwa, the one who ruled the world. He'd focused his entire summer studies on The Last Battle, when The Sovereign defeated Chancellor Ben-Shaachar about a thousand years ago, an event that reset the calendars to ASR, After Sovereign Returned. The more he read in this ancient tome, the more convinced he was that his theory was right.

He sat up on his bed, the scenes coming alive in his mind as he read about the battle that took place the day The Sovereign returned . . .

The Chancellor raised his periscope and surveyed his armies, all assembled in the broad parched plains to the north of The Sovereign's capital. From his armored command vehicle he could clearly see the capital mount only a hundred kilometers away. He had personally masterminded this complex military strategy, ensuring that each among his upper echelons knew his or her part.

Ben-Shaachar turned and perused the computer screens displaying the exact position of every man and woman who had come to defeat those who remained faithful to Yehowshuwa. Each combatant's vital signs were transmitted through satellite technology and microchips implanted in man and machine. Those flashes on the screen showed him they were all alive and ready for action. His generals were also controlling elaborate systems with their thoughts, eliminating cumbersome manual interfaces, which wasted precious time.

If any of his minions were too slow or stupid to compensate when certain forces were destroyed or disabled, The Chancellor could instantly update the computers with altered battle plans. The communication system was so sophisticated that he could send orders back to each soldier or vehicle with a single thought.

The Chancellor gave the mental command for his generals to prepare their troops for the attack. He watched the vital signs of his forces jump as the soldiers were pumped with adrenaline and other artificial stimulants that forced the recipients to obey orders unconditionally, ensuring their confidence and coordination. The monitors indicated that bombs, rockets, lasers, sonic cannons, and other offensive weapons were armed and ready.

He looked through the periscope again, squinting as the sun gleamed off the newly developed alloys, which could stop the best armor-piercing rockets. *There is no way this army can fail.*

He gave the attack signal to his generals. Each person, vehicle, and aircraft started precisely at the same time. Millions of feet stepped forward—left, right, left, right. Hundreds of thousands of armored vehicles advanced in unison. Aircraft broke their holding patterns to race toward their targets.

Suddenly the sky grew so dark Ben-Shaachar could only see a few meters ahead. Lightning flashed, illuminating the valley. The rumblings of thunder shook his command vehicle.

The earth trembled violently and swallowed many of the soldiers and vehicles. Thousands of vital signs disappeared from computer consoles.

The Chancellor bypassed his generals and redirected forces away from the crevices, cursing loudly.

He heard his pilots complaining that the clouds were so thick they couldn't see their targets. Lightning bolts pulled stratospheric bombers from their heights. Lower-flying attack aircraft collided with hailstones weighing as much as a hundred pounds. Dot after dot on the consoles blinked off.

Chancellor Ben-Shaachar pounded his fists on the arms of his command chair. His face grew hot, his stomach knotted, and his throat constricted with anger. *This can't be happening—*

"Robert! What are you doing up there?" his mother screeched in her usual annoying tone.

"Aw, Mom, I'm just reading." *Here we go again!*

"When are you going to finish school and get a job? All you ever do is bury your nose in those musty old books. Who cares what happened way back when?"

Musty old books? Where does she get these clichés? I haven't seen a book for over ten years.

She added her latest barb: "What makes you think anyone is ever going to want to read another book on The Last Battle anyway, much less one that a youngster like you would write nearly a thousand years later?"

Robert folded his twenty-four-by-thirty-centimeter Electronic Communication Device into a ten-by-eight-by-two-centimeter packet and slipped the ECD into his shirt pocket. Floods of self-doubt washed over him. Years of his mother's belittling was wearing him down with even greater precision than any of the previous era's mighty weapons of war.

He regretted sharing his latest dream with her. Each year added to the pattern, repeating itself over and over. He would leave for another year of school and return pumped up by a brilliant and gifted educator who inspired him to do his best and reach beyond his thoughts of mediocrity. In his enthusiasm, he would share with his family his latest goals and ambitions. His mother would ponder his assertions and slowly pick them apart until he returned to school with his head hung low, searching for new direction.

It started the first year, when he was positive he would become an artist. Back then, his mother was right. He didn't have any artistic talent and wasn't particularly creative by nature. Marilyn Maskil didn't want her son to be hurt. So she gently prodded him to think through the logic of his desires. In the end Robert appreciated what Mom had shown him about himself and the world around him. He was older now; this time, he knew exactly what he wanted to do with his life.

"Your father just got home," Mom yelled up the stairs, "so put that book away and get ready for supper."

"OK, I'm coming." Robert sighed loudly enough for her to hear. He knew that agreeing with her was the only way to get some peaceful conversations in the next few days before he returned to school. Once she had made up her mind that one of his projects was lame, he wouldn't hear the end of it until he acquiesced and gave it up. He wasn't going to do that. Not this time.

He also knew that she had been working on his father to try to get him to be more in agreement with her. In the past, Dad had been supportive of Robert's goals, but he was obviously getting tired of hearing new ones and never seeing any come to fruition.

Justin Maskil was an important man in the community. He served on the Board of Elders and managed the local hardware store, which provided a wide range of merchandise, including repair kits for automatic doors, kitchen cabinet knobs, plumbing fixtures, miniature power units for camping, and other sporting goods. His work and ministry kept him quite busy—too busy to be involved much with his youngest son. It wasn't that he didn't love Robert. He had already spent considerable time raising Robert's five older siblings. Robert was the only one still technically living at home yet was away at school most of the time. Besides, being on the Board of Elders was an important responsibility.

The proof that Dad was doing a good enough job as a father was that no family Enforcers ever showed up at their home. The Enforcers had an uncanny knack for appearing just before things got out of hand, putting families back on track.

Robert thought again about the "musty old book" he had been reading. The nagging thought that had plagued him for the last couple of years kept torturing his mind. *What if that isn't the way it really happened?* All the books, whether novels or documentaries, were in such complete agreement, it seemed as though there must be a conspiracy to hide the truth. Survivors of the battle, people who were loyal to The Sovereign, wrote all the initial reports. Most books written since then had been based on interviews with survivors or compilations of other writings. *Has anyone ever questioned these accounts? Would we continue to measure our years ASR, After Sovereign's Return, if something scandalous was involved?*

Robert pulled the ECD out of his pocket. He had to get in just a bit more reading before heading downstairs for supper.

June 23, 997 ASR

Chancellor Ben-Shaachar stared into darkness so deep and thick it seemed as if it could be poured out like black paint. The silence was equally unbearable. If he had been a normal being, the sound of his heart and the blood rushing through his veins would have been like the roar of a mighty river. However, The Chancellor was no ordinary person.

Ever since his defeat, he had been held prisoner in this detestable dungeon without sight or sound. He had been isolated from every living creature for 997 years, with only his own thoughts to keep him company.

Day and night (though it was impossible to tell one from the other), he had gone over his defeat, analyzing each step that he had carefully planned and orchestrated to liberate the masses of humanity from the clutches of The Sovereign. If only he had predicted the earthquake and the violent storm. If only he had moved a day earlier. The regrets resounded through his mind until he thought his head would explode.

He turned his thoughts to his backup plan. I wish I had put more time and attention into it. Had it been implemented sooner, perhaps I would be free now.

Ben-Shaachar hadn't risen to power based only on his charisma and natural charm. He had powers of the mind that went far beyond the realms of man. During his imprisonment these powers had enabled him to remain sane. They alone had kept him from falling completely into the downward spiral of self-incrimination. When the "if-onlies" came flooding in, he turned to meditation and attempts to contact his lieutenants.

He remembered experiments people had done on frogs to study muscle atrophy. They had tied a frog down so it couldn't move, with one leg restricted and one free to kick. Researchers had expected the restricted leg to atrophy because it couldn't move. Instead the muscles grew stronger as it tried to kick against the restraints. It became larger than the free leg, which had no resistance. Like that restricted leg, The Chancellor Ben-Shaachar's mind was growing more powerful every day that he was kept in the smothering darkness and silence.

May 15, 998 ASR

Captain Chuck Andrews of His Sovereign's Star Ship Ramah strolled along the beach, gazing at the bleak landscape before him. Forty kilometers ahead, barren foothills gently rose from the plains and led up to rugged mountains capped with snow. The plains were covered by sand and littered with rocks. A small river flowed down the mountains, spilling into a great ocean within a hundred meters of his ship.

He'd expected to find mud in these flatlands, but had discovered only sand and rocks worn smooth by the waves. While some of the sand was fine enough to be considered dirt, there wasn't a trace of anything that could be classified as soil since there were no nutrients from the decomposition of animal or vegetable life. The crew's analysis of the samples taken before they landed didn't turn up one little microbe, not even a virus. *There's no evidence of any life here except for the crew.* He kicked over a small rock, disgusted that a bug didn't scurry out from under it.

He looked at his crewmembers, all either relaxing on the beach or splashing through the shallow waters. They were supposed to be supervising the pumping of water into the ship. They would need that water for fuel as well as for their consumption to supplement what they could recycle from the hydroponic crops.

"Get back on those pumps," Chuck barked. The crew, unaccustomed to hearing their Captain bellow, scurried to follow his order.

Chuck started back toward the ship—the only man-made object in view. It hovered a meter off the ground. Twenty-five stories high, one kilometer long, and one kilometer wide, it was the largest craft ever designed to fly among the stars. Each towering wall was covered with sensor antennas of various shapes and size, hatches leading to the inner corridors, powerful lights, and access panels for equipment maintenance. *Whatever possessed me to come this far in that ugly piece of junk?*

Chuck ascended the ship's ramp. As he trudged to his office, he paged his science officer with his ECD.

He stared out the virtual porthole behind his desk. His crew had returned to their frolicking on the beach. *We've been out here exploring the cosmos for twenty-five years, three months, six days, and thirteen hours. I guess a bit of free time on the first inhabitable planet out of the 120 we've visited isn't out of order.*

All of the planets had looked inhabitable according to long-range sensors. *I'm tired of this wild goose chase. I want to go home.*

Science Officer Commander Zophia Assir's ECD chirped and she picked it up. *I wonder what Captain Andrews wants so urgently.* She rose from her station on the bridge, which consisted of a simple desk, fifty centimeters by forty centimeters, with an imbedded display panel and a keyboard she seldom used.

"Computer," she said, "let me know when the water supply tanks are 99.9 percent full."

The computer acknowledged her request both on screen and audibly in her earpiece. She removed the earpiece and placed it in its receptacle, closing the panel over the computer.

Zophia turned from the view screen that filled the forward wall and exited through the automatic door. She crossed the corridor and knocked at the Captain's office door.

"Come in, Zophia," she heard as the door opened.

The Captain stood with his back to her, staring out his porthole. Andrews was of medium height and build. The bald dome of his head was surrounded by rusty red hair that covered the tops of his ears, and then curled up at his collar. Few people lost their hair these days, and most restored it with simple medical treatments. Zophia had often wondered why Andrews didn't, though she never felt comfortable asking him.

She walked past the five plush visitor chairs and approached his desk. "You wanted to see me, Captain?"

"How long would it take us to get home from here?"

Zophia quickly calculated the answer. "One year, five months, and eleven days, give or take a few hours, at our normal cruising speed." She wondered why he wanted to know.

Andrews turned and spoke softly. "I'm 175 years old. That's more than fifty years older than anyone else on this ship. Few people over a hundred had a desire to leave Earth to explore the universe. Did we make a mistake? Have we wasted the last twenty-five years?"

The Captain sat in his chair and adjusted its height up. Apparently, even after twenty-five years of working together, their height difference still made him uncomfortable. His eyebrows knit together and his brow wrinkled.

Zophia took her cue and sat in one of the visitor chairs quickly adjusting its height down. "If you keep scowling like that, your eyebrows will intertwine so badly it'll take a barber to get a smile out of you."

Andrews laughed lightly.

"So, what's wrong?" she asked.

He leaned forward as if to take Zophia into his confidence. "I think our journey has been a waste. Every time we reach a new planet, we analyze the soil, air, water, and other liquids on the surface. When our detailed analysis proves that the planet is uninhabitable, we hop in the ship and do it all over again somewhere else. All with the same results."

"Why is this bothering you now?"

"This place is different from any other planet we've visited. It's almost a perfect match to Earth in size and temperature and composition, but it's totally barren of life. I'd hoped we'd find a planet with plants and animals."

"The Sovereign told us we wouldn't find life out here," Zophia reminded him. "That was never the goal."

The Captain stood, clasped his hands behind his back, and paced behind his desk. "Right, but the way he phrased it, I thought he was referring to intelligent life. I got the feeling he was hinting that we'd find at least a tree someplace."

"He only approved this voyage because we hounded the Administration until they got tired of saying no. The only thing that swayed them was the idea of finding a planet to colonize," Zophia reminded him.

"I know. However, when he christened the ship H.S.S.S. Ramah, which means 'to shoot,' I took that to mean that he was shooting us out into space. It's as if we had his explicit approval and sanction to find something. I'm beginning to think there isn't anything out here after all."

Andrews stopped pacing and looked at Zophia. "How much more time before we're scheduled to return?"

"Five more years. Sir."

"Maybe we don't have to wait. After all, we did discover one place we could colonize."

"So, now that we've found a planet on which a tree could grow if we supplied some fertilizer, you're saying you want to head home and stop looking for a place where The Sovereign may have already planted a tree?" Zophia hoped he hadn't decided to return early. *I like exploring.*

Captain Andrews raised his hands. "If he had planted a tree somewhere out there, why didn't he at least give us a hint about where to look?"

Zophia stood quickly. "Maybe he did." She stared into space as she tried to recall a past memory. "I vaguely remember something in The Sovereign's launching speech that puzzled me at the time. I'd like to study the transcript in our database before you make a final decision."

The tension in His face eased. "All right. Let me know what you find out."

As she darted out the door, she heard him call, "Oh, and you're dismissed, Commander."

August 18, 998 ASR

Robert put a large bowl of mashed potatoes on the dining room table. Mom always put just the right amount of butter, garlic, and parsley to tantalize his taste buds. His father arrived home from work just in time for dinner. Mom had fixed Dad's favorite: broiled steelhead so juicy and rich that it practically melted in his mouth. She served fresh long green beans which would also add color to the plate along with the lettuce, red onions, tomatoes, olives, and peppers in the salad. *Mom only prepares a spread like this when she wants to make points with Dad.*

If he played his cards right, Robert would be able to escape to his room without having any meaningful discussion about his continuing school or his desire to write a book about The Last Battle.

Robert sat at the table as his father pulled a chair away from the table for his mother. After they were all seated Dad bowed his head and prayed, "Thank you, Sovereign, for all you provide, amen." He reached for the steelhead and glanced at Robert. "Well, Robert, how was your day?"

"If we had sautéed mushrooms, I think the setup would be complete," Robert replied. Over the years he had developed the art of dodging issues by distraction.

"What do you mean?" asked Dad sharply.

Robert reached for the salad bowl. "This is the first night you've been home on time for dinner in almost two weeks. Not only that, but you've got that look on your face that says, 'It is a father's noble role to discuss his son's future, guiding him and helping him make important decisions so that all will be well with him because he has had the best counsel available.'" Robert lifted his chin, turned his head, and gave just a hint of knitted eyebrows, hoping to provide an accurate imitation.

His dad's face turned bright red, as if he had a fish bone stuck in his throat. He almost tipped over the water glasses as he lunged forward in his chair. "Why, you ungrateful brat! How dare you speak to me that way? I've worked hard to provide for this family." He pointed a boney finger at Robert. "I've helped each of my kids get the best education and find significant positions in the Empire. What have you contributed to the family except discord?"

Robert waited a second or two to get the right timing. Then he scooted back in his chair. "Discord? You're the one who always flies off the handle and can't have a decent conversation with his own son."

Dad stood; his hands in the air. "Why, I've half a mind to—" He stopped suddenly and sat without completing his sentence.

"Justin, are you all right?" Mom asked.

He wobbled his head left and right then up and down slowly. "No, uh, yes. Yes, I am. I'm . . . I'm sorry. I was out of line, Robert. Please forgive me."

Robert's jaw dropped and he stared at his father. *How can I storm out now?*

"You're right. I haven't had a decent conversation with you for years. I've done many things *for* you, but not *with* you. I've done what I thought you needed without talking things over with you. I even intervened with the Board of Elders, without consulting you, so you can continue your studies." Dad hung his head and didn't look directly at Robert.

"You what? Are you saying I've been allowed to study, not because of the merit of my work, abilities, and potential to contribute to society, but only because you intervened?"

"Son, I think it's time I started over." His voice was calm and compassionate. His eyes met Robert's with a steady gaze.

Robert couldn't remember the last time his father had called him Son.

"You have every right to be angry with me. I haven't been honest with you, and I need to clear the air. I hope you'll hear me out."

Robert felt all hope of escape melt away.

"Last week your mother and I had a long talk about your future and where we thought you should go. For a long time I've been in favor of keeping you in school. Perhaps we've been afraid that you would fail if you got a job. However, we believed a full education was best for you, so we were determined to make sure you got it. I've been trying to protect you. At least that's what I thought I was doing. We haven't really been listening to you."

"You were . . . protecting me?" Robert swallowed hard. "From what?"

"I've been shielding you from the Board of Elders and using my influence to convince them to keep you in school." Dad paused, looking down at his plate. "Today I had a consultation with the Board and they've asked you to come by tomorrow at two o'clock for an interview. I won't be participating as a Board member this time, so their decision will not be influenced by me."

Mom inhaled sharply.

"Tomorrow?" Something between fear and panic churned in Robert's stomach. His mind raced, trying to imagine what the Board was going to ask or say or do. *How can I be ready in such a short time?*

What would his life be like if he were forced to stop his education and get a job? He felt unprepared to transition from studies to eight hours a day behind a desk—or worse, in a factory assembly line. *How could this be happening to me? What did I do to deserve this?* "I need more than one day to prepare."

"I apologize for not talking to you sooner about this or including you in our thoughts. However, the meeting is already scheduled. You know that can't be changed without some kind of disaster."

Dad was right. The Board of Elders didn't look kindly on anyone who missed an appointment.

How did this happen?

"Thanks a lot, Dad . . . for messing up my whole life." Robert threw his napkin on his plate, left the table and headed for his room.

"Where are you going?" Mom shrieked after him. "You can't talk to your father like that and walk out. Come back here this—"

"Let him go, Marilyn," Robert heard his father say as he stormed up the stairs. "He's got a lot to think about."

Justin folded his napkin carefully and laid it down beside his plate while he thought about his own character. He was beginning to realize how much he had become like his own father. Now he may have passed his faults on to another generation. Justin felt sorry for his youngest son.

As soon as Robert's door closed, Marilyn's compassionate gaze turned to a glare. "We need to talk. Now!"

Justin looked at her, knowing full well what was coming.

"I can't believe you took yourself off the Board for this interview. Don't you care what happens to our son? He's never going to make anything of himself if he doesn't get away from that school where they keep putting crazy ideas into his head. What were you thinking?"

Justin half listened to his wife while his thoughts drifted back to a comment an Enforcer had made when checking up on his family. He had quoted an old Scripture—something about the sins of the parents being visited on the children for several generations. He hadn't known what it meant at the time. Now, he was beginning to realize how much Marilyn was like his mother—a matriarch in every sense of the word. His mother had taken control of the family while his father devoted himself to work. Justin had rebelled and forced conflicts between his parents. Truth be told, the men in his family for several generations followed the same pattern: neglecting their families to attend to business and abdicating the responsibility for raising the children to their wives.

I never wanted to be like my dad. I hated him for letting Mom walk all over him. Now here I am with a rebellious son and a wife who wants to control his destiny.

Justin turned his attention to Marilyn, stopping her in mid-sentence. "I know how disappointed you must be. We did agree that I would be on the Board for Robert's review. I'm sorry I didn't discuss the change of plans with you. In a way the decision was taken out of my hands."

"What do you mean?" Marilyn looked ready to explode.

He proceeded with caution. "Most of the time I can get the Board to see things my way. Yesterday, I brought them up to date regarding Robert's educational accomplishments and started talking about his future; Henry interrupted me."

"The senior Elder?"

"Yes. He said he had already been considering Robert's case. Apparently Markus, the statistician, had a private conversation with him recently about Robert's education being way outside the norm. He felt it was time for Robert to quit school and become a contributing member of society. The other ten agreed."

Marilyn exhaled and relaxed. "That's wonderful. It's exactly what we wanted. Why aren't you going to be on the Board when the decision is given?"

"It was Henry's idea. He thought there might be some suspicion that I had unduly influenced the Board. Besides, Robert knows how we think. He'll have to make a case for what he wants to do with his life—continue to go to school or write that book of his."

"Did you warn them about that?"

"I mentioned that he had some ideas about writing a history book about The Last Battle. They said it was the most ridiculous thing he could come up with. That would only help them justify their decision."

"Sounds like they've already made up their minds." Marilyn's demeanor relaxed.

"They still have to consider what Robert has to say. They'll probably give him a few days to come up with a plan for the next few years of his life. Then he'll have no choice but to go along with the Board's decision."

Chapter 2

The Chancellor felt a surge of power flowing over him as he meditated, sharpening his mind. Something was happening. He couldn't tell for sure, but it appeared that his backup plan was starting to kick in. While he relied mostly on his own powers, he knew that other forces in the universe were beneficial, too, and he had groomed others to aid his cause when the time came. *Perhaps my increased strength is enabling me to contact the others.*

"Abathar, can you hear me?" Ben-Shaachar forced every fiber of his mind to focus on transmitting the message into the darkness.

"Excellency. Is that you?" came the immediate and startled reply.

The Chancellor Ben-Shaachar's heart pounded. He had not only successfully sent the message, but had transmitted the means to reply and contact others, in spite of the gloom that had imprisoned him for so many years.

"It is good to hear your thoughts again, Abathar." Abathar was the brightest and most loyal of all his forces. His admiration for The Chancellor would have taken him almost as far in his position in Chancellor Ben-Shaachar's government as his abilities.

"I had almost given up hope of ever hearing from you again, Chancellor. This isolation has been so severe, I thought I would die. If it hadn't been for your excellent training, I'm sure I would have given up."

If Ben-Shaachar hadn't felt such a sense of urgency, he might have let Abathar continue his praises for a while. "Time is short. We must contact the others, one by one. We must make sure the enemy does not detect our communications. I focused on you alone for this first contact. You now know how to penetrate the enemy's interference. Do so carefully. We can't risk global communication until we have assessed the strength of the enemy and his current abilities. Much time has passed and we can't assume that he hasn't been strengthening himself, as I have."

"Oh, Excellency, why would he be concerned? He thinks he has us in prison, isolated from one another. He has made grandiose claims about his strength. Wouldn't he think he has been completely successful?"

"You are right, Abathar, but he is a deceiver. He holds back information about himself and reveals aspects of his capabilities at the most unprofitable of times for us. It is better to overestimate rather than underestimate him."

Ben-Shaachar knew the dungeon didn't exist on a purely physical plane. It didn't have walls and bars or corridors between cells. He had always imagined it as a three-dimensional honeycomb, with each of his subordinates in cells surrounding his. As he expanded his powers and successfully contacted Abathar, he confirmed his position in this alternate realm.

"I'm sending you my coordinates. You are only a few meters away from me. As you contact the others, map out their locations. I will search out the enemy's vulnerabilities. My success in contacting you has opened other doors that I must now explore. We will soon escape and reassemble our forces."

Chancellor Ben-Shaachar abruptly closed communications with Abathar and immediately started probing and pushing his psychic abilities against metaphysical barriers and obstructions, looking for tiny cracks. As soon as he found one he would prod deeper and expand his energy to force a larger opening until he could wiggle his spirit through and continue the process of searching out his enemy's weaknesses.

August 18, 998 ASR

Kevin leaned against a broad weeping willow tree trunk. He watched his favorite mare kicking up her heels in the lush green pasture as his son ran beside her. His delight at this scene was tempered as he mulled over the communiqué from his superior, J'Bar Mohamed. It had been several weeks since Kevin had an assignment. Now, the Matthews were at it again. He knew without reviewing the details the cause of the problem with this family and how long they had been fighting. He also knew how each family member had blown things out of proportion.

He didn't need a watch to tell time even though timing was critical. He must step in when his intervention would have the most impact. He took a deep breath, waiting patiently until the optimal moment arrived.

He used his wait to reflect on how he came to be an Enforcer in service to The Sovereign Yehowshuwa. He was a successful corporate executive before The Last Battle, dedicated to his career and to the company. He'd been amply rewarded for his achievements. He owned a huge estate with a twenty-two-room mansion, riding stables, guesthouse, and Olympic-size swimming pool. However, he spent most of his time at the office, leaving little time to enjoy the benefits of his position.

He hadn't spent much time with his wife and three children, either. However, he was more fortunate than many. His wife, Rachel, was a patient and tolerant soul. That hadn't stopped them from fighting. Her dedication to The Sovereign had prevented her from leaving him, although she had threatened it many times.

Several years before The Last Battle, The Sovereign had made a dramatic retreat and pulled all his subjects out of The Chancellor's territory. The move had taken Kevin off-guard. His loyalty to Yehowshuwa had been barely evident because his job had always taken precedence over his sense of duty for The Sovereign's Administration. Many even thought he was working for Ben-Shaachar.

Assigning him as an Enforcer for family intervention seemed fitting in the eyes of The Sovereign. In retrospect, Kevin saw the wisdom of the decision. He now had to excel in areas he had earlier neglected. In truth, he was thankful that he had been considered for this job. He felt honored to be in this position in the Administration. Now he could help others in areas where he himself had failed.

It was time. Kevin raised his hands in front of his chest, closed his eyes, took a deep breath, and popped in at the Matthews' modest home in the older part of what had once been a large manufacturing city.

Whump! Kevin caught the vase that had been aimed at Clyde Matthew's head. If he had appeared a second later Clyde would have been on his way to the hospital with multiple lacerations on his face. Kevin set the vase on a nearby table. "What is it this time, folks?"

Clyde and Charlotte stood frozen. Their jaws hung wide open. These instantaneous entrances always unnerved the families, but were an effective way to get their attention and stop hostilities. Not every entrance was as dramatic as this one; however, many broken bones, stabbings, scaldings, and other abuses had been averted when Enforcers used this technique.

Family intervention Enforcers never showed up without an invitation unless there was an imminent threat of serious bodily injury to a member of the family or a severe violation of Administration laws. Kevin had visited this family several times and had been invited back for extensive counseling, which apparently had minimal long-term impact on the family dynamics. Since their behavior had mushroomed into violence, their future counseling would not be by invitation, but was required by law.

He led them to the couch and had them sit together. "Clyde, you're the head of the household, so you start."

Kevin listened, comparing Clyde and Charlotte's stories with his mental notes of what had actually happened. At various times he interrupted one of them to clarify a point and help them get back to the situation. They both knew from previous interventions that Kevin had a better understanding of what had happened than either of them, yet they always tried to shade the truth in their favor. A major breakthrough would occur if they could put their own interests and defensiveness aside.

This young couple accepted the Administration and the rule of Sovereign Yehowshuwa over their lives. They had no choice; otherwise, an Enforcer would compel them to comply. However, only if they yielded their will to The Sovereign would they be able to overcome their problems and get their family straightened out.

At times Kevin wanted to grab them and shake them until they came to their senses, to see the benefits of yielding their lives. Yet, he couldn't force them to change their wills. All he could do was enforce outward compliance with the rules and demonstrate a better way to live.

Unfortunately the Matthews were becoming more the norm than the exception in society. People were less diligent in teaching their children about The Sovereign, instead concentrating on following regulations in order to avoid intervention from an Enforcer.

After two hours of counseling, Clyde and Charlotte had made enough progress to hold them over until follow-up sessions could be started.

Kevin returned to his abode as quickly and silently as he had left.

September 2, 997 ASR

Ben-Shaachar continued to explore the enemy's vulnerabilities. His mind had finally broken through the prison wall and he was able to gather information. As he had suspected, while the population of Earth grew, the enemy's control had diminished. *There's no way he can maintain constant surveillance over billions of people.* This was to The Chancellor's advantage, of course, because the enemy's efforts were taking resources away from the dungeon. *That must be why I was able to reach Abathar sooner than I expected.*

"Chancellor," Abathar thoughts interrupted his search with a report, "I have some astounding news. Some of our people have already escaped. I'm relaying their coordinates to you now."

"Excellent, my friend. That verifies what I suspected." He would soon enable Abathar to hack into the enemy's systems and plant data so the backup plan could be implemented.

☙◉◈☙

August 19, 998 ASR

Daylight chased the moonbeam away that Robert had watched slowly inch its way across his bedroom floor. All night long, he tossed and turned, imagining every possible scenario before the Board. His mind had been in an endless loop of questions and answers that always led back to the initial question: *What can I say to convince them that continuing school and writing this book are of any benefit to society and the Administration?*

He could hear their questions. "What have you contributed so far? What kind of job have you been preparing for? Have you considered getting married and raising a family?"

Robert couldn't figure out how being married was such a great contribution to society. He hadn't met any ladies he would want to live with for the rest of his life. Sure, he'd had a few romances, and they were wonderful. Sooner or later, the women all started sounding like Mom. *"What are your plans for the future? When are you going to finish school?"*

Can't I just be myself and do what I want? Why does the Board have so much control over my life?

He knew why. The Board members represented The Sovereign Yehowshuwa. Their authority had been established by the Administration to guide the community in an orderly and peaceful manner for the benefit of society. Or so the basic civics classes taught. In reality, they held the purse strings and the connection with other Boards in other communities around the world.

I need to convince them that my education and my book are important to society. Robert feared they would badger him until he became so frustrated he couldn't communicate clearly. If he'd read his father correctly last night, they'd already made up their minds. All the questions would be for show and Robert would be stuck looking for some dumb job behind a desk.

He finally gave up on sleep and rose early, took a convy out of the suburbs so he could take a long run in the country to clear his head. There was something about a 10K that had a cleansing effect on his mind.

He started out at a good pace, but he was concentrating too much on his breathing to be able to focus on what he was going to say to the Board. Then the usual pains cropped up. The knees started complaining first. *Just keep running,* he told himself. *They'll get used to it.* Before he knew it, 2K had passed and his body was complying with his will.

Robert liked getting out and enjoying the beauty of the countryside. The Administration insisted that everyone kept things well maintained, and people took pride in integrating their homes and businesses with nature. Most streets were lined with trees and shrubs that bloomed throughout the year; in addition, some blossomed at a different time to provide a never-ending display of color. All roads were paved except in remote wilderness areas. Every country road had a separate paved bike path that made it safe and enjoyable to ride, run, or walk.

Robert liked looking at the farms with their cottage-like houses. This particular community had built their homes based on ancient Dutch patterns, each one even sporting a functioning windmill. The houses all stood about a hundred meters apart. The buildings were octagon shaped with a white stucco exterior. The roofs were round and sloped upward sharply to a round brick chimney in the center. The chimney was used only for venting since it had been hundreds of years since burning fuels had satisfied heating needs. Above each of the eight walls was a dormer window that revealed more rooms and an upper floor.

Parallel to the road and the running trail were rows of brilliant tulips, highlighted by a short white picket fence. Crisply cut dark green lawns were lined by petunias, pansies, hollyhocks, and other assorted flowers. All bloomed throughout the year.

Robert ran past the historical marker that explained the origins of this community. Having read it before, he knew that the designer had chosen a theme that reflected the long-extinct Dutch nation. He had chosen the theme because of the functional nature of the houses that fit in the farming community but mostly because he liked the style. Some of Robert's friends had grown up here, but few of them could trace their ancestry back to that nation.

The church in the middle of the village, which also served as a community hall, was the center of the town's social activities. Robert's two o'clock appointment was at his own community hall.

As he approached the building, Robert felt refreshed and alert in spite of his restless night. He still hadn't figured out the best argument to achieve his goals.

Keep it straight and to the point. My goal is to write a book. However, he also needed to finish this last quarter of school first. One class was essential. Professor Robison's sub-ancient philosophy class analyzed the prevailing thoughts and motivations of those who opposed The Sovereign before The Last Battle. The professor was the leading authority on the way people thought before the war. Robert had read his books, but that wasn't the same as sitting under his tutelage and searching his mind.

Certainly the Board would ask why he wanted to write the book. As Robert thought about his reasons, those nagging thoughts returned. *What if that isn't the way it really happened?*

The younger generation, those who were furthest removed from The Last Battle, had been taught how beneficial The Sovereign was to society and what great bounty he had provided. A few young people, like Robert, harbored doubts about the truth of those claims. *Would we still have these things even if he weren't ruling us? What price have we paid for the bounty?*

When he got together with others of like mind and talked through the night, they discussed many things that his elders seemed to take for granted. At the heart of it all was what happened before, during, and immediately after The Last Battle. Those things had shaped their society and who they had become as a people. *Somehow, I have to convey the need of our generation to be assured that our history is correct . . . or if it's not, determine what really happened.* How could he do that without offending the Board Elders by insinuating that he didn't trust or believe them?

Robert stopped running as a new thought occurred to him. What if he shared with the Board his knowledge about other students who were questioning history and The Sovereign Yehowshuwa? If he presented himself as someone who could put the record straight for them, the Board just might let him do it. That sounded like a job with a positive contribution to society. *I'll file a motion to become a historian!*

Robert reached the conveyance stop. He pushed the call button and started his post-run stretches while he waited for the convy. Less than two minutes later, the cab appeared out of the underground ramp and stopped before him. The doors opened quietly. As he stepped inside he spoke his home address so the computer would process his destination.

The small convy had only four seats, all of which were empty. Robert chose one, and the cab plunged deep underground, picking up speed as it raced down the conveyance tubes. Commuter traffic was taking most people into the city from the suburbs, so the cab linked up with a train, which took Robert close to the city. From there the computer found a vacant tube going to his house. Robert's home was only thirty kilometers from the end of his run, but it took nearly ten minutes to get home.

He jumped out of the convy a block from his house. He jogged home and rushed to his room to see if he could find a boilerplate for a motion that he could adjust to file with his arguments.

November 29, 997 ASR

Gloria was the first of Chancellor Ben-Shaachar's operatives to escape from the dungeon nearly 75 years ago. Her break out occurred just as The Chancellor had planned. When other troops gained their freedom, they reported to her for their assignments. All operations outside of the dungeon were in her domain. She relished her position.

Shortly after her escape her forces were too small for the task of recruiting the human population without direct involvement. Gloria took on the form of a forty-five-year-old woman with pale skin and long black hair. The body was attractive enough to catch the attention of the males she recruited, but not so much as to lose the respect of the women. She grew accustomed to the body and kept it even though she seldom contacted humans.

Deciding to focus mostly on university students, she took a small office near the Scottsdale University campus as a base of operations. She needed nothing more than her plain wooden desk painted black and her comfortable but modest chair. Two hard wooden chairs were provided for appearance. They were seldom used.

As she sat behind her desk and looked over the recruitment statistics for the fall quarter, a ghostly wisp appeared before her desk. *A new escapee.*

"What is your name?" she asked.

"Jonathan."

She looked through her ECD for an assignment for this newcomer. "Let's see what I can find for you to do."

"I already have an assignment," he said. "I am to be the line of communication between you and The Chancellor, Ben-Shaachar." The wisp pulsated. "What news do you have that I can pass on to him?" His voice dripped with arrogance.

Gloria's stomach knotted up immediately. It felt as if her heart had done a flip and dropped to her gut. "So, Ben-Shaachar is finally able to communicate with us? Well, it's about time. And you are the go-between." She snorted in disgust. "Well, I've got some instructions for you, and you'd better follow them. When you show up around here you belong to me. You will take the form of a human and act like a human. We don't want anyone reporting ghosts to the Administration."

The wisp immediately became a young, athletic Asian man dressed in running shorts and a Scottsdale University T-shirt.

Gloria smiled. "Good choice." She stood. "You can tell Ben-Shaachar that everything is proceeding as planned. Recruitment on the campuses is almost complete, and we will meet his goals in the next year and a half. The general population's psychological state is exactly as he predicted, so recruitment outside the campuses will not be a problem when the time comes."

Jonathan bowed slightly. "The Chancellor will be pleased to hear this."

She was pleased at Jonathan's attitude adjustment but maintained her scowl to make sure he knew who was in charge. "Tell Ben-Shaachar that his planning and wisdom in keeping our current leaders and me in the background before The Last Battle have proven most effective. I have been able to operate without any apparent detection from the enemy, as have the others who have escaped. Everyone is eager for action. They have all gone to work with a zeal that surpasses anything we knew before our imprisonment." She was pleased with her accomplishments.

Jonathan stood motionless at attention. "Yes Ma'am."

Gloria's snapped, "You can go, now!"

He quickly turned, opened the door and left.

She sat back down and noticed her hand shaking. It was not Jonathan's attitude that bothered her. *If Ben-Shaachar had allowed me to do my best instead of remaining in obscurity we could have won The Last Battle. Then I wouldn't have to be doing this all over again.*

Chapter 3

Maria tamped down the soil around the base of the new rhododendron hybrid she had developed in her spacious garden. She planted it next to her dolphin fountain, the center of the Northwest-theme section.

Sensing in her spirit that her supervisor, Benjamin, had arrived, she stood and turned. His dark complexion and round, swarthy face contrasted with his cream-colored turtleneck. He wore the white yarmulke that was worn only by those who belonged to The Sovereign's nationality. As he approached, he took time to examine one flower, smelling another. She guessed that his presence wasn't an emergency, but not likely a social call either. Though the two of them were good friends, this was the first time Ben had ever come unannounced.

"I like what you've done with the garden Yehowshuwa has provided for you, Maria. It reflects the beauty of our father's heart. The fragrance of the lilies reminds me of The Sovereign himself."

"It wouldn't be fitting any other way," she replied, then added, "Our Sovereign lives forever"—the standard greeting among Board supervisors.

"Indeed he does."

No more pleasantries. I need to know why he's here. "What brings you to my humble home?"

Benjamin's face grew solemn and his voice low. "I have a special communiqué for you. This message is of the greatest importance, and the utmost secrecy must be maintained."

Secrecy? Here in eternity, where everyone's thoughts are open to The Sovereign and he reveals all to us as we need? This was most puzzling. "Please continue."

Maria closed her eyes as Benjamin touched his hand to her temple. She felt a tingling all over her body as the message was transmitted to her mind. The communiqué was directly from Yehowshuwa. She was told about future events that must take place. She was given instructions about her role in making sure they happened, and as much detail as she needed to make decisions on her own. Some of those details include a young man by the name of Robert Maskil and his desire to write a book.

As the Administration's supervisor over Robert's Board, Maria was in charge of the other twelve members—all respected and wise members of the community. Most of the time they conducted their affairs without Maria, though she always paid close attention to all their meetings. Her presence was only required if the Board strayed from the wishes of The Sovereign Yehowshuwa or encountered decisions that proved too difficult for them.

She hadn't attended a meeting in several years. The Board had been doing well without her guidance. The Elders were well trained and fully able to function independently. She only stopped by occasionally to encourage them as individuals or as a group. It let them know that she was aware of their proceedings.

According to this communiqué, however, it was vital that she sit in on Robert's motion for occupation.

Her mind raced to absorb everything that was being transmitted. When she had finally done so, she opened her eyes.

Benjamin placed his hands on her shoulders like a father commissioning his daughter for battle. "I had no idea what was going on until this came. As you saw in the message, we need to be careful about any nonverbal communications with The Sovereign since Ben-Shaachar may intercept them."

She nodded, still overwhelmed and unable to speak.

"You have work to do. I'll leave you to it. The Sovereign Yehowshuwa be with you."

"And with you," Maria replied as Benjamin disappeared from her view.

August 19, 998 ASR

Jim lay back in the sand, staring up at the delicate cirrus clouds floating across the sky. When he was a child he'd seen the shapes of animals in the clouds. As he got older all he could see was clouds. He could identify and classify each one without half thinking about it. They all just looked like clouds.

Education takes some of the wonder out of seeing things that aren't there, he mused. However, education was necessary to accomplish the goals of the Administration. Summer break had been great, but Jim only had a couple of weeks before getting back to the grind. Worse, he'd have to go to work after this session.

He wished he knew how Robert had managed to go to school so long without his Board getting on his case. *Maybe because he gets better grades than I do, and because his dad is on the Board.* Still, he'd expected Robert to get nailed by the system sooner or later and have to "contribute to society."

Jim was looking forward to seeing his friend before heading back to school. He missed their late-night bull sessions and eagerly anticipated having some good ones at the cabin Robert reserved in the mountains. He'd never been in the "wild" before. He couldn't imagine anything beating the sand and the surf.

I wonder if being a professional beachcomber would be acceptable to the Board. I could pick up a little trash here and there and then ride the waves all day.

He chuckled. Undoubtedly, they'd tell him they invested too much in his education to let him waste his life like that. *Maybe I could be a physical therapist and teach people how to surf.*

A cool breeze wafted off the ocean as the sun set. The clouds in the west changed colors. Brilliant yellow flames melded into pastel salmon, followed by undulations of orange smattered with pink. This led to deepening purple robes stretching from north to south, covering the majestic mountains that subtly reflected the fire. *If this sunset could tell a story, I wonder what it would be.*

February 8, 998 ASR

All of The Chancellor's probing and pushing, power and psychic hadn't enabled him to shed one bit of light in his cell. The gloom remained. However, he was able to communicate in thought with his faithful lieutenant, Abathar. He chose two-way exchanges with him to minimize the risk that vile Yehowshuwa would know how much headway he had gained.

"How long has it been since the first of our troops escaped?" Ben-Shaachar asked.

Abathar's thoughts pierced the shadows. "Sir, it has been seventy-three years since Gloria made her way out. She has not been detected. She is rallying the troops as they report in to her. They are carrying out their assignments with complete success. Your plan is being carried out to the letter."

"Excellent." The Chancellor Ben-Shaachar knew he still had one more chance, and he was thrilled to hear this confirmation that his plan was in motion and succeeding.

"She wants you to know that she is in awe of how well you had this planned more than a thousand years in advance. She has expressed praise to you for your wisdom in restraining her before."

"That's funny. Gloria complained for thousands of years that she was being underutilized. However, if I had freed her to fight to her full potential at any time leading up to The Last Battle, she would still be in the inner parts of this dungeon with you and me. Per my plan the enemy must have considered her a lowly peon and not worthy of increased security. Instead she was placed in custody on the fringe, where she was able to escape sooner."

"You are invincible, Chancellor," said Abathar with a respectful quaver in his mental voice.

In this darkness The Chancellor couldn't see a thing. He couldn't tell if Abathar was bowing as he spoke or thumbing his nose. He had better bow. I can't imagine how human beings ever communicated effectively by phone. Vocal inflections can be so misleading without facial nuances or body language.

"Please continue with the report," he commanded.

"Your strategy on the university campuses is working extremely well, sir." Excitement and awe oozed from Abathar's voice. "Your plan enabled Gloria to prepare a large segment of the population for recruitment. She will soon be able to set up training camps and start recruiting outside the universities."

"Very good. Let her know how pleased I am with her work. Now, what about my interplanetary forces? Have they been freed?" Their release was crucial to his victory.

"Their leader escaped. She reports that all the preliminary work has been done and she is able to operate freely." The enthusiasm in Abathar's voice waned. "However, her troops are still incarcerated."

Ben-Shaachar's fists pounded into the empty blackness of his cell. He wanted to break something, but there wasn't anything for him to hit, not even physical walls. "What's the holdup?"

Abathar' voice quavered. "The enemy's lockdown in that section of the dungeon hasn't been cracked yet. The information you've provided hasn't enabled us to release them."

Remembering that his anger had opened up vulnerabilities to the enemy the last time, The Chancellor restrained himself from telling Abathar what he really thought about him. He took a deep breath. "I used the interplanetary forces extensively before The Last Battle to free many from the enemy. His Despicableness must have viewed them as a greater threat than I had realized; otherwise they would be out by now. I will see personally to their release."

"Sir, may I speak freely?"

The Chancellor allowed his silence to communicate his disinterest one way or the other.

"Sir, you seem . . . different."

He laughed. "I am. I have grown more powerful. Before I was imprisoned I was overly concerned with my success, but I have come to realize how selfish that was. The key to this coming showdown will be our service to the people when we free them from the enemy's clutches and show them true freedom."

The Chancellor imagined that his new approach had Abathar rolling in his cell with laughter or so choked up with shock that he couldn't answer.

"While we wait for more of us to be released, pass my attitude adjustment on to Gloria and the troops. It is my latest plan enhancement. Be sure to let them know that I expect all to adjust their outlook as well, no matter how difficult it may be for some of the less disciplined troops to master"

"Yes, Sir."

As Ben-Shaachar terminated the communication link, his heart swelled with satisfaction. Excellent progress was being made – except with the interplanetary forces. His spirits dampened. If he were not able to free them soon his plan would fail.

He had to find the key that would unlock and free this vital contingent of his militia.

August 19, 998 ASR

Robert and his parents slipped into the community hall a few minutes before their appointment. He would have been happy to sit at the back until his case was called, but his dad strutted down the center aisle and took a seat in the front row on the right side. Mom sat beside him, looking proud to be seen in the hall with her husband, the Board member. Since custom dictated that families sit together in the community hall, Robert had no choice but to follow them.

His father had taken the seat on the aisle, so Robert had to scoot between his parents' knees and the front railing. After he sat down, his mother leaned over and whispered, "If you hadn't dawdled down the aisle, you wouldn't have had to climb over us."

"Yes, Mom." He turned away from her so she wouldn't see him rolling his eyes.

A large oak conference table, shaped in a half ellipse, took up most of the space between the railing and the back wall of the hall, where a gigantic picture of The Sovereign hung. When the Board members arrived, they would sit at their assigned places along the curved side of the table, where they could see one another and the audience. Petitioners would be seated along the straight edge of the table, with their backs to the audience.

For informal cases one or two of the Elders usually sat at one end of the table with the petitioners, which was less intimidating. At this moment, Henry sat in an end seat, with two elderly ladies sitting close to him. Marge and Thelma lived beside each other about two blocks from Robert's house. When he was in high school he had done chores for them. Marge was short and often cranky, hard to please. Thelma was older and taller but independent and wanted to do most of her own chores.

"Thelma isn't trying to do anything," Marge's voice was cracking as each word came out louder, "and it's driving me crazy. Can't you make her take better care of her dumb chickens?"

Robert stifled a snicker. Still the same old Marge. Always looking for something to complain about.

"I've told you, Marge," Thelma retorted as she shook her finger in Marge's face, "I'm doing all I can, but they get out no matter what I do. You didn't have to drag me into court."

Marge's face flushed and she grabbed at Thelma's finger but Thelma pulled it back.

"OK, ladies," Henry said, "simmer down. I'll send Tom over to look into the situation. He's good with chickens. You know, Thelma, you could have asked him to check it out in the first place."

Thelma squirmed in her seat and looked at her folded hands in her lap. "I know, but I don't want to be a nuisance. Tom is always doing things for me. Besides, I'm feeling old and useless these days. I can't get around like I used to. I'm not a spring chick myself, you know."

Robert let out a quiet chuckle. His mom elbowed him and shushed him with an index finger over her lips. He looked back at Thelma. She seemed to have aged quite a bit since Robert had last been to her house. He felt sorry for her, losing even more of her independence.

"Tom likes helping you out," Henry said. "He'd do it just to hear your stories of the old days, not to mention those chocolate-chip cookies you bake."

A tear trickled down Thelma's right cheek and her lower lip quivered.

"Besides, you've served this community for years. It's time you let other people serve you for a change." Henry reached over and squeezed her hand that she had placed on the table.

Marge sniffed back tears. "I'm sorry for dragging you in here. I didn't realize you were feeling poorly. Why don't we go to the spa together? We'll have tea and talk, without any chickens bothering us!"

"I'd like that," said Thelma as she took Marge's hand with her free hand.

"OK, ladies," Henry said, smiling broadly, "you two get on out of here. The Board has some formal business to take care of."

Marge helped Thelma up and they shuffled out as ten other Board members entered and took their seats around the curve of the table. A few people strolled in and sat at the back of the hall; others got up and left. Robert noted about twenty five people were being busybodies. He couldn't imagine that the Board had very much public business.

Henry picked up his gavel and whacked it once on the table. The recorder stood, his blank facial expression revealing an apparent lack of interest. He was young and slender, with pale skin.

I'll bet he just got out of university and had to find a job. Now he's stuck in here all summer. Oh, please don't let that happen to me.

"All rise." The audience obeyed the recorder's monotone command. "The August 19, 997 ASR, meeting of the South Cottage Grove Board Number 23 is now in session. The first and only agenda item for today is a motion for occupation by Robert Maskil."

That confirmed to Robert that most of the people attending were busybodies. No other official business was scheduled.

His parents stared at each other. "Wasn't this supposed to be an informal meeting?" his mom whispered.

Robert was pleased that he'd managed to get something past his mother. With an informal meeting, his parents would have been allowed to offer unsolicited comments at any time. Since Robert had filed a motion for occupation, the meeting would be run by a stricter set of rules. The formal motion kept his mom and dad from having any input during the discussions.

Robert knew he was taking a gamble. If the Board rejected his motion, he would have only a few weeks to submit a new one. If the second motion failed, he would be at the mercy of the Board. They would select an interim occupation of their choice until he "found himself." Translation: five to ten years of hard labor. There was no way he could complete his last year of school and write his book in his "spare time."

"Let us bow," Henry intoned.

Robert dropped his head but kept his eyes open while Henry prayed.

"Lord Sovereign, we are here today to decide the future occupation course of one of your people, Robert Maskil. Please give us wisdom and peace as we consider the outcome of his motion."

The room resounded with the automatic response: "Amen." Everyone sat.

"Robert Maskil, please approach the Board." The recorder moved one of the chairs the two ladies had used off to the side and placed the other at the center of the straight edge of the table.

Robert and his parents stood. His mom and dad moved into the aisle so he didn't have to crawl over them. Robert looked straight at Henry as he ambled past them.

Henry stepped around his end of the table and shook Robert's hand. "Good to see you, Robert. Have a seat." He motioned to the chair the recorder had positioned.

Henry looked at the audience. "Since this is a formal meeting to discuss Robert's motion for occupation, we'll need to have his background read." He turned to the far end of the table and pointed his gavel at the Elder seated directly across from him. "Markus?"

The Board's statistician was middle aged with a hint of gray in his reddish hair. His dark suit coat was draped over the back of his chair. His pastel blue bow tie was crooked on his white shirt with rolled-up sleeves.

As Markus stood, he nodded to Henry, flashed his teeth to the audience, and read from his ECD. "Robert Maskil, son of Justin and Marilyn Maskil, son of Gregory and Judith Maskil, son of Herbert T. Maskil III and Samantha, survivors of The Last Battle. Age: sixty-nine. Marital status: single. Occupation: student. Education: BS in chemistry from Pueblo University, MA in art from Milino University, doctorate in psychology from Faust University, PhD in archeology from Southwestern University, doctorate in ancient languages from University of Midrib, doctorate in recent history from Far East University. Currently working for a doctorate in sub-history culture at the University of Midrib. Has served as part-time assistant professor at the University of Midrib for five years and for two years at Far East University while working on his studies. He has also served as a teacher's assistant at each university except Pueblo. He has participated in thirty archeological digs during summer breaks."

The Elder next to Markus yawned.

"Quite a bit of schooling you've piled up there for a youngster, Robert." Henry smiled. "Thanks for the introduction, Markus. Well, Robert? What are you aiming to make out of all this education?"

May 15, 998 ASR

Zophia sat at her workstation. She reviewed The Sovereign's speech before they left Earth and found nothing that sparked her memory. *There was something somewhere, I just know it.* She started searching all the communiqués and documents associated with the exploration project that included planet coordinates. Her terminal displayed a list of 64,688 references.

"Eliminate all planets we have already visited."

The list shrunk. The soft, even-toned male voice confirmed, "Your query has found 48,765 documents."

"Keep all references where the gravity is within .9 and 1.1 times the gravity of Earth and that meet the expected life-sustaining conditions listed in the databases. Eliminate duplicate references."

The display size decreased. "Your query has found 786 matches."

"Keep only those that The Sovereign has spoken about or alluded to."

The list displayed only one reference. "Your query has found one match."

Zophia's heart skipped a beat. *Is it true, we had the location of a planet all the time and we just didn't ask?* "Display the details."

The terminal brought up a picture of Earth along with physical detail about gravity, atmospheric content, temperature ranges, and other data. "Display completed."

"Stupid machine," she groaned. "I already know about Earth. Why did you show it?"

"I'm sorry; you did not instruct me to eliminate Earth."

"Fine," she hesitated. The computer's response seemed odd to her. Then she snapped back at it. "Eliminate Earth from all lists. Go back to the previous list. Keep only references that are in documents that originated from the Administration's World Ministers."

The display showed a blank screen. "Your query has not found any matches."

Zophia tapped her fingers on he desk. "Apply the same criteria to every document in every database we have."

"Please wait. Don't be surprised if the lights dim."

Zophia jerked her head back when she heard the computer respond with an attempt at humor. "Who's been messing with your response algorithms?"

"Dave Bowman was the last to modify my program," came the written and verbal reply. I knew Dave was doing some routine maintenance but I wouldn't have expected that to cause such a smart aleck reply.

An empty screen displayed again. "Your query has not found any matches."

Zophia rubbed her chin and stared at the terminal. "I should've gotten something out of that last search. Why not?"

The computer responded without emotion, "Redefine your search parameters so they are less restrictive."

Zophia pursed her lips. "I wasn't talking to you, but that might work. Define World Ministers."

The display responded with the definition as she listened to the voice response. "World ministers are people who are part of the Administration but are not listed as living members of the Earth's population."

"How many documents do we have from World Ministers in the month before our launch?"

"16,288,012."

"Eliminate all technical communiqués."

"74,543."

"How many personal messages, not from relatives, were received from World Ministers within 24 hours before the launch?" Zophia felt like she was looking for a needle in a haystack. Any clues would help. "Launch from Earth," she added quickly.

"271."

That worked out to about six per crewmember. "Makes sense," she said thinking out loud, "presumably, one would have come from the local Board Elder, one from the regional, one from national, one from continental, one from the world, and one from Sovereign Yehowshuwa. Did anybody get more than six messages?"

"You were the only one to receive more than six," droned the computer.

"Me? Which one was not from those I just listed?" She wondered why she would get any more messages than anyone else.

The screen displayed a message from a person named Berekiah.

"Who's that?" she asked quickly.

"He is a World Minister."

"What's his capacity?" she snapped. She wished computers were a bit more intuitive and had a faster interface. The Sovereign had refused to allow mental interfaces with computer and she had always hoped he would change his mind. Talking was faster than typing but she would have preferred a brainwave link.

"Unknown. He isn't listed in the databases."

"Then why do you think he's a World Minister?" she asked as quickly as she could.

"He isn't listed as a living person or a person who was alive at the time the message was sent. Therefore he must be a World Minister to be able to send the message." The computer's voice always spoke at the same speed which was much slower than Zophia would have liked. She read the response before the voice finished.

The only reasonable explanation was that Berekiah was part of The Sovereign's Administration. Zophia had heard of a group called Encouragers who occasionally showed up in peoples' lives to impart some kind of support when circumstances were weighing them down. They seldom stuck around long enough to get registered in the databases.

"Show me the detail."

The monitor displayed the text of the communiqué from Berekiah.

Greetings, Zophia.

All of us lend you our support in this historic journey on which you are about to embark. You have an important path set before you. You must not deviate from it but travel it to the end. Along the way you will face many difficulties and you will be tempted to depart. Keep on the path. When you are tempted to return before the allotted time, choose the fourth of five and try again. Do this and you will find success.

For your encouragement,
Berekiah

"What did he mean by that?" Zophia wondered aloud.

"Please clarify your inquiry."

"I wasn't talking to you. Well, since you asked maybe you can help. What did he mean by, 'choose the fourth of five and try again'?"

"I do not have sufficient data to compute an answer to that question."

"What would you need to answer my question?" she asked, hoping it could filter the message sufficiently to develop a formula or command.

"I would need five things so that I could select the fourth for you."

Zophia pondered what to give the computer. "OK. Get the list of planets and add the ones we've already visited. How many are on the list?"

The monitor displayed 905, an even multiple of five.

"Did you remove Earth from the list?"

"Well of course I did. You already instructed me to do so."

Zophia narrowed her eyes at the third anomaly in the computer's responses. She had only expected a yes or no answer. *Was it my imagination or was the tone of voice different too?*

She made a mental note to look into it later and continued, "Divide the planets into five groups based on their distance from Earth. Select the fourth group. Divide that group into five based on the same criteria. Continue until you only have one planet."

Coordinates appeared on the screen for one planet. "Request completed."

"Now go back to the list of 905 planets and divide them into five groups based on their absolute deviation from Earth's gravity. Select the fourth grouping. Continue selecting until you have only one planet."

The coordinates for the same planet from the previous search appeared on the screen. "Request completed."

"Go back to the list and divide into five groups based on the probability that they could sustain life. Continue selecting until you have only one planet."

The coordinates for the same planet appeared again. "Request completed."

Zophia sat back in her chair and whistled. "What is the probability that the same planet would be selected from all three of these searches?"

"It would be one in 7.41 times ten to the eleventh power."

She stared at the screen trying to comprehend the tremendous odds that this one planet could meet the criteria she had provided and was selected based on a communiqué sent to her some twenty five years earlier. "That is amazing! Transfer these selection criteria to my ECD." Zophia had to see the Captain right away. "Thank you, computer."

"You are welcome. Please, call me Hal."

"That does it! Tell Dave to see me first thing on his morning shift." She spun on her heels and left to talk to Andrews.

Chapter 4

The Sovereign Yehowshuwa called a special meeting of his High Council, summoning them to his special conference room atop the tallest building in his capital, Yeruwshalayim. The ceiling and walls were a pure crystal dome that provided a 360-degree view of the city. The rising sun cast long shadows from skyscrapers and the temple to the east on either side of the building. There were no doors in this room.

Before making his appearance, The Sovereign watched the members of his High Council materialize inside the room, all dressed in white robes, and take their places along the curved side of the semi-oval oak conference table. They faced Yehowshuwa's throne, which sat at the straight edge of the table so that his back was toward the temple.

Since the twenty-four members could all communicate mentally, they didn't need to meet in person. However, they enjoyed one another's company, and it seemed natural to give their reports verbally, discussing issues, and getting their assignments. The Sovereign always knew ahead of time what was in their reports, but he too preferred the more intimate contact with his loyal and trusted subjects, all who had been with him before The Last Battle.

Yehowshuwa gave them some time to talk among themselves, letting them speculate about why this special meeting had been called. He hadn't provided them with an agenda in advance.

"This is the first meeting we've ever had where we haven't received any advanced communiqués regarding the topic," observed Bartholomew Washington, one of the recent additions to the High Council.

The Sovereign liked Bartholomew, who had been a slave on a cotton plantation . . . hardly what some would have considered qualification to be a High Council member. However, The Sovereign had different ways of measuring a person's qualifications. Bartholomew's dedication under adverse situations had not gone unnoticed. In that miserable life, he converted many from Ben-Shaachar's rule to become guerrilla fighters for Yehowshuwa. He also trained them to recruit others, which severely hampered The Chancellor's activities.

The Sovereign appeared in the room in a soundless flash of light. All members of the council immediately slid from their chairs and bowed before his throne with their faces to the floor. In unison, they called out, "Our Sovereign lives forever. You are holy. We worship and adore you."

Yehowshuwa's face glowed with pleasure at the semicircle of heads bowed before him. "Arise, my brothers and sisters."

All stood to their feet. The Sovereign walked up to each one, greeting him or her by name and giving everyone a tight hug. Then he took his seat on the throne and picked up his golden scepter. Once he sat, the council did as well.

"My friends, there are stirrings in the dungeon, and Ben-Shaachar is gaining power. He is now able to intercept some of our communiqués. That is why I did not inform you in advance of the purpose for this meeting. I didn't want him to know that we would be talking about his activities."

Tsvar raised his hand. Yehowshuwa held his scepter out toward the short man with a long square trimmed black beard and white turban. Tsvar had kept the true ways of The Sovereign alive when he served The Sovereign in his ancient Asian home country. In Tsvar's lifetime people claimed to be the only representatives of The Sovereign but were really servants of Ben-Shaachar. They persecuted and killed Tsvar and others who tried to free people from the clutches of The Chancellor. Yehowshuwa respected Tsvar's sharp mind and dedication.

"Sir," said Tsvar, "how can he be gaining power? I thought he exhausted every trick of his trade during The Last Battle."

"In actuality he isn't gaining power. He still only has the powers I gave him at his creation. However, I hid many of his abilities from him and only now have allowed him to recognize them. As he uses those abilities, he is finding ways around the restraints I imposed for his incarceration. It won't be long before he is free to mobilize the recruits that his forces are gathering." As he spoke, The Sovereign felt a sad anticipation for future events.

"Sovereign Yehowshuwa, do you mean it's almost time?" asked Petros. The large man still wore a first-century fisherman's robe, though now that robe was pure white.

Thomas said, "Ah…That explains why we've allowed some of Ben-Shaachar's forces to escape."

Others made similar comments as The Sovereign opened their minds to see more of the impending situation.

"The Last Battle wasn't really the final one. We will soon be facing another, and we need to be prepared. We must be especially careful about our communications. All normal business of the Administration will be communicated as usual so that Ben-Shaachar will observe what he wants to believe. All conversations about our offensive and defensive tactics will be done in secure locations, such as this room. All of these communiqués will be delivered personally; no mental contacts or written memos. Bartholomew has already delivered my first message in this manner through his chain of command to Maria."

Bartholomew remembered the thrill of receiving that message from Yehowshuwa through his touch. The Sovereign was also pleased that Bartholomew didn't somehow feel special because he was the first to know the depth of The Sovereign's plans.

"I trust all members of the Administration to follow these rules. Unfortunately, we can't expect mortals to be so faithful. The Chancellor will draw away many who have pledged their allegiance but whose hearts are not fully with us. Many who do have their hearts with us can be deceived or distracted for a time. Our immediate goals will be to protect the latter and change the hearts of the former before Ben-Shaachar gets to them."

Yehowshuwa looked at each member meeting their eyes with a steady gaze, glowing with pride in the ones he had selected. He knew that none of them would fail him, even though each in his own way had done so while they were mortals.

"Let's join hands and I will give each of you your tactical assignment." He stood and moved to the other side of the table.

His council stood and formed a circle with The Sovereign, all closing their eyes. He closed his eyes as well and felt power flowing from him as the effect of his mind and thoughts were transmitted to his council members. For several minutes he kept them entranced as they received details beyond anything they had known or even imagined. He heard oohs and aahs, amens and halleluiahs, deep mournful sighs and laughter as his closest followers absorbed the coming events and their responsibility in keeping the future on course.

When he was finished, The Sovereign Yehowshuwa released his grip, the power ceased, and everyone opened his or her eyes, looking expectantly at him.

"Go now," he commanded. "Carry out your missions with determination and trustworthiness. I know you will exercise wisdom in all decisions ahead of you. Go with my blessings."

August 19, 998 ASR

Robert did his best to sit still until Markus finished his spiel. Then he turned and looked at the audience. His mother and father wore sour looks on their faces. He smiled, wanting to assure them that this was his show, not theirs.

"You may begin your presentation, Robert," Henry said.

He turned back to the council. "Thank you, sir." Feeling a sense of confidence that even amazed himself, Robert puffed out his chest slightly. "Most people in universities are quite a bit younger than I am, working on their first degree. Those who are older have families and jobs, and are returning for multiple degrees. Since I have an uninterrupted forty years, I am viewed by the younger students as a peer."

Robert scanned the faces of the Elders, looking for a clue about their disposition toward him. Their faces all looked rather deadpan and bored, except for Henry, who kept his eyes on Robert with his mouth curving up slightly. He made a quick decision to cut out a lot of the statistics he had planned on giving them regarding longevity and population growth after The Last Battle. *I need to wake these guys up.*

"This younger generation, which represents nearly 50 percent of the world population, is expressing doubts about the Administration. They are questioning The Sovereign's right to rule as—"

The Board member that was second from the end of the table at Robert's right jumped to his feet. "Treason!" he exclaimed. People in the hall murmured to one another. Robert glanced at his parents, who were staring at him in shock and disbelief.

"Blain, please sit down," Henry said with a stern look. "Robert hasn't said anything treasonous. We need to hear him out and see where he's going."

Blain slowly sat back down, his jaw pulsating. The voices behind Robert quieted.

"Thank you, sir," said Robert. "However, Mr. Caucus' reaction is precisely the reason I've brought this motion for occupation. You see, many people who are younger than fifty think quite differently than most of those who are over a hundred. They mistrust the older generation, so they don't speak their minds to their elders; thus, the more senior population is unaware that a shift in philosophy has occurred."

Robert felt that he now had the Board's attention, even if it was negative. Henry was constantly glancing back and forth between Robert and the other members of the Board. *I've got to convince these guys that they have a potential crisis on their hands and that I can help them out of it.*

"Since I am between these two generations, and have earned the trust of the young people, they have spoken to me about their doubts. The biggest issue, in their minds, is The Last Battle. Their question is simple: what if The Last Battle didn't really happen the way our books say it did?"

Three Board members started to rise but Henry stopped them with a scowl and a thump with his gavel. He could not, however, stop several people in the audience from standing. His penetrating look and another crack of his gavel communicated clearly that he would not tolerate any outbursts or interruptions. Everyone slowly sat back down.

Robert stood and leaned over the table, speaking quietly. "Gentlemen, I respect you all highly. I appreciate the concern you have for The Sovereign Yehowshuwa and his Administration. That is why I want your approval to write a new history book about The Last Battle. Today's young people are afraid of what might happen to them if their doubts are made public. Based on the strong feelings displayed here, they may have reason to fear. However, no Enforcers have intervened when they've discussed these topics among themselves. That tells me they are not a threat to the Administration . . . at least not yet."

Robert examined Blain's expression. His jaw had relaxed but his brow was still furrowed. Robert hoped he was now thinking instead of reacting.

"I think the best method to erase their doubts is to write a book that will be accepted by this new generation. It must be written from a different perspective from all the others; otherwise, they will see it as just another one of the Administration's books. If they can see the truth of what happened, they will stop their questioning. If not . . . can you imagine what this world would be like if half the population rejected The Sovereign's rule just because they doubt his account of The Last Battle?"

Blain turned to Markus, who was sitting beside him, and whispered something in his ear. Markus shook his head back and forth. Walter and M'Karin, two other Elders, also started whispering to each other and shaking their heads. Robert hoped they were all pondering the fate of society if a major rebellion broke out.

Henry cleared his throat loudly and the others gave him their attention. "Robert, if this course of action were approved, how would you proceed?"

"In order to do the proper research for this book, I must finish my last quarter of school and get my doctorate in sub-history culture. That will give me the credentials I need, not only to satisfy my fellow students but also for the benefit of the older citizens. The younger generation needs to see that this book is written by one of them, but it also needs to be authorized by the Administration. That is why I am requesting your approval for this endeavor." Robert sat back down.

Henry turned to the Board members. "Any questions for Robert?"

Blain's clear blue eyes seemed to pierce Robert as he sat back in his chair; an elbow on each armrest, with his fingers interweaved except for his index fingers, which were pressed together, pointing upward. He looked at Robert over his two fingers. "If this younger generation you speak of is really questioning The Sovereign, don't you think someone would have said something to us? Surely out of ten billion people, someone would have spilled the beans to a parent or local Board member, who would have alerted us so we could counsel the students."

"That is a good question, sir. However, in order to answer it, I have to ask that only Board members be present. I would like to invoke the confidentiality clause."

Gasps and mumbling filled the hall.

"It must have been a hundred years since anyone has asked for confidentiality." Henry gave a deep sigh. "Since you've asked for it, I must allow it." He pointed his gavel at the recorder and asked him to clear the hall. Then he leaned close to Robert. "This better be good, son."

Robert turned and saw people leaving out the back door of the hall. His dad stood to go but his mom sat tight. The recorder edged his way over to her and leaned over the rail, speaking quietly. She shook her head. His dad put one hand on her shoulder and whispered to her. The recorder gestured toward the back door. Finally Mom stood, shot one thin-lipped glance at Robert, and then marched out the door while Dad scurried to keep up with her.

After everyone left and the recorder closed the doors as he left, Henry addressed the Board. "Under the rules of confidentiality, you cannot divulge anything to anyone about what is said here. That includes wives and families. Understood?"

Each Board member nodded.

"Alright," He turned to Robert. "You may continue."

"Thank you." He sat back in his chair and folded his hands under his chin. "An underground paper, containing articles that express the views that are prevalent on university campuses has been in circulation for over thirty years. It is passed out to university students all over the world, but only after 'recruiters' have made personal contact. At every university I've attended, I have been approached to receive a copy soon after my arrival. The first time, a recruiter asked me questions, trying to determine whether I might be sympathetic to the ideas presented. I was curious, so I played along and was given a copy. Each month thereafter I found a new encrypted copy in my inbox. Groups gather at night to discuss the issues brought up in the paper."

"You have to be kidding," Walter said. "You want us to believe that for more than thirty years subversive groups of students have had clandestine meetings all over the world and we never heard about it?"

"Absolutely! One of the requirements to receive the paper is not to share it with 'the establishment.' By divulging this information to you today, I am running the risk of losing the trust I have established with the younger generation." Robert glanced around the room to make sure no one other than the Elders was present. "In truth, I fear for my life."

Blain straightened; his eyes wide.

"The Sovereign would never allow anyone to take your life," said Henry.

"Nevertheless, I know some of these people. I believe they would do whatever they could to stop me or retaliate if they found out . . ." Robert pulled his ECD out of his shirt pocket and unfolded it. "Gentlemen, I have brought a copy of the paper to show you." He opened a recent issue, then walked around the table and showed it to each member.

He explained that the article was encrypted so he had to hold the ECD. If an unauthorized person touched it, the screen would not even display the existence of *The Question*. The encryption was based on the recipient's DNA and brain waves. If a person were forced to share the data under duress, his brain waves would reveal the pressure and the encryption mechanism would prevent divulgence of the data.

Each Board member looked at the article briefly. Each one was visibly shaken by what he read. One covered his mouth to suppress a gasp; another dropped his jaw. As Robert moved on to the next Elder, the previous began whispering to his neighbor. Markus, the last, asked to page through to a couple of the articles listed in the table of contents. Robert obliged him. Then he folded the ECD and slipped it back into his pocket.

"I wasn't aware that anyone outside the Administration had this kind of encryption capability," Blain mumbled.

Robert marched back to the straight-edged side of the table. "You may have noticed that the rate of Enforcer appearances seems to have decreased in the last two decades. In actuality the number of interventions hasn't decreased; the population has simply increased. I believe the Administration is being stretched too thin. They don't have time to deal with people who are expressing doubts . . . even if those doubts could lead to treason."

Henry's face sagged. "Any more questions?"

None of the Elders said a word. Walter fiddled with his beard and looked down at the table. Blain sat back with his arms folded. M'Karin had one elbow on his armrest and his head cocked sideways, resting his head on his hand. He stared at Henry blankly. Markus fiddled with his ECD, probably trying to verify Robert's claim about the rate of Enforcer appearances.

Robert tried to make eye contact with each Board member, hoping to discern his thoughts. *If they believe that I sincerely intend to steer this generation to faith in The Sovereign, I'll have it made.* He hoped they didn't realize how undecided he really was.

"OK, Walter," Henry said. "Let the recorder and everyone else back in."

As Walter made his way to the door, Henry walked over to Robert. He put his hand on his shoulder and whispered, "Go ahead and take your seat. When everyone is back in, I'll let them know that we are going into deliberations." He sat back down, closed his eyes, and rested his head in his hands

Robert passed back through the gate in the railing but turned to his right instead of his left. He glanced back and noticed Henry's bowed head. His lips were moving but not making any sound.

May 16, 998 ASR

Captain Chuck Andrews came onto the bridge of the H.S.S.S. Ramah and looked around to make sure everyone was in position. Zophia sat at her station, her dark brown eyes glued to the monitor showing Ramah's systems. Zophia's brother-in-law, Dr. Ntari, had been instrumental in developing the antigravity engines that enabled their space travel. Her close association with him and his work gave Chuck confidence that if anything went wrong during their journey, she would be able to repair the engines.

Chief Navigator Buckly Ramstad sat at his navigation console. He was one of the youngest crewmembers but was a good chief navigator because of his background in four-dimensional space physics.

Helmsman Irene Glover, a diminutive lady, was at the helm. She excelled in eye-hand coordination, which made her the best pilot ever to graduate from the space academy.

"Is everyone ready to lift off?" he asked.

"The computer still wants to be called Hal," said Zophia with unmasked irritation. "However, all the diagnostics indicate that we still have full control of Ramah."

"Irene, take us twenty thousand kilometers outside the atmosphere. Use backup protocol in case 'Hal' has any quirks." Chuck said.

"Yes, Sir." Irene placed one hand on the horizontal-control joystick and the other on the combination vertical-control stick and throttle lever. "Ready for emergency backup control, Captain."

"Roger that. Proceed." He turned his attention to the view screen that had several different inserts showing views from the exterior of the ship as well as the status of the ship's critical systems.

Irene gave the computer the command to lift off, "Take us to a distance of 20,160 kilometers above the surface and hold us steady there." Nothing. She quickly added, "Hal."

Indicator lights showed the deflectors coming online. An insert on the view screen displayed clouds forming around the top of the ship. The deflectors punched a hole through the atmosphere to outer space, clearing the way for a high-speed takeoff. The ship creaked and groaned as internal gravitation fields stabilized all 25 decks of the ship against the high G-forces that would otherwise have crushed the ship as it accelerated. A slight tremor shook the ship as it slowly lifted from its hovering position just above the beach.

Captain Andrews sat down in his command chair, paying careful attention to the view screen with the external sensors. One insert showed sand, gravel, and boulders flying away from the ship as they slipped out from beneath the gravitational thrusters. It always amazed him how far and fast the boulders would fly. The great ship gradually gained speed, and the barren landscape rapidly shrank, displaying the planet's oceans and continents.

As the ship approached its designated position, it decelerated and adjusted external gravity fields to hold it steady.

Chuck turned to Zophia. "See if we can get confirmation that our target planet will meet our specifications to support life. If it checks out OK, we'll be leaving tomorrow."

"Yes, Sir." Zophia gave the computer the coordinates. "I'll have our sensors focused on the target and recording data within the hour. At this distance we will be able to get more details than the sensors on Earth's moon did before we left."

Chuck left the bridge, marveling at the technological advances that had occurred over the last millennium. Even after twenty-five years, he felt a thrill during every takeoff.

Chapter 5

Robert leaned against the rail at the front of the community hall as Walter marched up the center aisle after the conclusion of the Elders' confidential session. As he swung the large double doors open to let in the spectators, Robert's mom was the first to cross the threshold.

Robert stood near a seat on the opposite side of the aisle from where he had originally sat with his parents. As they came forward, Mom shoved Dad toward Robert. As a result Robert found himself again edged to the inside of the row, but next to his father who was glaring at him. As he sat down, he noticed a stranger enter the room and take a seat in the back row.

She was only about 152 centimeters tall and looked very young. Her olive brown skin, dark almond eyes, and flowing black hair contrasted with her white linen suit. Her countenance glowed, giving her an irresistible allure. She sat leaning forward slightly as if ready to spring into action. Her eyes were fixed on the front of the room.

Robert elbowed his father. "Who's the good-looking lady in the white suit?"

Dad looked back and saluted her with two fingers above his eyebrow. She raised her hand from her lap and returned his greeting with a wave. He faced forward regaining his frown. "That lady, my son, is Maria, our Board supervisor."

Robert quickly faced the front, his heart pounding. The last thing he wanted was to have an Administration official involved with his case. If she got wind of the sensitive topics that had been discussed in the confidential session, a huge investigation would likely follow. That could reveal the more subversive topics he hadn't shared with the Board, which would probably be the end of his chances. He could be facing time in a retraining camp.

"What do you suppose she's doing here?" he whispered to his dad. "You don't think she's going to get involved with my motion, do you?"

He shrugged and growled quietly, "I have no idea. She hasn't been involved in any Board meetings for several years. It's probably just one of her drop-in calls to let us know she's still ultimately in charge." Dad paused, obviously still irritated, and added, "Maybe she learned that a Board member's son is trying to pull off a smart stunt and she wants to make sure he gets his comeuppance."

Robert shuddered at the thought as well as Dad's sharp tone. He ventured one more glance back. She looked even more poised to strike.

As soon as everyone was seated, Henry announced, "We have completed the initial phase of Robert's motion for occupation. We will adjourn now to deliberate our decision and reconvene in one hour."

Maria stood and marched to the front of the hall. Her speed astonished Robert. "You gentlemen wouldn't mind me joining you for the deliberations, would you?"

"What—" Robert started, but stopped when his dad kicked his ankle.

Maria turned at the railing and looked at Robert, raising one eyebrow with an air of unquestioned authority.

"Glad to have you, Maria," Henry said as he opened the gate for her. She followed him to the side door then led the Board into the conference room.

"What's going on?" Robert's father asked his son as soon as the door closed. "How dare you file a formal motion of occupation without telling us? Then you pull this confidentiality rule out of the archives. On top of it you start to question an Administration official. Have you taken leave of your senses?"

Mom leaned across Dad's lap and opened her mouth, but before she could speak, Robert stood. "How can that woman sit in on the deliberations when she didn't even hear what we talked about? Doesn't confidentiality mean no one outside of those present have the right to know what I said? I can't believe Henry let her go in with them."

His dad snorted and looked up at Robert. "You don't have much appreciation for the Administration's abilities, do you? I'll bet she knows every word that was spoken. That aside, you still haven't answered my questions."

"I don't want to talk about it." Robert threw his hands up, and then scurried down the row of seats to the side aisle and out the back door.

"How can you let him walk out like that?" Marilyn demanded, taking her anger at Robert out on her husband.

Justin took her hand and looked her in the eye. "I'm just as upset as you are. He's a grown man, capable of taking charge of his own life. I don't like his methods any better than you do, but his motion has removed any influence I might have had with the Board."

Marilyn glanced around to see if anyone was staring at them.

Justin continued quietly talking through a fake smile and clenched teeth. "I suggest we continue this discussion at home. I don't want the whole community knowing our business."

Marilyn straightened and put on her public I'm-with-my-husband-the-Board-member-aren't-we-great expression. "You're right, dear." *But when we get home, I'm going to give you and Robert a piece of my mind.*

Henry sat next to Maria with the other eleven Board members at the round oak table in the conference room. Justin Maskil's chair remained empty. Though Henry was pleased that Maria had chosen to join their meeting, he felt under a great deal of pressure.

"Maria," Henry said, "I'm a bit perplexed by your presence here. According to the rules, we are not supposed to discuss any of the confidential information with anyone. Not even you."

Maria smiled and extended her hand. He took it and she clasped her other hand over his. "I'm glad you stick to the rules, Henry. It's important to make sure everything is done in order and with propriety. You don't need to reveal to me a single word. I already know what you were talking about, even in the confidential session."

Henry relaxed. "As I expected."

Maria gave Henry's hand a pat then turned toward the rest of the Elders. She put on her strictly-business, stern expression. "The Administration has known about *The Question* from its inception. The Sovereign Yehowshuwa knows what is in each issue, and he has been waiting for the right time to deal with it. We work on a need-to-know basis, and I was brought up to speed myself only yesterday."

Henry agreed. The Sovereign often worked in ways he didn't understand; this situation was one of those times.

"You may speak freely about Robert's motion without repeating anything that was said in private." Maria passed control of the meeting back to Henry with a hand gesture.

He cleared his throat. "Well, on with business, then. Who would like to go first?" He looked at Blain, who had been the most agitated during the meeting. Blain was calmer now.

"Frankly," Blain said, "I am in shock. If Robert is right about this generation and its philosophy, there is treason in the works. I'm not convinced that Robert isn't in on it. He says he wants to write a book to set the kids straight, but I'm not sure." Blain glanced around the table. "He's been in the university setting almost his whole life, and if Markus hadn't blown the whistle he would be headed back there without any concerns. Justin tells his kid the free ride is over and suddenly we have this motion sitting in our laps. I think we ought to deny it. Get him out of those crazy universities and into something that will bring him back to earth." Blain leaned back.

Walter raised his hand and got the nod from Henry to proceed. "I agree with Blain. I can tell when someone is using his psychology degree to try to push my buttons. I don't think Robert has pure motives about setting this generation straight."

M'Karin stopped twisting the end of his mustache to raise his hand. "I think Robert is on the up and up. He's articulate and knows more about the ancient world than most of us do. The young people might listen to him. If he can write a book they will read, he may be able to turn this generation around . . . providing he prints the truth."

"I think M'Karin is on the right track," Henry said. "We haven't paid much attention to what's happening with university students these days. Robert may not have been completely forthcoming with us; however, I sense that he's looking for the truth. I'm confident he'll find it and that it will have a tremendous impact on the students."

Henry waited a few seconds to give others a chance to contribute. When no one spoke, he asked, "Anyone else have an opinion?" Silence. "All right, then, let's vote. All in favor of granting Robert's motion for occupation raise your hands." Five hands rose. "All opposed?" Five more hands.

"Markus," Henry said just a bit miffed, "why didn't you vote?"

"I'm a numbers guy. If this were a matter of budget or resources, I wouldn't have a problem making up my mind. However, I don't feel like I'm a good judge of character. I need to abstain."

Henry turned to Maria. *I'll bet she knew this was going to be a tie vote.* "What do you have to say?"

"I have processed my thoughts and weighed the possibilities, just as you all have. If the only thing I had to go on was what you have heard, I'd be hard pressed to make a decision. However, I have been fully informed about *The Question*, and it's time to do something about it."

Every eye in the room focused on Maria.

"The Sovereign Yehowshuwa has chosen Robert to be instrumental in accomplishing his will concerning the direction of the younger generation. Therefore, he wants you to approve this motion for occupation. When you tell Robert the news, you will let him know that there are two conditions on his motion. The first is that he must complete the educational prerequisites exactly as he outlined. The second is that he must write the book in the next year and a half. The Sovereign doesn't want this to become a lifelong pursuit."

Henry tried to stifle a chuckle, and Maria's questioning glance stopped him completely.

"Sorry," he said. "When I read Robert's motion, I got the impression he wanted it to be a lifelong job."

Maria turned her head to the right and winked her right eye. "I think you're right. He's probably not going to like the time constraint, but he doesn't have a choice." She paused and covered her mouth as she chuckled slightly. "Yeah, that will definitely rock his boat a bit. However, to make it up to him, he will need access to resources that aren't normally granted without going through formal application processes. The Sovereign doesn't want anything to slow his progress. He is to be given priority access to all resources of the Administration."

Several jaws dropped in amazement. Henry had never heard of anyone being granted such privileged support from the Administration.

Maria took a thin lithinium card, about the size of a business card, from the side pocket of her jacket. "Give this to Robert. Tell him only that it will provide him with what he needs. It will be up to him to learn how completely he is supported by the Administration."

"I guess that settles the issue about Robert's motion," Henry said. "Why don't we take a break and meet back here before we reconvene?"

"Sounds good to me." Markus stood. "I've got some figures to work on before the budget meeting." He fled out the back door.

The rest of the group exited in twos and threes without comment, leaving Henry and Maria alone in the conference room.

Henry looked at Maria with tight lips. "It's almost time, isn't it?"

"Yes. I knew you would understand. If there are some in your community who aren't prepared, I hope you will help them get ready." Henry detected sadness in her voice.

"Many proclaim their loyalty to Yehowshuwa," he said, "but don't really understand what it means to be loyal. There isn't much I can do that hasn't already been done." He looked down at his hands.

"I know. You've overseen this community very well, and The Sovereign is proud of you. However, each person's mettle will soon be tested."

Henry relaxed. Her words had soothed his spirit. He couldn't wait to hear The Sovereign's final, "Welcome home, my good and faithful servant."

Maria stood. "I must be going. The Sovereign Yehowshuwa's blessing be upon you."

"And on you."

As she disappeared, Henry stared at the place she had just been. I will visit every single person in the community. I can't bear to see anyone lost. I sure hope Robert's book will help.

May 16, 998 ASR

The Chancellor Ben-Shaachar was almost grateful for the darkness of the dungeon. There were no physical distractions to interrupt his meditation or his mental excursions beyond his cell into enemy territory.

"Chancellor," Abathar cried, interrupting Ben-Shaachar's meditative state. "I bring you good news!"

"Have you come to tell me that the interplanetary forces have been released and are ready to embark on their mission?"

Abathar had a mental flicker. "Yes. That is exactly what I came to tell you. Did you already know they had escaped?"

Ben-Shaachar sighed; disappointed at having to explain himself to his underling. "I'm the one who secured their release. The Sovereign doesn't even know they're gone. They have been replaced by phantoms that look just like the forces he incarcerated."

"I am impressed, Your Highness," Abathar gushed. "You continually amaze me. Is there no end to your abilities?"

Ben-Shaachar warmed to boasting about his proficiency. "No, there is not. I have accomplished more than you can imagine. At one time I thought I might be limited in some ways, but not anymore. Given enough time, I will see Yehowshuwa become like a toy in comparison to the powers I am developing. However, I must be cautious about alerting him to my abilities."

Ben-Shaachar communicated a series of instructions to Abathar. "Please relay these instructions to the troops who are waiting for their assignments."

Jonathan was glad he had escaped the dungeon a few weeks earlier and had the opportunity to pass back and forth between the physical realm and realm of spirits. However, when he was in the physical, Gloria made him take on a physical form. That was distasteful to him.

He stiffened as he received a long, detailed communiqué from inside the prison, and then relaxed after he heard the details. *I'm glad I don't have to take on human form to deliver this one.*

Jonathan had to take this message to troops that were hiding in the spiritual realm where the enemy couldn't find them. This job was particularly challenging since the enemy could be around any corner.

He took flight as a wisp passing through a dark and dreary mist as he started his journey to the coordinates he had been given. He zigged and zagged in a crazy, erratic flight path to avoid any enemy that might be watching for a purposeful messenger. Jonathan circled obstacles, passed through narrow caverns, scaled vertical cliffs, and dodged vicious blows of mighty weapons wielded by shadowy beasts as he darted past them in the gloom.

He arrived at the entrance to a vast, dark gray valley, barren of all vegetation. Surrounded by jagged rock outcroppings towering thousands of meters above him, he cautiously proceeded to the center of the flat, sandy area strewn with rocks and boulders.

"I come in the name of The Chancellor Ben-Shaachar!" His shout rattled the crags, causing a small avalanche of sharp, jagged boulders to crash down the mountainside. After the echoes and rumbling subsided, the rocks slowly changed into creatures of various shapes and sizes. Some were small, gray, spindly things with large heads and sad-looking oval eyes but no ears or noses. Others looked just like humans. Some appeared as globes of light or balls of fire. Others looked to be gargantuan inanimate objects of various sizes and shapes. Thousands of what appeared to be a child's spinning top and metallic cylinders hummed in mid air. They all approached Jonathan and closed in around him.

"The Chancellor wishes to congratulate you on your past achievements," he said. "Centuries ago, when you were called into action, you set the stage for what you are now about to finish. The enemy had already planted his seed in mankind so that they had a desire for something greater than themselves. The enemy wanted that seed to point people to himself, but you were successful in turning mankind's desire into a wish to find other intelligent beings in the universe. You appeared at the right times and places so that people all over the world began to look to the stars for their origins, kinsmen, and even saviors."

Cheers erupted from the crowd, along with flashes of light and pulsating colors from some of the metallic-appearing creatures.

"You did this so well that even today, with The Sovereign living among them, they are still looking for someone other than him. Humans have mastered the ability to travel through space and are, at this moment, searching for life in other worlds. It is time to give them what they expect to find!"

The crowd again yelled and screamed in affirmation. A chant started and welled up in unison "Go, go, go, go."

My, aren't they eager to get on with their mission? Jonathan had to change his wisp features to a huge red dragon with seven heads to regain their attention. The chant abruptly stopped.

"I have Ben-Shaachar's assignment for each of you." He mentally transmitted the instructions to the hoard that encircled him. "You know what you must do, and you have the resources to accomplish it. Be on your way, in the power and strength of The Chancellor Ben-Shaachar."

With obvious glee and anticipation, they disappeared, leaving the valley looking as if it had been swept clean of even the sand that had covered the barren, rocky plain.

Jonathan was amazed at this army's enthusiasm. He had learned from the communiqué how difficult it had been to get them released. He now knew why.

He flitted on a more leisurely route back to the dungeon to await another assignment.

August 19, 998 ASR

Robert stormed down the hallway away from the council chambers. He couldn't remember when he had felt angrier. His face was flushed, his ears hot, and his throat constricted and sore. He was sure all his plans had gone down the tube, never to be seen again.

"Robert!" cried an unfamiliar voice behind him.

He turned to see a short, stout man wearing a faded, loose-fitting floral print shirt, baggy trousers, sandals without socks, and a small light blue cap on his head. His full beard was wiry but somewhat groomed. Robert was about to resume his brisk pace but noticed a twinkle in the man's eyes that, together with his smile, immediately soothed Robert's anger. He stopped and let the man catch up with him.

Panting, he spoke between breaths. "I saw what happened back there. I can imagine what you're going through right now. It looks like you need a friend. If I can, I'd like to lend you some support."

"That's very kind of you, but what can you do? They've already made up their minds by now."

"Maybe I can be of more help than you think. First, let's walk." The stranger's mouth seemed to stretch in an upward arc almost to his ears as he smiled.

The two followed the path around the gardens surrounding the community center at a leisurely pace. Robert didn't know why, but he felt he could trust this strange little man. So he began to unload all his fears for the future, even the frustrations he felt at the way his mom had been trying to control his life. After a few minutes he felt much calmer.

He stopped and faced the stranger. "Who are you? Why were you here today? I don't remember seeing you in the community hall."

"My name is Berekiah. I was sent to encourage you." He grinned. "You have a most important path set out before you. You must not deviate from it, but persist to the end. Along the way you will face many difficulties. You will be tempted to depart for various reasons. Keep on the path. When you find five options, choose the one that is to the left of the one that is on the right. Do this and you will find success."

Robert wondered how the riddle could have anything to do with finding success. Even though he felt better he still doubted that his future would be approved.

"So that you may know that what I say is the truth and that you can rely on it, I can also tell you that your request will be approved." Berekiah abruptly disappeared.

Robert wasn't surprised when Berekiah vanished. He'd heard about Encouragers, though he had never met one. Now he knew what they were like and what it felt like to be encouraged.

The strange command about the five options continued to puzzle him. However, as he wandered back to the community hall, he felt soothed, comforted, as if all was right in the world. If the man's prediction proved true in the face of such overwhelming odds, Robert was determined to do as he said.

May 16, 998 ASR

Zophia typed furiously on her seldom-used keyboard after Captain Andrews left the spaceship's bridge. She enjoyed the mathematical challenge that was required to enter the correct formulas for the computer to point the sensors at the right location. It wasn't a simple matter of directing the arrays to a specific location in space and taking a picture. Space had more than three dimensions. She liked to think of it as a carpet that was folded and twisted but in three dimensions appeared to be flat. The data would be received through the folds, a much shorter distance, instead of along the surface of the carpet.

After the entries were complete, she instructed the computer with simple voice commands. "Hal, when the sensors are aligned with the planet's coordinates, begin data collection."

The smooth respectful voice responded, "Sensors have been aligned and data is being received. Do you wish to be notified when the analysis is complete?"

"That would be nice. Thank you." She was starting to like the modifications Dave had made when he corrected the machine's response algorithms. It wasn't smart-alecky but now seemed more human. She was even getting used to calling it Hal.

Twenty minutes later Hal completed the calculations and signaled Zophia that they were complete. She took a few minutes to verify the readings and called the Captain on his ECD.

"Sir, we have the data on the planet ready for review."

"Thanks, Zophia, I'll be right there."

Five minutes later Andrews arrived on the bridge and sat in his command chair. "Show me what you've got."

Zophia pressed a couple of buttons on her monitor, and the large view screen lit up with an image of a planet rotating slowly before them. The planet bore a remarkable resemblance to Earth.

The Captain stood and took a few steps closer. "This is fantastic. The clarity is amazing."

The screen showed obvious areas of ocean and land covered by layers of clouds. In a smaller side panel insert on the main screen, a view of the star was filtered so that it looked like a glowing orange, with tiny flames representing solar flares. Above it another panel showed a barren, pockmarked sphere without any atmosphere labeled "moon." Six other panels on the screen surrounded the planet in the center. Each contained views of other objects in the star system. Under each panel text displayed the vital statistics of each object in the system: distance from the sun, mass, circumference, atmosphere, number of moons, mean temperature, and other data.

"Captain," Zophia eagerly explained, "the information we received is much more than I would have imagined. The warps and twists in space between the planet and us are so small it's almost as if we were just outside of its system. As you can see, the planet has only one moon. That is vital in keeping the oceans moving so that life can exist in them. The planet is approximately 150 million kilometers away from the sun, which has the same mass and energy output as our Sol. The other planets in the system resemble the planets in our solar system in mass and distance from the sun. The system contains two huge gaseous planets that protect it from comets and rogue planets. The mean temperature of the planet makes it a virtual Garden of Eden, provided we actually find flora and fauna there."

Captain Andrews gave Zophia a stern look. "Are you saying this place has everything needed to support life?"

Zophia had held the best for last. "We can't be 100 percent positive that there is life on the planet. However, the presence of carbon dioxide and oxygen in the atmosphere does suggest it."

The Captain beamed. "Very impressive. This planet was located all on the tip from that Administration guy, what's his name?"

"Berekiah."

"I see no need to wait. Let's get out of here. Buckly, set a course for that planet. Irene, when he's ready, take us out of here at maximum power. If we push this ship for all it is worth, how long will it take us to get there?"

Buckly's keyboard clattered as he typed on his computer terminal. "If we run the Extra-Light-Impulsion drive at our current maximum...it will take about six weeks, Chuck."

Zophia scowled. It still bothered her when other crewmembers didn't address their leader as "Captain" or "Sir." However at the moment she was more concerned about the wear and tear on the ship. "Sir, we've never sustained ELI drive at full power for more than a few hours. I feel it's a bit risky to run this fast that long."

"Maybe," he conceded, "but we need to find out what's there and get back to Earth as soon as possible if we find life. You and Demetrius have done a superb job of enhancing our ELI drives so we can travel three times faster than when we left. I have full confidence that you'll be able to keep this ship moving. Still, I want you both to devote your full time to see if you can pull anything more out of it."

"Yes, Sir!" Zophia forgot about the risk when she heard the challenge to increase speed. There was nothing she liked more than working with a talented engineer like Demetrius to apply science at a practical level to accomplish what others believed to be impossible. "What about refueling, sir? The cold fusion reactors will be consuming a lot more H_2O than before."

Captain Andrews waved his hand, dismissing her concern. "Don't worry about efficiency. We've found water and ice in enough locations that we can stop to refuel if we need to. The time saved by traveling faster will more than make up for the refueling time."

Buckly announced that he had programmed the course to the new planet.

"Irene," Andrews said, "you have control."

She used her keyboard to enter instructions for Hal to start acceleration. She glued her eyes to the ship's systems monitor. She rested her hands lightly on the manual override controls. At maximum ELI the computer had to adjust the gravitational fields on all decks to compensate for the extreme acceleration. If either the acceleration or the gravitational fields were out of sync for even a fraction of a second, the entire ship would be torn apart as easily as an origami box in the hands of a two-year-old. Given the unusual verbal communication skills Hal had exhibited lately, Zophia had instructed her not use voice commands for such a critical maneuver.

A slight vibration slithered throughout the ship as it began to move away from the planet. The view panel showed that they were approaching the speed of light. Stars and planets blurred then disappeared from the visual spectrum, leaving the screen black. *We are now as invisible to the universe as it is to us.*

Pleased with the safe transition to hyper-light, Zophia used her ECD to contact Demetrius as she headed out the door. "Demi, we've got an assignment, high priority. Meet me in the lab in five minutes."

Chapter 6

Robert delayed his entrance back into the community hall as long as possible. He wanted to avoid his parents until the outcome was announced. When he saw the recorder come in he hurried to a seat across the aisle from his parents. The Board members were already seated; their expressions sober. Maria was nowhere in sight.

"The South Cottage Grove Board number 23 is back in session," the Recorder announced without emotion. Then he turned to face Robert. "Robert Maskil, the Board has finished deliberating on your motion for occupation. The chairman will provide the results."

Henry stood. "Robert, we have decided to grant your motion."

Robert tried to restrain himself but succumbed to an under the breath "Yes!" and a thumbs-up toward Henry. One glance at his dad's surprised open mouth and his mom's horrified and distorted face was enough to know that they were not rejoicing with him.

"There are two conditions," Henry added. "The first is that you complete this next quarter of schooling as you outlined in your motion. The second is that you finish this book in the next year and a half."

Robert didn't have any problem with finishing his degree by the end of the quarter, but he was apprehensive about being able to complete the book in only a year and a half.

Henry must have noticed the surprise on his face. "That seems pretty quick to me too. However, the Administration wants to turn this generation around as much as you do. Therefore, to help you out, Maria has provided an access card for you to use. It should facilitate getting anything you'll need."

Henry walked to the railing and shook Robert's hand then gave him the access card. "Congratulations, Robert. May our Sovereign Yehowshuwa bless you in this endeavor." Henry addressed the audience. "This concludes all scheduled formal business for the day. Anyone with informal requests may now approach the recorder."

As the handful of spectators exited the room, Robert whispered to Henry, "Sir, I'm very thankful that you approved my motion. To tell the truth, I thought for sure Maria would quash it."

"You don't need to call me Sir, Robert. Henry will do just fine. Actually, you have Maria to thank for the approval. It was a tie vote with one abstention, and Maria broke the tie."

Knowing that Maria had cast the deciding ballot unnerved Robert. He was afraid Maria might know his involvement with *The Question* and the underground. If they did, he couldn't imagine why the Administration would have intervened. "Thank you, Sir—er, Henry. That's good to know." He stared at the access card in his hand. His name stood out in a bold font. A long string of numbers appeared below. "So, how did you manage to get this for me? I would have at least expected a bunch of red tape."

"Again, you can thank Maria. She brought it with her."

"How did she know to bring it?"

Henry chuckled with a twinkle in his eye. "You haven't been around Administration people very much, have you? She had your motion before we did. It didn't really matter that we tied on the vote. Your motion was as good as approved before we started."

Robert was amazed then thought of Berekiah. "That explains the old guy who talked to me outside. I was really disheartened. He said my motion would be approved...then he disappeared. I figured he must be an Encourager, because I felt a lot better afterward."

"An old guy, you say?" Henry cocked his head to one side.

"Yes. He was a lot shorter than me, dressed casually, in kind of faded clothes. Oh, he also wore a small beanie-like cap."

"A yarmulke?" suggested Henry.

"Yes, that's what they're called."

"Interesting." Henry stroked his chin. "Seems like odd dress for an Administration official."

Henry's attention diverted toward the gate in the rail. The Recorder had just opened it to let an older couple enter. "Looks like someone's waiting for me. Take care."

Robert and Henry shook hands. Henry joined the couple that was waiting for him. Robert turned to see his mother standing across the aisle, tapping her foot. His dad stood behind her, avoiding eye contact.

He crossed the aisle to them, feeling confident for the first time all day. "Let's go outside where we can talk privately." He led his parents outside before they could say anything.

Once they were a fair distance from the community hall, Robert stopped.

"How could you do such a thing?" his mother spat out. "You knew I was dead set against this foolishness. When are you going to start doing as I ask and become a loving, obedient son like the one you used to be? I have a mind to throw you out of the house." She folded her arms tightly across her chest and turned her back on him smacking into Dad who was standing right behind her. He held her.

Robert tried to put his hand on her shoulder, but she jerked away from them both. "Apparently the Administration doesn't think my plans are foolish," he said.

She wheeled around and glared at him, her body shaking. "I don't care what the Administration thinks. The Sovereign himself could have ordered you to write your book and I'd still say it's foolish."

"Marilyn!" Dad interjected.

She turned to him, buried her face in his chest, and started crying. "Make him stop this, Justin."

He put his arms around her again and motioned for Robert to leave. "We'll catch up with you later," he whispered to Robert.

Robert took a deep breath, then turned and walked away. He'd won a major battle today, but the war was far from over. *I should be elated but Mom sure knows how to keep the conflict raging.*

August 20, 998 ASR

Samantha Spell shuffled into her parents' kitchen, rubbing her eyes. She was greeted by the smell of fresh-baked biscuits and coffee. On the opposite side of the island counter, which also served as an informal table, her mother Emerelda stood at the stove, scraping scrambled eggs in a large pan.

"Good morning Samantha," said Mama without looking up from her cooking. "Did you have a good night's sleep?"

"Not very," she said, stretching. "Guess I'm a little anxious about leaving for university." She'd never been away from home for more than a few weeks.

"Now, honey, The Sovereign has always been good to us. I know he'll take care of you at university."

Samantha sat on a stool at the island. "You're right Mama. I know that too, but sometimes it is just hard to stop thinking about things when they are so new and will be so different. So, how'd you sleep?"

"Oh, seems like most mornings I wake up with more aches and pains than when I went to bed. I can't complain. I'm doing quite well for someone 722 years old." She turned down the heat on the burner and stirred the pot of sausage gravy.

"Is Papa still out slopping the hogs?"

"Yep." Her mother chuckled. "Sometimes I think he likes them animals better than he likes us." Mama took a cantaloupe out of the refrigerator and put it on the counter. "Breakfast will be ready in a few minutes. I'm sure the aroma will bring him running."

Samantha laughed as she selected a knife from the knife holder beside the refrigerator. She started cutting, cleaning and slicing the melon. Her papa always put his family above all other things, right after his loyalty to Yehowshuwa. Still, he loved his animals, even the ones that went to market.

At that moment Samantha's papa, Merlin, a tall, wide man in bib overalls, entered the kitchen. "How are my favorite ladies this morning?" He took one large step to Mama and gave her a big hug, pulling her off the floor and turning her around, then put her back where he'd picked her up. He planted a big kiss on her lips then headed for his daughter with a gleam in his eye.

Samantha playfully ducked his hug." You're going to have to be quicker than that to crunch my ribs, Papa." Then she threw her arms around his neck and lifted herself off the floor. As he swung her around, Samantha's feet flew out and almost knocked over an island stool. They both laughed heartily.

"You know, I think I understand now why my aches and pains are increasing." Mama waved her spatula at them.

Samantha rested her head on her father's shoulder. "I'm going to miss you and Mama."

"Me, too, Sam. I'd be pretty disappointed if we didn't. It shows how much we care for each other." He patted her back.

"Your papa is right. We've been very blessed to have such a loving home. Not all families know Yehowshuwa the way we do; they don't have his peace and love in their hearts. You'll see when you get to university."

"That's hard to imagine, Mama." As far as Samantha could tell, every family in the community was very much like her own. "How are others so different?"

"Not everyone is like us, Samantha, even in this community. Some put on a good show, but their families aren't as well adjusted as you'd think. It really boils down to their relationship with The Sovereign." Mama poured sausage gravy in a bowl and set it on the island.

Samantha dished the scrambled eggs into another bowl and set it beside the biscuits that were already on the island while Papa brought a pitcher of milk from the refrigerator.

The family sat down to breakfast and Papa reached his big hands out to Mama and Samantha on each side of him and bowed his head. Samantha closed her eyes and bowed her head. He asked The Sovereign Yehowshuwa's blessing on their meal and the activities of the day. Samantha felt secure and loved by her Papa and by The Sovereign. She was very thankful for her family.

"So," Papa asked his daughter as they dropped hands. He took two biscuits and put them on his plate, "are you ready to go to town this morning and get the things you need for school?"

"Sure am, Papa," she replied. She was looking forward to the shopping trip, even though she didn't feel prepared. "I've been trying to put together my list, but I'm not sure what all I'll need."

Papa held the plate of biscuits first to Mama then Samantha. Mama and Samantha each took one.

"You still have a little over a week before you have to leave," said Mama as she dished up some gravy and poured it over her biscuit. "Also, you don't have to get everything here. I'm sure you'll be able to pick up whatever you need at school." She passed the gravy to Papa.

"I'm afraid I won't have time once I get to university. I've signed up for a huge workload. That bothers me too. I don't want to be a failure and embarrass you two." Papa dished up a huge portion of sausage gravy and passed the bowl on to Samantha while Samantha took some eggs and passed them to Papa.

"Don't you worry about that. We'll be proud of you no matter what." Papa took most of the eggs and passed the bowl to Mama.

Samantha was concerned that it would be easy to slip away from her faith. "I've heard horror stories about what happens to some people who leave home for the first time and wander away from what's right."

"You've been raised in a conservative family, Sam," her father reminded her. "Just remember how we've lived and what you've been taught, and you won't have any problems. Your older brothers and sisters have done just fine. I'm sure you will too."

Samantha put her hand on Papa's shoulder and leaned her head on top of it. "Thanks, Papa. You two will pray for me while I'm gone, won't you?"

Papa nodded and Mama answered, "Of course we will. We pray for you every day. We won't stop just because you're not here."

Papa wiped a tear from his eye and changed the subject. "After chores, we'll load up the truck and take some produce and a couple of hogs to the market. That'll take your mind off university for a few minutes."

Samantha appreciated her parents' love and encouragement. She thanked The Sovereign Yehowshuwa for both of them.

May 16, 998 ASR

Tia-le surveyed her troops. They were just released from the dungeon and were under her command once again. Here, at their designated rendezvous, they were all assembled. It was a rock about a third the size of Earth's moon, beyond the orbit of Pluto. She surveyed the ranks at attention before her. Her chosen form, a biped with spindly arms and legs, seemed to move in opposition to her frail body. She chose a large head with oval eyes, no visible ears or chin, and a small mouth at the end of an elongated jaw. She paced in front of the troops, examining their various forms.

She was pleased with what she saw, "Fellow aliens," Snickers rose and quickly subsided as she continued, "yes that is what we are as far as humans are concerned and what we will be again."

Tia-le's assignment was to encourage the troops, then lead them into battle. She believed a brief reminder of past victories would help negate the past nine hundred plus years of imprisonment. "We were very successful in our missions before The Last Battle and that is why we were not released earlier. We are now going to take advantage of our past experiences to bring great glory to The Chancellor Ben-Shaachar."

She raised her spindly three-fingered hand to quiet the cheers.

"When we last appeared to humans," she said, "we successfully planted seeds in their minds and culture that there were other intelligent beings in the universe. That is the truth, since we are intelligent beings."

"Amen! Sister!" blared a top-shaped being with lights rotating around its middle.

Tia-le enjoyed the encouragement as well. "Their desire to know superior beings other than The Sovereign Yehowshuwa made our job easier. They accepted us in many forms, some of which are represented here today." The front rows of the troops could have been her spindly siblings. If she didn't know better, she would have believed that the next ranks were actually human, except that they were much better looking.

"Some of the humans thought we were their long-distant ancestors who had evolved to higher life forms. Others believed we were higher life forms who had genetically engineered their ancestors to produce intelligence on Earth and that after several millennia we had returned to see how our experiment had gone. Still others believed we were simply explorers from distant galaxies. While some thought we could be malicious, most believed that since we possessed superior intelligence and technology we were benevolent."

She waited several minutes for the snickers and guffaws to abate.

Her voice rose in volume and fervency. "The people we are about to encounter have had these seeds implanted in their subconscious by the first forces that escaped from the dungeon. This proves that their nature hasn't changed in a thousand years. That will enable us to carry out our mission flawlessly. Since they have not acknowledged that The Sovereign is the only one who can satisfy their desire, we have the opportunity to take over his role in their lives and eventually free them and ourselves forever from The Sovereign's tyranny."

Tia-le paused, relishing the cheers and shouts of victory.

She thrust her bony arm in the air. "You have all been versed in what you must do. The Chancellor Ben-Shaachar has relayed his instructions. He has endowed us with more power than we have ever had before. Nothing can stop us from bringing victory to our king. Follow me!"

Tia-le departed from the physical realm, followed by thousands upon thousands of Ben-Shaachar's interplanetary forces.

August 20, 998 ASR

Jim hopped out of bed at 6:00, wide-awake. Bounding into the kitchen, he saw his parents' breakfast dishes in the sink. *I can't believe they've gone to work already. Didn't they remember that I was leaving for the mountains today?*

Then he remembered that he hadn't told them. They probably still would have gone to work without seeing me off.

Then again, Jim wasn't very good about being available for his parents either. When they were home he was usually out with friends. Their contact since his teen years had been barely enough to be classified as a family. He believed this had prepared him to accept the independent atmosphere he'd found when he first arrived on campus.

Jim muttered, "Still it would have been nice of them to at least acknowledge my existence," to himself as he ate a piece of toast with peanut butter and raspberry jam. He was really looking forward to this trip to the mountains. It would give him a chance to spend time with Robert, who had become his mentor as well as his best friend.

After adding his dirty milk glass and butter knife to the dishes in the sink, he returned to his room to get ready for the trip. *What do I pack for a week at a mountain cabin?* Figuring it couldn't be much different from going to the beach, he tossed some shorts and T-shirts into an overnight bag. He tossed in some underwear, too, but didn't feel a need for socks since he was wearing sandals. *Nobody to impress, so no point in taking a razor.*

He vaguely recalled Robert mentioning something else, but couldn't remember what. *Oh, well, I'll just get whatever else I need at a store on the way.*

At 6:30 he started on his two-block walk to the nearest convy stop, which was about two blocks farther than he would have liked. An early-morning mist filtered the sunlight that gleamed through the trees lining the street. The air was a bit cool. Jim wished he'd brought a light jacket.

He headed north past neat brick townhouses with small front yards. In the shade of the homes, the temperature dropped a couple of degrees, making him reconsider going back to the house for his jacket. He continued on. By the time he reached the convy stop, he was shivering.

A convy popped up from the tubes within a minute after pressing the call button. The second the door opened Jim leaped inside. "Delta Nature Reserve," he instructed the computer.

The mechanical female computer voice responded, "You will need to transfer at the Hampton regional center to reach that destination."

"Yeah, I figured," Jim grumbled.

"Enjoy your trip," replied the computer.

"I wonder why they always use women's voices for these things," he pondered aloud as he surveyed the empty seats in front of him.

"Women's voices are generally easier to understand than men's," said a man's voice behind him. "That's because the tones are at a frequency that our ears can discern more easily."

Jim jumped and turned around quickly and stared at a kindly-looking old man in a seat behind him. His small stature and wrinkled face posed no threat but Jim hadn't realized anyone else was already on the convy.

"I didn't mean to startle you, Jim. Have a seat." He said as he pointed to the empty seat across the aisle.

Jim sat, eying the elderly man suspiciously. "How do you know my name? Who are you?"

"I'm Akahito Takarabe, the senior Elder of your Board. I know the names and faces of everyone in our community." He shook Jim's hand.

"I wouldn't have thought you had time to get to know everyone," replied Jim. He was skeptical that this guy would know much about him.

"It is not difficult for us. If it were too much for us to handle, our community would divide and we would have two Boards instead of one," said Mr. Takarabe with a smile.

Jim wanted to be polite but he wasn't too interested in talking to a Board Elder, "Uh huh. That's interesting."

"So, how is university going for you?" Mr. Takarabe asked.

"Fine." Jim really didn't want to talk about school. The work was boring and his grades were mediocre. Nevertheless, he would rather stay there than have to get a job. "It looks like I'll be finishing my bachelor's in meteorology this year. I've considered going on for an advanced degree."

"I see."

Jim resisted rolling his eyes. The regional station was a good thirty minutes away. He hoped Mr. Takarabe's stop came sooner.

"You need to work a bit harder this next year. You're a smart lad. You can get better grades than you have been. You'll need to improve to continue for an advance degree." Takarabe said matter-of-factly.

The convy popped up out of the ground and the door opened.

"This is my stop." Mr. Takarabe stood and patted Jim's shoulder. "I'll be seeing you. The Sovereign Yehowshuwa bless you."

"Yeah, you too," Jim mumbled as Mr. Takarabe departed and another passenger got on. *Great. Our senior Elder knows who I am and my grades, no less. I'm doomed.* He slouched in his seat, folded his arms, and scowled, hoping his body language would communicate to the new passenger his desire to be left alone.

August 20, 998 ASR

Samantha and her father left the house to load the produce they would take to town in conjunction with her school shopping trip. She glanced around, absorbing the sights of the farm so she could take them with her to university. They passed some storage barns where she had played hide-and-seek with her cousins and the farm hands' kids when she was young. Inside, huge melon harvesters sat idle.

Papa had related much of the farm's history to her, since he had been the farm's director for the last five hundred years. During his first years, there had been a big push to increase automation, much of which he implemented. Now, she saw hundreds of workers in the fields, tending and harvesting the crops by hand. With the burgeoning world population the need for much of the farm automation had been eliminated.

Samantha had come to know many of the farmhands well when she worked with them during summer breaks and doing daily chores throughout the school year. She waved to the nearest ones and caught their attention. They straightened and returned her greeting.

Helping her dad before going into town was the most natural thing she could think of doing. As she and her father walked to the hog pens, she couldn't help thinking about how much she would miss the farm and her family while she was away at university.

"Sam, would you cut out that big red from this pen?" Papa pointed out the pig he had in mind. "I'll open the chute when you get him over here."

"Sure enough, Papa."

Samantha jumped in the pen, swinging both legs over the top rail and launching herself over the fence with one hand. She reached back over the fence and grabbed a two-handled wooden gate, which she would use to help guide the hog to the chute.

The eight critters in the pen milled around her, looking for a handout or just being inquisitive. Unlike the days before The Last Battle, pigs had no fear of people and would never intentionally harm anyone. In some ways that made the job easier; in other ways it was harder. If they had been afraid of her, she could have used that fear to direct the hog to the chute when it tried to get away from her. On the other hand, she didn't need to worry about them trying to bite her . . . unless they mistook her toes for food, which was unlikely since she was wearing knee-high barn boots.

Samantha's immediate job was to try to convince a ninety-kilogram hog that he needed to move in the direction she wanted him to go. She put the gate between her and the barrow that had been selected for market. With the gate square in his face he obediently started to turn away, but not toward the chute. Samantha deftly pressed the chute against his shoulder while sticking the bottom protrusions in the ground.

Things seemed to be progressing well until the hog changed his mind and started running in the opposite direction. Samantha blocked his path with the gate but she was thrown slightly off balance. He started a pushing match with her, and soon one of his sisters decided to play too. The gilt came up behind Samantha and rubbed her rump up against the back of Samantha's legs so she couldn't step back to brace herself from the barrow's push.

Samantha floundered backward. She flopped over the second hog and fell on her back in the muck, with her calves still on top of the female. The rest of the hogs rushed over to greet their new wallow mate with grunts and squeals, nuzzling her in the ribs with their snouts.

"Hey, Sam, you need a hand in there?" Papa laughed.

"Not funny, Papa." Samantha jumped up, grabbed the gate, and went after the hog with a vengeance. He didn't stand a chance this time. She whacked him firmly on the back end and sides to steer him toward the chute. Papa opened the gate, and big red gratefully trotted through the opening, up the chute, and into the transportation cage.

The second hog proceeded into her cage without incident. Samantha watched her father load the hogs' crates onto the flatbed of the truck with a forklift. He also loaded ten five-hundred-kilogram bins of melons that had been hand picked the day before. He directed two of the farm workers to load up forty bushels of lettuce and twenty bushels of green beans.

As each item was loaded, Samantha used Papa's ECD to check it off the request manifest. When they were loaded Papa climbed into the truck's cab while Samantha stepped on the running board and grabbed a handhold on the truck bed.

"I'll just ride out here to the house so I don't mess up the cab," she said, glancing at her mucked-up clothes.

"That's a good idea." Papa engaged the anti-gravity reactor, raising the large transport machine and its cargo about sixty centimeters off the ground. He maneuvered the joystick on the right arm of the driver's seat to glide it silently forward, steering it to their farmhouse, where he set it back down.

Samantha went into the house to clean up. After taking a shower, she replaced her barn chore attire with a light pink floral dress. She curled her still-wet hair against her nose, relieved that she couldn't detect any pig smell.

As she hopped into the cab alongside her father, she started thinking that maybe she wouldn't miss some aspects of the farm after all.

Chapter 7

Chuck sat on the bridge of the H.S.S.S. Ramah, waiting for Zophia and Demetrius to arrive and give him their daily progress report. He swirled around in his command chair when he heard the swoosh of the automatic door open behind him. "Good morning," he greeted his two assistants.

Tall, dark Zophia, with her short-cropped black hair took one stride for every two of short, round Demetrius, the chief engineer, who had a fair complexion and bushy blond hair. He couldn't imagine two more dissimilar people.

"What have you got for me today?"

Demetrius spoke first. "Our systems remain stable after three weeks of pushing the ELI drives at maximum speed, which is better than we hoped. There are no indications that we can't maintain this during our deceleration phase, which means that we should arrive at Eden right on schedule in three weeks."

"Did you say Eden?" Chuck cupped his right hand over his ear.

"After seeing the reports on the planet, a lot of the crewmembers have dubbed it Eden. Guess you hadn't heard that, Sir," said Zophia soberly.

"I like the sound of it. Still, we'll have to wait and see if it turns out to be that good." Chuck stood up. He wasn't comfortable talking to them while he was sitting down. It wouldn't have been so bad if it were only Demetrius but Zophia... that was another thing. "How's it going on the speed enhancements?"

Demetrius launched into a rapid-fire report mode that Chuck referred to as engineer-speak. "I have good news there as well. We've enhanced our monitors of the gravitational thrusters and ascertained data we hadn't previously been able to gather. With a few more modifications of our circuitry, we can probably achieve another 100 percent increase in power to both the thrusters and the deflectors. That will give us a 20 percent increase in speed since the drag increases exponentially. The actual reconfiguration will take about one week to build and install, which can only be done when we aren't cruising. With the boost and the fact that we won't be returning to Earth by the same route, we should be able return to Earth in about seven months after we leave Eden."

"That's fantastic." Chuck turned to Zophia. "So, what have you—"

Loud static from the bridge's speakers interrupted him. He spun around and the view screen showed streaks of color, then random checkerboard patterns.

"What's going on?" Chuck shouted above the noise.

"I am receiving an unknown communication from outside the ship," Hal announced in its calm voice.

"Hal, turn down the volume before we all go deaf," Zophia yelled.

The volume dropped to white-noise level.

"Where is this communication coming from?" Chuck asked.

Zophia sat down at her station and typed in a few commands. She looked up at Chuck with wide eyes. "Five small objects, about the size of farm transports, have matched our speed and direction. They're cruising around us, each about five hundred meters away. It appears they are beaming some kind of signal at our sensors in an attempt to communicate with us. Hal is running multiple analyses against the beams in an attempt to correlate them with intelligent speech or video signals that we can display."

The screen slowly transformed from the block patterns to spirals, whirls, and loops, blurring and fading at different rates like an old-fashioned screen saver gone mad.

An image appeared on the screen. The speakers quieted at the same time. Below the image a series of strange figures and characters streamed in a horizontal line from right to left as a strange language came from the speakers.

The image on the screen showed a man seated in what could have been the cab of a private transport. He was dressed in a long-sleeved white jumpsuit. Chuck noticed a familiar-looking insignia on the left side of his chest: a six-pointed star similar to the one used by The Sovereign Yehowshuwa.

The man appeared to be of Middle Eastern decent, with a swarthy face and dark brown eyes overshadowed by bushy black eyebrows. His black hair was cropped close to the sides of his head, while the top was left long, protruding slightly over his forehead and over his ears. His mouth moved in sync with the audio and the character stream at the bottom of the screen.

"He is transmitting simultaneous textual signal and audio," explained Zophia. "Hal is still trying to correlate the audio and text so he can translate the language."

"How long do you think it will take?" Chuck asked as he sat down in his command chair.

"Perhaps another three or four minutes, sir. The longer our visitor keeps talking the more accurate our translator will be."

The speakers began transmitting intelligible words, bringing everyone's attention to the man on the screen. "Greetings, Captain Andrews and crew. I see that you have finally made progress in your ability to receive my transmission. I have sent instructions to your computer on how to respond to my transmissions so that we can have a two-way conversation. If you instruct it to make the necessary technical modifications to your sensors, you will be able to transmit as well as receive."

Chuck glanced at Zophia. "Have you looked at these instructions?" *How did he know we had translated his language?*

Zophia looked up from her monitor. "Yes, Sir. It appears the modifications will not harm the sensors in any way. I find it quite intriguing, actually. They have managed to modulate the sensors to emit energy particles that are unaffected by our speed."

"OK, Zophia. Set it up so we can talk with this guy and find out what's going on."

Zophia typed in a couple of commands, and the ship's computer processed the instructions. Within a few seconds Zophia informed him that the modifications were complete.

"Oh, hello, Captain." The stranger smiled warmly. "It's good to be able to see you. Thank you for making the modifications. This will make it quite a bit easier for us to deliver our message. I expect this is quite a surprise for you, having us show up here in the middle of the universe."

That was an understatement. "You seem to know who we are," Chuck said, "but we know nothing about you. Who are you, what are you doing out here, and what is this message you have for us?"

The stranger's countenance immediately changed to a stern gaze. "Ah, the inquisitive human race, always asking questions and seldom ready to obey." He spoke crisply with a slight sneer on his face. "We will answer your questions because we know you will not receive our message in a positive light without additional information."

Chuck shifted in his command chair. He didn't like what the stranger said or how he said it.

"My name is Rol-el. My team and I are representatives of your Sovereign Yehowshuwa, but we are from an alternate realm and are his allies. Because you have traveled farther than expected and passed beyond his jurisdiction, he has sent us to intercept you."

Chuck closed his eyes briefly taking a second to process what he had just heard. "How could we have gone past The Sovereign's jurisdiction? I've always believed his jurisdiction extended throughout the universe." Chuck's hands shook. He felt a bead of perspiration drip from his armpit. Rol-el's statement rattled his faith to the foundations.

Chuck looked around the bridge to see if he was the only one in shock. Demetrius was shaking. Zophia had both hands over her mouth. Irene stared blankly at the monitor. Buckly's knuckles were white gripping his armrest tightly.

"Easy, Captain. I can tell this is a shock to you, and I don't want to cast aspersions on Yehowshuwa. Perhaps he let you believe he was sovereign over the entire universe because that is what you wanted to think. However, the fact is that you are now in the jurisdiction of Sovereign Jehov." Rol-el sneered briefly.

"Why did The Sovereign send you instead of one of his Enforcers or other Messengers to give us this communication?" Chuck asked, still unsure what to believe.

"Having no jurisdiction in this area he has certain restrictions. His people cannot travel in this realm without previous arrangements with Jehov. So Jehov decided, in agreement with Yehowshuwa, that it would be best if he sent his own people to contact you."

It appeared that Rol-el was enjoying every statement that caused Chuck and the crew discomfort. He dreaded what the message might be. "So, what's the message?"

"It is simple. You are to turn back now and return to Earth."

Zophia put her index finger to her lip, then waved her fingers across her throat and put her finger over her ear. Chuck understood her gesture to mean that she wanted to speak to him without Rol-el hearing.

"May I put you on hold for a minute? I'd like to talk with my officers in private."

"Certainly, Captain," replied Rol-el as he raised his eyebrows with a hint of a smirk.

Zophia switched off the camera and microphones. "Captain, I've been able to adapt the particle emissions and our sensors beyond the instructions provided for us. I can give you visual pictures of our visitor's spacecraft. There are some things about them that I don't like."

"Show me what you've got."

Zophia punched some commands on her keyboard and the view screen divided into two sections, with Rol-el on one side. The other section showed five cylinders with three short wings extending perpendicularly from the rear third of the cylinders. The nose of the cylinders obviously had deflectors; however, among the various sensor arrays on the hull Chuck saw some appendages he couldn't identify.

"Captain." Zophia's voice was strained. "The readings I'm getting indicate that these ships are expending far more energy than they could sustain to arrive here from the nearest star system. They must have a mother ship nearby; otherwise, they would never have been able to reach us."

"Agreed." Chuck shifted in his seat. "What do you make of those appendages?" he asked, pointing to the right section of the screen.

"Power readings indicate they are some kind of weapons. The Sovereign doesn't use physical weapons. Maybe we should ask them for some kind of proof that they are his representatives." Small beads of perspiration formed on her forehead.

"Good observation. Take them off hold."

"Rol-el," Chuck said, "we have a bit of a problem. We—"

Rol-el cut him off. "You are questioning whether or not we really represent Yehowshuwa. You would like proof that we are delivering his message to you. I know you have detected our weapons."

Chuck choked, "How did you know that?"

"This may be difficult for you to accept, Captain, but the rules you played by in Yehowshuwa's realm have no effect here. We have powers you couldn't imagine because we have no enemies as does Yehowshuwa. As a result the physical and extra-physical realms are more tightly coupled."

"What proof do you have of all this?" Chuck asked.

"The fact that I know what you discussed on your bridge should be sufficient evidence, don't you think?"

Chuck's head was swimming. The Sovereign isn't sovereign. There isn't supposed to be any intelligent life in the universe outside of Earth and this thug-like guy from some other planet is telling him to turn around in the name of The Sovereign Yehowshuwa. He wished he could just wake up and this would all be a bad dream. *I'm the Captain. I need to stay focused.*

"So, are you ready to comply and turn your ship around?"

Chuck stiffened in his chair. "That sounds like a threat rather than a message from The Sovereign."

Rol-el's face steeled into a hardened frown.

"What if we decide we'd like to visit Eden before we turn around?" asked Chuck.

Rol-el's face reddened. "We have been instructed to deliver the message and see to it that you comply. If you don't, we are authorized to use force. We are authorized to destroy both you and your ship."

Chuck felt his cheeks getting warm and his blood pressure rise. "This ship is designed with the structural integrity to sustain anything your pea-sized vessels are capable of dishing out. So why don't you just get out of the way and let us continue on our course?"

Immediately a huge fireball came from one of the ships toward Ramah. Alarms blared on the bridge. Damage control monitors appeared on the view screen, showing that the fireball had struck the ship in the middle of the western wall at deck fourteen.

"Captain," Zophia reported, her voice choked, "sensors show the temperature in Dave's quarter just reached one thousand degrees Celsius. Sprinkler systems aren't functioning." Tears formed in Zophia's eyes.

"Where is Dave?" Chuck asked, fearing the worst.

Zophia shrugged. "He hasn't responded to my queries. His latest reported position was in his quarters."

"Do you still think you are invulnerable to our weapons, Captain?" Rol-el sneered. "You need not look for Dave; he is no longer with you."

Chuck jumped to his feet and yelled, "No…you didn't. How could you do that?"

"See what your impertinence and disobedience has cost you?" Rol-el emphasized the words "your" and "you." "There will be no more warnings. You have five minutes to plot your course for Earth and begin your return voyage. If you have not complied by that time, your entire ship will be destroyed."

With a heavy sigh, Chuck turned to his navigator. "Buckly, plot a course for Earth. And please don't tell me it will take longer than five minutes."

August 20, 998 ASR

Gloria sat at the small desk in her small office staring at her ECD. She scanned page after page of requisitions and responses, tasks yet to be started as well as those completed, memos, edicts, status reports, shortages and overages. *I'm glad I didn't have to do this back before The Last Battle.* Since they'd been able to tap into the Administration's computer system and create phony IDs, their operatives looked just like normal human beings to the system, so they could get almost anything they wanted. That made it simple to describe a project, approve it, and then move material from The Sovereign's system to theirs.

Her pondering was interrupted by a knock on the door.

"Come in, Jonathan," she called out without taking her eyes off the screen.

Jonathan stepped through the closed door as if it were a holographic projection. He still assumed the same Asian features he had before.

Gloria looked up and scowled. "I have instructed you on proper procedures, Jonathan. You know you should open the door. If a human were watching, you could have compromised our cover. If you breach protocol again I will lock you so deep in the dungeon you'll never see the light of day."

Jonathan gave her a sneer. "I thought The Chancellor said our new attitude should be kinder and gentler than before we were imprisoned."

Gloria squinted her eyes into narrow slits, imagining Jonathan flying backwards and slamming into the closed door, and then sliding down onto the floor. When she opened her eyes, she was pleased to see him picking himself up off the floor. "If you screw anything up because of your lackadaisical attitude, our kinder and gentler Chancellor will have you for lunch. Now, why are you here?"

Jonathan brushed himself off. "Ben-Shaachar wants you to know of his latest plan enhancements. Oh, there was something else. He wants you to deal with a Professor Robison."

Gloria was pleased to note that he appeared less cocky than when he arrived. "Tell me about the professor."

"The Chancellor's archives operatives reported a potential problem. They were successful in guiding the primary target, the human Eric, to the proper location. However, Eric surprised them by contacting his boss, Professor Robison, who immediately joined him."

"Those idiots. They knew Eric was a loose cannon. They should have been more forceful in their guidance." Gloria had little use for the mistakes of others.

"The Chancellor said the professor couldn't be trusted to deliver the goods into the proper hands."

Gloria snorted. "He's right about that. Have the professor and Eric found the archive yet?"

"No. Our operatives managed to keep them distracted. However, the professor compiled extensive notes and returned to the University of Midrib. The agents believe that he will make his findings public. Ben-Shaachar says his plans will be ruined if the professor sends hundreds of archeologists to the site." Jonathan's voice carried a concerned tone. "He said you would know how to deal with the situation."

Gloria felt vindicated. "You can tell our illustrious Chancellor I will take care of his...the problem." *So he comes to me when his other flunkies fail. Fine, I'll show him.*

Jonathan continued relating what he had been told to explain to Gloria. When he was finished she dismissed him. He opened the door and left.

August 20, 998 ASR

Jim's convy popped up from the tubes twice, picking up more passengers. Then it linked up with a train of other convys. The 120-kilometer trip to the regional center took only twenty-five minutes.

Jim and the other passengers exited the convy amid the bustle of the regional transit center. Most people were dressed causally, while a few wore business suits or more formal attire. He wondered why business people bothered traveling when it was so much easier to conduct virtual meetings with holographic images. Then again, with virtual meetings, it was impossible to tell who was a live person and who was merely an image. He chuckled to himself, remembering attending his first virtual class dressed only in his underwear but projecting his image fully clad in a suit.

The huge room contained ten large carousels with booths around the perimeter. Each carousel contained twenty booths. Each booth could hold ten people, enough to fill a regional convy.

He located the carousel that would take him to the northwest coastal region of the continent, which was the closest regional hub to the Delta Nature Reserve. He stepped into an empty booth and stated, "Northwest regional center." As he waited, he watched convy cabs popping up like prairie dogs, and then ducking back into their burrows.

A convy appeared before him with a man and a woman sitting together near the front. He stepped in and sat down at the opposite end. The convy dropped back into the waiting area. Two minutes later it popped up again to take on a family of four, including a small child. As it dropped the third time, Jim felt a slight jolt. They had hooked up with other convy cabs, forming a train.

Jim watched the monitor at his seat, which showed the cab's status. Jim's cab was represented by a little green light; the others were yellow. The lights appeared to be moving down a tube, just as the train moved through the underground tunnels. The convy reached a cruising speed of a thousand kilometers per hour. When it approached a junction, the speed dropped to 800 KPH, and the lights veered into a side tube, where more yellow lights joined with Jim's green one.

Knowing he had a four-hour trip ahead of him, Jim settled down to catch up on the sleep he'd missed by getting up early. He took a pair of headphones from his seat's entertainment center and selected some contemporary mood music to mask the conversations of his fellow passengers. He pulled a pillow from underneath the seat and adjusted the seat back to a semi-reclining position. He was soon fast asleep.

June 7, 998 ASR

The bridge of the H.S.S.S. Ramah was quiet. The only motion was Buckly's fingers as he hurriedly entered commands so Hal could calculate a course that would take Ramah back to Earth. Chuck sat in the Captain's chair at the center of the bridge. He held his head in his hands, resting his elbows on his knees.

What have I done? I questioned a command from Sovereign Yehowshuwa and it has cost the life of a crewmember. How will I ever explain this when we get back? How will I explain it to Dave's family? Sovereign, how could you let such hideous people speak and act on your behalf? What are we doing here in the first place? Hundreds of doubts and questions raced through his mind as the burden of guilt crashed upon him.

He was startled out of his thoughts by Zophia's voice." Captain, there are twelve more ships approaching. I detected them at twenty thousand kilometers.

They will be here in two more minutes at their current speed." Alarm was evident in her face as she twisted her chair to look at Chuck.

He groaned and raised his head. "Don't they think five is enough annihilate us?"

"Sir, the five ships are pulling away in the opposite direction from the approaching ships. Eleven are closing on the five and one is coming toward us."

"Put it on the screen." Chuck's curiosity overcame his distress.

As the picture came up, he saw the aft section of five ships veering away from the ships coming into view. Flashes of light surged out from the two leading ships of the eleven. One of the pulsating streaks of light caught up with and engulfed one of the retreating ships. The shrapnel from the explosion tore through another of the squadron's ships. The two disappeared from the screen.

Chuck jumped to his feet. "I hope that was Rol-el that got blasted."

The remaining three craft returned fire but the fire balls were deflected by the pursuing ship's deflectors. Soon fourteen ships passed beyond the range of the sensors, leaving the one that had veered off to approach Ramah.

The view port changed to show the image of a woman-like creature. Her skinny body was topped with a head that was much too large for her body—clearly not human. She was completely hairless, without even eyebrows or lashes. She had no chin and a mouth so small it looked like a sock puppet. Her nose wasn't much more than a slight protrusion. Her eyes were large, dark ovals without any evidence of iris or pupil. They tilted down toward her nose and upward on the outside, pointing to where one would have expected ears. Her three fingers were much too long, with too many joints. She was dressed like Rol-el, but her uniform was jet black. She, too, had an insignia on her uniform, but it didn't resemble the one that was on Rol-el's.

"Captain Andrews," she said with sympathy, "my apologies for arriving late and my condolences for the loss of your crewmember. You must have a lot of questions about what has just happened. We are here to assist you and to ensure your safe passage to Eden."

Zophia showed another insert on the view port that displayed the newly arrived ship. Unlike the cylindrical ships that Rol-el commanded, this one was shaped like an Olympic discus with an upside-down soup bowl on top, providing a taller top section. As the woman-like creature spoke, the other eleven ships returned and flew in formation about five kilometers away.

"Thank you for your rescue," Chuck said. "If that is what it was. Our previous visitor also sounded friendly when we started talking. Do you have any messages or commands we need to follow? I don't feel much like being a target for anyone who claims to be The Sovereign's representative but doesn't act the way we know him to be."

"Rol-el did indeed speak for Sovereign Yehowshuwa and acted on his behalf. However, we believe he intended to destroy your ship whether or not you turned around. He has been known to toy with his prey. Your initial refusal to comply simply gave him an opening to initiate his plan. You could not have prevented the death of your crewmember. If you had complied immediately, he would have destroyed you later. Your delay may have cost one life, but it saved the lives of the rest of your crew."

Chuck sat down, not sure whether he should trust this strange being or not. Yet part of what she said made sense.

"My name is Tia-le. My task force was sent to ensure your safe passage by our Sovereign Rof, who is in direct conflict with Sovereign Jehov. However, we encountered resistance from Jehov's forces and were delayed. Once we got past them, we were able to monitor your communications with Rol-el as we approached. Much of what he told you is the truth. Yehowshuwa doesn't have jurisdiction in this area, and his powers are indeed limited. What Rol-el didn't tell you is that there is a Council of Enlightened Beings from which Yehowshuwa and his father have alienated themselves because of their actions on Earth. This council sent help to Earth, and for several millennia a battle has been fought between the council's forces and Yehowshuwa's. The Chancellor Ben-Shaachar is not the evil person Yehowshuwa has made him out to be. In fact his mission has been to free humanity from the bondage Yehowshuwa has imposed on your people."

"Hold on right there!" Chuck threw his hands up. "Are you saying The Sovereign is evil and that The Chancellor represents good in the universe?"

"Easy, Captain," responded Tia-le.

"Look, I'm not a history major, but everything we've ever been taught is that when The Chancellor Ben-Shaachar was loose, the earth had wars, disease, suffering, pain, and evil." Chuck stood shaking his finger at the forward view screen. "After The Last Battle, when The Chancellor was imprisoned, the earth was restored to a garden-like state. There haven't been any more wars. Disease is unknown. People live in harmony with each other. How can you say we are in bondage?"

"I'm not here to change your mind, only to make sure you get to Eden and return to Earth without harm. If you decide to return without visiting Eden, that is your choice. Unlike Rol-el, we will not force you to do anything against your will. However, when you reach Eden you will find answers that I am not able to provide. In addition, we believe Yehowshuwa has no intention of letting you return to Earth with the knowledge you now have. The only way you will be allowed to return is to make sure that every crewmember denies this encounter ever happened."

That stopped Chuck. He raised his hand. "I need some time to confer with my crew. Do you mind if we continue on toward Eden and get back to you in an hour or two? Oh, is my request going to cost anyone their life?"

"Not only will we give you time to consult with your crew, we will remain on guard and protect you. We will not attempt to monitor your conversations, as Rol-el did."

"Thank you."

"May your deliberations be inspired by the truth."

When Zophia cut the communication link with Tia-le's ship, Chuck sighed with relief. "Zophia, assemble the senior officers in my office. I want everyone there in five minutes."

Chapter 8

Samantha and her father cruised along the country road, enjoying the scenery as they took their produce to town, where it would be delivered to the world-wide food distribution network. Papa had switched the transport to automatic and was staring out the side window. Samantha turned her attention out her window. As far as she could see were fields of row crops: beans, peas, beets, carrots, squash, watermelons, and many others. Workers and equipment dotted each field, weeding, harvesting, planting, or plowing. Across the broad prairie clusters of trees surrounded farm buildings and the homes of each farm's non-commuting staff. Farther in the distance she made out larger communities, where most of the workers lived.

Samantha turned to her father. "Papa, we've been told in school that the farming country wasn't always this way. That we didn't always get just the right amount of rain every night, and the temperature hasn't always been just right to keep the plants growing year round. I even heard that people didn't used to change crops each year for six years then let it lie fallow the seventh year before starting all over again. I can't imagine that."

Papa turned and faced his daughter when she addressed him. "I can't imagine it any other way either. The Sovereign has designed the whole earth with different regions that produce certain types of food in abundance. Only a couple of thousand kilometers east of here, for example, the climate is perfect for wheat. If they got the constant rains we do, their crops would be ruined. Thanks to Yehowshuwa's organization, there has never been a lack, not since The Last Battle. It's been that way all of my 751 years on Earth."

"Some of the kids at school say they don't believe it was different before The Last Battle. They think our history books are only stories that have been made up to help keep us in line. Have you ever had thoughts like that?"

Papa paused. "It had crossed my mind a few times when I was much younger—about your age or a little older. I was afraid to say anything because admitting it would be doubting The Sovereign himself. Finally, I screwed up my courage and talked to my mama about it. She got a strange look on her face. I wasn't sure whether she was going to call down fire from the skies on my head or banish me from the family. Instead, she took a deep breath and smiled as if she'd just received a revelation. 'Son,' she said, 'let's go visit your Grandma.' The next thing I knew we were on an airplane headed for my grandmother's house."

"Great-grandma was a survivor of The Last Battle. So she would have known first hand, wouldn't she?" asked Samantha.

"That's right." Papa's eyes took on a faraway look. "For four hours I listened to Grandma relate to me about life on this planet before The Last Battle. We stayed the night, and the next morning Grandpa took me fishing. He told me that both he and Grandma had been devotees of The Chancellor until about four years before

The Last Battle. Everything they'd heard about The Sovereign up to that time they had dismissed as fairy tales, or the fabrications of a society that wanted to control people so they could stay in power and lord it over them."

Samantha understood. "That's what quite a few kids at school are saying."

"Grandpa told me he met a man who changed his mind about it all. As a result of that conversation, he changed sides and went over to Yehowshuwa's camp, even though it could mean a death sentence for desertion."

"What caused him to change his mind?"

"He finally understood that The Sovereign really was looking out for his best interest and didn't want to be a tyrant who ruled over him. Yehowshuwa was looking for people who would trust him, people he could know as friends. A lot of people in those last few years before The Last Battle didn't want to have anything to do with The Sovereign. They didn't want him to have any say over what they did. Ben-Shaachar offered them exactly what they wanted . . . or so they thought."

Samantha couldn't imagine how anyone would not trust Sovereign Yehowshuwa. She knew and trusted him since she was five.

"I came away from that fishing trip caught by a vision of Yehowshuwa that I didn't have before. I realized that my loyalty to him couldn't be based on fear of getting caught doing something wrong. I had to trust him with all my life and obey him out of gratitude. I finally came to know him, not just know about him."

Samantha squeezed her father's hand. "I'm so glad you taught me that since I was a tiny tot!"

"Me too. When my mama realized that she and Papa had missed the boat with me, she was determined to raise the rest of my brothers and sisters differently. Like I raised you."

Samantha sat quietly for a moment, pondering what her father had said. "Why didn't you tell me about your conversations with Grandma and Grandpa before?"

Papa's face turned a bit red. "I guess I felt embarrassed that I didn't understand everything sooner. Mama learned a good lesson and she passed it on to me. You and your brothers and sisters all became loyal as a result."

Samantha wrinkled up her nose. "Do you think some of my school mates' parents aren't teaching them thoroughly?"

Papa nodded. "Maybe they haven't taught their kids because they weren't taught either."

When they arrived at the distribution center, it was a beehive of activity, with transports from the surrounding farms coming and going from the various loading docks.

"I'd better check in and see where they want me." Papa switched on the truck's com center and registered his presence in the queue of trucks and transports waiting for a dock. The screen lit up, and a stern-faced young woman appeared on the screen. Behind her, people sat at other screens while a constant stream of people hurried past.

"Spell farms number 758870," she said in a flat monotone, "you are late and your docking schedule has been relinquished. You will be placed on the waiting list. You will be notified when space is available."

Samantha thought most computer voices had more warmth in their interactions than this lady.

She leaned forward, about to switch to another truck, when a man's grinning face came into focus on the com.

"Uncle Merlin, is that you, you old codger?" When he saw Samantha, his eyes lit up even more.

"Sir," objected Stern Face, "I need to manage this queue; there are people waiting."

"Cool your nanoprocessor, Helga; I'll only be a second. Merlin, I'll switch you to my post. Hang on; I'll be right with you." The screen in the truck blinked showing an empty position.

Papa beamed. "It looks like we'll be able to talk to your cousin, Tom while we're waiting."

Samantha was looking forward to seeing him again. Tom was much older than she was, but he had always been like a brother to her.

As Tom turned to go, Helga challenged him. "I suppose you're going to give him priority just because he's your uncle even though he's over thirty minutes late."

He stopped; amazed that she had challenged him. "Do you know who that man is?"

"I have no idea."

What's wrong with this lady? Doesn't she remember that she works for me? Tom tried to decide whether to lecture her or to try to teach her. "If our director were to come in here, would you tell him you don't have time to be nice to him because there are too many trucks in queue?"

Helga shook her head. "Of course not."

"If a farm director brought in a load, would you treat him the same as our director?"

Helga squinted one eye and cocked her head sideways. "Why would a director do that? Wouldn't that be beneath his station?"

"Many farm directors come into town to drop off a load when they have other business to attend to here."

She lifted her eyebrows. "Really? Who?"

Tom sighed. "Helga, you were just talking to Merlin Spell of Spell farms."

The woman turned a bit pale.

"How many other directors do you think you may have talked to as if they were chamber maids?"

Her lower lip quivered slightly, "Y-you don't think he's going to report me, do you?"

"No, but I will if you continue talking to drivers the way you just did. We are here to serve. You shouldn't let a busy schedule pressure you into being short with the drivers... or anyone else."

"Yes, Sir. I understand," she said, avoiding eye contact.

Tom lightly touched her shoulder and smiled. "Get to know these guys and lighten up. You'll enjoy your work more and they will too. We can start here. My name is Tom, not Sir."

Helga mumbled, "Ok," and turned back to her station.

Tom proceeded to his post and sat down in front of his terminal. "So, Uncle Merlin, Cousin Sam, how are you guys?"

"Just great," Merlin replied. "It's been a while since I've seen you. How have you been?"

"Very well, considering..." Tom's eager spirit dropped a bit. "I have to admit it seems to be getting harder every year to find dispatchers who are people oriented, and that makes my job harder. That and the increased demand as the world grows more populated have added more stress. Things sure have changed since I was out in the fields a couple hundred years ago. Maybe I should go back."

"Who would keep the distribution center running? You know that place would fall apart without you."

Tom brightened. "Thanks, Uncle, but we both know I'm only small potatoes here." He glanced at the monitor in front of him. "Hey, I've got level 10 bay 18 available in five minutes. Why don't I meet you there and we can talk while you unload? I can get one of your bear hugs too."

"Think you can break free for a cup of coffee with Sam and me afterward?"

"Sounds good. See you in five." Tom clicked off, feeling more light-hearted than he had in a long time.

Samantha watched the com in Papa's truck light up as it beeped clearance to the dock.

Papa glanced at her. "How would you like to take it in?"

"Really?" Samantha was thrilled that her father trusted her to guide the big transport into the dock. "Thanks, Papa."

She switched controls to her seat then brought the truck up to thirty-six meters, the height of the tenth-floor docking bays. She slowly curved around the great, round building until she came to the east side, where bay 18 was located. Outside the bay she rotated the truck until the tail faced the bay, then backed in. Inside the bay she dropped the truck and gently set it on the floor.

Samantha and Papa hopped out of the cab as Tom came running up. They greeted one another with hugs, Samantha being lifted off her feet by Tom. A fleet of forklifts approached the truck from every direction. In two minutes the truck was empty and the com beeped, signaling them to leave and make room for the next transport. All three scrambled into the cab, with Tom in the backseat.

"Take us out, Sam," said Papa.

"If I'd known Sam was driving, I would have met you at the coffee shop," Tom kidded. Samantha reached back and swatted him on the arm.

August 20, 998 ASR

Professor Robison returned from his summer dig and went straight to his small studio apartment near the University of Midrib. He plopped down on his cluttered couch and stared at the ceiling for a few minutes. His mind raced back to the events that led up to his summer.

The previous winter he placed Eric, his most valued assistant, on an extended leave. The professor's demanding schedule had worn Eric out. For years the professor used him to coordinate every detail of his digs. The equipment they needed, the students who did most of the physical labor, temporary housing, food, and transportation were all under Eric's supervision.

When Eric contracted a minor illness, the professor suggested he slow down. Instead he continued his schedule. The combined work and illness weakened him to the point that he collapsed.

It shouldn't have happened. Even in The Sovereign's near-perfect environment, people can wreak havoc on their own bodies by ignoring sensible lifestyles.

He felt responsible for pushing Eric so hard. Once the young man recovered physically, the professor insisted he take an extended leave. Eric took a long camping trip before returning to work. He selected an area eight hundred kilometers to the northeast of the world capital. The rugged mountains had long been considered the most unlikely place to find anything of archeological value, which is precisely why Professor Robison suggested it. He didn't want Eric to get sidetracked when he was supposed to be relaxing.

March 24, 998 ASR

Eric started his leave by hiking in the mountains that The Sovereign Yehowshuwa had named *Haunt for Jackals*. The hike was easy as he followed game trails through lush green trees: apple, pear, cherry, mango, avocado, orange, banana, and many other non-fruit trees. Some were in full bloom; others were in various stages of ripeness. He didn't need to go far to find a snack or a meal. He planned to live off the land but had expected it to be more difficult.

He set his sights on a particular mountain, determined to reach its peak in two days. When he reached that objective, he surveyed the mountains and valleys before him. He picked out a valley with a crystal blue lake about thirty kilometers to the north as his next target.

Eric took almost two months before he was able to stop conquering peaks and setting goals for how much territory he could explore each day. He had no schedules imposed on him and stopped creating them for himself. Instead he took time to meditate about life and to look within himself to find out what was important. He felt that this was now the most significant time of his life. He slowed down to examine the beauty of creation and meditate.

As he looked within, he felt a strange sensation, as if the land were reaching out to lead him. Every day, he let his feelings guide him from mountain to valley, from tree to river. He felt as if they were calling to him so they could show him what they had in store.

He was meditating early one morning when he felt that the mountain was warning him of danger. He looked up and saw a violent storm sweep up the valley toward his camp on the mountainside. The wind increased in strength, snapping and uprooting trees as it moved toward him.

Eric grabbed his pack and crawled under a rock outcropping just as a tree flattened the ground where he had been camped. Another tree fell onto the outcropping with such force that it broke off a large slab that had been his main protection. The last thing he remembered was dropping into the earth and losing consciousness.

When Eric came to, he discovered he was in the entrance to a cave, and it was calling him inward. He found the solar-powered lamp in his pack and spent a few hours exploring the cavern, going several kilometers into the depth of the mountain.

The beam of light from the lamp reflected off something metallic. He found twisted pieces of steel and other debris that could only have come from a building of the previous era. *This could be one of the most important archeological finds ever. I've got to reach Professor Robison.*

Eric scrambled back to the surface, where the storm had subsided. He rummaged through his pack for his ECD, which he hadn't used for over a month except to keep a journal. He opened it, logged his present position, and sent a priority message to the professor. Because of the time difference, he knew the professor would probably be inaccessible immediately. The next hour and half seemed like an eternity to him. Finally his ECD beeped.

Professor Robison's unshaven face appeared on the screen. "Eric, I just got up and saw your priority message. Are you OK?" He rubbed his eyes.

"You won't believe what I just found," he said, his words tumbling over one another. "I've been wandering all over these mountains and got knocked into a cave by a storm, and I explored the cave and found what must be a pre–Last Battle city buried under the mountain. I've checked the coordinates and I believe it could be The Chancellor Ben-Shaachar's capital! You have to get here as soon as you can and take a look."

The professor's eyes flew wide open. "We need to verify that before we tell anyone about this."

Eric agreed that they should keep it quiet until they could verify the find's significance. Eric said he would hike out part of the way and the professor promised to send a private craft to get him.

May 12, 998 ASR

Professor Robison arranged for a colleague to supervise his previously planned dig. He said only that he needed a break and that Eric had found incredible refreshment in the mountains, so he planned on joining him for the summer.

Two and a half weeks later, after he finished his last lecture for the year, Professor Robison hurried to the regional transport center and left for Lashib in the Middle East. He had already packed his clothes, so there was no need to return to his apartment before starting this mysterious journey.

Early the next morning Eric met the professor at the Lashib transportation center. Professor Robison inventoried the supplies Eric had already loaded into the private transport. Satisfied that they had what they needed, the professor engaged the automatic navigation system to depart for the *Haunt of Jackals*, about a hundred kilometers away. At the edge of the small town, a couple of startled residents stared at them as they passed.

"I'll bet they've never seen a private transport in this sleepy little village," said the professor as he waved to them and they waved back.

Once they came to the mountains, the transport soared over the trees and hills into the center of the region where the cave was located. As they approached the cave, Professor Robison took over controls. Eric pointed out the clearing he had prepared, and the professor set the transport down in the middle of it. Robison licked his lips, certain that he was about to engage in the most thrilling discovery he had ever experienced.

Over the next three months the two men mapped out numerous caverns and passageways through a city that had been turned upside down and buried for a thousand years. As they worked their way deeper into the caves, they found the charred remains of the city that had been closest to the surface when it was destroyed. Everything they found suggested that this had indeed been Chancellor Ben-Shaachar's capital. This was the most important find in recent history.

August 20, 998 ASR

Professor Robison sat in his messy apartment, wondering how best to break the news to the world. Would this change people's perspective of the past and reshape their future? *The first thing I need to do is compile our findings and share them with the archeological community.*

Professor Robison's thoughts were interrupted by his doorbell. He stood, still weary from his return trip. *Who could that be?* He opened the door and was greeted by two men in black suits, white shirts, narrow black ties, and faces that seemed to glow.

"Professor Robison, you need to come with us," they stated in unison.

"Who are you?"

"You will find out in a few moments," they answered again in unison.

He looked into their eyes and felt as if he were being transported into another realm. He started to relax. "Is this my time? But I have so much left to do."

"You have completed your mission quite successfully," they both said. The two men each took one of the professor's elbows, and one picked up his ECD. Everything around him blurred as he passed out of the physical realm.

June 7, 998 ASR

Chuck, Demetrius, and Zophia hustled across the corridor to the Captain's office. Chuck opened the door and marched to his desk, then turned and sat in one of the plush visitor chairs. He motioned for the others to be seated. He looked at the floor, discouraging any conversation until the others arrived. Zophia and Demetrius whispered back and forth.

Chuck looked up when Marti, the operations officer, came in. She had smudges of soot on her face and her jumper. She looked at the others and sat beside Demetrius. Neither made a comment.

Alex, the biological officer, arrived next, a pair of surgical gloves poking out of his shirt pocket. He sat in the remaining visitor chair.

"Marti, Alex," Chuck asked, "how much of what just happened have you been following?"

"Sorry, Chuck," Marti answered. "I've been mopping up after the fire in Dave's cabin, so I haven't been able to follow much. All I know is that some weird space pirates wanted us to turn around, and they blew Dave away to make a point. Then someone else showed up and chased them off."

Chuck groaned inwardly. "I'm glad your people are well trained; otherwise, that fire could have finished us off. Thanks."

"I only know as much as Marti," Alex said. "I've been taking care of Dave's remains." He choked back a sob. "I've never seen a death before, much less one caused by the purposeful act of another."

Chuck sniffed back a tear too. "I think you both need to hear everything that went on today. You may want to take notes."

As they took out their ECDs, Chuck turned to Zophia. "Play back the entire confrontation, starting with the first words we were able to understand from Rol-el. Use as many screens as you need to display our visitors and the bridge."

"Sure. Hal, play back the bridge log, from when you were first able to translate Rol-el's transmissions until I cut off the transmission with Tia-le. Put the bridge conversations and video on one half of the screen and everything that was on the bridge's view screen on the other side."

The view screen in Chuck's office came to life, with Rol-el on the right and a view of the bridge on the left, the Captain sitting in his chair in the center.

For the next few minutes they all sat quietly as the entire encounter was replayed before their eyes. At each revelation about The Sovereign, Marti and Alex squirmed in their seats. For Chuck, it didn't sound so far off the second time around, but it was still unnerving each time he heard the accusations against Yehowshuwa. When the replay stopped they all sat in silence for a couple of minutes.

Chuck broke the silence. "OK, people, we have some decisions to make. The first is whether or not we continue on to Eden. This will be a brainstorming session. We'll record everything without comment then discuss the options after we've run out of ideas. We'll start with the reasons for going on to Eden. Hal, record these pros on the screen under that heading. Everyone, speak up and say whatever is on your mind."

"We've come this far," said Zophia. "It would seem a shame to turn back now."

"We have a promise of more answers to questions," contributed Demetrius.

"This may prove whether or not these claims about the real nature of The Sovereign are true," ventured Alex.

"We owe it those on Earth to find the truth," said Marti

Demetrius spoke again. "Tia-le risked her life to enable us to continue."

Alex's face reddened. "I'd do it just for Dave."

"If The Sovereign doesn't want us to find out what's there, maybe that's a good reason to continue," said Zophia. A few eyebrows rose at that comment but no one objected to the contribution.

Zophia's comment sparked a thought in Chuck's mind. "We don't know for sure The Sovereign sent Rol-el to stop us."

"Whether we go or return," Marti added, "we may face the same problems when we eventually return. Once we're out of Tia-le's protection, we could be dead meat."

"If we don't go, and The Sovereign wanted us to, we will have missed a great opportunity," said Zophia.

The comments kept coming for another minute or so, as Hal displayed them on the screen in a neat column. Eventually the room grew quiet.

"OK, Hal, set up another column. This one will be reasons to return to Earth immediately."

Alex provided the first reason. "More people may die if we are disobeying Sovereign Yehowshuwa, so returning could save lives."

Demetrius rubbed his chin. "Tia-le may be lying about what we will find. It could be a waste of time."

"We haven't found life anywhere else," offered Zophia.

Chuck grimaced. *I don't need to be reminded of that.* He thought back to the blasphemies he had heard spoken by both Rol-el and Tia-le and added, "This may prove whether or not the claims abut the real nature of The Sovereign are true."

"Hey, you can't use the same thing for both pro and con," Alex said.

Chuck frowned. "Remember, discussions come afterward. For now, let's keep going."

"We could be walking into a trap." Marti trembled. "If we return now, and it is what Yehowshuwa wants, he may forgive our reluctance to obey when we were first told to return."

That seemed to be consistent with The Sovereign that Chuck knew.

"Tia-le may not be able to protect us from a heavier attack," Demetrius offered.

The ideas slowed until everyone sat intently looking at the screen.

"I think it's time to start discussing the reasons. Let's take the first reason to go on. 'We've come this far; it would be a shame to turn back now.' Do we need any expansion or clarification on that?" Chuck looked expectantly at the others.

Zophia started. "We've spent a good chunk of our lives going from place to place and haven't found anything. It makes sense to me to continue on our mission. I hate to leave anything undone, especially when we've spent so much time on it."

"I concur," said Alex, "it's a good reason to keep going."

Chuck moved on to the next point. "Tia-le promised we will have our questions answered more fully once we arrive at Eden."

Demetrius fidgeted. "I don't think we can base our decisions on Tia-le's comments and Rol-el's actions against us. How can we be sure these guys aren't in cahoots with each other and this is some kind of setup?"

"We can't be sure of anything they tell us," Marti responded. "They would have to be conspiring together to both have essentially the same concepts of the universe. Why would Rol-el get himself blown up if it was a trick?"

Chuck agreed. He couldn't imagine how Rol-el and Tia-le could be aligned in any way. "They have a lot more fire power than we do. They could force us to stop at any time, board us, and take whatever they want. If they're leading us into a trap, they're wasting a lot of time."

Demetrius' knee jostled up and down. "Good points, but what if Tia-le isn't able to protect us? What if some of Rol-el's buddies come back with a bigger force than Tia-le can handle? If we head home, we might be able to make it before they catch up with us."

Chuck wasn't sure they were making any headway. "I think the most difficult thing is that all this directly challenges everything we know about The Sovereign. If what they are saying is true, what should we do? Would anyone believe us if we returned now and told this story? No. They'd think we were all crazy for challenging who he is."

Marti stared at Chuck. "I agree. The credibility of The Sovereign is what's really at stake here. If he isn't who he says he is then we need to do whatever we can to reveal that to the world. If these guys are all lying, we need to alert the world to the fact that there's something going on out here that is in direct opposition to Sovereign Yehowshuwa." She hesitated. "You know, I really miss Dave right now. He would have been able to help us sort out all this stuff about The Sovereign."

Demetrius poked a pudgy finger toward Marti. "I know what you mean. He was the only one of us who knew Yehowshuwa personally, or at least that's the way he described it. I don't know if he ever met him in person, but he certainly talked about knowing him. He was a pain in the neck sometimes because of it. Remember the time he came down on Henry and Barbara about their relationship? We didn't think anything wrong was going on, but he knew, just as if The Sovereign himself had told him they were out of line."

"You're right," Chuck said. "He kind of became our spiritual leader after that incident." He took a deep breath. "I know what Dave would do at a time like this. He would pray. Before we go any further, I think we should too." He slipped out of his chair and knelt on the floor. The other four also knelt in a circle.

"Dear Sovereign," Chuck prayed, "we call you sovereign because that's what we've always believed you to be. Now we have people telling us that you are limited and that you are holding us in bondage. I guess if you are sovereign you already know that. If you aren't, you can't even hear our prayers. So if you can hear us, we need your help in understanding what to do and where to go. Help us to make sense of all this."

When Chuck stopped speaking, Marti stammered through a brief prayer. The others, in turn, expressed their doubts. When it came to Zophia's turn they all waited for her to pray.

After a long silence she spoke. "Sovereign, this would be a good time for you to send an Enforcer, an Encourager, a Messenger. Maybe Berekiah. I mean, if it wasn't for his clues we wouldn't even be in this mess."

"Amen," Chuck said with a groan.

Chapter 9

Jim woke with a start as the computer interrupted his music to inform him that he had arrived at the Northwest Coast Regional Center. It told him that he would need to transfer to a local convy to get to the tri-cities area.

He stopped at a restroom then decided to get a snack at one of the many cafeterias that surrounded the regional center's hub. As he moseyed by each café, he scanned the menu, hoping to find something exotic he hadn't tried before. The first two cafeterias only offered sandwiches, vegetables, and fruit dishes. *Boring.* The third advertised a promising-sounding dish: Kentucky Burgoo. The ingredients were beef, veal, chicken, and squirrels (when available) along with mixed vegetables, brown sugar, and flour. Then again, that sounded a little too much like stew. Jim kept looking. The next café had Boeuf a La Mode. *Beef with ice cream?* It turned out to be pot roast braised in red wine. *Probably very tasty, but not eclectic enough.* He continued on until he found a menu that listed Anquilash: baby eel cooked whole, served in sizzling olive oil with garlic and bits of red-hot peppers.

Now, that is weird! He entered the cafeteria and picked up a tray. After placing his order, he selected a pre-made salad and an iced tea, then found a seat and waited for his entrée.

After a few minutes a wrinkled dark-skinned man with brown eyes and white hair brought his order, placed it on the table, and sat opposite him. Jim stared at him in amazement. The older gentleman looked so much like him; he could have been his father.

"You must be Quebash," said the old man as his eyes roved over Jim's face. "Why else would someone so young ask for such a dish?"

"I was just looking for something different to eat, and this was the most unusual thing I could find in the station." Jim wondered why this man would sit with a customer and ask such a blunt question. "What is Quebash anyway?" he asked as he took his first bite of eel.

The old man's eyes brightened. "We are a very small race of people who have remained pure from the beginning of time. Our ancestors and our language have survived from the time when the Earth's one language was turned into many in the far ancient past. We alone have kept the original language spoken by the first man and woman—the language of the Creator. We predate The Sovereign Yehowshuwa's own people by several thousand years. Where they pride themselves in keeping their lineage pure, we have accomplished it far longer without flaunting it . . . and without The Sovereign's protection."

The old guy likes to talk, Jim thought, considering his boastings to be a bunch of old folks' tales. He continued to relish the ethnic dish as the old man babbled on.

"When Chancellor Ben-Shaachar was at the height of his power, our people steadfastly resisted him. While some were aided by Yehowshuwa, most of us hid in the mountains and caused great damage to The Chancellor's forces using our own resources. We did as our ancestors had whenever our land was invaded by those who would bend us to their will."

As he continued to tell the history of the Quebash people, Jim felt something stir inside him. Though he had never heard about these people, he felt somehow that he belonged with them. Yet he also felt cautious, not wanting to be drawn in. "Why are you telling me this?"

The old man sat back and smiled. "I wanted to see for myself who would ask for this dish. The moment I saw you, I knew you had to be Quebash. Not only that, but I perceive that, like most people, especially those in these last generations, you have lost your roots. Hardly anyone today can trace their ethnicity, so I like to tell folks about ours."

This guy really, really likes to talk.

"My name is Josu Taratoricakena. Before The Last Battle, my grandmother of six generations ago was well known among our people. She sparked a renewed interest in preserving our culture and led the way for establishing our transnational and cosmopolitan identity. Many of us believe that had this not been done, we would have been completely absorbed in the years before The Last Battle."

What makes him think I need or even want to know all this?

"So, what is your name?"

He looked at his near-empty plate. "Jim."

"I mean your family name."

"Arizna."

Josu rubbed his chin. "Could be Quebash. Perhaps it is only half a name."

Jim chewed on an eel and thought for a second. "Yeah, it is. My dad shortened it to make it easier for his coworkers. Our full name was Ariznabattera. My mom's parents' name is Iturri. That was shortened from Iturri-berry-gory or something like that."

Josu almost hopped up and down in his seat. "Iturriberrigorrigoikoettoraqueoera! It is one of the longest surnames of all our people!" He clapped his hands. "Your parents and grandparents distanced themselves from our people. Do you know why?"

Josu was being awfully blunt for someone he had just met. Even so, Jim was warming up to the old man. "I haven't been close to my parents and have seldom seen my grandparents. I don't even know if any of their family is still alive."

Josu leaned closer. "The Quebash are closely knit, but we are also an independent people who tend to be rebellious. That rebellious nature has overcome the cohesiveness of our people in recent years." He raised one eyebrow and squinted with his other eye. "Tell me; are your parents and grandparents relatively young, all less than sixty years old?"

Jim did a mental calculation. "Yeah, so?"

"As I thought. I sense the same thing in you, Jim: rebelliousness and suspicion, especially of older people. You are probably suspicious of me. Right?"

Jim sat back in his seat. "You're right. I am suspicious of most older people. I don't want to be molded into someone else's idea of who I am or what I should do. I want to be free. Yet I feel strangely drawn to what you've told me about the Quebash."

Josu pointed at Jim's heart. "It's in your blood, son. You are indeed Quebash. We call out to one another, even those who are unaware of who they are. As for your lofty philosophies, how do you expect to be your own person in this world, with The Sovereign in control? I suppose you are even suspicious of him."

Jim looked around to see if anyone might be listening to their conversation. He lowered his voice. "We're in public. Are you trying to get us in trouble?"

Josu laughed. "Don't worry. It is no crime to be suspicious. Besides, if anyone were to get into trouble, it would be me, not you. I am the one suggesting you could be suspicious of The Sovereign. However, I can see from your reaction that what I've said is true. I, too, have many unanswered questions but few people to share them with."

Jim was shocked but also excited to find an older person who expressed things so close to his own heart. "I thought everyone over a hundred were all dyed-in-the-wool Sovereign loyalists," he whispered.

For the next hour Jim shared with Josu some of the things he had learned at school from *The Question* and related discussion groups.

"I have not heard of this newsletter," Josu said. "I have little contact with people your age outside my own family. I would like very much to learn more. Do you think I could get on the mailing list?"

Jim hesitated. "I don't know. I'll have to talk to one of the guys who enroll new people. Someone would have to meet with you first. They implement a lot of security to ensure it doesn't fall into the wrong hands and get us all in trouble."

Jim looked at his watch and gasped at the time. "I've got to get going. Give me your ID and I'll get back to you about the newsletter."

Jim and Josu exchanged their ECD IDs and then stood to leave. Josu gave Jim a bear hug. It caught him off guard, but he returned it with enthusiasm.

June 7, 998 ASR

Tsvar and Bartholomew were having lunch together in a small café near the center of New Yeruwshalayim, The Sovereign Yehowshuwa's city in his alternate realm. Tsvar had selected a small table in a corner where they wouldn't be noticed. He had long ago discovered that members of The Sovereign's High Council tended to draw attention in public.

The Sovereign appeared and stood between them at the edge of their table. His dark brown eyes sadly matched his down-turned mouth that was almost hidden by his short black beard. Before they could get on their knees, he reached out his muscular arms and touched each of them on his shoulder.

"Remain seated, my friends. I have come to show you what is taking place far off in our galaxy."

In an instant all three were watching the drama of the spaceship and its encounter with Rol-el. Tsvar saw everything unfold as if he were on H.S.S.S. Ramah's bridge as well as suspended in outer space along with the monstrous spaceship and other vessels, both at the same time. He never lost his sense of awe when Yehowshuwa gave him a glimpse of what it was like to be aware of events from multiple perspectives.

As Rol-el discussed his relationship to The Sovereign, Tsvar could feel the agitation of the crewmembers on the bridge.

Tsvar was feeling his own outrage at what he heard as well. "I would be upset, too, if I were in their place."

Tsvar and Bartholomew jumped slightly when the fire ball emerged from one of Rol-el's ships and crashed into the Earth vessel.

Dave found himself floating in outer space, his heart filled with joy and calmness. Floating along with him were three other people. One's curly dark brown hair covered the tops of his ears and blended with his beard. His hooknose, long face, royal white robe, and golden sash clearly identified him. *Ah, Yehowshuwa, my Sovereign is here, no wonder I feel too good to be real.* He didn't recognize the others, but somehow knew their names were Tsvar and Bartholomew. *That's the way it works in dreams.*

Dave enjoyed being able to realize that he was having a dream without waking up until he was ready. He liked seeing how the dreams played out without fear of falling or other things that caused most people to open their eyes in panic. In fact he delighted in the sensation of falling from a great height but landing softly . . . with the exception of the time he rolled out of bed and was rudely awakened.

In this dream he was looking at his ship, accompanied by five other crafts, each of which was so small it could have only held one person. The Sovereign was intently observing the confrontation between Ramah and the aliens.

Dave wanted to approach Yehowshuwa but held back. He turned his attention to the conversation between Chuck and Rol-el.

Oh, my. They think I got zapped by space desperadoes claiming to work for The Sovereign Yehowshuwa!

When Tia-le's rescue occurred, Dave cheered her guys on. "That's the way to show those fakers and teach them to malign The Sovereign," he yelled.

He watched in disbelief as she confirmed Rol-el's story. *I don't like this dream anymore. I think I'll wake up now.* But Dave couldn't wake himself up. The vision continued.

"Sovereign, what is going on?" he finally asked.

The Sovereign turned and gazed at him. His eyes twinkled and his face radiated a soft soothing light. His white robe sparkled as if it had millions of sequins reflecting rainbows from every angle... except he was the source of the light. "Wait and see. I'll explain everything in a few minutes," he said calmly.

Dave's peace and calm immediately returned.

His vision followed Chuck off the bridge and took him through the deliberations with the ship's officers. After he watched the crew kneel and pray to The Sovereign Yehowshuwa, the vision changed. Dave and his three companions were now floating among the stars while the H.S.S.S. Ramah and its escorts sped away.

"What you have seen is the view from the crew's perspective," said Yehowshuwa, "not mine."

"Are you really going to let them get away with that, Sovereign?" the one named Tsvar asked.

"For now, yes," answered Yehowshuwa. "I have no doubt things will work out the way we want."

"Lord," said Bartholomew, "I know you'll make it right. However, this just sticks in my craw! Ornery bunch of disobedient Yahoos. I never would have let them go in the first place. Now I'd wipe them off the map." He snapped his fingers. "Like that."

"That's what James and John said once, too, but I had other plans," said Yehowshuwa. "Their time will come."

Bartholomew and Tsvar disappeared, and Dave found himself standing on the grassy bank of a gently flowing river. Yehowshuwa faced him. Behind The Sovereign Dave saw a huge building in the distance, at the top of a hill that appeared to be the source of the river. He felt certain he'd been here before, many years ago.

Dave looked into Yehowshuwa's glowing eyes. "This isn't a dream, is it?"

"No." He put his arm around Dave. "You and I need to have a little chat." The two walked upstream. Dave had never felt such joy. He felt completely at home, with the one person in the universe he wanted to be with forever.

August 20, 998 ASR

Marilyn awoke to loud noises from the kitchen. She groggily sat up in bed, having tossed and turned most of the night. She finally fell asleep only an hour earlier and now someone seemed to be rattling every pot and pan in the house. She threw on her robe and stumbled downstairs, only to find her son cleaning the seeds out of a cantaloupe.

He looked up as she entered the kitchen and almost tripped over a huge backpack lying on the floor. His fine brown hair was slightly mussed but neatly trimmed around his ears. The clean-shaven, strong jaw and piercing brown eyes made her proud to be his mother when he was dressed up in a suit like yesterday, but not when he wore those baggy trousers with too many pockets and ugly University of Midrib T shirt. He looked wimpy and bottom heavy. *Yesterday? Something isn't right.*

"Robert, what are doing?" She glanced at the kitchen clock. "It's six in the morning."

"Don't you remember?" he chirped. "I've booked the cabin in the Delta Nature Reserve and I'm leaving today. Jim and I are spending a week there before school starts."

Vague memories from a dream she'd been having before the sounds woke her up filtered through her subconscious. She couldn't remember any details . . .

except that a loved one had died. She could still feel pain and anger stirring deep inside.

Marilyn's blurry mind cleared slowly as she remembered why she'd had trouble falling asleep. It wasn't a dream, it was Robert. After the family got home from Robert's hearing with the community Board, he refused to listen to her and give up his silly idea about writing a book on The Last Battle. In her agitation she yelled at him even more than usual. He fled to his room, slamming the door. Marilyn went to bed frustrated and angry with Robert over his insubordination.

"You aren't going anywhere until we get this book mess straightened out," she demanded, now wide-awake.

Robert's shoulders sagged and his cheeriness disappeared. "Sure, Mom." He sliced off a chunk of cantaloupe. "Want some?" he asked, holding up the slice.

"Not now, thank you," she answered sharply.

Robert flinched and then sighed as he put the melon on his plate. "Well, I think the first step in getting this 'mess' straightened out is to define what the mess is. Then we can formulate a plan of action to resolve the problem. Make sense?"

Marilyn didn't like it when her son used logic against her. "You went against my wishes, pursuing more education and writing a book that I believe is nonsense and a waste of time instead of getting a job and contributing to society." She stared him in the eye.

Robert turned away, continued slicing the cantaloupe and didn't look up again. "So you have a plan for my life, and I haven't followed that plan. You also figure the only way to get out of the 'mess' is for me to get on the road you have established for me."

Marilyn decided to fight Robert's cynicism with some of her own. "By golly, I think you hit the nail on the head," she said in a happy tone.

Robert put the knife and melon on the kitchen counter and replied in an overly cheery voice. "I'd really like to try, but I don't know how to undo all that happened yesterday. The book is a stupid idea, I admit. I probably couldn't get more than one chapter done anyway. So what can I do about the Board's decision? They expect me to go back to school then work on that book. How can I get out of that?"

Marilyn eyed Robert warily. "I know you're putting me on. So knock it off and get serious."

Robert put a slice of wheat bread in the toaster. "I am serious, well, kind of. Even if I wanted to, I don't think there's any way I could get out of this. When I filed for a motion for employment and it was approved, I entered into a legal contract with the Board, the Administration, and even The Sovereign. I can't go back and say, 'Oops, sorry, I made a mistake. My mommy doesn't want me do this. Please excuse me and let me try something else.'" He raised the pitch of his voice to imitate a child.

Marilyn stomped her foot and smacked a hand on the counter. "Don't talk to me that way."

Her son met her intense stare and spoke evenly and quietly, "I'm a grown man, Mother. I have a contract. They aren't going to let me out of it unless there's sufficient cause."

Marilyn changed tactics suddenly. "I have an idea."

"What?" The toaster dinged that his bread was ready, but he kept his gaze on her.

"Go back to school but do something that invalidates your contract. Like forget to register. Or miss your required classes. That way you won't have to write the book and you can start some other employment."

He rolled his eyes and turned to get his toast. "I'm already registered for the class, so I'll have to go to school for at least the first session next week. Maybe I could skip enough classes to get kicked out. Or flunk the tests on purpose."

Marilyn felt her face get warm. "Don't patronize me."

"Yes, Mom. I'll take your desires under serious consideration." He appeared serious. He opened the refrigerator and put a plate of butter on the counter. "Look, I'm still heading off to meet Jim for our before-school getaway. If, after this week, your idea makes sense to me, I'll do as you wish and find a way out of the contract."

"Thanks, Robert."

"I love you, Mom, but I really need to get going." He gave her a hug, picked up his pack and headed for the door.

"I love you too," Marilyn called after him. "And please be careful!"

She watched the empty doorway to the kitchen until she heard the front door close. She turned and looked at the plate with a slice of melon and toast on it beside the butter dish. *Dang, he did it again. He escaped. I'll bet he's going to go right ahead and make a fool of himself trying to write this book. He'll embarrass himself and our whole family.*

June 7, 998 ASR

Chuck got off his knees and returned to his seat. The other officers followed suit.

I'm out of my area of expertise when it comes to prayer. The others avoided eye contact with one another, as if they were thinking the same thing. He wondered if Sovereign Yehowshuwa had heard what they said and whether he would answer their requests, especially Zophia's asking for Berekiah to show up and help them sort out what to do.

Zophia's eyes widened as she looked beyond Chuck. Marti and Alex turned slightly and stared in the same direction. Chuck followed their gazes and saw a short, stout man wearing a faded, loose-fitting floral print shirt, baggy trousers, sandals without socks, and a light blue yarmulke. His full beard was wiry but well groomed. He grinned from ear to ear.

"Hi. My name is Berekiah." He stretched out his hands, waist high, a bit wider than his hips, palms facing the crewmembers. He cocked his head to one side, raised his eyebrows, and rotated his hands slightly as if to say, *"Well, folks, what are you waiting for? I'm here. Start asking questions."*

Chuck cleared his throat. "Are you the one who sent the clue to Zophia before we launched?"

"I am. I am also here in direct response to her prayer to The Sovereign. So, is there anything I can help you with?"

Chuck groped for words. "Yes . . . uh . . . I don't know where to begin."

"How about at the beginning?"

Berekiah's cavalier attitude irritated Chuck. *He seems to be enjoying our distress.* "Hey, this is serious business. We've already lost one crewmember and we don't know what could happen next."

Berekiah toned down his facial appearance a bit. "I know. I'm very sorry that you lost a respected crewmember. Still, perhaps the beginning of this unpleasant encounter would be a good place to start."

Chuck relaxed a bit. "OK. Who is this Rol-el guy? He says he's working for Jehov and that Jehov and The Sovereign are in league with each other. Is that true?"

Berekiah answered with a straight face. "Yes."

"How can that be? He said The Sovereign didn't have any jurisdiction here," Demetrius pointed out. "Yet you're here in response to our prayer. How can both be true?"

The edges of Berekiah's mouth curled up slightly. "You have drawn two incorrect conclusions. The first is that I'm with Yehowshuwa's Administration; the second is that he sent me."

"If you aren't with the Administration," asked Marti, "who are you with?"

Berekiah's face beamed as he broke into an ear-to-ear-toothy-eyebrow-raised-wide-eyed grin. "I work for The Chancellor Ben-Shaachar."

Chuck drew back slightly.

Demetrius spoke what Chuck was wondering. "The Chancellor and his minions have been imprisoned since The Last Battle. How could you be working for him?"

The corners of Berekiah's face dropped, letting his jowls droop. "Yes, he is still in prison at this time. Nevertheless he will soon be freed. My colleagues and I escaped over forty years ago and have been working on his plan to free him ever since. That is why your message from me had to be a clue instead of blatant directions that might have been filtered out by the Administration. The fact that I'm standing here before you proves that Yehowshuwa isn't totally sovereign."

I'm not sure whether to believe this guy or not.

"I know this is quite a shock to you. However, we have gained a great deal of power since I first escaped. We are now able to move freely without being detected. The Sovereign doesn't have any idea I'm here talking to you."

"What about Tia-le?" Chuck asked. "Is she who she says she is? Is the man she works for one of Ben-Shaachar's friends?"

"I wouldn't necessarily call Rof and The Chancellor friends. A better description would be allies. They both report to the Council of Enlightened Beings. Each has his own assignment and carries it out with a certain amount of autonomy. Seldom is there a need for cooperative efforts such as this."

"Is she able to protect us if we continue to Eden?" Zophia asked.

Again Berekiah's countenance erupted with his characteristic huge grin. "Tia-le and her forces are quite capable of ensuring your safe conduct to Eden and back to the borders of Yehowshuwa's domain. You see, Rol-el was far from home when he intercepted you, and Jehov's forces are sparse in this area. Rof is more powerful than Jehov, and he wouldn't risk another attack while you have an escort."

Berekiah stepped forward a bit forming a semicircle with the officers around him. Demetrius, who stood beside the Captain, wrung his hands. "You said she can conduct us to the borders of The Sovereign's domain. What happens when we pass those borders? Won't Sovereign Yehowshuwa be upset with us for going to Eden, not to mention going under Rof's protection? Sounds like we could be charged with treason."

That thought had also been at the forefront of Chuck's mind.

"That would appear to be a problem, wouldn't it?" Berekiah stroked his beard with his thumb and forefinger. "Well, let me assure you that The Chancellor will provide you with all the protection you'll need to keep your fact-finding trip to Eden concealed from Yehowshuwa. He will also assist you in disseminating any information you gather to the rest of the population on Earth."

Chuck couldn't imagine how Ben-Shaachar could help him distribute treasonous information to the rest of the world even if he wanted to.

"I will not deceive you, though. There will be great risk once the data has been released. Yehowshuwa will not be happy. If you decide to continue on to Eden and then choose to reveal what you have found to the rest of the world, you will join in a cosmic battle that has been going on for millennium. However, we believe the end result will be an Earth that will be like Eden. Mankind will be completely free. Chancellor Ben-Shaachar and his servants, me included, are committed to that outcome."

Alex looked warily at Berekiah. "What's so important about Eden that we need to go there?"

Berekiah's eyes narrowed. He looked directly into Zophia's eyes, paused, and then went around the room looking intently at each person, finishing with Chuck. "I'll let you know in a moment, but first, tell me, if I were to ask each of you right now to report what you've seen and heard so far, risking punishment as traitors, would you do it?"

The officers looked at one another. Chuck answered first. "No way! It appears to me that you are claiming that The Sovereign isn't omnipotent and omniscient. Even worse, you are implying that he is some kind of bad guy, the exact opposite of everything we have believed all our lives. I'd need more concrete evidence that what you and Tia-le have been saying is true. So far all we have is five hostile ships, eleven friendly ships manned by some strange-looking people, and your testimony. I don't think that would be enough to convince billions of people that The Sovereign is evil and that we should jump on your bandwagon to help you do that. Are you saying there is something at Eden that will convince us and sway the population of Earth?"

Berekiah clapped his hands. "Yes. Yes. Yes. At Eden you will see proof. A planet populated with people who have lived outside The Sovereign Yehowshuwa's rule and influence for thousands of years. You will be able to conduct interviews with leaders and common people. I believe you will be thoroughly convinced by the time you leave. The documentation you bring back will be believable. Most importantly, your evidence will corroborate other evidence that will soon be prepared for publication on Earth. To be frank, if you don't bring back this evidence, our efforts may not succeed. Your decision may affect the future of mankind more than any other single event in history."

After a long silence, Chuck asked, "If we decide not to align ourselves with you after we visit Eden, what will you do?"

"Nothing. You are not a threat to us, so we have no reason to harm you. However, we will have no reason to protect you either. You will have to face The Sovereign and explain yourselves, assuming he lets you return."

Chuck shifted his weight, trying not to appear too nervous to his officers. He wondered if he could trust Berekiah. Everything he had been taught about the evils of Ben-Shaachar and his forces said no but everything he had seen in the last hour told him that reality might be different. "Thank you for your input, Berekiah. We will need to confer with one another before making a decision. We will also have to inform the rest of the crew. Some may not want to partake in this adventure, assuming we take that direction. In that case we would have to make provision so that they neither harm our plans nor treat us as conspirators. Will you be willing to wait outside for our decision?"

"Oh, I think I'll just head on home to finish some work I have to do. I trust you will make the right decision and that I'll see you when you return to Yehowshuwa's domain." He waved good-bye and disappeared.

Chuck shook his head. The others looked bewildered as well. The idea that enemies of the Administration could appear and vanish at will was unsettling, yet at the same time strangely comforting.

Chapter 10

Robert arrived at the Tri City Transportation Center an hour late, having missed a couple of connections due to the time he had spent trying to smooth things over with his mother. The small center only had a half dozen convy stations. The waiting area, which wasn't even half as big as Robert's community hall, had a dozen tables with four chairs each, a couple of padded benches, and a sectional L-shaped couch with a coffee table. He lowered his pack to the floor and stood by the convy booth he had just exited. It felt good just to stand after sitting for so long.

While he felt good that his mom was no longer angry with him, he felt uneasy with telling her a half-truth. There was no way he would reconsider his plans, although technically he could do it in a split second and say he had.

He looked around for Jim, but didn't see him. That didn't surprise him, since Jim left a message saying he was going to be late. As he was about to give his friend a call, a convy arrived, scarcely a meter from where Robert was standing, and Jim hurriedly stepped out and ran into Robert.

Robert grabbed Jim to keep them both from falling over. Jim's long, thick, wavy dark brown hair bounced and fell into its usual disarray as his head bounced backward. *That's Jim, jumping before looking.*

"Whoa, sorry, I didn't see you. Hope you haven't been waiting too long," Jim said. "I got sidetracked talking to an old guy. He was kind of weird but had some great things to say. I think we may have some common ancestors. Boy, am I hungry. Have you had anything to eat?"

"I just got here myself. There's an eatery a couple of blocks from here."

"Sounds good to me."

Robert glanced at the small bag in Jim's hand. "Hey, where's your equipment?"

"Right here." Jim held up his bag.

"You can't possibly have everything I told you to bring in there. Where's your sleeping bag? Hiking boots? Backpack?"

"Uh…I remember you giving me a list, but that was a couple of weeks ago. Besides, what do I need hiking boots for? We're not going to do that much walking, are we?"

Robert rolled his eyes. "Man, sometimes I wonder about you. Come on; let's get something to eat. Then we can pick up the things you'll need."

The two strolled from the transportation center down the small town's narrow streets. Robert admired the brick buildings, none of which was more than two stories high except for one two blocks ahead, which is where he was headed. It was the only restaurant in town.

Jim paused before the marquee over the sidewalk that advertised "Rosey's: The Best Place to Eat in Town." Next door was the entrance to a hotel that filled the four floors above the restaurant. Its narrow sign above the doorway simply read, "Rosey's Hotel."

"Why is this place named Rosey's?" Jim asked.

"Let's go in and ask." Robert opened the door and walked into the small dining area. A large dining table with twelve chairs stood at the back of the room. Two people sat in a booth along the left wall. A long, narrow bar took up the right two thirds of the room. Robert sat on a padded green swivel seat perched on a shiny metallic post. Jim took the seat next to him.

A short, round lady came out of the kitchen, wearing a simple pink dress covered by a white bib apron, her face encircled by white hair. As she approached her two new customers, she pulled a pad of paper and pencil out of her apron pocket and scooped up two menus, handing them to Jim and Robert. Her broad smile seemed to push her cheeks closer to her eyes, intensifying their rosy glow. "Well, if it isn't little Bobby Maskil come looking for the best burger in the world! Who's your buddy, Bobby boy?"

"Rosey, meet Jim Arizna, a man who has never met a real burger."

"Welcome to Tri City, Jimmy. It's been many years since Bobby was here. Has he promised to take you out into the wilds of the old west for a week of rest and relaxation?"

"He sure has," Jim said with a chuckle.

"Well, be careful. There are some mighty wild animals up there," said Rosey with a wink at Robert.

Robert knew what she meant. He quickly got back to the food subject. "So, Rosey, can we have two super deluxe burgers with fries?"

"You bet." Rosey scribbled the order on her pad, ripped off the top page, then turned and clipped it to a small chrome drum hanging in the window between the bar and the kitchen. She spun the drum so the paper was inside the kitchen then slapped her hand on a small chrome bell on the windowsill. "Order," she yelled and turned back to the counter.

"So, Rosey," Jim said, "I'll bet you can tell me all about this place."

She leaned her arms on the counter. "Sure can. Tri City's been around since long before The Last Battle. This restaurant and hotel were part of the downtown area. The marquee and signs then were just as you see them today. The bricks in the building are the originals. We've tried to keep them looking almost exactly as they did over a thousand years ago. My several-greats-grandmother Rosey was the original owner. That would've been around 1950 AD by the old dating system. This building is one of the few that survived The Last Battle."

Jim took a quick look around. "That's amazing."

Rosey glanced back at the kitchen, and then continued. "Rosey passed the restaurant and hotel on to her daughter, Rosey and so on. When the Great Time of Trouble came, the Rosey that owned the place wasn't loyal to The Sovereign, but she and many others in town switched their allegiance to him a few years before The Last Battle. It was just before the great earthquake hit. The Tri Cities were all destroyed, with the exception of this one block in the center of town. It was somehow protected from destruction. Rosey credited it to their new allegiance to Yehowshuwa."

Robert hadn't talked to Rosey for a long time. He forgot how much she had credited loyalty to The Sovereign for preservation of the town.

"The mountains to the southwest of here were much farther away before the quake. The river that ran between the cities was thrown off course. It now flows 140 kilometers to the west of where it did before. There were no airports or highways left for the few survivors to use."

Changing a large river so that it now runs so far away must have been a mighty big earthquake. I can't imagine that kind of destructive power being unleashed and not leveling or turning this city upside down. Could this be another one of those altered histories? Robert felt as though he was now listening to Rosey with a new set of ears.

"Chancellor Ben-Shaachar's government wrote off this area as a complete loss and ignored it. Meanwhile, hostilities between The Sovereign's loyalists and The Chancellor's forces intensified. The loyalists were hunted down and destroyed. What was left of the Tri Cities became a safe haven for loyalists who managed to escape from other regions. They renamed the town Tri City to honor Yehowshuwa's family."

Robert had heard the story many times but enjoyed watching Jim try to take it all in.

"After The Last Battle, when Earth was restored and the new economics of The Sovereign's Administration were established, all privately owned businesses were transferred to the Administration. Yehowshuwa let Rosey's daughter, also named Rosey run the business. A Rosey has been in charge ever since."

"Ah," said Jim as he raised his chin, "that explains the quaint interior design. But what's with the order pad, the bell, and the spinney drum with the clips? I've never seen anything like it."

"All of us Roseys wanted to preserve the way things were before The Last Battle. Waitresses back then would write orders on a pad of paper then pass it to the cook in the same way as you just saw me do it. In the kitchen the cook takes the order and prepares everything the way it was done over a thousand years ago. There are a few exceptions since the old technology of cooking with gas hasn't been available for centuries."

Ching went the bell.

"Order up!" came a voice from the kitchen as two plates appeared on the windowsill. Rosey turned around, scooped up the plates, and deftly placed them in front of Jim and Robert in one smooth motion.

Jim stared at the huge wheat bun covering his sandwich, then leaned over sideways, lifted one edge of the bun, and peered underneath at the layers of lettuce, onions, tomatoes, and a beef patty resting on the lower bun. Rosey pushed two jars in front of him. "You might want to try some ketchup and mustard. We make these ourselves."

Jim looked up at Rosey. "I feel like I've stumbled into a time machine."

Robert laughed. "You're supposed to eat it, not study it."

Jim picked up the sandwich and took a small bite. "Hey, this thing is good," he said, then took another mouthful.

While the two men ate, Robert reminisced with Rosey about the many times he and his family had visited over the years.

After lunch, he and Jim continued down the street toward the hardware store. As they took their time, Robert reminded Jim of the conditions he'd already warned him about for their camping trip: like rocky trails and the need for adequate foot protection, as well as bunks without linens or blankets in the cabin. They also needed food to supplement what they could forage during the week.

The hardware store was small compared to his dad's, but it had the necessary items they needed. Fortunately, the only pair of hiking boots happened to be Jim's size. The store clerk helped them find a good sleeping bag, backpack, and enough freeze-dried food to supplement what they would find in the wild for their weeklong stay in the mountains.

"Are you sure we need all this?" Jim asked.

Robert assured him they did.

"That freeze-dried food doesn't look like it'll last us a week."

Robert assured him it would.

As they continued past the city center with their goodies, Jim rambled. "The way Rosey was talking, in the olden days we couldn't have just walked into the store and picked up the stuff we needed. We would have had to pay for it with money we'd earned for the work we did at some other place. If we didn't have enough, we wouldn't be able to get the things."

Robert listened patiently. He knew that Jim would slow down as soon as he had processed his newfound information.

"I think I'd have a hard time living in a society like that. Especially since I've tried to avoid working as much as possible." He chuckled nervously. "Guess that's going to change after this year. When I'm done with my degree I'll probably have to get a job since my grades aren't that good. That reminds me, you haven't told me how things turned out with your Board meeting."

Robert slapped him on the back. "I'll bet you only want to know how my Board meeting went so you can get some tips on how to convince them to let you stay in school and avoid getting a job."

The two friends laughed.

August 20, 998 ASR

Samantha guided the transport out of the distribution center bay, back to the surface streets of the city, and onto a one-way arterial parallel to the one she and her father had taken when they arrived. "So, Tom," she asked her cousin, "where is this coffee shop you mentioned?"

"Take a left at the next street and go two blocks. You'll find a parking lot there with spaces large enough for the truck. We can walk to the coffee shop from there."

Samantha turned the corner off the busy arterial laden with trucks and larger transports moving away from the distribution center. When she turned onto the side street vehicular traffic became almost nonexistent. Many people were on the sidewalks along the street lined with trees and small shops. The parking lot had only a few trucks and a couple of personal convy cabs. She guided the truck into the lot and parked near the walkway.

"The place is just around the corner." Tom led the way.

The small coffee shop contained half a dozen round tables with chairs, three low tables surrounded by plush couches and loungers, and a bar with eight stools. Samantha selected a papaya from the fruit selection of the cafeteria-style food case. Tom took a bagel then stopped at the coffee bar. Papa opted for a gooey cinnamon roll.

When Samantha and her dad joined Tom at the coffee bar, her cousin spoke to the young barista behind the counter. "Cindy, I'd like you to meet my uncle Merlin and my cousin Sam. Merlin, Sam, this is Cindy. She has some of the best blends of coffee ever to tantalize the human palate. What's the specialty of the house today?"

Cindy enthusiastically gave her spiel. "For you and your family, I have a new blend that was developed yesterday by master barista Garida and delivered overnight to only a handful of shops around the world. The blend takes 80 percent of its beans from the first crop of a new hybrid he's been working on for the last eighty years. The other 20 percent is from an ancient line of Colombian beans. The Colombian beans date back some two hundred years before The Last Battle. I'm sure the subtle floral aroma will heighten your anticipation and reward you with its winey flavor, which is somewhat on the tangy side."

"Sounds good to me," said Papa.

"Make it two." Samantha raised two fingers.

"Nope…three," said Tom with three fingers in the air.

"Very good. Have a seat and I'll bring them to you in a few minutes." Cindy motioned toward an empty table.

After they settled down at the table, Tom asked, "What are you going to study at university, Sam?"

She took a breath as she thought about the classes she had scheduled. "I'm leaning toward a degree in history. I've always been fascinated by the changes in our society from the centuries before The Last Battle up through the present. We aren't taught much about people's mind-set back then. I'd like to dig deeper and find out more about the way our ancestors thought."

Tom nodded. "Everything is going so well under The Sovereign that we seldom look back at the times before he took over. How do you think this study will prepare you for future employment?"

Samantha chuckled. "I can tell what generation you come from! No one my age ever asks what we're preparing for with our studies. It seems most of us have the idea that we are owed an education, and that in itself is reason enough to continue in school. That's not how I've been raised." Samantha glanced at her father to acknowledge his influence over her. "I've been thinking about becoming a teacher. Other than that, I haven't figured out how I can use this major yet. I'm hoping that as I pursue the studies I'll be able to find my place in society."

Tom applauded quietly. "Well spoken, Sam. So, what have you been doing to get ready for university?"

She thought back to Tom's visits on the farm when she was younger. His questioning and purposefulness, combined with his fun nature, had always inspired her. "I completed as many history studies as possible at school, but found them all shallow. So I enrolled in online studies at University of Midrib, which has the best history courses. I've completed the first three years of my major already. If it wasn't for all the required courses and the number of credits needed, I'd be able to get my bachelor's degree in only a year. As it is, I'll pick up those credits over the next four years and end up with both my bachelor's and master's."

"I'm impressed. Where is the University of Midrib?"

Papa answered in a sad voice, "About as far away from us as it could be. Southern hemisphere, opposite side of the world."

"That is quite a distance from home. Seems like an awfully big step for a farm girl," Tom said with a twinkle in his eye.

"Farms are great places to raise kids, Tom," Papa shot back. "Why, I'll bet the most important things you learned in life were learned from a cow. Like 'live life to the udder-most'?"

Tom laughed. "You're right. I've learned that to be successful we need to be more than 'moovers and shakers.'"

Samantha joined in the familiar banter. "Well, that fits with the motto, 'If you follow The Sovereign he will *steer* you in the right direction!'"

"That's right, Sam," Tom added with a grin. "The best things I know I've *herd* from The Sovereign."

Cindy arrived with their coffee and set the glass coffee mugs before them. "If you *milk* those jokes for all they're worth, you won't need any of our cream." She winked. "Guess I'll get back to work so you folks won't think I'm trying to *horn* in on your conversation." As she turned to leave, she flipped her head, swinging her ponytail close to the back of Tom's head.

"I think we've been outdone," Samantha said. In a more sober tone, she added, "You know, one of the things I found out in my studies is that coffee shops like this were even around in the previous era. Coffee has been a staple beverage for about 1,300 years."

Papa swirled his coffee cup under his nose and inhaled. "Ah, that sure smells good. I can see why coffee has been around so long." He took a sip and smacked his lips. "Life sure was different back then. People only lived eighty or ninety years at best, and most of them treated their bodies as if they thought they'd last forever. I'm in better shape than someone in their seventies would have been back then."

Samantha agreed. "Another thing that seems strange about that latte craze is that some of the people who were lower paid spent an inordinate amount of their income on them."

"Now you're talking about money, right?" Tom asked. "That's one thing I remember from history classes but never really understood."

Samantha found the concept hard to understand, too, but she'd spent quite a bit of time trying to comprehend it. "It's difficult for us to imagine the way their economy worked since we can go into any store and get whatever we need without paying or trading. Back then, a person was valued by what he or she did for an occupation. The higher value society placed on a particular job, the more money the person got for doing it. For instance, in their society, since Papa is the director of a large farm, he would be paid a lot more than the people who do the harvesting.

So he would be able to trade the money he made for more things than the person who made less money."

Tom wrinkled his brow. "Still doesn't make sense to me. So Uncle Merlin has all this money and can get more stuff. So what? He has a house, clothes, food, and an ECD. What more does he need?"

"Apparently they felt that having more things added to their sense of worth. It wasn't based on what they needed but on what they perceived was needed to show others that they were successful and worth more," said Samantha between sips of coffee.

Tom sat back and folded his arms. "So you're telling me that to feel good about themselves, gifted people acquired more and more stuff whether they needed it or not, while some people went without basic needs because they didn't have the same abilities?"

Samantha sat back and put her cup down with a clunk. "Now you're getting the picture."

Tom threw his hands up. "It just doesn't make sense."

"I agree," Papa said. "Each person has worth not because of his or her job, abilities or position in society, but because they are valued members of society under Sovereign Yehowshuwa's rule. We give each other the fruits of our talents and labors and take from each other the things we need."

Samantha listened to her father's wisdom. She was proud to have a man with his understanding guide her as she bounced ideas off him.

Papa continued as he wagged his finger in the air. "But, if it wasn't for the strict enforcement of the Administration, I fear we would soon revert to a self-centered, materialistic society like the ones that existed before Yehowshuwa took over. Each generation must be taught, and obedience to The Sovereign's teachings must be enforced."

He looked his nephew in the eye. "You've raised a couple of kids. When they were tiny tots, did they naturally share things with each other?"

"No way. They were always grabbing things, pulling toys away from their siblings or playmates, and yelling, 'Mine!'"

"When they became teenagers, did they become selfless and willingly share with others without your guidance and instruction?" asked Papa.

Tom rolled his eyes. "No way!"

Samantha thought about a few times when Papa had to correct her selfish ways with her younger cousins. She remembered the big difference in her own behavior after she declared her loyalty to Yehowshuwa and he changed her heart. But she still had selfish tendencies.

Papa took his cup in both hands. "From what Sam has been telling me, it seems fewer and fewer youngsters are developing loyalty to The Sovereign. They are rebellious at heart while maintaining outward conformance due to fear of reprisal." He finished his coffee.

"Yeah, sounds like an employee I have." Tom's forehead creased and his eyes looked sad.

Papa looked at his watch. "I'm glad we were able to get together for a few minutes, Tom. But we need to pick up some things for Sam and get back to the farm."

Tom stood "I've got to get back to work too. Sam, may you have a blessed time at university. Let me know when you've figured out why people were the way they were."

Samantha laughed. "If I ever get it totally figured out, it won't be in this life." She had enjoyed the stimulating conversation. She hoped she would find people at university as logical and questioning as her father and her cousin.

Chapter 11

Chuck sat in a visitor chair in his office after Berekiah vanished. He motioned for the others to sit as well. He looked at the view screen, which still showed their list of reasons to go to Eden or return to Earth. He was leaning toward continuing to Eden but wanted to get everyone else's opinion first.

"OK, people, we have some decisions to make. I want each of you to let me know what you would like to do and why. Reverse alphabetical order. Zophia?"

"I vote we go on to Eden. Once we get there, we will be able to test the veracity of Berekiah's word. If it's true, we need to let people know. If it's not, The Sovereign has some problems with Ben-Shaachar that we need to let him know about." She put her hand to her chin. "Then again, if he doesn't know, that proves Berekiah is right."

Marti glanced at Demetrius and Alex before responding. "I don't know how you can make it so cut and dried, so emotionless, Zophia. But I have feelings and they tell me we're entering into something much bigger than we are. If we aren't careful, we're going to get squashed. I'm scared... Still, I don't think we have much of a choice except to go to Eden."

Demetrius fidgeted. "I don't want to be charged with treason and this certainly sounds like it would be in that category. If we lose, we're dead. However, I too think we should continue to Eden, if for no other reason than to verify what we've been told."

Chuck motioned for Alex to go next.

"No question in my mind. The only way we can verify any of this is to visit Eden."

"Thank you all for your input. It seems we're in agreement. I'll inform Tia-le that we are going to continue to Eden. I want an all-crew briefing in the mess hall in thirty minutes. Please take care of assembling everyone in your departments."

When Chuck arrived on the bridge, he sat in his command chair and told the computer to let Tia-le know he was ready to talk to her. The view screen switched from a display of the escort ships to Tia-le.

"We've finished our deliberations," he said without enthusiasm. "We will take you up on your offer of safe conduct to Eden."

Tia-le smiled as much as her small mouth and fixed features would allow. "I'm glad you made that decision, Captain. I'm sure you won't regret it. You will see the value once you reach Eden. In the meantime, do not be alarmed if you see several of us right beside you. We will be going back and forth to our support ship, which is much larger. For safety reasons it is now cruising some distance away. If you need to contact us for any reason, you can call me."

Chuck scowled. "Why can't your support ship come as close as you are?"

"Since both your ship and ours are large vessels, the deflectors could cause significant disruption. If we were to deflect an asteroid while we were close to you, it could be pushed aside with a vector that your deflectors would miss, and it could strike your ship from the side. Of course the reverse could happen to our ship. The smaller ships wouldn't deflect anything big enough to hit your ship."

Chuck nodded. *I should have thought of that. Being alone in space for so long has made me careless. I can't let that happen again.* "Is there anything we should be considering to make sure we don't have an accident?"

Tia-le slowly blinked her large eyes. "You will have to be careful as you approach Eden. They have limited space travel; however, they have a few satellites and some ships. You will need to make sure your speed and power levels are very low if you come within 150,000 kilometers."

Chuck stood. "When we get near, you could transmit positions to us so that our computer systems will know where they are. Earth has a lot of satellites, so we're used to traveling without knocking them out."

"Very well."

"If we have any questions or concerns, we'll contact you. Right now I've got to brief the entire crew."

"Good day, Captain."

Chuck watched the view screen switch back to show the escort ships. "Hal, you have the bridge. Everyone else, down to the mess hall for our briefing."

Irene and Buckly raised their eyebrows. This was the first time the computer had ever been left alone to pilot Ramah. In the twenty-five years they had been in space, someone had always been on the bridge, monitoring the ship.

Chuck motioned with his hands low, as if to push them out the door. They obediently rose and exited ahead of the Captain.

As Chuck entered the mess hall, he saw that the night-shift workers had been awakened and were sitting with the rest of the crew. The buzz of conversation died away as he walked swiftly to the far end and stood in front of the room's view port. He looked at the forty-eight expectant faces before him.

Chuck asked Zophia replay the events on the mess hall's view port. While the events replayed, he watched the crew to see their reactions. Most of them watched quietly and soberly. When Tia-le confirmed Rol-el's comments about The Sovereign Yehowshuwa, there was a lot of foot shuffling and squirming in chairs.

At the conclusion of the bridge scene, Chuck asked Zophia to show everyone the deliberations that occurred afterward.

She again used her ECD to play a log of what had occurred in Chuck's office. The screen showed the officers brainstorming their reasons to go to Eden or return to Earth. Chuck watched as he and the senior officers knelt to pray. He felt his face flush as he heard his own prayer. *That was lame.*

The screen showed two views of the room, so he was able to see everyone's face when Berekiah appeared. *I wasn't the only one shocked when he arrived.* After Berekiah disappeared, the log provided the comments and the choices the officers had made.

When the ship's logs finished, Chuck said, "We are going on to Eden. This decision could lead to charges of treason for disobeying The Sovereign's command to turn around. Since the order was confirmed by Tia-le and Berekiah, we do believe it truly came from him. If anyone disagrees with this decision, say so, and it will be recorded in Ramah's logs that you are continuing on under duress. I will give you thirty minutes to ponder your decision. Then I'll take a roll call. Everyone's vote will be recorded. If a majority of you decides not to continue, we may have to rethink our decision. Do you have any questions?"

Chuck searched each face. "Alright, I'm going to start the timer. You may talk among yourselves or ask me or the other officers any questions you have. If you would like to leave and come back, make sure you are back here in time for the roll call."

The noise level in the mess hall ascended sharply as people started talking. Chuck wandered around the room, eavesdropping enough to understand that most of them faced the same fears and concerns as were voiced among by the officers. Gradually, the chatter died down and they sat in silence as the thirty minutes came to an end.

Chuck pointed to the back left of the room. "We'll start on that side and go across the back. State your name for the record and say yes if you agree to go to Eden and no if you don't."

"Henry Edgar—yes."

"Barbara Edgar—yes."

"Michael Edgar—yes."

The role call continued back and forth across the mess hall until everyone had given his or her vote. Only two people voted no.

Chuck was pleased that the crew was mostly in agreement. He didn't know what he would have done if there had been a majority of no votes. "After we reach Eden and gather more data, we will meet again to decide what to do. You will all have the opportunity to change your vote at that time. Any questions?"

Raymond, one of the crewmembers who had voted no spoke up. "What happens if I continue to disagree with your course of action after we have visited Eden?"

Chuck sighed. "Raymond, you know I'm a fair man. I'll make sure you don't get into any trouble. The ship's log will show your loyalty to The Sovereign."

Raymond didn't look happy about it, but didn't say anything more.

August 20, 998 ASR

In the gloom of the dungeon, The Chancellor Ben-Shaachar thought back to his previous planning a year before The Last Battle.

June 15, 1 BLB

Ben-Shaachar sat in his executive chair, looking out over his great capital city. The sun cast an eerie reddish glow over the skyscrapers, even at high noon. He reviewed his dominion and contemplated the deterioration of the environment as one hideous disaster after another decimated the globe. In the past few months it seemed as if all of nature had rebelled and orchestrated a clever plan to test and stress his reign. The sun increased its output, scorching the earth so that all the grass burned up. A third of the trees died. After that a comet crashed through

Earth's atmosphere, contaminating a third of the fresh water sources with arsenic. Millions of people died before they could be warned. Without any explanation the sun became dark, plunging the earth into gloom. Only yesterday the murkiness dissipated and now this feeble sun seemed a relief.

He whirled around to face his desk and touched the intercom's call button.

A female voice came from the intercom, "Yes Sir?"

"Find Abathar and send him in here pronto!" he barked.

Five minutes later the intercom buzzed and the voice stated, "Sir, Mr. Abathar is here to see you."

"Send him in," he snapped as he looked again out the window, his back to the door.

The huge walnut door opened and Abathar poked his head around it. Then he entered and tiptoed without sound up to The Chancellor Ben-Shaachar's huge walnut desk. "Sir, you called for me?"

"What took you so long?" The Chancellor Ben-Shaachar growled. "What do you make of this latest development with the sun?" He waved his hand at the window before him then turned to face Abathar.

Abathar bowed at his waist then straightened. "It could be a natural reaction due to the dust in the air from the comet. I'm sure it will return to normal when the dust settles."

The Chancellor slammed his hand on the desk. "Are you some kind of idiot? Haven't you read the prophecies? This is another attack by my archenemy. I'm doing everything in my awesome power to defeat him and neutralize his followers, and I am confident that I will succeed. Even so these events dictate that I have a backup plan. I'm putting you in charge to establish the groundwork for it."

Abathar shook his head. "Sir, you are invincible. Surely you don't need a backup plan. You are omniscient and know the beginning from the end. You will persevere against our enemy and imprison him forever. You will—"

Chancellor Ben-Shaachar pointed his finger at Abathar. "I appreciate your praise. However, if I know the beginning from the end, doesn't it make sense that when I tell you I want a backup plan you had better do as I say?"

Abathar hung his head and bit his lip "Yes, sir. I live to serve you and will do as you wish."

Ben-Shaachar grinned. If it wasn't for my magnificence, charisma, magnetism, and incredible power, I doubt this worthless creature would put up with my tirades. He doesn't realize that he is nearly as powerful as I am. I must keep his esteem low or he may strike out on his own.

He continued. "Should we lose our pending confrontation; the enemy will put his spin on the circumstances and make it look as if he is the savior of all mankind. He will make me out to be a butcher and the vilest being ever created. He will so malign our cause that for hundreds of years people will believe he has freed them from tyranny and suppression, though in fact he will enslave them and make them think they are free."

Ben-Shaachar paced before the window. "Therefore, I want you to make a documentary detailing the atrocities that the enemy's attack on the environment has caused. Start with the famine that raged early in my reign and show how we were able to abate it. Include the great earthquake that followed nearly three years ago. Finish up with the last three disasters that have come upon us. I want explicit footage showing the horror that was visited on people around the earth. Make sure it is graphic; none of the gore and suffering is to be held back. I want people to see exactly what these things did to the population of Earth. Include the numbers of people who were killed in each of these attacks. Rouse the emotions of the viewers so that they will be utterly disgusted and revolted at the crimes that have been poured out on us."

He snapped his fingers as he thought of more to add. "Interweave this documentary with quotes from the enemy's own people. Many of them have acknowledged that he has caused these catastrophes, so you shouldn't have a hard time getting what you need. With each claim of responsibility show what I have done to aid the suffering. Show how I have restored order where chaos reigned."

He was starting to enjoy the thought of releasing this to Yehowshuwa's followers and watching them squirm at the horror their master had wreaked upon the Earth. He turned to Abathar to make sure he understood his final instructions. "After you have completed this portion of the documentary, set up a shoot here in my office where I will present an epilogue."

He pointed his finger again at Abathar and growled. His voice lowered and became guttural. "Now, as far as anyone other than you and I know, this is simply a documentary. If anyone hears of the real reason you're doing this, there won't be enough left of you to fill a thimble. Is that clear?" Ben-Shaachar glared at his underling.

Abathar bowed at the waist with his face to the floor. "Yes, Sir."

"Now, get out of here and get started. You have two months to show me your first cut." The Chancellor turned and looked out the window again. He heard the creak and clunk of the large door as Abathar left.

There has to be some way to alter those blasted prophecies. If I can't, then this backup plan will be necessary. He kicked his chair in anger, sending it crashing into his desk.

August 20, 998 ASR

Kevin stood before the Tree of Life in the New Yeruwshalayim, admiring the large pink blossoms dangling over the river, inhaling the strong, sweet fragrance. The tree had many trunks and exposed roots that dipped into the River of Life. It spread along the opposite bank of the river as well, where many other people walked and talked around it, or paused to admire it, just as people were doing on his side of the river.

He plucked one of the many fruits that weighed down the branches. This one resembled something between a mango and a nectarine. He bit into it and savored the sweetness and fragrance. He felt The Sovereign's strength flow through his body. This was one of his favorite places to come when he wasn't working as an Enforcer with errant families.

He heard a voice behind him. "Greetings, Kevin, I come with news."

He turned to see a young man dressed in a flowing white robe. His face was radiant, and stoic. "I don't think I've met you before. What's your name?"

"My name is Rafael," the Messenger stated mater-of-factly, "and I need to show you something of great importance. Please come with me."

Kevin didn't think he would ever get used to the Messengers. They never beat around the bush or engaged in small talk when they are on the job.

He wondered why a Messenger would come to him. Sovereign Yehowshuwa usually spoke to him directly or through his supervisor when he was needed to intervene in a domestic squabble. "Where are we going?"

Rafael reached to take Kevin's hand. "You will see."

The moment they grasped hands, Kevin saw a bright flash of light, as if a door had opened and closed in the blink of an eye. The Tree of Life and the river were replaced by a grassy meadow surrounded by a dense forest. Kevin wondered why he would be brought out into the wilderness without any visible souls around.

Rafael broke the silence. "Tell me, Kevin, what do you see?"

He tried to quell his need to get things moving, knowing that Rafael would reveal his message in the way The Sovereign wanted. "I see a small grassy meadow that is relatively circular, about two hundred meters in diameter. I see a forest of fir trees with a few cedars and hemlock mixed in. There is dense undergrowth with bushes I can't identify. Some look like they could be some kind of berry bushes. Beyond the trees I see mountain ranges that make me believe I'm a long way from civilization. I can't see any signs of roads. Is that enough or do you need more details?"

Rafael's furrowed brow showed a hint of puzzlement. "Very good, Kevin, now I will tell you what I see. I too see a meadow surrounded on three sides by a dense forest with underbrush and mountains in the distance. However, I can identify all the bushes. To my left I see a tall vertical cliff that starts at the edge of the meadow. It is an imposing sheer rock wall that rises about two hundred meters straight up. I can't see any mountains beyond it because it is too tall to see past its top. How do you explain the fact that we are seeing two different things?"

Kevin was stumped and curious. "I don't know. Do you?"

"No. I was only told to ask you what you saw and tell you what I saw and to tell you to take a closer look. Can you see anything else to my left?"

Kevin stared in the direction the Messenger indicated. He looked up and down. He looked at different trees, bushes, and the grass that led up to the edge of the clearing. He looked back and forth, trying to see if something changed or shifted. He felt as if he were trying to find the difference between two almost identical pictures. "I don't see anything unusual, just the shimmering of heat waves near the edge." His words, once spoken, sparked a question in his mind. "Wait a minute. It's cloudy and cool. Why would there be heat waves shimmering at the edge of the clearing?"

Kevin hurried to the edge of the glen, where it appeared as though a transparent sheet was suspended in the air and could only be seen when it swayed back and forth in a breeze. When he arrived at the edge, he realized there was no sheet. Kevin passed through the wispy barrier then turned to look back at Rafael, who had a bewildered look on his face.

"What do you think about this?" Kevin asked.

Rafael stared straight ahead to the place where Kevin had gone through the curtain. "I can hear you but I can't see you. It looks like you just walked right into a solid rock cliff." He stood a few centimeters from the shimmering air, staring intently at it.

"I can see you clear as day," Kevin said. "Why don't you join me?"

"I can't."

"Come on. Where is your faith?"

Rafael rolled his eyes. "You know Messengers don't have faith. We have always walked by sight because we can clearly see all that is in The Sovereign's universe and on Earth. This is something I've never run across before. I am at the end of my instructions. I am to wait until you want to return."

Kevin chuckled. "That sounds like faith to me. You didn't know what was going to happen, but you did as you were told."

"You have a point, Kevin," said Rafael as he reached forward tentatively and touched the wavering air with his finger. His eyebrows shot up as his finger went through what he must have seen as rock.

"Fine, I'll just help you out then." Kevin reached back through the curtain, grabbed Rafael's hand, and yanked him through to the other side.

Rafael raised his other hand as if to ward off hitting his face against an impending collision. Stumbling, he passed through the curtain of air.

"Now it's my turn. Rafael, what do you see?" asked Kevin. He took pleasure in becoming the inquisitor.

The Messenger gazed about, turning in a full circle. "I see exactly what you described earlier. A clearing surrounded on all sides by forest, and mountains in the background as far as the eye can see. I also see a faint shimmering where I just saw a cliff of rock." Rafael stepped back through the shimmering and looked at Kevin. "Now I see a cliff that should be solid rock." He stepped into the cliff and almost knocked Kevin over.

Kevin held up his hands. "Whoa, that was close. It's a good thing you didn't step in a few meters to your left; you would have smacked right into that tree." Kevin laughed. "What is here has been hidden from you, but not from me, for a reason. Why don't we take a little hike to the top of that next rise and see what we can find?"

"As you wish." Rafael's face became stoic once again.

Kevin led the way through trails in the underbrush. Prints from deer and elk marked the trail. As they got farther from the clearing and higher up the hillside, the bushes cleared and Kevin had an easier time hiking. He looked up at the tall trees whose leaves were turning brown, then down at the path. He no longer noticed any recent animal droppings.

"Why is everything so dried up?" asked Rafael.

"I'm not sure, Rafael, but it looks like there hasn't been any rain beyond the veil for a long time," said Kevin as he kicked the ground on the dusty trail.

The rise was a lot farther away than Kevin had expected. It took them forty-five minutes to reach an area where he had a clear view of the next valley. In the broad, brown, dry valley, he saw something that looked like partially constructed buildings.

Rafael touched his arm. "As we were climbing this hill, I started to get an uneasy feeling that I haven't had for nearly a thousand years. In addition, my body is not responding in the way it should. As we came closer to the top, I had more and more difficulty putting one foot in front of the other."

"I've felt something unusual, too, that remind me of long ago before Yehowshuwa returned. There is something evil nearby."

Kevin looked up and down at Rafael. His usually robust face looked gray and pasty, as if he were about to experience a heart attack. "You don't look well. If you were a man, I'd say you need to get to a hospital right away. Do you think you'll be OK for a bit longer? We can beam out of here right now if you want."

Rafael sat down. "You may be able to leave, but I have lost contact with our realm and no longer have the ability to move back there. If you have contact, you could take me back. However, my physical symptoms seem to have stabilized now that we have stopped."

"If you're OK, I'd like to get a better look at what's going on in the valley. Can you see those buildings?"

Out of breath, Rafael panted. "Yes, but it looks like objects are moving through the air by themselves, as if carried by people who are invisible to me."

"You mean you can't see the people carrying the building materials?

Rafael shook his head.

"There seems to be something here that is messing with your abilities but doesn't affect mine. If you feel up to it, let's try a little experiment. Let's walk down the hill about a hundred meters and see how you feel. Let's stay out of sight. Since those guys working on the building are invisible to you they probably don't even want you to see the work they are doing and we shouldn't let them know we're here."

"Agreed."

Kevin and Rafael moved down the hill, staying behind trees to make sure no one in the camp could see them. After about fifty meters Rafael stopped. "I can't go on any farther. I can barely move my arms and legs, much less stand."

Kevin took Rafael by the arm. "That's what I thought would happen. Let's see if you can move back up and over the hill."

"I will try," Rafael answered, gritting his teeth.

With Kevin helping the Messenger, they slowly made their way up the hill and back down the other side. With each step they took away from the camp, Kevin felt Rafael gaining strength until he didn't need any assistance. His normal color returned to his face.

As soon as Rafael reached the meadow and emerged from behind the shimmering curtain, he announced, "I am again in contact with our realm and will be able to return on my own power. What do you make of our adventure?"

Kevin's mind raced to put it all together. "It seems to me that those people I saw and you couldn't are some of Ben-Shaachar's forces. My feelings are consistent with what I felt when The Chancellor was in control and we returned with The Sovereign to do battle. I hadn't felt them before we were evacuated from Earth, but only when we returned to Earth with Yehowshuwa. When Ben-Shaachar was locked up, the sensations disappeared. I expect we have seen some escapees from the dungeon."

Rafael pursed his lips then stated, "Not having ever experienced physical weakness, I was concentrating on what was happening to me. I missed everything that should have told me the enemy was near."

Kevin chuckled. "Sounds like you're becoming human."

Rafael frowned. "This isn't a laughing matter. If I had a body that could tire, I would also be susceptible to temptations."

Kevin didn't like the sound of that. "Here's what I think might have happened. When the enemy escaped from the dungeon, they had to get past the guards without being seen. Since the guards are all your people, the enemy developed powers that can affect your mind. It's probably like the mind blindfold they used on me when I was a mortal. They're probably not aware that my mind can't be affected now that I've been transformed from Earth's realm to The Sovereign's. I am now more like Yehowshuwa, so I suspect I'm immune to their power. I also think that the last thing we should do is reveal to them that I can see them and that their blinding doesn't work on me. I think we need to report this to the one who sent you."

"Please take my hand," said Rafael.

When Kevin took Rafael's hand, he saw a flash of light, as if a door had opened and closed in the blink of an eye. Inter-realm travel thrilled him beyond measure because he knew that he traveled the same way as Yehowshuwa whether he or Rafael initiated it. He felt The Sovereign's power course through him.

Chapter 12

Chuck sat in his office staring at his ECD. Space travel usually bored him. It was day after day, doing the same thing, reviewing the same reports. Time seemed to drag even more the last two weeks. They were still about a week from Eden, and Chuck could hardly wait to get there.

He received a call from the bridge. "Captain, Tia-le has contacted us and would like to talk to you," said Buckly.

He wondered what was up. They hadn't talked for a week. "Put it through to my office."

Tia-le's face appeared on the view screen. "Good afternoon, Captain."

It amazed Chuck that Tia-le and her counterparts had adjusted to Ramah's time, always greeting him with a good afternoon, morning, or evening whenever they contacted him. He had kept the ship's clocks on Earth's SMT, Sovereign Mean Time. The regular schedule helped people feel like they were not in timeless space. At Alex's advice he had Ramah's internal lighting dimmed in the evening and brightened during the day, giving the impression that the sun had gone down and risen again.

"I hope I'm not interrupting you."

"Not at all. What can I do for you?"

"We are approaching the end of Rof's jurisdiction and will soon be entering Adon's jurisdiction, so we will be leaving you until you come back this way."

Chuck sat up straight. "I thought you were going to escort us to Eden. What if we're attacked between here and there?"

Tia-le blinked her big eyes slowly. Chuck had learned that was the way her people usually smiled. "There is no cause for alarm, Captain. Adon is one of the most powerful sovereigns in the universe. There is no way he would allow you to be attacked once you are in his space. You will be safer than any other time in your life."

Chuck still felt uneasy about leaving his escort. "Can't you come along?"

"We can, but we may not. Each sovereign, with a few exceptions, honors each other's territories and boundaries. That is why we choose not to continue. We do so with complete confidence in Adon. You need not fear any of Jehov's forces. He would not attempt to extend himself this far or risk retaliation from Adon. Adon is quite capable of snuffing out any invasion, even at this distance." She slowly blinked her large eyes. "Farewell, Captain. I will see you again on your return voyage."

"How will you know when we are returning?" The view screen went blank. Chuck banged his hand on the desk.

He decided not to share this last communication with the crew. People were jittery enough as it was.

June 24, 998 ASR

Chuck felt a minor shudder in the ship as it adjusted to the reduction of power on the gravitational thrusters. Its speed began to drop, rapidly at first, then slower as the counter forces of the deflectors produced less drag. Chuck went to the bridge to review Buckly's navigation plan to enter Eden's star system.

When he arrived on the bridge, he discovered that Buckly already had Eden's sun and its planets mapped on the view screen. He sat in his command chair and turned to Buckly. "Let's see your approach pattern."

Buckly traced the ship's proposed route on the screen with a pointer. "As Ramah approaches Eden's star system, we will slow to a point where we can safely turn the ship around and use the gravitation thrusters to decelerate and navigate closer to the planet." A blip showed on the screen where Buckly indicated. "Tia-le transmitted the coordinates of the few satellites surrounding the planet. We received word that the Edenians will halt all space travel in order to receive us, so we don't have to worry about flight plans. As you can see, the planets in Eden's system all align in a plane circling the sun. We will come in above the plane, avoiding planets so we can achieve maximum speed until we turn the ship around."

Chuck recognized the wisdom of that plan. "I like that. Should shave off two days from our travel time. Let me know when we're in orbit." He stood and patted Buckly on the back then he left the bridge.

Back in his office, Chuck tried to finish reading his reports. He was more interested in their arrival at Eden. After a couple of hours that seemed like a day, Buckly called to inform him that they had slowed to sub-light speed and entered orbit around Eden.

Chuck returned to the bridge and saw Eden displayed on the view screen. The first up-close picture made the planet appear to be everything he'd expected and more. Part of the view panel showed a close-up of the surface; the whole planet was displayed in another section. It appeared to rotate, showing abundant water, lush forests, and ample signs of animal life. Brightly lit cities dotted the night side of the planet.

"Zophia, can you contact the Edenian ambassadors?"

Chuck heard Zophia's keyboard clicking. Then the faces of a man and a woman appeared on the view screen.

Zophia and Irene gasped. "What a hunk!" Irene whispered.

The man was extremely handsome, with dark brown hair, blue eyes, light but tanned complexion, square jaw, white teeth shinning from his smile; a captivating expression.

The woman was an astonishing beauty. She had long, shining black hair that fell out of sight, dark brown skin without a sign of blemish, deep hazel eyes, high cheeks, also with extremely white teeth radiating from her gentle smile; an intoxicating appearance.

"Greetings, Captain Andrews," the man said. "We've been awaiting your arrival with great anticipation. My name is Minelumanathar and this is my wife, Anahamathala. You may call us Mine and Ana. We have been chosen as representatives to greet you and be the guides for you and Science Officer Assir during your visit. Each of your crewmembers will have a guide to answer questions and show you whatever you desire here on Eden."

"I hope I get Mine," Zophia whispered.

Chuck ignored the comment, but was thinking he wouldn't mind spending his time with Ana. "Thank you for your gracious welcome. Please call me Chuck. I believe Science Officer Assir would like to be called Zophia."

Zophia nodded.

"We are eager to begin our visit," Chuck said. "First we need to make sure we won't contaminate your planet and that there aren't any contagions or pathogens that would cause us problems. With your permission I would like to launch and retrieve sterilized probes to collect air and soil samples. It may take us a day or two to complete preliminary studies on them."

Mine and Ana looked at each other then back to Chuck. They didn't change their confident expressions. "We appreciate your concern about our safety, but we can assure you that there are no microbes or other diseases with which you could possible infect us. We are invulnerable to anything you could have brought with you. You will see why after you are here. As far as us posing a threat to you, there is nothing in our environment that could cause any problems. You see, we live in a perfect world."

Despite Mine's positive attitude Chuck didn't want to be the one to unleash a pandemic on an unsuspecting world.

"However, we understand that you need to run your tests, and we'll be glad to help you in any way we can. When you are satisfied that it is safe, let us know. We've prepared a landing port for your ship so that your whole crew can enjoy Eden."

"Do you know how big our ship is and how much structural integrity a port would require to hold it?"

Mine waved his hand past his face as if shooing away a fly, "We are able to construct buildings much larger than your ship. When we were notified that you would be visiting, we began construction of a port specifically for your ship. We have included piping so that you can replenish your water supply while you are here. We also know that you would like to make thruster modifications, which would be easier if you could completely shut down your systems. Hal has already been given the coordinates, so you can come down whenever you are ready."

Chuck was impressed with the Edenian's hospitality. He was also getting used to aliens knowing more than they should, like their plans for thruster modifications and a computer named Hal. "Thank you. We'll run our tests and let you know when we're ready."

"We will be looking forward to seeing the results, Chuck. We will keep in contact."

The screen went blank, but Chuck could still see Ana's image in his mind.

Zophia and Alex supervised the collection of samples and the analysis from the ship's lab. The drones passed through a series of isolation chambers to become sterilized then Hal launched them into space. The returning probes passed through another set of isolation chambers that would detect any life before being brought into the chambers where the sample would be processed. Then the drones were placed back in the queue to get another sample.

The first probes checked the upper atmosphere; succeeding waves worked their way down toward the surface of Eden. After two hours samples were being processed in the lab from rivers, lakes, and oceans in the first pass.

After the decontamination cycle, the probes returned to get soil from mountaintops, valleys, plains, and even from the bottom of the ocean. The final wave of probes came back with grasses, tree leaves, fruit and bug-like creatures.

Zophia took alternate shifts with Alex and the department analysts so they could work around the clock examining the specimens. She watched the process eagerly, excited to finally be able to see and eventually touch alien life. She had waited for this kind of work for twenty-five years.

June 26, 998 ASR

Chuck studied Zophia's and Alex's faces as they entered his office to report the findings of their analysis. He didn't like what he saw in their sober expressions. Zophia stood at-ease with her hands behind her back. *Always the proper first officer.* Alex's hands hung limply at his side.

"Have a seat." He waited for them to pull their chairs closer to his desk then asked, "Are we going to be able to talk face to face with these people or not?"

Alex began after looking at the floor then at Zophia then finally at Chuck. "I'm not sure. What we've found is perplexing and we can't totally explain it."

Chuck leaned forward expectantly.

Alex took a deep breath. "We can't find any evidence of viruses in the samples. This planet is completely sterile from that standpoint."

"That's good news, isn't it?" asked Chuck as he cocked his head to one side making sure he heard right.

Alex extended his hands, palms up, and moved them up and down as if he were trying to determine the weight of two objects. "For us it is good news. It means we can't get any kind of viral infection. However, for them, it could be bad news. Since we still have viruses, how do we know we won't infect them?"

Chuck sat back. "I guess we don't."

"There's something else that's strange. Out of all our samples we found only a handful of microbes, and nothing we could identify as a parasite. The microbes we did find are completely harmless. I'm not sure why they're even in the environment," said Alex as he shrugged.

"What does that have to do with our ability to go down to Eden?" Chuck asked. He was still looking for some bad news.

Zophia cleared her throat. "Without microbes we don't know how the animals or people on this planet are able to digest their food. We don't know how a dead blade of grass decomposes and returns to the soil to provide nutrients for the next blade that grows. This planet's mountains, forests, plains, flora, fauna, and people shouldn't exist without microbes."

Alex's face remained serious as he patted his fingertips together lightly a few times just below eye level. "That's not all. We wanted to see if any of our bacteria would harm anything we gathered from Eden. So we took some of the cultures and exposed our everyday germs to them."

"What happened?" asked Chuck. He was feeling like he was going to have to drag everything out of them.

"The germs died. There's something about the cells of plants and animals on Eden that make them impervious to anything we have that could cause a disease," replied Alex as he bit on his left thumbnail.

Chuck rubbed his brow. "Everything sounds perfect. So what's the bad news?"

Zophia stood and put her hands on her hips. "It's too perfect. If we breathed their air or ate their food, whatever kills the bacteria that enable us to function might be killed, and then we could be killed too."

"Ah! Why didn't you just say so in the first place?" exclaimed Chuck.

Alex pointed to himself and then Zophia twice. "We aren't done. We've run tests on some of the lab animals we brought with us, but they're inconclusive." He held out one hand palm out and gestured with the other as if placing things in his hand. "We took some of the air, water, soil, and plants we collected and built a closed ecosystem with the lab animals. So far, we haven't seen any harmful effects, but it may take a week or more before we see anything go wrong."

Chuck groaned. "So what's your conclusion?"

Alex glanced at Zophia then returned his attention to Chuck. "We strongly suggest that we wait another week before we attempt to land."

Chuck had to admit they were right. He couldn't jeopardize their mission or the crew just because he was impatient to mingle with the natives. "I'll let them know we're delaying our schedule."

August 20, 998 ASR

Robert and Jim continued up the street to the transport lot. They needed surface transportation to get to the trailhead where they would begin their hike into the wilderness area. Five transports, including two trucks, sat on the lot, but there was no one in sight.

Robert went to a tiny booth, where he found a note written on a white board signed by Alice. It provided the attendant's ECD ID and said it would take her about fifteen minutes to get to the lot.

"Looks like we'll have to wait awhile," Robert said as he lowered his backpack and hiking equipment to the brick pavement.

"Talk about crummy service," Jim grumbled. "These guys would never make it in the city."

Robert put his hand on Jim's shoulder. "This is the normal way of life out here. There aren't as many people and no one is in a hurry. This is the way things were over a thousand years ago, except for the technology." Robert then pulled his ECD from his pocket and unfolded it. He instructed the computer to connect him to the attendant's ECD ID. Alice answered and said she would be there in a few minutes.

Jim dropped his equipment next to Robert's. He paced for a couple of minutes then sat on his new sleeping bag. "I'm just not used to waiting for things." He fidgeted with the zippers on his new backpack. "How much longer do you think it'll be?"

Robert shrugged. "Beats me. Why don't I tell you about my Board meeting while we wait?" He related his experience of the past two days, including how his parents had tried to set him up. He didn't tell Jim how much information he had revealed to the Board about *The Question.*

About twenty minutes after Robert's call, a short, young blonde lady dressed in a brown work shirt and shorts rode up on a bicycle. "Hi, fellas," she greeted them a bit out of breath. "Sorry it took so long, but we don't get many visitors. There's no sense in me sitting here all day, so I work over at the feed store too. What can I do for you?"

Jim jumped up and started to explain how long they'd been waiting, but Robert interrupted him. "That's OK, Miss, I understand. We're going out to the wilderness area beyond Lone Mountain. We need something to get us to the trailhead and bring us back in a week. What do you suggest?"

She looked at the equipment on the bricks. "That little two-seater is a fun ride, but if you're looking for something more comfortable, the purple cruiser would be fine. The limo hasn't been moved for the last two years, but you could take that if you want."

"The two-seater looks just right," Jim said.

She gave Jim a thumbs-up. "The two-seater it is then. I'll just need you to sign for it and let me know when you expect to return. That way we can send out a search party if you don't come back on time." She winked at Jim then went into the booth.

"Maybe small town isn't so bad after all," whispered Jim while he stared at the young lady.

A moment later she returned with a signature pad.

Robert filled in the blanks on the form and pressed his thumb in the signature area.

She looked at the pad. "If you decide you'll need it any longer, just use the extension form that'll be in your ECD in-basket. Do you need any familiarization with this model's controls?"

Robert meandered around it and looked inside. "No, I've driven one like this before. Thanks, Miss, you've been very helpful,"

Robert opened the canopy, which was made from a transparent aluminum formula. Hinged at the frame behind the passenger seats, it opened at the dashboard and came up over the passenger compartment. He flipped the ON switch, energizing the electrical systems, and it rose up to cruising height. He popped open the hatch of the tiny rear cargo bay, which also hinged at the frame behind the passenger compartment. *From the side, it looks like a bird with two misshapen wings.* The vehicle was a sleek teardrop shape when the canopy and hatch were closed.

Jim ran his hands across the near-frictionless surface.

"I thought you were in a hurry," Robert teased. "Haven't you ever driven one of these?"

Jim put his pack in the back. "Can't say that I have. Although, I haven't been around as long as you have."

"In that case, I'm driving. Hop in." Robert stepped into the right side of the vehicle and set the switch for right-side control. When he lowered the canopy the air conditioning came on. He dialed in the coordinates of the trailhead, waved good-bye to Alice, and pressed the Go button. The transport moved slowly to the street, then accelerated to the town's speed limit.

Jim glanced back at the booth on the lot. "She is a pretty gal, isn't she? Maybe there's something to be said about small-town life after all."

Robert laughed as they turned a corner, taking her out of view.

Jim pointed to the control panel and snorted. "Some driving! You're doing it all with auto control. I could've done that."

Robert folded his arms and leaned back in the bucket seat. "Wait till we get out in the boonies a ways. Then we'll put it on manual and see what kind of driving skills you have."

Within five minutes they cleared the outskirts of town. Robert felt the two-seater bounce and sway slightly as the speed kicked up to 250 kilometers per hour. Wheat farms flew by as the mountains in the distance grew in height, reaching higher and higher into the sky. Uncultivated prairie took over as the wheat farms disappeared. Robert brought the two-seater to a stop and switched the controls to the left side.

"Go ahead, Jim. Just remember, this thing responds more quickly than the larger models."

Jim wrapped his hand around the joystick and gingerly moved it forward. The sleek vehicle jerked forward and wobbled back and forth. Robert set the joystick sensitivity down several points, and soon they were traveling smoothly at about fifty kilometers per hour. The road veered slightly to the right and Jim navigated the change easily.

"There's a side road just up ahead on the right," Robert said. "Why don't we go off on that, and you'll get some time on a winding road with lots of curves and turns?"

Jim pulled back on the joystick as he approached the side road, slowing for the turn. He then pulled the stick to the right, but his execution was too quick. The vehicle cut the corner, cruising over the ditch and across the side road. He overcorrected and ended up about forty meters off the side road on the other side.

Robert switched the controls back to the right side. "So, Jim, just how many times have you driven a transport?"

Jim looked sheepishly at Robert. "This is the first time. I thought it would be easy. I do great on those video games where you race around the track and obstacle courses. This was different. We were really moving."

Robert laughed. "You should have seen the look on your face when we went over the ditch." Jim joined in the laughter.

After switching the control back to Jim, Robert said, "Why don't you get the feel of driving this thing before we get back on the road? Do some figure eights for a while, and increase your speed until you feel comfortable."

Robert gave the controls back over to Jim. For the next hour he watched Jim carefully as he wound the vehicle around the prairie, going up and down the rolling hills, faster and faster.

"Looks like you've translated your video game experience into real life," Robert said, admiring how quickly Jim was able to maneuver the small craft. "I think you might well be doing better than me now."

"Thanks, man," said Jim as he did a quick figure eight.

Robert glanced at his watch. "Sorry to be a killjoy but we need to get back on the road or we'll be hiking in the dark. Whenever you've had enough fun, reset it back to automatic."

Jim raced back to the road then kicked in the auto control. As they returned to the road toward the trailhead, Robert sat back and enjoyed the scenery. The prairie gave way to foothills with broadleaf trees and underbrush covered with colorful flowers and berries.

They arrived at the trailhead where the mountains abruptly towered above the foothills. Robert let Jim enjoy the magnificent scenery while he parked in a small, vacant lot.

"Years ago, when I came here with my family," said Robert, "there were always three or four transports in the lot. Guess people don't have time to get out here much anymore."

Robert recalled pleasant memories of past trips as he viewed the steep mountains covered with large evergreen trees, clinging tenaciously to the nearly vertical slopes. To his left sheer rock cliffs were covered with moss and vines hanging down hundreds of meters, draping the rocks like long-neglected curtains in an abandoned house.

As he stepped out of the vehicle he drank in the fragrance of the bright pink flowers that adorned the vines. He heard water trickling over a cliff nearby and the distant crash of a waterfall. Multicolored birds flew in and around the trees, adding their plumage to the awe-inspiring scene.

Jim stood outside the transport, looking all around. "This place is beautiful. I never knew places like this existed. Nothing on the beach matches this."

Robert was pleased that his beach-bum friend was enjoying the scenery. "I thought you'd be impressed, but we'd better get going. It's getting late and we have a long hike ahead of us."

Jim slowly turned from the view and retrieved his equipment from the trunk. "Where are we headed first?"

Robert pointed. "You see that valley? The trail leads up along the river and then it rises steeply to get above the cliffs. It's an eight-hour hike to the cabin, so we won't make it before dark. I'd like to get in about two hours tonight. There's a place we can camp just before the rise to the top starts." He looked at his friend's feet. "Better change out of those sandals first."

Jim put on his new socks and shoes and Robert helped him adjust his backpack. After snacking on some ripe peaches from a tree beside the river, Robert led the way down the trail, winding around boulders and trees that grew in the narrow valley. The trail was well maintained by wilderness personnel. Robert was especially glad to see sturdy railings where the trail edge dropped sharply to the river and rocks below. The trail rose and fell, but stayed pretty much at the same level as the river.

Robert liked everything about this trail, but one of his favorite areas was where the trees offered a canopy of moss-covered branches. Sunlight barely filtered through, providing only a few spots where direct light reached the ground.

After two hours on the trail the sun began to set. They rounded a bend and all direct sunlight disappeared. Robert gazed into the impending twilight. The moss glowed a fluorescent yellow green in the reflected sunlight from the cliffs high above them.

He stopped at a small clearing. "This is the base of the upper trail that will take us to the top of the cliffs. We can camp here for the night. You want to cook us up some chow or set up the tent?"

Jim looked at the equipment they had just put down. "I think I'll cook. Wouldn't want the tent to fall during the night." Jim turned around in a circle. "So, where's the stove? How do you cook out here?"

Robert tossed his pack to Jim. "I have a portable heater in my pack. You can get water from the creek or that little waterfall to your right."

Robert erected the small pup tent. He was sure he would enjoy the savory stew he smelled that Jim had simmering on the portable hot plate. He plugged a lamp into the heater, satisfied with the rosy glow the light cast over their campsite.

They sat down on their bedrolls and ate in front of the lamp.

"You're a good cook, Jim. I don't think I've ever tasted trail rations this good before."

"Eh, no big deal. My parents are hardly ever home for meals, so I learned to cook by necessity." Jim curled one side of his mouth up as he spoke. "My older brother and sisters went off to university while I was still in grade school. After that Mom and Dad got even more absorbed in their work. Guess they figured I could raise myself."

Robert wished his mother had been around less. "What's it like not have parents around?"

Jim wagged his head back and forth shrugging each shoulder toward his head. "I hung out with school friends a lot. Most of their parents weren't around much either, so we could always find a place to go where there weren't any parents home. We always covered for each other."

Robert sensed Jim's sadness but avoided eye contact. He wanted to know more about his friend. This topic had never come up at university before.

"How do you feel about your parents now?"

Jim stared at the camp lantern. "I think I'm beginning to understand them better. They try hard to impress people by putting in a lot of extra work time. They want to earn more important positions, I think because they believe that will give meaning to their lives. Problem is, older people tend to keep their positions, even if they aren't as capable or qualified as younger ones."

Jim looked up at Robert. "You know, I think that old economy that used money makes sense. Maybe we're getting the short end of the stick because there aren't any monetary rewards for doing a good job. I mean, where's the incentive to do your best and prove to others that you have some worth other than what the Administration says you have?"

Jim picked up a stick and broke it in two. He held up the short piece.

"Look at me, for example. What am I going to do after I get out of school? Try to find out what's available in society so I can be a 'good contributor'? I can't do what I want because I'll be forced into some job without any meaning. Frankly, that scares me."

Robert took the short stick and scratched in the ground with it. "I've been struggling with the same things. I've never felt like I was worth anything. I've got more degrees than you can count on one hand, but I still feel like there's something missing in my life." He looked up at the clouds that were starting to hide the stars. "The Board gave me an access card so I can get whatever I need for my assignment. I haven't used it yet, but I've thought of some interesting possibilities. I mean, if I can get anything, maybe I could get a two-seater as my own personal transport. Having the card gives me a sense of power, knowing that I have something that others don't." He thought about The Sovereign Yehowshuwa's power. *What would it be like to have that much control?* "Maybe, instead of a capitalistic society, we should have one that's based on assigning some kind of authority as a reward."

Jim slipped off his sleeping bag and stretched out on the ground with his head propped up on one elbow. "Isn't that what we already have? The Board members have control. When a community grows and they divide into two councils, who gets the new positions that open up? Only those who've held authoritative positions in different Administration organizations, or their buddies. They exercise power over others, whether it's food distribution, the transportation authority, even the local hardware store. Board members are also responsible for making sure everyone has a 'suitable' position in society. With a capitalistic system, only truly capable people would have the wealth and, therefore, the power."

Robert felt a bit dumb. Jim's comment was right. "I see what you mean. When power isn't manifested in something tangible like money, those who have the influence use it in the way they want instead of letting people's abilities determine where the control lies. So do you think the way the Administration is set up is wrong?"

Jim dropped his voice to a whisper. "You're starting to sound like Josu."
"Who's that?"

Jim's eyes appeared to brighten in the dim light. "Josu is an old man I met at the Northwest Coast Regional Center. He runs one of the cafeterias there. I ordered this exotic dish with baby eels in it, and this old guy sits down and starts talking to me. Spooky, he looked exactly like me, except three or four hundred years older. He said we must be related, and after we talked awhile, I had to agree it sounds like our ancestry could be the same."

Jim looked around quickly as if to see if anyone was listening. "He asked me a lot of questions about myself, but I felt like he already knew the answers. Then he asked me if I'm suspicious of older people. When I said yes, he asked if I'm suspicious of The Sovereign."

"He asked you that right there in a public place?" It was hard for Robert to imagine an old guy asking that question.

"Yeah." Jim shivered. "Now you're asking me point blank if I think the Administration is wrong. We've beat around the bush about this stuff but this is creeping me out."

Robert puffed out a quick breath. "Lighten up, Jim. How many times have we met on campus to discuss controversial subjects and never had any Enforcers show up? I doubt that what you and I are discussing here is of any importance to the Administration. So, do you think the way the Administration is set up is wrong?"

Jim took a few seconds to think about it. "Yeah, I do. When my mom and dad were spending more time at home, they had conversations about stuff they had learned at university, outside their classes. They talked about how things could be different and how society could be reformed. What they said made sense to me. That's why I joined the groups when I got to university. Suddenly, one day they stopped talking about those things. They told me they had to go to meetings and seminars for business training. That's when everything changed. They started spending more time at work, and it seemed they lost the ideals they had. Personally, I think an Enforcer got involved and brainwashed them to the Administration's goals."

A queasy ripple tightened in Robert's gut. "I've heard people talk about that happening, but I never knew anyone who went through it."

Jim's voice quivered slightly as he quietly talked, "Ever since my first day on campus, when I got my first copy of *The Question,* I've been waiting for an Enforcer to show up and escort me to a brainwashing center. I don't know why my parents got caught and I haven't. I don't know how the groups can continue to meet and use *The Question* as a guide to discussions. I don't know why *The Question* hasn't been shut down. Why do you think we haven't been busted?"

Robert thought about his revelation to the Board. "Either they don't think we're a threat or they're powerless to stop us. From the meetings you've been involved with, do you think the groups are a threat to the Administration?"

"I do. People who've done less to instigate dissatisfaction with The Sovereign's policies have been locked up for treason." Jim shuddered.

"So millions of people have been involved in treasonous activities, yet no one we know has been confronted by an Enforcer, much less locked up."

"It doesn't make sense to me. I can't help feeling that they're going to get us sooner or later." Jim jabbed his stick into the ground.

"I think it all goes back to what happened in The Last Battle. When we find the truth, it will transform society. For now, I think we're safe talking about whatever we want." Robert waved his hand from one side to the other. "Especially out here."

Jim looked at Robert out of the corner of his eye. "I hope you're right. I can't shake this feeling that someone's looking over my shoulder. I don't want to end up like my parents or become a grunt in some factory, cranking out coffee cups for Board meetings. On the other hand, I like the discussions in our clandestine meetings. They give me hope that there may be alternatives for my life." Jim glanced furtively over his shoulder. "Then again, I don't know how much of a difference they'll make."

Robert pulled Jim's stick out of the ground and held it up. "I think they've already made a difference. We can question policies and meet together. I've studied enough ancient history to know that many oppressive governments had to make concessions when the multitudes demand it." *It feels good to be making a difference even if we haven't seen the effects yet.*

Jim took the stick, scoffed and stuck it the ground again. "But didn't some of those revolutionaries get killed for their ideas?"

Robert hesitated. "True, however, this is different because of the number of people involved. As I've said before, we don't know the whole story yet. When we find out, it will be liberating. Believe me, things are going to change."

"Who's there?" Jim jumped up and shouted pointing into the darkness.

Startled, Robert stood and peered where Jim indicated. "I don't see anything."

"No. I saw a person. A very tall, slim guy. I caught the reflection of the lamp off his shiny jacket and sunglasses. For an instant I could see his face too. It looked real pale then he just kind of dissolved and disappeared." Jim stopped and scratched his head. "Oh man, I sure hope that wasn't an Enforcer or maybe an Informer."

"You have to be seeing things, Jim. Besides, sunglasses at night? Informer? I've never heard of that before. It was probably just an animal."

Jim stretched. "You've got some good points." He grabbed his canteen, took a step toward the river, and stumbled. "Hey, I thought these were good hiking boots!" He sat back down and pulled off his left boot and sock. "Look at the blister on my big toe. I'll never be able to hike up the mountain tomorrow."

Robert looked at the bloody mess on Jim's sock. "Stop whining. I have balm in my first-aid kit. That'll be healed by morning. What did you expect with new boots?" Robert got up, pulled a small box out of his pack and retrieved a squeeze tube from it. He handed it to Jim.

Jim took the salve and rubbed it on the wound.

Robert stretched. He looked up and couldn't see any stars. "I think it's about time to turn in. The air is getting damper and cooler. It won't be long before the rain starts."

The two men put their equipment inside the pup tent and settled in. Within a few minutes rain pelted the tent.

In the dark, Jim asked, "Are you sure this is waterproof? How long will the rain last? I'm not sure I can get any sleep with all that noise."

Robert muttered just loud enough for Jim to hear as he crawled into his sleeping bag. "Everything is under control. The tent is secure. The rain will only last an hour or so. When it stops, you can get some sleep. Unless the sounds of the night animals keep you awake." Robert bet that would shake Jim.

Jim sat up quickly. "I thought we were going to be in a cabin, not surrounded by some flimsy piece of cloth. What happens if one of those animals decides to come snooping in our tent?"

Robert rolled over. "Go to sleep."

Jim shoved Robert's shoulder. "This isn't the beach, you know, with sand and surf and a nice, soft bed in a cottage by the bay."

Robert flopped over on his back. "If you were out there surfing and a big shark came up beside you, what would you do?"

Jim was quiet for a few seconds. "That's never been a problem. Fish stay out of the way."

Robert turned away again. "The animals here will stay away too. Now, go to sleep."

Chapter 13

Chuck sat behind his big mahogany desk, his chin propped on his hands as he looked at the view screen across the room. Eden rotated slowly as he watched the seconds tick off the digital time display at the lower left corner of the screen.

The past week had dragged by endlessly. Each day seemed longer than the one before. Now that the possibility of finding intelligent life had become a reality, he couldn't bear to wait even a few minutes longer. He bolted for the lab.

Four crewmembers' heads quickly looked at the door as it swooshed open and Chuck burst into the room and asked, "What have you got?" He marched over to the sealed ecosystem labeled *Little Eden* and stopped short. There was only one gray mouse in the sophisticated cage. "Where is Bernie? Why is Ebert alone in the cage?"

Zophia looked back at her monitor and replied, "We had to perform a detailed examination on Bernie to make sure there were no ill effects of his stay in little Eden. We aren't quite finished."

"So where is he?"

Zophia looked at Alex, who gestured for the Captain to follow him to a monitor. There he punched in some commands and the results of the examination displayed on the screen. "This is Bernie's liver. Several cross-sections have been examined down to the atomic level to verify that there hasn't been any necrosis. Hal will show you everything we've analyzed so far. If you'll excuse me, I need to finish some more tests before our briefing." Alex returned to his work.

Chuck stood transfixed before the screen as slide after slide of the necropsy displayed before him. He shifted his weight from foot to foot and rubbed the top of his head. His head felt…different.

Zophia was glad Captain Andrews was engrossed in the results so he wouldn't interrupt them with questions she wasn't prepared to answer about the results of their tests.

When the tests were completed, she quietly suggested to Alex that they sneak off to a conference room to go over the results. The last thing she wanted to do was compare notes and try to reach a conclusion in front of the Captain.

Alex took a glance at Andrews standing in front of the monitor rubbing his head and quickly led the way around a corner down a short passageway to a small conference room. They sat down at the small metallic table. "That was a good idea to get away from Chuck. It would take us twice as long to figure out what we have with him interrupting every two seconds."

He started talking faster as he turned his ECD and pointed to the screen. "If we hadn't taken samples before we put Bernie in there, I wouldn't have believed these results. Look at this. He was actually in better health now than when we put him in *Little Eden* last week. Even the scars from the biopsies disappeared. It actually looks like the aging process may have been reversed to some extent. Chuck is going to be ecstatic"

Zophia was trying to get her mind around the possibilities of reversed aging. "If something seems too good to be true it probably isn't. All this data indicates that if we went down to Eden we'd come back younger than when we left. If we stayed there long enough would we become teenagers? Would we continue going backward until we were babies?"

Alex's eyes widened. "That's a scary thought. Here's another one. We need to make sure that whatever is in Eden doesn't come with us when we leave. What if we put Bernie's ecosystem buddy, Ebert, into another isolation chamber? This time, it will be a normal Earth environment and we'll give him a new friend that hasn't been exposed to any of Eden's environment."

"Another week?" Zophia closed her eyes and put her hand on her forehead. She didn't want to be the one to tell the Captain he would have to wait another week.

Alex must have read her mind. He took a long-handled disposable chemical ladle out of shirt pocket and broke it behind his back. He presented the two ends of the handle between his thumb and index finger. "Draw straws to see who tells the Captain?"

Zophia lost.

Chuck finished looking at all the slides from Bernie. He looked around the lab eager to hear the result but discovered that Alex and Zophia were missing. He felt his patience wearing thin. He turned to a technician and asked, "Barb, did you see where Alex and Zophia went?"

"I thought I saw them go down that corridor a few minutes ago," she answered pointing to her right.

He paced back and forth to the corner of the passageway until he saw them coming back toward him. He folded his arms and tapped his foot. "Where did you guys go? I've been looking at all this medical mumbo jumbo, turn around and you're gone. From everything I've seen here, I could have been on the surface enjoying a walk in the park by now. Well? Do we have a go or not?" His patience was well past worn thin.

Zophia grimaced then explained what she and Alex had discussed in the conference room. "I'm sorry; we need another week, Captain."

"You guys are being so super cautious that I'm seriously considering taking a shuttle down there and letting you play your 'what if' games 'til kingdom come." Chuck again rubbed the top of his head.

Barb approached the three officers. "Excuse me, but before you make any decisions there is something else you need to consider."

Chuck felt that Barb's intrusion was a breach of protocol until he saw the concern on her face. "What do you have, Barb?"

"I had Hal compare the results of Arnie, the control specimen that was in the *Little Earth* ecochamber with Bernie's slides. They're almost identical. If I didn't know that they came from two different mice. I would have thought they were both from Bernie."

"Let me see that." Alex took the ECD from Barbara and studied the notes.

"How could that happen?" Chuck asked. "Are you saying that Arnie looked as if he had been in *Little Eden* with Bernie?"

"Yes," Alex answered with a puzzled look. "I'm not sure what to make of it. My theory is that we've all been contaminated, and that whatever is causing the changes are already throughout the ship."

Chuck broke into a huge grin and rubbed the top of his head. "Guys, look at this." He bent over slightly. "In the last two days, I've started to grow hair! I've been bald for years. You're right. Something has affected the crew. That may be bad news or good. Since it appears we're already 'contaminated,' is there any reason we shouldn't go on down?"

Alex, Zophia, and Barbara stared in silence until Alex spoke up. "Arnie bears testimony that any contamination occurred before he was put in the isolation chamber."

Chuck pointed to Alex and Zophia. "You two, come with me. Barb, don't tell anyone about Arnie or my bald spot just yet. I don't want a panic on my hands."

"Yes, Sir. I won't say anything until you give the word."

He smiled to let Barbara know that everything would be OK. "Thank you. Now, let's go to my office."

When the three arrived in his office, Chuck sat in his chair behind his desk. Alex and Zophia took two visitor chairs. "Hal, get me Mine, and let him know this is important."

Hal established the connection but Mine wasn't in his office.

While his assistant went to find him, Chuck told the officers his theory. "Four days before we arrived here, Tia-le informed me that we were about to pass from Rof's territory to Adon's and that she couldn't accompany us any farther until our return trip. She assured me that Adon would have everything under control and that we would be safe in his space."

Alex's and Zophia's expressions indicate they wanted to interrupt but neither said anything and Chuck wasn't going to let them.

"When we got here, Mine assured us we wouldn't have any problems coming to the surface. After you guys came up with this Bernie and Ebert idea last week, I told Mine we would be delayed another week. He wasn't bothered about the delay but assured me our experiments would prove that Eden was beneficial to our health. When I pressed him for details, he told me to wait and see."

Chuck leaned forward. "These guys on Eden really believe that Adon has so much control over everything here that not even a microscopic piece of space dust can enter his domain without him knowing about it and without his permission. Mine also said that Adon would be giving us a little surprise."

Before his officers could respond, Chuck's view screen came to life with Mine's beaming face. "Hello, Chuck, Alex, Zophia, it's good to see you. I'm guessing by the looks on your faces you've finished your tests and found our little surprise."

Zophia folded her arms. "If it's your surprise, why don't you tell us what you gave us? That would help me believe it came from you."

"Zophia!" Chuck began to reprimand her but Mine interrupted.

"It's all right, Chuck. Zophia, I understand why you might be apprehensive about this. You come from a planet that isn't perfect and have taken this trip expecting to find hostile life in space."

It was more as if we didn't expect to find any life but here we are almost face to face with aliens. Let's get on with it.

"The gift that our sovereign, Adon, has bestowed on you is eternal life. It isn't really anything unique to you. He grants it to all who come into his dominion. I know that on your home planet, people have illnesses, age and die. We don't. Adon gives us eternal life, and as long as you are here you will have it too. It applies to all life, including your lab mice."

Alex scowled. "Are you saying that Adon is causing this to happen?"

Mine raised his eyebrows. "Is that so hard to believe? Wasn't Earth miraculously restored after The Last Battle? Hasn't Earth and its inhabitants enjoyed near-perfect health ever since? Hasn't your sovereign claimed to have done all this for you? Why then should you doubt that Adon has done the same and more for us and for visitors while they are here? Or is the real problem that you now suspect that your sovereign has been holding back on you? Are you afraid that when you return to Earth you will eventually age and die?"

Chuck was getting used to aliens challenging the integrity of The Sovereign Yehowshuwa. He didn't like it but the shock had worn off. However, he saw the muscles in Alex's jaw twitch and his eyes narrow.

"We have much to talk about. Why don't you come down and see for yourself what a truly perfect society is like?"

Chuck turned to Zophia and Alex. "Unless you two can come up with a scientific reason for not getting on with this mission, I'm going to give the order to land." *Please, please don't find any reasons. I just want to move forward.*

Zophia looked at Mine's face on the screen for what seemed a long time. She appeared to be studying his features. The screen only showed his face with square jaw, deep blue eyes, perfect white teeth, angular nose and flawless tanned complexion. Her glare disappeared and she unfolded her arms. "I believe we can trust him. I'm all right with landing. How about you, Alex?"

Alex remained tight lipped but agreed.

Chuck jumped up. "Mine, when can you accommodate us?"

Mine's showed even more of his perfect teeth. "We will be ready within the hour. All I need to do is let your escorts know it's time to come to the port and welcome you. Would you like to have lunch with us as our first official function together?"

Chuck rubbed his hands together. "That would be great. I'll see you in an hour."

"We'll be ready," Mine replied and the view screen went blank.

"Hal, get me Barbara."

The view screen came back on with Barbara.

"You can tell our secret now. We haven't been infected. Adon, the sovereign of Eden, has reversed the aging process. We'll make a general announcement in a few minutes that we are going to put down on Eden firma."

The lines on Barbara's forehead melted away. "Thank you, Chuck. I'll let our team know."

He turned to Alex, who had stood. "I'd like you to prepare a formal statement of our findings and make a ship-wide announcement in ten minutes. You don't have to make it too detailed, but do include that we believe Adon is responsible for the reversal of the aging process. I'll follow up with an announcement that we are invited to lunch. I want to be on our way down in twenty-five minutes at the latest."

Chuck pointed to Zophia, "Make sure Irene and Buckly are on the bridge. Meet me there as soon as you can."

Zophia whipped out her ECD as she hurried out the door after Alex.

Chuck did a little jump and clicked his heels together before he followed them and crossed the corridor to the bridge.

August 20, 998 ASR

The convy that Samantha and Papa took from the coffee shop deposited them in the middle of the mall. It always intimidated Samantha to be suddenly surrounded by people since she spent most of her time in the country. They stepped out of the cab amid hundreds of people walking in every direction.

Samantha took a few steps from the convy stop and stared at the circular building, five stories high, surrounding a large open-air inner court filled with flowering trees, shrubs, walkways, grass, park benches, picnic tables, and food courts. As she watched people going up and down on transparent elevators and escalators on the interior side of the court, she imagined that some were on their way to shop, meet friends, or run errands of importance. The signs above the shop entrances identified sellers of clothing, business supplies, household goods, art, electronics, hobby supplies, fabric, personal care products, and pets.

"Papa, is it my imagination or is this mall at least twice as big as the last time I was here?"

"It always is overwhelming unless you lived here. When were you here last?" Papa asked.

"I'm sure it's been at least six months."

"They have been adding on because of the growth in the city but it couldn't be that much bigger. Anyway, what's first on your list, Sam?"

Samantha put her fists on her hips. "First we have to look around and see what's here. You know Mama and I don't pull out the list until we've checked out every shop."

He lifted his hands in surrender. "My mistake. It's been a while since I've been shopping with you or your mama. I wouldn't dream of rushing you."

Samantha pivoted around in a small circle, looking at all the shops within view. "A complete survey would take half the day and not even get through a third of them. So...let's start with that clothing store."

They walked across the courtyard into a small shop of women's clothes. Samantha went to a rack of blouses and sorted through various colors and patterns while Papa wandered around.

After a few minutes, Samantha motioned for Papa to come look at a particular blouse. "Papa," she said in a low voice, "look at this. It's supposed to be a blouse, but can you imagine me wearing something like this?" She held it up in front of her. It was short, sleeveless, and had a low-scooped neckline.

"Not unless it includes something underneath." He looked around the store and quickly returned his attention to Samantha. He motioned with his head for her to look where he had.

Samantha looked in the direction indicated and stared at a young woman who wore a blouse just like the one Samantha was holding. She was wearing a skirt that covered only a minimal portion of her lower body. "What do you say we look in a different store?" she blurted out.

Papa hurried Samantha out of the store and back into the courtyard as she whispered, "I thought clothes like that were banned!"

"I would have thought so too. I don't recall ever seeing designs that were intended to invoke a man's attention like that. I'm shocked. Guess I don't get off the farm much."

Samantha was puzzled. "The styles at school have been getting a little weird, but nothing like that. The dress code has always been strict. We can't expose any body parts above the knee, below the neck, or over the bicep. I'm surprised The Sovereign allows this."

They continued meandering around the first level of the mall, looking at the various shops, but Samantha was more cautious about which stores to enter. She found two more new shops that provided questionable clothes. Other shops that had been open longer didn't appear to have any of the skimpy clothes. She picked out a few articles there.

While browsing among some pants, she asked, "How come I don't see any indiscrete clothes for men?"

Papa laughed. "That's a good question. Maybe we just haven't found any yet." His mouth turned downward abruptly. "I spoke too soon. I just saw a guy on the other side of the court wearing skintight pants. His top is like the woman's blouse we saw in the first store. I hope the guys at university don't dress that way."

Samantha didn't look. Her father's description was enough. "I guess things are changing and we've been oblivious to it. If that's the case, whether I go to university or a trade school I'll run into the same things."

"Well, things will always stay the same on our farm," Papa stated. "I wouldn't allow anyone to show up for work dressed like either of those people. It isn't my job to teach folks decency but I don't have to tolerate a lack of it."

Samantha put her chin on the clothes rack. "If they aren't learning basic decency before they get to the workforce or to university, it sounds like something has gone amiss in our society. Does that mean The Sovereign is losing control or doesn't care or can't keep up with everyone?"

Papa elevated his eyebrows. "Do you really think Yehowshuwa can lose control or that he doesn't care?"

"Of course not. I just don't understand what's going on. It doesn't make sense that he'd allow this."

Papa looked down at the floor and scuffed the carpet with one foot. "I'm sure there's a logical explanation for what's happening. Maybe the time is just about here and we need to be ready, as well as help anyone who isn't ready."

Samantha contemplated what her father had said. "If that's the case, maybe the best thing I can do is go to university. Maybe that's where Yehowshuwa can use me."

Papa's shining eyes let her know he was proud of his daughter. "Let's get an ice cream before we head home."

Samantha finished shopping quickly. Suddenly some of the things she thought she needed didn't seem as important as before. She did need some new clothes, though, and she chose items that were neither so conservative that she would alienate others on campus nor so provocative that she would appear to have questionable morals.

Chapter 14

Chuck marched onto the bridge of the Ramah and plunked himself down on the command chair. He felt more like a starship captain than at any time in the previous 25 years. He was ready for the adventure. "Hal, open a channel for an all-ship announcement." He set a bottle of the finest Earth wine, his present for Mine, down on the floor beside him.

Hal responded, "The channel is available, Chuck."

He announced, "This is Andrews. In seven minutes Alex is going to give us the results of his Eden tests. I want everyone to hear this announcement, so be prepared. That is all." Chuck switched off the channel.

The timing couldn't be better. H.S.S.S. Ramah ran with three shifts. The 11:00 PM to 7:00 AM shift normally slept in the morning, and the other two shifts normally slept overnight, which meant that everyone was awake in the afternoon. In addition, most of the crew found that they required much less sleep than usual. He had attributed it to the anticipation of arriving on Eden. Now he figured it was due to the improved physical condition Adon had provided for them.

Chuck watched the clock on the view screen. Alex's face showed up right on time. He made a brief and very positive summation of the studies, Adon's surprise, and the conclusion.

As soon as Alex signed off, Chuck announced, "We've all been invited to lunch on Eden. In a few seconds we will leave orbit for a quick descent to the pad they've prepared for us. Forty minutes from now we will be on the surface of Eden. Hal will monitor all systems while we meet our hosts. Irene, take us down."

Chuck switched off the channel, and the view panel switched to an exterior view of the planet. Clouds were blown away as the ship plunged into the atmosphere. The ground rushed toward him as fields, cities, buildings, trees, and streets got closer. At five hundred meters above the surface the landing pad was about the only thing visible on the screen. Chuck responded, "Hal, switch to side views."

The view screen changed to four panels that showed the vantage from each side of the ship. He saw buildings, landscape, and crowds of people who had come out to welcome the visitors from Earth. The walls of the landing pad filled the lower half of the scene, blotting out all but the distant tall buildings.

The last few meters seemed to take an eternity, but Ramah slowly settled down. Chuck heard a grating noise as it made contact with the surface of the pad. The ship shuddered as Hal shut off the gravitational fields. Chuck breathed easily as if a weight had been lifted from him as well.

"Everyone report to the north disembarkation hatch," Chuck instructed over Ramah's system. He picked up his wine bottle and started for the exit.

Irene, Buckly, and Zophia hesitated at their posts.

"Well, come on. Don't you want to see your hosts?"

"Sir," Irene said, "we have to make sure everything is shut down and—"

He cut her off. "No, you don't. Hal has complete control of the environmental systems."

"The Captain's right," Zophia said as she stood. Buckly joined her but Irene held back.

"You two go on down," he told Zophia and Buckley. "Irene and I will catch up with you. As soon as the whole crew is assembled, we'll open the door."

"I know we haven't talked to anyone other than the crew for 25 years but I've been talking with them quite a bit since we arrived. These people are very hospitable," Chuck said. "And good looking," he added with a wink.

"I'm nervous," Irene responded.

Chuck extended his elbow toward Irene. "Would it help if you were my date? Would you care to accompany me to the ball, m'lady?"

Irene shyly took Chuck's arm. "Don't mind if I do," she stammered. He could feel a slight tremor in her hand.

"You can sit with me at lunch if it would make you more comfortable," he said as they promenaded down the corridor with her hand on his arm.

"I may just take you up on that. Let's wait and see what things are like. It might not be as bad as I expect."

When Chuck and Irene arrived at the disembarkation hatch, the rest of the crew was present. Chuck felt compelled to make a short speech. "Ladies and gentlemen, we are about to embark on what could be the most significant event in human history. We are about to meet, face to face, intelligent beings that are not human. What we learn from them may change the future of mankind. However, right now, we are going to have lunch and just get to know them. So enjoy yourselves. Tomorrow, we'll get down to the business of fact gathering."

Zophia handed out small earpieces to the crew as she explained to them, "These are transceivers that will feed the Edenians speech back to Hal. He will translate it so you can understand our hosts."

At Chuck's command, the hatch opened. The blast wall had been pulled away and folded down to form a large patio, where the Edenians had assembled. Music from a hundred-piece orchestra on the left side of the patio greeted the crew with a melody that was smooth and lofty.

As Chuck descended the ramp with Irene on his arm, a 500-voice choir joined in with a reception song that hailed the visitors in Eden's native language. He felt as if angels were serenading him. After the first verse, they continued singing in The Sovereign Yehowshuwa's universal language.

Chuck was glad that at least he had brought a token gift of wine. However, it seemed terribly insignificant in light of the grandeur of the Edenians' welcome.

Chuck led the way down the ramp with Irene next to him, followed by Alex and Marti, then Zophia and Demetrius. The remainder of the crew followed in ranks. They had not brought formal uniforms since they'd been told they wouldn't find any kind of intelligent life. Right now, he wished they had something fancier to wear than jumpers.

As they approached Mine, Ana, and the others, Chuck stopped thinking about his appearance. "Now I know why they only showed their heads on the view screens," he whispered to Irene. At a hundred meters away it became obvious that their welcoming committee didn't have skin tight body socks but that they were all stark naked.

Chuck heard several gasps behind him but didn't want to turn and see how the rest of the crew was reacting. They were the first humans to meet aliens on their grounds and didn't want to make a political blunder.

"I don't know if I can go through with this," Irene said without moving her lips.

"Just look them in the eye," he whispered back.

Chuck continued to the reception line forcing a smile on his face but with his teeth clenched. "Welcome to Eden, Chuck," said Mine. "It's good to see you." He looked Chuck up and down. "It appears that you are rather tense. Is something wrong?"

Chuck answered, barely separating his teeth. "Thank you for your warm welcome. We were not expecting such a formal reception. But mostly we were not expecting you to be . . . well, nude. Your, uh, dress code is significantly different from ours. You must have seen from our video meetings that we wear clothes."

Mine didn't change his expression. He showed no signs of being nervous or uncomfortable. "I'm sorry you are uncomfortable. However, would you have come to lunch if you'd known we would be unclothed?"

Chuck hadn't thought about it that way. "Some of us may have decided to stay on board."

"We were certain the only way to introduce you to this facet of life on Eden was to let you show up and find out. Besides, we don't have any clothes to put on. This seemed easier than asking you to come without clothes." Mine's kept his eyes on Chuck's.

Chuck reflected on how absurd it would be to ask his crew to strip bare for a luncheon. He couldn't hold back a quick laugh.

Mine's mouth straightened along with his eyebrows. "During your time here you will find many uncomfortable things. The only way to overcome them is to face them. Nudity is a minor thing compared to what you will find out about Adon and Yehowshuwa."

Chuck wasn't sure how many more uncomfortable things he or his crew would be able to handle. "I'm sure you are right. But nudity is a significant moral issue on Earth."

"With us there is no embarrassment or shame. Our bodies are perfect and we have no need to cover some parts and expose others. However, there will be plenty of time to discuss that later. Are you still willing to join us for lunch?"

Something about Mine, his eyes, his ever present smile and voice, were almost hypnotic. Chuck felt comfortable after only a few words. "I believe I will be able to adjust. However, I would like each of my crewmembers to decide for themselves."

Mine bowed slightly. "Certainly. We would expect no less than to give you the choice."

Chuck led Irene a few meters to the side and turned to his crew. He motioned for them to come around him. "I apologize for what you see here. If anyone would like to return to the ship, you may go. I will be going to lunch because that is my duty, but I don't expect any of you to do anything that is against your principles.

I'm afraid there may be other things that will shock us as we get to know these people."

The crew looked around at one another, apparently waiting to see what everyone else would decide. Irene turned and eyed the waiting dignitaries. Chuck followed her glance to see the Edenians smiling back. Their calm nature set Chuck at ease but he wondered how they could appear so happy all the time.

Irene must have felt the same soothing effect. For the first time since they left the bridge her hand wasn't trembling and she let go of Chuck. "I don't know about everyone else, but I'm hungry. I also want to see what their food is like."

One after another voiced or nodded their agreement. As Chuck turned to tell Mine that they were all coming to lunch, he felt as if their nudity was completely natural. There was something almost infectiously attractive about these people and their openness. Perhaps Adon was affecting more than just their health.

"It appears you were correct in your assessment of us, Mine. We are ready for lunch and the beginning of a great relationship." Chuck reached out for a handshake.

Mine extended his hand and shook Chuck's firmly. "No problem, Chuck. Getting to know people of other cultures is always difficult, especially for someone who has never before had the opportunity. I'm sure Adon has already softened your hearts toward us and will continue to influence you as you learn more about us." Mine held up his hand, wiggling his fingers. "Oh, I hope you don't mind, but we eat almost all our food with our hands instead of utensils."

Mine motioned for his team to step forward. "Before we go to the dining area, let me introduce your crew to their guides. During your visit, these guides will show you Eden and answer your questions. Each morning for the first week, we have a group tour planned. In the afternoons you are welcome to follow up with individual tours. As you learn more about us, you may want to take some extended tours to other parts of Eden or stay here and explore our capital city, Adonlon."

Mine introduced his guides. Chuck didn't think it odd that Mine knew the names of his entire crew. That freed him to mingle with the crew and see how they were getting along with their guides.

Irene was matched with a guide who appeared to be a young woman. As the two talked, Chuck discovered she was over twelve hundred years old. The shyness Irene had exhibited before leaving the bridge was quickly evaporating and the two were soon engaged in conversation.

Other animated conversations between Edenians and humans convinced Chuck that his crewmembers and their guides were quickly becoming friends. The warmth of the Edenians' hospitality and their winsome personalities melted any barriers.

Once introductions were over, they proceeded to the luncheon. Chuck would have described it as more of a picnic as it was held in a large grassy area surrounded by flowering trees whose fragrance perfumed the air. Low tables accommodated twelve people each. Instead of sitting in chairs, they reclined on pillows.

Chuck felt very much at home.

August 20, 998 ASR

The Chancellor Ben-Shaachar was so thrilled with the reports he received from his interplanetary forces he almost forgot about the gloom of the dungeon. He laughed loudly. His plan was coming together. He reflected on the formation of his backup plan that was now being set in motion and the documentary that would be at the heart of his plan. His mind took him back nearly a thousand years.

August 22, 1 BLB

"OK, Abathar, let's see what you've got this time," said The Chancellor. "If it isn't any better than the last cuts, you are going to be in big trouble."

"Yes, sir, I understand. I've added the segments you requested with your narration of history. I'm sure you will like it." Abathar handed the remote to Ben-Shaachar. He clicked it and the 180-by-120-centimeter screen in his office lit up.

The title "The True Story" faded in over a background of stars and swirling cosmos. Haunting, unearthly music increased in volume, filling the room and giving Chancellor Ben-Shaachar an overpowering sense of a divine presence. The music reached a crescendo as the title was replaced by an implosion of swirling gasses, resulting in the formation of Earth. The scene zoomed in rapidly upon Earth, drawing him into the screen as if he were falling from a great height. Clouds approached at an alarming speed but became a mist which disappeared, yielding the great ocean beneath. The rate of descent continued as the ocean came up but he plunged beneath without a splash. The water appeared to expand and then come under a microscope. With each passing second he saw deeper and deeper into the structure of the water, seeing molecules of dissolved minerals and chemicals.

He blinked as a lightning bolt shot through the waters. Some of the minerals fused together to form a chain of a denser and more complex structure. Another flash and the molecule became even more complex. Several molecules joined together and the scene started to draw back. He could no longer see individual chains but a small mass of a jelly-like substance that changed, moved, and grew as his view kept backing up. The jelly became a cell that sucked in nourishment from the water and divided over and over again, filling the water. Other cells joined together as he retreated even more.

Small plants and animals formed and swam in the waters. A plethora of animals and plants developed in the ocean. Then he withdrew from the water to dry land. Myriad creatures and plants came from the water and covered what had been barren land. Trees grew tall while animals covered the plains and frolicked in the lush forests. Lions grazed peacefully among antelope.

People appeared without clothing and walked alongside the animals, all as tame as domesticated pets.

The camera panned back to reveal The Chancellor standing in front of a screen that looked much like the one he and Abathar were watching in his office. The scene behind his image froze as he spoke. "Dear children, it saddens me deeply to realize that there can only be one reason you are watching this documentary. It is because I, Ben-Shaachar, have failed in my efforts to restore Earth to its natural and beautiful beginning, which you have just seen. I humbly ask for your forgiveness. Yet because you are viewing this presentation, I am hopeful that I, with your help, still have one more chance to restore the true purpose of Earth and free mankind once and for all. To do this I will show you the true story of the history of your people, a history that has been hidden and repressed by one who has posed as your friend. What you are about to see is shocking. It strikes at the very heart of everything you have been taught since you were born. There is no way I can completely prepare you for this, but I do ask you to keep an open mind."

The Chancellor watched himself motion to the screen, extending his arm as if to embrace the whole world. "This is what Earth looked like millions of years ago. People lived in harmony with nature. There was no death or evil in the land. You continued to evolve in knowledge and wisdom without any restraints on your mental and physical abilities."

The scene behind him in the film changed as beautiful cities with magnificent architecture appeared. He lowered his arm. "You were destined to grow to the point that you could ascend to enlightenment and create perfect environments and planets. You would continue to live in harmony with all nature for eternity. You were to grow and have the potential to join those who are in alliance with the Council of Enlightened Beings in our realm. However, Yehhovaw, the one who fashioned this world and you through the methods shown, saw you as a threat to his existence. He knew that at some point you would become as knowledgeable and powerful as he. He feared that someday you would even surpass him."

The camera panned in on the screen again and dark clouds formed over the cities. Lightning flashed and thunder crashed. Ben-Shaachar felt vibrations in his chest from the thundering speakers as violent winds, earthquakes, and hailstones reduced the cities to rubble. People and animals ran in every direction, seeking shelter. He heard his own voice narrate, "Yes, Yehhovaw struck this planet and destroyed all the accomplishments of man and almost eliminated all life. The destruction was so complete that no future generations could find even a trace of these magnificent cities. He also infected the world with disease and radiation so that for the first time your forefathers knew death instead of immortality and enlightenment. Even as I speak, your mental capabilities have been suppressed by his powers. If that were not enough, he also appeared to the remnant, demanded that they worship him and blamed them for the disaster he had wrought. He said that since they had disobeyed him and thus failed to worship him, this was a consequence of their actions. So that they would not be able to pass on to their children the true history, he erased their memories and replaced them with a myth that the first two people had been alone in a garden and had disobeyed his command not to eat the fruit of one of the trees."

Chancellor Ben-Shaachar was delighted when the camera came back to show a close-up of his face. "In another realm, innumerable immortal beings exist. As time passes they are constantly growing more powerful and wise. However, a few have created physical realms before they were ready, as did Yehhovaw. In this realm there is a Council of Enlightened Beings that tests each one before they are given permission to create beings like you and me, who can then grow and evolve to become like them as well. Nothing escapes the knowledge of this council, and it was appalled that one who aspired to the Council would have done such a despicable deed. From many volunteers, I was selected as the commander of a rescue team that was sent to your physical realm to free you from this tyranny. I wish it were as simple as attacking with weapons or hand-to-hand combat. When trying to defeat immortal beings that have advanced to the point of Yehhovaw, these kinds of weapons don't work. We needed to work with your ancestors, the victims of this crime, to defeat him and free you."

The Chancellor Ben-Shaachar sat back in his chair with growing satisfaction. The documentary was developing just as he wanted.

The screen again came into view and he watched angelic beings helping people dressed in animal skins to make fires, and then use clay tablets to read and write. His image on the screen continued the narration. "We came to break through the limitations that Yehhovaw placed on you and give you the power needed to break free. We taught you how to be free from his lies and develop your true capabilities, especially in the realm of the mind. Our plan was to regain your freedom in these areas. Then you could use your restored abilities, linked together with ours, to reverse the disease and radiation that had devastated the planet."

Chancellor Ben-Shaachar leaned forward in his chair, his hands under his chin, as the screen showed civilizations beginning to flourish again. Villages of thatched huts developed into more imposing brick-and-stone buildings. *I like the sound of my voice. It has a trusting, soothing quality.*

"Some of us even intermarried with you, and their children helped us advance faster than we would have been able to without them. However, not all of you were open to our help. Some violently attacked and resisted us." The screen showed handsome giant men with broad shoulders and bulging biceps leading armies of well-groomed men standing erect with their shoulders back and chins held high. Each was dressed with battle array, bronze breastplates, and steel swords glistening in the sun. They faced hordes that had sloping foreheads and large protruding eyebrows. They were dressed in rags and carried clubs.

Ben-Shaachar looked at Abathar and pointed to the screen. "That's a good touch, showing The Sovereign Yehowshuwa's followers as physically inferior and stupid brutes to match their spiritual disposition."

He turned back to the screen as the camera suddenly appeared to submerge under water. Twisting whirlpools of debris from buildings and bodies floated past. The Chancellor's voice in the film was somber. "Unfortunately, the enemy again attacked with the forces of nature to flood the Earth. He killed nearly all the inhabitants except for a few whom he shielded from the floods. Our children, along with our wives and our allies, were wiped out. We mourned for many years, but awaited the right time to start again the process toward freedom. We decided the risks of intermarriage were too great. We were sure Yehhovaw would simply kill our physical descendants again, so we abandoned this direction to seek new ways to overcome the enemy. While our new methods have taken longer, we would not and will not give up."

The Chancellor paused the film. "Abathar, I think we need to show more gore in this scene. There aren't enough bodies. Show them bloated or mangled, buried alive under the mud and silt. Use your imagination." He pressed Resume.

"Not long after Earth began to be repopulated we found people who were unwilling to submit to Yehhovaw and his enslaving tactics. Our rescue plan was engaged anew. It seemed we were gaining substantial ground until we discovered that he had been selectively breeding a people to become a super race. While they never did become this superior race, he managed to develop them into a nation that was fiercely loyal to him. His intent was to subject the entire world to them, and through them to force his restraints on all people. The heart of this plan included forced worship of him. He had them build edifices in which his worship would take place." The screen displayed an ornate three-story temple with a huge altar before the entrance.

People led animals to the altar, where richly dressed priests slit the throats of the animals and caught the blood in bowls. They burned portions of the animals on the altar and poured the blood at its base. A steady flow of blood ran from the compound into a valley. "His worship demanded the revolting slaughter of many animals to appease him. He was claiming to be their loving benefactor, but he was simply bloodthirsty."

Chancellor Ben-Shaachar clapped his hands with glee and stopped the film. "Killing those poor animals should start people thinking, shouldn't it? It helped us solidify our followers recently and it will again." He restarted the film without waiting for a reply.

"As this people became stronger and more numerous, they expanded their territory, enslaving or committing genocide against unsuspecting people. As entire races of people were wiped out, we had no choice but to engage them in every method of physical warfare we could muster."

Battle scenes played out as Ben-Shaachar spoke of the many wars his followers had fought to save the human race. "We have always been able to find some among Yehhovaw's people who were not loyal to him. They were self-sacrificing to the point that they sabotaged their nation so others could be free. At one point in history we had a decisive victory and were able to scatter the remnant of these people among many nations. Even though we knew they could one day become a renewed threat, we were unwilling to annihilate them as they had done to other peoples."

Ben-Shaachar slammed his hand down on his chair in anger. If I had managed to wipe them out, I wouldn't be in this fix today. But they don't need to know that.

"After many years they managed to come together again and become a nation, but we kept them subjected to the rule of nations that were aligned with our cause. We also placed people in their ranks that were sympathetic to us. We seemed to be making good progress educating the rest of mankind and getting them ready for a final assault on the enemy when he made another unexpected move."

He knew that the next segment had to be done right. In all of history, this was the turning point. It was the part he hated the most.

"Unlike our intermarriages in the past, Yehhovaw forced himself upon one of his people and impregnated her. It soon became clear that his offspring had many of the same powers he had. He became known as the Son and used his powers to make his intention known to his father's nation that he was to become their ruler, uniting them to overthrow the rulers we had placed over them and eliminating those sympathetic to our cause among their own leadership."

Ben-Shaachar seethed behind his desk as he watched a tall, handsome man saunter among crowds as people thronged to be near him. He held rallies where he miraculously fed thousands from a single loaf of bread. Finally the film showed him riding a white stallion as thousands lined the road, chanting allegiance to him as king.

Again, The Chancellor paused the film. He took a deep breath. "You know, Abathar, this next part has to be done perfectly. Our whole backup plan depends on the right spin on this event so future viewers will reach the correct conclusion. Are you confident I'll like this?"

Abathar shuddered slightly but answered strongly. "Yes, Your Greatness. It has been put together just as you have directed."

Chancellor Ben-Shaachar pressed Resume and turned back to his narration of history.

"I personally tried to dissuade the Son from this course of action, even offering some compromise solutions. However, he rebuffed me and made it clear that his intent was not only to enslave the human race but also to imprison my forces and me in the process. We had no choice but to try to stop him. We urged our sympathizers among his people, who were still firmly in control of their nation, to arrest him. They tried him before their highest council, where he was convicted of treason and quickly executed."

Seventy Elders of the nation in flowing robes intently questioned witnesses and the would-be king. The head of the council pounded his gavel and the scene faded, replaced by a tomb carved in a hillside with a huge stone rolled in front of it.

On screen, Ben-Shaachar explained, "We thought this would be the end of this phase of the battle. However, Yehhovaw had cleverly concealed from our sympathizers the fact that his son had not died but had gone into a self-induced hibernetic coma. While he was in the tomb, his father revived him and enhanced the powers that he already had so that he entered into our realm as an enlightened being and became as one of us. After escaping from the tomb, he appeared to a few of his followers, convincing them that he had indeed died and been resurrected. A handful embraced his story, and he taught them that they too would be transformed as he was, providing they worship him and his father." The Son could be seen meeting with a few of the people who had followed him in the previous scenes.

Ben-Shaachar squirmed in his chair. He didn't like what he had seen but couldn't think of anything better to replace it.

He continued to listen to himself on screen. "This new turn of events at first seemed alarming, but it helped us immensely. Our sympathizers among the enemy's people ostracized the few followers of the Son and converted almost their entire race, directly or indirectly, to our cause. While many still swore allegiance to Yehhovaw, he disavowed them unless they would also worship his son. Without his support for their nation, it soon collapsed and his former people had little or no influence against us."

The Chancellor cheered as he watched the temple burn and crumble on the screen.

"With the other nations firmly aligned with us, we were almost ready to go to our final phase of liberation. We had, over the previous centuries, slowly taught many to expand their minds and tap into the same power we possessed. Many scrolls had been published detailing the techniques needed to find the power within themselves and how to link it with our power."

Groups of people wearing long robes with hoods studied scrolls, and then moved together into a large room, where they chanted and swayed around candles illuminating an ornate tiled pentagram on the floor. As they joined hands a glow came from beneath the hoods that hid their faces.

"Do you remember, Abathar, how strong we were? Look at the power we had." Ben-Shaachar pointed at the figures around the pentagram. "We would have won then if it hadn't been for those—" The Chancellor Ben-Shaachar excavated from his vocabulary the strongest epithet he could find—"Son worshipers."

He kept his fixed eyes on the screen.

"Unfortunately, those who worshiped the Son had been endowed with some of his power, and they used it in direct confrontation with those who had mastered our techniques and expanded their powers. They began to tell lies about the character of the Son and his father, Yehhovaw. Their teaching spread like wildfire throughout the rest of the world. I am sorry to say, the incident with the Son became another defeat for us, but we didn't know its full impact for another two centuries. For a time we were able to contain the damage. We never guessed that the Son could give powers to his followers as quickly as he did. However, this power also enslaved them like a drug addiction, in addition to his false promises of a paradise in the future."

Ben-Shaachar breathed easier. "That drug-addiction thing worked out better than I thought it would."

In the next scene a processional of men in red robes advanced down the aisle of a cathedral packed with men and women dressed in black and white garb. The leader was wearing a long, flowing robe decorated with purple. Many jewels glittered from his vestments and from the tall hat he wore.

The onscreen narration continued. "After a few hundred years we were able to infiltrate their ranks and for many years neutralize their efforts at their highest levels. The Son then abandoned the organization he had established and started a new one that again threatened to unite the world against us. Still, we found that infiltration was one of our best defenses as well as an offensive move. Over several hundred years the battle ebbed and flowed. For a time we were winning, then for a while the Son. Each time we battled to the top we became stronger."

Chancellor Ben-Shaachar rocked in his chair, bobbing his head up and down as he remembered how he'd used the gullibility of his enemy's forces to infiltrate and neutralize them.

"In the final years before we defeated the Son, our people became closer to nature than they had since the beginning. This gave us great strength. Yehhovaw's people, in collusion with his son, did all they could to destroy this globe. They supposed it had been given to them to rule as they willed. At this time the Son, in his arrogance, became known as The Sovereign Yehowshuwa because he taught that his people were to rule over nature. Their rule consisted of a total disregard for all other forms of life that were created along with people to share the Earth. We were able to convert a large majority of people to our cause as they became disgusted with The Sovereign's policies, which continued to exterminate one species of life after another."

Ben-Shaachar gave Abathar a thumbs-up as he watched dead fish and otters floating down an oily stream.

"With his people rapidly losing ground, he staged an evacuation, transforming all of his loyal subjects into our non-physical realm. This caused significant chaos to the world as millions of people vanished. At that time I entered the physical realm to restore order and became known as The Chancellor Ben-Shaachar. However, with his people safely out of the way, The Sovereign Yehowshuwa began systematically destroying Earth. First, he brought a devastating earthquake that affected the whole globe. This caused unprecedented damage and loss of life. Look at the suffering and pain this caused to mankind."

Abathar jumped up and down as he watched the graphic close-ups of destruction on the screen. Thousands of bodies were dug from the rubble and prepared for burial. Men, women, and children wept for their loved ones and cursed The Sovereign.

"To our utter dismay, we found that The Sovereign Yehowshuwa was still recruiting people after his evacuation. He even brought two obnoxious spokesmen from our realm to Earth to try to condemn us and unite his new followers. These two proclaimed that Yehowshuwa was indeed responsible for the earthquake and the subsequent disasters he perpetrated on those who were only trying to escape from his slavery. See for yourselves what he did." The earthquake victims were replaced by people in hospitals with terrible burns.

The screen displayed brown plains and farms with withered crops. Forests full of dead and dying trees. Bodies of animals scattered over the plains.

A sudden mighty roar from the speakers shook Ben-Shaachar and his desk. The camera turned to the skies, where a huge meteor entered the atmosphere and crossed the sky. Ash and dust fell over the surface of the Earth as it burned. Ben-Shaachar on screen explained, "What you are seeing is a comet that The Sovereign diverted to pass through the upper atmosphere of the Earth. Its composition contained deadly poisons that polluted our natural water sources. Before we knew it, millions of people were dying horrible, cruel deaths."

A woman went to her kitchen and took a drink of water. She suddenly clutched her stomach, retching and writhing in pain on the floor. The same sort of death flashed on the screen multiple times as people drank from different contaminated water sources.

The Chancellor enjoyed scene after scene of people who developed strange sores. They tried to pick up knives to cut their wrists but were too weak.

His on-screen self spoke somberly. "We now faced the greatest challenges we had ever seen. We were not just fighting for the freedom of mankind but also for your existence. We were finally able to silence Yehowshuwa's two spokesmen but he only intensified the misery that he poured forth upon the world. We knew there would have to be a confrontation of forces to stop him, as he had promised to come back to Earth and take control after he reduced to ashes all who opposed him. For three years we prepared our forces in spite of being forced to live under adverse circumstances. Because we had already suffered great losses, we realized that there was a distinct possibility we would not be able to overcome his forces, who would be coming back from his non-physical realm to aid him in battle."

On screen, The Chancellor Ben-Shaachar paced when the scene behind him went black and he summarized the documentary. "There is only one reason you are viewing this documentary. It is because we have lost the battle. We hid this disk and protected it in every way we knew how. Now that you have found it and are watching it, we know that The Sovereign Yehowshuwa is in power and that he has thoroughly brainwashed the entire population with his own version of history. Since you have found this disk and have gone to the trouble of restoring the technology needed to view its contents, we believe you have been destined to carry on this battle and spread the truth to mankind. The battle for freedom and truth will not be easily won but we are confident that as you do your part to inform your brethren, we will also be able to implement our backup plans and escape the prison where The Sovereign will have incarcerated us."

Freedom and truth. Two ideals that humanity has sought since the beginning of time. The bait that will once more give me opportunity. Ben-Shaachar rubbed his hands together in glee.

"We have included on this disk detailed documentation supporting the summary you have viewed. Please review it carefully. We don't want you to be misinformed since we are now asking you to help free mankind. We have provided you the means to contact us should you decide there is enough evidence here to convince you that the future of mankind is indeed in your hands and that you desire to become part of a glorious destiny. We trust you to make the right decision. May you seek ascendance to become one with the universe and find your true destiny in eternity with me."

The screen went black. Ben-Shaachar walked around his desk to stand face to face with Abathar. "I never thought I'd hear these words coming out of my mouth." He grasped Abathar by the shoulders. "Well done, my good and faithful servant." The Chancellor thought he saw a tear in Abathar's eye. "Now, go and secure the disk in the vault as we have planned, and do everything in your power so that we don't have to use it."

Chapter 15

Jim woke to the smell of hot coffee. He poked his head out the tent door and saw that Robert had sliced fresh nectarines on top of steamy oatmeal. Direct sunlight was still a long way away, being blocked by the high mountains. The air felt chilly, and he was glad Robert had talked him into getting a jacket and a pair of long pants. As he sleepily dressed and put on his shoes, he noted with pleasure that his blister had healed overnight.

"About time you woke up, sleepy head. I was ready to throw in a bucket of cold water to get you going. Go soak your head in that little waterfall and you'll be wide awake in no time." Robert took the coffee pot off the portable stove.

Jim shuffled to the bubbling waterfall at the edge of the cliff and stuck his head under the water, then jerked it out quickly. "That's cold!" He was wide-awake.

"Here, have some hot oatmeal and a cup of coffee. It's just what you need before we start up the mountain. There's a hot spring about a hundred meters up that trail. The park rangers have rigged up a shower system."

Jim took the cup of coffee. It tasted good. "Where'd you get the nectarines?" He took a bite of the oatmeal.

Robert pointed to the trail leading to the hot springs. "There are all sorts of fruit trees by the hot springs and some berry bushes as well. We could have had blueberries, boysenberries, raspberries, peaches, apricots, apples, pears, kiwis, and other fruits as well."

After breakfast, Jim grabbed his towel and started up the trail to the hot springs. As he rounded a bend he saw that it opened up into a box canyon much wider than the valley. The walls were almost vertical. The glassy rock of the western cliff reflected the early-morning sun into the flat valley floor. *I was wondering how all those fruits could grow here. This is like a gigantic hothouse.* Beyond the trees, Jim noted row after row of cultivated vegetables and a vineyard.

Near the entrance to the garden Jim entered the shower facilities. He admired the craftsmanship of the hewn stone and sections that were carved into the cliff. He pondered whether he wanted a shower or to soak awhile in one of the tubs that had hot water flowing through it. He decided a shower would be quicker. He soon emerged feeling energized but still a bit grubby because he hadn't brought a razor.

When Jim arrived back at camp, Robert had everything packed up and ready for their climb up the mountain. He was sitting on a rock by the small waterfall, reading something on his ECD. "What are you reading?"

Robert glanced up and folded his ECD. "The morning news."

Jim looked up in the sky. "So the satellite communications systems even cover this valley, huh?"

Robert stood and grabbed his pack. "As far as I know, every centimeter of the Earth is covered, and I've been in some pretty remote areas. Power cell should last a month without recharging even if you used it constantly. There isn't any reason to be disconnected from the rest of the world."

Jim followed Robert up the steep trail leading to the top of the mountain. Vines and moss were now within easy reach instead of hanging high above them.

He started breathing harder as the trail became steeper. He placed one foot after the other on the steps that showed chisel marks. It looked like the trail had been carved by hand. In most places it followed natural ridges in the cliffs. Occasionally they entered tunnels through sheer walls. Even with the guardrails he shied away from getting too close to the edge of the cliff. As they climbed higher and higher, the rushing of the river below faded away and the roar of a waterfall grew louder.

As they rounded a bend, Jim saw a 300 meter waterfall that dropped from the top of a cliff to the river below. He gazed at it in awe.

Robert suggested they take a break. Jim welcomed the opportunity to catch his breath and to drink in the beauty of the cascading water thundering to the rocks below.

"I think you'll like this next part of the trail," Robert said pointing to the path ahead. "It takes us behind the waterfall."

"Looks kind of scary to me." Jim was glad that the trail leading behind the falls was railed. The cliff glistened in the mist. He was sure the rock would be very slippery.

Robert insisted they take off much too soon for Jim's liking.

"Slave driver," he grumbled.

As they passed behind the falling water Jim peered into the solid wall of water dropping past his face. Air sucked him lightly toward the water as it fell. He gripped the rail tightly. A mixture of fear and respect gripped him as he realized how frail he was compared to the overwhelming power of nature.

When they exited to the other side he looked down the valley past the bend they had rounded. Squinting, he could barely make out the parking lot. Beyond that, in the distance, he recognized a portion of the prairie they had crossed the day before.

He peered over the edge of the railing and saw a near-circular rainbow in the mist that came up from the crashing waters. He'd never seen anything like it.

Four hours later they emerged from the canyon trail and entered the higher mountain area. The climb seemed to level off after the steep ascent out of the valley, but they were still going uphill.

As they reached a clearing near the top of a rise, Robert called for a break. They took off their packs and sat down for a brief rest. The energy bars Robert produced from his backpack hit the spot.

"Take a look behind you," Robert said. "This is one of the most spectacular views so far."

Jim looked back to the west at the prairie spread out before them. To the north in the distance he saw green wheat fields fading into a haze at the horizon. Robert pointed out Tri City. Farther to the left he identified a portion of the great river that had been diverted from the small town.

"Can you see the cabin?" Robert asked, pointing in the opposite direction. "It's just to the right of that clump of trees near the river."

Jim followed his direction due east halfway up the valley. "That little dot is our cabin? How far away is it?"

"We've only got about ten kilometers to go. The trail wanders a bit but pretty much follows the tree line."

Beyond the cabin higher mountains with scattered trees rose from the grassy plateau that lay before them from their vantage point. Animals grazed in the highland to the north of the cabin, though they were too far away for Jim to identify.

"What kind of animals are those? Are they dangerous? They look awfully big."

Robert chuckled. "Don't worry. They eat grass, not people. They're not as big as you might think. We could wander right among them and they would barely acknowledge our presence. If you wanted to, you could probably throw a rope on a deer and lead it to the cabin. If you've got the stomach for it, you could even butcher it. Wild deer have some of the tastiest meat in the world."

Jim felt revolted at the thought of killing a deer. "That is the grossest thing I've ever heard. You wouldn't really do that, would you?"

Robert laughed. "That's not really my forte, but one of my uncles is a butcher. When we came up here with him and a couple of other aunts and uncles, that's what he did. Some of my cousins and I watched him. I was about twelve at the time. It was two days before I could eat any of the venison, but when I did, I thought it was the best meat I'd ever tasted."

Jim stuck out his tongue. "I don't want to think about where my meat comes from. It's enough to spoil my appetite."

"My uncle says the process is a lot better than before The Last Battle. Back then animals were far different than they are now. Most were afraid of people, except ones that had been domesticated, like cows. They ran or hid at the smell or sound of a person approaching. People had to hunt and shoot them."

Jim felt a bit queasy. "Spare me the details. I've heard of guns."

"Even so, people usually killed the animals more quickly and less painfully than when the animals killed each other. A lion, for instance, would stalk its prey; run it down until it got close enough to claw it and drag it to the ground. Then it would puncture or break its prey's neck."

Jim shuddered.

Robert stood. "According to my uncle, the Administration has strict specifications on how animals are supposed to be killed so they aren't traumatized."

Jim picked up his pack. "Enough! I think we should get going to the cabin now." He hoped there would not be any more gory stories along the way.

They continued on the path. It took a while before Jim could resume his normal chitchat. He never liked the sight of blood and talking about butchering and killing animals was just as bad.

"I think we're being followed."

Robert sounded alarmed, which put Jim on edge.

"I could swear I saw something in the woods to our right, but I haven't been able to get a clear look at what it is."

Jim stared into the woods.

"Don't look," Robert said between clenched teeth. "Just keep walking. The cabin is close. We can make a run for it if we have to. Better loosen your pack; we'd never make it carrying them."

The trail turned away from the trees, and Jim saw the cabin about five hundred meters away. Robert picked up his pace, looking over his shoulder. Jim glanced back and caught a glimpse of a cougar creeping through the tall grass. The animal emitted a soft growl.

"Run for your life!" Robert yelled. He threw down his pack and raced past Jim.

Jim dropped his pack and sprinted past Robert. He glanced back over his shoulder when he heard a roar and saw the mountain lion bounding along the path, quickly closing the gap between it and Robert.

"Get to the cabin," Robert yelled, gasping for air.

The cougar leapt into the air, then bowled Robert over into the grass. Jim stood frozen as Robert thrashed beneath the cougar, punching and pushing. In seconds, he was lying limp on the ground with the cat straddling him.

The lion raised its head and fixed his gaze on Jim licking its chops. It slowly stepped away from Robert's near-motionless body and advanced in a low stance, as if daring Jim to make a run for it.

Suddenly Robert got up yelling like a banshee, running faster than Jim had ever seen him move. With blood smeared all over his face, he threw his arms around the cat's neck, leaped over its back, and pulled the animal off its feet. The two rolled off the trail and into the grass.

"Run, Jim! Now!"

Within seconds Robert was lying on his back again, with the lion standing over him.

This time, Jim took off for the cabin, adrenaline, and fear pumping his heart hard against his chest.

June 28, 998 ASR

Tsvar paced in front of the temple, careful to avoid bumping into the many people who were ascending or descending the steps of the shrine. Sunlight gleamed on the golden walls and pillars of the magnificence structure. If he had not been pondering the events he had reviewed at Yehowshuwa's request, Tsvar would have gladly joined the others in worship, but The Sovereign had asked him to wait here.

Before Tsvar arrived, Yehowshuwa had given him a vision of the H.S.S.S. Ramah's meticulous research and their subsequent landing on the planet. The discussions he'd heard aboard the ship about Adon and his abilities annoyed him.

"Your face conveys a deep concern," The Sovereign Yehowshuwa said as he appeared beside Tsvar.

Tsvar bowed before him. "Lord Yehowshuwa, I am in awe of your abilities and your patience." He straightened. "However, I think Bartholomew may have been right in wanting to wipe out this threat right now."

The Sovereign spoke soberly. "Believe me, it has crossed my mind. However, the time isn't right."

Tsvar took a deep breath. "It seems to me that Captain Andrews and the crew have been positively affected by Adon. They will believe he is the supreme being of Eden. All the sensors on the spaceship find Eden to be absolutely beautiful. It appears to them much like what your Eden would have been, had our first parents not disobeyed. Mine and the others are beginning to convince the crew that you are the most despicable being in the universe."

Yehowshuwa confirmed Tsvar's assessment. "You are right. The crew will also gain powers that make the magicians of Mitsrayim – ancient Egypt - look like amateurs. In addition, they will return next year with a different attitude." He took three steps up toward the temple then turned back. "We need to be prepared. You know what to do."

Tsvar watched The Sovereign climb the stairs and enter the temple. *Feed my sheep. The sheep need to be warned to recognize the wolves. Not an easy task when many don't show up for feeding.* He left to go tell the others on the High Council what The Sovereign Yehowshuwa had revealed to him about the crew of the Ramah.

Chapter 16

Kevin found himself standing before The Sovereign under a crystal dome. Sovereign Yehowshuwa sat on a golden throne inlayed with ivory crosses along the top and sides of the high back. Light radiated from his face. He wore a white robe with a golden sash across his chest. The members of the High Council were sitting on smaller thrones facing him in a semicircle. Rafael and Kevin stood in the open area between The Sovereign and the High Council. Kevin and Rafael dropped to their knees and bowed.

"Arise, friends," Yehowshuwa commanded, "Kevin, tell me of your adventure."

Kevin stood. He knew The Sovereign was already aware of everything that had happened. However, he answered without questioning. "Sir, I believe the time you predicted is almost here. Some of Ben-Shaachar's forces have escaped from the dungeon. They are able to hide their activities from my friend Rafael."

He extended his right hand toward Rafael who bowed. "He can't see them. Some kind of visual shield makes their entire camp appear as if it were behind a cliff. In addition, he grew weak as we approached the camp. I, on the other hand, did not experience any effects, as far as I could tell."

"Thank you, Kevin. You have accomplished your mission exactly as I wanted," said The Sovereign as he raised his eyebrows. "Still, you have a question."

Kevin felt relieved. He always appreciated his informal conversations with The Sovereign because he was so willing to take the time to answer Kevin's questions. It was good to know that even in the formal setting with the High Council present Yehowshuwa didn't change. "I'm sure you know exactly who has escaped from the dungeons and where they are. So why did you want us to infiltrate the camp?"

"It's part of the plan. Let me show you what is occurring even as we speak."

The Sovereign's throne faded. Everything went black. A faint light grew, revealing only a shadowy figure lurking in the darkness.

Kevin heard a disembodied voice. He couldn't tell where it originated. "Chancellor Ben-Shaachar, can you hear me?"

The shadowy figure stood erect and answered, "Yes, Abathar." He rubbed two boney hands together. "Do you have news for me?"

"Camp twenty-two reports an intrusion by one of our enemy's agents."

"Were they successful in protecting the camp?" Ben-Shaachar's voice sounded edgy.

"Yes, sir," Abathar said in an excited tone. "Everything worked exactly as you said it would. The agent appeared outside our perimeter, then apparently leaned against the shield or accidentally fell through. He hiked some distance inside and started to approach the construction area. As he came closer, he became weaker and finally turned around and left"

The Chancellor clapped his hands and danced in his cell. "Very good. I've been waiting for a test like this to make sure all of our defenses are intact. Let the others know that our camouflage is perfectly functional. We can now speed up the process to our victory."

The vision faded and Kevin again found himself in the presence of the High Council.

"This was a two-fold test," Yehowshuwa explained. "Not for my benefit because I knew what would happen, but for the benefit of Ben-Shaachar and his legion, as well as for you. I'm sure you noticed that Abathar only mentioned one agent and described Rafael's fatigue."

"Why didn't they see me?" Kevin asked.

The Sovereign stood, approached Kevin, and put an arm around his shoulder. "Ben-Shaachar was imprisoned before he had an opportunity to interact with anyone who has been transformed. He has no concept of the powers that you have or how I can shield you from him. You possess more power than any of them because I live in you."

Kevin dropped to his knees.

The Sovereign Yehowshuwa turned to the High Council. "Summon the others who are to be sent on the same assignment as Kevin."

They all disappeared in poofs of light.

The Sovereign laughed. "I was going to ask you to kneel before me as I gave you your next assignment. Since you are already kneeling, here it is." He placed his hands on Kevin's head.

Immediately Kevin understood his complete assignment. He left in a flash of light.

June 28, 998 ASR

Zophia and her guide, Ana, reclined on the pillows at the same table as the other officers and their guides near the center of the luncheon area. She took a small glass of yellow juice from among the multicolored glasses a servant brought to her. She took a sip. "This is very good. It tastes a bit like peach but also somewhat like kiwi."

"The different juices are made from various fruits found in Eden," Ana explained. "Since there's such a great variety here, they're served in sampler-sized glasses. Guests can request a larger glass of whatever beverage pleases them the most."

Following the beverage waiter another servant brought a tray of appetizers. He set the tray in the center of the table so each one could be dished up family style.

For the next three hours Eden's magnificent culinary abilities were showered upon the guests. Many of the dishes tasted somewhat familiar to Zophia but the flavors were different from anything she had ever experienced.

"I feel as if I'm truly tasting and smelling for the first time in my life. Like I've been living in a shadow land and have now emerged into the real world."

"This is what a perfect world is like. Because you are now under Adon's influence, you can experience things as we do. Before, you were limited because of The Sovereign's restraints on your physical body. Here, those restraints are removed and your body is adapting."

Ana leaned closer to Zophia and spoke quietly. "Soon, you will notice your mental abilities improving as well. On Earth your race was restricted to using about 10 percent of your abilities. After The Last Battle The Sovereign Yehowshuwa allowed you to use about 20 percent. Your ancestors deemed that a significant improvement. However, if you were allowed the use of 100 percent of your mental faculties, you would be like us."

"You mean you actually use all of your mental powers? Can you explain what that's like to someone who only has 20 percent?"

Ana whispered, "I can tell you some things. For example, you use translators to understand us. Your computer translates our language and transmits our conversations to your ears." Ana removed the translator from her ear and didn't speak in her native language. "This device we put in our ears is a replica of yours but it neither transmits nor receives. We have already learned your language."

Zophia eyebrows arched, "That is totally amazing. You don't have any accent. I wouldn't be able to tell you from an Earthling. I've tried to imagine what scientific breakthroughs we could accomplish if we could use all our mental capacity. Oh, wow. It boggles my mind."

"We don't even normally use audible communication. We are capable of telepathic communication with each other."

Zophia drew closer to Ana and grabbed her hand. "Tell me more!"

"We have other capabilities as well. I suspect that the longer you stay here, the more you will tap into these mental abilities that have been forbidden for you to use."

"What kind of forbidden things are you talking about?" asked Zophia as she drew back slightly.

Ana frowned mildly. "What do you know of something on Earth called the occult?"

Zophia shook her head. "I've never heard that word."

"Look it up in your records," Ana urged. "When we meet again, we can compare what you have learned with what we have been permitted and even encouraged to do. I don't want to steer you down a path that you may later find . . . distasteful or prohibited."

Zophia was puzzled but decided not to press the matter further until she had looked up the occult. "When we get back to Ramah, I'll find out all I can about the occult. In the meantime, I'd like to know more about you." Zophia looked at Ana's perfect naked body. "You and every other woman here have gorgeous bodies. I'm only a hundred years old, but compared to you, I feel ancient. I have to admit, I'm a bit jealous."

Ana laughed lightly. "We don't experience jealousy here, but I can see why you might. That will disappear as you grow here."

A course of soups was served in small porcelain cups. Each cup was a different color and Ana explained that the color represented the spiciness of the broth. Ana took two pinkish cups and handed one to Zophia.

"How old are you?" she asked, accepting the bowl of steaming broth. She could smell a hint of ancho peppers.

"2,056 years old. Mine is six hundred."

Zophia was having a hard time grasping the concept of living that long. "How long have you two been married?"

"325 years," Ana said, stirring the soup with her finger

"Do you have any children?" asked Zophia then took a sip from her cup. The light spicy flavor was very pleasing.

"122." Ana tossed the contents of her small cup into her mouth and downed it in one gulp.

Ana's method of eating her soup slowed down Zophia's mental calculations. "That's nearly one every two years for you and Mine."

Ana chuckled, "Oh, Mine and I haven't had all those children together. I've been married four other times. Mine is my fifth husband. I've had one child about every twenty years. Some have been close together and others were further apart."

Zophia couldn't believe her ears. *I thought people didn't die here.* "What happened to your first husbands?"

"Nothing has happened to them, but I understand your confusion. On Earth, Yehowshuwa has imposed restrictions on marriage. On Eden we get married for an agreed-upon time, and then we are free to marry again. Marriage to the same person would become a burden instead of joy if it lasted for all eternity, don't you think?"

Zophia hadn't thought of marriage that way. "I guess I can see your point, but that raises another question. If you live forever in a perfect state of health, there's no limit on the number of children you could have. It seems like sooner or later this planet would fill up and become overcrowded."

Ana took a bright red cup from a waiter as he passed by. "Even though we are born with perfect bodies, our intellect continually advances and grows. As we develop our mental powers, telepathy seems like child's play. At some point, usually between twelve and fifteen thousand years old, we are able to transform our physical bodies so we can ascend into the eternal realms, where Adon lives. In fact, Adon was once like us until he ascended and eventually joined the Council of Enlightened Beings. As we take some tours together, I will introduce you to some of those who have advanced beyond those you see around you." Ana waved her hand toward those seated nearer to her. "Many are nearing the point where they will soon be leaving us."

Ana downed her second cup as she had the first. Her face flushed. "Whew, that was good but I don't think you will want to try it unless you are used to really hot spices."

Zophia decided to try a light blue cup instead. It turned out to be very mellow with a sweet rather than spicy flavor.

"Before we reach the point of enlightenment, we stop having children and marriage relationships. The physical aspects of our lives, even like spicy food," Ana wiped a tear from one eye, "become less important. Once we have attained the ability to ascend into the eternal realms, other possibilities open to us as we evolve and grow."

It was hard for Zophia to imagine this process of evolving and growing into an eternal realm or what she would do if she were to do the same.

"Some become guides for those of us who are still limited but are reaching out to expand our minds. They tell us what is on the other side. This gives us incentive to look inside ourselves to find the power to grow and expand. Meanwhile, they too are looking to those who have gone ahead of them to encourage and exhort them, providing power and energy to each generation. Many, like Adon, have advanced far enough to establish worlds like Eden, where they have created life. The universe simply continues to grow as more worlds are created."

A waiter took Zophia's soup cup and replaced it with a salad of fruits, nuts, sprouts, pods, and leaves. "So everyone on Eden will someday have the ability to make a planet and everything it takes to support life and even create beings?"

Ana met her gaze. "That's exactly what I'm saying. Even though it is an eon away, I look forward to the day when I will have a new kind of children. Not ones born of my flesh and blood, but of my spirit. I love the children I've borne here but my love for them is only a shadow of how I will love as a creator."

Zophia picked at her salad. "Ana, if I were to stay here instead of returning to Earth, would I continue to grow like you and eventually become . . . a sovereign?"

"From all that I know and understand, the answer is yes. Adon is already working in you to enable you to grow to be just as we are, and eventually just as he is." Ana plucked some salad from her bowl using two fingers and a thumb. She leaned her head back and dropped it in her mouth.

Zophia rolled back on her cushion and stared into the sky, gazing at a few high, wispy clouds. She imagined that these clouds were like the spirit of Adon; gently moving her toward a fuller understanding of a reality she had never known existed. "If I go back to Earth, I'll be under The Sovereign's rule and control. He promises us eternity with him in heaven after we die. What's the difference between that and enlightenment?"

"You are more perceptive than I expected. I did not expect these questions to arise for several days."

Ana's assessment assured Zophia that she was on the right track. She couldn't help but think that her ability to absorb new truth and to question was being aided by Adon.

"There is a big difference between heaven and enlightenment. On Earth you will experience death. That isn't natural. Yehowshuwa has imposed this on you as his method of transforming you into his eternal realm. However, because you have not advanced to the point of being able to ascend yourselves, you will enter into the eternal realm as crippled beings. You will always be dependent on Yehowshuwa to sustain you. You will not be able to advance as we do because he will never let you grow beyond a certain state; otherwise, you would become as he is, and that is a terrible threat to him. You will always be his servants. Therefore, you will never reach your true potential."

Wow, that is very disturbing, if what Ana is saying is true. "Tia-le said that we are in bondage to The Sovereign. She also said that The Chancellor had been sent by some council to free us. How does all that fit together?" asked Zophia.

Ana sat up from her reclining position and turned to Zophia, sitting cross-legged. "That would be The Council of Enlightened Beings. It was established eons ago by five of the wisest and most powerful beings in the universe. There are now more than a hundred on the council. They decide which enlightened beings are ready to create new worlds."

"So how does this relate to The Sovereign and why he keeps humanity in bondage?" asked Zophia as she sat up to meet Ana's gaze.

"Unfortunately, a few rogue beings have circumvented the council and created planets before they were ready. Because they are flawed yet nearly omnipotent, the slightest flaw in their character causes distortions that engulf galaxies. Jehov and The Sovereign's father, Yehhovaw, are both examples of rogues who thumbed their noses at the Council of Enlightened Beings. As a result of Yehhovaw's imperfections he created a twisted and abhorrent version of Eden. Yehowshuwa, his son, is unique in all creation. Yehhovaw raped one of his own created children to produce an offspring who could aid him in his combat against Ben-Shaachar. He became, what shall I say, an instant sovereign and so is even more flawed than Yehhovaw but just as powerful. Together, they are a formidable force to overcome."

Zophia covered her eyes with one hand. *Ok, that was way harsher than any other claim I've heard so far.* It was several seconds before she could look at Ana again.

Ana slowly pointed her finger at Zophia. "You are here, Zophia, as a part of the hope for returning Earth to the way it should have been in the first place. Ben-Shaachar and his forces had compassion for the souls of Earth. So they entered Yehhovaw's domain to free mankind from his oppression. The only way a renegade can be overpowered is to have enough of his followers embrace a path to enlightenment and gain sufficient power to bind him in his own realm. Over many centuries they taught mankind the true way to enlightenment."

Servers brought the main course on platters and in bowls, setting them in the center of the tables. The platters were layered with flat oval white loaves that looked something like chicken breasts and round brown one that resembled beefsteaks. The bowls contained various vegetables; most of them were most likely tubers. Large plates were placed before each person around the table.

"I see," said Zophia, "but The Chancellor has been imprisoned by Yehowshuwa so there isn't anyone to teach us how to progress in any way other than what Yehhovaw has allowed." This was too important to bother with food. She paid no attention to the main course as others at the table filled their plates.

Ana leaned forward and touched Zophia's hand, "Exactly! With Chancellor Ben-Shaachar imprisoned Yehowshuwa has been able to tightly control people and hide the truth from them."

Zophia wondered if would be possible for her to become enlightened enough to assist The Chancellor but that seemed too absurd. "Why are we so important to the plan? How can we possibly help?"

"You will be able to take the truth back to Earth. We can provide you with a complete, detailed history of your planet recorded by the Council of Enlightened Beings. You can take these documents with you and share them with people on Earth."

Zophia turned her head away from Ana to consider this. She returned her eyes to Ana's. "It would take more than just our crew and a bunch of documentation from outer space to convince the world that The Sovereign isn't who he claims to be. Yehowshuwa could claim we were all suffering from some kind dementia"

Ana touched Zophia's shoulder. "You are right. Or he could brand you as heretics if you simply started propagating what you have learned here. However, The Chancellor has freed many of his companions. They have been laying the groundwork for a powerful assault on The Sovereign that will free Earth. When you arrive home, you will be met by someone who has unearthed similar documentation, which has been safeguarded since before The Last Battle. Ben-Shaachar has prepared the framework for disseminating this information, as well as training all who will rally to the truth so that they will have the power to stop Yehowshuwa."

Zophia scoffed. "What makes you think there will be enough people rallying to the truth to be able to overcome The Sovereign? His Enforcers would keep people from joining any training efforts."

Chuck and Mine had stopped eating and were engaged in a very quiet conversation. Zophia glanced at Marti and her guide. She couldn't hear them either even though they were reclining next to Ana and her. *I wonder if everyone else is talking along the same lines. It sure has quieted down.*

The edges of Ana's mouth curled up slowly into a smile. "The Sovereign and his Administration have been very busy lately. He hasn't been able to keep up with the burgeoning population on Earth. He is unable to monitor everyone. This, in combination with Ben-Shaachar's enhanced powers, has provided the perfect opportunity to overthrow this evil regime. A lot has happened in the twenty-five years you've been gone. Many have grown distrustful of your Sovereign Yehowshuwa. Some will soon be in training toward enlightenment."

Zophia put up a hand. "You said it takes thousands of years to become enlightened. How does Ben-Shaachar expect to get enlightened beings in just a few years?"

Ana returned to a reclining position and then leaned on her elbow. "He doesn't need enlightened people to overthrow Yehowshuwa. He only requires those who are on a path to enlightenment. They can draw on his power and that of the other enlightened beings who are under his command. This symbiotic relationship is similar to what we have with our spiritual guides. When billions of humans work together with The Chancellor's forces, they will achieve the necessary power to win the battle."

"Billions? Are you saying that a majority of the Earth's population is going to join forces with Ben-Shaachar?"

Ana took Zophia's hand and patted it gently. "I have no doubt in my mind that this will happen if your crew returns to Earth. If you don't, this opportunity will be lost, possibly forever."

"That's a heavy responsibility to lay on us."

Ana's hazel eyes felt like they were penetrating Zophia's soul. "Indeed it is. But it is your choice whether to accept it or not."

Zophia looked away quickly. *That was a bit intense.* She took a breath and was about to look back when the servers quickly started removing the main course dishes. As each dish was taken, another waiter placed dessert trays on the table.

Zophia's attention turned to a parfait of swirled dark chocolate brown amid white and cherry. It was a welcome break from the deep conversation.

The evening sun reflected off the windows of tall building of the city to their east. The picnic area was showered with sparkling reds and yellows. Zophia felt that it helped her contemplate the challenge Ana had presented. She considered the consequences if they decided to help The Chancellor and they failed. As far as she understood she would end up in The Sovereign's hell forever. If they decided not to help, then mankind may very well be enslaved forever, but was that enslavement all that bad?

August 21, 998 ASR

Robert lay flat on his back in the prairie grass, feeling the pressure of the cougar's paw on his chest and the wet, raspy tongue licking his face. He opened his eyes and saw the animal's nose a few centimeters from his own. He laughed so hard he thought he would burst.

"OK, Hobbs, you can stop now. Your tongue is going to take off all my skin." He pushed the cat away and slowly rose to his knees. He wrapped his arms around Hobbs's neck and gave the mountain lion a hug. It purred gently.

The two strolled up to the cabin, where Jim stood on the porch with his jaw agape.

"Jim," Robert said, "meet Hobbs, my boyhood friend. I was hoping he'd still be around so I could show you our man-eating lion game. You know, sometimes he even lets me win." Robert put his hand behind his back and stretched. "This is lot tougher on the body than last time, though. I think I'm getting old."

Jim threw his hands up. "You almost gave me a heart attack!" He plopped down on the porch steps, shaking.

"Don't they teach you anything in school? Animals don't eat animals anymore, much less people. They're vegetarians." Robert slapped Jim on the back.

"Yeah, well, your hunting stories didn't help. It's hard to remember that these critters aren't supposed to hurt you when a seventy-kilogram cougar is charging you full bore. You looked dead after that first encounter. And where did you get all that blood on your face?"

Robert wiped his face and looked at the red on his hands. "Berry juice." He licked his fingers. "Come on and say hello to my lion friend."

Jim cautiously descended the steps. Hobbs rolled over and Jim gave him a belly rub, making the furry creature purr. "He feels soft."

Fond memories of camping trips flashed through Robert's mind. "Hobbs was just a cub when I first ran into him and his mother out in the woods. I got lost and she led me back to the cabin. She hung around for the rest of the time we were here. Hobbs and I would wrestle in the woods together, and his mother kept watch over us. Each year, when my family and I came back, Hobbs would find me and we'd go through this ritual greeting. My mom freaked out just like you did the first time she saw it."

"I sure am glad to see you, old buddy." Robert gave the mountain lion a pat on the head.

The two men went back up the trail and retrieved their backpacks. Hobbs walked between them, rubbing up against one and then the other.

He flopped down on the porch when Robert and Jim returned to the log cabin and stepped into a large front room. Robert looked at the circular glowstone fireplace in the center. He remembered warming himself with the radiant heat in winter and spending summer evenings sitting around enjoying the heat-free glow.

Most of the furniture had been replaced since his last visit. Three large semicircular couches surrounded the fireplace. Around twenty upholstered chairs, many with reading lamps on side tables, circled the room.

He noted the four round tables with chairs that he and his cousins had used for board games and cards. He gazed at the large picture of The Sovereign Yehowshuwa on the wall at the rear of the room. Additional scenic paintings and portraits adorned other walls.

Jim wandered around the central room. "When you said this was a rustic cabin, I wasn't expecting something this nice." He pointed to his right. "It looks like you could seat forty people in that dining room.

"Right, and the kitchen has a restaurant-style cooking range, griddle, and oven. It also has a walk-in refrigerator."

"How are the appliances powered?"

"There's a miniature cold fusion reactor out back. Like the ones used in transports." Robert pointed to the door at the back. "There are four sleeping rooms, each with a double-sized cot and four double bunks. Each bedroom has two bathrooms and shower facilities." They carried their packs into the first bedroom. "There are also two public facilities behind the building, so swimmers can rinse off before coming into the building." He threw his pack on a cot.

"I'll just take a cot in the next room," Jim said.

After getting settled, they went out back and found a garden growing almost every vegetable they could imagine. Robert picked a zucchini squash and pulled up a couple of carrots.

Jim dug up a few potatoes and snapped off some green beans and peas. He started reaching for some lima beans when Robert stopped him. "What are you going to do with those?"

"I'm going to put them in the stew," answered Jim. "You'll love it."

"Not if you put those things in there." Robert laughed.

They went back inside, without the lima beans, and soon Jim had a scrumptious stew brewing, using the dried beef they had brought and the vegetables they'd picked.

After dinner they devoured a whole watermelon while they swung on the porch swing, seeing who could spit seeds the farthest. Jim won.

Robert closed his eyes, enjoying the warmth of the evening sun as it dropped in the western sky. "Tomorrow I'll show you around the neighborhood. We've got a great swimming hole at a bend in the river. There's a big oak tree with huge limbs about one meter in diameter stretching several meters out over the river. My cousins and I tied a rope to it so we can swing out over the river and drop into it. It's quite a thrill."

"Now that sounds like fun. When can we do that?"

"Tomorrow, the next day, maybe every day. There are a lot of hiking trails around too. We can go out and see some of those herds up close. Besides that we'll have plenty of time to relax, play chess, snooze, and get ready to head back to school."

Jim slugged Robert on the shoulder. "You sure know how to break a mood, don't you? Promise you won't mention school again this week."

Robert put his hands up in mock defense. "Alright, no more mention of the 'S' word. Now, what do you say we try a game of chess before we turn in?"

He hadn't met many who could play chess as well as Jim, so he welcomed the challenge. When they played together, the outcome was often a draw. They had first met at a chess tournament. If it hadn't been for their common love of chess, a meteorology major and an archeologist wouldn't have crossed paths.

The next morning, while Jim slept, Robert took a ten-kilometer run across the flat lands. It gave him a chance to scope out where the different animal herds were located. As he came back along the river, he looked over the majestic mountains that rose a few kilometers on the other side of the river.

"I don't remember that mountain being there," he said to Hobbs, who had been running along with him. "I thought it was much farther away, and the canyon seemed a lot longer than it is now." He stopped at a better vantage point but the view was still different than he remembered. "Must be getting old," he muttered.

When he got back to the cabin, Jim was up and they ate breakfast while planning their day's activities.

They took a hike among the grazing herds on the plain and through some of the trails in the lower mountains, arriving back at the cabin for lunch and a siesta. When the air turned warmer, they went to the swimming hole and had a contest to see which of them could make the largest splash.

Jim devised a point scheme for their rope dives. Points were awarded for height, the most graceful exit from the rope, and best entrance into the water. Belly flops and back slaps were automatic zeros but brought a huge laugh from the opponent. They both got pretty good at creative dive formations and were even able to turn a flip or two before hitting the water.

They spent the evening playing chess. Robert felt like a kid without a care in the world.

The second day was spent much like the first. On the third day Robert wanted to cross the river and check out the mountain at the end of the canyon, which he had viewed on the first day. He led Jim past the swimming hole and found a small boathouse with several canoes and a couple of rowboats for visitors.

"Let's take a canoe up the river about two kilometers. There used to be a trail on the other side leading up the canyon to that mountain that looks too near."

"Sounds good to me," Jim said.

As they paddled Robert watched Hobbs explore the shoreline, pausing frequently to munch on berries, other fruits, or tender clumps of grass.

Robert pointed out an eagle on a high branch above the river. Jim turned quickly to look and nearly dumped them both.

When they reached their destination on the opposite bank and started their hike up the trail, Robert whistled to Hobbs. The mountain lion plunged into the water and swam to the other side, then bounded up to them and shook violently, spraying water all over them.

"You did that on purpose, didn't you?" Jim sputtered.

"Now what makes you think I had anything to do with that?" said Robert. He patted Hobbs on the back. "Good boy, you remember everything I taught you, don't you?"

"Great! I can't wait to see what else you taught him."

The trail took them to the base of the two mountains that formed the canyon. It continued to wind up the steep canyon, which was heavily wooded and shaded by towering trees on either side.

"This is a neat trail," Jim said. He pointed out the moss growing on the trees, hanging down like an old man's unkempt beard. "What was that?" he asked, pointing again. "Those birds are all different colors: blue, green, yellow . . . and there's a violet one."

Jim continued to give a running account of everything he saw or heard that was new to him. "Hey, look at Hobbs. It looks like he's scouting the terrain around us then coming back for a reward." He patted Hobbs on the head. A second later Hobbs bounded off again.

Robert managed to interject a comment between Jim's run-on sentences. "We must be near the top, where it levels off. As I remember it, we should come to a clearing in a couple of minutes. From there we'll be able to see the cliff that's the base of the far mountain where the valley ends. I think the cliff is still another twenty kilometers away, but I'll be able to tell better from up here."

Forty-five minutes later they arrived at the top.

"There's your cliff," said Jim. "I'd guess it's about five kilometers, not twenty. We should get there in less than an hour."

Either I'm getting old or that mountain moved. I sure hope the mountain moved.

They continued on. About 200 meters from the cliff, the trail veered off to the right and started up the steep mountainside.

Robert looked up at a pile of rubble nearly ten meters high piled up at the base of the cliff "I don't remember those boulders and rocks. They must have fallen from the face since I was here last." He pointed to the path. "The trail up the mountain doesn't seem familiar either. How could things have changed this much in twenty years?"

Jim gave him a little shove. "You probably thought it was a lot farther because you were a kid."

Robert stared up the cliff and shook his head. "I was 49 years old. Hardly a kid." He sat down and opened his lunch pack, still feeling puzzled but enjoying the view down the valley, where he could see parts of the great prairie. The previous day they had found a hazelnut tree and harvested enough to roast and grind into butter for today's lunch, spread thickly on biscuits Jim had baked. They didn't have any jam so they'd mashed up a variety of berries and distilled them until they had the right consistency.

After a brief rest they started back down the trail. By late afternoon they returned to the cabin. A ranger transport was parked in front. Two rangers were tending the garden behind the cabin, one was picking ripe fruit from some of the trees, and a fourth was making minor repairs to the roof of the cabin replacing some tiles that had cracked. Pieces of the old tile were still lying on the roof.

"Howdy, folks," the roof ranger called as he climbed down the ladder. "How are you enjoying your stay?"

"It's been a real pleasure," Robert replied. "The trails are well maintained and the garden and orchards have some of the best produce anywhere on the planet. The cabin is immaculate. You guys sure make it a treat to stay here."

"We aim to please," said the ranger. He shook Robert's hand.

"You really like this job, don't you?" Jim asked. "Was it hard to get?"

The ranger scratched his head and shrugged. "Oh, I had to go through the usual Board review hoops, just like any other job."

"I'll have to keep that in mind."

Robert read the ranger's name from the badge in his shirt.

"Say, Mack, it's been about twenty years since my last stay here. I seem to be a bit mixed up about the layout of the land. You see that mountain over there on the other side of the river, between the two higher peaks? Do you know how far it is to the base of the cliff?"

"It's about fifteen kilometers from here, but it takes a while to get there because you have to take the river to the trail head."

Robert kicked the dust. "I could've sworn it was a lot farther away. We took a hike up there today and it seemed a lot closer than I remembered."

Mack rubbed his chin. "You aren't the first person to wonder about that. This is my first year here and I've been asked the same question by three or four people who've been here in the past. One old guy actually accused me of moving the mountain! So I took him inside the cabin and showed him how to look up the old photos and visitor logs on his ECD. Some date back to when this area was first established as a retreat. We looked at some of those old pictures and every one of them that was taken from this vantage point looked just the way you see it now."

Jim snickered. "I told you, Robert. You aren't as young as you think you are."

Robert held up his hand. "OK, OK, it's all in my mind. I can't help wondering how I got it all screwed up. Thanks, Mack." Robert and Jim went into the cabin to clean up.

Robert looked out the window at his mountain that was too close. He connected to the cabin's database with his ECD and pulled up several old pictures. He wasn't getting old. It still bothered him, pictures, or no pictures.

Chapter 17

C huck and the crew marched up the ramp and back into the H.S.S.S. Ramah. Inside the small disembarkment area, Chuck got the crew's attention before they returned to their duties.

"We are going to adjust the ship's clocks to fit the local time here on Eden. At 6:30 tomorrow morning we will have an all-crew meeting before breakfast. The Edenians have promised to serve us all our meals during our visit. They also said that their food will be simpler fare than the elegant banquet we just attended."

Chuck heard someone in the back say, "Too bad." He wouldn't mind more meals like the last either but knew they couldn't afford to spend a half day sitting around eating.

"Senior officers, please join me in my office. I'll see the rest of you in the morning."

Chuck, Zophia, Alex, Marti, and Demetrius spent the next two hours comparing notes about their conversations with their guides. They sat in Chuck's visitor chairs and briefly related the high points of their conversations during lunch. Everyone asked questions about enlightenment and the difference between Eden's view of eternity and Earth's. The conversations converged on the Edenians explaining that the Ramah's visit to Eden would be crucial in the future defeat of The Sovereign.

"I get the idea that they are positive we will join forces with Ben-Shaachar and they want us to return to Earth quickly," Chuck observed.

Zophia turned her ECD so that all could see it and ran her finger down the edge, scrolling through a display. "I had Hal make a transcript of all the conversations he translated and then run a topical analysis. You are right, Captain. Eighty five percent of the crew's conversations contain the same topics. The top two indicate that the Edenians want us to join forces and not delay our return to Earth. From my conversation and these excerpts, they believe that we are approaching a pivotal point at which The Chancellor has to make his move or he won't be likely to succeed. If we decide to do this, we don't want to cause a delay that would result in failure."

Demetrius rubbed his chin, "Ah, let's not jump to conclusions. We haven't agreed to join Ben-Shaachar, have we?"

Chuck held up both hands. "Oh no. We haven't taken that leap yet. At least I haven't. Even if what Berekiah and everyone here say is true about The Sovereign, I wouldn't go along with them without solid proof that will convince people on Earth to rebel."

Chuck looked around at his officers.

Alex folded his arms. "I agree, Chuck. I'm not becoming a mutineer without more compelling data."

Marti stopped twisting a lock of her hair. "Me neither."

Everyone looked at Zophia. She looked at the others one by one then responded. "My conversation with Ana today was quite compelling but she promised they would provide more than enough information to convince us as well as people on Earth."

She paused and leaned in toward the circle. "I found that they have powers like mental telepathy. When I questioned Ana about them, she said I should look up something called the occult. Then we could compare their abilities with it. Have any of you ever heard of this?"

"Can't say that I have," Marti said.

"Not I," said Alex.

"I think I have heard of it before." Demetrius shivered. "All I remember is that it was spooky."

"I don't know anything about it. Hal," said Chuck, "give us a definition of the word *occult* and a brief history of it."

Everyone looked at the view screen as Hal provided a definition.

Occult:

1. The practice of mystical arts: magic, divination, astrology, alchemy, or any supernatural powers.

2. Practices that involve gaining knowledge or power beyond human understanding or abilities.

History:

These practices were common among people on Earth before Yehhovaw gave his selected nation their original land. During the takeover of the land, all who practiced these and other abominations were to be annihilated. However, not all were eliminated and these practices were eventually taken up by Yehhovaw's nation, along with worshiping other gods. This led to the dispersal of the nation as punishment. After the nation was restored, the occult was still a problem on occasion, but never as it had been before the dispersal.

At the time The Sovereign Yehowshuwa first appeared on Earth in the flesh, these practices were still common among many other nations. As loyalty to The Sovereign increased, his people made great strides in removing these practices.

Before the great transformation, when The Sovereign Yehowshuwa took his people from Earth, these practices reached their highest level of practice in history. During the period between the transformation and The Last Battle, all who were loyal to The Chancellor Ben-Shaachar engaged in the occult in one form or another.

Yehowshuwa's official position on the occult is as follows: "You shall not practice divination or sorcery. You shall not turn to mediums or seek out spiritists, for you will be defiled by them. These are done in accordance with the work of Ben-Shaachar before The Last Battle and were displayed in all kinds of counterfeit miracles, signs, and wonders. Let no one practice divination or sorcery, interpret omens, engage in witchcraft, or casts spells. Let no one consult the beings in other realms. Anyone who does these things is an abomination to me. I will cause calamity to come upon the person who turns to mediums or spiritists by following them, and I will remove him from among the inhabitants of Earth."

Demetrius exhaled loudly. "That sounds ominous. However, I'm not familiar with some of the terms in there, like sorcery, divination, witchcraft, mediums, and spiritists. Can we find out what they are?"

"Hal," Zophia commanded, "give us definitions of those terms."

The computer displayed the response:

Sorcery: employment of supernatural agencies such as Ben-Shaachar or his associates to accomplish remarkable or unexplainable feats. Synonyms: witchcraft, magic.

Divination: the act or art of trying to tell the future or the unknown, especially by contacting supernatural agencies such as Ben-Shaachar or his associates.

Witchcraft: the practice of sorcery, usually in association with Ben-Shaachar or his associates.

Medium: a person who is supposedly in contact with or controlled by the personality of someone who is deceased. In reality the person is in contact with or controlled by supernatural agencies such as Ben-Shaachar or his associates.

Spiritist: a person who believes that the spirits of the dead who have not been translated to The Sovereign's Administration communicate and manifest themselves to the living.

Chuck felt as if there were another person in the room. It was eerie. He couldn't put his finger on why he thought someone might be there. However, as he sat back in his chair and read everything a second time he sensed his thinking becoming sharper. "Wow, this is really something! I can see it now. The occult is one of the paths to enlightenment that The Chancellor was trying to teach people. No wonder The Sovereign wanted this stuff stopped. It fits right into what we've been told today. I believe that someone is helping us think these things through and draw the right conclusions."

Alex slapped his knee. "That's it. I couldn't identify it earlier, but I know what you mean. While I was talking to my tour guide, I got the strangest feeling. Like I'd been searching for the truth for a long time but didn't know it. What I heard from him made sense like nothing else. I asked questions about things that must have been buried in my subconscious all my life but I was afraid to ask. When he told me about our potential it just seemed right."

Marti pointed at Alex. "That's very close to what I've been feeling as well. If everything continues to check out here, I think we should definitely go back to Earth and engage in direct conflict with Yehowshuwa. That could be dangerous, of course. However, as I dwell on the possibility of a future that far surpasses anything we've ever even imagined, I am filled with peace. I think we are doing what we were destined to do."

"You guys are scaring me." Demetrius pushed his chair back away from the circle a few centimeters. "What's going on here? This goes against everything we've ever been taught. How can you suddenly jump on Ben-Shaachar's band wagon?" His hand was clamped securely on the arm of his chair.

Zophia reached over and lightly touched Demetrius' white knuckle. "Today I became aware of Adon's spirit moving on me, giving me a fuller understanding of cosmic realities. I'm sure that it is Adon who is even guiding our conversations right know. Don't you feel it?"

Demetrius pulled his hand back. "Yeah, I've felt it too. It gives me the creeps. Conclusions a lot like yours have been popping up in my head …but I've been fighting them. I don't want to end up on the wrong side of The Sovereign and die."

Chuck leaned toward Demetrius and spoke softly. "Don't worry, Demetrius. We are going to be careful." He leaned back, looking around to the others. "What we need is something that will convince Demetrius. If it doesn't convince him the people back home won't believe us either."

Zophia turned to Demetrius. "I was concerned that you hadn't experienced this spirit moving you the same way we had, but I can see that you are like a stabilizer. If we can't find enough to persuade you then I'll stand with you."

Demetrius' eyes got large and his grip on his chair relaxed. "You would do that? Really?"

"Yes, really," said Zophia as she gazed into his eyes without any flinching.

A tear welled up in Demetrius' eye as Chuck said, "Me too." He sensed the spirit assuring him that Demetrius would change his mind.

Chuck clapped his hands together. "Ok, then let's get on with deciding what we need to convince our doubter here. Zophia, you mentioned Ana had promised something."

Zophia glanced back at her ECD. "Yes Sir. Apparently they have some kind of cosmic library that recorded Earth's history from their Council of Enlightened Beings' perspective. She said it will match some documentation that was hidden on Earth before The Last Battle. We also have Ramah's logs, which recorded our encounter with Rol-el and his claim that The Sovereign sent him, as well as Tiale's claims. We have a whole planet of people who have given us a totally different perspective on history. Their claims seem plausible considering their perfect environment."

Chuck thought the library sounded intriguing. "Hal, put 'cosmic library' on the screen as a point of interest for tomorrow. I'd really like to see that library."

Zophia looked at the screen. "I am curious about these occultic powers that have been forbidden to us. They may prove useful to back up documentation from the library. Hal, put 'explore occult' up there. I want to follow up with Ana on that."

"I want to meet some of their people who have approached enlightenment but haven't yet ascended," said Alex. "I'm a little surprised that they weren't in our welcoming committee. Hal, put 'meet near enlightened' for me."

Demetrius wrung his hands. "Put 'interview ascended Edenian.' I want to see one of these guys for myself."

Chuck turned to Marti. "Marti, is there anything you would like to discover from the Edenians?"

"I've mentioned before that any alignment with Ben-Shaachar could be dangerous. If they have occult powers then they may be able to warn us about future dangers. Put 'future danger' on the list."

"I think you've all hit on the most important things that are left to see," said Chuck. "Is there anything else any of you want to add to the list?"

"I'd like to know how we're going to get our modifications done if everyone is out on tours," Zophia responded.

"Oh, no problem. At lunch I arranged for some of Mine's people to work on the modifications while we do the tours," Chuck said. "Any other questions?"

No one else indicated he or she had anything more to contribute.

"Tomorrow I'll brief Mine about these five things we would like to dig into since he is coordinating all tours. I'll look into the documentation at the library. I'd like each of you to follow up with the things you brought up. In the morning I'll brief the crew on all this at our meeting in the mess hall before breakfast. It's been a long day, and we'll start a few hours earlier tomorrow to match their time, so let's get a good rest tonight."

Chuck stood up and followed his officers as they left his office.

After only four hours of sleep, Chuck entered the mess hall feeling refreshed. His crewmembers looked refreshed as well.

He outlined the discussion he had with his officers the night before and the goals each had for the next few days. He polled the crew to see if anyone was getting a different impression. Without hesitation, by a show of hands and some verbal comments, everyone reported similar conversations and conclusions. *It can only be Adon's spirit that is bringing this kind of unity.*

Chuck had Hal display the five main areas they wanted to investigate.

Cosmic Library
Explore Occult
Meet Near Enlightened
Interview Ascended Edenian
Future Danger

"These are the things we are investigating to validate what we've been told. Look for anything that you feel will convince people back home that what we've been told is the truth. If any of you finds anything that makes you suspicious of what we are learning here, I want to know, even if it seems insignificant. Most of us have been getting good feelings about what we are being told. If anyone gets any negative feelings, hunches, or anything that leads you to believe something isn't as it appears, I want to know. OK, let's go out there and be alert."

Everyone reported to the North ramp and proceeded to the same area where they had their luncheon the day before. Chuck wondered how the naked natives could brave the cool of the morning and the slight mist from the damp ground. As the crew approached the grassy area, Chuck saw a canopy with tables and chairs. Several Edenians were setting places, bringing beverages, and loading the tables with dishes containing a variety of fruits, breads, cheeses, and eggs.

The guides arrived, and they all greeted one another as they sat down for breakfast. After Chuck's waiter took his order for an omelet, Chuck told Mine, "My crew and I had some discussions last night and this morning. It appears that all of us had similar experiences at lunch yesterday. We have some concerns that need to be clarified; things we'd like to see. I know you had some tours planned for us, but unless they're related to gathering what we need to convince any skeptics left on the crew and people on Earth that things aren't really as they've been told, I'd like to make some alterations to the tours. We believe that time is of the essence and we'd like to move ahead full speed."

Mine listened quietly as Chuck spoke. His mouth curved upward more with each sentence. "I'm delighted that you are so eager. We also had debriefings after lunch yesterday and compared our notes. We were amazed that your people were so receptive and inquisitive. Let us know what you would like to see and we will satisfy your requests."

Chuck told Mine about the five points upon which he and the officers had agreed. "After breakfast, I was thinking the crew and guides could break up into five groups, each group exploring one of those five areas."

Mine agreed. Chuck was pleased that everyone seemed to be on the same track.

August 29, 998 ASR

On Saturday, Robert and Jim rose early, ate breakfast, and started for home. They had packed everything the night before so they could get back to Tri City before evening. Going downhill made the trek quicker, especially since they weren't carrying a week's worth of provisions.

When they got back to the trailhead, they climbed into the sporty transport. Robert set the auto controls to take them back to the lot where they had picked up the vehicle.

Jim leaned back as far as the seat would allow. "This was a great vacation, Robert. I'm glad you invited me. I don't think I've ever been more relaxed after a time away."

"We should do this again next year," said Robert. "Maybe make it an annual tradition."

Jim sat up. "I'd like that, but I don't know if it'll work out. I'm going to have to get a job next year, and being a rookie, I won't be able to choose my vacation dates."

"I've got an idea." Robert tapped Jim's elbow. "When I start my book I'm going to need a research assistant. You could work for me."

"Wouldn't you have to get authorization from the Administration for something like that?"

"I can hire as many people as I need. All I have to do is file a form. However, there is one problem. I only have one quarter left of school before I start writing. I'll need an assistant sooner than next year."

"No problem," Jim said. "I can postpone my last two quarters. I've got plenty of time to finish my education. I'd much rather run around with you and dig up dirt on the Administration."

"Let's do it!" Robert grabbed his ECD, unfolded it, and set it on voice-command mode. "Computer, I want to file a form to become an employer."

"Authorization code," it responded in a monotone.

Robert fumbled in his pockets for the access card. He pressed it up against the electronic paper. "Try this."

"Authorization accepted. Form submitted and accepted."

"Great." Robert rubbed his hands together. "What do I need to do to hire an employee?"

"You must start with job titles and requirements. Do you wish to enter them now?"

"Yes." The job description form appeared. "Title is Research Assistant. Requirements are minimum three years of university in . . ." He looked at Jim.

"Meteorology."

"Meteorology major. Because he will be assisting me personally and traveling with me, the applicant must be a male. Able to hike eight hours with a 27 kilogram pack and wrestle with a puma." Robert stifled a chuckle as he watched his words appear on the form.

"That doesn't sound like something a research assistant would have to do," Jim interjected. "Isn't someone going to be a bit suspicious?"

"The backpack stuff is legitimate. If we have to go out to some digs, you'll need to be able to carry that much. The puma is a bit out there, but if we have to go back to the cabin to finish compiling the book, I can guarantee my assistant will have to wrestle with Hobbs." Robert winked at Jim.

"Sounds logical to me. What else do you need to put in?"

Robert directed his attention back to the ECD. "Computer, is there anything else needed?"

"Beginning date of employment, posting date, and how long the posting will be open."

"Beginning date: January 1, 999 ASR. Posting date: today. Posting close date: now plus 45 minutes. Submit."

"Posting A66508RTZ862B has been confirmed." The ECD beeped.

Robert handed his ECD to Jim. "You'd better snatch up this choice job before some out-of-work meteorologist grabs it."

"Computer," said Jim to Robert's ECD, "sign on James Thaddeus Arizna, voice recognition *anzira mij*."

"Welcome, Jim. What do you want to do?"

"I want to apply for job posting A66508RTZ862B." Jim sat back as the computer entered his request.

"Application submitted . . . waiting . . . rejected. Availability conflict."

"What conflict?"

"You are enrolled at University of Midrib in January. That is when the job is to begin."

Jim rolled his eyes. "Computer, cancel my enrollment at Midrib effective January first."

"Cancellation rejected. Board authorization required."

Robert handed him his access card. "Try this."

"Use this for authorization." Jim pressed the card against the ECD.

"Enrolment canceled."

Jim gave Robert a high-five then told the computer, "I want to apply for job posting A66508RTZ862B again."

"Job application has been sent. You will be notified of interview schedule by the employer."

"Excellent. Log me off." Jim handed the ECD back to Robert.

Robert immediately received a message that Jim had applied for the job. "Accept applicant."

"Applicant accepted and notified. You will be notified when applicant accepts job."

"Your turn again," Robert said. Jim signed back in.

Within five minutes all the paperwork had been completed, and Jim was Robert's research assistant effective January first.

When they arrived back at the transport lot, the sun was starting to set, silhouetting the mountains west of Tri City. Robert parked by the booth. Jim pulled out the backpacks while Robert found the check-in form in his ECD's in-basket and told the computer to fill it in with the date and time.

"Do you want to stop at Rosey's for another burger?" Jim asked.

"I'd like to, but I want to get home before dawn. I'd like to get a couple hours of sleep before Mom and Dad haul me off to worship."

"I'll head home too then. It wouldn't be the same without you."

They walked the four blocks to the transportation center, then each took a separate convy for home. Robert tried to sleep, but setting Jim up as his employee had made him excited about his future work. He started planning what he needed to do to get his book started while he was still in school.

June 29, 998 ASR

After breakfast with the Edenians, the Ramah's crew and their guides broke up into five groups. Those who wanted to interview people who were approaching enlightenment gathered together with Alex.

Once his group was formed he explained their request to the guides. "We've heard that people who are near enlightenment have come to a point where they don't marry or have children. Their focus is less on their physical lives and more on the spiritual or eternal realm. We'd like to meet with some of them, hear what they have to say, see if they have any advice to offer."

Alex's guide, Kalamarathanor – shortened to Kal, spoke for the Edenian guides of the group. "We thought this would be one of your requests, so we have arranged for a visit with a colony about 250 kilometers from here. A bus is waiting for us on the other side of those trees."

The group proceeded to the bus. It looked much like a bus transport on Earth, but with a clear dome top. Once everyone was on board and seated comfortably in the plush seats, it rose up a few centimeters and moved toward the city.

Kal stood at the front of the bus, facing the passengers. "We should arrive at our destination in about twenty minutes. If you have any questions, please feel free to ask."

Martin, one of the crewmembers raised his hand. "When we got on board, I didn't see any bus controls or means to tell a computer system where we want to go. How is it controlled?"

Kal pointed to his head. "We interface with nearly all mechanical devices using our telepathic abilities. If you were to take a tour of our city by yourself, you would be restricted in your ability to move about. While you could walk the streets, you wouldn't be able to use any of the transportation vehicles or even take an elevator."

When the bus entered a tunnel, the dome seemed to close. "The dome is darkened during underground transport," Kal explained, "so that the tunnel does not cause any distractions. Some travelers have been known to experience vertigo."

"Why do the people nearing enlightenment live in a colony?" asked another crewmember at the back of the bus. "Do they live like monks, isolated from the rest of society?"

Kal spread his hands apart. "In a sense they are isolated. They become one with each other and thereby closer to oneness with those who have already ascended. When they approach this state of unity, they withdraw and join a colony. In the colony they receive the support required to continue on their journey. They are completely self-sufficient. Occasionally someone will return to visit relatives, but our most frequent interaction is when one of our relatives is ready to join a colony. That is a great time of celebration, both for us as we send them off and for those in the colonies to welcome them."

Kal continued to answer questions until the bus emerged from the tunnel in a rural setting. Beyond a few farms Alex saw what appeared to be a medieval castle surrounded by a stonewall about twelve meters high. Through the dome Alex gazed at four tall towers, one at each corner of the wall. When the main gate swung open, the bus entered. Alex didn't see anyone on the grounds or operating the gate.

As the bus made a loop around the central building, Kal said, "The walls are twenty meters thick and provide quarters for the residents. The large structure in the center is five stories high and includes more quarters and meeting rooms in addition to a communal kitchen and small eating area."

The bus stopped just before the back gate. Everyone got off and followed Kal into what looked like the main entrance to the center building. Kal took them to a large room. "We will wait here for a resident to greet us."

Alex sat on one of the hard wooden benches in the austere stone room. The only light came from a small open window with wooden shutters. He couldn't see more than a meter through the partially open door at the front of the room. The word *draconian* popped into his mind as he squirmed on the uncomfortable bench.

The door at the front of the room opened, allowing a sudden shaft of brilliant light to blaze in from the hallway beyond. Alex shielded his eyes. A glowing figure glided into the room and hovered in midair before them. Alex could make out the form of a person but the light obscured his ability to see any details of face or body.

The glow pulsated as he spoke. "Greetings, people from Earth, in the name of our Lord Adon. My name is Parathanos. I understand that you have come here to meet someone who has advanced near to transformation." Alex heard the voice but couldn't see his lips move because of the brightness of his face. "Your purpose is to see if what you have heard here on Eden is true and, more important, verifiable when you return to Earth. Rather than have you ask me questions, I will simply read your thoughts and answer the questions that are deepest in your hearts."

Alex sat up straight. He wasn't sure he wanted anyone reading his thoughts. *That seems like a major violation of privacy.*

"Don't fear, Alex. I can understand your thoughts but it isn't something we do without care. We respect the privacy of those outside our community. I am looking into your minds in order to demonstrate that we are capable of powers beyond even normal people here on Eden. My intention is not to frighten you, so please, accept my peace. We are brothers and friends."

Alex could hear Parathanos' thoughts, though not a physical voice. The response to his fear came so peacefully that all concerns vanished. Alex understood that his thoughts were being shared with someone who was a friend, who had his best interests at heart. He was reassured that there was no threat from this strange person.

Parathanos turned toward a woman crewmember in the front row opposite Alex. "Amanda, you are wondering about the light that is emanating from me. As we get closer to ascension, the power that is in each of us manifests itself in the glow you now see. When we are transformed and enter the eternal realm, the light will reach its highest intensity. It would be too bright for us to remain in your presence."

The figure raised an arm and pointed toward the back of the room. Alex turned to see crewman Martin's eyes widen. "Yes, Martin, we do move without walking. We can levitate to any height we wish, but that doesn't come right away. It is a slow process as we learn to use the powers within us and combine them with the power of the community and the eternal realm. An important part of the process is discovering what has been inside us all along. Our maker has put these abilities in us, and they are in you too.

He bowed slightly to Philip, who sat beside Alex. "You're right in what you've been told about our focus on the eternal and lessening our focus on the things of Eden. We trade our personal relationships with others for a communal relationship that surpasses the intimacy of a marital relationship. In a sense we are all married to each other. We learn to share our minds, our thoughts, and our goals. Physical things become less important to us. There are no material comforts here because we don't need them. You were told there is a kitchen and small dining area. This is for the convenience of those who have recently arrived and haven't yet gained sufficient power to sustain themselves without eating."

Alex's thoughts turned to their return trip. He wondered if Parathanos could shed any light on the future.

"Alex would like to know if I can predict the future. No, I cannot. That ability comes after ascension."

Bummer! Alex thought he heard a chuckle but he wasn't sure. No one else seemed to hear anything.

"Yes, Philip, your sovereign's father, Yehhovaw, did go through a stage similar to what I'm going through. So did Chancellor Ben-Shaachar."

Parathanos pointed to Amanda. "Amanda would like to know if there are any women who are sovereigns. The answer is yes and no. You see, as we are transformed, we no longer retain a gender. I still appear to you to be a male, but since I am close to ascension I could appear as a female as well." The figure before them changed to the outline of a woman. "We refer to sovereigns with a male pronoun because your language doesn't have a correct translation, and 'it' depersonalizes the nature of an enlightened being. You will note that on Eden a woman's name always ends with the letter A and a man's name always ends with the letter R. My name ends with the letter S, indicating that I have moved beyond gender. When I become a sovereign, I will change my name to one that reflects the person I have become."

After a few more questions the delegation returned to the bus and left the compound. On the way back, Alex sat quietly. He was deeply impressed by this highly evolved being. While the mind reading was amazing, the way he was able to put Alex at ease was more impressive. *If this is what enlightenment is like, I want a piece of the action.*

Chapter 18

On Sunday morning Samantha and Papa rose an hour earlier than they did on weekdays to help their farm hands feed the livestock before attending worship.

As Samantha approached the pigs, they came running to the fence to see her. She strolled along the fence and patted several heads. The animals were friendlier during feeding time than loading time.

When she rounded the corner of the pen they followed her, squealing and grunting and bumping into one another, each one trying to get ahead of the others. She stepped up to the control panel, two hundred young porkers staring at her expectantly.

Samantha entered the code for the computer to measure the correct combinations of ingredients. She pointed to the feeding troughs and announced dramatically, "Behold, your food cometh." The pigs all ran to the trough, where they jostled one another until they were evenly distributed in a row. When they all turned their heads and looked at Samantha, she punched the button to start the feed flowing. The pigs began devouring the mixture.

She moved on to the sheep, which were not as smart as pigs. Many came to the side of the pen to get a few pats on the head, but none waited for her hand signal. When the feed was properly delivered she continued to the other animals.

At the horse corral, Samantha hand-fed her favorite steed some carrots and patted his neck. The horse nuzzled back.

Papa came and pressed the numbers on the computer interface to give the horses their usual feed of alfalfa pellets mixed with oats. A few seconds later the mixture rolled into the trough.

They hurried back to the house, where they cleaned up and then met in the kitchen for the hearty breakfast Mama had prepared.

After Papa pronounced the blessing Samantha took a few slices of honeydew and cantaloupe.

"I love Sundays," Samantha said as she stacked a couple of buckwheat-blueberry pancakes on her plate, sniffing the aromatic steam puffing up from them.

Papa smothered his pancakes with butter and maple syrup. "What is it about Sundays that make them special for you?"

Samantha added two sausages to her plate. "You mean besides feeding the animals, eating Mama's wonderful breakfast, driving to the community hall with the rest of the people on the farm, and having our big fried chicken dinner with all the friends and relatives who drop by?" Samantha crossed her arms over her heart and closed her eyes. "I love gathering to worship The Sovereign in the morning and again in the evening. There's nothing better than joining with his people to honor him and learn more about him."

"I couldn't agree with you more." Papa rocked back in his chair. "We've been blessed with a Sovereign who cares for us. He has given us to each other. We owe everything to him, and we look forward to a glorious future with him in eternity."

After breakfast they went outside, where others had gathered in front of the main storage barn. Kids were climbing inside and around the flatbed transport that had been converted to a bus.

Papa told the kids to be seated. The parents and other workers piled on. Soon all fifty-seven of them were on their way to the community center. Mama started a song about The Sovereign Yehowshuwa and the rest of the group joined in.

As soon as the transport bus stopped, the kids scrambled off and ran into the community center. The adults milled around outside, talking to people as they arrived.

When Samantha heard the bells ring, she entered the auditorium along with the others who were still outside. The worship band started playing a lively instrumental. The congregation swayed and clapped to the rhythm as they made their way to their seats. The auditorium was almost half-full when Samantha sat down.

The worship leader invited everyone to stand and sing. Lyrics appeared on a screen behind the stage, but Samantha didn't need them. The volume grew as the auditorium filled. Many raised their hands and sang loudly. Even though not everyone sang on key, it was a joyful noise.

Some of the songs were over a thousand years old; others had been composed that week. Samantha loved them all.

At the end of the singing hour, when the pastor stood to teach, the auditorium was almost full.

The tall, bearded pastor bounded onto the stage. "Good morning, brothers and sisters. It is good to see you here this morning. I know Sovereign Yehowshuwa is pleased with what he has heard here today. This morning I'd like you to turn to the sixth book of the writings of Yehowshuwa's servants, the second chapter. Read along with me, starting with the third verse and ending with the eleventh."

Samantha unfolded her ECD and entered the passage.

Pastor Steve held his ECD. "I'm going to read from a translation that is more than fourteen hundred years old. It may not match your translation, but follow along." He read:

Let nothing be done through strife or vainglory; but in lowliness of mind let each esteem others better than themselves. Look not every man on his own things, but every man also on the things of others. Let this mind be in you, which was also in The Sovereign: who, being in the form of Yehhovaw, thought it not robbery to be equal with Yehhovaw: but made himself of no reputation, and took upon him the form of a servant, and was made in the likeness of men: and being found in fashion as a man, he humbled himself, and became obedient unto death, even the death of the cross. Wherefore Yehhovaw also hath highly exalted him, and given him a name which is above every name: that at the name of Yehowshuwa every knee should bow, of things in heaven, and things in earth, and things under the earth; and that every tongue should confess that The Sovereign Yehowshuwa is Lord, to the glory of Yehhovaw the father.

Pastor Steve lowered his ECD and placed it on the transparent pulpit in front of him. "Our whole society is based on these verses. We are not a people who seek to have more than others do. We put others first. This is the ideal. To a large extent, with the help of The Sovereign, this is how we operate as individuals and as a society. Of course we are weak and succumb to temptations. Yehowshuwa, in his wisdom, has put people in authority over us who ensure that we don't get out of line. This was predicted by Daawiyd when he said, 'You will rule them with an iron scepter.' Ioannes wrote about it also when he reported the vision given to him: 'She gave birth to a son, a male child, who will rule all the nations with an iron scepter. And her child was snatched up to Yehhovaw and to his throne.'"

This point reinforced Samantha's belief that she had been on the right track about the economy and the need for enforcement during her discussion with Papa and Cousin Tom a few days ago.

Pastor Steve left the pulpit and paced to the left. "The child of Yehhovaw, our Sovereign Yehowshuwa, gave up everything he had in the spiritual realm and became a humble human being. He always considered others before his own comfort. If he hadn't, he would not have died for our transgressions. His death is what Ioannes saw when the child was snatched up to his father, Yehhovaw, and to his throne."

He marched to the other side of the stage. "Now that The Sovereign has returned to carry out what was predicted so long ago, he is exalted. His name is above every name on the earth or in the spiritual realm. Paulos said that Yehowshuwa was set 'far above all principality, and power, and might, and dominion, and every name that is named, not only in this world, but also in that which is to come.' That is why we he has the title The Sovereign."

A shout of "Amen" rang out from a man behind Samantha and a couple of people clapped. Pastor Steve walked back to the pulpit.

"However, not every tongue confesses that he is Lord. Not every knee bows before him. Oh, you don't hear anyone denying it in public or refusing to kneel when he appears. There are hearts that have not yielded to him. There are people who are not loyal to him, even though he is physically among us. At some point in the future, those who have not bowed their knees to The Sovereign will have no choice but to do so. They won't be able to hide anymore and they will be exposed for who they are."

Samantha wondered when that would happen. After her discussion with her papa, she felt unprepared because it might be soon.

Steve slapped his hand on the pulpit and turned quickly to the congregation. "Considering the insolence of many people, as demonstrated in their work attitudes and the way they dress, I suspect the time is drawing close. Soon, The Sovereign will end evil once and for all." His mouth turned down at the corners. "Any who have not made up their minds to follow him by then will be lost to an eternal punishment that is more horrible than any of us can imagine."

A woman called out another, "Amen." Samantha wondered if the vocal agreement was because the time was coming soon or because the speaker wanted to see the rebellious punished. Samantha wanted to see evil eliminated, too, but she didn't want to lose anyone in the process.

Pastor Steve wagged his finger back and forth in front of him as he stooped forward. "The Sovereign Yehowshuwa does not want to punish people. As Petros said, 'The Lord is not slack concerning his promise, as some men count slackness; but is longsuffering to us-ward, not willing that any should perish, but that all should come to repentance.' The Sovereign is giving everyone a chance to know his love and accept his sacrifice for them."

Steve put his open hand above his eyes and looked across the audience. "We need to be on the lookout for those who haven't bowed their knees and confessed from their hearts that Yehowshuwa is Lord and do whatever is in our power to bring them the good news. We need to tell people who may not know him personally how to know him while they still have a chance; before it is too late."

Samantha continued to take notes and consider how The Sovereign's reign had created a near perfect environment and how there would be a day in the future when he would remove it and replace it with his completely perfect eternal universe. She had mixed feelings. On the one hand she couldn't wait; on the other hand she felt a need to warn as many people as possible.

The Pastor went on to expand on the coming new world that Sovereign Yehowshuwa had promised, then wrapped up his discourse. He pronounced a blessing on the congregation and stepped off the platform. The worship team came back up and started another song. They sang for thirty minutes.

She joined in the worship expressing her gratitude to The Sovereign in song along with the rest of the worshippers. While she sang, she also thought about how inadequate she felt about her ability to share her faith with others.

After the service was formally concluded, Samantha left, thinking about the family meal and get-together that awaited her. Since Pastor Steve was coming to their place for dinner she hoped to get some time to talk to him about her inadequacy.

Samantha's family and the others who had come to the service together climbed back on the bus. Papa set the controls to head back to the farm. Mama, Papa and Samantha discussed the sermon until the bus pulled into the farmyard and everyone clambered off.

Samantha helped Mama and the other ladies get ready for the afternoon outdoor potluck, setting the tables as fast as the guys set them up. All joined together hauling the food out from the kitchen. Within an hour more than a hundred people were eating, talking, and playing games on the large lawn in front of the Spells' house.

Samantha waited for an opportunity to talk to Pastor Steve. She caught him on the return from his second pass through the buffet. "Pastor Steve, can I talk to you for a minute or two?"

He fumbled with his plate to get it out of the way, and then put his right arm around Samantha's shoulders and gave her a small squeeze. "Certainly, Sam, this wouldn't happen to be about a young lady I know that's just about to leave for university, is it?"

Samantha appreciated Steve's warmth. It set her at ease. "Well, yeah, it is. Your message this morning was great but I'm not sure how to share what I know about

The Sovereign with someone who doesn't know him. Some people are ambivalent and I can't even tell if they are loyal or not. What do you suggest?"

Steve pointed to a couple of empty seats at the end of a table. "Let's sit over there and I'll give you some quick tips and then let you know where you can follow up with more detail.

He led the way and sat down. "Here are some questions to help you find out if someone knows him. Ask, 'If the world were to end today, where would you end up?' If a person doesn't know, you get to tell him how to end up with Yehowshuwa."

Samantha got the idea. "So that's a qualifying question to see if he knows The Sovereign Yehowshuwa?"

"That's right but it isn't enough. Some people think they know him but only know about him. The second question is the clincher. Ask, 'Suppose The Sovereign asked you, "Why should I let you into my new world?" How would you answer?'"

"I know Yehowshuwa. I came to know him when I admitted I'm not perfect and asked for his forgiveness. He already paid the penalty for all my disobedience to him so when I pledged my allegiance to him he gave me the right to enter that wonderful new creation," replied Samantha. Calmness and peace swept over her as she recalled the day she made her decision to follow The Sovereign.

"That is a very good answer, Sam. Usually, if someone doesn't personally know Yehowshuwa, he will most likely say something about trying his best to obey all the rules and regulations." Pastor Steve paused and thought for a moment. "The answers vary so you have to be discerning. If the person responded, 'Because I love The Sovereign,' do you think that would be a good answer?"

Pastor Steve picked up a chicken drumstick and took a bite while Samantha thought through the question.

"Well, no, I don't think that would be a good enough answer. He is depending on his own love to qualify him for eternal life instead of what Yehowshuwa has done for him," she finally answered.

He waved his drumstick toward her. "Excellent! You picked up on that nuance between a good sounding answer and a correct answer. I think you will do well at university."

Samantha felt good about the compliment but wasn't done yet. "Ok, I've got a pretty good idea that I'm talking to a guy that doesn't know The Sovereign Yehowshuwa. How do I proceed?"

Pastor Steve put down his chicken. "If this guy says he lived a good life, it shows he is not trusting in The Sovereign's mercy to let him into his future world. Set him straight. Let him know that Yehowshuwa loves each of us so much that he bore all our sins in a horrible death so we wouldn't have to be punished. He needs to see that he is an offender and that there is only one way to eternal life, through Yehowshuwa and his sacrifice."

He thumped his forefinger on the table. "He may insist that he is good enough to be accepted. If so, ask him if he has ever lied. One lie, even just a little fib, makes a person a liar. Lying breaks the ninth commandment that Yehhovaw gave to Mosheh."

As Pastor Steve mentioned a fib, Samantha hung her head. She recalled that just that week, she had told a friend she was busy and couldn't meet her when they were scheduled. She wasn't busy; she was angry over a hurting comment her friend had made.

Steve waited for Samantha to look up again. "See, it's convicting, isn't it? You can also ask him he has ever been angry with someone or called someone a hurtful name. Yehowshuwa said if anyone is angry with his brother and calls him contemptuous names, he will face the same judgment as if he killed him. That kind of anger is murder in the heart."

Wow! Two strikes at one time. Samantha held up her hand. "Ok, I get the point. I'm guilty. What's next?"

Steve pushed his plate aside. "Ask this person what he thinks Yehowshuwa will do with murderers on judgment day."

The Pastor held his chicken bone out toward Samantha. "These simple questions expose where a person's loyalty lies. If he is not loyal to The Sovereign, tell him how he can change that. Don't push him into a decision. If he is obstinate let Yehowshuwa's words do their work. If he recognizes his need to be saved from the eternal consequences of his offences, let him know he can ask The Sovereign to forgive him and take control of his life just like you did."

Samantha was sure she would be able to use this information when she went to university. "Thanks you very much, Pastor Steve, for helping me out. I'd better let you go. I'm sure there are others that would like some of your time today."

"Always glad to help. Have a great time at school." Pastor Steve got up and took his plate. In a couple of minutes he was in another conversation with a couple. Samantha wondered how he ever managed to finish a meal at a get-together like this.

Samantha found herself a drumstick and munched on it as she took in the scene: adults seated at tables, kids sitting on the ground, a few people standing and talking. She wanted to remember this day. It was going to be her last Sunday with her family until the holidays.

August 30, 998 ASR

"Robert, aren't you going to get up?" Mom pounded on the bedroom door like a sonic disrupter. "Robert, can you hear me?"

Robert pulled his pillow over his head, but the noise wouldn't go away. He tried to understand why his mom was being so insistent about getting him up. Then it hit him. His parents expected him to go worship The Sovereign with them whenever he was home. He didn't want to go after getting only a couple hours of sleep, but feigning illness would only cause Mom to become super protective and he didn't need that.

"Robert, it's time to get up." The pounding now seemed only a bit more than a normal knock, and the screech in her voice sounded just a smidgen louder than required.

"Yeah, Mom, I'm awake." If he said he didn't feel good, his mom would try to baby him. Besides, it wouldn't be the first time he'd gone to a worship service dead tired. He forced himself to get up and shuffled to the shower.

A few minutes later Robert sat at the breakfast table with his mom and dad, ready to eat. He was a bit wary, wondering if Mom would bring up the book again. He was hoping that she would still have the impression that he would be doing something to get out of his commitment to the Board to write his book.

"Morning, Mom and Dad."

"Good morning, Robert," Mom said as she poured him a cup of coffee. "You certainly were hard to wake up this morning. When did you get home?"

Robert took the coffee cup. *I need this.* "About two hours ago. Jim and I had a terrific time up at the old cabin. Did you know Hobbs is still roaming around up there? When I spotted him I pulled that old wild lion trick on Jim, and he fell for it. You should have seen his face!"

Dad laughed. "I remember when you first pulled that on us. I thought the laws of nature had reversed back to before The Last Battle. You sure had me going."

Robert kept chatting about his trip, stopping at Rosey's, the mountain that seemed to have moved and other things they had done. He was pleased that the book was not mentioned.

After breakfast the three strolled to the community center and entered the main hall. The large oak table where the Board had met with Robert was gone. The rail had been moved to accommodate the choir and worship band behind it. As they entered in they passed people who were standing around talking with one another. Robert spotted Henry near the front, chatting with some older people. As they headed toward their customary seats in the front row, Dad greeted several of his friends and Mom donned her broad public smile.

Robert couldn't see any of the people he'd grown up with fifty years ago. He recognized some of the parents but none of his childhood friends was there, even though several still lived in the community. Apparently very few younger people were loyal enough to The Sovereign to attend worship. If his dad hadn't been a Board member, Robert wouldn't be there either.

The worship director, Abisur Jerahmeel, stood at the front, between the railing and the picture of The Sovereign. The choir took their seats to his left, and a small group of musicians with horns, woodwinds, stringed instruments, and electronic keyboards assembled to his right. As soon as they were in place, he raised his arms. After a dramatic pause, he brought his arms down quickly. Most of the choir started clapping their hands, while others produced tambourines. A loud, long note similar to the blast of an ancient ram's horn blared from the horns. It was the call to worship.

The congregation ceased their conversations and took their seats. The choir sang a rousing song. The chorus appeared on view screens on either side of Sovereign Yehowshuwa's portrait. The congregation joined the choir, singing all eleven verses.

Robert enjoyed the song because of its tempo and beat. He didn't pay much attention to the lyrics, but sang along anyway.

Joy comes to those who sing his praise.

He is worthy.
Joy comes to those who proclaim his name.
He is worthy.
Joy comes to those who walk in his ways.
He is worthy.
Joy comes to those who spread his fame.
He is worthy.

Abisur then introduced a new song he had written. The music was slow and the words unfamiliar. Robert didn't like new songs because he had to pay more attention to the lyrics, and that was too much thinking for a Sunday morning.

Abisur asked Henry to pray for the people. During the prayer, most sat, others knelt, and one couple stood. Robert drifted in and out of sleep, thankful that he didn't jerk or snore when the stirring of the congregation woke him up at the end of the prayer.

Henry made some announcements about community affairs and gatherings that were coming up. Then he relinquished the podium.

Abisur pointed to an ornate chair in front of the large portrait. "Yehowshuwa is with us at all times in spirit. Let us continue to worship him as if he were physically here and seated on the throne."

The choir sang a familiar song and Robert clapped to the rhythm. He was getting into the mood of the music when a bright light flashed at the front of the hall. The choir stopped singing. The musicians lowered their instruments and stood gaping. To Robert's shock, he saw someone sitting on the throne. It was The Sovereign.

Some people dropped to their knees. A few in aisle seats fell face down on the floor. Most just stood and stared. Robert didn't know what to do.

He heard a commotion behind him and looked back. A couple of women had fainted. One slumped in her chair; the other had been caught by her husband, who was easing her back into her chair. Several people near the back made a hasty exit.

Robert felt Marilyn tugging on his pant leg. He turned and saw her on her knees, so he knelt as well. Soon everyone within Robert's vision was either prostrate on the floor or kneeling.

The Sovereign Yehowshuwa stood. "Please, my children, arise and continue your worship. I'll just sit here and enjoy. Abisur, if you please." The Sovereign motioned to the choir director and sat back down.

Abisur got the singers and musicians to their feet and resumed the song that had been interrupted. As the worship continued, Yehowshuwa glowed, light emanating from his face.

Robert looked around. Henry sang louder and more on tune than Robert had ever heard him, rocking back and forth, with his hands extended toward his master. His eyes were glued on The Sovereign.

Dad was missing several notes as he sang and stumbled over some of the words. He was singing much better before Yehowshuwa appeared. During one of the verses he just stood and stared at the floor.

Mom looked down at her skirt and straightened it after she stood up. She continued adjusting it and picking something from it. Robert looked but couldn't see any lint or anything. She patted the ends of her light brown hair curling in toward the back of her neck. *If she takes out a mirror and starts checking her makeup I'm going to find another seat.* The first verse was completed before she joined in singing and clapping. He recognized her forced smile, the one that didn't change when she talked to someone she could barely tolerate. He was amazed that she could also sing without changing expression. When The Sovereign started to shine her smile faded from her face.

Robert couldn't get back into the mood of the music either. He felt intimidated with The Sovereign seated a few meters in front of him. He had never seen Yehowshuwa in person and doubted that many in the congregation had. He wanted to look at The Sovereign but didn't want to stare, so he looked past him or at Abisur.

Why would he show up here during our worship service? Robert felt resentful that The Sovereign had shown up, ruining the program. He was enjoying the music before he appeared.

Robert wondered about the light emanating from him and concluded that The Sovereign must be drawing his power from the worship. *I wonder if his power is diminishing lately because fewer people are worshiping him.*

After a few more songs Sovereign Yehowshuwa stood and clapped his hands. "Thank you very much for your worship. It does my heart good to see and hear you in person, even though I see and hear you every morning, just as I see millions of other congregations who are worshipping. Every day, I visit a few communities when they assemble together."

He held his hand out toward Jotham, the congregation's teacher. He wore a yarmulke signifying that he was of the same lineage as The Sovereign. "It is Jotham's responsibility to make sure you receive proper religious instruction. As my representative here, he has complete authority over the spiritual life of this community. Usually at this time he would bring you some instructions. However, if it's all right with him, I'd like to say a few words."

Jotham bowed. "Who am I to say no to an opportunity to sit at your feet, Master?" he stammered. "Please let us hear what is on your heart."

Robert pulled out his ECD and switched it on to record. He also enabled the writing pad so he could jot down his thoughts in conjunction with what was recorded or highlight points that made an impression during a lecture.

"Thank you, Jotham. I have always appreciated the clarity with which you have taught my people, but I often like to say some things myself."

Yehowshuwa turned to the congregation. "My people, hear my voice and heed what I have for you today. I am the one who created the heavens and the Earth. Everything in the universe is the work of my hands. There is nothing that exists that I didn't mold and shape. Look to the heavens and see the starry hosts. How did they come about other than by my hand? Have I not made them all and know their names? I tell you the truth, there are wonders even beyond all that you have seen or will ever see that I have placed in the heavens."

Robert glanced at the words being displayed on his ECD as they were being recorded. He highlighted "I am the one who created..." Robert jotted down, "Why would he be emphasizing that?"

"I created Earth from nothing. I called out with my voice and it came into existence. I was there in the beginning with my father and brought it about as he willed. Other than our spirit, no one else was involved. I am The Sovereign and there is no other. I formed the Earth to fit my purposes and my desires. I hold all things together and keep the universe in place. Without me there would be nothing and without my will everything would disappear in an instant."

This is some really basic stuff. He highlighted the last sentence. He tightened his jaw to suppress the yawn that was trying to escape.

"I declare to you, as I did to my people thousands of years ago, there is no other supreme being."

Each time Robert looked up from his ECD, it seemed The Sovereign was looking at him alone. He wriggled in his seat. *I sure hope he didn't come here just to give me a boring refresher course in theology 101.*

"All that is living is alive because that is my will. I created you from nothing. Who has caused the dust of the earth to live? The creatures of the world are as I have made them; they have not changed. Have you ever heard of a blade of grass deciding that it would turn into a tree, or a duck become a platypus? These things cannot happen because I made them to continue as they are. They do not have the ability to change."

Robert tried not to look up too often. He wanted to appear to be taking notes to avoid The Sovereign's eyes.

"I have reshaped this world twice and I will do it once again. Jotham has told you about the flood, how the mountains were reshaped as I poured down the rain and loosed the mighty waters beneath the surface. You also know of the punishment brought upon the inhabitants of the earth just before The Last Battle. The world you see today I restored for your enjoyment and mine. Do not forget that it is this way because I determine the laws of physics and maintain the behavior of all the creatures."

The more he heard, the more Robert felt a critical spirit rising up within himself. Discussion subjects from *The Question* popped into his mind for each point The Sovereign had made so far. He was no longer bored but perceptive.

"The nations of the earth are mine. Even when nations rebelled against me ages ago, I guided them, determining which would prosper and which would decline. I gave power to one and reduced others to dust. I have shaped all generations from the beginning for I am The Sovereign, the first and the last, the beginning and the end. I have preserved my nation even in dispersion while all others have changed."

According to Jim's old friend, Josu, The Sovereign's nation wasn't the only one that remained intact. Maybe that should be another subject for The Question to pursue.

"You alone, my children, are created in my image. You are the crowning glory of my creation. You have not always walked in my ways or followed my decrees. The transgressions of your fathers were an abomination, yet I have removed the reproach from you. Is there anything you need that you don't have? Is there anything that harms you? Am I not in your presence day and night to lead and direct you in the way you should go? Do I not say to you to turn this way or that? I lead you with a rod of iron lest you turn to the ways of your fathers."

Another late night conversation theme came to Robert's mind. *I haven't heard him tell me what way to go. If I had, wouldn't I have a say in what I could or couldn't do?*

"I have done these things so that you would know that I alone am sovereign and that you can trust me because I love you. Are there any who disbelieve these things? Let them come forward and we will discuss the matter. Let them explain what has been and what is to come. Are there any who deny that I am the creator and can prove it? Do I not control the seasons, bringing forth the rain in its time? Do not the great plains bring forth an abundance of grain and the broad valleys bring forth fruits and vegetables? Is there not always enough fodder for your animals as well as for those that roam the earth? I do this because I love you."

How can someone who is so busy with the environment and regulating society have the time to love people? He's a lot like Dad, working late and serving the community. How can he say he loves me when he doesn't even know me?

"A time is coming when many people will not put up with sound teaching. They will turn to myths and fables because that's what suits their ears. They will make claims that have no foundation. They are blinded by their own desires and seek to become what they are not and cannot be. They will turn to promises of powers beyond their understanding. Once again there will be a new heaven and a new Earth."

Is he getting a little paranoid? Or does he know there is more to the underground movement? Robert felt a shiver run up his spine as it dawned on him that almost every point The Sovereign Yehowshuwa had made countered an article in *The Question.*

"I will give the fountain of the water of life to him who overcomes, even the sure promises of my eternal love, which I promised to Daawiyd, the king of my nation."

Is that an offer of amnesty if I bail out of the underground? Maybe I'm being paranoid. There's no way he could have known about those commentaries.

"I have kept you beyond your usual time, but for those who would linger for a while, I will walk among you and talk with you." The Sovereign caught Robert's eye. For an instant he had the strongest impression that Yehowshuwa wanted to talk only with him.

"Thank you, Abisur, for leading the delightful worship. I have enjoyed it immensely. Thank you, Jotham, for relinquishing your time to me."

The Sovereign looked at Henry, smiled, and nodded, then walked to the rail that had previously separated the Board hearing table from the audience. He stopped in front of Justin, Marilyn, and Robert. "I'm glad you were able to come this morning, Robert, even though you only had a couple hours of sleep. Marilyn, your son has an important task ahead of him. Support him and pray for him so that his work will accomplish what is needed for our future. Justin, take care of Marilyn and nurture her. She is the most important person in your life other than me. Robert, you are going to have some unique challenges in the next few months. You will face dangers you know nothing about and you will have to make a lot of difficult decisions. If you remember everything you have been taught about me, and act upon it, you will not be harmed. I know your potential and I want you to fulfill your greatest purpose in life."

"Uh," Robert stammered, "thank you for your confidence in choosing me. It's an extreme honor and pleasure." He had no idea how to respond in a one-on-one impromptu meeting with the supreme ruler of the world and self-proclaimed creator of the universe.

His parents mumbled something like, "Thank you, I will."

"If you folks will excuse me, I need to talk to some others before I leave." The Sovereign leaned over the rail and gave Robert a good-natured slap on the shoulder. "Make sure you don't miss that class you need."

Yehowshuwa took about six steps to where Abisur and Jotham stood, and waved Henry over. Henry quickly joined them.

The room was quieter than normal, so Robert eavesdropped on their conversation. "Time is running short. I do not need to tell you what's about to happen. It gives me great joy knowing that you are ready. However, I need to reiterate what Maria told Henry. There are many people who aren't ready. Did you notice how many slipped out when I appeared? Many more didn't even come this morning. I'm not finding fault with what you have been doing. You are my friends because you know what I want and do it. I am saddened, however, that so many haven't taken the time to know me."

We are right and he knows it, Robert thought. From what I've learned through The Question, a lot fewer people are loyal to The Sovereign Yehowshuwa than ever before.

As Robert's mom and dad exited the row, he continued to watch the group of men out of the corner of his eye. His parents stopped to talk with another couple, so he decided to hold back and listen a little more.

Henry's wife, Wanda, joined the small group as Abisur and Jotham left.

"Are you two hungry?" The Sovereign Yehowshuwa asked.

"Now that you mention it, I'm famished," Henry replied.

"Well, yes," said Wanda hesitantly.

"I know you have lunch prepared, Wanda, but how about having dinner at my place?"

Wanda's eyes lit up and she clasped her hands in front of her. "Just say the word."

"Great. After I chat with a few more people, I'll be back." The Sovereign mingled with those who had stayed and waited for him.

Robert caught up with his parents. He didn't want to get into another conversation with The Sovereign.

Chapter 19

C huck and the three crewmembers in his tour group strolled to a conveyance stop a few meters away from where Alex and his group boarded their bus. His group's destination was Eden's central archives library in the heart of the city. They were interested in looking up documentation on Earth's history from the Council of Enlightened Beings' perspective. Chuck didn't think it would be terribly exciting but it was necessary. They boarded a convy and within a few minutes were in the heart of the city, Adonlon.

As they emerged from the convy Chuck looked at the 500-story library, the base of which rested on five city blocks. The structure looked like six hexagonal crystals growing side by side. Each crystal was a different height and color, resembling the colors of the rainbow and blending into different hues where they joined together. The group entered the violet building, which opened into a large reception area.

Mine began the tour by explaining how the library system acquired its data. "All the sovereigns that are aligned with the Council of Enlightened Beings work together to keep accurate records of activities that occur in physical space as well as the eternal realm. The council even monitors and records the activities of Yehowshuwa and Jehov. The physical data is stored within the crystal matrix of these buildings. As data is added to the libraries, the buildings grow. Since terabytes of data can be stored in a small crystal, the growth is very gradual."

The crew's boots clicked on the marble-like floor and echoed back from the cavernous room's walls as they walked toward an escalator. *I'll bet they never thought about how noisy this place could be, since they are bare-footed and telepathic.*

"Each council member maintains one copy of the records on one of the worlds he has created. We have all the technical records, inventions, and discoveries of every world that has ever existed. These records enable us to learn from those who have preceded us."

Chuck raised his hand. "All of the libraries I've visited have screens to identify different subject areas and we can query them or use our ECD to find out where to go." He looked around the empty room. "How do you find your way around here?"

Mine pointed to his head, then the ceiling. "We use our telepathy to interface with the crystals' systems. When I entered the lobby, I inquired where to find the history of Earth. The system found the logical location of the data. I can inquire further and get more detail. If I wanted to review the data, I would be assigned a cubicle."

That sounds a lot like our systems except we use ECD's to dig deep unless we are looking up some ancient manuscript. "Can we use these cubicles even though we aren't telepathic?"

"No, you can't, so I have made arrangements to use one of the larger rooms. We have constructed what you would call a virtual reality complex where you will be able to experience the representation of the data almost as realistically as we can through our telepathy. These devices have built-in earphones, view screens, and olfactory units, so your experience will be almost as if you were there when the data was recorded. You will be able to hear, see, and smell history."

"How can we take the information with us? We can't take your devices with us, can we?"

Mine patted Chuck on the back. "What you see here will be translated into videos that Hal can store and play back on your view screens or ECDs. It will also be translated to interesting and colorful textual documents for those who still like to read."

Mine led the way up an escalator to a second-floor conference room. Several plush chairs filled the dimly lit room. Four helmets sat on a table beside the door. Mine invited Chuck to sit down. He put a helmet on Chuck and made sure it fit well, covering his eyes, ears, and nose.

After Mine fitted the others with helmets, he said, "If you can see me, raise your hand?" Chuck and his crewmembers all obliged. "Good. You are not hearing my voice but rather my thoughts, as I am now speaking to you telepathically through the library's system."

Mine explained the few simple verbal commands that would be required for them to mark points of interest, move forward or backward in time, or obtain more detail about a certain period of history. "You will see a time indicator to your right that will give you an idea of what period of history you are viewing at any time. Any questions?"

"Where's the popcorn?" asked one of the crewmembers.

Mine laughed. "We don't have popcorn; however, we do have other refreshments across the hall. Restrooms are just outside. Perhaps you'd like to take a quick break before we start."

They removed their helmets and went down the hall to get beverages and munchies, then returned to the conference room, where Mine put their helmets back on. When everyone indicated they were ready, the show began.

The title "Earth History" faded in over a background of stars and swirling cosmos. Chuck felt like a spectator in outer space. Haunting, unearthly music increased in volume and he felt an overpowering sense of a divine presence. The music reached a crescendo as the title was replaced by an implosion of swirling gases, resulting in the formation of the earth. He felt as if he were being drawn into the Earth and falling from a great height. Clouds approached at an alarming speed but became a mist, which disappeared, yielding a great ocean beneath. His rate of descent continued as the ocean came up and he entered without a splash. The water expanded until he was within the structure of the water, seeing molecules of dissolved minerals and chemicals.

He jumped when a lightning bolt shot through the waters. Some of the minerals fused together to form a chain of a denser, more complex structure. Another flash and the molecule became even more complex. Several molecules joined together and the scene drew back until he saw a small mass of jelly-like substance that changed, moved, and grew. The jelly became a cell that sucked in nourishment from the water and divided over and over again, filling the water.

Chuck's view retreated more, revealing small plants and animals forming in the waters. A plethora of animals and plants developed in the ocean. Then Chuck found himself on dry land. Myriad creatures and plants came from the water and covered what had been barren land. Trees grew tall while animals covered the plains and frolicked in the lush forests. Lions grazed peacefully among antelope.

People soon appeared, without clothing, which didn't bother Chuck. He was getting used to seeing naked people. They walked alongside the animals, which all behaved like domesticated pets.

The music was replaced by a woman's voice. "This is an overview of the creation of the system called Sol and the inhabitable planet Earth. It was organized from the existing matter and energy of the cosmos by Yehhovaw beginning 256,887,372.87725 ET, Eternal Time. He did this without the permission of the Council of Enlightened Beings, who determined that he was not yet ready to be a sovereign. On 256,887,657.54287 ET the first of his children with the potential of becoming eternal beings evolved and began to multiply and fill the Earth."

Beautiful cities with magnificent architecture appeared. "During the next twelve hundred years these people, called humans, achieved growth in knowledge and abilities faster than most beings with eternal potential. Yehhovaw became jealous and fearful of his creation."

Dark clouds formed over the cities. Chuck blinked as lightning flashed and he shuddered when the thunder crashed. He felt the violent winds, earthquakes, and hailstones that reduced the cities to rubble. People and animals ran in every direction, seeking shelter.

"In his fear, he utterly destroyed all the accomplishments of the humans so that nothing could be found by future generations to prove that these cities had ever existed. He also infected the world with disease and radiation so that for the first time human beings knew death. He suppressed their mental capabilities as well."

Chuck was upset. He had barely seen Adonlon but it looked a lot like the cities Yehhovaw had destroyed. *Earth should be even greater than Eden.*

"He appeared to the survivors and demanded that they worship him. Yehhovaw convinced the humans that the disaster was a consequence of their disobedience and failure to worship him. So that they would not be able to pass on to their children the true history, he erased their memories and replaced them with a myth that the first two of them had been alone in a garden and had disobeyed his command not to eat the fruit of one of the trees."

Chuck said, "Pause." He needed time to adjust to a new concept of the Garden of Eden. He reviewed in his mind the attack on the H.S.S.S. Ramah. *That was consistent with what I've seen.* He reviewed the discussions with Berekiah, Tia-le and Mine, people from different parts of the galaxy. *Either there is a cosmic conspiracy going on or The Sovereign Yehowshuwa has changed our recorded history. It seems to me that the latter would be easier to accomplish.* When he regained his composure he said, "Resume."

The narration picked up where he had paused. "The Council of Enlightened Beings was horrified that Yehhovaw would take such action against his own children, beings that possessed eternal capabilities. Volunteers among ascended beings were solicited to form a rescue team for Earth and its inhabitants. The largest rescue force ever assembled was dispatched under the command of Ben-Shaachar, who was about to become a sovereign but postponed his advancement in order to be of service in this confrontation."

"Mark," said Chuck. He wanted to be able to find this spot again when Ben-Shaachar was first introduced.

"By universal law, the only means of defeating Yehhovaw was to show his children how to find and use the power within themselves to advance toward enlightenment. If enough of them resisted Yehhovaw, he would be overthrown and all mankind would be freed forever."

Well that is consistent with what we've been hearing on Eden.

"Ben-Shaachar began to teach Yehhovaw's children how to be free from their creator's lies and how to develop their true capabilities, especially in the realms of the mind. As soon as enough regained their freedom in these areas, Ben-Shaachar was to use their restored abilities, linked together with the rescue team, to reverse the disease and radiation that had devastated the planet. This would bind Yehhovaw from further activity. However, not all of the humans were open to help. Some violently attacked and resisted those who were trying to help them advance."

Chuck felt as if he were moving among thatched huts of a village in the virtual reality. He could smell the smoke of wood fires and the shouts of barefoot children playing in the dusty street. The digits on the time indicator spun forward and the huts changed into imposing brick-and-stone buildings.

"Some of the rescue team married humans, and had children with them, in order to help them advance faster. Their offspring were giant men of great strength and noble character."

Chuck marched with handsome men that were heads and shoulders taller than him. They led armies of well-groomed men standing erect with their shoulders back and chins held high. They wore shining bronze breastplates and carried bronze bows. Quivers of arrows were slung on their backs. They faced hordes that had sloping foreheads and large protruding eyebrows. They were dressed in ragged clothes and carried clubs.

He was suddenly submerged in twisting whirlpools. He felt as if he were spinning out of control, no longer sure where up was. Debris from buildings and bodies rushed past or directly at him. His stomach started to protest as he clutched the armrests of his chair. "Pause," he said and quickly took off the helmet.

Mine hurried over. "Are you all right?"

He held up a hand. "I will be in a minute. That whirlpool was way too realistic."

He put the helmet back on and cautiously said, "Resume. Faster." Chuck wanted to get the flood over with before he felt nauseous again.

Fast forwarding through the worst of the flood didn't have the same effect on Chuck and he resumed normal speed when he saw the waters calm.

"Unfortunately, Yehhovaw again attacked with the forces of nature to flood the earth, killing all the inhabitants except a few whom he shielded. The rescue team's children, along with their spouses and allies, were wiped out. The team mourned its losses for many years but waited for the right time to resume the process toward freedom. The team decided that the risks of intermarriage were too great, believing that Yehhovaw would again wipe them out, so they abandoned this direction and sought new ways to overcome him."

Chuck identified more and more with Ben-Shaachar and his team as they tried different tactics through history to introduce paths to enlightenment to mankind. At times it appeared that Ben-Shaachar was on the verge of victory when Yehhovaw intervened. Chuck admired Ben-Shaachar's tenacity to try again and again.

The birth of Yehowshuwa was significantly different from what he had been taught. As Chuck watched the accounts of history, he could see how he had been deceived all his life about The Sovereign's true nature.

Chuck watched in fascination as a young man who excelled in cultic powers and enlightenment gave his body over to Ben-Shaachar. This occurred at the same time Yehowshuwa withdrew his followers from the Earth and started raining destruction on those who remained. Ben-Shaachar excelled politically so that he quickly took control of the world governments in an attempt to save Earth from Yehowshuwa's devastation. The narration explained that Ben-Shaachar was henceforth known as The Chancellor Ben-Shaachar.

"Yehowshuwa continued to try to destroy the Earth and all its inhabitants."

Chuck was sickened as he watched buildings crumble in earthquakes. He could see limbs and body parts in the wreckage. He smelled the rotting flesh of people in hospitals inflicted with horrible tumors. All these horrors and more were attributed to Yehowshuwa by his own people. Chuck couldn't imagine anyone giving his or her allegiance to Yehowshuwa while he was pouring out his wrath on the Earth.

"After Yehhovaw wiped out all who were on the path of enlightenment, he captured and imprisoned the rescue team."

He almost wept as The Chancellor's army lay in rivers of blood after The Last Battle. Chancellor Ben-Shaachar was seized and locked into a pitch-black dungeon cell.

Chuck watched the Earth restored to a near-perfect environment after The Last Battle ended. *I wonder why The Sovereign restored everything. Everything he has done in the past shortened life spans and made life on Earth more difficult.*

"Yehowshuwa, under the power of his father, rebuilt Earth to a semblance of what it had been originally. People were still restricted, and compliance to his will was enforced by transformed but unenlightened humans who had stayed loyal to Yehowshuwa during the preceding centuries. Because of his strict control he became know as The Sovereign. Even so, his followers were so impressed they thought he was benevolent."

Yeah, that's what I used to think too. It sure is a far cry from the way it was in the beginning and the way Eden is now.

"Under the new conditions, The Sovereign Yehowshuwa hoped to appease the Council of Enlightened Beings so that they would recall Ben-Shaachar and the rescue team. However, the council would accept nothing less than total freedom for humans so that they could ascend into true enlightened eternal beings."

Ah, now I see why he did it.

Civilization again began to flourish on Earth. The scene was very much like the original Earth, except that people were clothed and animal sacrifices were performed.

"Under The Sovereign's direct rule, civilization was rebuilt. However, he still demanded worship and reinstituted animal sacrifices like the ones required thousands of years earlier by his father, Yehhovaw. Death was still the means of transformation without achieving enlightenment, and beyond this there was no hope of higher evolution."

I never have understood why The Sovereign Yehowshuwa has those sacrifices at the temple in his capital. It just seems to be part of his twisted need to be worshiped.

"As the population on Earth grew, The Sovereign found that he couldn't maintain control because of the limited number of unenlightened Enforcers. At the same time Ben-Shaachar evolved well beyond the capabilities he had before The Last Battle. His imprisonment dramatically increased his powers. He freed many of his forces and awaited the right time for his own escape."

Chuck found himself walking briskly on a university campus with a tall, attractive young woman dressed in black with pale white skin and long black hair. The campus was bustling with students crossing one another's paths.

"Gloria was the first agent to escape. She has been coordinating the activities of the forces as they report to her. The main thrust of their work has been preparing people at universities to question the status quo. They have introduced an electronic newspaper that has been hidden from The Sovereign Yehowshuwa's view. It prepares activists for the next level of involvement so they will be willing to do battle against The Sovereign."

Berekiah appeared, busily working with an ECD. "For many years after Berekiah escaped, he worked in the background to encourage deep-space exploration. He successfully planted the coordinates of the nearest council library aboard the H.S.S.S. Ramah, authorized by Yehowshuwa for space exploration."

Chuck's jaw dropped as he watched his ship being launched just twenty-five years earlier. He hadn't considered his voyage a part of history or that it would be pertinent to his research. The accuracy of the event confirmed the validity of what he was watching.

Next, he found himself in a wilderness area in rugged, mountainous terrain. He appeared to be on a transport laden with building materials rapidly approaching a huge cliff. He ducked when the transport flew into the precipice, but he passed right through the rock face and emerged on the other side. He watched the transport being unloaded among new buildings that were being erected.

"The rescue team constructed shields that The Sovereign cannot penetrate. It is currently building training camps for human recruits for the battle for freedom. Preliminary work among university students is nearing completion. After documentation of the true history of Earth is disseminated, these students will be asked to report to the training camps."

Chuck's vision put him in his office on the Ramah. Zophia entered with the coordinates of Eden.

"Ramah met with resistance from one of Yehhovaw's allies, Jehov."

Chuck watched from outside the Ramah as Rol-el's ship launched the fire ball that killed Dave.

"Rof, a council confederate, was able to protect them from Jehov's attack. Tia-le's rescue followed, then the landing of Ramah on Eden.

"They arrived safely at Eden and are gathering information to use when they return to Earth."

Chuck watched a quick view of the luncheon the day before, then his group entering the library, going up the escalator, and starting the presentation.

He took off his helmet to find the other crewmembers had already finished and were talking with Mine. He got up and joined them.

"How did it go?" Mine asked.

"It was truly amazing. I'm stunned at the detail. The accuracy of the events surrounding our departure from Earth and arrival here vouch for its credibility. I would like to take some time to explore some more areas of our history if that's all right."

"Please, be my guest." Mine gestured back to the chairs.

Chuck instructed the three crewmembers to go back into the presentation and dig deeper into different aspects of Earth's history.

Chuck zeroed in on the birth, death, and supposed resurrection of The Sovereign Yehowshuwa. He weighed this against the version he had been taught on Earth. He had always been told that The Sovereign was conceived by the power of his father's spirit. On the other hand, this chronicle stated it was by Yehhovaw himself and without the 13-year-old mother's consent. He had been taught that Yehowshuwa had died to pay for the sins of humanity. These archives indicated that The Sovereign was indicted for trying to take control of the world. He didn't die but was transformed by Yehhovaw and taken into the spiritual realm in a last-minute rescue effort.

That blows apart the whole concept of sin.

Everything he'd seen in this presentation contradicted what he'd been taught all his life. How could he doubt information that had been recorded over centuries, accurate up to the last hour?

He took off his helmet and saw Mine standing by. "This certainly appears to be proof of what we are looking for. I must admit; it bothers me that this history is so up-to-date, right down to the minute. I'll bet if I put that helmet back on, I'd find this very conversation."

"You would, if you knew the right place to look," agreed Mine.

"It's pretty scary knowing that you could see everything I've ever done or said. Doesn't this violate a person's privacy rights?"

Mine put his arm around Chuck's shoulder. "That fear comes from your experience in an imperfect world. We have nothing to hide and no reason to use this information other than to improve ourselves or help people who are under bondage."

Chuck thought about that. While he didn't feel he had anything to hide he still felt uncomfortable that his entire life was recorded in this building.

"Do you think we are the only ones capable of gathering such detailed information? What you see here is merely a reflection of what has been recorded in the spiritual realm. Yehowshuwa has almost the same capabilities as the Council does to gather information. Haven't you ever wondered how he always knows what is going on? If he had the time, he could review every conversation in the world. As it is, he makes the information available to his Enforcers so they can monitor activities on Earth. However, they are limited in how much they can monitor."

Chuck felt a knot forming in his gut as he envisioned The Sovereign watching his conversation with Mine. "I never really thought about Yehowshuwa being able to see my every move. I guess I assumed he would only be interested if I were doing something big either for or against him. The rest of the time he would barely even know I existed. What if he's watching a replay of everything we've learned on Eden?"

"In a sense you are right. He has far too many people to monitor, so only important events are monitored. Regarding our conversation, Ben-Shaachar has been able to disable The Sovereign's information gathering to hide selected events from him, like the training camps. Despite what he claims, The Sovereign is not omniscient. He is significantly less powerful than Adon and you have been protected ever since you entered his jurisdiction."

Chuck felt his tension ease. "Whew, that's good. Enough of this musing. I need to get back to the ship and see how this information looks viewed through our video system."

August 30, 998 ASR

Robert and his parents walked home from the worship service quietly, but he felt like he was floating on a cloud. There was no way his mother could pester him now about giving up the book, and he didn't have to pretend to find a way to get out of it, not with The Sovereign's personal direction to Mom to provide support.

He hummed his favorite worship song.

When they arrived home Mom started preparing her usual Sunday dinner while Dad and Robert went into the backyard to relax.

Dad sat on the edge of a lounge chair and opened his ECD. The sound of a cheering crowd came from the speakers. Robert sipped on a cold juice cocktail he had taken from the refrigerator on the way out. "Dad, what did you make of The Sovereign showing up today?"

Dad set his ECD down beside him. "It was a shock at first, and it was hard with him being there, but after a while I got used to it. To be honest, it felt a little strange to be worshiping with him right in front of me."

Robert put one hand over his eyes to shield them from the sun. "I know what you mean. I couldn't get back into the music after he popped in. Also, what about his speech? I don't know why he would tell our congregation what he did. What was his point?"

Dad wrinkled his forehead and pursed his lips. "Hmm. Well, it reminded me of the words spoken by the prophets before his first appearance. Why us, and why now? I don't know. The last part sounded like a warning, though I don't really know what he was talking about. To tell the truth, I don't remember exactly what he said."

Robert pulled out his ECD, looked at the transcript of the warning, and summarized, "He talked about people turning to myths, foundationless claims, and wanting to become something they can't. What's that all about?"

Dad shrugged. "Beats me. I imagine Jotham knows, though. He'll probably explain everything to us next week."

Robert wondered why The Sovereign would speak in such a way that his listeners wouldn't understand, and teachers needed to explain what he meant. *We should be able to get to the truth without having to go to the Administration's mouthpieces.*

Dad closed his ECD. "Based on what he said to you, it sounds like you have some very important work ahead of you. When he came over to us right away, it was as if you were the main reason he showed up."

That thought had crossed Robert's mind but he didn't want to talk about it. "What about the things he said to you and Mom?"

Dad grunted. "I know quite well what he meant with his comments to me. I've been spending too much time at the hardware store and not enough with your mother or you. The hard part is going to be getting things working the way they should."

Robert was surprised by his dad's candidness. "You got all that from one little comment?"

"No. He just confirmed what I've been thinking about over the past week or so. You know, now that you mentioned it, I think I should help your mother with dinner." Dad stood up. "What did you make of his comment to you?"

Robert sat up. He really didn't want to pursue the conversation in front of Mom. "Before I left for the mountains, Mom tried to get me to throw my classes so the deal would fall through and I wouldn't have to write the book. After what The Sovereign said, I don't think she'll give me any more static about the book. Nevertheless, what he said to me caught me off guard. I know it'll be a challenge, but I wonder what dangers he was talking about."

Dad grimaced "Does sound a bit ominous."

Robert took a sip of his drink and stood up. "I can hardly wait to get going on the project. Jim and I talked about it quite a bit and he's excited too. I signed him up as my research assistant starting in January."

Dad raised his eyebrows. "Are you sure that's wise? I wonder about that young man's maturity sometimes."

Robert and his dad made their way back into the kitchen from the back yard. "You just have to understand Jim and know how to motivate him."

"The way he rambles on makes no sense."

"He just gets nervous around authority figures."

"He doesn't seem to have any initiative."

"He's a hard worker...on things that are interesting to him."

Dad snorted. "Well, good luck with him."

Marilyn turned as they came in the door. "What's this about Jim?"

"I've signed him on as my research assistant starting in January," answered Robert before he remembered he didn't want to bring up the book in front of Mom.

"Well, maybe you found a way out of doing the book after all. With that worthless boy's help, you'll never get it done in time."

Robert took a step back. "That was a bit harsh. Jim's my friend." He bit his tongue. He spoke too quickly and now he was afraid of what was going to come next.

Mom surprised him and looked at the floor. "You're right. I guess I'm just shook up over what The Sovereign said." She looked up with tight lips. "I was so sure this book was the biggest mistake you could have made. Then The Sovereign Yehowshuwa himself shows up and says I need to support you. I guess I'll have to bow to his wishes, but I don't have to like it."

Marilyn quickly turned and opened the oven door and peered in.

"Good luck, Dad." Robert was glad that he wasn't going to have to deal with his mother. *He's going to have a big job softening that heart.*

Chapter 20

Zophia was eager to explore the occult, especially after Chuck had tied it to the path of enlightenment. He hadn't shared that with the crew so she thought it odd that her tour group was the largest. She wasn't sure why so many of the crew wanted to find out more about something The Sovereign was dead set against.

"Irene, why did you want to investigate the occult?" asked Zophia as the crew left the Ramah.

"When Chuck listed the five areas to investigate I felt drawn to that one. It's hard to explain but I sense some kind of presence guiding me. It started sometime yesterday afternoon when I was talking with my guide."

Zophia thought that sounded a lot like the experiences the officers had shared the night before. "Did you talk to anyone else about this?"

"Yes, Buckly, Martin, and Barb. We all felt the same way. Is there something wrong?" Irene stopped and let others pass them by.

"No, I don't think so. Chuck, the other officers and I have felt the same thing. I believe that Adon is guiding us. This occult study tour may be one of the most important of them all." Zophia experienced calm even as they scurried to catch up with the rest of the crew.

During breakfast she told Ana they wanted to know more about the occult and, if possible, see some examples.

"Did you look up the occult in your archives?" asked Ana.

"I did," Zophia said, "but I didn't learn a whole lot except that The Sovereign is strongly against it. It seems to encompass several facets, including knowing what will happen, making things happen, and contacting the dead using the aid of supernatural forces or agents such as The Chancellor."

Ana nodded. "Your description is a good one but it is from Yehowshuwa's point of view. Today you will see what you have been denied."

After breakfast Zophia's group along with their guides assembled on the north side of the canopy.

"We have constructed two learning centers for you on the other side of that orchard." Ana pointed to two buildings that were partially visible on the far side of some trees. "Let's go over there while I explain a little more." As they strolled through the orchard, Ana said, "I want each of you to select an object that you would like to use during our demonstration. It can be something you already have with you or something you see on the way."

Zophia wondered what they were going to do with the objects, but she didn't want to interrupt Ana.

"Telepathy would fall into the category of the occult because it would be considered magical on Earth. However, there is nothing extraordinary about it. We all have brainwaves that can be recorded using electrical sensors. The physical operation of our brains is accomplished by electrical impulses. Even before the Great Time of Trouble, as you call it on Earth, your scientists were able to use paraplegics' brain waves to control computers, artificial limbs, and even robots."

"Then why haven't we developed the telepathic controls for computers that you have?"

Ana paused before answering, "It seems many of your questions and my answers paint The Sovereign in a bad light. How are you doing with this?"

"I think we are all getting used to it. It's been several weeks since our world was turned upside down. Go ahead; tell us how Yehowshuwa has interfered in this area too." Zophia was looking for the truth and if it rubbed the wrong way she still wanted to hear it.

Ana stopped, and then looked at the group, "You are a resilient people. Very well…after Earth's restoration there were no more paraplegics, no need for artificial limbs. So Yehowshuwa discouraged any further experimentation in that area out of fear that you would develop your natural telepathic skills. If you were trained you could contact Ben-Shaachar and his associates. Ben-Shaachar is more powerful than we are because he has ascended. Before his imprisonment, he and his associates were able to discern your thoughts and he could plant his thoughts in your minds. People who were called spiritists and mediums developed limited telecommunication with The Chancellor's forces after significant training."

A crewmember raised his hand. "One of the things our database mentioned about the occult was telekinetics. What is that?"

Ana picked a peach-like fruit from a tree and tossed it to the crewmember. "Telekinetics requires focused concentration on the power that is within you. A simple example is the ability to move an object by willing it to move. A more complex example is healing. On Earth certain people invoked something called spells to heal diseases caused by The Sovereign. Some of The Sovereign's followers used these skills to inflict pain and disease. He blamed Ben-Shaachar. As a result anyone who could do this was labeled a witch and was persecuted. People who were doing good and trying to free mankind were labeled evil and killed. Yehowshuwa often takes what is good and turns it into something bad."

After several weeks of contact with aliens, assaults on The Sovereign Yehowshuwa's character had little effect on Zophia and she presumed the same applied to the crew, since no one objected to Ana's comment.

"We built the two identical learning centers so we can conduct two different training courses at the same time. Today we'll use the one on the left."

Zophia and the group followed Ana into the small, five-sided building. The foyer was a hallway that went to the right and left. They followed Ana to the left, which followed the exterior walls to the opposite side of the building. The lighting dimmed as they progressed and finally stopped out of sight of the building's entrance.

"This is the central room in the building and it is where we will do all our training. We keep the lighting low to help us concentrate." Ana approached the door and it opened.

An ornate tile pentagram graced the center of the floor. Zophia felt as if it were reaching out and calling for her attention. Pillows surrounded the pentagram, enough for everyone in the group. Five glowing orange bulbs hovered in the air above the pentagram. Below each bulb a pyramid pointed upward.

As Zophia's eyes gradually adjusted to the low lighting she noticed that the walls were decorated with pyramids, octagons, and pentagrams separated by pictures of goat's heads and unicorns. *What a strange room.*

Ana approached the pentagram and turned to the crew that was now inside the training room. "Would each of you place your selected object inside the pentagram and then sit down on a pillow? It is most helpful if you sit cross-legged."

The crewmembers put their objects inside the pentagram. Zophia set down a fruit that resembled a grapefruit she'd picked along the way. Other items on the floor included two hair combs, six leaves, an ECD, four sticks of various sizes, one shoe, and a heterodyning gravitational stabilizer. Zophia rolled her eyes. *Leave it to Wilfred to keep a tuning tool in his pocket.*

After they all sat down, Ana said, "I will first demonstrate my ability to move objects without touching them. Then I will show you a few things that would have been called magic tricks or illusions on Earth. Here you will learn that they are not tricks or illusions, but reality."

Ana sat cross-legged on a pillow nearest the pentagram. "First I will organize your objects."

Zophia watched carefully. Ana didn't move a muscle while the six leaves swirled into a circle, with each stem pointing to the tip of the leaf in front of it. The two combs marched over to the circle and aligned themselves, teeth pointing together. The sticks formed a rough quadrilateral next to the combs. The shoe clomped over to the sticks and jumped into the center. The ECD lined up with the leaves and the stabilizer came up beside it as if it were making an adjustment to the ECD. The grapefruit rose up in the air about a meter and then came to rest in the middle of the circle of leaves.

Zophia was so excited that she didn't realize she had been holding her breath until she heard a couple of gasps, and then she exhaled.

"How did you do that?" a crewmember asked.

"I simply willed these objects to move to where they are."

"Is there something special inside the pentagram?" asked another crewmember.

"The pentagram serves a purpose in learning. Once you have mastered the ability to move objects, it isn't necessary." Ana lifted her hand palm up and chest high. "Hold out your hand like this and I'll toss the grapefruit to you, outside the pentagram."

The crewmember raised his hand and the grapefruit flew toward it as if it were a fast-pitched softball. It stopped just above his hand and landed gently on his palm.

"Go ahead and toss it up and down. You will see that it is the same as when Zophia picked it." After a couple of tosses, Ana sent it back to the center of the leaves.

"We can also fabricate flames without consuming anything." The sticks in the rectangle all stood on end and a small flame came up above each one.

Cute trick. It might dazzle someone when we get home but I wonder what good that will be.

"I'm keeping the flame low so you won't have to readjust your eyes." The flames went out and the sticks lay back on the floor.

"Are you going to teach us how to move objects?" Zophia asked.

Ana looked around the room. "I can guide you through the steps that will put you in touch with your inner powers, which have been awakened by Adon during the week or so that you have been here. Moving objects is not the first step. Would you like to give it a try?"

Enthusiastic affirmatives echoed around the room.

Ana's face glowed. "Good. For now, I'm going to remove everything from the pentagram so we can use it to focus." All the objects lifted and were deposited neatly by the door. "Physical contact with those already possessing power is helpful, so join hands with your guides and rearrange yourselves into a large circle around the pentagram."

Everyone moved around the pentagram. Ana took Zophia's hand and the hand of a crewmember on her other side. "The purpose of this exercise is to open your minds to your inner powers and to call upon the powers of the universe. Focus on the center of the pentagram. Relax, but keep your back straight, legs crossed, and head up. Your guides and I will chant in unison as we join our minds. Listen to the chant. It is in our language but it is simple. There are five words in the chant. Each is the name of one side of the pentagram as well as the name of one of the founders of the Council of Enlightened Beings. When you have learned the chant, join in with us. After repeating the chant a few times, close your eyes but keep the pentagram in your mind."

Ana paused and looked around the circle.

"All right, let's begin. *Harum Opparum Mararum Rorarum Amorum.*" Over and over the guides repeated the names.

Zophia quickly memorized the chant. Soon she felt her spirit rise as though she were being physically levitated. She felt her body tingle as if a small electric current was running through her hands as she held on to Ana on one side and another guide on the other.

She closed her eyes. To her surprise and enjoyment she could still see the pentagram as if her eyes were still open.

The chanting changed. Zophia realized that she was no longer hearing with her ears but in her mind. She was no longer using her voice to chant, but her mind. She was sure the others could still hear her. Soon it was as if everyone in the room had only one voice. She felt that she had lost her sense of self and became joined in one mind with the others in the room.

"Ana?" Zophia did not speak audibly, but she was confident Ana could hear her.

"I hear you," Zophia sensed in her mind. "You have amazed me. Within a short time you have accomplished what we thought would take many hours or even days. It is now time to go to the next step."

The chanting in Zophia's mind slowly faded and she opened her eyes. The others opened their eyes and looked around. She was surprised to find they had been entranced for over an hour.

Zophia wondered if she could communicate with other Edenians, and more important, with others from her crew, without needing to chant, hold hands, or sit in a circle. "Ana," she projected without speaking. Everyone in the room looked at her. "How far away can two people be and still communicate telepathically?"

Ana answered telepathically. "General communication, such as what is going on right now, is limited to about a hundred meters in a quiet environment without distractions. Private communication between people with bonds, such as husband and wife or parents and children, has taken place from opposite sides of our planet." She paused and added after surveying the crew, "Does everyone here realize that Zophia did not speak but asked her question using telepathy?"

Several people responded with telepathic yeses and a few with audible responses. Audible negatives came from two surprised-looking crewmembers.

Ana applauded the group quietly. "I'm impressed. Since everyone here is capable of hearing via telepathy; that is the method I will use for the remainder of your training. This will keep your ability fresh and enable you to participate more effectively. We'll take a short break for refreshments, as you will need your strength for the next session. Food and drink are just outside the door. Restrooms are on either side of the building, men to the right and women to the left. We'll reassemble here in fifteen minutes. When you return put your object back in the pentagram for the next lesson."

Ana and Zophia quickly refreshed and fortified themselves with a sweet fruit juice puree. They reentered the training room before the others.

"Ana, I am convinced that these powers were banned by The Sovereign simply so that we would not be a threat to him. If we were allowed to communicate quickly and efficiently, then we would have advanced way beyond our current state on Earth. I want to delve deeper into every aspect of the occult. Somehow, I know that not all of the crew will be able to keep up with me."

"Let's sit together." Ana sat down cross-legged and Zophia sat facing her. "I sensed from the very first time that I saw you on our view screen that you are special. I believe you have a special call on your life. I think some one-on-one training will greatly enhance your abilities."

Zophia studied Ana's face framed by the waves in her long black hair. The tinge of gold and green in her eyes appeared to flicker in the dim light. "I'll look forward to our time together."

When the others started entering and taking their places, Zophia and Ana joined them.

Ana outlined the second phase of their training. "I will now teach you how to move an object. This technique is similar to the connection we gained during our mental telepathy exercise. So let's join hands and chant to clear our minds and regain the momentum we had before the break."

Everyone joined hands and chanted. Zophia heard only a few people chant audibly. She soon heard them all only telepathically.

Ana let them know that the chanting should cease. Without speaking audibly she guided Zophia's mind, directing her attention to the middle of the pentagram, where the grapefruit sat in the center.

Suddenly, Zophia realized she was looking at it in Ana's mind. She didn't just see the fruit rise from the floor; she also saw how she lifted it. The grapefruit drifted back to the floor.

Ana directed each crewmember to face his or her guide and hold hands while still sitting cross-legged. "Your guide will help you levitate the object you placed in the pentagram."

Zophia turned and faced Ana. As they took each other's hands and looked into each other's eyes she felt a tingle go up her arms and through her whole body. She was sure her heart skipped a beat.

This is the most beautiful woman I have ever seen. I want so much to be like her.

"You are also a beautiful woman, Zophia," Ana said with her mind. "You are more like me than you know. For now let's concentrate on the task at hand. Focus on the fruit the way I showed you."

Zophia turned her head and concentrated on the grapefruit but nothing happened. She tried again and still nothing. Ana again impressed on her mind the technique necessary to raise the fruit. Zophia closed her eyes. In her mind she willed the grapefruit to raise one meter from the floor. She visualized it happening. When she opened her eyes she was shocked to see it floating in midair exactly where she had imagined. It immediately dropped.

"Excellent! Now, close your eyes and try again. Keep the object in your mind as you open your eyes this time."

After several more tries Zophia was able to lift the grapefruit and make it move around the room. She felt like a little child who had just learned how to ride a bicycle. However, she also found that she was exhausted.

"You have done remarkably well," said Ana as she let go of Zophia's hands.

Zophia missed her touch but she wanted to see how the crew was doing. She watched some of the objects in the pentagram hover in the air, drop, and rise again. She stifled a laugh when she saw the ECD shaking on the floor. None of the objects glided around the room the way her grapefruit had.

Several of the crewmembers had perspiration on their foreheads. A circle of moisture discolored the armpit of the ECD's owner.

"It is getting late," Ana announced, "and some of you are quite exhausted. This would be a good time to end our lesson for the day. Zophia, would you like to add any comments for your crew?"

"You've all worked hard and accomplished more than I ever expected. You should congratulate yourselves. We have an hour and a half before we need to rendezvous back at the ship. I'll see you there."

Everyone rose and left the training center. Some of the crew made a beeline to the ship while others stood around talking with their guides and one another.

Zophia turned to Ana. "Will these skills remain with us when we return to Earth? Or do you think The Sovereign will block them from us when we leave Adon's domain?"

"It is unlikely that Yehowshuwa will be able to reverse what you have learned. He will probably try to destroy you instead." Ana's lower lip protruded slightly as her eyes narrowed.

Zophia took Ana's hand and felt a shiver go up her spine. "It is scary but we know this will be dangerous. It's hard to explain, Ana, but ever since our luncheon yesterday I've had a feeling of peace. If everyone on the crew is trained before we leave, we may gain sufficient strength to unite with The Chancellor before The Sovereign has a chance to do anything. If we already possess these powers, we should be able help our people learn them."

Ana's cheeks glowed. "You have great courage. However, none of the others progressed as quickly as you have. There is something remarkable about your mind that I haven't seen even in our own race." She looked in her eyes. "While we were joined during the last exercise, I began to experience a unique bond."

Zophia put her free hand on her chest. "I felt the same thing."

"Perhaps we should explore this connection further...in addition to probing deeper into the powers that you are discovering within yourself."

"Let's do it right now. I don't have any pressing reason to return to the ship until our groups are scheduled to report to the Captain."

The two women returned to the pentagram and sat down cross-legged on two pillows, facing each other and holding hands. Over the next hour, they spent intimate time with each other. Ana showed her many of what she called the deep secrets of Adon. Zophia saw how he kept the Edenians young and enabled them to advance toward enlightenment.

Zophia was having a hard time separating the excitement of learning from the thrill of the closeness she was feeling with Ana. She stopped trying to compartmentalize her sensations and found that they then merged into a pinnacle of emotion and spiritual clarity.

Chapter 21

After the other groups left the breakfast table, Demetrius and Marti munched on pastries while they and their guides discussed how they were going to fulfill their assignments.

Demetrius' guide, Rana, picked up a cup of hot coffee-like beverage and addressed the small group. "Marti needs to know about the possible dangers ahead. I'm not sure how we can tell her without the help of an enlightened one. Since Demetrius wants to meet an enlightened one, I think we should combine our groups."

"Sounds good to me." Demetrius licked a bit of frosting off his thumb.

Marti nodded.

They called the two groups together and Rana led them through the orchard. Demetrius had to hustle to keep up with the tall Edenian. For a while, they followed the trail the previous group had made in the damp grass. When they approached the two five-sided buildings, they diverged from the tracks and entered the one on the right.

Everyone followed a corridor to the right which circled the outside of the building and entered a large room. When the dozen crewmembers along with their guides had filed into the room, Rana directed them to sit down on cushions on the floor on one side of a pentagram painted on the floor. The dim lighting came from some globes hanging in the air at each point of the pentagram.

Demetrius' guide introduced himself to the combined group. "My name is Ranathalomar, or Rana for short. I will be teaching you about the aspect of the occult that Yehowshuwa has restricted most: the ability to foretell the future. He condemned it for two reasons. First, if someone knew what was going to happen, that person would appear to be able to control fate. Since Yehowshuwa claims to be in charge of the future, this was a threat to him. The second reason is that this ability is available only to ascended beings. Therefore, anyone who sought to know the future had to have direct contact with one of these beings. There are no truly enlightened ones under The Sovereign's dominion. The only other option is Ben-Shaachar and his team. Yehowshuwa didn't want anyone contacting them."

I hadn't thought of Chancellor Ben-Shaachar as an enlightened being...just the opposite. Demetrius waved his hand. "That's the way it works on Earth, but how will you provide us with information about the future?"

Rana stepped into the center of the pentagram. "I will be introducing you to my spiritual guide shortly. Any information about the future will come from him. Contacting ascended beings should not be done frivolously. While they could come whenever we call, they are not what you would call magic genies that perform tricks at our beck and call. When we call them it is for a higher purpose than to satisfy our whims."

Demetrius wasn't comfortable sitting on the floor even with the cushion. *I wouldn't call our concerns frivolous.* His discomfort didn't help his attitude.

"We don't contact them until we have progressed to a certain point in our own development toward ascension. This is when we require a personal guide to learn the deeper and more complex nature of the eternal realm. Then we seek them on a regular basis. We are matched up with one who is the most suitable to train us in our own journey to enlightenment."

Come on Rana; let's just get on with it. We don't need all this enlightenment ascension mumbo jumbo.

"I will now ask my guide, Cleomanthas, to join us."

Demetrius squirmed on his pillow. There was something about asking a being from some other dimension to join them that bothered him. He had chosen this tour but hoped that they wouldn't really be able to produce anyone.

Rana took a pillow close to the pentagram and sat cross-legged, resting the backs of his wrists on his knees. With his hands partially open upward and his thumb touching his middle finger, he closed his eyes and began to breathe slowly and regularly. He chanted the name of his guide and some other indistinguishable words.

Demetrius blinked when a sudden flash of light sparked in the center of the pentagram. When his eyes adjusted he saw a rather good-looking but otherwise ordinary Edenian standing there with their trademark smile. Rana stood and they greeted each other with a hug. Rana took the man's hand and led him to the group.

"It is my pleasure to introduce you to Cleomanthas, my guide and friend for many years." Rana sat again on his pillow.

Demetrius wondered if there was a trap door under the floor.

Cleomanthas bowed slightly. "Greetings, my friends from Earth. It is my pleasure to visit with you and to reveal answers to your questions, as much as is in my powers. Ask what you will."

Demetrius stretched his legs out in front of him and folded his arms in front of him. "Except for your remarkable appearance out of thin air, you look like a normal person. How do we know you are an enlightened being?"

Cleomanthas looked at Demetrius. "Honesty, even in doubt, is an admirable quality." He then folded his hands in front of his chin. "As we approach enlightenment, we learn to control powers that you would have no way of comprehending even if I described them to you. These powers enable us to sustain ourselves without food or water. After we ascend we no longer have bodies as you know them. So when we choose to speak with you, we take on the appearance of a normal body. We do this to make you comfortable with us."

I may be more comfortable but so far I'm not impressed. He's going to have to come up with more than talk to convince me.

"However, we can move from one dimension to another at will." Cleomanthas disappeared. A split second later he reappeared at the far side of the pentagram. He vanished again and returned to where he had been before.

"We can also radiate light if we so desire." Cleomanthas began to glow. His radiance increased until Demetrius had to shield his eyes. Abruptly the brilliance stopped.

Then Cleomanthas' body changed into roaring lion. Just as quickly, he became a unicorn and then returned to his previous appearance. "Are you convinced now that I belong to a realm beyond your understanding?"

Demetrius still wasn't ready to buy into Cleomanthas' explanation. *This room could be set up with holograms.*

"Do I still sense some doubt, Demetrius? Perhaps we should take a stroll in the orchard. Would the rest of you wait here for a few minutes?" Cleomanthas walked up to Demetrius and touched him on the shoulder.

Demetrius felt the damp grass on his bottom and stood quickly. Cleomanthas was standing in front of him in the orchard.

"How did you do that?"

"That isn't important. Beside, you wouldn't understand if I told you. For now it is sufficient for you to know that I took you through the eternal realm and brought you back to the physical realm at this point. Since you can't perceive that realm, it seemed as if you were instantly transported."

Demetrius turned around and looked at the training buildings, then at the luncheon area in the opposite direction. "Ok, you got me on this one…unless I'm dreaming."

"When Ben-Shaachar tried to dissuade The Sovereign from his plan to rule Earth, he did something similar to take him to a high mountaintop and to the top of a temple."

Demetrius scratched his head. "Yeah, I remember something about that. Trouble is I thought The Sovereign must have imagined that because he hadn't eaten for forty days or so."

"You may still doubt but to prove this to your compatriots inside, please pick a fruit to take back with you."

Demetrius selected something that looked like a peach, then Cleomanthas again touched his shoulder. In the blink of an eye Demetrius was standing on the pentagram beside Cleomanthas.

Cleomanthas pointed to Marti. "Tell us what you've seen in the last couple of minutes so Demetrius will know what happened while he was gone."

"OK." Marti's mouth had been wide open and her eyes wide. "You touched Demetrius on the shoulder and he disappeared. Then you told us not to be shocked because you took him outside for a chat. You went back to the center of the pentagram where you are now."

"Marti," Demetrius interrupted, "are you saying that Cleomanthas was still in here while I was outside?"

"Yes. He said that if someone could see both places, it would appear as if he were in both places."

Cleomanthas turned to Demetrius with a smug look. "All right, Demetrius, tell everyone what just happened to you."

"Well," Demetrius stammered, "one second I was sitting here on the pillow, and the next second I was sitting on the grass in the orchard. I chatted with you for a couple of minutes. You explained that you had taken me through the eternal realm and back into the physical in a different place." He stared at the peach-like object in his hand. "Then you had me pick this fruit to prove that we had been outside. Then, poof, here we are again."

"Do you believe that you were really in the orchard? How do you know I was not simply playing a mind trick on you?"

Demetrius touched the seat of his pants and turned around. "My jumper is still wet from the dew." He heard a couple of snickers.

"So Cleomanthas was outside with you the whole time?" Marti asked.

"Yeah." Demetrius said.

"But all the time that you were gone, Cleomanthas was standing here," Marti said.

Cleomanthas took the fruit from Demetrius. "I did appear to be in both places at the same time. In actuality I was exhibiting a power that enables ascended beings to travel quickly and to carry on multiple conversations at one time. Our mental abilities are not restricted by our bodies so we can seem to be in multiple locations simultaneously. Let me demonstrate."

Cleomanthas, still holding the fruit, appeared at two corners of the pentagram. Each of his images spoke to the group. Then he appeared at three, four, five, and six places. At that point he looked like a wavering image on a view screen with poor reception. Demetrius noticed flashes between the images and could almost follow the pattern of appearances in a circle around the pentagram.

Cleomanthas resumed his single appearance. "When an enlightened being gains the power to become a sovereign, he can achieve thousands of simultaneous appearances. We are not truly omnipresent. No matter how powerful we become, we are really only in one place at a time."

I'm not dreaming. I was outside. He was in both places. What can I say? I haven't even heard of Enforcers being able to do that.

Cleomanthas bowed slightly. "Now, are there any more doubts about whether or not I am who I claim to be?"

Demetrius hung his head then turned and looked at Cleomanthas. "No, Cleomanthas. You have convinced me. I repent in dust and ashes for ever doubting you."

Cleomanthas exhaled sharply. "An old Earth custom for which there is no need in Eden. Only Yehhovaw and his son would have come up with such a demeaning method of groveling for forgiveness of alleged offenses."

Marti cleared her throat as Demetrius resumed his seat. "I want to know what dangers may lay ahead for us. Rana told us an enlightened one could provide that kind of information."

Cleomanthas rubbed his chin. "Are you looking for possibilities or specific dangers?"

"We'll be grateful for any help you can give us. From what we've heard so far, this mission may be mankind's last chance, and we don't want to blow it."

Cleomanthas closed his eyes and took a few steps, then looked at Marti. "I've just had a long conversation with others in the eternal realm. Your understanding is correct. This is so important that the Council of Enlightened Beings has provided me with some information about things in your future that you need to know."

Demetrius still had trouble believing that Cleomanthas could have a long conversation with the Council of Enlightened Beings in the blink of an eye.

However, he dared not express further doubts. Besides, he was curious to hear what this enlightened being had to say.

Cleomanthas took a cushion and sat down before the group. "On your way back to Earth, you will be attacked. During the conflict you will take decisive action that will save you. Tell Zophia to choose again the fourth of five. She will know what you mean."

I don't like to hear about riddles, especially when our lives depend on them. I sure hope Zophia understands.

"Your greatest danger will be people who either pretend to be sympathetic or switch allegiance after entering into your confidence."

A voice at the back asked, "That's pretty vague. Can't you tell us more?" Demetrius turned to see that it was Barb who spoke up.

"Unfortunately the details surrounding your return and your activities on Earth are vague because of interference from Yehhovaw and his son. However, we have seen that there will be two people, a young woman, and a young man who will be particularly dangerous. Also, you must avoid at all costs reporting directly to The Sovereign. If you do, you will be imprisoned and then executed. Anyone loyal to Yehowshuwa will attempt to apprehend you as well. The Chancellor Ben-Shaachar will be your only protection."

Demetrius had what he needed and wanted to get off the uncomfortable floor. "We figured we'd have problems if we went to The Sovereign when we returned. However, this attack on the way home is new, as is the warning about the two young people. Thank you for providing this information for us."

Cleomanthas stood and bowed. "You are quite welcome. Is there any other way I may help you?"

"What's it like in the eternal realm?" asked Henry, Barb's husband.

Cleomanthas' countenance glowed. "It is difficult to explain to someone who is bound to the physical world, but I will try. When we ascend, our bodies and our minds are blended together and become a pure spiritual being. We no longer require bodies to perceive our surroundings. The power of our minds enables us to know completely all that is around us. This produces a life that is beyond your comprehension."

"Isn't there any way you can relate it to what we already know?" asked Marti.

He held up the peach-fruit in his hand. "Outside, Demetrius picked this produce from a tree. He saw it and felt it and smelled its fragrance." Cleomanthas looked down at it then put it behind his back. "However, I didn't need to pick it to feel it. I felt it when it was still on the tree. I knew its aroma and tasted its sweet flavor. Your eyes can perceive variations of color, but I experience those colors and many more that you can't distinguish. Your brain compresses the color signals it receives so they can be processed. My mind is not limited, so that I can see every hue. All of my senses are so far beyond yours that I can savor life far more fully than the greatest joy you have ever experienced."

Cleomanthas' body glowed brighter and brighter as he spoke.

Demetrius shielded his eyes. Wow! It is as if just talking about the eternal works him up to a fever pitch.

"In the eternal realm we have intimate relationships with others that make anything you've known on Earth insignificant. We encounter exciting challenges as we encourage and help others toward enlightenment. We embark on missions to save those who, like yourselves, are enslaved by evil. We have parties and pleasures you wouldn't believe. When we become sovereigns, the fulfillment of creation far outweighs anything we have experienced before, or so I've been told. That is what the eternal realm is like."

Demetrius longed for these pleasures. "Is heaven part of the eternal realm?"

Cleomanthas' glow faded and his face grew dark. "Your concept of heaven revolves around being a slave to The Sovereign for eternity. In the true eternity we become Adon's peers instead of his servants."

"What about hell?" a crewmember asked.

A flash like lightening came from Cleomanthas' eyes as he scowled. "The greatest of Yehowshuwa's abominations. He cannot completely annihilate an eternal being such as yourself, yet he must do something with those who are disloyal to him when their bodies have died. So he created a horrible dungeon. In this blackest of pits each person is isolated from everyone else and kept from all light. This is where Chancellor Ben-Shaachar and his team have been held captive for a thousand years, ever since The Last Battle. This is where you will end up if you are captured by Yehowshuwa or if you fail to liberate mankind."

Demetrius gulped. "Have you been shown a vision of the future in which we are victorious over The Sovereign?"

"That is something I have foreseen." Cleomanthas glow returned. "Come, join hands with me and I will give you visions of the eternal realm and your future. These will be more accurate than words, though you will not be able to relate them to others any better than I could."

The group joined hands around the pentagram and closed their eyes. Demetrius saw The Sovereign's version of heaven, which appeared wondrous but paled in significance when compared to the glimpses of the true eternity he saw. The horrors of hell flashed through his mind. He felt completely alone. The darkness dissolved into light and joy beyond his dreams. He saw millions of people freed, becoming enlightened beings.

He was then ushered into the presence of a great body of glowing auras. They spoke to him in unison and identified themselves as the full Council of Enlightened Beings. He started to bow down to worship them but they quickly stopped him. "Stand before us. You are our peers. We are not to be worshiped."

Time raced forward. His vision continued as he developed power, created his own world, and populated it with beings who also evolved to ascend. Suddenly everything went black and he opened his eyes.

After the visions ended he contemplated what he had experienced. The memory quickly faded. Demetrius knew he would never be able to explain this fully to the Captain.

August 31, 998 ASR left off here

Robert arrived at his apartment in Midrib late Monday afternoon. The moment he entered, he could tell something wasn't right. Several items weren't quite where he had left them. The lamp on his desk was turned about twenty degrees. One of the sofa cushions stuck out a bit farther than the other two. He clenched his teeth as he saw other things slightly turned or a bit out of place, suggesting that someone had searched his apartment.

He went into the kitchen and looked in the cupboard. Someone had apparently removed all the dishes, glasses, and cups and put them back again. His hands started to tremble slightly as he looked under the sink and found a crumpled tissue in the trash bag.

The words of The Sovereign about facing dangers came back to him. Who would be searching my apartment? The underground? Only if they thought I've betrayed their trust. Why did I have to spill the beans about The Question to the Board? But the underground wouldn't know about that. Would the Administration search? Maybe they wanted to know more about my connection with the underground. Robert looped through the same thoughts twice more as he went to his bedroom looking back and forth furtively.

Robert went into his bedroom. He felt his armpits getting damp as he saw a wrinkle in his bed spread. He heard the door slam shut behind him. A blanket or bag covered his face and torso. He was pushed from behind. His face hit the bed. A belt or rope cinched over the blanket, pinned his arms to his side.

"Help!" Robert yelled.

"Shut up and you won't be hurt," said the intruder in a mechanical voice.

Robert felt his feet knock together as something was tied around his ankles.

"Now we will see what you are up to."

A second mechanical voice asked, "Who are you working for, Robert?"

"What do you mean? I'm not working for anyone." Robert squirmed and started breathing faster and harder.

Whap!

Robert felt something like a belt strike his rump. It didn't hurt much but startled him. "Everybody works for someone."

Robert felt his heart do a back flip in his chest. "I work for the University of Midrib. I'm an archeologist, researcher, and student teacher. Who are you? What do you want?" He needed to know who they were. *If they are underground I can't let them know what I've told the Board. If they are from the Administration I can't let them think I'm siding with the underground.* Robert's brain started to hurt.

Whap! That one stung more.

"We ask the questions, not you. So you aren't commissioned by The Sovereign Yehowshuwa?" asked Voice One.

"No. Well, I guess in a way I am."

"What is your mission?" asked Voice Two.

"I don't have a mission."

Whap! Another strap stung his backside.

"What has the Administration commissioned you to do?"

"You mean writing the book?"

"Yes, that sounds like something the Administration might commission a person like you to do. Now, what is your goal in writing this book? To stop people from questioning The Sovereign's rule or cause them to question even more?"

Robert had no idea what he should say. If these interrogators were from the Administration and he told them he wanted people to question The Sovereign, he'd be in deep trouble. If they were from *The Question* and he said he wanted to stop people from questioning Sovereign Yehowshuwa, he'd lose all credibility with the younger generation.

What am I going to do?

Chapter 22

Zophia, Captain Andrews, Demetrius, Marti, and Alex retreated to the Captain's office as soon as all the groups returned to the ship. They sat in a circle in the visitor chairs. Andrews poured cups of a coffee-like brew that he said Mine had provided during his review of Earth history.

Zophia listened intently as Andrews told about his trip to the library and briefly related the history of Earth they had observed. "After we returned to the Ramah and had all the data transferred to Hal, we divided into groups to study the different areas we reviewed in the library. The data is quite detailed. There were a few places where we hit limits. In the library we could go into minute-by-minute details of any time in history. Unfortunately, with Hal, we could only research things that happened in a single day, and only then if it was something significant that affected the course of the world."

"What conclusions have you come to at this point?" asked Zophia, eager to get to the point.

"If this data corresponds to the hidden documentation on Earth that Ana told Zophia about, we will have verified that everything we've learned since Rol-el attacked us is the truth, even though it contradicts every history book we've ever read. However, we don't know if it will be enough to convince people that we've all been duped."

I have no doubt that it will.

"Alex, why don't you relate what you've found out?"

Alex described his group's meeting with Parathanos. "The fact that he could read our thoughts and speak to us in our minds was a shock to me. Quite frankly, it frightened me too. Parathanos sensed my fear immediately and put me at ease. All in all I was impressed with the path they take to enlightenment. What we learned correlated with the other information we've gained about The Sovereign. Unfortunately, there wasn't anything we could take back to Earth to prove all the allegations against Sovereign Yehowshuwa."

As soon as Alex paused, Demetrius started explaining his experience. "Our visit with an enlightened being was similar as far as information goes." He explained the insight they had gained about the eternal realm, including his experience of being transported outside the building. "I wish you could have seen what we did. It was phenomenal."

"Did you feel any ill effects after being transported?" asked the Captain.

"I was a bit disoriented each time because my surroundings suddenly changed but I felt fine."

"That's good." Zophia laughed to herself as she imagined Demetrius' disorientation causing him to get sick all over an ascended being. "Anything else you can tell us?"

"Oh yeah!" His eyes got wide, he arched his eyebrows and he sat up straight in his chair. "The enlightened being gave us a vision of our future after The Sovereign is defeated. Unfortunately, within seconds, the memory of the vision faded. Like when you've had a wonderful dream that you can't remember in the morning. All we can remember is the gist of it and a few images. It was the most beautiful thing I've ever experienced." He slumped back in his chair and his voice lost enthusiasm. "It isn't anything we can take back to Earth as proof."

"Impressive, but what about the future dangers, Marti?" Andrews asked.

"Cleomanthas, the enlightened being, gave us some general information but nothing that's really helpful. The only significant thing is that there's supposedly going to be an attack on our way back. He said we'll need to take decisive action but he didn't give any details." Marti told everyone about the young couple and the advice that they avoid The Sovereign. She also mentioned that The Chancellor would protect them but there wasn't any explanation as to how.

Zophia had an impression of a thought in Demetrius' mind. "Demetrius, what did he tell you to tell me?"

Demetrius straightened back up again quickly. "Oh, that's right! I can't remember his exact words. Something about four out of five." He creased his brow. "How did you know he asked me to give you a message?"

"I could see it in your mind. His exact words were, 'Tell Zophia to again choose the fourth of five. She'll know what I mean.'"

Demetrius' eyes got bigger and he started fidgeting. "Don't tell me you can read my thoughts."

"No, I can't. However that stood out, probably because it was a message intended for me. Berekiah sent me the same message." Zophia explained how she had used the method of dividing planets into groups of five and choosing the fourth to select Eden.

She went on to describe the information they had received about the occult. It confirmed the Captain's suspicion that occultic powers were used in the path to enlightenment and that was why Yehowshuwa had squelched their use. She described the demonstration of occult power that had been provided.

"After the demonstrations we were given some training and learned to communicate with each other telepathically and even move objects."

"Did you learn how to levitate my coffee cup?" Demetrius scoffed.

"I can try." Zophia closed her eyes and settled back in her chair. Even with her eyes closed she could see Demetrius grab his cup. In her mind she started to chant as she focused on the pentagram in the training room. With her eyes still closed, in her mind she saw him wink at the Captain, his hand wrapped firmly around the cup. The other officers snickered silently.

She contacted Ana. "Do you see what I see?"

"Yes, Zophia, I see," Ana immediately answered.

"I'm not sure I have the power to pull the cup from his hand, but at least I want him to know he had a tug of war."

"I think it is time for Demetrius to become a believer. Here is what you can do. It's beyond what we practiced, but our time together has bound us together strongly. I am confident that you can do this." Ana gave Zophia a mental image of what she could do and how to do it.

In her vision Zophia watched Demetrius' cup shake slightly. He used his other hand as well. His knuckles turned white with effort. Suddenly he was yanked out of his seat. He moved to the center of the group, holding the cup at arm's length.

"Hey," Demetrius yelled. "I can't let go of the cup."

With both feet braced and his back bent, he tried to pull away. Suddenly a flame surged sixty centimeters up from the top of the cup. When Zophia released his fingers, he let go so fast he stumbled backward and plopped into his chair, out of breath and ashen.

The cup stayed in midair. Then a face appeared in the flames. "Demetrius," the face said, "I have been given one more thing to tell you. Your entire crew must be in complete unity in this mission. If you persist with your mocking attitude, your unbelief will cause untold damage to this ship and to your efforts when you return home." The face disappeared.

Zophia spoke telepathy to Ana. "That wasn't me. Where did he come from?"

"That was Cleomanthas, the ascended one that Demetrius and Marti contacted today. Apparently we weren't the only ones who thought he needed a rebuke. I think your demonstration will be enough. If you need me again do not hesitate to call."

Zophia opened her eyes. She took the cup out of the air and handed it back to Demetrius. The others stared with expressions of fear and amazement.

Captain Andrews took a deep breath. "That was quite a show."

Zophia bowed her head slightly. "I'm sorry, Captain. I had only intended to raise the cup up a bit and set it down in his hand again. Demetrius' scoffing upset me. When I saw that he was going to hang on to it I contacted Ana and she showed me how to enhance the show for his benefit."

"How did you contact your guide? I didn't see you use your ECD."

"My group learned how to communicate with each other via telepathy. Not everyone has gained the same capabilities, so I don't know how many of us will be able to do any significant demonstrations. However, the whole crew is invited for training over the next few days."

"I think we should take advantage of this opportunity. I'm sure that if even a few of us can do these things on Earth, people will have to believe us."

"The message from Cleomanthas wasn't in my plans or Ana's," Zophia explained. "In Eden, there are no secrets, and Cleomanthas was obviously aware of our deliberations. He took advantage of the situation to deliver an important message. When we get home we're going to have to be very careful. If we aren't united we could cause an opening for The Sovereign to stop us."

"You're right, Zophia. The Sovereign may not be as powerful as we once thought but any chink in our armor could be very dangerous. If the whole crew goes through this training I believe we will be strengthened and unified. What do you say? Any second thoughts, Demetrius?" asked Andrews.

Demetrius' face blushed, "I'm sorry, guys. That vision sold me that we should be on a path to enlightenment and that we need to help all of mankind. Nevertheless, this is still new and I had no idea any of us could advance so quickly. I agree. We all need to be trained and the sooner the better."

They all agreed that everyone on board should be trained as soon as possible. All other tours were cancelled.

Zophia was excited about the opportunity to sharpen her skills and to get closer to Ana.

June 30, 998 ASR

Zophia arrived at the breakfast table early. She enjoyed the cool breeze and the morning sun on her face. Her respite was interrupted when the Captain, Mine, and Ana joined her.

After a refreshing meal, the crew proceeded to the training centers to start their education. Those who had already received fundamental training would continue, and the others would start off with the basics.

Zophia's group reviewed the previous day's lessons then went on to refine their skills. Soon Zophia was able to move larger and heavier objects. The more she was able to accomplish, the more she wanted to learn.

"This is going too slowly," Zophia told Ana in her mind. "I'm distracted by what the others are doing."

Ana suggested they slip away from the rest of the group for private lessons and personal enjoyment of each other. Zophia found that the lessons incorporated a lot of physical contact that heightened her senses and pleasure.

When the crew returned to H.S.S.S. Ramah for the night, they discovered that they were able to communicate with one another telepathically. The mess hall was silent as the crew discussed what they had learned.

"Captain," Zophia thought to Andrews, "I've been doing some research into The Sovereign's ancient language, and I found something interesting. When Yehowshuwa named our ship Ramah, we believed it to mean "shoot" or "hurl," as if he were launching us into space for this mission. However, I discovered that the word could be figuratively interpreted to mean "delude" or "deceive." In light of what we've learned, I wonder if he meant to deceive us and keep us from knowing the truth. Since he never intended for us to go beyond his jurisdiction, naming the ship Ramah may have been his twisted way of making a joke out of our exploration."

"I think you may be right," the Captain said. "It galls me to think of traveling back to Earth in a ship named deceit."

"I suggest we change the name of the ship to the Chancellor Ben-Shaachar's Rescue Ship Aman. The root of *Aman* is *truth*. It includes the concept of building up and supporting, trusting and believing, being true or certain. Since we are now sure of the truth and will be supporting our brethren on Earth, I think it would be an appropriate name."

"I like it," Andrews said. "Let's run it past the crew and see what everyone thinks."

Using their newfound telepathic abilities, Zophia repeated what she had learned to the others. To her delight, they all agreed to rename the ship C.B.R.S. Aman before their departure.

July 6, 998 ASR

Zophia advanced more rapidly in her training than the others. She attributed her progress to the personalized attention she received from Ana and to the bond they had formed. Four days later, she was monitoring the rest of the crew's intensive training.

She and Ana stood in the orchard near the star ship port, watching the crew move objects with little or no perspiration. She took special pleasure in watching rocks, sticks, and other objects fly thorough the air, trying to dodge her fiery pulses and energy beams.

Zophia suggested a match between herself and five other crewmembers. The crew tried to get their two kilogram rocks from one side of the orchard to the other before Zophia could neutralize them. Captain Andrews and Mine observed the contest. Zophia toyed with the crew, purposely shooting beams in front of their stones to see how long she could keep them from advancing half way through the trees. After twenty minutes it became apparent that it would take another hour or two for the crewmembers to advance their objects to the center of the orchard. Not wanting to wait that long she summarily vaporized all five rocks at the same time.

The Captain and Mine joined Zophia after the demonstration. Mine voiced his astonishment at the crew's skills. "Chuck, the progress you've made in these last four days is amazing. I believe you are ready to return to Earth and that you will be effective in saving your people. The modifications to your ship have also been completed, so your journey will be considerably shorter than the time it took to get here."

"Thank you for your assistance, Mine. Eight weeks ago I thought I'd never find life in the universe outside of Earth. I certainly didn't expect to make dear friends. I wish we didn't have to leave, but we have become different people than when we arrived, and our destiny has changed. Our eyes have been opened. We now know the difference between good and evil. We owe you our gratitude forever."

Mine looked down and bowed slightly. "It is the least we could do for you. We will again meet together in the eternal realm."

"We are prepared to launch tomorrow after our farewell breakfast."

"I will miss your company, my friend."

Zophia thought about the time they had spent on Eden. She would miss Ana's physical presence but knew their bond would enable them to stay in communication during the trip back to Earth. She felt well on her way toward enlightenment.

August 31, 998 ASR

Kevin wasn't sure he would like going back to school and spending so much of his time away from home. Even so, he felt confident that this was what The Sovereign Yehowshuwa wanted.

Yet he wondered why Yehowshuwa wanted him to present himself as a pre-transformed person in order to protect Samantha Spell. *I would think I could do it better if I were an Enforcer. Then I could pop in whenever the need arises.* Then again, if that were the case, the enemy would probably get wise to her.

As he approached his dorm room he whistled an old praise song that he was sure no one from this generation would recognize. It was an expression of his contentment in his service to Yehowshuwa.

He threw his bag on the single bunk bed and looked around. Dark blue curtains bracketed a window above the desk. A small beige couch sat opposite the bed, with a coffee table positioned between the couch and the bunk. The beige carpet and off-white walls blended in with the dull blue bedspread. A tiny kitchenette divided the main room from a tiny bathroom with a shower stall.

He sat at the desk and started to familiarize himself with his new ECD. He felt glad that his knowledge and aptitude were greater now than when he was in school or even working in the business world. *I don't think I would have been able to understand how to use this ECD so quickly back then.*

Kevin looked up his class schedule and made sure he was enrolled in a number of obscure classes in addition to the sub-ancient philosophy class in which Samantha was enrolled. According to The Sovereign, that was where he would make contact with her.

He looked over the class roster to see what kind of academic competition he had. *This Robert Maskil guy looks like he should be teaching the class. Samantha is a remarkable young lady. She's a freshman and taking a post graduate course. This should be interesting.*

Kevin set the ECD to view data at high speed. He captured it all with his photographic memory. Within a few hours he felt confident that he could back up what his transcripts indicated he should know about archeology.

His next task was to bone up on the other subjects on his transcripts. He spent the next forty-eight hours straight making sure he had the knowledge necessary to present himself as an authentic student.

After standing to stretch, Kevin hung up his clothes and then went to the local store to get coffee, tea, and snacks. *The food selection here certainly isn't as good as back home.* He would miss the banquets, not so much because the food was so delicious but because he would miss his family and The Sovereign's presence.

When he returned, he looked at his ECD and realized he had missed his new-student orientation. *I'm going to have to use this organizer if I don't want to lose track of time.* It was a long time since he'd needed to do that. Kevin looked up the orientations in the archives and ran through them in a couple of minutes.

Samantha opened the door to her dorm room and glanced around. Her eyes were drawn to a floral bedspread with beautiful roses, then to the small couch with matching throw pillows. The walls were painted with light pastel green and rose colors. Frilly pink curtains graced the window. *I can make this work with a few changes here and there. Different color of paint for the walls.* She looked over the kitchenette and shower room then hung up her clothes in the tiny closet.

After putting away her toiletries and making a list of what she would need for the kitchen, she sat down at the desk and recorded a quick video message to her parents, showing them around her room. After it was sent she checked out her classes to make sure there hadn't been any last-minute changes.

She had arrived a couple of days early so she could join in the welcoming activities at the dorm and attend the orientation for new students. Feeling sufficiently settled in, she decided to take a jog around the campus before the first events started.

July 7, 998 ASR

Ana and Mine joined the crew of the H.S.S.S. Ramah for their farewell breakfast. Ana sat as close to Zophia as she dared without attracting attention from the others at the table. The table was filled with a large selection of pastries, fruits, nuts, cereals, and beverages. As she reached for a fruit she lightly brushed against Zophia's arm.

"Would you please pass me one of those rolls," she asked, pointing to a dark brown pastry with chocolaty frosting.

"Certainly." Zophia picked up a roll and handed it to Ana.

Ana's fingers lingered against Zophia's for a few seconds as she directed a tiny electric charge from her fingertips through Zophia's body. The pleasure on Zophia's face assured her that it had the desired effect.

"I'm going to miss you very much," Zophia said.

"I will miss you as well," Ana said.

After breakfast the guides gathered to watch the crew rechristen the ship C.B.R.S. Aman. Ana thought the name was appropriate. However, when Chuck smashed the bottle against the side of the ship near the gangplank, she felt they had wasted a perfectly good bottle of wine.

Mine gave a long-winded speech. Ana stood beside him with her body angled toward him and smiled as she knew she must. She paid no attention to his words, glancing occasionally at Zophia.

Chuck gave a speech, too, which she also ignored. Zophia stood beside him. Ana was pleased when Zophia glanced her way and their eyes met.

Ana hugged one crewmember after another and said good-bye to each. She gave Zophia a hug that lasted longer than the others.

The guides backed away from the ship, waving at the crew, who waved back at them. The ramp lifted and the hatch closed. The huge blast barrier rose into place.

Ana and Mine held hands just in case any of the crew tuned them in on a view port. They backed up for a better view. Clouds formed around the top of the ship as the deflectors pushed away the air in preparation for a quick lift to space. It quickly shot out of the port as howling winds of displaced atmosphere whipped the trees in the orchard. It rapidly disappeared from view.

"Were you able to complete your connection with Zophia?" Mine asked.

Ana thought about the secret intimate times she had spent with Zophia. "Oh, yes. I believe our mission has been quite successful."

July 28, 998 ASR

Chuck sat in his command chair on the bridge, looking at the view screen. He was glad that Tia-le's three saucer-like ships were still within viewing range. He'd felt more comfortable after they rejoined the Aman as escorts.

It had been three weeks since they left Eden and two weeks since Tia-le joined them. So far there'd been no sign of the attack that Demetrius' ascended being had prophesied.

His thoughts were interrupted when Tia-le's face appeared on the screen. "Captain, our long-range scout ships have detected an armada from Jehov headed this way. Our mother ship has launched all of our available fighters to intercept them. We expect to engage them in about twenty minutes. If I don't see you again, I want to say it has been a privilege to serve you in this worthy cause."

Chuck stood. "You sound as if you don't expect to survive the battle."

"We will gladly give our lives, if necessary, to protect you. We are outnumbered, but we are more skillful and have better equipment. What concerns me most is that it appears to be a suicide mission for them. We will transmit video so that you will be aware of the outcome immediately. May Rof be with you."

Chuck summoned the crew with his newly acquired telepathic abilities. "Listen up, everyone. The attack we've been expecting is about to happen. Tia-le and her forces will be intercepting the enemy in about twenty minutes. I'll put the whole thing on the view screens in the mess hall. In the meantime, I want all officers to report to my office."

Having all the officers together would bolster Demetrius' courage. Chuck didn't want Demetrius to falter in the heat of battle. He met Alex, Demetrius, Marti, and Zophia in his office and asked them, "It looks like this could be the real thing. Are you ready?"

"Most assuredly, Captain," Zophia replied.

"We've duplicated a pentagram in the mess hall to aid our concentration should the need arise," said Alex through tight lips.

"Demetrius, any doubts?" Chuck asked.

"None at all," Demetrius said without any quaver in his voice.

"Good. I hope Tia-le and her people do well. Nonetheless, it's nice to know we're ready for action if need be."

"Captain," Zophia said, "perhaps we should join the crew in the mess hall and watch from there. If we need to do something, we will be able to react more quickly if we are all together."

"You're right. I'll bring the bridge crew and meet you there. Hal will be able to keep us on course." Chuck went back to the bridge to inform the crew, then went to the mess hall.

Telepathic chatter in the mess hall stopped when the video feed came in from Tia-le's lead ships. Chuck sat at one of the tables beside Zophia and watched as several inserts showed the view from different ships.

"Hal, piece those together and give a three-dimensional detail of the battle arena," Zophia commanded. "Darken the mess hall so we can see it clearly."

Holographic projectors built a three-dimensional representation of the area filled with ships. Chuck recognized Tia-le's insignia on the leading defensive ship. He estimated she was followed by nearly a hundred other ships.

The first attackers appeared as tiny points of light. They approached in a conical formation with a single leading ship followed by four ships. Each of the four ships was followed by another four.

"Hal," he said, "give me a count of Tia-le's ships and the enemy's at the bottom of the screen." The number one thousand appeared on the bottom right of the screen. One hundred appeared on the left.

"They're outnumbered ten to one," Alex said. "It looks like Jehov's pilots may try to punch a hole through the defenses simply to get one or two ships through."

The leading Jehov ship fired bursts at the defenders. Tia-le and her forces avoided the first blast and didn't return fire. Fireballs, laser rays, energy beams, and lightning bolts flashed. The images shook and jittered as the ships providing the video dodged enemy fire.

"It looks like their deflectors are causing problems for both sides," Zophia said. "All that turbulence isn't just because they're dodging bullets." The advancing hoard's conical formation began to dissipate.

Tia-le's first volley passed through the lead ship without causing any harm. The lead ship and several others returned fire simultaneously. One of the blasts passed through the outer edge of her saucer.

She relayed an audio message to her comrades and the C.B.R.S. Aman. "I don't know exactly what we're up against, but it appears they have enabled some kind of reflection devices. Each ship has several duplicates and the lead was a fake. Fortunately, their fire power is also a reflection. I passed through an echo of the real blast. Though there aren't as many as it once appeared, we don't have any way of knowing which bogey is real. This means we'll have to shoot faster and take less time setting up."

Tia-le repositioned her ship. "I'm going in." She unloaded six quick bursts at different approaching ships. Her shots passed through the first two but the third one blew up in a fiery blast. Four others disappeared at the same time. Ships from behind the destroyed vessel advanced to take its place. The cone flattened and widened as Tia-le and her comrades picked off more attackers.

Chuck felt a knot in his stomach as the attackers started firing in waves, like ancient soldiers marching across the battlefield, discharging their weapons against the enemy but not taking specific aim at individuals. The sheer numbers guaranteed that some of the opposition would fall. Indeed some of Tia-le's forces succumbed to the onslaught.

The opposing forces were now so close that several members of Rof's lead defense squadron began to weave in and out among the enemy, firing at will. Others dropped back, picking off any ships that got past the initial battle line. Every time an attacker went up in flames, the crew cheered.

"It appears Jehov saved his best pilots for last," Alex observed. "The ones bringing up the rear are doing much better than the initial forces at the beginning of the cone."

The video feed from one of the lead ships blacked out, indicating another ally fell in battle. Other friendly ships replaced the lost connection. The cone, though much sparser than the original mass, penetrated beyond the front line of the defenders. Rof's rear guard continued to pick off the attackers as they came through the battle lines.

Some of the advancing enemy ships squeezed past the defender's last ships, requiring them to turn from the battle and pursue the death squad headed toward the Earth ship. Battles spread out over a large area as the number of defenders and attackers dwindled. Some tried to outrun the rear guard and were easy pickings. Other pilots executed sophisticated evasive maneuvers and returned fire while on the run. Both defenders and attackers disappeared one by one. Suddenly the hologram faded.

"What happened?" Chuck asked.

Zophia picked up her ECD. "Hal no longer has enough input to construct a three-dimensional picture. We'll have to make do with the flat screen and the feed from individual ships on different inserts."

Chuck stood up and paced, keeping an eye on the screen.

Eventually the vast armada was destroyed, except for twenty five ships that had managed to get past the rear guard. The remaining defenders turned to aid in the pursuit. Chuck felt helpless as he watched five panel inserts, each representing one ally chasing an enemy and its four reflections. He sat down, feeling a bit dizzy after following the bobbing and weaving enemies.

The main panel displayed the remnants of Tia-le's squadron. No more enemies were in sight in the original battle zone. "Hal, make the five inserts larger. We don't need a view that doesn't have any of Jehov's ships."

The inserts expanded, revealing fire balls flying past and through the defenders as the enemy's reflections fired simultaneously. When the pursuer passed through a blast image the crew sounded a collective gasp.

Chuck held his breath as the defender on one of the five remaining panels veered sharply as closely aligned shots converged in front of the ship. The blast appeared to go past the video camera but the panel suddenly went black. *That doesn't look good.*

When the last visible enemy was destroyed, the mess hall erupted into cheers and high-fives. Chuck wasn't quite as joyous as the rest of the crew. He wanted to know where the ship was that got away.

His attention was drawn back to the screen when one of the pursuit images flickered and the ship's pilot came on the screen. "Captain, we have bad news. One of Jehov's ships got past us. The other ships led us too far away to catch it before it reaches your position. We've calculated its last known position and believe it should be upon you within five minutes. It should be within your sensor ranges in a few seconds. I'm sorry; there is nothing more we can do."

"Many of your team members have given their lives for us, and we are grateful. If there is anything we can do for you in the future, let us know."

"Liberate your people," replied the pilot. "That's all the thanks we need."

The screen flickered and went dark.

"Zophia, start making preparations."

She contacted the crew telepathically, telling them to take their positions and get ready.

The crew cleared away chairs and tables and sat on the floor around the pentagram that had been painted in the middle. Alex, Marti, Demetrius, Chuck, and Zophia each sat on one of the five sides of the pentagram and took hands. The remaining crewmembers formed two more circles around them.

Chuck heard Zophia in his mind directing the crew. "Let us open our minds to the eternal."

The crew's telepathic chant echoed in his mind as he joined in. *"Harum Opparum Mararum Rorarum Amorum."* He imagined the mantra echoing across the ages through the ethers of space and time, raising the spirits of the unknown to infuse power into him and his crew. Chuck's mind melded with the rest of the crew and they became one as they entered into their trance together.

Zophia felt Ana's presence as the chant grew quieter. In her mind she saw five ships approaching.

"Remember," Ana transmitted to Zophia, "we have limits on our ability. We will only have one chance to eliminate this threat."

"I know. With you in me I know we will prevail. I can feel the power you are giving me. Our power is magnified because of our bond."

Zophia shared her vision with the rest of the crew so they could see the attacker and his four images. Suddenly she realized she could penetrate the pilot's thoughts. "The ship's pilot has armed its weapons. He is prepared to fire upon the Aman and follow through with a direct collision if necessary. Do not fear. We can defeat him when he gets in range. I will direct us to focus on the correct ship."

Zophia waited for her vision to show which ship was real. The patterns of the original and the false copies kept changing. When she first saw them, they were approaching in the pattern of an X, but quickly shifted from one random pattern to another. She saw the pilot's finger starting to squeeze the trigger. The pattern turned roughly into a line.

"There! The fourth of five starting from the left. That is our target."

Zophia directed each crewmember's mind to the one real attacker. "Focus on raising the interior temperature of the attacking craft."

The combined energy from each crewmember caused the ship to go nova in an instant. Too late, however, as its energy beam was already on its way toward the Aman. Zophia watched in horror as the pulsating mass of energy sped toward the ship. She remembered what a much smaller blast had done to Dave and his quarters.

The fiery menace raced toward them. Time seemed to slow as the impending doom approached.

Chapter 23

Robert was still laying face down on his bed when he heard the bedroom door open, then Jim's voice. "What are you guys doing in here?" Immediately the bed shook and he heard thumps, bumps, and bangs followed by Jim's yell, "Take this, you creeps."

I hope Jim can take those guys or at least scare them away.

Voice One groaned as Robert heard a large object crash against the closet door.

"Nice try, buster, but you're going to have to do better than that." Jim grunted and another dull thud came from the wall.

Robert felt the bed bounce, and he felt a large irregular object fall against him hitting his back and right leg. He rolled over to his left and fell to the floor, landing on his back

"Come on," screamed mechanical Voice Two. "Let's get out of here while we can." Robert heard footsteps fading away.

As he fell, the fastening that held the blanket over him loosened. Robert struggled in the small space between his bed and the wall to get the blanket off.

"Take that, you man-eating lion," yelled Jim. Robert heard another whump on the bed.

Robert sat up and peered over the edge of the bed. *Man-eating lion, what is going on?* He saw Jim standing at the foot of the bed.

Jim whacked the mattress with a broomstick. Grinning, he held his ECD up to his mouth. "So, Robert," he said, his voice sounding exactly like Voice One that Robert had heard, "does The Sovereign Yehowshuwa know you've been training cougars to eat people?"

Robert slumped on the bed. *Oh no, payback time for tricking Jim with Hobbs.* He tried to keep from laughing but couldn't. Soon both men lay on the bed, gasping for air.

"OK, I deserved that," Robert said when he finally caught his breath. "You really had me going there. I thought I was either going to end up ostracized by the whole underground or in one of the Administration's retraining camps if I said the wrong thing."

"When you sent that message about The Sovereign predicting danger for you I knew you'd be stewing about his meaning. That gave me the idea to stage this prank. How'd you like the way I shuffled stuff around before you got home to make it look like someone had been searching your apartment?"

"Yeah, that certainly set the stage. You better watch out. It's your turn next." Robert gave Jim a friendly whack on the arm.

"Hey, when you become my boss, are we going to have to be all stuffy and formal? Are you ready for classes tomorrow?" Jim launched into one of his stream-of-consciousness ramblings. "I'm glad we'll be starting a new routine in January. Going to classes doesn't sound nearly as appealing now as it used to.

Funny, a few weeks ago I was wondering if there was any way I could keep going to school, like you." Jim felt his stomach. "Say, are you hungry?"

"Yeah, but we'll have to go out to get something to eat. I don't have anything here."

Robert and Jim left his apartment to find a place to eat. On the way he thought about Jim's practical joke. It started him thinking again about what could happen if the Administration discovered how deeply he was involved with the underground. *Retraining camp, imprisonment or capital punishment.* He shuddered involuntarily. On the other hand, if the underground found out how much he had revealed to the Administration... *Well, he had told the Board that he feared for his life.* He felt like he was on a tightrope without a safety net. Yet he also felt alive, as if his life had more purpose now. He was more than ready to start classes and begin his documentation of The Last Battle.

July 28, 998 ASR

Zophia's heart pounded as the rolling ball of flames continued to rush toward the ship. It expanded and became more intense as it approached. There was no question in her mind that it would surely incinerate everyone aboard.

She heard Ana whisper telepathically, "You know what you must do, Zophia."

"I'm scared, Ana."

"You have all you need to protect the ship."

"It's all theory; I've never done anything like this."

"Just remember what you have learned."

"I won't survive."

"Give yourself now."

Zophia took a deep breath. She let go of the hands of the crewmembers on either side of her and broke her link with them.

Harum Opparum Mararum Rorarum Amorum aide me now!

In her mind Zophia visualized herself standing in front of the flare absorbing all its energy so that it wouldn't harm the Aman. She smelled burning flesh and felt her lungs explode.

Chuck abruptly came out of the trance with the crew. This was different from when they were in training. He felt confused and disoriented. He was still holding Demetrius' hand but not Zophia's. Marti's face was ashen and he followed her gaze to see Zophia lying motionless on the floor beside him.

Zophia's skin was blistered, her hair singed and her jump suit smoldering. He twisted around to kneel beside her. He felt her neck for a pulse. Nothing. He listened for breathing. Nothing.

"She's dead!"

Demetrius sprayed her with a fire extinguisher, cooling her suit.

Alex pushed Chuck and Demetrius away and checked her vitals. "Get a cardiac resuscitator," he barked at Henry. Henry immediately jumped up and ran for the door.

"Sick bay is too far away. It will take him over five minutes to get back. Her brain will die before then. Barb, help me with CPR." Alex gave Zophia mouth-to-mouth resuscitation, Barb unzipped Zophia's jumper and started doing heart compressions.

Chuck stood transfixed, hoping that they would be able to restart Zophia's heart. He then backed the crew away to give Alex and Barb room and made sure there wasn't anyone in the way when Henry returned.

After several long, agonizing minutes, Henry came flying through the door. He dropped to his knees and slid up alongside Zophia as Barb jumped out of his way.

Alex grabbed the oxygen mask and placed it over Zophia's mouth while Henry placed the shell of the medical unit over her upper torso.

Both stood up and Henry handed his ECD to Alex.

"What's going on? Why isn't that thing doing anything," asked Chuck as he grabbed Alex's arm.

"It's using gravitational fields to massage her heart and keep the blood flowing. It's also analyzing her condition to determine the best method to start her heart up again. I'll get a detailed cellular integrity status in minute or two. In the mean time it will probably give her an electrical shock." Alex kept his eye on the ECD.

"Probably?"

"I've never had to use one of these things before. People's hearts don't stop very often, and even then it's usually only as the result of freak accidents." Alex raised his voice and jerked his arm away from Chuck. "Just let it do its job."

Chuck cringed as Zophia's body jerked, her back arching up and then slumping back down on the floor. The ECD in Alex's hand showed a heart monitor with a flat line.

"It will try again." Jerk. Flat line.

"This is the last time it will try." Jerk.

Tears welled up in Chuck's eyes.

Alex shook his head. "It's no use. The analysis is finished. There is significant cellular decomposition in all her major organs. She's gone."

Zophia floated near the ceiling of the mess hall, watching her body convulse with each shock of the cardiac unit, amazed that she didn't feel a thing. The crew knelt or stood around her body, which was stretched out on the floor in the middle of the pentagram she had designed with Ana's guidance.

"Hal," Captain Andrews said as he sagged into a chair near the view screen, "show what happened while we were in the trance."

The view screen displayed the enemy ships approaching. The formations of the five ships shifted from an X into a line. They launched their energy burst a split second before the second ship from the right exploded. The four phantom ships and their plasma spheres vanished, leaving the one real flame speeding toward the C.B.R.S. Aman.

Zophia's image, as large as the ship, suddenly appeared between the ship and the fire ball. In another panel, the crew sat in their trance. Zophia released the hands of the two on either side of her and stood at the same time her image appeared in the other panel. Her image absorbed the fire. Then she collapsed on the floor of the mess hall.

"She gave her life to protect us," Marti said. "We have to try to get her back. Quick, everybody, let's all join minds again."

It's about time you guys decided to do something we've learned on Eden, Zophia thought. She knew that if there was any hope for her it would not be in the physical realms.

The crew joined hands around her lifeless body and called on the names of the original members of the Council of Enlightened Beings to restore her.

Slowly, Zophia's vision of the mess hall faded into a gray fuzziness. The chanting of the crew grew softer until there was nothing but silence.

She looked around but couldn't see a thing. She raised her hand in front of her face but couldn't see it. She felt weightless, as if still floating above her body.

Suddenly, her feet touched something solid, and the floating sensation stopped. She stood upright, surrounded by a dense fog.

When the fog dissipated she found herself standing before a magnificent white marble pyramid. At the top of the structure a bright light in the shape of an eye beckoned to her inner being. She started up the steps. As she went farther she had to shield her eyes from the brilliant light. At the top she encountered five glowing humanoid figures.

"Where am I?" Zophia asked.

"You don't know?" they answered in unison, their voices blending in pleasing and comforting harmonizing tones.

She shook her head.

"Open your mind, Zophia. Don't rely on your logic but on your feelings. Ana has been teaching you how to know us," they sang to her.

She searched her mind, but could not recall anything Ana had taught her that applied to this situation. She contacted Ana and showed her what she was experiencing.

"You've gone somewhere beyond my knowledge, Zophia," Ana said. "Just as you have opened your mind to me, now open yourself to these who are standing before you."

As soon as Zophia let the five beings fill her mind, they started instructing her. In rapid fire they took turns giving her visions and narrating instructions. For what seemed like several days, they gave her wisdom and understanding that went beyond anything she had ever imagined.

At last the five communicated to her, "It's time for you to return, Zophia. Remember what you've learned here and teach your brethren. Then you will be well-equipped when you return to Earth."

Zophia's vision vanished and she felt herself lying on the floor. Her face hurt and her lungs burned. She was both stimulated by her vision and discouraged by the reality of the pain in her body. She tried to move and sit up but the cardiac resuscitator stopped her.

"Hey, let me up!" she tried to yell through the oxygen mask covering her mouth and nose.

Alex opened his eyes first and stared at her with his mouth open.

"She's alive!" Andrews yelled as he reached over and pulled off the mask.

Alex pulled the cardiac unit off her and she sat up amid cheers from the crew.

"Look at her face!" Marti pointed at Zophia, looked at others and back again at Zophia. "Look, look"

Zophia felt her face and realized the pain was gone and she could breathe easily.

"She's healing, the burns are fading," exclaimed Andrews loudly.

"Why are you so amazed?" Zophia asked. "You asked for me to be returned and here I am. And boy, have I got a story for you."

Hal interrupted the joy in mess hall. "Captain, four ships are approaching."

"Put them on screen," the Captain responded.

"I can do better than that with a vision." Zophia gave Andrews and the crew a vision of the saucer-shaped ships approaching. Zophia recognized the ships as the remainder of their escort.

The pilot of one of the lead ships, a large-headed spindly alien, appeared to them. "Captain, my name is Nire-te. I see that you were able to protect yourselves from the ship that managed to get through our defenses. Unfortunately only fourteen of our ships survived. The other ten are still at the battle zone. Tia-le and her squadron were the first to succumb to the onslaught, but not without taking a great number of the enemy with them."

Captain Andrews bowed his head. "My condolences for your losses. Our debt to you is enormous. Is there anything we can do for you?"

Nire-te slowly closed and opened his large oval eyes. "No. We were all prepared spiritually. Those who are in the eternal realm prematurely will be greatly rewarded."

Zophia contacted Tia-le and brought her into the vision.

She appeared as swirling pillar of light and vapor that pulsated as she spoke. "Greetings, my friends."

"Is that you Tia-le? Aren't you dead?" asked the Captain as he stepped back quickly.

"Yes, Captain. I am Tia-le. In your realm I am dead. Thank you, Zophia, for contacting me here and being a conduit for me to wish you 'Rof's speed.' Though my ship and my body have been destroyed, I am alive and well here in the eternal. My comrades are also here, rejoicing with me that your mission is still on course. Even if some of you should die, as we have, in the attempt to rescue your race, you can be confident that you will be transformed and become as we are."

Andrews approached the swirling gaseous Tia-le. "Thank you, Tia-le. It is good to…ah …see you again, and in an even better place. I can see that Zophia's sacrifice has resulted in great powers that can only be attributed to the grace of Adon, Rof, and the rest of the Council of Enlightened Beings."

"You are right Captain. I am now just starting to discover the infinite powers of the eternal. Zophia has been blessed with abilities that most of us never acquire until we get closer to enlightenment. I look forward to seeing you all here in the distant future. It is time for me to go. Good-bye." Tia-le faded from the vision.

"Thank you for sharing your vision of Tia-le with us, Zophia," said Nire-te. "I will let the remnant of our forces and our mother ship know what she has said. Our enemy, Jehov, expended many more ships than he could afford. He will be severely hampered in maintaining control of his jurisdiction. He cannot risk another attack."

If he did try another attack he would have to face me. His forces would be crushed.

"We will be with you for another two weeks," said Nire-te. "After that you will not be passing through any hostile territory until you reach Sovereign Yehowshuwa's dominion."

After the vision faded the crew gathered around Zophia. She grabbed Chuck and gave him a big hug. She felt him stiffen. *Relax Chuck. You have a lot to learn before we get home.*

Zophia considered the job ahead of her, preparing the crew for their role before they reached Earth. She now felt fully prepared for the task. She was eager to get started. After all, the freedom of mankind depended on her and the crew.

Chapter 24

Robert arrived early at his classroom for his first Sub-Ancient Philosophy class. He sat down at a desk in the middle of the empty room and pressed the "Surface UP" button on the right armrest. The writing surface slid silently out of the armrest and extended in front of him. He unfolded his ECD and placed it on the desk top, then looked around wondering how much classrooms had changed in the last thousand years. The metallic alloy desk automatically adjusted its ergonomic design to fit his body when he sat down but the seat still felt hard to him. He heard the ECD beep which let him know that it had completed the connection into the classroom's system. It was ready to make a video recording of everything the professor or students would say, including anything displayed on the view screen at the front of the class.

As the time for the class to start drew near Robert watched students drift into the small twenty-seat room. He turned sideways in his chair to see better. He said hello or nodded as they came in. He knew most of the students in his major as classmates, as their teaching assistant, or colleague on an archeological dig. After seven others arrived Robert mentally calculated who would be in the class and expected that every one was here.

A young man entered whom he didn't recognize. He sat down several desks away. A very young woman was the last to enter and sat down right behind Robert.

Robert wondered about the last two. The man could be a newer student he hadn't yet met. He appeared old enough to have advanced this far but the young lady looked like she had just graduated from high school. *How did she get into this class? Oh well, it doesn't matter, she'll soon find out she's in the wrong place and will bug out. Too bad, she's really cute. I wouldn't mind getting to know her.*

Robert's watch showed him that it was at least three minutes past starting time. He turned to his classmate on his left and quietly asked, "Mike, have you ever known Professor Robison to be late?"

Mike frowned and shook his head. "No, this isn't like him. He's always punctual and insisted on it in others. I've had other classes from him and he would rake a latecomer over the coals."

"Yeah, me too," agreed Robert. I wonder what Professor Robison would say about me choosing Jim as an assistant. I doubt he would have even considered Jim with his unpunctual track record.

Mike and Robert continued to chat but after fifteen minutes Robert was getting edgy. He was wondering what would happen if the class was cancelled for some reason and how it would affect his ability to write his book.

Robert's thoughts were interrupted as a woman dressed in a dark business suit walked briskly into the room, marched to the front, and turned to face the class. "Good afternoon people. Welcome to Sub-Ancient Philosophy. I'm your instructor, Dr. Halverson. I'm sorry to inform you that Dr. Robison is not available to teach this quarter and I have been selected to replace him. Since I don't know any of you, I thought it would be a good idea to give you a test to see if you are up to the level this course will demand. Your tests are now available on your ECDs. You know the drill. Enter your course number and your ECD will be disabled except for the test until you finish. You have forty five minutes for this test. I will see you tomorrow." Dr. Halverson immediately marched out of the room, ignoring the raised hands.

Robert was stunned. Dr. Robison wasn't teaching. Dr. Halverson's abrupt manner on top of being ignored when he raised his hand offended him. Several things raced through his mind. *Will the Board accept a substitute for Dr. Robison as the professor? Who is this woman? I've never heard of her before and I know almost all the people in this field.* However, he quickly settled down and entered the course number on his ECD. *I'd better get this test out of the way, then I can get some questions answered. I've been around here long enough that they have to let me know what's going on.* The first question appeared on his ECD.

1. What was the predominant philosophy of the students on the Berkley California campus during the late 1960's?
    a. Free Speech
    b. Free Love
    c. Question Authority
    d. Fight Communism
    e. Use drugs to cope

The first question wasn't one that Robert liked. He knew that there were at least three possible answers but he wasn't sure which one was predominate. He skipped to the next question trying to find something in the following questions that might give a clue to answer the first question. This wasn't going to be a snap but he knew how to take tests and knew it was best to continue and answer the easiest questions first, then go back to finish the harder ones when he had time to think.

As soon as Robert finished his test his ECD was unlocked and he quickly sent a note to Henry, the senior elder for his Board.

Henry,

This is Robert. I have a question before starting on the book. You know taking the class 'Sub-Ancient Philosophy' by Dr. Robison as one of the requirement I set to finishing school. Today, I found out that Dr. Robison isn't teaching the class but they have a substitute. I'm wondering if there is a problem fulfilling the requirements if Dr. Robison isn't teaching. I just want to make sure that this development won't be a problem.
Robert.

Next, he started looking for data about Dr. Halverson. He entered a search argument that included her name and Midrib University. He received the standard public information that was available about all employees of the University. He scanned it to see if there was anything that would help him understand her ability and qualifications to teach the class. She was transferred to Midrib from Scottsdale just yesterday. *That might explain why she was so abrupt with the class and didn't want to stick around.* The bio listed several of her accomplishments at Scottsdale, including several books on philosophy and history. *Funny, I haven't heard of any of these books before. It looks like several are about the period which the class covers so that's good. Nothing in archeology so she isn't going to bring anything to the plate from that arena like Dr. Robison could have. Too bad.*

Robert folded his ECD and quickly got up to go, turned around and almost bumped into the young lady behind him as she stood up at the same time. He stared into her blue eyes and mumbled, "Excuse me, Miss. I should have looked before leaping," before averting his eyes from hers. *Young, good looking, blond. Ah, maybe too young. I'll bet Jim would like her.*

"No problem; my name's Sam." She extended her hand to Robert.

He turned his head slightly as if he hadn't quite heard her correctly and gave her a quizzical look.

She added, "That's short for Samantha."

Robert took her hand and shook it. "My name's Robert." As they left the room he remarked, "Samantha, it's good to meet you. I know most of the students that would normally be taking this class but I certainly don't remember seeing you before. Have you just transferred in?"

"Uh, not exactly; this is my first year. Please call me Sam. Samantha sounds so stuffy" she said as they stopped just outside of the door.

The young man Robert didn't know exited the classroom and paused for a second, then got a drink of water from the fountain beside the door a couple of feet from Robert and Samantha.

"Sam it is. You're a freshman?" asked Robert trying not to sound too surprised or superior.

"Yup, that's me," answered Samantha confidently.

"I thought you looked a bit young. How did you get into a post graduate class as a freshman?"

"I've been fascinated by history for years and enrolled in Midrib while I was still in high school. Apparently I took too many classes because there wasn't much left and the remaining classes I need aren't available this quarter. My counselor suggested that I could take some graduate classes and recommended this one. It fit right in with my other studies so here I am," she answered with a hand on the hip and the other palm up in front of her. "I'll have to admit that test was quite a challenge for me. Some of the questions were about obscure events or policies that I've barely heard about."

The young man turned to Robert and Samantha and smiled warmly. "I didn't mean to eavesdrop but did I just hear that you're a freshman?" he asked Samantha. "That wasn't an easy test. I would imagine that it would have been extremely difficult even with lots of lower level classes. Oh, by the way, my name is Kevin. How do you think you did?" He extended his hand toward both of them.

"Hi, I'm Sam and this is Robert. I'm not sure about the test. I hope it was just to see how much we still need to learn rather than requirements for being in the class."

Robert reached out and shook Kevin's hand. "Glad to meet you, Kevin. I don't remember seeing you around before but you don't look like a freshman like Sam here," stated Robert.

"No, I'm not a freshman but I'm new here. I just transferred from Kaketuchan primarily to take this class from Dr. Robison. I'm really disappointed that he isn't teaching. Do either of you know Dr. Halverson or why he isn't teaching?" asked Kevin with a concerned look.

"Not a clue. I just looked up her bio and she was just transferred here yesterday," answered Robert.

Other students were leaving and made various comment to Robert as they passed, "See you later, old timer." "Bet you aced that one, huh, Robert?" "Still in school I see, Dr. Maskil."

Samantha raised her eyebrows at the last comment. "Well, Robert, or should I say Dr. Maskil, it sounds like you've been here forever," she said.

"Yeah, that's pretty close." Robert hung his head and shuffled his feet in mock humility. "Let's keep it at Robert. Say, since you guys are new here, why don't we go over to the student union building and get a snack. I was going to meet a friend and you can see a bit more of the social life there."

"Sounds good to me," answered Samantha.

"Me too," chimed in Kevin.

While they walked to the student union building Robert got to know the others better. Kevin was a good listener, asking questions that made Robert feel comfortable and easy to talk about himself.

Samantha turned the tables on Kevin after a while, "Kevin, we've been talking a lot, but it seems to me that you have been studying more than history and philosophy in your years at Kaketuchan. Have you been studying psychology as well?"

Robert noted Kevin's hesitation before answering, "Well no, I haven't, but I've been, er, had, ah, quite a bit of experience with Enforcers. I've learned the hard way that there are more gentle ways of conversing than the way I used to. My retraining has made me a kinder and gentler person." He added a long pause before continuing, "On the outside anyway."

Robert was relieved when they arrived at the student union. It gave him an opportunity to change the subject. He wasn't ready to delve into Kevin's background too quickly but his comment whetted his curiosity. He might make a good recruit if he wasn't already involved in the underground.

Samantha didn't pursue the subject any farther either. Robert looked around the cafeteria where he agreed to meet Jim.

"So where is your friend?" asked Samantha.

"Late as usual would be my guess. Let's see what the chef has available for us while we're waiting," said Robert as he led the way to the cafeteria line.

Samantha picked up an apple and tossed it up and down in the air a few times while she waited for the others. Kevin took a while to decide and poured himself a blended fruit drink pureed with ice. Robert ordered a ham sandwich on rye with lettuce, Swiss cheese and mustard. When it was prepared he led them to a table near the area where Jim was supposed to show up.

As they sat down Jim arrived, carrying a small bag from a local donut shop. Robert made the introductions, explaining that Samantha and Kevin were new at Midrib.

"Good to meet you guys. Anyone want a donut? I brought a couple of extras but was only expecting Robert but you're welcome to have one. It looks like Robert has his hands full with that sandwich anyway. I can't believe how hectic my first day has been. I would have thought by now I'd be used to the beginning of a quarter but it seems like they never get easier. Like a dodo, I went and signed up for a 7:30 AM class. I just about missed it since I still can't get used to waking up to an alarm. At least I remembered how to set my ECD to wake me. You know, they should have some kind of shock thing on them so they could really jolt you awake. I must have hit snooze three or four times before I realized what was happening. Then I get to class and it turns out not to be what I expected and so I waded through about 55 screens trying to find the right class and change my schedule. I just barely got to my next class. That seems to be the way my whole day has been. Robert, have you told these guys about your book?" Jim stopped talking long enough to stuff half a donut in his mouth.

"No, I haven't. We don't talk as fast as you do, Jim. Since this is Sam's first year at university our conversations have taken more of a track about campus life and what we've been doing rather than future aspirations." Robert didn't want to introduce his book concept to people who were still strangers.

Jim abruptly changed the subject and started to ramble on, telling Kevin and Samantha about his broad experience of three years at Midrib. Robert mentally rolled his eyes.

Samantha sat back with a bit of a scowl on her face as Jim talked on and on, hardly taking a breath and still managing to down his donuts. Robert imagined that she was wondering why he valued Jim so much as a friend. Jim certainly didn't come across as shy around strangers but his rambling made him sound a bit like an air head. *I hope she sticks around long enough to get to know Jim once he gets past his rambling stage.*

Jim was quite the opposite of Kevin who was quiet and said very little. On the other hand none of them had much of an opportunity to talk since Jim arrived. Jim suddenly stopped talking and Robert knew they would now be able to have a normal conversation.

After a while Robert felt that they were developing a friendship. He had a bond with Samantha and Kevin because of the shared class. Jim seemed to fit in quickly as he was able to key in on the history and philosophy topics that came up and contribute insight from a non-historian viewpoint. Robert was glad to see that Samantha's scowl was replaced with smiles. She leaned forward instead of away. It was apparent that her first impression of Jim was quickly changing.

Samantha looked at the time and interrupted, "If you would excuse me, I need to get back to the dorm pretty quick. There's going to be some organizational meetings tonight and I've got some homework to do." Samantha got up quickly.

"What dorm are you staying at?" asked Kevin.

"I'm at Wycliffe," she answered.

"I'm next door at Huntington and we're scheduled for the same stuff tonight too. Why don't I walk you back that way?" suggested Kevin as he stood up.

"Sounds good to me. We'll see you tomorrow in class, Robert. Nice meeting you, Jim. I'm sure we'll be seeing you around," she said as she and Kevin started to leave.

"Hey, Robert and I usually meet here after classes. Why don't you join us?" Jim said very cheerfully with his eyes on Samantha.

"I may just do that," said Samantha tilting her head slightly with her eyes fixed on Jim.

Kevin just nodded. They both left while Jim and Robert stayed and talked.

Jim leaned over and elbowed Robert, speaking quietly, "Hey, Robert, that Sam is quite a cutie. I'm sure glad you're too old for her. What do you think? Could she be interested in a guy like me? I mean you know, like as a boyfriend? Did you see the way she looked at me when I invited them back? I wonder if I will have to compete with Kevin for her attention. He seems like a nice guy and is good looking. Nah! Watching his interaction with her I don't think that he is interested in Sam as a girlfriend. Of course that offer to walk with her might give him a chance to ace me out. Did you see those deep blue eyes?"

Robert started going over some class notes. He answered rather absentmindedly, "You fall in love with the first freshman you meet each year. What happened to Joan, Felicia, Eleanor and what's her name? Take a while before you jump in too quickly and scare her off. Oh, yeah, I did notice that she is cute but I decided she's too young for me so don't worry, I won't try to take her from you." He suddenly stopped and looked Jim in the eye. "Wait a minute. Sam is cute. She's really smart and mature too. She's way too smart and mature for you. Maybe I should turn on the old Maskil charm to make sure she doesn't break your heart."

There was a long silence while Robert waited for Jim to digest what he said. First Jim had a puzzled look on his face then his eyes twitched a little and squinted as he concentrated more. Slowly his eyebrows came down along with the corners of his mouth. Then his lips started to purse and his bottom lip protruded. In the mean time Robert returned to his studies and tried his best to not make eye contact or smirk as he watched out of the corner of his eye. Jim then stuck out his tongue and gave Robert a good old fashioned raspberry and they both erupted into laughter.

"Oh come on, Jim. I had you going there for a minute, didn't I?"

"No, only for 49 seconds, but it was long 49 seconds."

Robert and Jim stayed at the student union building another hour studying and talking until they departed. Jim headed for his dorm and Robert returned to his apartment.

July 29, 998 ASR

Zophia couldn't sleep. It was 2:13 AM. She tossed and turned on her bed in her stateroom aboard the C.B.R.S Aman. She kept rehashing her death experience. She laughed that Alex, the medical officer, had insisted on giving her a complete physical exam after her miraculous healing. Of course, it revealed that she was in perfect health.

The excitement of the battle and her voyage into the eternal realm after her death hadn't diminished. She kept going over and over what she learned from the founders of the Council of Enlightened Beings. Something was missing or didn't seem to fit. She felt both exhilarated and empty. Finally, she decided to contact Ana. *Perhaps some of the emptiness is my longing for her.*

Zophia shed her night clothes and sat cross-legged on the floor as she did in private with Ana while they were on Eden. Even though they were now several thousand light years from Eden, Zophia was able to contact Ana immediately by mental telepathy. She felt as if Ana were in the same room with her. *Ana, my beloved, how good it is to share my mind with you. My joy would be complete only if we were together physically as well.*

Ana responded, Indeed, I too desire to be together. However, I sense you are troubled. This seems strange to me. You have journeyed into the eternal. You have learned more in a few hours than I did in two thousand years. Why are you disturbed?

I may have gained much knowledge but you have wisdom. I feel unfulfilled as if there were a void in me. When we were together, I didn't feel that. When we departed, I missed you greatly but what I feel now is much stronger. It is like a black hole from which I can't escape. Zophia was able to share her emotions with Ana so that they could both feel the same thing.

There was a long pause before Ana answered. Zophia could see thoughts flashing across Ana's mind as she sorted through two thousand years of experience. She felt a deep sadness as Ana began to answer. *My dear Zophia, I have bonded with you closer than I have with any of my husbands. This makes it very difficult for me to say, but it is time I let you go.*

Zophia's heart sank as she heard Ana's conclusion. I don't know how I can continue without you. I was sure we would be linked together forever.

We will always be able to contact each other but this longing you feel can be only filled by an enlightened being, one who has already ascended and overcome all the limitations of a physical body.

Zophia received Ana's pain and her emotions and replied, I see your loss is as great as mine. I also see that you are looking beyond yourself and forward to the joy that you expect me to receive. What must I do?

You have advanced well beyond me in knowledge. Surely, Zophia, the Council of Enlightened Beings conveyed to you how to take the next step, answered Ana.

Zophia sighed deeply. So much information was provided that it is hard to sort through it all.

It seems that for now I must leave you so that you will not be distracted. I know you will find what you need. May the peace of Adon be with you.

Zophia was all alone. She slowly called upon her training on Eden to concentrate and remember her experience with Harum, Opparum, Mararum, Rorarum, and Amorum, the founders of the Council of Enlightened Beings. She recalled standing on top of the great white pyramid as she opened her mind to them. It became clear in her mind and the precise visions and instructions she needed were immediately available.

Zophia jumped to her feet and ran out the door. She ran down dimly lit corridors and burst into the chapel. There at the base of the wall-sized portrait of The Sovereign were a dozen candles in an ornate golden candelabrum. No one had used the chapel since Dave's premature death at the hands of Rol-el. She took five candles and a lighter.

She rushed to the mess hall. She was thankful that the tables and chairs were still pushed to the sides exposing the pentagram in the middle of the floor. Her burned body had been lying there just a few hours ago. She hesitated only a moment as she remembered the pain, then the healing. Quickly, she lit a candle, dripped some wax on one corner of the pentagram, and set the candle in the wax fixing it firmly to the floor.

Once she had a candle burning at each corner, she sat cross-legged in the middle of the pentagram, one wrist resting upside down on each knee, chin up and back straight. She started to chant the names of Harum, Opparum, Mararum, Rorarum, and Amorum. In a matter of seconds she was oblivious to her surroundings.

Chapter 25

Samyaza leaned his right shoulder against the back of Robert Maskil's apartment building one block from the University of Midrib campus. He folded his arms, watching the dimly lit rear door that opened into the alley. He was waiting for Robert to leave for his meeting. Robert always used the back exit. He was too predictable.

At 11:15 PM Samyaza heard the door open. He realized he was still visible and didn't want Robert to catch a glimpse of his thin, pale face and sunglasses as Jim had done in the mountains. He quickly faded from view and followed Robert, who hurriedly exited the alley and crossed the street to the campus.

It was easy for tall, thin Samyaza to keep up with Robert's brisk walk through the almost vacant campus. He already knew where Robert was going for a secret meeting of *The Question* discussion group. He was following only as a matter of protocol – properly recording Robert's movements.

Robert walked around the history building and started back the way he came, then took a left turn and circled the central fountain and rose garden. A causal observer would think he was simply getting some exercise. He alternated between jogging and walking, taking a couple of loops and abruptly reversing his direction. *He thinks this prevents him from being followed. If he only knew.* They passed Jim Arizna going the opposite direction. No one said a word.

At 11:33 PM Robert entered the gravitational engineering building's back door, descended into the basement, went down a dimly lit hall and into a storage room without any outside windows to reveal that it was being used late at night. Samyaza thought it was ironic that with The Sovereign Yehowshuwa's rule locks on doors were unnecessary but allowed the underground to commandeer unused rooms for their clandestine meetings.

Robert slipped through the door before Samyaza could squeeze in at the same time. It didn't matter. Samyaza simply glided through the wall and took his position at the back of the room, leaning against the wall.

By 11:53 PM Robert, Jim, and six other students had filtered in, each at a different time.

Gustav Jones, the cell group leader, called the meeting to order at 11:55 PM, "OK guys, we're all here so let's get started. Each of you has been here before but this is only the second year for Mike and Sandra so I'll go over our procedures and goals for the next year. It is very simple. Each of us will recruit one or two people that you believe have a questioning spirit. Someone who likes to be challenged to think beyond what you've always been told by the Administration."

Samyaza could recite the speech himself. He had heard it enough times. During the first few meetings we select basic subjects for discussion that will explore the recruit's potential.

"We'll eliminate any who would be a threat to us by showing an ingrained loyalty to The Sovereign. Those who quickly grasp deeper meanings and embrace new concepts will be invited back. Any questions?" Gustav looked around the room.

Robert popped up his hand but didn't wait to be acknowledged, "Yeah, Jim and I will be leaving after the end of the quarter. Who will look after our recruits since we won't be around to monitor them?" he asked.

"This is kind of abrupt, isn't it? I thought you were going to finish the full year. What happened?" asked Gustav.

Robert briefly explained how he had been boxed in by his dad and mom while he was home and how he used the Administration's own rules to ensure his class and his ability to write the book he was planning. He also related how he signed up Jim as his research assistant.

My superiors are going to want to know that Robert let his Board think that his book would bring about an increased loyalty to Yehowshuwa in the younger generation. It makes me wonder if he may be shading the facts with his cell group.

"We've talked a lot about writing this book and how it will help our cause. It's ironic that the Administration is actually going to help you expose its own beginning as the sham that they have hidden for hundreds of years." Gustav gave Robert a thumbs up sign. "Good job, Robert. Don't worry about any recruits you two drum up. We'll be able to cover for you."

Samyaza loathed Gustav. He made no bones about his agenda when he was with those he trusted but was noncommittal, just like Robert, when there were new recruits around.

"Are we going to have a discussion tonight?" asked Jim.

Gustav rolled his eyes and answered, "Well, of course we are, Jim. Didn't you read your bulletin?"

Jim's face took on a puzzled look at the question.

"Oh, right, in three years you've never read to the end of a bulletin. How could I have forgotten? Tonight we will be discussing sexual freedom, something in which you may be particularly interested. Why don't you start by telling us what you believe are the Administration's rules and regulations regarding sex?" asked Gustav smirking.

Jim immediately blushed and stammered, "Hey, why do you want me to start? I'm sure Robert would be quite a bit more capable than me. I just don't think I'm the best qualified to say anything. I mean I really like to look at, ah, I mean I have always liked girls but I haven't had any intentions, I mean I look for a long term, I mean why don't you ask Robert?"

Gustav laughed along the rest of the group then continued, "I asked you for a reason and I think you demonstrated it quite well. Look at all of you, not just Jim. The mention of sex and you all blush, and why is that? Robert, what do you think about that?"

"I think it has a lot to do with your first question about the rules and regulations that we have regarding sex. It has been established by The Sovereign Yehowshuwa that sexual relationships are strictly forbidden except between married couples. It has been stringently enforced and to my knowledge there hasn't been any violations for hundreds of years. Sexual relations are kept private and are not a matter for public discussion. While the biological process of procreation is taught in school, detailed instructions are reserved only for those who are about to get married." Robert squirmed in his chair.

He continued barely taking a breath, "A couple can only become betrothed when their union has been approved by their Board and once they are betrothed they may enter into this instruction phase. However, the betrothal is actually the first step in their marriage and the only way that a couple can back out of it would be for the same reasons for a divorce, namely, unfaithfulness."

Robert's face lost its rosy glow as he discussed the legal aspect of marriage. "Since their Board has already had the couple go through a significant amount of counseling and examination and since any unfaithfulness would be stopped by Enforcers, there hasn't been any divorces during the betrothal."

"Therefore discussions about sexual relationships are very private and I'd expect that none of us have had any more instruction than the biological facts." His cheeks glowed again at just the mention of sexual relationships.

"We have also had certain dress codes in our society that makes personal experience with the anatomy of the opposite sex unknown to the unmarried. However, we all know that we have attractions to the opposite sex that are physical and we are prohibited from exploration in these areas unless we are in a marriage relationship. When these things are brought up we blush because all the privacy makes these things seem shameful when made public." Robert spoke clearly without stammering but when he finished his face was beet red.

Gustav's nodded as he listened. "Very good, Robert. As usual you can articulate the Administration's position clearly, however you did leave out one thing and that is that The Sovereign has made it clear that we aren't even supposed to consider in our minds sexual relationships outside of marriage." He turned and looked directly at Hillary as he spoke.

Hillary wore a very short skirt exposing more of her legs than the usual dress on campus. She slowly crossed her legs and responded with a wink and a smile. Her dark complexion revealed only a trace of embarrassment. Samyaza made a mental note to include Hillary's dress and attitude in his report to his superiors.

Gustav's normally ruddy face reddened considerably. He smiled and continued, "When we meet together, one of the things that is at the heart of all our discussions is freedom; freedom to think and formulate rules that are relevant and not imposed because they have been made up by someone who thinks he knows better than we do. We have reasoning powers and we are able to determine what is right and wrong. Tonight, we are going to use these abilities to evaluate the rules surrounding sexual relationships. As you know, we do this by asking questions and seeking the answers."

"The first question is 'Why are sexual relationships restricted to marriage?' Can anyone give me the reasons for this? Yes, Mike." Gustav acknowledged Mike's raised hand.

Mike was also in Robert's Sub-Ancient Philosophy class. Both were being watched carefully.

"As I understand it there is something about sex that causes two people to become one and that according to Yehowshuwa, this relationship should be forever," Mike answered confidently.

"Good answer. And can anyone tell me how this 'becoming one' works?" Gustav paused and waited for an answer. After a brief time of silence he continued, "Jim, would you describe your parents as being one?"

Jim thought for a few seconds and answered, "My mom and dad are one if you think about their devotion to work but I don't see how that has anything to do with sex. They argue a lot when they're both home at the same time, which isn't all that often. I don't see a whole lot of unity. They like different kinds of food and recreation. No. I couldn't say that they are one. They are two distinct individuals married to each other and that is how they will remain. They don't have a choice because that's the way things are."

"How about your parents, Mike?" asked Gustav as he pointed back to Mike.

Mike scratched his head and answered, "My parents have quite a few things in common. They both like soccer and other sports. They've both been on teams for as long as I've known them. They don't agree very much about how to raise kids. My mom is very strict and my dad is very easy going. When we were younger she was always concerned that we'd be hurt while my dad would let us do stuff that was more physical and challenging. Mom goes to worship at least twice a month but Dad seldom goes, maybe every other month. Their adherence to The Sovereign's rules and regulations are quite far apart. I'm with Jim. I don't see how sex really has much to do with the unity they do have or the areas where they aren't unified."

Gustav turned to Robert. "Thanks Mike. Robert, your dad is a Board member, right? Wouldn't you think that someone with that high level in the Administration would demonstrate unity with his wife? They are also older than most of our parents and have been married about two hundred and fifty years, haven't they?"

"Yeah, Dad's a Board member and they've been married a long time. To be truthful, they are pretty much one in the way they think and act but that's primarily because Mom calls the shots and Dad does what she wants to keep himself out of trouble with her. Since I left home he doesn't spend much time at home or with Mom. If you call placating your spouse becoming one then they are indeed one." Robert paused and scoffed.

It seems that Robert didn't think it pertinent to the conversation that his dad has decided to work on his role as a husband. Samyaza made a mental note of his omission along with his other notes.

Gustav rubbed his hands together as he usually did when he wanted to wrap up a point and move on. "So far it sounds like three out of eight of us haven't been able to say much for this concept of oneness that is supposed to be the result of sexual relationships of married couples. Have any of the rest of us observed anyone, parents or otherwise, who they could say have oneness and explain how sex had anything to do with it?"

Again Gustav paused for input but received only silence and heads shaking no. "I thought not. So let's move on to the next question but first I'll clarify that marriages and the associated oneness aren't supposed to be forever but while both are still alive. According to the rules, if one person dies, then the other is free to marry and have sexual relationships and become one with another. Doesn't the possibility of remarriage after the death of one partner raise the possibility that someone can become one with more than one person? If so, then the next question is, 'Why should this relationship be for a person's life time?' Who would like to go first? Michelle, we haven't heard from you yet tonight."

Michelle swept her long red hair behind her right ear with one hand. She squirmed in her folding chair and answered, "Yeah, go ahead and give the guys the easy questions. However, from a logical point of view, since you haven't shown that a couple does become one, it appears to me that unless there is other outside documentation to prove that oneness is a result of sex then the question should have been phrased, 'Since we can't prove from our experience that sexual relationships produce oneness, why should sexual relationships be limited to a married couple and why should that last for the life time of the one which lives the shortest time?'"

Oh boy, Gustav should have known better than to give that one to Michelle. She can go on forever with the slightest opening. Samyaza yawned silently as he endured her spiel.

"Continuing on with deductive logic from what we've witnessed tonight, the concept of becoming one because of sexual relationships is a sham. Therefore if two people do not become one then there is no reason for the relationship to last any longer than it takes to perform the act. If that is true then there needs to be another reason for marriage and limited sexual relationships. Before we can draw a conclusion we should investigate other reasons that may exist for limiting sex to married couples and having the marriage last a life time." Michelle raised her hand above her waist and quickly flipped it over, signaling she had finished.

Samyaza watched Robert's uncharacteristic reaction as he slowly looked Michelle up and down, even though she was dressed in a baggy sweat suit. He made another mental note that Robert must have been affected by the evening's topic.

"I guess I deserve that for calling on you, Michelle. As usual, you cut through the flack and precisely laid out what we still need to address. What other reasons do we know about for restricting sex to marriage and marriage for a life time?" asked Gustav as he looked around the room.

"You mean other than because The Sovereign says so?" quipped No-neck Walter, a senior this year on the football team.

"Yeah! Other than that and since you piped up, why don't you tell us what else there is?" answered Gustav.

Walter shifted his weight, causing his folding chair to quiver under his weight, "OK. One of the big factors of sex is procreation. Along that line the Administration pushes the idea that a marriage provides a stable environment in which to beget and raise children. The family is the heart of our society and allowing sex outside of marriage would destabilize it, which in turn would also destabilize our society. That's one of the reasons the Enforcers are more active in maintaining families than any other area of society. If you raise the kids the way the Administration wants, then other problems with society are minimized."

Twila popped into the act and asked, "So the primary purpose behind limiting sex to marriage is simply to keep the Administration in power through rigorous rules being passed down from one generation to another?"

"Who would like to tackle that question?" challenged Gustav.

Robert spoke up, "Isn't that just about the basis of all our discussions? When we think through the questions that we bring up, whether it is the way a Board controls its community or some of Yehowshuwa's claims, we usually come to the conclusion that our society is structured the way it is to keep people in line and The Sovereign in power. This doesn't seem to be much different. From what I understand about sub-ancient philosophy, the concept of marriage was being challenged in the century that led up to the Last Battle. According to most of my research, family breakdown was blamed for most of society's problems. Documentation showed that people having and raising kids without being married presented 'twisted' role models."

Samyaza stiffened and concentrated on what Robert was saying. He may have to report, word for word, Robert's discourse.

"Sometimes the parents weren't married or they were married, divorced and remarried even multiple times. Some kids ended up being raised by a person that wasn't their biological parent. These kids grew up without the moral upbringing of the rest of their culture. They didn't fit into society's mold. They soon accounted for the majority of people incarcerated for crimes. Even the loss of ethics in businesses was traced to family breakdown. Each generation drifted from The Sovereign's ideal of a family and therefore society deteriorated. Yehowshuwa restored the traditional family when he returned and society has been in harmony ever since."

Gustav's eyes got big and his jaw dropped. "Do you really believe that, Robert?" he asked.

Robert laughed and leaned back with his hands behind his head. "If I did, you guys would have been turned into the Administration by now. See, this is what I'm trying to find out." He dropped his hands and gestured as if he had a large ball in his hands. "Everything seems to fit together just too nicely from all I've studied. Every book, every class points to the same conclusion, that The Sovereign Yehowshuwa was the only answer to the woes of the world. There isn't any dissension published after the Last Battle and references to opposition have been presented in the light of how ludicrous these ideas were. All sorts of statistics are used to show that life would have been much better if people had been aligned with The Sovereign. The Chancellor would have never gotten such a strong foothold as he did. I have yet to find any original documents that were written during that era arguing against The Sovereign's position, whether it's about sex, family values, social issues, or religion. It's as if everything was burned and then rewritten from his point of view. I just can't see how so many people can all come up with the same conclusion when we sit here and can come up with various other conclusions. The more I think about it, the more I'm convinced that it's a regimented rewriting of history. There. I've said it so lock me up for treason but there's got to be more and I want to find out," said Robert resolutely.

Samyaza felt his pulse increasing as Robert spoke. He was extremely grateful that he had committed Robert's every word to memory. If he didn't have previous orders he would have made himself known at this moment.

"I think I speak for the whole group and the hierarchy of those behind *The Question* when I say that I agree with you, Robert. However we must be careful or I'm afraid that we may actually end up being charged with treason. But it's getting late and we better move on. We don't want to linger in one place too long. So far we don't believe that any of our meetings have been detected and none of the leadership has been challenged in any way by the Administration," admonished Gustav.

Walter asked, "Gustav, who is the leadership? I've been in this group about three years and I've never heard of anyone other than you being a leader. Obviously the network is huge judging by the technology, planning, and everything else that goes into *The Question*. Why don't we know the leaders? Wouldn't that help spread the word?"

Oh, this is getting to be quite an interesting evening. Let's see if Gustav gives up some names. Samyaza moved to the front of the room and stood right beside Gustav, maintaining his invisibility.

Gustav shook his head. "We are organized in cell groups so that if any group is ever compromised then no one knows any other group. In a few cases, some of the leaders are part of other higher groups but this is quite rare. We don't meet personally with other leaders. I only know them by code names and we use virtual meetings. Information and directions come from our leader and so forth up the line. We really don't know who the top is but we've recently found that we've been getting some help from some very powerful people. That's one of the reasons why we haven't been detected so far. Because of our help it looks like we will be able to meet in larger groups without any danger. We are about to enter into some very exciting times in the next year or so."

Jim's hand shot up and his mouth engaged, "The idea doesn't sound very appealing to me. Why would we meet in larger groups? Wouldn't that jeopardize the whole organization? We've been so secretive so far, how could anything change so that we could risk larger groups? It just doesn't seem very wise to me."

Gustav shrugged his shoulders. "I hear you, Jim, and I don't understand how we're going to pull it off either, but I know the leadership wouldn't risk it if it weren't possible. They've simply told us that we need to continue to recruit, form new groups, and prepare the veterans for some deeper involvement. But that's enough for tonight. We really need to move out."

I'm not sure where Gustav got his information. I haven't heard of this before. But then again I'm not always kept informed of the latest Intel or my superior's plans.

With his last comment, Gustav got up and the others followed. Michelle and Twila opened the door, looked up and down the hallway then slipped out. They were followed two minutes later by Robert and Jim.

Samyaza stayed and watched as every two to three minutes another one or two exited the room. Finally Gustav left. Samyaza left to report to his superiors.

September 4, 998 ASR

Henry got up early and went to his study to start his time of prayer and meditation before breakfast. The flashing light from the ECD on his desk aroused his curiosity. He had a text message from Robert.

Henry read Robert's letter with interest. *I distinctly remember Maria saying that he must complete his education exactly as he said. Why would a class that was required by the Administration suddenly have a substitute professor?*

He quickly started some research into Robert's class and the reason for the substitution, using his authority as a Board member to access Administration records that were not available to the public. He soon found that Professor Robison was listed as missing and not available for the class.

Henry sat back and pondered how anyone in this day and age could be listed as missing. *Even if he were out in the wilderness and didn't have his ECD or had an accident that broke his ECD, Yehowshuwa must know where he is and if he knows, why wouldn't he let others working in the Administration know the professor's location?*

He found a long chain of documents from the administrators at Midrib and other universities. The first was a cancellation notice for the Sub-Ancient Philosophy class. That notice was followed by a short memo from the world director of education to nullify the cancellation. *Wow! That is really high in the chain of mucky mucks. Obviously Yehowshuwa wants that class to take place. All the rest of this stuff is just the dean at Midrib scrambling to find someone to take Professor Robison's place.*

Henry scanned the titles of at least a hundred different memos relating to the class. It was obvious that finding a replacement for the missing professor wasn't easy. The search continued until just three days before the class was to start. They found Dr. Halverson after a person by the name of Berekiah brought up her name. She was immediately approved by the world director of education.

Henry dictated a reply to Robert, "Dear Robert, I've done some research and your substitute teacher has been approved for this class at the highest levels. I have no doubt that the class taught by her will fulfill your requirements for the Administration. Your local Board doesn't have any problems with the change. Remember to keep in touch. May The Sovereign bless you and your studies, Henry"

He cleaned up the formatting of the note, pushing the words around with his index finger and sent it.

Henry closed his eyes and started his prayer time. "Lord Sovereign, protect Robert and keep him safe. Keep him in your love. This missing professor stuff is so unusual but I know you have your reasons for letting it happen. My confidence is in you and nothing will shake it."

September 4, 998 ASR

Dr. Halverson was already in the classroom when the students arrived. She stood behind the lectern, leaning on it with both elbows, and propping her chin with both hands. She watched carefully as her students entered noting their walk, where they sat, and interaction with others. She wondered who was who. Sure, she could have looked up pictures of each student, but she enjoyed guessing and seeing how well her first impressions matched her expectations from the pop quiz.

One young man entered the room with his head slightly down and sat near the back. Not too far to be obvious but clearly far enough that most people who were still to arrive would sit closer to the front than he. He glanced up once or twice but avoided eye contact with Dr. Halverson. *Mr. Timid.* She put a little check mark next to a name with a low score on the test on her list in her ECD.

An older student entered. He walked directly to a seat near the front of the room and sat down. He smiled and nodded to her. He was older than she would have expected of a student. *Mr. Oldguy.* She looked at her list, hesitated a moment, then made a check beside Dr. Robert Maskil.

Dr. Halverson had to make some quick checks as several students entered one after another. A woman with short brown hair dressed in a blue suit but with a very revealing V necked blouse and short skirt strode quickly to a desk a row behind and one to the left of Mr. Oldguy. She quickly set up her ECD, folded her hands, fixed her eyes on Dr. Halverson, and smiled as if she knew some secret. She reminded Dr. Halverson of herself when she was two hundred years younger. *Miss Self-confident-has-the-world-under-control. She would be Jammie Soute.*

A man and a very young woman entered together, smiling and looking as though they both enjoyed life. She had a perky walk while the man's was even and purposeful. Dr. Halverson was surprised at how young she appeared and how mature he looked, not like a student but more like a teacher. *Miss Youngster and Mr. Enigma.* They quickly walked in and took a seat on either side of Mr. Oldguy. The three quietly said hello to each other. She glanced over her list and checked off a name – Marsha Peterson – low score. She decided to wait before checking off a name for Mr. Enigma until other students arrived and she would see who was left.

When the last student arrived, a male, Dr. Halverson checked him in as Kevin Trimble then marked Mike Stevenson as Mr. Enigma. She straightened up and proceeded to take a role call.

"Kevin Trimble." She wanted to know right away if she had picked the most difficult to peg by elimination.

"Here," spoke up Mr. Enigma.

Without changing her expression she grimaced inwardly realizing how far off she had placed him. Unfortunately that meant that she had also missed another student. Her next objective was to find out which one of the women had scored the highest.

"Samantha Spell."

"Here," answered Miss Youngster, the person she had labeled as Marsha Peterson.

She hid another facial contortion. How could this bouncy young lady who looked like she was fresh out of high school be the highest scoring woman? That means Miss Self-confident-has-the-world-under-control had better be the number two woman. By pushing Samantha to the top it also meant that she missed at least one other woman in the class.

"Dr. Maskil."

"Here," said Mr. OldGuy.

Finally she had a right guess for the high scoring man. But then he was obviously the oldest person in the class and the most self confident; he was not timid. She did find it interesting that the high scoring man and woman were sitting together. *Could there have been some chance that Miss Spell looked over his shoulder during the test?* She remembered that Miss Spell had been sitting behind him and to his left yesterday. She decided to keep an eye on them.

The rest of the class fit neatly into Dr. Halverson's first impressions. She walked around to the front of the lectern and proceeded to pace back and forth in front as she started her lecture.

"Welcome to Sub-Ancient Philosophy. As I mentioned yesterday, Professor Robison isn't teaching this quarter. As a matter of fact we don't know if he will ever be teaching again. Last summer he took a well-deserved but unexpected summer vacation. He didn't tell anyone where he was going or what he was going to do. He was scheduled to return last week and when he didn't check in the dean checked his apartment. No one has heard from him or knows where he is. Rather than simply canceling this class, which was the smart thing to do, I was summoned to cover it. This is all I know about why I'm here instead of Dr. Robison so don't ask me any questions about it. If you are disappointed that he isn't teaching the class and that I am, then quite frankly, so am I. However, together we will be able to get over our mutual disappointment and I assure you that you will be able to understand the years before the Great Time of Trouble much better than you would have ever imagined."

She paused and looked at the class. There were mixed reactions to her announcement about Professor Robison's disappearance but Mr. Trimble was the only one that didn't show any surprise. *I wonder if he is the one that will get my little gift.*

"Your test scores have all been returned to you and you know where you stand with the rest of the class. With the exception of one person, you already have a significant knowledge of the facts of the era but you have little insight into why and how people thought back then. The purpose of this class is to shed light on their philosophies and hopefully understand what changed the way their world thought and therefore acted. With that out of the way, let's see how this all got started."

Dr. Maskil glanced at Miss Spell when Dr. Halverson mentioned the low score. Obviously Dr. Maskil's estimation of her knowledge was the same as mine. You are wrong, Mr. Oldguy, or she is a cheater.

Dr. Halverson returned behind the podium and adjusted her ECD to transmit Professor Robison's notes to her contact lenses. The words immediately appeared before her eyes in perfect focus. She had originally planned to memorize the notes each day but the material proved to be too difficult and voluminous for her. She had enough work altering his notes just enough to keep his blatant loyalty to The Sovereign from blasting through. Besides, her attitude stunk and she wasn't too concerned whether the students noticed she was reading notes or not. She returned to her pacing and started reading using a button-sized transmitter to scroll the notes up and down in front of her.

For the next forty five minutes, Dr. Halverson reviewed the works of philosophers and theologians during the years preceding the Last Battle. She started with Immanuel Kant. From Robison's notes, she showed how his reasoning set the ground work for other philosophers such as Søren Kierkegaard, Martin Heidegger, Jean-Paul Sartre, Sigmund Freud, Karl Barth, and others. She emphasized that while some were Christian and others were atheists their philosophies influenced each other. The philosophy of existentialism was formed and shaped the thinking and thereby the actions of everyday people, including those loyal to The Sovereign Yehowshuwa.

She tried not to make eye contact with the class to discourage anyone from asking questions. The pacing back and forth trick seemed to be accomplishing her purpose. She did note a few stifled yawns and Mr. Stevenson was fighting to stay awake. *Not too bad,* she thought, *this stuff is really boring.* She mentally sighed in relief as the summary for the day appeared in the notes.

"When Kant reasoned that we can't know anything except by experience he introduced the idea that our individual freedom lies in obedience to the moral law that speaks from within us. This opened the door for people to believe that there is no personal basis for accepting absolutes and that introduced relative thinking."

Dr. Maskil dropped his hand from propping up his head and sat erect. *At last, a sign of life.*

"Prior to this time most people believed and acted upon the presupposition that there were truths that could not be changed. Wilhelm Friedrich Hegel took up where Kant left off and introduced a system of logic in which a thesis could work against an antithesis to produce a synthesis. Before this system of logic, if you were to think logically about a problem, you would start from something that was true and could understand the cause and affect as applied to the truth. With relative thinking truth was changeable and therefore you would develop different effects for the same causes because the underlying truth had changed."

Miss Spell raised her hand a little way. Dr. Halverson ignored her. Miss Spell looked around then raised her hand farther, brought it down, then stretched her hand up high.

Dr. Halverson abruptly stopped pacing and glared at Miss Spell, "Yes, Miss Spell, you have a question?"

"Yes Ma'am, I do. I'm not sure I should be interrupting a doctor but I could really use an example to help me understand," Miss Spell pleaded with her eyes.

Dr. Halverson looked around the class and saw several expectant faces and a couple of nodding heads. She had hoped that this wouldn't happen. She could scroll through the notes without being obvious, but selecting the example icon beside the paragraph she had just read with the button transmitter was going to take some concentration. "Very well, if you insist," she said, buying time to pull the example up before her eyes.

The example popped up and she continued to pace and read, "Would you agree that it is wrong to murder another person for any reason? Yes? We believe that to be true and it is therefore absolute and unchangeable. It is because we all agree on the definition of murder as defined by The Sovereign and it doesn't depend on our own definition. With relative thought, we first reject The Sovereign Yehowshuwa's definition of murder because that is defined outside of ourselves and our experience. People argued that murder being wrong was indeed a universal truth because all societies had prohibitions about killing others and therefore the sense that it is wrong should be something that all people would experience. However," Dr. Halverson turned to the class, raised her hand pointing, to the ceiling for effect. "They also argued that since different societies approved of killing others under different circumstances, each person would have to define murder for themselves. We agree with The Sovereign's definition because that is how we've been taught. However, when we introduce Kierkegaard's philosophy, we must seek an inner affirmation that murder is what The Sovereign says and if we don't feel the same way as he does, then we change the definition, even if it is ever so slightly. You, Miss Spell, would then have a truth that is unique to you and Mr. Trimble would have a truth that is unique to him. Neither of you would then be able to say that it was wrong to murder another person for any reason because you allow it under circumstances that you have defined. You both still would be using the same word but your actions could be quite different depending on the situations. You would have then embraced relativistic thinking without realizing it."

Dr. Halverson looked at Miss Spell. "Good enough?"

She didn't wait for a response. She hadn't read the examples before class and was intrigued by them so she continued to read. "This process can be applied to any moral truths. For instance, some people observed homosexual behavior among a few seagulls. They then reasoned that since this was observed in nature among animals that didn't have any ability for moral reasoning it must be something that is natural among animals and therefore not a moral issue. If an animal could have homosexual instincts then so could a human being. If it were natural then there should be no prohibition against it. They then reasoned that they must have misunderstood The Sovereign Yehowshuwa's prohibition of homosexuality or that he was wrong in prohibiting it. Their experience trumped The Sovereign's declaration of truth."

Even Mr. Stevenson was wide awake after she read that example. She glanced quickly at the next example then stated, "I think you will really like this next example."

"Relativistic thinking leads to actions that can vary depending on circumstances instead of the truth. In those days a pregnant woman could murder her unborn baby if she felt that the baby would present an imposition to her life. More callously put, if she didn't want the responsibility of raising the child she could abort it before it was born. Because of relativistic thinking, she didn't consider it murder and neither did society. However if that same child was already born and the mother decided she didn't want to be bothered with it and killed it, she would be convicted of murder. Non-relativistic thinking sees the absurdity of treating the two situations differently. Relativistic thinking reduced the definition of murder even further in many areas of the world. Eventually babies born with even minor defects were killed because it was thought they would suffer or face other unacceptable trauma in life. Older people who became a burden to society were routinely over-medicated and died much earlier than they would have had they received care from someone dedicated to preserving life."

Dr. Halverson paused to see how the class had responded. Dr. Maskil and Mr. Stevenson both appeared to understand. The wonder on their faces indicated that they might have already considered relativistic thinking as a viable way of looking at life. Miss Spell's scowl, on the other hand, demonstrated her understanding but she didn't accept the concept. That was a start. Mr. Trimble was still Mr. Enigma. She couldn't read him.

She switched back to the conclusion of the lesson and resumed pacing and reading, "A point comes when you can't tell other people that they are right or wrong because you don't have the same experiences as theirs and therefore your 'truth' isn't the same as their 'truth.' To ensure that your truth is just as valid as theirs, you must all agree that truth is what each of you perceives. To insist that a truth is absolute is the only philosophy that is not allowed because it negates all the other 'truths' that everyone enjoys."

I really hope that these guys are getting the message even though I have to present this from Yehowshuwa's point of view.

"Søren Kierkegaard contributed to the philosophy of the era and introduced these concepts into the Christian Church. Mr. Kierkegaard reasoned that since we can't know anything beyond our five senses our faith must be blind. He also believed that since there is no absolute truth on which to base our lives, we must find relative reasons for our lives. He has been regarded as the origin of existentialism. Existentialism is one of the primary philosophies of the era and it shaped the thinking of almost every person whether they realized it or not. While it was taught as a philosophy during the era, it is not currently discussed or taught outside of a few obscure university classes such as this one."

Mr. Trimble sat and listened attentively and it began to bother Dr. Halverson. The others began to fidget; some were losing interest and Mr. Stevenson's eyes were getting droopy again. But not Mr. Trimble.

"Those who were not loyal to The Sovereign embraced existentialism without much question. A tenant of existentialism is that people are free to make choices and those choices establish the future into which they project themselves. Of course, those choices are made based on their own experiences. They don't need to answer to forces outside of themselves that they can't experience with their natural senses. This appealed to a person's sense that they were the center of their own universe. This affected the every day lives of people in the highest positions of business, government and the church. Ethics became situational so that profit was not based on what was right but on what produced the best return on an investment as long as there wasn't any law against it. Conformity to the law wasn't because it was the right thing to do but because of a fear of the consequences. In many cases even this did not deter those who, in their own sense of truth, believed that the laws were incorrect."

Dr. Halverson had the eerie feeling that Mr. Trimble was looking right into her soul. *I think he knows I believe this. I wonder how he will take this next part.*

"Those loyal to The Sovereign didn't escape the affects of existential thought either. The church once existed with a strong sense of community, but the concept of individual freedom and choice ravaged organized religion. People sought membership in congregations where they felt the most comfortable or where they felt their needs were being met. Many congregations didn't require any kind of membership but existed as people came and went, many times without being noticed. Without membership there was no accountability to leaders who supported moral decisions based on The Sovereign's version of the truth. Attending church functions but not becoming members also allowed people to decide what they thought was best for themselves and their families. After a few years, entertainment with morally corrupting content became common place. Service to others was done when it was convenient and didn't interfere with personal activities. Such service was considered as something that only the paid church staff was supposed to do as people pursued their own individual goals in life."

She didn't want to look Mr. Trimble in the eye. It was too unnerving but she relaxed when she saw him nodding in agreement. *Yes, it is looking more like he is the one to receive the package.*

"Hopefully you now have a spark of insight into how this came about. There are two requirements to complete this class satisfactorily. The first is to imitate the relativistic thinking of the twenty first century. You will be required to chose a moral issue of the day and write an essay from a relativistic existential viewpoint. You will not be allowed to argue your position from a viewpoint other than your own experience. In other words, you will have to develop your own truth. The second requirement is to write an essay that describes the effects on society if everyone adopted and accepted your viewpoint or other viewpoints based on their own truth."

Miss Spell curled the edge of her mouth displaying disgust at the assignment. Well, Miss Youngster, you will have to wrap your mind around this philosophy and hopefully you will be moved toward it in the process or, if you are as loyal to Yehowshuwa as I'm guessing, you will abandon this class.

"That wraps it up for today and you have your assignment. In our next class we will be digging deeper into the philosophies of Friedrich Nietzsche. Be prepared."

Dr. Halverson stopped pacing behind the lectern. She scooped up her ECD then marched down the aisle in the middle of the class and out the door. While she believed the philosophy, she was not prepared to go any deeper than Professor Robison's notes and didn't want to expose her lack of knowledge to the students.

Chapter 26

Zophia found herself standing in the middle of a great plain with low rolling hills covered with grass growing as high as her knees. Her bare legs tickled as the grass swaying in the mild breeze brushed against her. She was near the top of the highest hill in sight. A lone spreading tree devoid of leaves stood at the top of the hill. Under its gnarly black branches a man stood. He beckoned to her to come up the hill.

She began walking up the gentle incline. The breeze became stronger with each step. Black clouds formed all around the horizon. Lightning flashed in the distance and thunder rolled across the prairie. *This isn't smart. The last place we should be in an electrical storm is under a tree on the highest hill in view.* Zophia backed up; the clouds and wind abated.

The man again gestured to her to come up the hill. She took a few tentative steps forward. Again the wind picked up and the sky grew darker. She hesitated.

Come, Zophia. There is nothing to fear.

Zophia focused on the man under the tree. As she walked toward him she was struck by his magnificent physique. She remembered the first time she had seen Mine, Chuck's guide and spokesperson for the people of Eden. He was such a remarkably handsome man that she had wanted him to be her guide. But this man was taller, stronger, tanner, with an even more captivating smile.

By the time she reached the tree she could barely stand against the gale that whipped first from one direction then another. If her hair were long she was sure it would have been completely entangled around her face and head. Just as she was sure the wind was going to pull her off her feet, he reached out and wrapped his arms around her.

The peace that overwhelmed her was more than enough to ignore the tempest around her.

What is happening? Who are you? asked Zophia.

I am Mararum, one of the five original founders of the Council of Enlightened Beings. I am here in response to your meditation. Rebuke this storm, Zophia.

Zophia didn't know what to do. *How can I do that?* Her body tingled as lightning struck the ground ten meters to her right. For some reason her peace prevailed.

Let me be your guide and I will show you how to do this as well as many other great and wonderful signs, answered Mararum. All you need to do is to open yourself to me, invite me in.

I am open to you, come in and be my guide, I am here to learn and become enlightened.

Zophia felt Mararum's body merging with her own. His mind became her mind. Now, as if one with him she turned and stretched out her arms to the wind. She felt his arms in hers or was it her arms in his? She, no, they, proclaimed to the storm, "Peace, be still."

Immediately the clouds disappeared and the gentle breeze again wafted across the prairie sending gentle ripples through the grass. Zophia thought that nothing could have surpassed the pleasure she had enjoyed with Ana as they bonded and her powers in the occult grew. But this, this far surpassed what she knew with Ana. Not only did she experience supreme pleasure but power and the knowledge of how to use it as well.

Zophia, we are one and all my knowledge, power, and pleasures are available to you. Join me here daily in meditation and together we will ready the crew of the Aman so that they will be fully trained and capable when you reach Earth.

Zophia took a deep breath and opened her eyes. At the corner of the pentagram in front of her, a gob of wax was left where the candles had melted and gone out. Movable partitions were placed around the pentagram and her jump suit was draped over the one to her right. She stood and donned her clothes, laughing lightly to herself. *It seemed only a few minutes but I must have been gone for several hours. We got used to seeing nude Edenians but the crew is obviously not ready for nudity among ourselves.*

It was past breakfast time and the mess hall was empty. Zophia went to her cabin to retrieve her ECD. She passed Walter who blushed and avoided her eyes as he said good morning. She laughed again. *This is going to be fun.*

September 4, 998 ASR

Justin sat with the rest of the Elders around the oak table in the Board's chambers. They had just concluded the day's business and were folding up their ECDs. As everyone was leaving, Justin tapped Henry on the shoulder and whispered, "Can I have a bit of your time, privately?"

"Certainly." When Henry and Justin were alone, they sat beside each other. "What's on your mind?"

Justin put his ECD on the table and spun it around. "Well, this is kind of embarrassing, but I'm afraid this ruckus with Robert and his book brought out some problems in our family. I hadn't realized how controlling Marilyn's become. I've been getting the cold shoulder from her ever since the Board approved Robert's continuing studies and his book."

"Sounds like you need some lessons on how to love your wife. I know just the person to help. Let's ask Yehowshuwa to send him." Henry bowed his head and prayed, "Yehowshuwa, you heard what's happening with Justin and Marilyn. Could you send Albert Bailey to help them? Thanks." He looked up at Justin. "Now, go on home. Sooner or later Al will show up."

"Is that all?" Justin asked.

"Unless you need something else." Henry tilted his head.

Justin was puzzled. He'd thought Henry would counsel him or at least ask some questions. "I was thinking maybe you'd help me, not some Enforcer I don't even know."

"Al is far more equipped to help than I am." Henry stood and slapped Justin lightly on the back. "Just be patient."

"OK. I'll see you tomorrow then." Justin left, feeling discouraged. *It doesn't seem like Henry to treat something like this so lightly.*

As Justin left the community center he was approached by a young-looking man in a white linen suit. "Hi, Justin, I'm Albert Bailey. I came as soon as I could. I understand you finally realize you need some help getting your marriage working the way it should. Oh, and by the way, I'm an Encourager, not an Enforcer."

Justin pointed back toward the community center. "Henry and I just asked Sovereign Yehowshuwa for help. What do you mean *finally?*"

"We've known about your problem for quite a while. We were simply waiting for you to ask for help." Albert put a hand on his shoulder.

Justin stiffened. "What do you mean *we?*"

"Don't get defensive. The Sovereign, Henry, and I have been aware that things aren't well with you and Marilyn. I was asked to counsel you as soon as you admitted your need. Now, would you like to know what you can do to improve your marriage?"

Justin sighed. "Yes, I would. I'm a Board member, and I should have my own house in order."

"You'd be surprised how many people don't seek help because of pride."

"You don't hold back, do you?" Justin knew Al was right but it hurt to hear someone say it.

"We need to get down to business pronto. First, let me tell you my background. Way back before the Great Time of Trouble I counseled hundreds of couples and wrote a few books about marriage. I studied Yehowshuwa's scriptures carefully to make sure these principles were in alignment with his instruction, and my current assignment is still helping people with these same concepts." Albert motioned to the park beside the community center. "Shall we walk while we talk?"

"Sure."

They turned toward the park and Justin pulled out his ECD to take notes.

"I have four basic principles that sum up everything you need to do. These are action items, not just head knowledge. They can transform your relationship, whether or not Marilyn agrees to engage in counseling with you. At this time we know she hasn't; otherwise, I'd be talking to both of you."

"OK, I'm ready to do whatever is needed." Justin felt bad that he let the situation get to the point that Marilyn wasn't agreeable to counseling.

Albert held up a finger. "First, speak well of your wife in her hearing as well as when you talk to others about her. Do this even if she does not reciprocate. Then put your words into actions by being kind to her. Show appreciation for her. Also, speak to The Sovereign on her behalf. Ask him to intercede in her life and bring her closer to himself."

Justin thought he often spoke well of her to others, but he rarely told her how much he loved her or appreciated her.

Albert held up two fingers. "Second, make sure she is part of your life. Involve Marilyn in every aspect of your world. Share your thoughts with her. She needs to know what's going on in your mind. Develop common activities and interests. Give yourself to her and make her the most important person in your life next to Yehowshuwa."

Justin thought of all the time he spent at the hardware store or at Board meetings. Marilyn became only a small part of his life. He seldom shared what he was thinking with her.

Albert raised three fingers. "Third, accept your wife unconditionally. Encourage her. Your praise will give her emotional nourishment. If there is a particular area where she insists on having control that's probably where she feels insecure. Your job is to make sure she doesn't feel vulnerable in that area. Shore up her self-confidence by letting her know, through your speech and your actions, she has the freedom to grow and develop without fear of failure or disapproval from you."

Justin couldn't remember the last time he had encouraged his wife in any of her activities.

"Instead of dwelling on what she has done wrong or how she has hurt you, think about the things she does well and that attract you to her. Tell her often that you have been thinking about her."

I don't think much about her unless we're in the same room or there's been friction.

Albert popped up four fingers. "Fourth, touch her physically. Not just sexually. If you make sure she knows you love her, she will feel close to you. Hold hands when you take a walk. Give her back rubs or foot rubs. Give lots of hugs. You can't hug too much or too often."

Justin felt more pangs of his conscience. They seldom held hands or hugged.

Albert caught Justin's eyes with his own. "To help you remember these points think of the acronym SPAT. S: speak well of her. P: part of your life. A: accept her unconditionally. T: touch her. If you apply SPAT to your marriage you will have very few spats."

"That pun is pretty lame," Justin said, not wanting to admit how far short he had fallen.

"My humor may not be great, but I bet you won't forget the acronym."

"True -- and I see areas where I need to improve. What if Marilyn doesn't respond?"

Albert faced Justin and put his right hand on Justin's shoulder. "There are no guarantees that she will. A lot depends on where her heart is. She may even reject you at first. When she sees the difference in the way you treat her, she'll want to know what's going on. Then, if you share these principles with her, she'll probably want to put them into practice too. I'll be available to counsel you together. Whatever happens, your job is to be obedient to The Sovereign in the way you love your wife."

Albert and Justin continued to walk and talk for an hour. Then Albert gave Justin a reading assignment that included one of his books and scriptures that were referenced in the book.

Justin felt a bit scared. This was a stretch for him. It was a long time since he was in a learning-and-applying mode. He was determined to try Albert's suggestions.

September 5, 998 ASR

Robert woke up earlier than he wanted Saturday morning. Dressed in his blue and green plaid pajamas, at 7:09 he trudged into his small kitchen and pressed the coffee button on his beverage dispenser. The no-cup light blinked and he took a white mug from the cupboard. He liked white mugs; defilements were easily seen. It passed inspection but he rinsed it anyway and set it in the beverage dispenser. He pulled a stool up to the counter and retrieved the cup with steaming coffee two seconds later. Not as good as fresh brewed, but the aroma was pleasing, the flavor was rich, and best of all it was fast. He didn't like waiting for his morning coffee.

With sunshine coming in the kitchen window warming his back, Robert fiddled with his ECD. He planned his other classes around Sub-Ancient Philosophy from Professor Robison so that he could devote extra time and attention to spending time with him; however Dr. Halverson made it clear that she was simply going to present the material the missing professor left behind and would not be doing any other tutoring, mentoring, or get involved with the students. It took no longer than two days to become quite apparent that his class load was going to be a lot lighter than he expected. He entered this first weekend without any homework; something that he couldn't remember happening since his second or third year at his first institution, Pueblo University.

The caffeine caught his mind up with his body and he took advantage of the situation to do some research for his book. Remembering how easily he was able to set himself up as an employer, he asked his ECD to access the Administration's data banks. He immediately started looking for information about the oldest people. He received some statistical information indicating that the oldest living person was 865 and there were five people who were 864. The list continued providing demographic information about the Earth's population based on age.

"I want to know everyone who is 860 years old and older - who the people are, where they live and their contact IDs," he queried of the data bank through his ECD.

"You are not authorized to receive that information," was the verbal and written reply.

"Oh we'll see about that." He scurried back to his bedroom with his ECD and found the access card he had received from his Board when his motion to write his book was approved. "Use this authorization," said Robert as he walked back to the kitchen. He touched the card to the ECD. Immediately the information he requested rolled onto his screen.

"Well, I'll be," exclaimed Robert aloud. "Thelma is the oldest person in the world. I thought she looked up there in her years but I wouldn't have guessed she's the oldest." The times he did chores for her in high school flashed through his mind. Her problems with her neighbor about her wayward chickens suppressed his fonder memories. Her age was evident as she and her neighbor met with the senior Board member, Henry, just before Robert's hearing. "No wonder she has problems with her chickens. I wonder if she's sharp enough to count them all. I'm definitely going to have to talk to her if for no other reason than get some more of her home baked cookies."

Robert looked over the remainder of the list which contained 150 names. There was only one name that he recognized. Tazi Ntari was well known for having been instrumental in developing the anti-gravity drive that powered everything from space ships to the small two-seater he and Jim took to the mountains. *Hmm, I wonder if he would be up for an interview.*

Then he came upon the name Josu Taratoricakena who was listed as being 861 years old. *That name sounds familiar but I can't seem to recall where I've heard it before.* "Computer, give me more detail about," Robert touched the name on the screen fearing that he wouldn't be able to come close enough to pronouncing the last name.

A new page appeared, listing more information about him than Robert really cared to see. "I guess if I had lived this long my data would be as long too," he mumbled as he began to scan down the pages. Near the bottom of the biography he spotted what he was looking for. Current manager of the Iluna Quebash Cafeteria at the North West Regional transit center. *That's it. This is the old guy Jim was telling me about. I really need to talk to him.*

Robert continued looking at the list of people and checking out their biographies. Soon he compiled a list of ten people that he wanted to interview for his book. If he timed it right, he could leave Friday night and visit each one personally on Saturday despite the fact that some lived half way around the world.

Next, he drafted a letter of introduction explaining his reason to visit and interview them for his book. He made sure that he included information that his book had been commissioned by the Administration just to add an air of authority. He sent the letter to each of the ten except for Josu. He changed his letter and left out the part about his book being commissioned by the Administration. He also added a note about being Jim's friend and reminded Josu of his meeting with Jim at the end of the summer.

By the end of the weekend he had meetings with each of the ten interviewees. He would finish two weeks before the end of the quarter so there wouldn't be any conflict with finals. He was feeling very good about his accomplishments.

Chapter 27

Justin arrived home just before dinner time. He opened the door and he was greeted by the wonderful aroma of pot roast. He went into the kitchen where Marilyn stood at the sink in front of the window. She turned as he entered and he passed the kitchen table which only had a vase with violet flowers on it. He hid a long stemmed rose behind him, then brought his arms around her to give her a hug without her seeing it. As he hugged her he could see their best place settings and candles on the dining room table. The dinner may have seemed ordinary, but the dining room set instead of the kitchen table told Justin that Marilyn wanted something.

He was sure that she was getting used to him arriving home earlier and always greeting her with a hug and "I love you." After a few weeks of counseling with Albert, Justin believed he was beginning to improve in his ability to show his love to Marilyn and she seemed to appreciate it.

"Hi, honey, I love you," he said while he hugged her.

Marilyn squirmed in his arms and pushed him away. "Me, too, now just go and get ready for dinner. It will be ready in five minutes." She turned back to the sink and started to wash some lettuce when Justin presented her with the rose.

She looked at the rose then back up at Justin. "Thanks, that looks nice. Would you put it in a vase and put it on the dining room table?" Justin was overwhelmed by her lack of enthusiasm.

He shrugged, wondering why the colder treatment tonight. "OK, I'll be right back." He found a bud vase in the cupboard, filled it with water and plunked the rose in it. He left the rose on the dining room table as he went to change into some leisure slacks and shirt. When he returned Marilyn was sitting in her usual chair at the side of the table. Dinner was on the table.

Justin sat down at the head of the table and reached over to take her hand. Marilyn bowed her head and Justin closed his eyes. "Father, thank you for your provision. Thank you for Marilyn and that she is always diligent in taking care of me and preparing meals. She is wonderful. Amen."

Justin reached for the salad and started scooping out some onto his salad plate. "So to what do I owe the fine dining atmosphere tonight?" he asked. He was trying hard to be as cheerful as he could despite the dread he felt.

"Justin, we need to talk," said Marilyn. "You go first."

OK, I thought I'd been doing a pretty good job of sharing my thoughts with her and telling her about my day. This has me stumped. Justin paused long enough before saying anything to make sure he didn't blurt out something stupid. That lead-in surely meant she was troubled and he needed to find the key so she would let him know why. "Sure, honey, you know I really appreciate the way you speak your mind. What's bothering you?"

"You are. Something's going on and I want to know what it is." She didn't look at Justin and didn't reach for any food.

Justin sat the salad bowl down. "Could you be a little more specific? I'm afraid I'm a little dense here and need a hint to help me explain."

She turned and looked him in the eye. "You know perfectly well what it is. You've been spending more time at home, helping me out around the house, being really nice, giving me hugs and back rubs. A lot of things like that. I must say that it has been quite nice but I want to know why. What are you trying to cover up? Have you been kicked off the Board? Have you been encouraging Robert in that silly book? What's going on?" asked Marilyn.

Justin reached for her hand but she drew it away. "Marilyn, I love you and I just felt that we've been growing apart. So I've been learning how to love you and show it to you."

"You've been learning how to love me?" The pitch of Marilyn's voice rose. "And just how are you learning?"

Justin sighed. "I've been meeting with an Encourager by the name of Albert Bailey. He has counseled people for over a thousand years. He teaches them how to have better marriages and how to love their spouses according to The Sovereign Yehowshuwa's principles," answered Justin.

"So you don't think our marriage is good enough? I certainly hope you haven't shared any of this with the other Board members." Marilyn's eyes narrowed as Justin felt his right eye twitch slightly when she said it. "You have, haven't you? Who was it?"

"I talked to Henry and he set me up with Albert," sighed Justin. *This is not going where I want it to go.*

"So now Henry thinks we have a rotten marriage and we need counseling. That's just great, Justin. How do you expect me to hold my head up when we go to worship or the Board wives meetings? I'll bet Wanda knows too. He probably told her." Marilyn slammed her napkin down on the table, ran to their bedroom, and slammed the door.

Where did I go wrong? Justin put his head into his hands and leaned his elbows on the table. He sat there for several minutes contemplating why he failed. He lost his appetite. Eventually he got up, cleared the dishes from the table, and cleaned up the kitchen, praying as he worked.

Justin went to his study and found Albert waiting for him, sitting on one of the two recliner chairs in front of his desk. Justin plopped down in the other. He felt extremely tired.

"It didn't work out the way you expected, did it?" asked Albert.

"No, it didn't. Marilyn was responding just as you said. She was acting more loving and seemed to be softening until this. What went wrong?" Justin hoped that Albert could tell him how to fix it.

"She appears to be very insecure about her position in society. That's why she is focusing on who knows that you are being counseled. She sees this as a threat to her position which is very important to her. She is focused on who knew, not on what they knew. She perceived your desire to become a better husband as an indication of a flawed marriage which she believes will reflect poorly on her."

Justin nodded. As usual, Albert hit the nail on the head.

"Be patient, you still have a lot of work to do. Don't give up but continue to love her. The next few weeks will be the roughest because she will wonder if this is really you or if you are just putting on an act. Your new interactions with her need to be fully established so that she will feel secure in your love and not depend on her position in society for fulfillment."

Justin didn't feel much better but he knew he must be consistent. That was one reason he cleaned up the kitchen. He wanted Marilyn to know that her tantrum wasn't going to reverse the changes he made in his behavior toward her. However, he imagined that she thought her life was ruined.

"Thanks, Albert. I'll be OK and will stick with it," he replied without a lot of enthusiasm.

"Hang in there. We'll talk again later." Albert disappeared.

Justin hung his head and choked back some sobs that kept welling to the surface.

The next few days proved to be the hardest for him. Marilyn jerked away from him whenever he tried to touch her. Whenever he complemented her, she would just say, "Oh you're just saying that because Albert says you should."

September 11, 998 ASR

Justin met with Albert again in his office at the hardware store. They were sitting on the couch. Justin leaned forward with his elbows on his knees, propping up his chin with both hands. He was despondent about the situation. "I'm really trying to do all you asked, Albert. Tell me there's something I've done wrong so that I can fix it and we can get on with life." Justin was near tears.

Albert put his hand on Justin's shoulder. "I know how you feel. I've been down this road myself and so have many others. I'm sorry, Justin; you are doing everything you can. You are a quick learner and you are doing quite well. What you need to do is keep up what you are doing. Soon it will become more natural to you as it becomes habit," answered Albert.

Justin shrugged and scoffed, "Well thanks for that, but I'm not feeling all that great about Marilyn right now either. I don't know how long I can continue."

Albert nodded and answered, "It's interesting that in my day most people acted on their feelings and that tended to get them into a whole bunch of problems. They did that instead of acting on what The Sovereign made clear in his scriptures. When I counseled them, I would tell them that they needed to act correctly in spite of their feelings. As they obeyed they found that their feelings would change. This is no different. As you practice loving Marilyn the feelings will follow. You need to give it some time."

Justin bit his lip then responded, "Thanks, Albert, I'll continue. I know that Yehowshuwa gives me the strength to do this because it is his way." He was resolute that he would see this through.

September 11, 998 ASR

Robert decided to interview Thelma first because she was from his own community. He figured that she wouldn't provide any valuable input for his book but he could get some good practice with her. Besides, it would show that he had done due diligence and hadn't simply sought out people who would provide what he wanted to hear.

Home was just about as far away from Midrib as anyone could get so he planned to leave right after his last class on Friday, finish any studies he might have on the road and then sleep the rest of the way. Because of the direction of travel he would be racing the sun and would arrive early in the morning. He scheduled an early breakfast meeting with Thelma so he could immediately head back to school and get back late in the evening on Sunday.

As soon as class was over Robert told Kevin and Samantha goodbye for the weekend and headed for the closest convy station. He already had his backpack loaded with the necessities for the weekend trip.

September 12, 998 ASR

The trip went as planned and he arrived at the Central Region center about 5:30 in the morning after traveling nearly 24 hours. He took about a half hour to use the regional center facilities to shower and shave, then caught a local convy that took him into the city and back out to the suburbs on the other side. He arrived near the community hall with about twenty minutes to spare. He decided to take a walk to collect his thoughts and review his interview questions. He arrived at Thelma's house precisely at 8:00 AM and rang the door bell.

"I'm coming, Robert," called Thelma. It seemed quite a while before she came to the door and opened it wide. The most wonderful breakfast smells wafted through the opening to Robert's waiting nostrils. "Hello Robert. My, it's been a long time since I've seen you. I was delighted to hear that you're writing a book and I've been looking forward to your visit. Please come in. Breakfast is almost ready and we can start your interview while we eat." She stepped aside and gestured toward the small kitchen.

Robert stepped in and walked to the kitchen table which was already set with bowls of fresh cut strawberries, cream, and sugar. Fresh coffee was brewed, not from instant like the beverage dispensers provide, and ready to pour. He glanced toward the counter and saw steam coming from a waffle maker. He also heard the sizzling of bacon and eggs cooking on the stove. He thought that just about covered everything he had smelled at the door when he spied a plate of warm cinnamon rolls covered with a thick creamy gooey frosting sitting on the far side of the table.

"Wow, Mrs. Thornton, this is really quite a spread for breakfast. You didn't need to go through all this for me."

Thelma smiled. "Please call me Thelma, Robert, every one does. I know your Mom and Dad so I know you're still a bachelor. I thought you could use a good home cooked breakfast and I really enjoy cooking. Please, be seated."

Robert sat down and marveled at how gracious Thelma was. When he saw her talking to Henry she had been quite agitated and almost befuddled. Now she was in her own home and appeared confident even though she still wasn't moving very fast. She shuffled between the stove, table, and waffle maker setting down serving bowls with enough food for five people. After only a couple of minutes she sat down and bowed her head.

"Dear Sovereign, thank you so much for sending Robert over here this morning to share breakfast with me. Please give us wisdom as we talk about this book you want him to write and of course, we thank you for this food and all your provision. Amen."

"Amen," repeated Robert.

"So, Robert, how is that you got started with the idea to write another book about the Last Battle?" asked Thelma as she handed him the plate with fried eggs.

Robert took the plate and scooped off a couple of eggs while he answered, "I've always been interested in history, archeology, and psychology. These three pursuits have led me to read a lot and question a lot. It's in my nature to ask why and what if. As a result I met a lot of young people in universities who are also asking the same questions but aren't finding any answers. It appears that at the heart of the matter is the question, 'What if the Last Battle and the time before it didn't really happen the way we are told?'"

Thelma's left eyebrow shot up. Robert continued quickly, "They ask this question because there seems to be only one point of view in history and that just bothers people who expect to see different opinions and perspectives of history. As a result they mistrust the Administration and are seeking answers outside of the regular channels." He tried to emphasize *they* each time he used the word. "They see me as a person who can objectively research and confirm whether or not the historical accounts are accurate. That's why I've come to you. You are one of the oldest people on the earth and you have a perspective that is closer to the actual events than anyone else."

"So you think that there is a possibility that The Sovereign has been lying to us and covering up what really happened to make himself look good. Do you think perhaps that The Chancellor Ben-Shaachar may not have been such a villain in history as it appears?" asked Thelma now with knitted eyebrows.

Exactly, wow, she's really sharp. I'd better be careful with her. "No ma'am, Not me. I wouldn't put it exactly that way but there are some people who apparently are thinking that way." Robert was more than a bit shocked that Thelma had seen through his introduction so clearly and quickly. He didn't want to let on to her that he was leaning more and more toward this conclusion. Every discussion group solidified his conviction but he couldn't afford to let anyone who was strongly loyal to Yehowshuwa know his position. He suspected that Thelma was extremely loyal to him. "I'm just looking for the truth." Somehow he didn't quite feel as convinced when he said it as he tried to sound.

"Very well, young man, this is your interview. What would you like to hear?" asked Thelma as she relaxed and picked up her cup and took a sip of coffee.

"Great." Robert took out his ECD and pulled up his list of interview questions. "You don't mind if I record our conversation do you?"

"Not at all," she replied.

"Thanks. First of all can you tell me a bit about your parents or grandparents? The people you were closest to who actually survived the Last Battle," asked Robert as he placed his ECD on the table.

Thelma sat her cup down, then looked up as if she was trying to see some memory in the back of her head. "My mamma and papa were both about five years old when the Last Battle went down. They were born during the Great Time of Trouble while The Chancellor was in control of the world. Their parents were killed when The Sovereign Yehowshuwa returned. They were both sold out to Ben-Shaachar and were in complete rebellion against The Sovereign. You know that no one loyal to that villain survived. Mamma and Papa weren't old enough to choose sides before then." She emphasized the word villain.

Robert was a bit disappointed. "So they weren't really old enough to remember the events of the Last Battle or the Great Time of Trouble?"

She shook her head, "Oh no, surprisingly they did have vivid memories. When The Sovereign came they were living in squalor because their parents had pretty much abandoned them to their own devices while they indulged in drugs and other destructive behavior that were prolific during the era. My mamma wasn't sure who her papa was." Tears were coming to Thelma's eyes.

Robert picked up his ECD and noted the comment about drugs and destructive behavior. *Yup, standard non-specific generalization.*

"During the reconstruction after the Battle, they were both adopted by families who survived because they were loyal to Yehowshuwa. My adoptive grams and gramps were all in their thirties and forties when the Great Time of Trouble started. Mamma's new parents were married only a couple of years when the world was turned upside down as The Sovereign evacuated his people and The Chancellor took over. Papa's parents were older and had two young kids who were taken by The Sovereign. Some time after the change of administration they all were forced to make a choice between Yehowshuwa and Ben-Shaachar. Mama's parents had already made the decision but Papa's hadn't. They wanted to remain neutral but they had to hide from Ben-Shaachar because he was forcing people to be loyal to him. The only ones that would help them were followers of Yehowshuwa. So they, too, eventually made their allegiance to The Sovereign and were rescued when he returned and ushered them into this new era." Thelma continued talking as she picked at a waffle.

Robert was enjoying the food more than the story. The claim that The Chancellor forced people to be loyal to him was another standard aspect of the documentation he had already studied and questioned.

"There were millions of orphans that needed homes and everyone pitched in to take care of them. So that's how my mamma and papa came to live with my grandparents," explained Thelma.

That peaked Robert's interest. "Were you able to get to know your adoptive grandparents very well? Did they tell you about the Great Time of Trouble or the Last Battle?"

"Oh yes. You know that when the restoration occurred the whole world was healed from all the destruction that took place during the Great Time of Trouble and the eras before that. But it still isn't perfect as it was in the beginning. And likewise the people that lived through that time were not completely restored from the severe physical trauma of the time or all the imperfections of being mortal. Even so, they lived to be about 350 years old so I got to know them in my younger years. I was just a bit younger then you when Grams on my mamma's side was the last to pass away. Being as young as they were Mamma and Papa faired better than their parents and lived about five hundred years. Still a far cry from how long those of us born after the restoration live." She was looking toward Robert as she spoke but seemed to be looking past him.

He picked up his ECD again and noted the reference to ages. *If Yehowshuwa did all this restoring why didn't he take care of everything? Why is there still death? If he is so all powerful, why doesn't he fix everything?*

She still didn't pay much attention to her food as she continued, "We loved to sit and listen to our grandparents tell about the Great Time of Trouble and how The Sovereign helped them through that time, even though he wasn't manifested physically like he is now. They told stories of hiding for weeks and months from Ben-Shaachar's forces, then fleeing to another location. They thought they had finally run out of places to hide when Yehowshuwa came back and rescued them."

Robert held up his fork and interrupted her, "Thelma, I've read some of the stories from the survivors and I can't imagine that people could treat each other that way. Why did you love to hear those stories?"

Thelma nodded thoughtfully, "It may seem strange to say that. There was a lot of suffering and death. It was the worst time in all of human history. Evil was rampant and had no bounds the way they described it. We who have not experienced evil can't really comprehend what it was like. There was only one reason we loved the stories and that was because they always ended with The Sovereign's return and the triumph of right over wrong."

She paused and looked down, sadness etched on her face. Robert thought she looked very old as the smile disappeared from her face.

"The world was so dark and it seemed like humanity was doomed, then he came back. Within a few minutes of the sky lighting up, Ben-Shaachar's whole army was devastated. All people on the earth who declared their allegiance to Ben-Shaachar, whether they were at the battle site or elsewhere were killed. It was a joyous day for Yehowshuwa's people."

"That sounds terrible. How could the death of that many people bring joy?" interjected Robert taking notes in his ECD.

She looked up sternly at Robert. "As sad and horrible as that sounds you have to remember what they were all trying to do to us, to our ancestors. Without any conscience they tortured them mercilessly, doing things to them that couldn't even be mentioned, then they beheaded them. Their goal was to track down and kill anyone who had not declared loyalty to their leader, The Chancellor."

Robert nodded his head and muttered, "What a terrible time." *I wonder how much of that is true and how much is fabricated.* He was starting to lose his appetite for the interview.

Thelma kept eye contact with Robert. "Our ancestors rejoiced not because people died but because now evil was curtailed and locked away. It was unfortunate that so many died but they only received the just punishment that was due them. They rejoiced because now they would be living in the presence of The Sovereign. Under his rule all the atrocities of the past would be over and he would not allow that to happen again."

Robert sighed, "Well, you're right. I can't imagine anything that horrible. It must have been a most traumatic time for your grandparents."

He wanted to change the subject and get on with digging up something that would verify his suspicions. He knew his next question would have to be carefully worded to get any good information. "When they told you about these times did they ever give you any reason to believe that there was anything beneficial about The Chancellor's rule but that something went wrong?"

"Ha! Are you serious, Robert?" snorted Thelma.

He tried to hide his surprise at Thelma's reaction and reworded the question. "Well, they weren't always loyal to The Sovereign Yehowshuwa, were they? Did they tell you about that and why they didn't join him sooner?"

Thelma held up her boney finger and shook it at him. "Ah, now that's a different story. Yes, they did tell us some things about that time. However, they all had different reasons for their rebellion against Yehowshuwa."

Robert's hope that she would provide some insight to her grandparents' reluctance to join with The Sovereign melted. "Rebellion against The Sovereign? I don't think I've heard it put that way before. Just because they hadn't declared their position didn't make them rebels, did it?"

"I guess that depends on your perspective. He has said that anyone who isn't with him is against him. One of his first followers said that everyone follows Ben-Shaachar until they decide to follow The Sovereign. Of course people who haven't decided whole heartedly to follow Yehowshuwa usually deny they are committed to Ben-Shaachar. Anyway that's how my grandparents described themselves before they declared their position and joined The Sovereign," said Thelma as she took another sip of coffee.

Robert mentally rolled his eyes. I might as well sit back and listen. I knew she wouldn't reveal any skeletons in the closet.

Thelma refilled Robert's coffee and continued, "It's hard to describe what they went through because we've always been under The Sovereign Yehowshuwa's rule. He and his Administration have kept evil away. We just can't comprehend what it was like back then. We see some things that aren't right now but people are usually quick about setting them straight. You were there that day that Marge brought me to court because I couldn't keep my chickens in line. I was wrong not to ask for help when I needed it. Later, Marge admitted that she was wrong for getting angry and not trying to see my need. Both of us were putting ourselves and our feelings ahead of the needs of others. Now you multiply that by a thousand times and you'll get an idea of what it was like back then when they didn't have The Sovereign in control of their lives. People looked out for themselves first instead of others."

Robert was glad his ECD was catching everything she was saying. He was having a hard time focusing. It was just the party line. He could have been interviewing The Sovereign himself.

"Gramps Perkins, he was my papa's papa, said he was a businessman. He traveled the country selling some kind of software programs for their ancient computers. Before The Sovereign pulled his people out, he said he cheated when he thought he could get away with it. Usually by fibbing about how good the programs were or when they could deliver just to make a sale. He did it because he felt he needed to do it to earn enough money to pay for all the things he wanted. He said he was careful so that only the people that deserved it got cheated."

Robert sat back sipping his coffee. He could tell Thelma was on a roll. *I wonder how many times she's told this story and how much it's changed over time.*

"In the evenings in a hotel room he said he'd look at what they called TV and search for programs showing naked men and women doing things that people ought not to do, much less record and put on a video. He said he didn't think it was harming anyone so he just did it because it made him feel good. Later, he understood how much it hurt his marriage."

I wonder what Thelma would do if she had heard our discussion about sex the other night. Robert smiled as the thought of her exploding during an underground meeting came to mind. Thelma frowned and Robert changed his expression appropriately.

She continued, "Then all The Sovereign's people disappeared. Gramps said it was as if all the restraints had been taken away from him. He cheated and lied even more when he was selling and he didn't even care. It seemed like no one trusted anyone and they expected you to lie, cheat, and steal. Everyone was doing it. What was worse was that now when he went on a sales call he could easily find a woman in the office that was willing to do what he had only watched before. He had no loyalty to my grams and he was just out to fulfill all his pleasures."

Robert felt his face flush at the mention of elicit sex. *I wonder if I'll ever get over that.* He hoped that Thelma hadn't noticed.

Without giving any indication that she noticed Robert's reaction, Thelma continued with her story, "Grams had become just about the same as Gramps. They saw each other when he was in town and that was just about all of a marriage they had. They thought it was great that they offered each other the freedom to do as they wanted. They thought that they were being modern and were fitting into the new culture perfectly."

Robert was still wondering what was so wrong about this kind of freedom. He squirmed a bit and somehow felt excited by the story.

Thelma was moving right along with her narrative, "Soon they found that it took more and more to give them the excitement and good feelings that they desired. When they couldn't find a greater thrill, they got depressed. They turned to drugs and alcohol to help, but that only gave them temporary relief."

Robert was still thinking about the discussion his group had. He felt his heart skip a beat as he pictured Hillary crossing her legs in her short skirt. *I can't imagine needing more. Even this gets me going.*

She paused and took a bite of her waffle. "Grams tried to kill herself and ended up in a hospital. That in itself was a miracle because most people didn't care if you tried to kill yourself. They just let it happen or even helped you. In the hospital, a nurse told her about Yehowshuwa and how he could give meaning to her life."

Robert thought it was pretty stupid for someone to try to kill himself. *Maybe people back then just couldn't handle it.*

"About the same time Gramps lost his job, not because of his unethical behavior but because he simply didn't show up enough. They spent all their money on drugs. That's another story because people said that by legalizing drugs the prices would be lower and people wouldn't have to steal or sell everything to get them. But it didn't happen. Anyway, he found himself in the dirtiest hotel room in the scummiest part of town coming off a drug high and no way to get any more to counteract the withdrawal. In that messy place he found one of The Sovereign's books and started reading in the brief time between his high and the onset of hallucinations."

Robert was trying to imagine what these reactions to drugs were like. He couldn't relate it to anything he knew.

Like an ECD set on automatic, Thelma kept right on talking, "At almost the same time, Grams and Gramps discovered the same thing. They understood for the first time that they had a fatal problem in their lives. It was their own desire to rule themselves. They found that in their efforts to please themselves and have the good life that they had deeply offended The Sovereign's father who had made them. In total opposition to what they previously believed they understood that they were in enmity against Yehowshuwa and that they were reaping the consequences of not following his plan for their lives. What was worse, if they died without his forgiveness, they would suffer the consequences forever. At first that seemed even more depressing because there wasn't any way they could earn his forgiveness. The only way they could be accepted by him was to have lived a life of perfect obedience and they had blown that chance long ago."

It sure is different now. Enforcers and the Administration make sure we live in accordance with The Sovereign's plan. I'm not sure where this is going.

"Then they learned that The Sovereign already paid the penalty for their rebellion the first time he came to the earth. His father arranged it so that he became a man and lived as a man. The only difference is that he wasn't in rebellion. He obeyed all the laws his father established. No one else before or after could do that. Even people who think they've been good have to admit that they haven't been perfect."

Thelma paused and looked intently at Robert. His stomach churned. She continued, "Ben-Shaachar had Yehowshuwa framed and killed hoping that his death would alter the set end of times."

Robert nodded as he now recognized the story. Theology 101 – The old need-a-perfect-person-to-pay-for-the-sins-of-the-feeble story. I might as well let her go on.

"The Sovereign was the one person who should not need to experience death because he didn't deserve it. However, his father predicted this long before and said that because he died without blame his death was acceptable as the punishment for the rebellion of the whole human race. His father gave proof of this by raising him from the dead after three days."

"Wait a minute." Robert interrupted. "If he died for everyone's offenses and paid the price, why were there still consequences for your grandparents?"

"That's simple. The pardon for those offences is offered as a gift to anyone who will accept it. It's like any other kind of gift. It doesn't really become yours until you take it. His pardon comes only to those who accept it and you can't accept it if you don't think you need it," answered Thelma. "By accepting the gift you acknowledge that Yehowshuwa really should be your sovereign and you're willing to change so that he is. Many people are not willing to admit their need and others are not willing to change. They aren't willing to give up their wicked ways and they aren't willing to let The Sovereign be their lord, if you know what that means."

"You mean that's like he's the king and can do whatever he wants with you?" I don't get it. He IS king and he can do whatever he wants whether I agree or not.

Thelma took her coffee cup in both hands and turned it around on the table as she talked, "Yeah, that true, but it's more than that you are willing to do what he wants. While this is really at the heart of it there is also gratitude that he took our place, suffered, and died instead of us. That demonstrates just how much he loves us."

"Getting back to your grandparents, this is when and how they declared their allegiance to The Sovereign? What happened with them next?" Robert didn't see how all this was helping him write his book and he wanted to move on.

"Exactly. When they surrendered their lives to him he actually began to live in them through his spirit and empowered them to overcome their destructive behavior. For Gramps it was a miracle because he didn't suffer the usual withdrawal symptoms from the drugs. Grams was released from the hospital and they both set out to find each other. With so many disasters happening they weren't even sure if the other was still alive. They both joined The Sovereign's underground and after about six months they finally found each other. From that time until The Sovereign returned they were together, concentrating on surviving, running from The Chancellor's forces, and trying to sway others to The Sovereign's side."

Robert felt an involuntary shudder at the thought of having someone's spirit living in him. The rest of it seemed like a rehash of what she'd already said. *Maybe there would be something useful on her mother's side of the family.* "What about your grandparents on your mother's side. Were they also involved in all this evil?"

Thelma took another sip of coffee. "No, they weren't. Grams and Gramps Twill were quite different people. They were very involved in The Sovereign's organization before he pulled his people. While they thought they were members because of their activities and their exemplary lives, they had never accepted his remedy for their transgressions. You see, they thought that they didn't need his forgiveness because they were better than most people. They didn't realize that no one other than The Sovereign Yehowshuwa himself has ever lived a life good enough not to need his forgiveness."

In spite of the coffee, Robert was finding it hard to pay attention.

Thelma droned on, "When The Sovereign pulled all his people off the earth Grams and Gramps Twill were shocked to be left behind. They weren't alone but unlike some who got angry and never admitted their need, they started digging through his book and discovered the truth."

Robert stifled a yawn by clenching his teeth. He was pretty sure Thelma didn't notice.

Thelma's voice seemed far away, "It wasn't long afterward that Ben-Shaachar declared all of The Sovereign's organization illegal so they had to go underground. As The Chancellor's hatred for The Sovereign and his people grew, they lost their jobs and were excluded from participating in the economy in any way. They couldn't even legally buy groceries or raise produce and sell it to others. Ben-Shaachar escalated his persecution and eventually declared allegiance to The Sovereign to be a capital offense. My grandparents and others had joined together all over the world to establish a complex underground to aid and assist their comrades. Then like Grams and Gramps Perkins they did what they could to recruit the undecided to The Sovereign's way."

Robert was still fighting to stay engaged in the interview. He felt fortunate he had picked up something for another question. "Why didn't they try to convince those who had decided to follow The Chancellor?"

"During the last half of the Great Time of Trouble, Ben-Shaachar issued a decree that everyone must worship him. If they didn't then they would be beheaded. When they agreed they were given an identity mark that was tattooed on their forehead or hand. Everyone needed this proof of his or her allegiance to Ben-Shaachar to conduct any commerce. Inwardly it meant that they had sold their soul to Ben-Shaachar. It was an irrevocable decision that prevented them from changing their allegiance even if they wanted."

It impressed Robert that Thelma never missed a beat. She always had an answer and it led right into her story.

"At first some of Yehowshuwa's people tried to persuade those with a mark but it soon became evident that it was too dangerous. Ninety nine percent of the time they were turned in to the authorities and killed if caught. A few with the mark realized their mistake and became extremely despondent. They either committed suicide or buried themselves in dugs trying to escape the reality of their decision. No one was known to have the mark and change their allegiance"

"That's really interesting that they couldn't change their minds. I would have thought that The Sovereign could provide them with the ability to do that," commented Robert as he noted in his ECD that The Sovereign refused or was unable to rescue these people. *If he is all loving wouldn't he want to help them also?* "After all, he is supposed to be all powerful."

Thelma narrowed her eyes and tilted her head slightly before continuing, "Most assuredly he does have the ability to give people the power to change their minds. Otherwise none of us would ever be able to declare our loyalty to him. However, at that time and with his knowledge of each person's heart, he chose to let those with a mark forever live with their decision. They made such a definite choice to worship evil that he gave them the desire of their hearts. Even those who realized their mistake didn't want to correct it. You might say that Yehowshuwa respected their decision and let them live with the consequences."

Robert heard enough to know nothing she said would help him. He wanted to end the interview and move on. "Thelma, what you told me agrees very closely with what others have documented in the past. It's pretty general in nature. Did you have any specific stories that they told you that you could give me? You know, details that could be cross checked with other historical documents?"

Thelma sat back and raised her eyebrows. "Do you think I haven't told you the truth?"

Robert put up a hand in surrender. "No, not at all. It's just that historians look for more than details to make the stories interesting. We also look for details that are different in various stories which show that different people have different perspectives. You see that even in the four historical narratives about The Sovereign's first visit to the earth."

Thelma chuckled slightly. "I kind of thought you might like some more details so I dug up some of my grandparents' stories out of my archives. We recorded them when they were still with us. As the years have gone by and technology has changed I've been able to transfer them from one recording media to another. There are about twenty to thirty hours of stories here all recorded in their own voices. I think you'll be able to see that they match up with other stories that have been recorded." She leaned over and handed a data module to Robert.

He took the button sized module and stared at it in awe. He was embarrassed that he hadn't thought of looking up the actual audio and video stories of the Last Battle survivors' stories. He had read many accounts but didn't realize that they might have come from recorded interviews. Then the idea struck him that there might be audio and video archives that were recorded during the Great Time of Trouble. If so, then he might have the opportunity to see the opposing viewpoint as well. "Thank you very much, Thelma. This is really valuable and I know it will be very useful for my research. Thank you so much for your time and the wonderful breakfast. I'd like to stay longer but I need to return to Midrib for classes on Monday." Robert got up to leave. "Say hello to Henry for me if you see him."

Robert was disappointed. He didn't find anything that suggested that her grandparents colored their stories to paint The Chancellor Ben-Shaachar in a worse light or covered up anything to make The Sovereign look better. Everything she related had the same remarkable consistency with everything he had already read and that was what bothered him the most.

September 13, 998 ASR

Robert navigated the return trip to Midrib and arrived home late Sunday afternoon. He was quite tired but also very excited about the possibility of finding witnesses from the past to help him write his book.

Chapter 28

Chuck sat at his desk staring at the blank view screen on the wall beside the door. He couldn't get the image of Zophia out of his mind. He could still see her sitting naked in the middle of the pentagram in the mess hall, a short candle flickering at each point of the pentagram. He was in a quandary wondering what he should say to Zophia when she reported to him. It was one thing to see the Edenians but he wasn't sure he wanted his crew to become nudists. His thoughts were interrupted by a knock on his door.

"Enter," he responded, still trying to get the vision out of his mind.

Zophia entered, fully clothed and stood before his desk appearing rather stoic. Chuck was both relived and disappointed to see her in her jumper. "You wanted to see me, Chuck?"

She called me Chuck! When did she start that? It's always been Captain, Sir, or Captain Andrews. "Ah, yes, have a seat. We need to talk about your, uh," Chuck paused. This nudity subject is just too awkward.

Zophia took a visitor chair and adjusted the height so the she was at his eye level. *Well, at least that hasn't changed.*

"I suppose you want to talk to me about why I was sitting naked in the mess hall when everyone woke up this morning." Zophia's face burst into a grin and she leaned forward. "There was no need to erect the partitions around me. I wasn't distracted by you or the rest of the crew. Did you like what you saw?"

Chuck felt his face grow warm. The thoughts he had about her were not what the captain of a star ship should have, much less admit to his subordinate.

"You don't need to answer, Chuck. I can read your mind and thank you very much. However we have much more important things to talk about. We need to get started training the crew so that everyone will be fully equipped to train others when we get home." Zophia sat back in her chair.

Her dark brown eyes glowed and her face was radiant. He couldn't picture a more alluring woman. *I've been able to repress these thoughts for 25 years, why not now?* He shook his head trying to focus his thoughts back on the subject at hand.

"Ah, yeah, training. Well, it seems like you have the inside track on what it will take. What do you need?" he asked.

Zophia's smile and wink let Chuck know that she was enjoying his difficulty but she made it easier for him as she started to outline her plan. "First we need a training center similar to those we used on Eden. It doesn't have to be as large so I would like to convert one of the empty storage rooms."

"Sure, that makes sense. We've used up most of the supplies we started with. I think the room on deck 22 above the hydroponics gardens would be the best place.

It's in a central location and more than big enough to accommodate half of the crew if you wanted to train that many at one time." Chuck felt a bit more under control making an executive decision.

"Can we get started right away? I don't want to lose any time," she asked with the most serious expression she'd had since entering.

"I'll notify Marti to meet with you and some of her crew. You can tell her what you want. Do you have any idea who you want to train first?"

Chuck was caught off-guard as Zophia quickly stood and leaned over his desk. She extended her right arm and touched his left ear lobe with her long brown finger. She drew it back, rubbing the tip of her finger down his jaw line and to his chin. "I think maybe you should be in the first class," she said as she cocked her head slightly to the left, then stood straight.

His heart was racing. In all of his 175 years as a bachelor he had never felt this excitement at the touch of a woman. He wasn't sure what to do. Something kept him from returning the affection. "I, ah, think maybe I should pass on the first rounds and concentrate on running the ship until we're closer to home."

She turned and started for the door, then stopped and looked coyly over her shoulder. "Suit yourself, Chuck. I can wait." She winked and left the office.

Chuck used his mental telepathy to contact Marti. *Marti?*

She didn't answer. It wasn't the first time he hadn't been able to contact someone. He used his ECD.

"Yes, Chuck, what is it?" she responded almost immediately.

"Zophia is headed down to the central storage room on deck 22. She needs to use it for training. Can you get a couple of your people and meet her there? She will let you know what needs to be done. Make this a top priority."

Marti hesitated slightly. "OK. I can be there in about five minutes. Ah, she is wearing clothes, isn't she?"

Chuck laughed, "Yes she is. But you might keep an eye on her. She does seem to be acting a bit differently since her near death experience."

"Different? How?"

"I don't want to color your observation. Just let me know if she doesn't seem her normal self." Chuck couldn't tell Marti what just transpired in his office, not in a million years.

"OK, I'll keep on the alert. Should we tell Alex? Maybe she isn't completely healed and needs some medical attention?" asked Marti.

"She appears quite physically fit. This is more personality-wise. Check in with me after your meeting." Chuck closed his ECD.

Chuck folded his hands behind his head and looked at the ceiling. *Where is this going?* A few possibilities passed through his mind as he wondered what a more intimate relationship with Zophia might be like. On the other hand that might not be good for the crew. He needed to maintain their respect for him as the captain. Then again he let them address him by his first name for the last 25 years. *Maybe it would be OK.*

September 18, 998 ASR

Robert and Jim sat in a corner of the student union building cafeteria before classes Friday morning. Their small table only had room for two, which suited Robert for his topic of conversation with Jim. The cafeteria was noisy with many students clanking dishes on the tables, scooting chairs in and out of the many tables, and loud but indistinct conversations buzzing.

Robert leaned closely to Jim, speaking only loud enough for him to hear. "Jim, we've been meeting with Kevin and Sam almost daily after classes for the last couple of weeks. What do you think about introducing them to *The Question* and seeing if they're interested in the sample topics?" asked Robert.

Jim scratched his head. "They certainly seem like they would be interested. I've never heard as much 'what if' talk from anyone before. I suppose it has a lot to do with that class you guys are taking but it sure has sparked many interesting conversations. I think we've already talked about things that have been in *The Question* so I don't see any reason why we shouldn't invite them to look at the samplers," replied Jim.

"I agree, however, we need to make sure that both of them are ready and won't expose this to the Administration. So how do you rate them?" asked Robert, munching on his egg, sausage, and cheese muffin.

Jim scrunched his mouth to the side then answered, "Kevin is a bit hard to read. He's really smart and it's almost like he's holding back at times so that we won't feel inferior. That's kind of nice, thinking about our feelings and all but on the other hand, I sometimes wonder if he's only saying things that we want to hear. You'd think that he'd slip up and say something that wasn't consistent. The more I think about him though, he does seem to be very insightful and ready to listen to new ideas. I guess I can't hold being smart against him so I'll say sure. He's ready."

Robert agreed with that assessment. Kevin wasn't transparent and was hard to read but he would make a good recruit.

Jim's eyes lit up as he continued, "Now on the other hand, Sam is pretty transparent. She seems to be loyal to The Sovereign but is always questioning things. That questioning is exactly what we're looking for. We want people who are ready to question, learn, and stretch. There's no question she's smart. I've never met anyone quite like her before. I think she's even more wonderful now after two weeks than when we first met her. Oh yeah, I think she would be great." Jim nodded eagerly.

Robert shook his head slightly at Jim's obvious infatuation with Samantha but he did agree with him. "Good observations, Jim. I don't think either would be alarmed at the sample material and by the time they are involved more deeply they wouldn't think of exposing *The Question* or our meetings. If they did, they would be just as culpable as we are and that's a good deterrent against blabbing. When we meet them this afternoon you can do the honors."

Robert sat back, pleased with the way Jim analyzed Kevin and Samantha's personalities and the potential impact *The Question* might have on them. Jim was developing well under his mentorship.

After class Robert, Samantha and Kevin found their usual table in the student union cafeteria. It was nearly vacant which would allow Robert and Jim the opportunity to introduce the others to *The Question* without worrying about being overheard. Jim arrived late as usual.

Jim sat down, wasted no time after the pleasantries of a good afternoon, and then jumped right into the pitch to introduce newcomers to *The Question*. "You know a lot of the stuff we've been talking about lately is really quite provocative. Robert and I are part of a group that meets regularly to talk about these things and other stuff too. I'd like to show you some of the topics. Do you think you might be interested?"

Kevin responded with a slightly bored expression, "Depends on what you've got. If it's mind-expanding, challenging, and not just a bunch of sophomoric game-playing, I might be interested."

Robert was alarmed by Kevin's comment. What started out as a routine recruitment became more complicated and was going to need his full attention. Samantha started to interject something but Jim replied too quickly.

"Sophomoric? I'm talking serious stuff here. I know you guys are ahead of me with this sub-ancient-philosophical-analyze-to-death-the-way-people-used-to-think stuff, but this will invigorate your brain cells a bit too," snapped Jim.

"Easy Jim. No offense. It's just that there always seems to be different debate clubs and organizations on campus that promise to enrich your lives but turn out to be time-wasters. What do you have that these others groups don't have?" Kevin raised his eyebrows slightly and look Jim directly in the eye.

"Yeah, what are you talking about? I wouldn't mind seeing what you've got but I have a lot of classes and they take up a lot of time. I've already gotten involved with a couple of dorm groups and I'm starting to feel a bit overloaded," added Samantha.

Jim bit his lower lip and looked at Robert as if he was unsure how he should proceed then continued, "Perhaps I should show them one of the initial discussion topics rather than a sampler, Robert. The samplers are pretty generic and don't have much meat in them. Do you think we can skip the preliminary stuff?"

Robert mentally rolled his eyes wondering why Jim always had to be in such a hurry. Now he had committed well beyond what he should have. How can you put a teaser out like that and not follow up? Robert carefully looked back and forth at Kevin and Samantha, trying to get a reading on what they were thinking. He decided to commit. After all, these two certainly couldn't get him in any more trouble than the risk he took with his Board meeting.

"OK," responded Robert as he leaned forward, "but before we show you this I want you know that this isn't an authorized campus group that publishes these discussion topics. These topics are distributed to university students all over the world and some of the larger high schools. Now this may sound a bit weird, but the group doesn't want us to show this stuff to anyone unless they promise not to tell others about it. I know I can trust you two to not freak out or blab this all over the place but I must get your promise."

Samantha frowned. "So what could be so mind-expanding that we can't tell others and why are you able to tell us?" she asked.

Robert looked around to see if anyone was listening, then continued, "Jim and I have been through training to screen new people. If we thought you weren't receptive or were obviously opposed to the discussions then we wouldn't have invited you to even look at the samplers. And Jim is right, they wouldn't challenge you enough to even consider going deeper. I can't tell you anything more about the discussion subjects than what we've already said. They will challenge your thinking."

"I still don't see why it has to be secretive. Do they think that they might get students expelled for brain strain?" Samantha said with a chuckle. She shrugged her shoulders when no one laughed. "I guess it couldn't hurt to look. OK I promise I won't tell anyone."

"What about you, Kevin? Do you want in or are you afraid you might be bored to death?" asked Jim.

"Sure, I promise I won't tell anyone that doesn't already know about your discussion topics. What you've told us makes it sound quite intriguing." Kevin appeared eager enough, more so than when the subject was first mentioned.

Jim rubbed his hands together. "Great! Then I'll give you software for your ECD that will allow you to view the first discussion topic. This software will only allow you to view the topic while you are holding the ECD. It works by sampling your DNA and your brainwaves, then authorizes the document to be un-encrypted. So after I transfer the software to your ECD you can start it," explained Jim. "Are you ready?"

"My ECD can do that?" asked Samantha.

"Sure. It already has a thumb print and retina scanners, voice recognition inputs as well as radio frequency receivers. The people who invented this software found out that the thumb print scanner also recognizes DNA. The radio receiver is able to detect your brainwaves. When you start the installation it will ask you to read some random words then scan brainwaves in the vicinity of the ECD. Since the random words don't relate to normal communication it is able to distinguish your brain waves from other nearby people."

Robert laughed at the blank stares on Samantha's and Kevin's faces. "Trust me," he said, "it will work just fine and protect the data so than no one will be able to see it or force you to reveal it to anyone."

Jim transferred the software from his ECD and Kevin and Samantha started the installation sequence. "Just follow instructions and let me know when you are finished."

"All installed," Kevin announced.

"Me, too," agreed Samantha.

Jim pushed a few digital buttons on his screen. "All right. Now I register you with the central server as new accounts and you'll receive your first discussion topic in a few seconds. After you read it over, we'll get together to discuss it and then move on to the next topic. If you are amenable you can then join us in our larger group for more advanced topics," explained Jim.

Robert was pleased with the way Jim handled the introduction and that neither Samantha nor Kevin became alarmed at the confidentiality he imposed.

Kevin arrived back at his dorm, plopped down on the small beige couch, and put his feet up on the scarred coffee table. He took his ECD from his shirt pocket and looked at the first discussion topic that arrived. It observed the supposed decrease in Enforcer activity in recent years. He had already read it during his briefings along with almost every topic that the underground developed since the first publication of *The Question*. This one was carefully crafted to make a person question whether or not The Sovereign was indeed omniscient and omnipotent without stating it directly. He remembered with disgust that all of the topics took the same approach but questioned various characteristics of Yehowshuwa and the Administration. Some attacked the way society was organized, others what was truly right or wrong. Kevin marveled that people would be sucked into the underground meetings and let themselves become brainwashed so easily. He reminded himself that without the mind of Yehowshuwa, he too would be just as susceptible as anyone else. However, he reasoned that Samantha was too sharp and spiritually discerning to buy into this stuff.

He quickly checked with the Administration to see if Samantha had started reading the first discussion topic. They informed him that she was about halfway through and she was already quite irate over what she read. He contacted his superior to see if he could drop by for a short visit.

J' Bar said it was OK. Kevin watched everything around him blur in a flash of light, then in an instant he was standing in J' Bar's residence. "Our Sovereign lives forever," said Kevin.

"Indeed he does Kevin. What brings you here today?" replied J' Bar. His pearly white teeth accentuated the smile spread across his black face.

"Samantha and I have made contact with the underground and received the first of their discussion topics. I've also gotten to know Samantha better since we first met and I was sure she would see right through the first topic. She is already alarmed that it is treasonous. I thought it best to do some preemptive planning to make sure she doesn't back out before the right time. We need to act quickly since she is already halfway through the document. She is probably also upset because she promised to not tell anyone about it," explained Kevin.

"I see. The Sovereign has made it clear that these matters must be communicated physically so bear with me for a few seconds." J' Bar closed his eyes, vanished and reappeared before Kevin could say anything. J' Bar continued as if he hadn't left. "Ah, yes, I'm also told she will come to ask your advice. Tell her to call her Board's senior Elder and we'll take care of the rest," he said.

"Sounds good to me. Thanks J' Bar. I better get back. She'll be coming around pretty quick." J' Bar blurred as Kevin returned to his dorm room.

Malcolm Gregapalous woke up earlier than usual. His wife was still asleep beside him. He sniffed and inhaled deeply. The smell of freshly brewed coffee was certainly calling him to the kitchen. He went downstairs and stopped in the doorway when he saw the back of a man dressed in white slacks and a white polo shirt pouring himself a cup of coffee. Malcolm rubbed his eyes and asked, "Is that you, Wilson?"

The man turned and smiled, "Good morning Malcolm. Have a good night's sleep?"

Malcolm was quite used to Wilson appearing at odd times and places. It was one of the things that goes along with being the senior Board Elder. However, it had been a long time since Wilson had contacted him on official business. "Hi Wilson, it's really good to see you. What brings you here this time of day? Social visit or business?" he asked, knowing that it was business. Wilson would have checked ahead of time to make sure a pre-breakfast social visit would be OK.

"Business and rather urgent at that. However, when we're done I wouldn't mind sticking around for breakfast if you're cooking," answered Wilson.

Malcolm's face brightened since he really liked making breakfast. "I thought that your transformed body wouldn't be tempted by my pancakes, eggs, and bacon. But I'm delighted to have you. Why don't I get started while you tell me what's up?" Malcolm opened the pantry door and started getting the ingredients for his buckwheat pancakes.

"Here's the story. You know Samantha, Merlin's daughter, is at university." Wilson filled in Malcolm about her post graduate class and becoming friends with Kevin, Robert and Jim. He included all pertinent facts that Malcolm needed to know. He explained *The Question* and the Administration's interest and knowledge of it. Finally he related how she was recruited by Robert and Jim but that they skipped the preliminary assessments which probably would have excluded her from even seeing the first discussion topic.

"Right about now, she'll be knocking on Kevin's door. It would be an understatement to say that she's a bit upset by what she read. Besides that, she's a bit scared. The fact that she promised not to tell anyone about the discussion topic is going to be weighing heavily on her since she has always been told to keep promises. This is the first time she's ever gotten into a situation where keeping such a promise could force her to do something against her conscience. Kevin will suggest that she call you and get your input on what to do and that's where you come in. So let's eat while we wait for the call," said Wilson as he cracked a couple of eggs for Malcolm.

Malcolm pondered what he heard before making a comment. "It sounds like the time is almost here and our Samantha is right in the middle of it. The Sovereign has one smart girl working for him. I feel privileged for being a small part of this."

Three loud angry knocks rang out on Kevin's door.

"Come on in Sam." yelled Kevin from the tiny kitchenette of his dorm room. He was fixing two of cups of coffee. He turned to enter the main room and hesitated.

The door swung open quickly and would have smacked him in the face if he hadn't stopped. Samantha stood there face flushed and both fists on the hips of her jeans. "How'd you know it was me?"

"Oh I just figured that it would take you about this long to finish your studies, read the topic discussion, stew about what you read, and then walk over here. How about a cup of coffee while you unload?" he said as he pushed the door closed enough so that he could step out of the kitchenette, then swung the door open to make sure that he met the dorm requirements to keep the door open when there were only two people of the opposite sex in a room.

Kevin hoped that his calm nature reassured Samantha. She took a deep breath, flopped down on the couch, and took the cup that Kevin offered. "I'm that predictable?" she asked.

"No, but that's what I would do in your situation. I take it that you weren't very sympathetic with what you read. Let's hear your opinion."

"Ugh, it makes me angry when I think about it. I think that they make many key observations but I'm not sure how much of it is factual. I know that it seems like Enforcers aren't around as much as they used to be based on some of the things I've seen before coming here. The way some people dress on campus and even at home is evidence of that. Their statistics could be accurate. It isn't what they said that bugs me so much as what they imply," Samantha sat her cup down and gestured wildly with her hands as she talked. "They are trying to convince me that The Sovereign has lost control and I know that just isn't possible. It didn't take me long to figure out that if he lost control then all that we know about him would be a lie. How can anyone seriously get sucked into this stuff?"

She stood up and started pacing quietly, then stopped and turned to Kevin who was still sitting on the couch. She leaned over with her hands in the air as if she were about to tear out her hair or make fists to beat on Kevin. "What really bothers me is that I promised not to tell anyone and I think that the Administration really needs to know what's going on." She turned around and stared at the ceiling. "I'm so frustrated. What am I going to do?" She whirled around and looked at Kevin. "What are you going to do? You made the promise too."

"What makes you think that I agree with your assessment of the topic or that I have a problem not telling the Administration about it?" asked Kevin trying to keep a straight face.

"Say what? Don't tell me you can't see where these topics are leading? If this is number one what do you think number 275 is going to be about? I'll bet that it is nothing more than a blatant denunciation saying that The Sovereign is a phony and it's now time to overthrow his Administration and set up a new government. I've gotten to know you fairly well over the past couple of weeks and I thought you'd see through this lightly veiled attack on The Sovereign Yehowshuwa."

Kevin chuckled to put Samantha at ease, "Just putting you on, Sam. You nailed it on the head. However it appears you are in quite a quandary. If you remember carefully, I said I wouldn't reveal these to anyone who didn't already know about them. My bet is that the Administration already knows about them so I don't think I have any problem discussing them with any of our superiors. You want to take me up on the bet?"

Samantha stopped and stared at Kevin before speaking. "If what you're saying is right and the Administration already knows, then it proves that their premise in the very first topic is flawed. Does it also mean that the Administration already knows we've been contacted so we don't need to tell them?"

Kevin folded his hands thoughtfully in front of his chin. "This bring up a moral dilemma that many people have to face. If you make a promise and later find out that you have to violate ethical behavior to keep the promise, what do you do? Maybe we ought to suggest that as a discussion topic and see what happens. In the meantime, I think that you should contact your senior Elder and confirm your conclusion. If he already knows, then you shouldn't have to say anything specific that would break your promise."

"I'm sure going to be more careful about what I promise in the future. That's for sure. I feel better already. Hmm, with the time difference between here and home, maybe I can reach Elder Gregapalous now. What do you think?" She was already reaching for her ECD.

"Better now than later. I'm sure you'll sleep better if you do."

Samantha sat down beside Kevin, opened her ECD and told it to connect her to Malcolm. A second or two later His face appeared on her screen. "Hi Sam. I was expecting your call. What's on your mind?"

"Why would you be expecting my call?" Samantha stammered at his opening. It appeared she almost forgot why she was calling. "Uh, Elder Gregapalous, I, um, don't really know where to start but I need some advice about some reading material I've come across on campus. I'm not sure where to start because I promised I wouldn't tell anyone about it. And this is Kevin. He suggested I call you."

"Hi, Kevin. Your name was also mentioned in the information provided to me. No need to go any further, Sam. Apparently you are exactly where The Sovereign wants you. I was told that you would call. I'm also fully informed about *The Question* and the Administration's position on it. There is no need for you to report the contents of their discussion topics or their activities so you don't have to break your promise to them. However, we don't want them to know how much we know, therefore don't let on about anything I told you." It looked like Malcolm was enjoying telling Samantha how much he already knew.

Samantha's mouth was hanging wide open until she replied. "I'm so relieved that you already know, but I guess I should have known that anyway. If you already know, then what purpose could I possible serve being involved with these discussions?" she asked.

Malcolm's countenance became more serious as he answered, "There are many people on campus who are being contacted by other cells. Some of them will fall for their philosophies. Your job is to find recent recruits and start your own discussions with them. Show them the fallacies of these topics and where they lead. More importantly, introduce them to The Sovereign. If they are led astray by these philosophies they probably don't know him. You will rescue some from the fire and warn others so that they won't be able to say they didn't know."

Samantha put her hands on her cheeks. "Wow! I'm awed that The Sovereign would have this in mind for me. I don't know what to say. But Elder Gregapalous, what about those that are already involved and are recruiting others? Is there something that I can do to help them? I've become friends with the two who introduced us to these topics. I'd hate to see them lost." Samantha looked at Kevin then back at Malcolm. "And how does Kevin fit into this?"

Malcolm glanced away from his screen for a second or two. He then focused back on the ECD. "I believe that Kevin will be able to lend you the technical help needed. As for the others, Sam, this may be hard but you need to do everything you can to make sure that Robert and Jim don't know what you are doing. If they find out they will quickly disassociate themselves from you and you will no longer be able to get more discussion topics. The key to reaching others will be your ability to get these topics and analyze them so that you can intelligently discuss them with those who haven't yet committed themselves"

Samantha was a bit startled, "You know I'm talking about Robert and Jim?"

Malcolm laughed, "Of course. As I said, I'm fully informed abut your situation." His face grew solemn as he continued, "There are others who have been assigned to deal with recruiters and people who are already deeply involved in discussion groups. They are playing in a different league where the stakes are higher. Quite frankly, if Robert's leader were to discover your true mission, it could become dangerous. You need to be cautious during your discussion when you are introduced to his group."

"What do you mean that it could be dangerous?" said Samantha with wide eyes.

Malcolm's voice remained calm as he explained, "We are dealing with entities that will stop at nothing to further their goals. Some people have already disappeared; Dr. Robison for one. I know your next question is how could that happen with The Sovereign in control? Just as in ancient times, he allowed people to go their own way to test them, so it is time to allow it again. Good people get hurt in the process. However, you can rest assured that he hasn't changed but will work all things to the ultimate good of those who are loyal to him. In summary, be careful but also trust The Sovereign."

"Thank you Elder Gregapalous. You've taken a load off my mind and yet I have a lot to contemplate. I think I'll seek The Sovereign's wisdom about how to accomplish this task." Samantha sat back on the couch.

"May he guide you and direct you. He will be with you always. If you need anything please call. Goodbye, Sam." Malcolm waved goodbye.

"Thank you again, goodbye," replied Samantha.

Samantha closed her ECD and let her head fall on the back of the couch.

"So what are you going to do now, Sam?" asked Kevin.

She sat up and stared at him as if she were looking right through him. "I'm thinking about how to find out who has been contacted by the underground on campus. I'm not sure what would happen if I just started asking around. I might raise the suspicion of some die hard undergrounders or get reported to their leaders." She focused on Kevin. "What do you think? What would be a good way to find others? I could post something on the bulletin board saying, 'Anyone getting sucked into the treasonous philosophies of the underground please contact Samantha in room 1445 for help in thinking straight.'"

They both burst into laughter at the same time.

"As Malcolm mentioned, I've been able to develop some technical expertise with the way our communications systems work. I can trace their discussion topics and find out who else has received it. If I gave you a list of people that have only received the samples of the first topic you could contact them and see if they are willing to meet with you. Chances are that many of them are a bit confused and would welcome a conversation with someone who doesn't have a mind warping agenda," volunteered Kevin.

"Oh, that would be great!" Samantha's enthusiasm quickly faded. "But how can you do that?"

Kevin flipped open his ECD and entered a few commands. "I'm looking at data that is available to anyone. Every ECD is constantly monitoring the network. It does this to enable it to receive the data that is meant for its address. Take a look at my monitor." Suddenly the screen was filled with numbers and letters flowing across the screen. He touched the screen and the data stopped. "Look at this data here. You see these numbers and letters? That is the header information for a new message. Within this header information is the address of the ECD that is supposed to receive the message and the supposed sender of the data. The message follows the header information and is encrypted and compressed. I can't tell what the content of the message is but I can tell from the header that this is part of a video conversation between two people." He touched the screen again and the data continued to flow until he stopped it.

Kevin entered a few more commands on his ECD as he explained what he was doing. "I'm now going to ping the ECD that was involved with the video conversation we looked at and request its identification. I'm entering the data I got from the header of the message." After he finished the name of the owner of the ECD appeared on his screen. "Now it's a simple task to find out where John is at on the campus by looking him up on the university's directory. There he is. John is in this dorm in room 1857."

Samantha took the ECD and looked at it then Kevin. "So you're telling me that someone could have been eavesdropping while I was talking to Elder Gregapalous?"

Kevin shook his head. "No, they couldn't eavesdrop but they could tell that you were having a video conversation with him. Well, to be more exact, they could tell that whoever was using your ECD and whoever was using his ECD were having a video conversation. Unless they developed a way to decrypt the Administration's data, they wouldn't be able to determine what the data represented."

Samantha wrinkled her nose and asked, "If the data is encrypted, how do you know that John, for instance, was getting a discussion topic? Can you tell who is getting topics by checking the sender of whoever sent us the topics?"

"Good conclusion but the senders alter their address so they can't be traced. I can determine discussion topics by the encryption code in the header. The ECD has to know what decryption program to use so that is in the header too. As soon as I received the first topic, I had the code and could monitor the network for other messages with the same code. I've been able to find three other people on campus that have received discussion topics since then. One is a woman in the dorm next to yours." Kevin closed his ECD and put it down on the coffee table.

Samantha folded her arms and smiled. "How did you know how to do that?"

"Well, I'll have to admit that I had some help from some technical people in the Administration who are a lot smarter than I am. But once they showed me how, it was simple to do."

Kevin took a drink of coffee. I came close to divulging my position in the Administration. That can't be revealed until the right time.

"Sam, this was technically simple. What comes next will be harder. We need to prepare ourselves to participate in the discussions without violating our conscience," explained Kevin.

Samantha exhaled sharply, "Oh, that doesn't sound like it's going to be very easy. How can we participate in these discussions without letting them know that we think they are way off-base? If we tip them off we will soon be uninvited to further discussions and will lose the advantage of knowing what they're teaching and how they think."

Kevin stared contemplatively into his coffee cup before answering. "No, it won't be easy. However, I think if we concentrate on asking questions rather than giving opinions we may be able to go a long way without showing any commitment. Another thing we can do is make non-committal comments that appear to express our feelings but don't really say anything. They will read into our comments what they want to hear."

Samantha wrinkled her nose. "OK... I think I know what you're talking about but I'll need an example, if you please. Say I'm in one of these discussion groups and someone says 'I think that this evidence proves that The Sovereign really isn't in control, which means that we need to reevaluate our loyalty to him. What do you think Sam?' How would I handle that?"

Kevin thought for a moment then replied, "I would reply something like this. 'That's a very interesting observation. Based on this evidence what you are saying has some serious ramifications for our society. Harry, what do you think the repercussions would be if more people knew this?' I used the word interesting, which is a neutral word rather than saying it was exciting or thrilling. I didn't tell them that what I thought was interesting is that this person could ignore all the evidence that The Sovereign really is who he says he is and come up with such an outlandish conclusion. However, I did affirm the person by saying the evidence did support the conclusion and that is simply because the underground only provided information that would lead to that conclusion. I then shifted the focus away from myself to another member of the group so that I wouldn't reveal any more of my thoughts. Let's pray that they don't fabricate evidence and then ask us outright whether or not we believe the veracity of what they presented. At that point we'd have to answer yes or no and that may give us away."

"Hmm. That's an interesting position, Kevin. It appears you've put a lot of thought into it. What other techniques do you believe will help us, especially if we're asked a point-blank yes or no question?" asked Samantha, obviously testing her own ability to put into practice what Kevin had introduced. "How's that for engaging in the conversation without being committal, except for the last part of the question? I really would like to know that answer."

"Very good, Sam," said Kevin as he laughed. "As far as getting stuck with yes or no questions we can always trust that The Sovereign will keep us out of trouble. He still is in control despite all they say. As long as we are where he wants, I believe that we'll be all right. If we start doing something that isn't in his will or in his way, then we could get into trouble."

"You're right, of course. We can't lose sight of his ability and working; otherwise we also would be lured right into the underground's lies. I'm ready to begin. How long before you can give me a list and I can get started?" asked Samantha.

"It's getting kind of late and you better get back to your dorm. I'll send you a list in the morning."

"Ooh, I didn't even notice how late it was. This evening has been so exhilarating. Just think. We are in service to The Sovereign! What could be any better than to know that you have a purpose for your life and it's exactly what he wants? I don't know if I'll be able to sleep but I do need to get going. Thanks, Kevin, for your guidance. It seems like you were sent specifically to guide me." Samantha got up to go.

"If I'm doing what The Sovereign wants then I guess you could say that I was sent for that purpose. Have a good night and I'll see you tomorrow in class." There would be a time in the future when she would find out Kevin's full purpose, but it wasn't time yet.

Chapter 29

Chuck threw his covers off and leaped out of bed. "Lights," he commanded but they didn't come on. He stared into the darkness trying to see what made the noise that yanked him out of a peaceful sleep. He was trembling. There it was again! It was a tooth-aching scraping combined with a rumbling noise like a large metal sheet being ripped in two and thrown to the wind. Chuck covered his ears. It was behind the bulkhead at the head of his bed.

Suddenly, curled claws punctured the wall. It buckled and tore away. Chuck felt himself sucked into the adjoining room. He was now standing in the middle of the pentagram in the training room that Zophia had constructed. He was facing a red dragon-like creature with seven heads on the ends of necks twice as long as the body. Blood was dripping from its talons where it had ripped out the walls around it. Zophia straddled its broad back two meters from the floor. She held the reins from each of the seven heads. Above and beyond her he saw the stars racing past through the blackness of space.

"Chuck, come up and join me. Together we will rule. The Earth will be ours and our descendents forever."

Fear gripped him as never before in his life. Words involuntarily came out of his mouth. "Why don't you come down here and get rid of that ugly beast? We'll be wed by The Sovereign himself and live forever." *Did I just say that?*

Chuck leaped backwards just in time to avoid the gaping jaws of one head as it swung down from his right. It collided with another head that came from his left. They fell to the floor, no longer supported by their long rubbery necks. He covered his ears again as the remaining heads and Zophia roared in anger. He turned, fled through the wall into his cabin, out the door and into the corridor.

The beast was right behind him. Zophia was kicking its sides with the long star spurs on the heels of her black leather boots. *How can they fit in this passageway?*

Crewmembers of the ship snickered and backed away into other corridors as he stormed full speed ahead. *Why are they laughing?* He looked over his shoulder to see Zophia effortlessly jogging along behind him smiling as she had in his office when she taunted him. No dragon, no clothes. He almost stumbled and fell but regained control and turned a corner.

There was nothing before him except blue sky and puffy clouds. He tried to stop but it was too late. His next step was in midair.

Chuck found himself falling through the clouds toward a broad grassy field on the side of a hill. He could clearly see a river running from a large golden building at the top of the hill down through the field to a sea several kilometers away. Somehow he landed in the grass, rolled and stood up unhurt. Looking back up, he could see Zophia falling toward him with the Aman hovering in the sky behind her.

As she landed Zophia changed into a gargoyle. She became a primate with long powerful frog legs, long arms, and bloodied curved talons on her hands – like the dragon's. Her catlike ears laid back, eyes glowed, mouth wide exposing long fangs. Her two leathery wings flapped to soften her landing. As soon as she hit the ground she sprung toward Chuck like a frog.

Chuck ran backwards up the hill keeping an eye on the beast. Somehow he easily kept ahead of her until he collided with something and turned around. The Sovereign grabbed him and kept him from falling.

"You are safe with me. I won't let anything harm you if you will trust me." The Sovereign's voice was soft and strong. Chuck felt secure.

"Don't let him trick you, Chuck." Chuck turned to see the beast transform back into Zophia. "Your destiny is with me. We will ascend together. The pleasures that we will enjoy will overshadow anything he has to offer." She reached out her long beautiful brown arms to him. She touched the tip of her finger to his cheek and drew her long bloody talon down to his chin. His cheek burned where she touched and blood dripped onto his shirt.

Chuck sat bolt upright in his bed. He was sweating and his heart was racing. *OK, no more thoughts about an intimate relationship with Zophia!*

September 19, 998 ASR

Robert was very thankful that Dr. Ntari lived closer to Midrib than his previous interviewees. He was able to get a good night's sleep Friday night, had a leisurely breakfast, and still arrived on time for his Saturday afternoon appointment. It would give him more time to talk to the distinguished scientist. He had to juggled a couple of the other interviews around in order to meet with Dr. Ntari but it was worth it.

He exited the convy stop and proceeded to Dr. Ntari's house. He didn't like this neighborhood. Each house had two seven meter tall trees in front. Each single story house was faced with a reddish brown brick. Some had the front door, shielded by a small porch, on the right, some on the left. The monotony of the houses was off-set by planting areas filled with the flowers and blooming shrubs providing copious color. *I would have thought that with Dr. Ntari's fame he would be living in a community with more variety – a more worthy location.*

Robert knocked at Dr. Ntari's door and it opened about a minute later. A relatively young-looking woman who was nearly two meters tall greeted him. She was very slim and dressed in a light brown jump suit which accentuated her height, light brown skin and thinness. Her soft brown eyes and a joyous smile captivated him immediately even though she was significantly taller. "Hi, you must be Robert. I'm Mavis and my husband will be with you in just a couple of minutes. Come on in and have a seat." She led him into the cozy but crowded living room and pointed him to a plush maroon couch and chair. Robert sat on the couch and Mavis took a seat on the chair. He had a hard time not staring at this woman.

"I would suspect by your expression that you were expecting someone older to be married to Tazi." Mavis met his stare with a kind smile.

"Uh, yes, I was. I've been interviewing people who are 860 years old or more and those that are married have wives much closer to their own age." *Not only that but you are so incredibly good-looking that I'm having trouble thinking straight.* "Please excuse me, I don't normally stare at women, but I, uh, maybe I better just shut my mouth." stammered Robert. He wasn't even sure why he was so mesmerized by her.

Mavis just laughed, "I may have simply shocked your system, visiting with older people so much."

Dr. Ntari entered the room. "No, I think it's because Mavis must be the most beautiful woman in the world. There's no need to be concerned, Robert. She has that affect on just about every male she meets. She certainly affected me when we first met. That was about fifty years after my beloved Bali passed away. However, for some reason that is still a mystery to me, this lovely woman has eyes only for me."

Robert stood to shake Dr. Ntari's hand as he extended it. Robert could see why Mavis had eyes for him. He was slightly taller than she was with broad shoulders and bulging muscles showing through his tight knit short sleeved shirt. His white hair and lined face betrayed his age but there was nothing else that would indicate how old he was. He stood straight and tall and had a deep booming voice.

"Welcome to our humble home. Please sit down."

Mavis got up and asked, "Can I get you gentlemen a cup of coffee, tea or something else?"

"I think a cup of joe would be great. How about you Robert?" answered Dr. Ntari.

"I think I'd rather have a cup of coffee, thank you."

Mavis disappeared into the kitchen.

"Some historian you are, Robert. I'll bet you don't even know what a cup of joe is, do you?" asked Dr. Ntari with a twinkle in his eye.

Robert could tell that he was being teased and he felt a bit embarrassed. "No sir, I'm afraid I don't."

"Well, way back when, long before the Last Battle, people called coffee lots of stuff. Joe was popular for a long time, then java became more common." Dr. Ntari sat in the chair that Mavis vacated.

"I didn't know that. How is it that one of the preeminent scientists in the world is acquainted with the nicknames of coffee from an era some two hundred plus years before he was born? Are you also an historian?" asked Robert.

"Not so much an historian as a lover of coffee. But you aren't here to find out about coffee, are you?" Dr. Ntari settled back in his chair.

"No sir, I'm not. As I explained in my letter I'm writing a book about the Last Battle and I'm looking for people who have first-hand encounters with people who lived through the Great Time of Trouble." Robert sat upright, almost on the edge of the couch.

"Well, you came to one of the right people. My mother and father both were survivors and I'd say that is about as close of a first-hand encounter as you can get."

Mavis came in carrying a serving tray with two cups of coffee, cream, and sugar. "Here you go, two cups of joe. Would you care for cream or sugar, Robert?"

"No thanks, Ma'am, I like it natural and this really smells great. I wouldn't want to mess it up with additives." Robert took a cup and set it on the coffee table on a coaster that Mavis provided.

"Ah, now that's a real man who knows the way coffee should be relished.

Mavis served a cup to Dr. Ntari then interrupted, "If you gentlemen would excuse me, little Timothy will be getting up from his nap pretty soon and will need his mommy. Two-year-olds can wake up a bit cranky. I don't think you'd want him running through here while you try to talk."

Robert was relieved that Mavis didn't stay. She was very distracting. He opened his ECD and started it recording. "That is amazing. I wouldn't have thought that a two-year-old could be only one generation away from the Last Battle. You don't mind if I record this, do you, Dr. Ntari?"

"By all means, go ahead and record."

"Thank you. Now, can you tell me more about your parents? Specifically, I'm looking for any stories that they related to you about their life during the Great Time of Trouble and the things that happened to them. Can you also describe their loyalty to The Sovereign?"

"OK, down to business. My mother and father both lived in an isolated area of East Africa. When The Sovereign took all his people I think only one or two people in their little isolated village were taken. It wasn't strange for people to go missing in that area so no one really knew what happened there or elsewhere. They had very little contact with the rest of the world."

"I'm curious that no one missed them. In most other stories I read, all the children disappeared also. That would have caused a lot of commotion even in a primitive society and it sounds like your parents were in a primitive society."

Dr. Ntari nodded his head thoughtfully. "Primitive society. Hmm, yes that would be a good description of the little village. However the part about all children disappearing, my dear friend, is a misconception that most people have about The Sovereign's recall of his people. Many children did leave but it was only the children who had at least one parent loyal to The Sovereign Yehowshuwa and who were not old enough to make their own allegiance decision. The remaining parent was usually quite devastated, which publicized the stories and made them popular. When both parents were left behind so were their children. As evil increased child abuse also increased. Many children died from neglect or outright abuse. It was convenient to explain the loss of a child to the disappearances even years later. As time went on those who later placed their trust in The Sovereign remembered the stories of the children being taken by The Sovereign, even though a few still had their children with them."

Dr. Ntari wrinkled his brow and grunted, "Hump, if people were a bit more familiar with Yehowshuwa's book they would have found a passage that explains that the children are set apart when either of the parents makes his or her allegiance to The Sovereign. This explains why some children were taken and others weren't."

"I certainly hadn't heard that before. Thanks for the clarification." Wow, he's sort of a history buff and a theologian in addition to being a scientist.

Dr. Ntari continued, "My parents first figured out something was wrong when the weather patterns started changing dramatically. Now there were already more droughts but this was much worse than before. They also suffered through the same maladies that beset the rest of the world and those who weren't loyal to The Sovereign. Since they were isolated, they didn't know what was wrong but believed that the spirits were out to get them."

He paused to take a sip of coffee. "Ah, that is good."

Robert wiped that comment from his ECD.

"One day refugees escaping from Ben-Shaachar's evil empire found their way to my parents' village. Apparently The Chancellor cared little about some of the more isolated tribes and that offered a haven for a few of The Sovereign Yehowshuwa's people. The refugees brought the truth about the destruction of the environment as well as the truth about Yehowshuwa and the impending Last Battle. Once they heard and understood The Sovereign's forgiveness and love for them, most of the villagers pledged their allegiance to him but a few, including my parents, held out. They were skeptical and wanted to wait and see how events transpired before declaring their allegiance. They even cursed The Sovereign because of the plagues he was pouring out on the earth."

Robert pricked up his ears at this comment. Wow! This has to be the first example of someone who was not loyal to The Sovereign making it through the Great Time of Trouble. This might be what I need.

"Fortunately for them The Chancellor Ben-Shaachar's forces never made it that far in their efforts to eradicate The Sovereign's followers or his race. When Yehowshuwa returned it was very evident to my parents he was more powerful and they quickly bowed to his sovereignty over their lives."

Robert held up his hand to stop Dr. Ntari. "So when The Sovereign returned your parents hadn't actually declared their allegiance to him, yet he spared them and killed others. Why was that?" asked Robert. "I thought that anyone who hadn't declared their allegiance to The Sovereign before he returned was killed." *That is one of the reasons I have a hard time with his bloody policy of the time. We've covered that in our discussion topics.*

Dr. Ntari leaned forward. "Not very many people were in a similar position to my parents. Most had already made up their minds to worship Ben-Shaachar or Yehowshuwa. Yup, The Sovereign spared my parents. You see, cursing Yehowshuwa didn't carry a death penalty but worshiping Ben-Shaachar did. It was consistent with what he told his followers about blasphemy while he was here during his first visit," replied Dr. Ntari.

"Did your parents tell you why they were so skeptical and hesitated aligning with The Sovereign?" Please let there be something here that will support my theory that we haven't gotten the whole story.

"Yes, they did. They grew up with witchcraft and medicine men who guided their entire outlook on life. They had deep spiritual beliefs. They were sure that the rain came or not based on whether or not they properly appeased the spiritual forces around them. Health, wealth, good crops, and healthy animals all were determined by the various spirits they worshiped. When the plagues started they were confused because they didn't know which spirit to placate. The Sovereign's followers arrived and told them that he was in control of all nature."

Robert laughed lightly, "That must have shook them up."

Dr. Ntari cocked his head sideways and added a nod. "Yup, it sure did. The first thing the whole village wanted to know was how to appease this new being that was revealed to them. When they were told that they needed to repent of their pagan practices and put their trust only in this Yehowshuwa they didn't buy it. They knew that animal sacrifices were the only way to satisfy the spirits so they protested. Of course the next thing they heard was that The Sovereign previously came to the earth as a person and sacrificed himself. They understood that and that's when many of the villagers put their trust in The Sovereign."

Robert looked down at his ECD. He had a feeling this wasn't going to help his book.

"The villagers also heard about The Chancellor Ben-Shaachar and the war between him and The Sovereign Yehowshuwa. My parents didn't have any first hand knowledge of The Chancellor but from what they heard they figured out that he was definitely an evil character. However, from their perspective they knew that most spirits had sinister natures so they just considered both The Chancellor and The Sovereign as two warring spirits and very pragmatically decided to wait and see who was victorious. Even if The Chancellor was evil and he won they thought he wouldn't be much different than some of the local spirits they worshiped."

Hmm, The Sovereign is just another warring spirit. Maybe that is an angle I can use. I also need to check out some other stories I heard like this.

"If I remember the stories correctly, didn't The Sovereign send one of his messengers who flew around the whole world declaring his sovereignty to all these isolated people? Did they hear him and still not align with The Sovereign?" asked Robert.

"Oh, yes they heard, but that didn't faze them. They previously saw fire produced by Ben-Shaachar coming down from the skies, even though it was from a great distance. When it came to deciding who was more powerful, a voice from the skies didn't impress them enough to make a decision. Fortunately for them none of The Chancellor's militia came to force a decision. Besides, Yehowshuwa is merciful."

Robert decided to speak the party line to see Dr. Ntari's response, "Yeah, especially the merciful part. Otherwise they would have ended up with those who received The Chancellor's mark of loyalty. But it appears that they didn't actually see his atrocities or understand completely who he was until it was all over. All they really knew of the Great Time of Trouble throughout the rest of the world was what they were told by the refugees."

"That's a pretty good assessment of what happened," agreed Dr. Ntari.

About that time Robert reasoned that he wasn't going to get anything from Dr. Ntari that would reveal anything different from what he already had. He kept finding that same consistency that bothered him more and more. However, he didn't want to be rude and cut the interview short either. "Dr. Ntari, your parents were relatively uneducated people living in the wilderness. Did they move to a more civilized area or were you born there and moved?"

"My parents had a pretty rough sustenance existence even before the Great Time of Trouble. They were always on the verge of starvation and saw more than one child die. After The Chancellor took over and the Great Time of Trouble started, their remaining two children died during the drought and scorching heat that came. They were living in a near desert area and had nothing when it was all over."

Robert sat back with his coffee cup and frowned dutifully when he heard that Dr. Ntari's older siblings had died. *I might as well enjoy the story.*

"Then Yehowshuwa came and the land miraculously bloomed with grass, trees, flowers, and even wildlife reappeared in a matter of hours. They told me how they watched the miracle unfold right before their eyes. The ground around them became moist, then was covered with fine green fuzz that turned into grass within five minutes. They were awestruck and sat down in the lush grass and enjoyed its coolness for the first time in years. As they sat there just outside the village a shoot came up out of the ground. It stretched heavenward and broke into two then six then twelve branches. They lost count. The trunk became thick and sturdy while leaves sprang out from all the boughs. Blossoms quickly followed but within a few seconds fell to the ground, covering them with their delicate pink color and fragrance. They were astounded as the fruit grew and ripened. It took less than an hour from the first hint of green until the cherries turned a deep burgundy red."

I wonder how much of this story is a result of their superstitious history and how much is true. I can't imagine a cherry tree growing, blooming, and producing fruit in an hour.

"That's when The Sovereign appeared in front of them. He reached up, plucked a handful, and held them out to them. 'I've grown these just for you. Take and eat,' he said. As hungry as they were they fell flat on their faces, worshiped him, and asked for his forgiveness. They didn't need to be told who he was and they knew they should have been worshiping him all along. Yet there he was offering them something to eat."

Robert remembered the worship service just last month when The Sovereign appeared in a flash. *Yeah, I can believe that part.*

"Then Yehowshuwa sat down with them and they talked as they ate together. He told them how he wanted them to participate in the reconstruction of cities and reestablishing society. They were more than eager to do whatever he asked."

Robert sat up more attentively. "I thought that he restored the cities when he restored the rest of the earth."

Dr. Ntari calmly answered, "No, he cleaned up a lot to make sure that there wasn't so much dead stuff lying around that it would stink up the environment, but he left much of the rubble. He took care of the things we couldn't. There was a lot of plain old physical work to be done and that's what he wanted people to do. While my parents helped clean up and rebuild they also went to school and learned to read and write. I had several brothers and sisters arrive before me; I was the last of the clan. We took lots of vacations back to what used to be the wilderness, but I was a city kid. My parents retired back in the country after the rebuilding was finished."

Robert liked Dr. Ntari's calm nature and deep voice. *I might as well get to know him since I'm here. He doesn't give many interviews.* "What made you decide to become a scientist? Did it have anything to do with where your parents came from and who they became after the restoration?"

Dr. Ntari put down his coffee cup. "I would have to say it was because of who my parents became after they met The Sovereign face to face. Their devotion to him inspired me to find out more about the universe he created. He created this world and everything in it in only six days. He restored it in a matter of hours. Not many people have seen a tree grow up before their eyes and that story made a deep impression on me. So I decided to find out everything that I could about the universe."

He paused and tapped his finger on his temple. "Just think about it. He was able to create matter from nothing and organize it to form mountains, plains, rivers, streams, and oceans, not to mention stars and galaxies. For a long time people believed that he created everything and then let it stew until life formed by the natural laws that he established. They believed that given the right combinations of chemicals and the right introduction of energy, these chemicals formed amino acids. From that DNA some living cells formed. Those cells divided and generated billions of single-celled animals and plants. Given enough time, as these cells divided, they were influenced by just the right environment or chemicals and energy to mutate and form more complex living entities. But that is entirely impossible."

"Why is that?" asked Robert. *From what I've read in The Question evolution makes sense, especially if you give it enough time.*

Dr. Ntari raised one finger, "First, there hasn't been enough time. The Sovereign created the universe as he said, in six days. Poor theologians said the term he had used for a day really could be interpreted as an era or any long period of time. He did use the same word in his writings to mean an era. However, The Sovereign was very explicit when he said that it was a twenty four hour period of time. He immediately established a day as a period of dark and a period of light. Each day he created something he said there was an evening and a morning – then numbered the day. If he had taken eons to create the different aspects of the universe and referred to them as a day, he wouldn't have emphasized that there was an evening and a morning. Based on what he said, the universe wasn't much older than six or seven thousand years when the Great Time of Trouble started."

Robert remembered much of this from another of his discussion topics with the underground. "But didn't the layers and composition of the rocks imply that they were much older than a few thousand years? You know, radioactive decay of some elements would suggest that Earth was much older. For instance, uranium-238 naturally decays into thorium-234 and then into other elements, including isotopes of lead, until it eventually becomes stable lead-206. Based on the amount of uraium-238 versus stable lead in the rocks, scientist once estimated that Earth was somewhere between 3.6 and 4.5 billion years old. Doesn't this evidence contradict what The Sovereign said?"

Dr. Ntari straightened up in his chair. It appeared that he was enjoying the challenge Robert provided. "That is precisely the argument many scientists used in the past to either deny that there was a creator or that creation wasn't done as described by Yehowshuwa. Even scientists loyal to The Sovereign bought into this theory before the Great Time of Trouble. However, as with other key points this is also flawed. Tell me, Robert, do you know what the ratio of uranium to lead was when matter was first created?" asked Dr. Ntari.

I think he's trying to trap me. But we've covered this too. "Well no, but I think they compared the amount of lead-204 which does not occur as a result of radioactive decay to the amount of lead-206 and other lead isotopes. With some complicated formulas they were then able to determine how much of the lead isotopes came from uranium decay and thus the original amount of uranium."

Dr. Ntari smiled and nodded. "Very good, Robert. You've done your homework on the misguided sub-ancient scientist.. But that has one very fundamental flaw. They assumed that all the lead-206 came from uranium and worked their way backwards. How do you know that the earth was created without any lead-206?"

"I don't get it. The formulas seem to be very foolproof. While they give some opening for error of a billion years or so they can't possibly get down to six thousand years," responded Robert. *I thought* The Question *had this nailed down really well.*

Dr. Ntari made a box in the air with his hands. "You missed the point. Let me illustrate for you. Suppose I showed you a sealed room with a single candle burning in it. The candle is now fifteen centimeters high. How would you determine how tall the candle was when it was first lit?"

Come on Doctor, this is a very basic experiment with controlled data. What are you getting at? "Well, I'd measure the amount of oxygen, carbon dioxide, water, and soot in the room. From that I determine the difference between that in the room and that occurring outside the room to determine how much oxygen was used and carbon dioxide, water, and soot produced. That tells me approximately how much of the candle was burned. Or more simply I could just measure the rate of burn and factor in the decreased amount of oxygen then extrapolate to determine how high it was when it was first lit."

"That sounds good," said Dr. Ntari as he leaned forward and pointed a finger at Robert, "but you assumed that the oxygen, carbon dioxide, water, and soot in the room before the candle was lit was the same as in the outside air. I didn't tell you that it was the same as when I closed the door. I could have altered the initial quantities of any or all of the ingredients. Since I built the room, filled it with air there is no way for you to determine from the contents of the air in the room how much of the candle has burned. In the same way there is no way to know if any lead-206 existed at the beginning of creation or not."

Robert raised his eyebrows. "Are you saying that when The Sovereign created the universe that he included isotopes of lead and other elements in ratios that made it appear, using these formulas, that the universe had been created 4.5 million years ago?" asked Robert. *Doesn't that make The Sovereign a deceiver?*

"Exactly!" Dr. Ntari slapped his thigh. "He created the universe as it is, not in a big bang that started expanding. There weren't hot gasses or clouds of dust that started cooling and collecting into planets and stars. If so, why would some collect into balls of rock and metal forming solid planets or gaseous giants? Why would some collect into larger balls of hydrogen forming stars? Yehowshuwa says he set the moon and the stars in place with his fingers. When he set those stars in place he also set all the photons in place between them and Earth so that the first time man looked up to the skies, all the stars were there to see. He created the earth with a molten center mostly of iron to make sure it had a magnetic field to help shield it from particles from the sun. It has layers of rocks with deposits of metal ores so that we would have them for our use."

Dr. Ntari closed his eyes and raised both hands above his head. "He created mountains, valleys, and oceans so that the climate would be able to sustain the diverse vegetation that he created. He put everything together in a way that would be consistent with the natural laws he established. If he had not created those isotopes in the quantities he did, then when we observe the radioactive decay it would produce inconsistent results. We would not be able to correctly understand the working of physics or anything else." Dr. Ntari opened his eyes, now glistening with moisture as he finished, "Glory to The Sovereign Yehowshuwa who has done all this."

The Doctor's confidence and obvious devotion to The Sovereign shook Robert. *This isn't new.* The Question *has kept us up to date with the Administration's arguments. I just need to word my response carefully.* He waited a few seconds to gain his own confidence before asking, "So the evidence indicates that Earth is 4.5 billion years old but The Sovereign says that is only around seven thousand years old. If he created it to look that old, hasn't he purposefully deceived us?" *Ugh, that response wasn't very careful. Oh well, now I'll see how an eminent loyalist scientist handles an accusation against The Sovereign.*

Dr. Ntari eyes narrowed and his smile was replaced by a scowl. "I think you're starting to believe those sub-ancient philosophies, Robert. That is one of the arguments used to deny a creator during that era. The point is that Yehowshuwa said he made everything in six days. However, if you carefully observe his creation you will come to the understanding that he had to make it with apparent age for the laws of physics to continue from that time forward."

Robert never heard that explanation before and he didn't like it.

"People in that era also believed that only what is observable is the truth. They discounted miracles or supernatural events, such as when Yehowshuwa walked on water, because they are not repeatable events. This is why many sub-ancient era scientists were atheists. They steadfastly denied the supernatural even though they couldn't explain where matter or energy originated. Some claimed it came from previously collapsing universes, but how did the first universe come into existence? They chose to believe that the first matter or energy appeared by chance or some other metaphysical phenomenon."

Dr. Ntari continued on for some time relating how biologists tried to prove that life was created by chance. They mixed chemicals and passed electricity through them to re-create proteins that could then form DNA. He refuted their research, which *The Question* had clearly confirmed.

Robert tried to keep a straight face, nod in agreement, and not reveal his confusion. What Dr. Ntari was saying started to make sense but...

Dr. Ntari continued "The difference between then and now is that The Sovereign is among us and reassures us that what he did in the beginning is true. He proved it by restoring the earth in much the same manner as he created it. For a brief period of time he set aside the rules of physics. The truth of the restoration continues to this day. I have lived over 800 years when my grandparents would have thought one hundred to be miraculous. Look at the wild animals; lions eat grass instead of hunting and killing other animals for their food. Their nature, their DNA, was changed overnight. Maybe you don't believe they used to eat other animals? Where does your faith lie, Robert?" Dr. Ntari paused, looking steadfastly into Robert's eyes.

"You're right, Doctor. I heard that question before and being a student of sub-ancient philosophy, I was interested in what you had to say. This will make excellent material for my book." Robert attempted to mollify Dr. Ntari in order to not expose what he really believed.

Dr. Ntari paused. Robert wasn't sure if he was convinced or not. "Think back about that tree that grew up right before my parents' eyes. The Sovereign was able to do in one hour what normally takes many years, not to mention the spring and summer to produce the fruit on a fully grown tree. It pointed out to me that The Sovereign is in charge of more than just creating things, but life itself."

Robert watched as Dr. Ntari leaned forward again smiling and almost looking past him. *Here we go again. The old man is getting excited. Maybe with some more breakthroughs in science we can produce life.* Robert wasn't ready to completely give up on what he'd learned from *The Question.* He nodded politely.

"You see, life originates with The Sovereign. He is the author of life and without him life doesn't and can't exist. Life and the universe were originally designed to last forever. The first two people would still be alive if they had obeyed him. He clearly told them that their disobedience would result in death."

Oh-oh. Here comes the theology lecture.

"Ben-Shaachar got in there and messed it up by lying to the first man and woman so that they willfully disobeyed. They should have known better but they listened and the result is that The Sovereign changed the universe to start to decay and death entered. Everything slowly started to proceed to lower states of organization so that without intervention from an outside force everything essentially rusts away. Living organisms which would have continued to replenish worn out cells suddenly started growing old. Eventually their cells couldn't reproduce correctly and they died."

"If everything were perfect, why would cells even wear out and need replacing?" asked Robert as he spotted a flaw in the argument.

Dr. Ntari cocked his head to one side then answered, "Good point, Robert. Either way, people would live forever. But even that relies on the laws of physics. All that we see and know follows laws of physics that The Sovereign Yehowshuwa has established. Yet he has changed those rules twice now. Once when the first man and woman disobeyed and then again when he restored the earth he altered that rate of decay as well as the basic nature of animals. I set out to learn everything I could about these natural laws and how they interacted with each other. I've studied the textbooks from the past as well as the current era. Few people realize it but he made quite a few seemingly minor changes in the physical laws from before the Last Battle. It took us a while to put it all together but the result is our ability to control gravity which has resulted in providing the power for our civilization. The rest is history."

Robert was still not convinced. "Dr. Ntari, I don't understand something. The Sovereign made the universe and all life. That includes The Chancellor. Now somehow The Chancellor deceives the first two people and The Sovereign then punishes the entire universe by changing the laws of physics so that death occurs. Since The Chancellor is part of his creation and caused all the problems, it seems rather unfair to punish all creation for his rebellion. Isn't this a denigration of The Sovereign's character?"

Dr. Ntari laughed, "Who is defining your concept of fair, Robert? Doesn't the creator have the right to establish the rules and carry out the consequences when those rules have been broken? Doesn't the fact that all creation suffers as a result of the disobedience of the man and woman tell you something about the importance of the human race in The Sovereign's plans? Doesn't the fact that The Sovereign himself paid the penalty for their misdeeds tell you something about the purity of his character?"

Robert felt quite chagrined by Dr. Ntari's answering him with a series of rhetorical questions. "I see your point, Sir. I think I have the material I need and I'll be able to incorporate it my book. I really appreciate the light you've shed. It will be most useful." *There's no way I'm going to put this stuff in the book. It's just a bunch more of the same Administration propaganda. If it is included, it will be just a demonstration of the brainwashing The Sovereign has used on his people.*

Robert stood to go, thanking Dr. Ntari for his time and then beat a hasty retreat, not wanting to get any deeper into the character of The Sovereign or his own belief of his character.

September 21, 998 ASR

Marilyn stood up at the center of the head table in the North East banquet room of the community hall after she officially closed the *Ladies of the Community* meeting. She relished the position of President. She felt powerful and in control. People looked up to her. As the clean up crew started to clear the fifty tables she saw old Thelma shuffling toward her. *One of the duties of President is to be sociable.* She put on her public smile as she walked forward to greet Thelma.

"Hi, Thelma. How are you doing today?" she asked.

"Hi, Marilyn. I'm doing OK for an old lady. That Robert of yours is such a sweet young man, Marilyn. Have you talked to him lately?" asked Thelma.

"Why no, I haven't, Thelma. Why do you ask?" replied Marilyn, wondering why Thelma would be interested in Robert.

"I'm a little concerned about his, humm, how would I describe what I'm feeling? Well, I would say I'm concerned about his direction in life."

"You mean because he has somehow turned into a perpetual student?" asked Marilyn, deciding to take the offensive. *Great! Now everyone in the community knows about him. What an embarrassment.*

"Oh no, heavens, no, Marilyn. I don't care about that. When he dropped by last week and interviewed me I was a bit concerned about the questions he asked me and I was just wondering if you had noticed his bent."

Marilyn shook her head as if to clear out the cobwebs. "Robert interviewed you last week, in person, here?" she asked, not really sure she just heard what she did.

"Oh no, not here at the community hall. He stopped by my house for breakfast." When Marilyn's jaw dropped she added, "Oh, didn't you know he came to interview me?"

Marilyn regained her composure quickly. Oh no, a Board member's wife and President of the Ladies of the Community shouldn't appear to be this out of touch with a member of her own family. Let's see, why would Robert want to interview Thelma? The book! Of course, that must be it. Thelma is really ancient and he would want to talk to people who might have known people who lived through the Last Battle. "Oh, well, of course, he wanted to talk you about his book, didn't he? You know The Sovereign seems to think it is important so I've been trying to encourage him. So how did the interview go?"

Thelma took Marilyn's hand and patted the back of it. "That's just it, my dear. I got a strong feeling that Robert was looking for something that would contradict the books and historical documentation we have about the Great Time of Trouble and the Last Battle."

He's doing what? Marilyn pulled her hand back hoping it wasn't too fast. "I know that he immersed himself quite deeply in the historical records but he never mentioned anything like that to me before. I'm sure he's just trying to make sure that he is getting all the information and that it is accurate." Marilyn was trying to reassure herself more than Thelma.

Thelma nodded thoughtfully. "Well, you might want to keep an eye on him," she said as she turned to go. "Good meeting, Marilyn. You are one of the best presidents we've had. See you next month."

Marilyn hurried out the door, ignoring whoever called her name as she left. On the way home she called Robert, even though she would rouse him up in the middle of the night.

He answered sleepily, eyes half open, "Oh, hi Mom. I hit my ECD three times before I realized it wasn't the alarm. What's so important that you're calling now? Do you know what time it is here?"

"I don't care what time it is. You are going to give me some answers or I'm going to come and get you, drag you home, and call a Board inquiry about you and your activities. So listen up and listen good. First I want to know why you interviewed Thelma and didn't even let me know you were in town," demanded Marilyn.

Marilyn was pleased to see that her threats got Robert's attention and he appeared wide awake. "Mother, I am doing interviews for my book and going to school at the same time. I barely had time to talk to Thelma before turning around and getting back to Midrib in time for classes. I'm sorry I didn't let you know I breezed through."

Marilyn paused as she pondered his answer. "I guess that makes sense, but I want to know what you are doing or where you are going with this book. Thelma seems to think you that you are specifically looking for anything that would contradict The Sovereign's accounts of the Great Time of Trouble and the Last Battle. So what's going on? I don't want my son hauled away by Enforcers. Can you imagine the shame your father and I would face if that happened?"

"Don't worry, Mom. The Sovereign knows exactly what I'm doing." She saw his eyes roll. "He must have forgotten it was a video call. "What I'm trying to do is find out if there are any heretical documents hidden away that someone might believe. Once I find any I can debunk them in a way that will once and for all settle these issues in questioning young minds. If I were to just walk into someone's living room and ask them if they had any stories that would prove The Sovereign to be a liar and they did, they wouldn't trust me. So that's why I approached Thelma with the questions I did. I was giving her the opportunity to reveal anything she might know but hadn't told anyone before."

Marilyn paused again. "I guess that makes sense too. You know that you should keep me informed about what you are doing, then I wouldn't have to call you at all hours of the night. I'll make sure Thelma knows your approach so we don't have to worry about any gossip."

"Thanks, Mom." Robert looked genuinely relieved.

Marilyn disconnected just before she arrived home. Justin had been getting home a lot sooner than he used to so she expected him to be home now. "Justiiiin, where are you?" she called.

His voice came from the back yard, "I'm out here, Sweetie."

As she came out the back door, Justin got up from his gardening and gave her a hug. "Hi, my love, welcome home."

Rather than return the hug she put her arms up in front of her so that her fists were beneath her chin and her folded arms were between them as Justin drew her into his arms. "Yeah, whatever." She let him hold her for a second or so then pushed him away. She was getting used to Justin's renewed devotion to her but she still wasn't ready to let him know. "Did you know that Robert was here recently to interview Thelma for his book and he didn't even stop by?"

Marilyn could see that her rebuff hurt Justin as he flinched, but immediately smiled warmly at her. *He appears to be growing fonder of me every day in spite of my attitude toward him. Maybe there is something to this counseling. We'll see how he handles this.*

"No," he said shaking his head. "I didn't know. How did you know?"

She eyed him for a second before answering, "It's a good think you didn't know. If you had known and didn't tell me you would be in some deep trouble." Her demeanor improved a bit as she explained how upset she was when she heard that Robert visited Thelma. She didn't confess that she was more concerned for her own reputation than for Robert's direction with his book; however she did relate her call to Robert with him.

"Marilyn, it was good that you called Robert to make sure he isn't going weird on us. I'm also glad that he reassured you he's continuing along paths that are not in conflict with The Sovereign. I'm proud of you." Justin put one arm around her shoulders and squeezed her lightly.

That felt good. She looked up and Justin and smiled at him, perhaps for the first time in two weeks.

Chapter 30

After class Robert, Samantha and Kevin took their usual stroll to the student union building to meet Jim in the cafeteria. When they arrived Jim was already there to Robert's surprise. It was the first time he arrived ahead of them.

"Jim, what brings you here so early?" asked Samantha.

Jim stood up as they approached. "Hi guys. I wanted to make sure I caught you early enough to see what you thought of the first discussion topic, but we can't discuss it here in the cafeteria. It's too easy for others to overhear us. So I reserved a small meeting room downstairs if you would like to come down and chat about it. This is sort of an informal interview to see if you'd like to go further and meet with others of our group. What do you say? Can you get away now?"

Robert was impressed that Jim took the initiative to get a private room for the follow-up discussions. He planned to do it himself but didn't feel like it was necessary to move so quickly. Maybe Jim would be much more valuable as a research assistant than he thought. "Sure, I have time. How about you two?" he asked of Samantha and Kevin.

"Sure, I was planning on kicking around some of Dr. Halverson's lectures with you but this sounds good, too," responded Samantha.

"Count me in," said Kevin, "I'm glad we don't have to wait any longer. I've been looking forward to this."

"OK, follow me." Jim led the way to the stairs and proceeded down one flight to the floor that housed offices for many campus organizations. It also had a few conference rooms where different groups could meet. As he entered his room he pulled out his ECD and punched in a few commands. "All clear. There aren't any listening devices in this room."

"Say what?" questioned Samantha as she wrinkled up her nose. "What do you mean there aren't any listening devices? What are you looking for?"

"It's just a precaution we always take before talking in depth about any discussion topics. We want to make sure that the Administration hasn't planted any listening devices that would report what we've been talking about," explained Robert.

"Have you ever found any bugged rooms?" asked Kevin, wide-eyed.

"Huh? What do bugs have to do with this?" responded Jim.

"Sorry, in sub-ancient times, listening devices planted in rooms were referred to as bugs. I think it came from the idea that the devices were small enough that they could look like a fly on the wall or something like that." Kevin's redden slightly as he explained.

That's odd. I don't remember reading about anything as obscure as that. I wonder where he dug that up, thought Robert.

"Oh, no we haven't, at least not that I know of, but that doesn't mean they wouldn't and we can't be too careful," Jim said.

The four sat down in purple upholstered arm chairs around a small round oak conference table that would comfortably seat six people. Jim opened up the discussion, obviously expecting them to fully embrace the direction that the topic had led, "So what did you think of the evidence that was presented in the topic?"

Samantha and Kevin looked at each other then both started to talk at the same time. Each then excused themselves and offered the other the opportunity to start first. After another false start Robert laughed and interjected, "Kevin, how about you starting?" He made a note to himself to counsel Jim a bit more on how to lead discussions.

"Sure. I was fascinated at the statistics that were provided. It looks like someone has done a lot of research to find out how many encounters there are with Enforcers. I certainly have to give credit to your organization for their detailed homework. Are all the discussion topics this well documented?" Kevin looked back at Jim with raised eyebrows.

With Kevin's question Jim was spurred on to talk for several minutes about how much detailed information all of the discussion topics contained. "The hierarchy of the underground assured us this is accurate and taken from the Administration's own data." He spoke quite authoritatively and with confidence.

Robert's mind briefly drifted off to his own conversation with Jim on the way to the mountains last summer. What a change had come over Jim since then . He felt quite proud that Jim's fears abated and he became bold in his convictions. However, Jim did tend to ramble and Robert had to interrupt to ask Samantha what she thought.

Samantha smiled. She looked so innocent when she smiled like that. If I didn't have this book on my mind and Jim wasn't interested in her I might consider…I should pay attention to what she's saying and not her good looks.

"Kevin took the words right out of my mouth," she answered. "These statistics are mind staggering. How do other people on campus react to them?"

Robert jumped in ahead of Jim to keep the meeting shorter. "Most people are also surprised by the data and welcome this knowledge. It helps them make informed decisions about their own lives and gain freedom." He then nodded to Jim to ask the next question.

"So, Sam, after reviewing the topic what do you think about the Administration's ability to maintain control of society?"

She paused for a moment before speaking, the smile faded to a slight frown. "Based on what I read it appears that the Administration is far from the all-knowing and all-powerful organization that it touts itself to be. Wouldn't you agree?"

Jim's face brightened and Robert knew he was thinking the same thing. They were looking for precisely that kind of answer.

"I'll let you know in a minute, but I'd like to hear from Kevin first," said Jim.

Good job. Robert saw that Jim picked up on his clue to get both of their answers and not run off with explanations too soon.

Kevin nodded thoughtfully, "Well, I agree with Sam. This certainly demonstrates that they are no longer maintaining the same control over society as in previous generations. What does this mean for the future?"

"I think that I can speak for both us in that we agree with your conclusions." Jim looked at Robert to get the go ahead, then proceeded after Robert nodded, "As far as the future is concerned, that is what we'll be discussing in some of the more advanced topics. We usually review more topics with people but we believe there isn't any need to screen you anymore. Would you like to come to an introductory meeting tonight for new members of our group? What do you say? Do you want to join and learn more about things you'll never hear from the Administration?"

"I think I'd really enjoy that. Thanks for the invitation," Samantha quickly answered.

"Count me in too," added Kevin..

Robert interrupted, "I didn't know our next meeting was tonight."

"You've been in class. The notice appeared about forty five minutes ago," replied Jim.

"Oh." Robert looked at his ECD and nodded. That explained why he was so eager to do the introductory interview.

"Great; that's settled. We're really excited that you'll be joining us. Kevin, I'll stop by your dorm at 11:55 tonight and take you to the first meeting. Sam, a lady in our group by the name of Hillary will stop by your room at 11:50 to show you the way. The leaders are very cautious and you will not know the location or times of the meetings until you have more or less proven yourselves to them. You might call this a probationary time. Once they are confident that you are aligned with us on the program you will receive the time and location of the meeting along with the discussion topic. Any questions?" Jim concluded.

There weren't any more questions so they decided to work on their homework and go over Dr. Halverson's last lecture in the conference room since it was already reserved.

At precisely 11:50 Samantha heard a loud knock ring out from her dorm room door. Opening the door, she was greeted by a stern-faced Asian woman who could have been either eighteen or eighty years old.

She had short straight black hair that covered her ears. Her bangs were perfectly straight across the middle of her forehead, giving her face the appearance of a square, except for her chin. If she wasn't scowling she could be pretty. She reminded Samantha of some of the Chinese red brigade that wreaked havoc in China long before the Last Battle. "Who are you?" she asked dryly.

"I'm Samantha Spell, you can call me Sam. Who are you?" replied Samantha as cheerily as she could, hoping to break the gloomy spell that the woman exuded. She extended her hand and was about to say pleased to meet you but the woman had already turned away.

"I'm Hillary and we don't use last names. Let's go," she snapped as she started down the hall.

OK, this is going to be a real fun meeting. Samantha scrambled to catch up with Hillary.

"So how long have you been going to these discussion groups Hillary?" asked Samantha as she caught up.

"Long enough to know not to answer newbes' questions." Hillary didn't look back.

"Well, excuse me! Is it against the rules to be friendly? If so, then the guys that invited me must really be in trouble." Samantha caught up and came alongside Hillary.

"Look, Sam," she emphasized Samantha's nick name. "I read your bio and I was opposed to inviting you. Cute little smart farm girls generally get freaked out by the introductory stuff if not by the first topic. Jim probably fell in love with you at first sight and convinced Robert to let you in. I'll be watching you very carefully. One sign of sympathy for The Sovereign and you'll be out."

Samantha was shocked because they did a background check on her as well as this woman's blatant hostility toward The Sovereign. However she was determined not to let this or any other intimidations keep her from her responsibility. "Little farm girl, huh? So what does that make you? You're at least fifteen centimeters shorter than I am. You're living proof that The Sovereign isn't able to monitor everyone." Samantha figured it wasn't going to hurt her chances any to let her know that she wasn't a docile farm girl.

"What do you mean that I'm living proof?" Hillary stopped and turned to Samantha.

Samantha was pleased that she bit on that jab. "Why should I let you know since you've been going to these meetings long enough to know why?" She reflected Hillary's icy personality with a bit of smugness added in.

"Look, girl. I don't have to take you to this meeting so don't start getting smart with me," growled Hillary as she started to turn from ice to fire.

"And just how are you going to explain to your leader if a new recruit doesn't get to the first meeting? You think he's going to be pleased, especially if the reason is simply petty envy? I may be young and fresh off the farm but that doesn't make me stupid. So just cool your jets and lead the way," said Samantha coolly.

Samantha retained her calm and even an authoritative aura while Hillary was visibly grinding her teeth. Hillary resumed her speed walk and Samantha easily matched her pace. Her countenance slowly softened as they quietly exited the dorm building. About five minutes later Hillary broke the ice.

"Maybe I was a bit hasty in my judgment, Sam. You certainly don't sound like a Sovereign sympathizer. Do you think we could call a truce?" Hillary's voice was softer but still stern.

Samantha hesitated long enough to make sure that she didn't seem like a pushover, then answered cautiously, "I think we could do that."

After a bit of an awkward silence Hillary asked, "Uh, what did you mean when you said I was living proof of The Sovereign's inability to monitor us."

Samantha couldn't keep from laughing. "Well, I may have to eat those words. I was thinking that anyone so rude and so blatantly anti-Sovereign would have been nailed by an Enforcer by now, but it now appears you may not be half bad."

Hillary joined in the laugh. "Sorry about being so rude but you're right about being anti-Sovereign. And I don't doubt you will be, too, after you dig into the dirt that the underground has. This will be my third year at university but I was introduced to the first topics my junior year in high school."

Within a few more minutes they arrived at the meeting location smiling and chatting amiably. Hillary introduced Samantha to a guy who looked like he was in charge. "Sam, this is Gustav, our cell leader. She's cool, Gustav, even pretty sharp."

Gustav shook Samantha's hand. "Welcome, Sam. I'll have to admit I'm a bit surprised to see you two getting along so well. Hillary was quite vocal about her objections to invite you. I assigned Hillary to escort you to the first meeting figuring that if anyone would be able to snoop out a Sovereign sympathizer she would."

"Pleased to meet you, Gustav. Yeah, Hillary and I came to an understanding on the way over. I'm glad I passed the first test." Samantha felt fairly confident but knew she would feel even better when Kevin arrived.

When everyone arrived Gustav had each person introduce him or her self. There was a recruit for each of the original members. Next, Gustav opened the meeting, "Welcome to our little study group. Each of you has expressed an interest in gathering together with like-minded students who are eager to explore topics beyond those provided by the university. You were all given some sample material which was a test to see how you would respond to more controversial subject matter. Since you all responded favorably to those, you were then introduced to our first topic. As you may have gathered, the theme of this material paints a slightly different picture of The Sovereign than you get from the Administration. I'll be up front with you right now. The rest of the topics will open your eyes to many more inconsistencies between The Sovereign's claims and our discoveries. We meet in secret because our discussions would be considered treasonous if the Administration were to find out about them. So far no Enforcers have appeared at any of these meeting, which is a confirmation of the subject of our first discussion, that Yehowshuwa really can't keep track of everything that happens. To ensure that we are not interrupted by Enforcers and charged for treason, each of you agreed to not disclose this information to anyone without authorization from us and we trust that you will keep that promise."

Gustav paused and looked each recruit in the eye.

Samantha looked Gustav straight in the eye and smiled. She was so thankful that she already settled the promise issue; otherwise she would have averted her gaze. She would be out of there right now. No, she would not have even attended.

Each of the others also looked expectantly as Gustav scanned the recruits. He smiled and appeared pleased.

The discussion group broke up later than usual thanks to some interesting questions that Kevin and Samantha asked. The new recruits seemed to be invigorated and excited to be accepted by this group. Samantha was relieved that she was able to participate in the discussions and not reveal her mission.

September 23, 998 ASR

Samantha walked down the hallway of Edgar Pavilion. It was on the opposite side of the campus from her dorm. The walls were a cheery pink and the carpet had rose patterns. It was definitely a woman's residence. Still, she felt like it was dark and oppressive.

She was nervous. This was her first contact with a new recruit to a cell outside of her own. She wasn't here to discuss the deficiencies of The Sovereign but to introduce Ellen to him. She carefully used public records to ensure that Ellen wasn't in any class with anyone else in her cell. If the meeting took the wrong direction she didn't want anyone in her cell finding out what she was doing.

Samantha paused at room 87078. She took a deep breath, asked The Sovereign for guidance, and then knocked on the door.

A few seconds elapsed before the door opened. A young woman, about the same age as Samantha held the door. Her blue eyes and a freckled face were surrounded by wavy auburn hair. There was no smile and she seemed sad.

"Are you Ellen Blake?" asked Samantha.

"Yes, who's asking?" Ellen replied coolly.

"Hi, my name is Amanda." *OK it is my middle name but I don't need to let her know that.* "I'd like to talk to you about a discussion topic you received a few days ago and the follow-up meeting. Do you have some time?"

She glanced up and down the hall, then replied, "Yeah, I suppose. Come on in." She quickly closed the door as soon as Samantha was in the room. "You aren't in my cell. How did you know I received a discussion topic? We were told no one knows except our leaders." She looked Samantha up and down. "You aren't old enough to be a leader."

As Samantha stepped into the room, she looked in the mirror. She didn't recognize the brunette staring back at her. Samantha would never be caught with that color or style. The dull brown eyes hid her normal bright blue.

"A friend gave me your name. With some help from the Administration, he got your ID off the network when the topic was sent to you." *Oh, my, I shouldn't have said that. If she rats out to the underground they will know we can detect the transmission of the topics and I've blown the whole mission.*

The color drained out of Ellen's face and she sat down on her small couch. "I knew it. I knew I should have never gone to that meeting. I'm in trouble, aren't I?" She put her face in her hands and started to sob.

Samantha sat down and put her arms around Ellen. "No, you aren't in any trouble. I've come to help you clarify what is true and what is false."

Ellen looked up through tear-filled eyes. "What? I don't understand. Aren't you with the Administration?"

"No, I'm not. I'm a student just like you. I've been to my first meeting also. The only difference is that I wasn't blindsided by the discussion topics and I have a more mature friend who helps me with them." Samantha was very thankful she could discuss them with Kevin.

"I'm so scared. I promised not to tell anyone about the meetings and topics and they said we are now engaged in treason. How can you help? You're stuck just like me." Ellen rubbed her eyes with the back of her hands.

"No, we aren't stuck and no, we aren't going to be charged with treason. Think about the primary premise of the first topic. They say that The Sovereign is not able to monitor everything as he claims and that he knows nothing about this underground. Yehowshuwa is The Sovereign that I know and I know that he knows all about the meetings and every single topic that has ever appeared in *The Question* or that will appear in the future. He is all knowing." Samantha's faith grew as she talked about The Sovereign. She was no longer nervous.

"Are you saying he knows we were in underground cell meetings? Then why hasn't he stopped them? These people are clearly against him and his Administration." Ellen shook her head.

Samantha thought for a second then felt a prompting within her to take a different approach. "We can talk about that later, but first I really need to find out why you are so afraid. I think that is the key to all your questions."

"OK, I'm listening."

"Ellen, this may seem like a strange question, but if the world were to end today, where would you end up?"

Ellen looked at Samantha quizzically but answered, "I suppose it would be in The Sovereign's new kingdom."

"OK, now suppose he asked you, 'Why should I let you into my new world?' how would you answer him?"

Ellen's mouth opened but nothing came out. She finally mumbled, "Well, until now I'd say I've been following all his rules. But this treason would knock me out of the running."

Samantha felt sorry for Ellen. She didn't know Yehowshuwa and his wonderful grace. She only knew him as a stern tyrant without compassion. She hoped that was about to change. "Have you really been able to follow all his rules? Have you ever told a lie?"

"Well of course I have. Hasn't everyone? But what does that compare to treason?" Ellen's knitted eyebrows revealed how perplexed she was at Samantha's question.

"It's simple, Ellen. If you want to be accepted based on your performance, then The Sovereign's requirements are perfection, 100% obedience 100% of the time. If you disobey in what seems like the least of his commands then you have fallen short of perfection." Samantha drew an imaginary target in the air with her finger. "If we both threw darts at a target but missed the bull's eye with even one dart, neither one of us gets a perfect score."

"Then no one will be in his forever kingdom. We've all messed up at some point. Doesn't he forgive us?" asked Ellen.

"He will forgive you if you ask him. His forgiveness is based on admitting that we have disobeyed and that our disobedience deserves eternal punishment. We need to realize that when he died, he took that punishment on himself. He didn't deserve it but we do. Since he didn't deserve it, he exchanges his punishment for ours. If we believe that, then we finally understand that we owe him our lives. Our response is to pledge our loyalty to him so that he really *is* our sovereign. It isn't just a title we give him anymore." Samantha put one hand on Ellen's shoulder. "Would you like to surrender to him?"

Ellen nodded her head. "Yes I would. You know, I've been taught all this before but somehow, tonight, this is the first time it makes sense. I guess it's the first time I've ever admitted that I've offended The Sovereign. I know what to do."

She bowed her head and spoke to The Sovereign, "Yehowshuwa, I know you are listening to me now the same as last night when I was at that meeting. I'm sorry, I know I've failed you and it wasn't just last night. I'm yours completely and totally."

Ellen lifted her head and smiled. "Amanda, I've never felt better in my life. The fear is gone, but what now? What's next? How do I get out of this underground?"

"First of all, welcome to The Sovereign Yehowshuwa's forever family. He will take care of you and protect you. However, I think the best approach is to tell the person who recruited you that you are no longer interested. If she asks you why all you need to do is to follow an outline I'll give you. Who knows, maybe you can rescue her too."

Samantha transferred the outline and some reading material to Ellen's ECD. "I've also given you a contact for a study group that meets in your dorm. Meet with them and you will learn more about The Sovereign than you ever dreamed possible. Just tell them Amanda sent you. Because I could be a threat to the underground I can't give you my ID or meet with you again. They may watch you to see who led you out of their conspiracy. If they found me out, my efforts would be hampered or they may physically try to stop me."

Ellen's eyes widened. "This is serious, isn't it?"

"Yes, it is. People's lives are at stake and I don't want to blow my opportunities. I need to leave now. Be sure to meet with the group right away. You have a lot to learn."

"OK, I will."

Samantha gave Ellen a big hug then left. When she walked back down the hallway it was no longer oppressive. She had a spring in her step and she felt almost as if she were walking in the air.

December 3, 998 ASR

Jim walked lazily across the campus main square. He wasn't in a hurry; then again, he seldom was in a hurry. He enjoyed the sounds of the chirping birds, the fragrance of the flowering trees, and the blue sky with only a few puffy clouds floating lazily along. *They look like they are in about as much of a hurry as I am.*

He entered the student union building and made his way through the cafeteria to the corner where his friends were studying. "Hi, guys, how're things going?" asked Jim as he sat down with Robert, Samantha and Kevin. "Hey, what's with all the quiet?"

"In case you haven't noticed finals are coming up in another week and unlike some of us around here we have to study to pass," Samantha informed Jim without looking up.

"Are you all ready for your finals?" asked Robert.

"Oh, I'm as ready as I'll ever be. I'm not going out with a blast but I'm doing well enough to pass. How about you? You haven't been around much these last few weekends. How're your interviews going?" inquired Jim.

"I'm almost finished with the ones I've scheduled during the quarter," said Robert lowering his voice to a whisper. He turned away from Kevin and Samantha. "They really aren't going all that well. So far each of them has been singing the party song and won't budge an inch. I discreetly try to toss out some questions that would let them open up but they steadfastly give me the same story. I swear they've all been brainwashed."

Jim understood that Robert didn't want to share that with Kevin and Samantha so he responded quietly, "Isn't that basically what Gustav has been telling us all along? With a few exceptions, people over one hundred years old are going to be sucked into everything The Sovereign has said."

"Yeah, that fits but sometimes I get a bit discouraged. That interview with Dr. Ntari is still bugging me. I guess I was just too hopeful that his scientific background would give him better reasoning powers. If anything, he's bought into the Administration's line even more than the others. Most of them have been touchy-feely about what they believe but Dr. Ntari was so adamant that his belief and science agreed that I really felt sorry for him." Robert shook his head.

"Yeah, it's too bad when they place their faith above their reason. So who's next on your agenda?" asked Jim.

"If you have time, I'd like you to come along with me on this weekend's interview. I have a feeling that it might be different and you would be especially interested." The concern on Robert's face melted into a smile.

"Sure, like I said, I'm good for the quarter and we can always study on the road. So, who are we going to visit?" asked Jim.

"I was saving it for a surprise. We'll be interviewing your old buddy Josu." Robert leaned back, his voice returned to a normal conversational level.

"Really! That would be great, but I thought you were only interviewing the oldest people on the earth. Why'd you pick him?" Jim was already looking forward to seeing the friend he made on his way to his summer camping trip with Robert.

"Because he is one of the oldest people on the earth. He never told you, did he? He is 861 years old."

"Whoa, that is old. We've kept in contact and I've gotten to know him better but I had no idea he was that old. When are we leaving?" asked Jim.

"Tomorrow after class we can take off and get there Saturday morning. I didn't tell Josu you were coming because I wasn't sure you'd be able to make it. We can surprise him."

Robert and Jim continued to talk until everyone was done studying and then let the others know their plans for the weekend.

December 4, 998 ASR

The next day Jim hurried to the student union building with his backpack to wait for Robert. He was eager to visit Josu since he was almost a father figure. His own father hadn't talked to him during his previous three years at university but Josu and Jim exchanged calls almost weekly.

When Robert showed up, he also had his pack and they immediately left for the convy station to proceed on their trip. Once they made their connections for the North West Regional transit center they settled back for the long trip.

"What will you do if the interview with Josu turns out to be the same as the rest? From everything you told me so far it doesn't sound like you found anything that would be book material unless you plan on writing another book just like the rest that tell the same old story," asked Jim.

"If all I get is the same dribble from Josu I'm not sure what I'll do. But from what you told me I think he's going to give us a different picture of the Great Time of Trouble. But even if he doesn't, I still need to do a lot of research to find documentation that must still exist from that and the previous era. As I learned from Dr. Halverson's class, there are philosophies that subtly direct people away from The Sovereign. There must be some documents that will show that there were benefits to society and not just the subversion and destruction that we've been told. I mean, why would they continue to follow these philosophies if they were so detrimental? People aren't so dumb that they would continue in self-destructive ideologies and behaviors, are they?" Robert threw up his hands.

"That makes sense. I read somewhere that we're born with a deep sense of self-preservation. Even now, when there is a little threat to us, like a man-eating lion, we do what we must in order to protect ourselves." Jim laughed as he remembered the fright he had when Robert tricked him with the cougar he trained to fake a battle to the death. "If we had a belief structure that caused us problems I would think that we would figure that out and make adjustments. Anyway, where do you plan on finding these mysterious documents?"

Robert joined in the laugh at the lion incident, then became serious. "I have some theories. If these documents still exist, then they are held by The Sovereign where most people can't find them. I've run across some references to royal archives in my studies. Once I was curious about them and tried to follow the data trails but finally ran into an access block. The explanation said that the documents I wanted were not online and I needed an access code in order to get them out of storage and online. Since everything checked out to that point I didn't have any reason to doubt that the originals would reveal anything different. However, I'm no longer convinced that these authors saw the originals. More important, even if the originals check out, there may be other documents that people don't quote because they disagree."

Jim shrugged his shoulders. "Why haven't you tried your access card to get some of the document?"

Robert grimaced, "I've been busy with the interviews and school so I don't have the time to look up books that I read, then follow the sources in the bibliographies. These lead to other books and bibliographies and those to other books and on and on. There are nearly a thousand years of quotes before we get back to the originals. I haven't been looking forward to that task."

"Hey, isn't that why you hired a research assistant? Give me a book and I'll get to the originals for you." Jim put out his hand as if to take a book from Robert.

Robert laughed, "Sure. How about starting with the textbook for my class in Sub-Ancient Philosophy? Look up the quotes of Søren Kierkegaard in it and see if you can find some books that quoted him from the early twentieth century, or even better, try to find his books. That should keep you busy for a while, Mr. Got-all-my-classes-under-control."

"No sooner said than done," replied Jim quite confidently.

Jim curled up in his chair, opened his ECD and started working feverishly. Robert reclined in his chair and quickly dozed off. After about thirty minutes Jim smiled, folded up his ECD, leaned back and did what he did best. He slept.

December 5, 998 ASR

Six hours later Jim tried to ignore Robert's beeping ECD alarm. He couldn't ignore Robert jostling his arm or his questions. "We're almost at our next transfer. You think fifteen minutes is enough time for you to wake up? How late did you work on the research?"

"Oh man, there has to be a better way to wake up than listening to your questions. What are you talking about – research? Can't a guy get a little rest?" Jim tried to roll over but the chair didn't recline far enough to allow that. He pulled his blanket up over his head and started to go back to sleep.

Robert shook his arm again. "Come on Jim, wake up. Don't you remember doing the research before you went to sleep? How late did you stay up?" Those question were threatening to jumpstart his brain.

"Leave me alone. I went to sleep about a half hour after you," moaned Jim.

"So how far did you get in a half hour? I'll bet you couldn't have gotten more that five or six books deep in that amount of time." That sounded like a challenge from Robert.

Jim was starting to come around. "Huh? What do you mean? I only looked at your textbook last night."

"So Mr. Research-assistant, in one half hour all the further you got was the one book I gave you? How long do you think it will take to get to the source?"

Now Jim was wide awake and he opened his ECD. "OK Mr. Dig-in-the-dirt-but-never-a-computer, I'll tell you." He glanced at the screen. "Well, it looks like I got far enough to hit your access block. Look at this."

"Say what?" Robert looked at the screen that showed a blinking panel asking for an access number to open archives for 687 books and put the data online. "How did you do that?"

"You don't think I was actually going to look all these up by hand, did you? I just asked the system to follow the links back from book to book for me. So how about trying your access card to see if we can get this show on the road?"

Sometimes I really wonder how smart Robert really is.

Robert handed Jim the access card and he pressed it against the screen. The ECD responded with a message that the card was accepted and that the requested books would be available online within a week.

"I'm really impressed! Good work!" said Robert as he slapped Jim on the back.

Jim and Robert transferred for the last leg in their journey and arrived at the North West Regional transit center. They stopped at the travel comfort station where they showered and shaved, then went to the Iluna Quebash Cafeteria to meet Josu.

"Jim, what a surprise that you have come with Robert for this meeting! It is so good to see you." Josu ran up to Jim and gave him a big bear hug. "Welcome my son, I am overcome with joy that you could come."

"It's good to see you again, Josu. I've enjoyed talking to you but it's always better face to face."

"Indeed it is. And this must be your friend Robert. You've told me so much about him." Josu turned toward the kitchen and called out, "Zuma, Jim is here with Robert, we'll need another omelet for him as well."

"Welcome my friends. Please come and sit. My daughter is preparing for you the most exquisite breakfast, zumentralagra omelets. You will enjoy these immensely. Then we can talk."

The three went to the back corner of the cafeteria where it was private and they could talk without being overheard. After about five minutes a young girl, perhaps fifteen years old, approached the table. She was quite slim, almost as if she were underfed, with long black hair and smooth dark skin the same shade as Josu's leathery face. She smiled broadly, exposing her shiny white teeth as she placed three plates before them. Each plate contained a large round golden omelet surrounded with slices of light green honeydew melon. She also brought three cups of freshly brewed, strong smelling coffee.

"Mr. Taratoricakena," stammered Robert trying to pronounce his name.

"No, no, please call me Josu. I may be old but we are friends."

"OK, uh Josu, Jim told me about your cuisine and I have a question. Are there eels or squid in these omelets?" asked Robert.

Josu laughed loudly. "Oh, Robert, you would not make a very good Quebash. Yes, we do love seafood but you will only find potatoes and eggs in these delicious omelets. Most Quebash cuisine is not complicated but the uniqueness is in the preparation. The potatoes are first cooked in a special oil that ensures that there is not even a hint of crispness." Jim knew that Josu left out the fact that the special oil was pig fat. "Then they are set aside to cool while the chef beats the eggs. The two cannot be mixed while the potatoes are warm; otherwise the eggs start to cook and would not be the right texture when they are cooked together. Then they are completely blended. The mixture is cooked in the pan until the bottom is the golden brown you see. The chef then slips the omelet into the lid and turns it over to cook the other side. None of this lazy turning half of it over the way many cook omelets. I'm sure you will enjoy it."

Jim dug into the omelet while Josu was describing it. "This is really great, Josu. You really know how to tickle a person's gastronomical fancy. Say, did I hear you say that the girl who served us is your daughter? I just found out you are 861 years old. Aren't you a bit old to have a girl that young?" he asked while he was wolfing down the omelet. "Hey, this is really good. I've had omelets with potatoes before but they've always been chunky. These are blended together so well that you can't tell that potatoes are in here."

"Zuma is a great cook, isn't she? Someday she will make an excellent chef. This is one of her favorite recipes, partly because one of her ancestors was named Zuma as well and tradition says that she was the one who invented this delicacy. She is my daughter just as you are my son, Jim. She is my direct descendent to the twentieth generation as are you."

"Say what?" Jim stopped eating.

"Yes, Jim, I've been tracing some of my errant family and found your parents. You and Zuma are 32nd cousins." Josu smiled broadly like a proud parent.

"Oh wow, then that means you really are my father. This is really cool. I had this feeling after we first met you that we were related. You know my parents never introduced me to my great grandparents. For some reason they and my grandparents never mentioned them." Jim felt a longing being partially filled.

"Ah yes, they decided along with others to break from the Quebash traditions and assimilate into the rest of society. That's why they wouldn't let you know your great grandparents or any of your other ancestors. You'll have time to get acquainted with the rest of your family but I see Robert is nearly finished eating and he has important business. What would you like to know?" asked Josu.

Robert wiped his mouth on a napkin. "Thank you, Josu, this was a great breakfast. First I'd like to know if either your parents or grandparents lived through the Great Time of Trouble and what stories they told you about the time. Jim already told me about some of your conversations and that he set you up to get *The Question*. So I can let you know that I'm looking for anything that will confirm what it says about The Sovereign."

"I see," said Josu, nodding thoughtfully. "Well, my grandparents were adults when they came into this new era. They didn't live as long as many who survived so I didn't get to know them. My parents were teenagers when The Sovereign recalled his people and let The Chancellor take control. Fortunately, our people have a long tradition of teaching our children our ways and history, so they informed me in much detail about the events leading up to the Great Time of Trouble and of that time itself. I think you will be very interested in our perspective."

Robert smiled broadly. Jim knew he was looking for this perspective.

"As I've been telling Jim, our people have always been very independent. We've had many people over us who tried to impose their sovereignty on us. Through it all we maintained our uniqueness and fought when needed and pretended subservience when required only so we could wait for more opportune times. Many times we were able to hide in the mountains and wait. We are a proud people and our allegiance has always been to our own kind. Very few of us were taken by The Sovereign. The ones that did go were weak and weren't missed all that much. They didn't support the strong affinity to our people."

Robert took some notes on his ECD.

Josu put his elbows on the table and clasped his hands together under his chin. "When The Chancellor Ben-Shaachar first took control he instituted many reforms that guaranteed our independence. Many of the social restrictions that The

Sovereign's followers imposed on us were released and we were able to enjoy life more than in the previous two thousand years when Yehowshuwa's influence brought limitations upon most of the world. However, we didn't trust The Chancellor just as we haven't trusted any other government but our own. Then, of course, when he tried to combine the whole world under his control we fled to the mountains to resist him."

Josu's eyes grew dark and angry. "When The Sovereign Yehowshuwa began his attack on the environment the mountains provided our people some safety as well. Many people in the world were destroyed and Ben-Shaachar had his hands full trying to maintain order under such terrible circumstances so we were left to our own resources."

His eyes brightened. "Even during the terrible ecological attacks my people found a freedom that was almost intoxicating and they attributed this to The Chancellor's new administration, even though they didn't submit to him. I've not experienced anything in all my years within this bland 'perfect' environment that could match the description of the way they lived during that time."

Robert was almost frothing at the mouth with excitement as he inquired, "Josu, I've been told over and over that The Chancellor was evil and that he promised freedom but actually turned people into slaves for himself. We were told that as a result of his reforms people became deviants, drug and sex addicts, and that society was worse off than before. Yet you are telling me that your people had freedom and enjoyed life even more than before. How do you account for the difference in these perspectives?" he asked.

Josu shrugged. "Our people were relatively isolated from the rest of the world. It is possible that since they escaped The Chancellor's direct influence over them they were not affected. However it is also possible that since those who told the other stories were loyal to The Sovereign that they made it sound worse than it was. They would do this to maintain The Sovereign's control over society today and perhaps because they have no choice if they want to remain loyal to him. According to those stories, the loyalists were hunted down and beheaded by The Chancellor and his forces. But it stands to reason that subversives need to be controlled. My parents were told that the loyalists were trying to undermine The Chancellor's authority and were applauding the catastrophes that The Sovereign was pouring upon the earth. They were deriding The Chancellor's reforms."

Josu lowered his head and shook a finger at Robert. "I'll be honest with you. My people were not enthused about those who had become loyal to The Sovereign and his policies after the Great Time of Trouble began. They were especially upset with the way Yehowshuwa waged war against the majority of the people in the world with earthquakes and other hideous disasters. There were a few among my people who became loyalists but they were banished from their inheritance. No one knows what happened to them. They were obnoxious in the way they were trying to force their beliefs on others. My people were also afraid that they would draw attention to our people and implicate us with their cause so that The Chancellor would come looking for us. Eventually many of my people aligned themselves with The Chancellor. However, they only turned in those who aligned themselves with The Sovereign."

"So what happened when The Sovereign returned and The Chancellor was defeated? Did it happen the way we've been told over and over?" asked Robert.

Josu nodded. "Most of what you've been told is the same as what I was told by my parents. However the perspective is different. The stories you've read and heard are all from the loyalists' viewpoint. They thought of Ben-Shaachar's regime as being totally evil. They believed anyone aligned with him was lost, without hope, and willing to do the vilest things to harm Yehowshuwa and his people. My people didn't see it that way. They saw what The Sovereign was doing to the earth and saw The Chancellor as one who was trying to stop him. Yes, he did some things that they didn't like but it appeared that he had little choice. The books say that The Chancellor drugged his soldiers so that they could continue to fight even though seriously wounded. That may be true but he was facing a last ditch opportunity to once and for all defeat The Sovereign Yehowshuwa and restore the earth to the way he said it should have been all along, with freedom from The Sovereign."

Jim sat back and covered his mouth. He had never heard, even from the underground such a direct accusation against The Sovereign. He was shocked. *How did Josu manage to live this long with his attitude?*

"When the Last Battle started, my people were hopeful that The Sovereign would be defeated and that they would be left to live in peace. However it didn't go that way. The Sovereign has powers that they didn't know about. Millions were slaughtered within minutes of the engagement. Many tried to surrender when they saw they were utterly defeated but Yehowshuwa didn't take prisoners. He wiped out every single person in opposition to him on the battle field. But he didn't stop there. Around the world the majority of the population of the earth was wiped out. Those that had sworn allegiance to Ben-Shaachar pleaded for mercy but found none."

"Yet your grandparents were spared. How did that happen?" asked Robert. His eyes were wide, evidently this was as surprising to him as it was to Jim.

Josu paused and took a drink of his coffee. "Yes, they were told that they were spared because they were among those who had not sworn allegiance to The Chancellor. With such a deadly display of power, they quickly bowed their knees but not their hearts to Yehowshuwa. For a brief time they thought they would be able to hide in the hills and maintain their independence but that was quickly quashed as the Enforcers showed up to establish the Administration's structure over them. Quite a few of my people disappeared when they refused to cooperate. Those who survived were the ones who saw the futility of resistance. They decided to bide their time and see if they could wait out The Sovereign and pass our heritage on to those who might eventually break free from his dominion."

He looked down at his coffee and sighed, "My grandparents all died at a relatively young age. Most of those who came through the Great Time of Trouble lived two and three hundred years, but not my grandparents. They were all just under a hundred when they died. My parents fared somewhat better but still only lived about three hundred years."

"That is young. Why do you think they died so young?" asked Robert.

"I think it was a direct result of their disobedience to The Sovereign. They were continually running into problems with Enforcers and were still rebelling. I can't help but believe that they were punished by The Sovereign," replied Josu.

"Josu, you sound as rebellious as your parents yet you are one of the oldest people alive right now. Why do you think you've been spared?" asked Jim.

"I believe it's because I've been compliant. I observed my parents and paid attention to what they told me of their ancestors. I realized that if I ever wanted to see true freedom for my people again I would have to be patient and wait for the right time. I would never have dared to tell you these things when I was younger for fear of reprisal." Josu shook his head. "You don't know what it's like to live 800 years in fear."

Robert leaned forward and asked quietly, "And now it's different?"

Josu nodded. "Yes, the teaching elders of our people have also been very careful while conveying our history to each generation. We kept what we learned about the Great Time of Trouble secret until now. We speak more feely now than years ago because we see that Yehowshuwa's power is slipping. He doesn't have as much control now as he did just a hundred years ago. We see in it in the way some of the younger people flaunt their bodies with styles that would have never been permitted before. You can also see it in their attitudes. They aren't subjecting themselves to The Sovereign's definition of social acceptability. I personally have seen this because I've worked here at the regional center for nearly two hundred years. I found that it's a good place to observe people and bide my time. It hasn't been until the last few years that I've felt free to speak openly with people. Now, our elders are educating our people about what happened during the Great Time of Trouble from our grand and great grandparents' perspective."

"Josu, how long ago did the elders start teaching the truth? I mean, would it have been about the time that my grandparents' changed their names and departed from their heritage?" asked Jim.

Josu looked sadly into Jim's eyes. "Yes, my son. When I did my research looking for you I found that they left at that time. Not everyone is able to accept the truth. Some are quite brainwashed by The Sovereign Yehowshuwa, even though we tried to raise our descendents carefully. We wanted to give them a sense of independence but not so much that we would risk the ire of The Sovereign. Others simply were afraid and also left. I don't know the reason your grandparents fled from our flock. From what you told me, it appears that after separating from us, they didn't embrace the way we raised our children. Otherwise, your parents would be much more involved with you and less so with achieving positions within the Administration. If they were following The Sovereign's way it points out that his methods are not always the best."

Robert whispered, "Josu, what you've told us corroborates many of the things that we've been studying in *The Question*. We need to get you in contact with the underground so that this can be told not only to your people but everyone in the world who is seeking the truth," His voice raised then became quiet again. "This is the biggest breakthrough in proving that The Sovereign isn't really all he makes himself out to be."

Josu laughed, "Why are you whispering, Robert? If we had been overheard before don't you think The Sovereign would have his Enforcers all over us for what I've told you already? I would be glad to do what I can to help the cause. Perhaps my people and others will be truly free sooner if we join together."

The three continued to talk and plan how they would get together again after Robert ran the news up the chain of command. He explained how the underground was structured to protect the participants and the leaders. Soon it was time for Jim and Robert to return. Josu sent them off with some house specialties in takeout containers.

Jim was thrilled that Robert finally had some concrete evidence for his book and that he was a part of helping him find it.

Chapter 31

Zophia briskly entered the mess hall. Chuck was at his table by himself looking down at his food. He didn't look up or acknowledge her entrance. She grabbed a tray at the service counter and surveyed her options. Cold drinks were soy milk, orange juice, or water. She could have hot cereal, fake bacon and eggs, pancakes, or toast. She already felt in a nasty mood and the options didn't help her out. *Too bad we didn't take up the Edenian's offer of some of their fruits. This homegrown stuff from our hydroponic gardens just doesn't compare at all to theirs.* To make matters worse, she had a deep craving for a very rare steak.

She took two pieces of toast and put several slices of fake bacon and eggs in between. She added a glass of soy milk and orange juice to her tray. She spun around quickly, marched over to the captain's table, and sat down across from Chuck. She was sure he avoided her look when she entered. She spoke audibly, "So, Chuck, why haven't I been able to contact you telepathically? Have you been shutting me out?" She identified the source of her spiteful frame of mind.

He looked her squarely in the eye. "I haven't heard you call. As a matter of fact, I've tried to call you and was wondering the same thing." He looked away, then back at her, shaking his head. "Then I realized I can't hear anyone."

Zophia was alarmed. "When did this happen?"

"I don't know. I think my abilities have slowly waned since leaving Eden, but I lapsed back into verbal communications and didn't really notice until this morning." He pointed his chin toward another table. "Look at Barb and Henry. They are talking. Don't you think a married couple would use telepathy if the could?

Zophia leaned forward. "Chuck, I'm sorry, I should have been more aware of what is happening. We can get your abilities back when we start up training. The room is ready and we should start immediately. Maybe you should reconsider and be part of the first class." Zophia reached out and touched Chuck's hand. "Or better yet, we could have private lessons." He quickly withdrew his hand.

She leaned back in her chair and smiled at him. *In time you will be mine, Chuck, then nothing will be able to stop us.*

Chuck stood. "At our staff meeting this morning, I'll have each of the department heads submit their choices for training from their subordinates. I'll see you there. You can start training today if you would like." He took his tray and left.

Zophia watched him walk away, admiring his strong yet relatively short body. His loose fitting jumper left plenty of room for her imagination.

She closed her eyes and concentrated on Mararum. She needed to check in with him regarding the crew's diminished abilities. Immediately she found herself under the denuded tree on the hill overlooking the prairie where she had first contacted Mararum. He stood waiting for her. As gorgeous as he was, it was the first time she notice how much he looked like Chuck, only much taller.

Welcome, Zophia. He stepped forward and wrapped his strong arms around her, pulling her close to his chest. She returned the embrace and laid her head against his shoulder.

You know that the crewmembers are losing their abilities as we get farther from Eden, she stated.

Of course. When they were under Adon's protection they were able to function as they should. They were no longer suppressed by Yehowshuwa. However, Adon's positive influence is wearing off. Soon they will be back to their original state. The only way to regain and keep their powers is to receive a personal guide and let us train them. Divide the ship's crew into five companies for training. Mararum showed Zophia how to initiate the training.

She trembled in his arms as he opened his mind to her. His power and wisdom was awesome. After what seemed like a few minutes he released her and she opened her eyes.

She saw Chuck exiting the mess hall. Yes, as soon as he gets his guide I won't need to imagine anymore what's under that jumpsuit.

December 7, 998 ASR

"Ah, here is a man after my own heart!" exclaimed The Sovereign as Daawiyd arrived in his throne room. He got up from the throne and threw his arms around Daawiyd as he tried to bow before The Sovereign.

After the embrace Yehowshuwa continued, "Thank you for coming on such sort notice. I know you are busy with Administration affairs but I desired to talk to you about Josu and his people."

"After all these thousands of years I'm still amazed that you thank me for coming when you ask. Every time in my life that I asked you to come to my aid you were there instantly. The relatively few times you've asked me to come to you I've been delighted and your command is my desire," said Daawiyd as he bowed low.

"I know, but since I can be in many places at one time and you can only be in one it's much more of a burden for you to come to me than it is the other way around. But enough of this. Isn't this the way we always greet each other when you arrive?"

There was a moment of silence as they seriously looked each other in the eye, then burst out laughing.

Yehowshuwa smiled as he pondered their relationship. The two had been close friends for over three thousand years. Daawiyd had been the first king of The Sovereign's people from whom The Sovereign could trace his physical lineage. This relationship stumped many of those aligned with The Chancellor after The Sovereign was born. Yehowshuwa easily silenced his opposition when he had asked them how it was that Daawiyd, whom they respected, called The Sovereign his lord even though The Sovereign was his descendant.

"I take it that Josu has decided to make connection with the underground and will be throwing his support to The Chancellor," said Daawiyd.

"Yes, it grieves me deeply that after all these years of being patient that he has stepped further from the truth and believes that his independence from me and alliance with The Chancellor will bring him the freedom that he desires." The two walked to the crystal window-dome and looked out over Yeruwshalayim.

Daawiyd shook his head. "If he only knew the true freedom that he could experience if he submitted to you. Unfortunately this promise of freedom is the same lie The Chancellor has been feeding people since he rebelled against you. Little does Josu know that he is already under The Chancellor's power. When The Chancellor breaks free I fear it will be too late to change his allegiance."

The Sovereign put his arm across Daawiyd's shoulders. "As I look out over this city and the people that have sworn allegiance to me, I'm overjoyed. Yet at the same time I know there are billions who haven't. They are all around us. But nowhere is there a greater percentage as among Josu's people. It saddens me."

Daawiyd turned to face The Sovereign Yehowshuwa. "But you have a plan, don't you?"

"Yes, of course. Come, I've prepared a small feast for us. We can eat as we discuss what the Administration must do regarding Josu and his relatives."

There was a flash of light and they were both standing at the head table of a large banquet room. The High Council members seated around the table fell to their knees.

This is going to be a good meeting.

December 10, 998 ASR

A week before the end of the quarter Robert sat in his usual seat in his Sub-Ancient Philosophy class. He glanced at his watch before class was to begin. He leaned to his left and spoke loud enough for Samantha to hear, "30 seconds until dear Dr. Halverson comes marching in."

Kevin looked over his shoulder toward the rear classroom door and Samantha nodded her head.

On cue, Dr. Halverson briskly strode into the classroom, turned, and faced the class. "I decided to give you your final exam today instead of next week. You must start the test in the next two minutes and you must finish it in 54 minutes. I will let you know who should return for the final class tomorrow if you want to pass this course."

She abruptly left the room as the students scrambled to open their ECDs and begin the test in the two minute allotment. Robert mumbled under his breath, "She certainly knows how to avoid any questions about her testing decisions."

Robert had grown to expect the unexpected from Dr. Halverson. He sighed deeply, thinking how glad he was that this would be his last quarter in school for a while. He opened his ECD and entered the code to start the test. He took his usual approach, reading the questions and answering the ones he knew, skipping anything that he didn't know. After twelve apparently easy questions he stopped, completely puzzled about the next one.

13. For which of the following was the Zeigler administration of the EU best known?
   a.   Chastity was strongly enforced
   b.   Homosexuality was prosecuted
   c.   Divorce was outlawed
   d.   Occult activity was prohibited
   e.   Pornography was eliminated

This simply didn't make sense. If anything the Zeigler administration had encouraged moral decay rather than promoting anything like the answers available. Had she incorrectly worded it or any of the answers? Nothing indicated that she made a typographical error. Was it a trick question? No, there simply wasn't a correct answer. *Well, according to testing theory, don't waste time, just take a guess.*

When you find five options choose the one that is to the left of the one that is on the right. Remember this. Do it and you will find success. Robert recalled Berekiah's words as if he were right inside his head. Berekiah's voice was so clear that he looked up from his ECD expecting to see the short man standing in front of the class.

Robert started to apply the counsel to his problem. OK, we read left to right and top to bottom and he didn't mention up or down. But we kind of think as up and left as the same thing so that would mean I need to select the answer that is above the bottom one. Hmm "D" it is. Robert didn't hesitate any longer and continued going through each of the questions. Five questions later, he ran across another with no correct answer. Eight questions later he found another weird question with all answers clearly wrong. Robert continued to mark each strange question with a "D." Normally, he would vary the response. Normally I wouldn't find any questions without answers.

Robert saw Samantha shaking her head and putting her hand on her forehead several times during the test. He believed it was her reaction to the strange questions. In the meantime, Kevin had blurted out a laugh and quickly stifled it. *I wonder how they are picking answers.*

Robert was the first to finish and he waited outside for Samantha and Kevin. As the students finished and filed out they congregated around Robert and started talking about the weird questions. As each voiced a theory about the questions, Robert wondered if there was anything in the questions that would reveal her purpose. He could see how someone in a hurry, as Dr. Halverson was, could make a mistake but with that many stupid questions he couldn't help but think she was up to something. As soon as Samantha and Kevin arrived, Robert motioned to them and they broke away from the group to leave together.

Samantha asked, "What did you make of that test? There were several questions on it that didn't appear to have any right answers. That seems just a bit weird to me. Was it just me or did you see them too?"

Kevin commented, "Oh I'd say weird isn't a strong enough word for that test. Dr. Halverson has been a bit of an enigma from the very beginning but this certainly put the icing on the cake today."

Robert agreed, "It's most definitely not standard modus operandi for a university professor. It isn't something I've ever done with any of my classes. You know, it isn't just the test. There was also that comment about returning to class to pass the course. I'd sure like to know what she has up her sleeve."

Kevin stopped where the path split to go to the student union building and the dorms. "I guess we'll know in a little while who gets invited back and passes the course. Hopefully I'll see you both in class tomorrow. I need to run some errands so I won't be able to meet with you at the student union today. Say 'Hi' to Jim for me, will you?" said Kevin as he excused himself.

Robert and Samantha continued on their way to meet with Jim. When Jim arrived, Robert explained the weird test. He didn't mention his method of answering the questions as he didn't want to sound foolish. Yet he had the unmistakable feeling that he provided the exact answers Dr. Halverson wanted.

December 11, 998 ASR

Dr. Halverson sat at Professor Robison's desk. She hadn't bothered to clean up the messy cluttered office. She knew that she only had one quarter to fulfill at Midrib. Let the next scholar to inherit his office clean it up. She simply pushed everything on his desk into a box and left it beside his bookcase.

She started reviewing the tests and wasn't too pleased to be doing it. This whole affair had grated on her nerves from the very beginning. If it weren't for the weird questions she wouldn't need to review any of them. Her ECD would simply provide the scores for each person and she would be done and on her way home. She was feeling more irritated with each test. *But no, those guys just had to run this whole silly charade. They knew who they wanted but for some idiotic reason they didn't tell me. So I had to teach the class then throw in those stupid questions with no answers on the final. If any of my colleagues found out about this they'd laugh me out of a job.*

She leaned back in her chair and reflected on how she came to Midrib in the first place. Only four months earlier she had been approached by a woman as she sat in her office preparing for her classes at Scottsdale University.

August 28, 998 ASR

Dr. Halverson's door was open and she was interrupted by a knock on the door jamb.

"Good morning, Dr. Halverson, may I come in?" asked a rather attractive looking woman with long black hair who appeared to be about forty five years old. She was standing just inside the doorway. She wore a black dress with a high buttoned collar that made her very white skin stand out in stark contrast. She was also very tall, even without the extremely high heels she wore.

"I am preparing for my classes next week but I can take a few minutes if this is important. You would be?" she replied glowering and folding her arms to be sure that her body language reflected her reluctance to get engaged in anything other than a question about the location of the nearest restroom.

"My name is Gloria and I'm sure you will have time for me," said Gloria as she closed the door behind her and proceeded to take a seat in one of the visitor chairs across the desk from Dr. Halverson. Dr. Halverson was about to raise her objection to the uninvited intrusion when Gloria scooted the chair up to the desk and leaned across it, looking deeply into Dr. Halverson's eyes. "You do know my name but you've never met me before, have you, Bristol?"

Until this point in Dr. Halverson's involvement with the underground "Gloria" had been a whispered code name for the head of the organization. Even at her high position she still shouldn't have known that name. She was shocked when Gloria introduced herself as the head of the underground by using Dr. Halverson's code name of "Bristol." Only other members at Dr. Halverson's level should have known that she was Bristol.

Dr. Halverson changed her demeanor, erasing any signs of irritation. Now she was nervous but hoped it didn't show. It wasn't just the fact that the leader of the underground had come to see her but there was something in her eyes that struck apprehension into her heart. "I'm sorry, Gloria, what can I do for you?" she said as calmly as possible.

Gloria settled back in her chair with a smile, half closing her eyes before opening them completely again. "First of all I need to know if you have received our advanced training to prevent the Administration from eavesdropping on our conversation. It should have reached your level by now."

"Ah, yes I have. It was just last week that I attended the seminar."

Gloria spoke sternly as she looked Dr. Halverson in the eye, "Then I suggest you start using it immediately. You are protected because I'm here but you must always be on guard whenever any of our business is being discussed, whether you know others are using it or not."

Dr. Halverson felt a bit sheepish. She realized that as soon as Gloria revealed her identity she should have immediately locked her mind and her office with the techniques she was taught. She blinked her eyes as she did so. "Forgive me, it is done."

"Good. We have a bit of a situation that has come up and we need your expertise to complete some work for us. It appears that one of our high ranking members disappeared before his time. We believe that The Sovereign arrested him, however we can't be sure. He has simply vanished without a trace. You will complete his mission."

Gloria paused and Dr. Halverson's mind raced. *How could someone just disappear? What does this have to do with me?* She brushed a bead of sweat from her forehead.

"In two days you will be at Midrib teaching his post graduate Sub-Ancient Philosophy class. We were able to retrieve some of his most recent research which needs to be put in the hands of one of the students in this class. However, you can't openly approach this person or deliver this information until the class has been taught. You can reveal this information to the student only if he or she answers all of these questions on your final with an answer of 'D.'" Gloria handed Dr. Halverson a sheet of paper with fifteen questions written on it.

As Bristol, she was used to receiving communications from the underground written on paper. This was quite unusual in the rest of the world where nearly everything was transmitted from ECD to ECD. She scanned the questions and answers and then looked up at Gloria. "There aren't any right answers to any of these questions. What's the deal?" she asked as she waved the paper in front of her.

Gloria lowered her chin and squinted her eyes. "You're correct in your assessment, however these must be scattered throughout your final exam exactly as they appear. After the exam you will meet with the one student that has answered all the questions with a 'D' and give that student this data module. It is encrypted and only that student will be able to retrieve the data." Gloria handed Dr. Halverson a data module.

Her cold stare kept Dr. Halverson from protesting.

"The Administration has graciously arranged your temporary transfer to Midrib. You will get your official notification shortly. You are expected there the day after tomorrow. Oh, by the way, you should also familiarize yourself with your new bio. You have written some books that you haven't read yet to make sure you appear completely qualified to teach this class. And this is the course material that Professor Robison used. You will find it quite interesting and we know you are capable of teaching it. I must go now." Gloria handed Dr. Halverson another data module. She abruptly got up and headed for the door, then stopped and turned. "Oh, and tell the student that Gloria says 'Hi.'" She was out the door before Dr. Halverson had time to ask any questions.

After Gloria left Dr. Halverson felt privileged that she had been visited by the head of the underground and entrusted to complete a mission that went awry. However, as she thought it over it sounded more and more stupid. *If Gloria knew my code name and the data was encrypted for the student, then why go through the charade of teaching the class? Just give him the data and get on with life. Didn't she say him?* By the time she finally finished packing and was on the interregional convy she had worked herself up into a fairly nasty mood that returned every time she thought about her temporary assignment.

December 10, 998 ASR

She remembered it as if it were just yesterday, including the mood. How strange. I now recall that Gloria implied that Professor Robison was a high ranking member of the underground, yet I had to revise his class notes so that the class didn't appear heavily biased toward The Sovereign. A lot of this just doesn't make sense.

Whoa, this is odd. I have two students that have answered "D" to all of the questions. Now what am I supposed to do? Dr. Halverson looked again at the two tests and was relieved. Oh whew, Mr. Trimble only picked "D" on fourteen of them. Oh well, I should have suspected that Dr. Maskil is the one to get the data module, not Trimble. She sighed, I guess that wasn't all that bad. I'll be on my way home tomorrow.

She removed all the bogus questions from the test scores and entered each student's grade into her ECD. She composed a form message to each student other than Dr. Maskil.

To: <student name>
From: Dr. Halverson
Subject: Final Exam
Your final test score was <final test score Sub-Ancient Philosophy>. This score and other assigned work earned you a <n> "<grade for Sub-Ancient Philosophy>" for the course. Do not report to the last class as only those with questionable test scores will be required to attend.

"Send the message one hour before Sub-Ancient Philosophy is scheduled to start today," she instructed her ECD. She sat back in her chair feeling relaxed for the first time in months.

December 11, 998 ASR

Robert sat in the library trying to review his interview notes from Josu. He was having a hard time concentrating, wondering when he would be notified whether or not to report to the last Sub-Ancient Philosophy class. He stared out the window looking across the commons at the Archeology building where he had spent much of his student life. If he didn't get a message in the next few minutes, he made up his mind to go anyway.

"Buzzzzzz, buzzzzzz" the vibration of his ECD startled him and he quickly opened it to see a priority page. It came from Dr. Halverson.

To: Dr. Robert Maskil
From: Dr. Halverson
Subject: Final Exam
Your final test score was 100%. This score and other assigned work have earned you an "A" for the course. However, you will need to report to the last class to receive this grade.

Robert was pleased with himself and even more confident that Berekiah's predictions of success would come true. It would only be one more week before he could devote full time to working on his book.

He hurried to class, arriving a few minutes early, eager to find out what was so important about this last class that everyone needed to come after the final. No one else had arrived when Dr. Halverson walked in right on time. Robert was very concerned that he was the only person in the class. In particular he was wondering about Kevin and Samantha. They both exhibited a superior grasp of the subject and he was sure they had passed. As a matter of fact, he couldn't name a single person that he thought would have failed except for the one woman who dropped out after two weeks.

Dr. Halverson entered and sat down next to Robert. "I suppose you are wondering why you are the only one here."

"That just might be an understatement. From what you said yesterday, I expected that everyone who passed would be here. I can't imagine that I'm the only one who passed."

"You, Dr. Maskil, are the only one that answered 'D' on every one of those stupid, idiotic, foolish questions. Everyone else except for Mr. Trimble had the common sense to vary their answers or left them blank. He, however, changed his answer on the last one which left you as the only one to win the award for answering stupid questions consistently. Congratulation and here is your reward." She handed Robert the data module. "I'm told that you will know what to do with it. Apparently it's some research notes that Professor Robison put together just before he and his assistant Eric disappeared. And Gloria says, 'Hi.'"

He squinted his eyes and looked at her suspiciously when she mentioned the name Gloria. "I don't know anyone named Gloria and why would anyone want me to have Professor Robison's notes?"

"Surely you've heard the name Gloria before? If not, maybe I've got the wrong person." She reached out to take the data module.

Robert pulled his hand back with the module. "Well, yes, I've heard the name but I don't know her. Are you referring to the code name of the leader of some organization?" he asked cautiously.

"Yes, that would be the person. Gloria, the head of the underground. The name that we really aren't supposed to know, but I suspect it has filtered down to all the cells. She gave me this data module personally and also devised those silly test questions insisting that it was the only way for the right person to receive this data."

Robert was a bit dumbfounded as he listened to Dr. Halverson. First because she was so blatantly ignoring underground protocol by openly talking without being sure of her audience and secondly because he couldn't believe that the head of the underground would have Professor Robison's notes and would want him to have them. "Why didn't Gloria just have someone give me the data module instead of going through all this folderol?"

Dr. Halverson scoffed, "She didn't say and didn't stay around long enough to answer me. The whole thing has left a sour taste in my mouth because it simply doesn't make sense but I went along with it anyway. Oh, there was one thing that chilled me but also encouraged me to follow the procedure no matter how silly I thought it was." Dr. Halverson paused and pursed her lips, "Gloria said The Sovereign was behind Professor Robison's disappearance but they were able to retrieve this data. You can close your mouth now. Your slack-jawed expression isn't becoming to a person with as many degrees as you have."

Robert closed his mouth. It was difficult for him to believe what he heard. It made all the warnings from Gustav suddenly become personal. "Sorry, it's just a bit of a shock to hear all this," he whispered, "I'm also concerned that you are telling me this in a public classroom. Aren't you afraid the Administration will hear and try to retrieve the data or even arrest us?"

"Humph." She shook her head. "You take the Administration way too seriously. Besides, we at the upper levels have received training on how to secure our immediate surroundings and our minds from their prying eyes and ears. There is no way they can monitor our conversation while you are in my presence. Your training will come soon enough."

"If that is so, then why was Professor Robison taken?" asked Robert.

"Maybe he was sloppy. I don't know. My turn for a question. Why did you answer 'D' on those questions?" asked Dr. Halverson.

"My Board was about to yank my school and other plans. After I pleaded my case before the Board I had a visitor appear to me while the Board was in recess. His name was Berekiah and he gave me some encouragement and instructions about how to decide between seemingly incomprehensible choices. Then he disappeared. Until now I believed he must have been an Encourager. Now, I'm not sure," answered Robert.

"An Encourager, huh? What did he look like?"

"Uh, let's see, he was short and kind of chubby. He had a wiry beard."

"What was he wearing?" snapped Dr. Halverson.

"It was some dumpy-looking shirt, faded with flowers on it. I don't really remember much else except that he looked very casual. Oh, yeah, he wore a yarmulke. What do his clothes have to do with it?"

Dr. Halverson rolled her eyes. "Well, Dr. Maskil, let me say that you need to get better acquainted with the Administration's people. You're still young but haven't you noticed that all of them are well dressed and typically wear white or very near white linen? It's one of their 'religious' things. It's supposed to demonstrate their purity, integrity and whatever," she said with a wave of her hand and just enough disgust in her voice to make it clear to Robert that she didn't believe for a moment that they deserved the honor. "I have a feeling he was one of Gloria's 'helpers.'"

Robert remembered Maria when she showed up at his review and how smartly she was dressed. "I haven't had any personal contact with the Administration's people and I have only seen a handful of them. I hadn't put that connection together about the way they were dressed. And I'm not following you about being one of Gloria's helpers."

This time Dr. Halverson's jaw dropped. "I'm totally amazed that they picked you out for this mission, whatever it is. I thought that you would be more knowledgeable about our organization and capabilities. I'm not sure how much you need to know or how much I should tell you. However these 'helpers' are an enigma to most of us who have met them. They are quite mysterious like your Berekiah. They appear and disappear just like Administration people. They inexplicably show up at cell meeting saying that Gloria sent them. In the past they trained us with various meditation techniques that help us analyze the Administration's activities and capabilities. Recently they taught us how to keep the Administration from monitoring our conversations. They promise future training to give us mysterious Administration-like powers. They tell us that all this has been available to us but The Sovereign has prevented it until he started losing control."

This was a lot more than Robert could imagine. "Are you saying that some people have been able to develop the same capabilities as the Administration's people and that we can do the same?"

Dr. Halverson nodded her head slowly. "That's the best description I've heard. They promised that very soon we'll all be able to start training and will be able to recruit millions and even billions to assure our true future, not ultimate death as The Sovereign has promised."

Robert felt his eyes get wide and his heart speed up. "Wow. I've seen some hints about new possibilities in the future from some of the discussion topics, but I never dreamed that it would lead to anything like this. You're talking about a full scale rebellion in the near future. We could be part of that. What else can we expect?"

She held up her hand. "I've said enough, maybe too much. You aren't prepared for this. I have to leave now. Good luck with your mission, Dr. Maskil, whatever it is. I do hope it will speed up the process to free us from The Sovereign." With her usual abruptness Dr. Halverson got up and marched out of the room.

Robert sat quietly watching her leave, then looked at the small button of a data module in his hand and proceeded to tumble it between the tips of his fingers as he had done with coat buttons when he was a child. How simple life seemed then. He wasn't sure what was in store for him but he was beginning to feel like he had just been catapulted into a deep dark void where he had no control over his life.

Chapter 32

Zophia entered the training room and was pleased to see nine crewmembers waiting for her. She walked to the center of the room and stood in the center of the pentagram, turning slowly. The unicorns, goat heads, and stars painted on each of the five walls were exactly as Mararum directed. The crewmembers were all wearing the long brown hooded robes she had made in accordance with his instructions.

"Please take a seat on the pillows around the pentagram and we'll begin our first training session." She motioned to the cushions.

After everyone sat down, Zophia raised her hands above her head and a pillar of fire rose from above her and ascended to the ceiling of the room. The roar from the flames was nearly deafening and the light nearly blinding. Everyone immediately closed their eyes and put their hands over their ears. Just as quickly the flame disappeared and there was silence.

"In case there is any doubt in anyone's mind regarding the power you have within you, I hope this little demonstration will alleviate them and any fears. First we will contact my enlightened leader. He will be working through me during the initial phase of the training, then you will be instructed how to contact an ascended being to be your own guide. Each of us on the Aman will have one of the five original founders of the Council of Enlightened Beings as a contact. When you finish today you will be able to contact your guide at any time.

"Let's begin by putting up our hoods, sitting cross-legged, closing our eyes, and concentrating our minds on the center of the pentagram." Zophia looked around the room. Everyone was sitting with eyes closed. "Very good. Now we will begin the mantra."

"Harum Opparum Mararum Rorarum Amorum." The chant began and continued for a few minutes as Zophia began extending Mararum's influence as he had previously shown her, like a large bubble growing from herself and extending to include the crewmembers seated around her.

As Mararum's influence extended she could see the pentagram clearly in their minds. For the next three hours Mararum and Zophia jointly re-instructed the small congregation in the art of communicating telepathically with each other so that they could again share thoughts with the people around them. Mararum was delighted with the progress and announced that they could take a thirty minute break.

They reconvened and started their second session, but this time everyone immediately connected with Mararum through Zophia. He used Zophia as a conduit to announce to them all, *Next we will introduce each of you to your personal council representative. He will become your guide. We will now give you the name of the guide you are to contact. Each of you will then use that name and the techniques we teach you to contact them and they will then instruct you from that point on.*

Mararum implanted the name of a council founder into the consciousness of each crewmember using Zophia as a medium. Harum, Opparum, Rorarum, and Amorum were each given to two of the crew. Mararum was given to the remaining member. They then followed up by providing everyone the mantra that was required to contact his or her guide. *You now have the name of your guide and the mantra to summon him. After you have called upon him you are to obey him as we instruct you and help you release the power that is within you. When you have fully developed your powers at the end of the ten days of training your guides will be available to you whenever you need them. Do not hesitate to call upon them. Now contact your assistants.*

Zophia found herself on the edge of a vast dark plane without any visible horizon ahead of her. She heard the name of Mararum being called from the center of the plane. It was Henry's voice, the crewmember assigned to Mararum. Her face, hands, and feet began to glow, emitting a bright light toward Henry. As he continued to chant she felt herself gliding toward him as he stood in the center of the plane.

His eyes got large, then he bowed his head and dropped to his knees. He asked as he had been directed, *What do you require of me?*

Zophia sensed Mararum answering, Open yourself to me and I will teach you all you need to know. I will direct you and show you things too wonderful for you to imagine. You will grow and become like me and we will grow together and become even greater. Invite me in. She approached closer to her subject until they were face to face. Invite me in.

Henry stood and responded with enthusiasm, *Come in.*

Zophia felt her consciousness along with Mararum's merge with Henry. Just as it had happened when she had allowed Mararum to enter into her being, she now experienced it from Mararum's viewpoint. At one point, she was standing face to face with Henry and then she was inside him looking out with his eyes. She then separated from him and they sat down cross-legged together. For the next fourteen hours she and Mararum showed Henry how to move objects by his will. They reviewed how to throw flames, laser-like rays, and lightening bolts from the power that was within.

We learned all this back on Eden but it faded. We lost everything we had gained. How is it going to be different this time? asked Henry.

Mararum answered, When you were within Adon's influence he gave you the ability to overcome The Sovereign's suppression of your natural abilities. Now, I live in you. As long as I am with you, you will never loose your abilities. When we return to Earth, you will assist me by introducing guides to those being trained, just as Zophia has done with you today.

Henry faded from Zophia's vision and she was alone on the vast plane with Mararum. He turned to her. Your work for this session is finished. You have opened the portal to their minds. We will guide them just as I am guiding you.

What comes next? asked Zophia. What do you want me to do?

You will join your crewmates for more practice with your new skills. For the next nine days you will meet in the hydroponic gardens, the largest open area of the ship and you will practice not only how to use your psychic abilities as weapons but also how to shield yourself from the enemy's weapons. When you have completed your ten days of training, you will then introduce the next group and observe their training. Mararum smiled and drew Zophia close to himself. You know that we wouldn't be able to do this without you.

She felt completely secure in his arms, yet she still had visions of Chuck. Her work with Mararum gave her great satisfaction but she wanted to share that and more with the Captain. She was sure that when he completed training they would be together.

December 11, 998 ASR

Robert took a deep sigh and shook his head as he watched Dr. Halverson exit the classroom. He pulled his ECD from his pocket, opened it, sat it down on his desk, and placed the data module on the screen. He had no idea how he was going to decrypt the data. A small box immediately appeared on his ECD with the words "Verify Identity." It was the same box that appeared when he opened a discussion topic without being in contact with the ECD. He picked up the ECD. The box disappeared. It was replaced by Professor Robison's written, verbal, and some video notes which appeared to be excerpts from his journal.

"Well, I guess that makes sense." Robert mumbled to himself as he began to read the notes. *I don't know why I was so concerned.* He was immediately intrigued when he read the first paragraph describing the professor's conversation with his assistant, Eric. Eric discovered a cave in the Haunt of Jackals Mountains that they believed to be the entrance to the buried capital city of The Chancellor. *Wow, what a find, but why does the underground want me to have this?* Robert skimmed through several pages of details about the professor's preparation, travel, and arrival at the cave. When the notes started relating details of the caverns and the artifacts that they found, Robert slowed and carefully read the descriptions, admiring the professor's keen eye and attention to detail that only an experienced archeologist would exhibit.

Descriptions of the caves revealed that they were not formed naturally but were the results of a great city that was burned, toppled, and turned upside down. Nine centuries of water seeping through the remains had washed away the lighter materials and left tunnels and caverns in the remains of the buildings. The professor navigated deep into the earth without using any significant earthmoving equipment.

Unfortunately, the city had been charred and twisted beyond recognition. Very little was left beside twisted steel, concrete, and stone. It wasn't until several durable artifacts such as metal and stone plaques were found that they confirmed that it was part of Ben-Shaachar's capital city. Professor Robison and Eric explored only a portion of the city that appeared to be near the business center, about twenty kilometers from The Chancellor's headquarters.

As Robert continued to read the notes he realized that even though vast areas of the city were now accessible, it was producing little of significant value. Anything recorded on perishable material had vaporized in the intense heat when the city was originally destroyed. Anything that might have survived would have been damaged in the earthquake or deteriorated by moisture that made its way through the heart of the city. Robert's enthusiasm waned as he realized that the possibility of finding any documentation to help him write his book would be nothing short of a miracle.

Robert continued to sort through page after page of notes looking for something that would indicate why Gloria wanted him to have them. The further he proceeded the more depressed he felt. Some fragments of sculptures had been found and a few that were nearly intact. These would prove to be very important finds to the archeological world but it didn't help him any. After two hours he was about to give up when he read that the professor and Eric found a bank vault that was still secure. However, they were unable to open it. It was made of the best stainless steel and was at least seventy centimeters thick.

Ah, now that vault could reveal some important information if we could only get it open. Robert's excitement was returning. Even if this safe doesn't reveal anything there may be other fireproof vaults that could. I wonder if we might even be able to find some of The Chancellor's archives. People back then had an obsession with storing backup data in secure locations. This, coupled with Josu's relatives' testimony, could really have an impact on the underground's cause.

He closed his ECD and popped the data module into his pocket, quite surprised that he had browsed through the notes for over two hours. *It looks like it's my turn to stand up Jim and the others.* Robert hurried out of the class building and over to the student union building.

Robert found Jim, Kevin and Samantha at the student union building just about ready to leave. "Sorry I'm late guys, I lost track of time. You'll never guess what just happened to me," he said excitedly.

"OK, you were in the john and accidentally locked your self in the stall and had to call security to come and get you out," said Jim.

"Oh, that's just swell, Jim," admonished Samantha. "I'll bet you were so thrilled about not having to go see Dr. Halverson that you decided to celebrate by taking a nap and just woke up."

"Let me guess too," said Kevin, "You actually did go to see Dr. Halverson because you flunked the final and you were the only one. You begged for mercy and from the kindness of her heart she decided not to count those stupid questions against you and gave you a passing score. Then in your deep gratitude you took her to lunch and swept her off her feet with your great charm. You asked her to marry you and now the wedding date is next week and you are here to invite us all to the wedding," Kevin said. There was something about Kevin's smile and wink that made Robert feel that Kevin knew he had seen Dr. Halverson.

When the three finally stopped laughing Robert started to explain, "I'm not sure why I put up with you guys. Yes, I did go to see Dr. Halverson but it wasn't because I flunked. I got all those stupid questions 'right' and she wanted to know why."

"Get outta here. There weren't any right answers to those questions and we all knew it. What was she really up to?" asked Samantha.

Robert put up his hands in defense, "OK, I gave her the answer she was looking for on each question. Apparently I was the only one to put 'D' down for each one so I was the only one that got a message to come to the last class. She told me that she is part of the underground and said that Gloria gave her this assignment. She was to give this to whoever answered each question with a 'D.'" Robert showed them the data module. "This contains all of Professor Robison's notes from the summer before he disappeared. Apparently his assistant made a very important archeological find and they spent the summer exploring and cataloging their findings. The underground believes that The Sovereign didn't want the findings made public so he made the Professor and his assistant disappear."

"You think The Sovereign would do something like that?" Samantha blurted out. "I--- ouch!" she stopped and glanced at Kevin.

Robert frowned, and continued. "It depends on what we find at that site. If it is something that supports what we've been learning from our discussion groups and what Jim and I found out from our last interview, then it could very well be that he has something to hide."

Kevin leaned forward and spoke quietly, "So what's your plan? Are you just going to head off to the site, look around and hope to find what's so important to The Sovereign, bring it back and then let the world know? If The Sovereign took the Professor out of the way, what makes you think he won't do the same to you and your assistant?" He slowly turned his gaze to Jim. "I realize that our discussions have shown that he is not as capable as we once thought, but if this is really that important wouldn't he watch the site to make sure no one else has access to it?"

Jim sat up straight and tapped Robert on the shoulder. "OK, Robert, Kevin's got a point. I don't exactly like the sound of this disappearing stuff," Jim's face was pale. "I mean, what if this is so important that he's been tracking your little data module there just to see if it would lead to you? It could lead him to everyone in the underground that has access to it. By now, he'd know that Dr. Halverson was a higher up, would know the leader and whoever gave it to her. Everyone who touched it would be exposed."

Kevin sat back, raised his eyebrows and nodded toward Jim. "I think you better listen to your assistant."

Samantha was just sitting there with her mouth hanging open a little, staring first at Robert then at Jim. Everyone was quiet for a few seconds until she spoke slowly, "Do you suppose that because of this," she pointed to the module, "The Sovereign might be listening in on us right now? Maybe we should be more careful. Do you think it will be safe to go to our meeting tonight?"

Jim's color quickly returned and asked for Robert's ECD and the data module. He put the module down beside the ECD and typed in some quick commands, smiled, and looked up. "There aren't any signals coming from the module." He placed the module on the ECD and typed in a couple more commands. "No programs were included in the data so there wasn't any way for it to send a trace over the network when Robert opened it. The module is clean and can't be traced here."

Robert sighed with relief, then leaned forward and spoke very quietly, "I was concerned that Dr. Halverson talked so freely to me in the classroom so I asked her about it and she said that the higher ups in the underground are all trained in some kind of mind technique that hides their thoughts and speech from the Administration. It was also possible for her to protect me when I was in the same room with her. I don't think any of the underground has been compromised."

Everyone was leaning closely in toward the center of the table like small children sharing a secret. Kevin whispered, "I'm glad the underground hierarchy is safe, but what about right now?" He added a wink. "Is this whispering helping us so that no one in the Administration will pay any attention to us?"

Samantha was the first to start laughing, followed by Kevin and Jim. Robert joined in when it dawned on him that they had spoken freely about treasonous topics at the very same table for months and hadn't heard a peep from the Administration.

When they stopped laughing Robert continued in a normal voice. "Still, if we want to get to Professor Robison's dig site unobserved we'll need some help. I'm going to talk to Gustav tonight about getting us this training. Between what we may find at the site and what Josu told us, I think we may be on the verge of a great breakthrough for the whole world."

The other three nodded solemnly.

"It's getting late and I need to make some preparations before our meeting tonight so I'm going to take off. See you tonight." Robert got up to leave after the others responded with their see-you-laters.

Jim was still nervous even though he pronounced the data module clean. He felt that he needed some more reassurance. "Kevin, what do you think of this? Do you think we'll be safe? Roberts seems to have a lot of faith that The Sovereign isn't going to find out so that we don't suffer the same fate as Professor Robison, whatever that was."

"Jim, I can say for sure that everything is going to work out OK. From what I know of The Sovereign, I'd say you don't have anything to worry about at this time. Do you remember what Robert told you about what happened at the worship service on the last Sunday before he came back to university?" Kevin paused.

Jim scrunched his eyes. He couldn't remember Robert telling him anything about the worship except that he had to get home in time to go with his parents. "No. Not that I remember."

Kevin appeared to tense up. "Hmm, I thought for sure he told you. Anyway he couldn't get out of going to worship with his mom and dad. When the congregation was worshiping, The Sovereign appeared right there in the chair reserved for him."

Jim felt his eyes opening wider. He heard stories about that happening but never knew anyone who actually saw it. *I wonder why Robert didn't tell me?*

Kevin continued, "Robert said he was bothered by his presence at first but what happened after the service was what really unsettled him. The Sovereign came over, talked to him, and affirmed his mission to write this book. If this archeological site has anything that will help then I don't think The Sovereign will do anything to stop him. Now are you sure that Robert didn't tell you about this?" Kevin seemed tense.

Jim thought hard. "No way! He told me that The Sovereign had predicted danger in the future but I assumed it was in some kind of message on his ECD, not in person. Wow!" He shook his head, trying to get over the shock. "So if you knew this, why'd you start all this stuff about The Sovereign watching the site and wiping us out if we showed up?"

Kevin breathed a bit easier. "Sorry, Jim, I just couldn't resist. It was obvious that Robert hadn't thought about that and I was just having fun with him. It turned out more serious that I thought. Bottom line though, we do need to be careful and not rely too heavily on what we've learned in the discussions. Just because the Administration seems unable to monitor everyone it doesn't mean that they aren't randomly monitoring people and we could get caught. Besides, when you and Robert show up at that site, he may start monitoring you full time."

"OK, I guess I'm alright with that as long as Robert and the underground figure out how to handle security." Jim needed to get away and think about this for a while. "Hey guys, I'm going to head out now and catch a nap. I'll be quite interested in what Gustav has to say tonight. See ya." Jim then got up and left.

Both Samantha and Kevin responding with a simultaneous, "See ya."

Samantha waited until Jim was safely out of earshot then turned to Kevin. "All right, Kevin, I know you're more astute than I am about these things but first you rattle them with this cockamamie stuff about The Sovereign snatching them if they show up at the site, then you assure Jim that everything's going to work out OK. What's going on?"

Kevin smiled and shrugged his shoulders, "Hey, I was just wondering how deep they were thinking. I thought it might be funny to see their reaction to some logic. It seems to me that Jim is thinking things through better than Robert."

Samantha wasn't completely convinced. Kevin always seemed to know just a little more about things than she thought was humanly possible. "OK, but what about this thing with The Sovereign showing up at Robert's worship service? I hadn't heard anything about that. Did The Sovereign personally affirm Robert's effort to write this book? It seems to me that the book will be nothing more than a rehash of the underground's heresy. From what he's said about his interviews it's obvious he was just waiting to find someone like Josu to confirm what he already decided is the truth. So everything is going to turn out OK?" Samantha was also miffed that Kevin would encourage Robert.

Kevin's smile and twinkling blue eyes soothed Samantha as he answered, "The Sovereign's servant put it this way, 'All things will be accomplished according to his purpose which is good for those that are loyal to and trust him.' I'm sure

Yehowshuwa wants Robert to work on this book. However, if Robert turns it into something evil, then The Sovereign will still be able to use it according to his plan in spite of Robert's intent or the underground's activities."

Samantha shook her head. "You have a lot more faith than I do. Either that or you have an inside informant in the Administration that feeds you information. I can't imagine how that book can be used by The Sovereign in any way, shape, or form. On the other hand, I know that he is completely wise and what you said is true."

Samantha half chuckled and harrumphed at the same time. "I expect that the underground wouldn't understand that, though, any more than they would understand that even now The Sovereign knows their every thought."

"That's right Sam. Hopefully they will understand before it's too late for them," replied Kevin.

"I think I need to prepare for tonight too. I almost slipped up when Robert make that stupid accusation about The Sovereign making Professor Robison disappear. Thanks for the kick under the table. See you tonight." Samantha stood to leave.

"OK, Sam, take care."

Samantha walked quietly back to her dorm, pondering how long she could keep up the ruse pretending to be sympathetic with the underground.

December 11, 998 ASR

Robert was eager to tell Gustav about Professor Robison's data module as well as what they learned from Josu. He wanted to arrive early but that would be a breach of security protocols so he met Jim a few minutes early and took a couple of extra turns around campus to insure they were not followed. They arrived at their designated time in the basement of the mechanical engineering building and proceeded to the janitor's office where Gustav, Mike, Hillary, and Twila were already talking.

"Gustav, you really need to hear what happened this week!" interrupted Robert. Gustav turned around. "I think we are on to something really big. It might even accelerate the underground's plans to enlighten people."

"Sure, Robert, we'll listen to what you have after everyone gets here and we've finished our regular scheduled discussion." Gustav turned his back to Robert.

"But you don't understand. I have information that has come from the top of the underground but I need some help to make sure we can make the most of it," Robert raised his voice to try to emphasize the importance of his information and to make sure Gustav would hear him.

"Fine, Robert, I heard you and we'll talk about it after the meeting," retorted Gustav a bit louder than he needed as he turned around.

Just at that moment Kevin and Samantha arrived.

"Hey, what's with the noise? I thought we were supposed to use our library voices during these meetings," asked Samantha.

Gustav rolled his eyes and answered, "It appears that Robert, here, wants to circumvent our normal procedures because he thinks he has something so important that it can't wait until after our normal discussion time," Gustav replied with a bit of a sneer. "Since this is my meeting, we will continue with the normal agenda. Then afterwards I will listen to what Robert has and will determine if it is important enough to bother the higher echelon." He again turned away and muttered just loud enough for Robert to hear, "As if anyone from the underground hierarchy would want to talk to him."

At that moment the broom closet door opened and from the shadows stepped a very tall slim man. He was wearing what appeared to be shiny black leather pants and a waist length jacket over a black shirt and tie. His very white skin stood in stark contrast to his black hair and dark glasses. "I would like to hear what Robert has to say and this would be the perfect time, Gustav."

By now everyone had arrived. They all turned to the closet and stood gaping at the stranger who stood before them. "Who in hell are you?" asked Gustav.

"A very interesting choice of words, Gustav. It appears that you have let your meager position in the underground go to your head. You should be more aware of your people and their potential. Instead of commanding their respect, earn it." His obvious displeasure with Gustav sent a shiver down Robert's spine.

"Robert, what have you found and how may we help you?"

There was something about this person that commanded respect and awe. Robert didn't want to take any chances of upsetting him. "Um, I don't mean to be disrespectful; you seem to know us but it would be helpful for us to know who you are."

"Please excuse me. Gustav's challenge made me forget to introduce myself. My name is Samyaza and I am the overseer for this cell. While you have been meeting I have always been nearby, ensuring that you were not being detected by the Administration."

Gustav stepped forward. "If you are our overseer, why haven't I been informed about you? Overseers have not been mentioned in any of our cell leader meetings. How do we know you aren't from the Administration?" challenged Gustav.

Samyaza turned slowly and faced Gustav. "Robert, if you had to choose between five leaders lined up before you and I was the fourth and Gustav was standing in the first position, who would you choose?"

Robert hesitated then recognized the pattern that Berekiah had given him to choose the fourth of five. He answered, "I would choose you."

"And if Gustav was standing in the fourth position and I was in the third position, who would you choose?"

"I would choose Gustav."

Still facing Gustav, Samyaza continued speaking, "Gustav, I care little whether you have heard about me or not. As I said before, your position in the underground is meager and you have been told only enough to function here. However, Robert can confirm my authenticity and that is what is important. Since you have doubted and have attempted to exceed your authority instead of recognizing the importance of Robert's information, you will not have the opportunity of participating further with his mission."

Samyaza turned to face Robert. "Are you convinced that I'm not working for the Administration?"

"Yes, sir. You certainly asked the right questions."

"And you answered as I would expect. Robert and Jim, we should go elsewhere this evening and discuss your needs." Samyaza turned back to Gustav, "Since I won't be here to shield you from the Administration, I suggest that you cancel the rest of your meeting tonight." He then turned and started for the door. "Shall we, gentlemen?"

Robert and Jim glanced at each other and quickly followed Samyaza out the door which someone loudly slammed behind them. As they reached the end of the hallway, Robert looked back and saw Kevin and Samantha leaving followed by Hillary. *I have a feeling this may be our last cell meeting with Gustav. Now I feel like we are really going to make a difference.*

Chapter 33

The chime on Chuck's office door sounded. It startled him as he was deep in thought about his latest alarming dream since leaving Eden.

"Come in." He announced as he looked across his desk to the door.

Squat Demetrius hurried in the door, sweat dripping from his forehead. His face was pale. "Chuck, do you know what's happening in the hydroponic gardens?"

"Yeah, Zophia asked if she could do some training there with the first class. Why?" Demetrius' panicked look alarmed Chuck.

"You better come and see for yourself. You wouldn't believe me if I told you."

Chuck stood up and Demetrius was already heading for the door. This must be important. *I don't think I've ever seen him move that fast before.*

Demetrius was running down the passageway to the pressure lift and opened the door as Chuck caught up with him. "Hydroponic gardens," he said as Chuck entered the lift. The door immediately closed and they were sucked away through the ship's mini convy tubes to the hydroponic garden deck.

The door opened. Chuck stepped out just in time to see a 2,000 kilogram water tank soar through the air toward five crewmembers at the opposite end of the atrium. Just as he thought it was going to crush them, a bright aura obscured them and a beam of light flashed out, vaporizing the tank.

Fruit trees from the tanks lay broken on the floor, their trunks sheared off just above the top of the tank. In the distance smoke was rising from what was left of some of the rice that was almost ready for harvest.

"Zophia!" Shouted Chuck at the top of his lungs.

"I'm right here, Chuck," said Zophia.

He turned to his right. She was standing only ten meters away with the other four members of the crew from the first training class. Each was wearing a brown floor length rob with a hood that was draped behind them. Zophia's countenance was much too calm for the destruction he observed as the group approached him.

Chuck felt his throat muscles tighten as he asked, "What is going on in here? What did I just see? How did all this equipment get destroyed? What? Tell me!"

"Oh, Chuck." She pursed her lips and shook her head. "I told you we were going to use the gardens for training. That's what we are doing. Our group just tried to kill the others by launching that hydroponic tank. They proved their abilities by vaporizing it. If you hadn't interrupted they would have retaliated and tried to annihilate us. We've been at it for hours." The edges of her lips turned up in a small smile. "It's been quite enjoyable."

The way she looked at him bothered Chuck almost as much as what he had seen. It was the way she looked in his dreams. *First things first.* "But you are destroying the gardens. What about our food supply? What about destroying the ship from within? Have you lost your mind?"

Zophia came closer and touched his forearm. "Don't worry, we have more than enough provisions to reach Earth. Everything that was ready for harvest was safely stored before we began."

Chuck stepped back. Her touch was much too familiar. "What about the ship? Aren't you the least bit concerned about fire and rupturing bulkheads? What if one of your missiles gets away from you and you kill someone?"

Suddenly Zophia's dark brown eyes locked on his. "It's OK Chuck. We are completely in control of our environment and won't let anything like that happen. You will see once you are trained." Her soft sweet voice made him feel as if he were being drawn into her soul until he looked away. She was having the same charismatic affect on him as Ana had when he was on Eden.

Demetrius tapped him on the shoulder. "Chuck, I think Zophia has everything under control here. Why don't we check back later to see how they are doing?" He was beckoning with his head toward the pressure lift door.

Chuck looked at Demetrius, then back at Zophia's gorgeous, radiant smile. "Ah, yeah, Zophia, carry on. I'll check on your progress later. I, ah, need to get back and go over Demetrius' reports with him." He started edging his way back to the door as Demetrius tugged on his left sleeve.

He turned completely around and entered the lift door. "Captain's office." The door closed and they were whisked away to the passageway near his office. They both walked briskly into his office and plopped down in the visitor chairs. Chuck was exhausted.

"Chuck, I'm scared. I know I was skeptical on Eden but that disappeared when I realized how much I wanted to be an ascended being and that I would never get there under The Sovereign. But now, I'm frightened by that decision and what I've seen of this training. I've had the weirdest dreams too." Demetrius' pudgy hands were shaking as he talked.

"Me, too."

"Really! Oh, I'm glad I said something." Demetrius' shoulders sagged.

"Yeah, just before you came to get me I was thinking about the dream I had last night. All of mine have been along the same line." Chuck hesitated; he felt embarrassed sharing this with Demetrius. "In them, Zophia is either trying to seduce me or kill me. She changes from one weird creature to another. Sometimes she's riding different animals, anything from a unicorn to a dragon. She wants me to join her and rule the Earth together. I end up freaking out and running with her hot behind me. I either wake up or run smack dab into The Sovereign who says he'll protect me."

"That seduction part isn't just a dream, Chuck. Everyone on board has seen the way she looks at you. I thought she was going to suck you in back there in the hydroponic bay." Demetrius pointed his thumb over his shoulder.

"Yeah, she's pretty obvious." Chuck shook his head. "But what about your dreams?"

"Mine are somewhat different. I find myself hovering over some beautiful planet, much like Earth. The next thing I know, I'm on the surface, either in a magnificent city, like Adonlon on Eden or in the country with forests, meadows, and sheep. There are always beautiful people around, naked like on Eden. They bow down paying homage to me as I walk among them. I feel great! Suddenly the people and animals turn into hideous monsters and attack me. Then suddenly everything disappears. I'm either in total darkness or a fog so thick I can't see my hand in front of my face. And horribly hot. Like you, either that wakes me up or I hear a voice telling me that he is the only way out. I think it's The Sovereign's voice." Demetrius was wringing his hands as he finished.

"I wonder if Yehowshuwa is trying to get our attention." Chuck stroked his chin as he pondered that. "Maybe it's just our own subconscious interacting with the lies he heaped on us before we came to Eden. On Eden we certainly didn't have any doubts or bad dreams."

"Well, you're a great help!" Demetrius sagged back into his chair. "I wonder if there is anyone on the ship that might have some insight."

Chuck sat up straight. "Why don't we talk to Raymond? He was the only one that voted not to go on to Eden."

"Humph, he joined in all the occult stuff on Eden just like everyone else. Why would he have any insight?" asked Demetrius without enthusiasm.

"Yeah, but as I remember he had fewer abilities than anyone. I lost telepathic contact with him before anyone else. If anyone else is having second thoughts it might be him. Let's not tell anyone else about this until we talk to him." Chuck pulled out his ECD to set up a meeting with the Raymond and Demetrius.

I feel almost like I'm a mutineer on my own ship.

December 11, 998 ASR

Robert, Jim, and Samyaza decided to go to Robert's apartment. Samyaza explained briefly that while he could protect them from the Administration, others could still overhear their conversation if they were in public. All were quiet as they continued walking briskly. Strangely, even though it was dark, Samyaza never took off his sunglasses and didn't seem to have any difficulty even in the darkest parts of campus, such as between buildings and under trees.

After they settled in and each got a cup of coffee, Samyaza asked, "Robert, what have you discovered?"

Robert quickly related his meeting with Dr. Halverson and receiving the data module containing Professor Robison's note about the archeological find. He shared that the Professor believed that he was actually in or around The Chancellor's ancient headquarters.

He felt quite important as he spoke about his book. "As you probably know, I've been commissioned by the Administration to write a new study of the Last Battle and I've been trying to find material that would show, as our discussion topics have maintained, that it wasn't the way The Sovereign reported it. While their goal is to vindicate his position once and for all, I've found from Jim's ancestors that the events leading up to the time of Great Time of Trouble wasn't as evil as reported. Putting this information together with what we could find at The

Chancellor's headquarters may provide what we need to expose The Sovereign as a fraud. The best part is that I'd be doing it under his authorization."

Samyaza rubbed his hands together eagerly, "This is what we've been hoping for, Robert. Now how can we help you?"

"We know that Professor Robison and his assistant disappeared and we believe that the Administration took him so he couldn't publish his findings. Jim and I don't want to end up the same. Perhaps you could tell us more about this training that Dr. Halverson had so that we could protect our conversations. That would be a starting point. Then we need to have some way to get to the site to do excavation work without being detected. I'm not sure what you have available so I hope there is a lot more to the underground than we were told by Gustav. Just the technology involved in publishing *The Question* without detection implies that you are capable of more." Robert felt as if he had been in a dungeon and was now starting to adjust to the light.

Jim held up a hand and interjected, "I think we also need you to make contact with Josu, my ancestor, and his clansmen. If I'm right they will become allies and will greatly help the cause."

Samyaza smiled as broadly as his slim face would allow and nodded, "You show much more faith than I was told. And with this we are very pleased. You are right about our abilities. While we have a long way to go, we are progressing more rapidly every day. I will work with both of you so you can protect yourselves. You both will be taking a leap beyond most people at your level in the underground but I can tell that you will make this transition easily."

Robert grinned and looked at Jim who returned the smile.

"We also have the ability to protect the site so that The Sovereign's observers will never see any activity there. We will make the necessary arrangements as soon as you are ready to go. We will also provide you transportation to the site in one of our own vehicles that is not registered with the Administration. You will be able to go anywhere you want and no one will know where you are. Oh, that reminds me. We need to add some additional software to your ECDs so that you can continue to use them without exposing your position."

"How do you protect the site?" asked Jim.

"Once you receive the training to protect yourself, you will understand that you have power within you to do amazing things. Things The Sovereign has forbidden for centuries so he could maintain his control. Jim, do you remember this summer how concerned Robert was about the position of the mountains?" Samyaza turned his attention to Jim.

"Oh yeah, he kept asking people about it and thought for sure that it should have been further away. Hey, how did you know about that?" Jim frowned.

"The Sovereign isn't the only one who can monitor people's activities. You have both been under our protection for quite some time. When you were there talking in the tent and Robert assured you that The Sovereign was too busy to pay any attention to everyone, I was there making sure that he was not interested in you." Samyaza leaned back in his chair. "I can assure you that I detected no monitoring, which I would have blocked had it occurred."

Jim pointed his finger at Samyaza. "I thought you looked familiar. I caught a glimpse of you in the dark before we turned in. The sunglasses in the dark!"

Samyaza laughed, "Yes, that's right. Anyway, the mountain did move, or it appeared that it had to Robert. The area beyond the cliff that you approached on your hike is enveloped in our shields and is being set up as a training camp. All around the world in wilderness areas we are currently establishing sites." His demeanor became quite serious again. "There we will train recruits to protect themselves and to regain control over themselves in the way it was intended before The Sovereign perverted the natural course of this world."

Robert felt his jaw drop as he uttered a quiet, "Wow! At least I was right about the mountain." He jabbed Jim in the arm.

Samyaza waved his hand, making what he said sound simple, "We will send people ahead of you who have the power to shield your archeological site. It will appear as vacant as the day Professor Robison left it. This will give you the freedom to explore without interference from The Sovereign."

"I had no idea that the underground was capable of anything like this. Why hasn't this been made know to more people?" asked Robert.

Samyaza shook his head. "We need to gain more power before we can reveal this to anyone other than the most trusted. You have earned our trust by answering the questions on the test as you did and by not buying into the fabrications that assaulted you on your interviews. Instead you kept looking for the truth and you found it with Josu."

Robert was feeling more elated with each detail that Samyaza shared.

Samyaza raised a long white finger with a long fingernail. "That brings me back to Josu. We believe as you, that his clan will be very valuable. As you know, they are very distrustful of outsiders. It is very providential that Jim met Josu and that their relational bond has formed."

Jim puffed out his chest with importance, obviously pleased with the recognition Samyaza gave him.

"Jim, would you set up a meeting with Josu to introduce one of my colleagues?" asked Samyaza. "We would be most appreciative."

Jim responded quickly, "Hey, I'd be glad to do that. When?"

Samyaza narrow mouth turned up again. "Just as soon as you two have received your training. Unless you have some objections, I'd like to start that tomorrow morning at 10:00. We can meet back here at your place, Robert, if that's OK with you."

Robert was more than willing to get on with the training. "Yes, sure. I don't have anything more important than that and here would be fine, too."

"Sure, you can count me in," answered Jim.

"Good. You should rest yourselves for this will be intensive training. I'll leave you now." Samyaza got up, shook Robert and Jim's hands and left.

Robert looked at Jim with a sense of awe, bewilderment and excitement. He could tell Jim felt the same way. They both flopped back down on the couch and took a deep breath.

"So what do you think, Robert? I feel almost numb and this seems be like a wild roller coaster ride. I'm pumped up but drained. What have we gotten ourselves into? Should we even talk anymore tonight without some kind of protection?" asked Jim with his rapid fire rambling.

Robert took another long deep breath, "I'm pumped too, Jim. I'm in awe of all that I learned tonight. It's a good thing we left the meeting. I don't think the others, including Gustav, would have been able to fathom all this. I feel like I'm called out for a special mission that will be instrumental to the future of mankind. And you too, Jim. It wasn't just chance that your grandparents left the clan. As Samyaza said, you are the key to uniting your clan with the underground. It's just too remarkable for words."

Jim added, "This implies that there's someone controlling our destiny other than The Sovereign, which means he isn't nearly as sovereign as he would like us to believe."

"You took the words right out of my mouth, brother. Hey, it's really late. Why don't you crash here tonight and save some time in the morning? We'll be ready for Samyaza when he returns. I'm really tired all of a sudden." Robert stretched and pushed Jim over.

"Sounds good to me. I'll just conk out on the couch here." Jim lay where Robert pushed him.

December 12, 998 ASR

Jim had trouble sleeping on Robert's couch. He had several short dreams about Samyaza appearing while he was at home, on a convy, or other odd places. Each time he woke and wondered just who Samyaza was. He had a hard time getting back to sleep. In addition, Robert was up early.

At 10:00 on Saturday morning Robert was hovering around the door. When a knock sounded, he immediately opened it. Samyaza stood tall in the doorway carrying a small briefcase. "Come on in, Samyaza."

Samyaza stooped slightly to keep from hitting his head as he entered. "I'm glad to see that you are so eager. Let's get started. First, draw the drapes and dim the lights so that we won't be distracted, then let's sit down around your coffee table."

Jim quickly went to the window and closed the drapes while Robert turned down the lights and they joined Samyaza, who had sat down on the couch. Jim sat on a pillow-chair and Robert sat beside Samyaza.

Samyaza unfolded a chart with a pentagram spreading it out on the coffee table. He took six small candles out of the briefcase and placed one at each corner of the pentagram and one in the center.

When he finished setting up the chart, Samyaza sat back. "First of all, I need to provide you some history that has been hidden or suppressed by The Sovereign throughout the ages. Since we don't have a lot of time, this is a crash course and won't cover all the details. We wouldn't normally go this quickly but you have already shown that your faith is ready to absorb this. We need to get you on your mission as soon as possible."

Jim couldn't imagine what Samyaza was about to present. However, what he said sounded similar to topics from *The Question*.

Samyaza glanced at Robert then Jim and continued. "When man was first created, he had the ability to communicate through telepathy with other people and with those in the eternal realm or spiritual world as you would call it,. The Sovereign's father, Yehhovaw, became jealous and fearful of what he created. He suppressed your abilities so that it was almost impossible for people to use telepathy. If anyone tried, he sentenced them to death. It is through these telepathic abilities that he is able to monitor us and it is only by engaging these abilities that we are able to prevent him from knowing our thoughts and our speech. Any questions so far?"

Jim spoke up, "Just to make sure I understand what you're talking about. You are going to teach us how to use telepathic powers, something that The Sovereign kills people for using?"

"Yes, that is correct," replied Samyaza.

Jim fidgeted in his chair. He didn't like the consequences of blatantly disobey The Sovereign Yehowshuwa. "If we are successful he won't know we are using these abilities. If we aren't successful he will know immediately and we're in deep trouble. Am I right?"

Samyaza sighed, "Correct again, Jim. There is a risk in attempting to use these powers before you are fully trained. That is one reason we have not trained more people. As long as you are with me, you can experiment and test your powers but you shouldn't try them alone until I let you know you are ready. Any other questions?"

Jim thought for a few seconds. *Is this really what I want? Are the risks too great? Am I really chosen?* He finally answered, "OK, let's continue."

Robert spoke up, "I have a question."

"Sure, what is it?"

"You said The Sovereign was jealous and fearful. Why would he be fearful of us if he created us?"

Samyaza spread his arms wide. "All created sentient beings, whether created by Yehhovaw through the evolutionary process or by any other beings, have the ability to progress to become like Yehhovaw and The Sovereign. His fear is that if you grow, you will find him to be a liar and will reject his authority over you. He craves worship and he would lose that if you were to become his equal. The ultimate goal of the underground is to free people to grow and become all that they were originally created to become. That can't happen as long as The Sovereign is repressing your abilities."

Robert's eyes widened. "So you are saying that each of us can become a being that can create other living creatures who can also in turn create beings? Where does it all stop?" asked Robert.

Samyaza rubbed his forehead. "I can see that the abbreviated version isn't going to be short as I thought, but that's OK. You need to know these answers before we move on. To clarify, not all living creatures can create other beings, only enlightened beings. Only those who are specifically created in the image of their creator and progress through ascension can do this. The beauty of the real universe is that it is always expanding as more and more beings ascend and create more and more galaxies, stars, planets, and people. The universe is infinite and has no bounds."

That boggled Jim's mind

"There are billions of enlightened beings who have progressed under the tutelage of their beneficial creators and the Council of Enlightened Beings. The Council of Enlightened Beings established guidelines and principles for those who ascend and gain the ability to create life. When someone has advanced to that point they petition the Council of Enlightened Beings for the right to create their own worlds. They are tested to see if they have matured enough to handle such a large responsibility, and if they are deemed worthy they are granted the right. Unfortunately a few beings have rebuked the Council's advice and created worlds while they still had character flaws. Such is the case for Yehhovaw, the creator of this world. Even a very minor flaw in such a powerful being can have horrific repercussions in their worlds"

Jim's head was spinning but he was starting to understand the concepts, but not without question. "If this Council of Enlightened Beings is so powerful, why didn't they simply stop Yehhovaw from creating the earth?"

"The nature of enlightenment is beyond the understanding of those who have not yet progressed to their level. In their wisdom they have determined that it is better to wait and see how the rebel administers his creation. Some have done well and others have not. When they haven't, the Council seeks beings who are in the process of enlightenment to rescue the children of the rebels. The Chancellor and his forces were sent to Earth for the rescue mission."

You have to be kidding! The Chancellor? This is getting really weird. Jim decided to hold his tongue and hear more of what Samyaza had to say before interrupting again.

Samyaza didn't appear to notice Jim's shock but continued with his speech. "Ben-Shaachar has been working for centuries to free mankind from Yehhovaw and his son, The Sovereign. The only way to stop the rebel is to free his children to become enlightened. They are the only ones that will be able to imprison him and prevent him from perpetuating his abuse."

Jim couldn't wait any longer and interrupted, "The Chancellor! But he's been imprisoned and out of the way. How can he help us?"

Samyaza frowned slightly and for some reason Jim wished he'd kept his mouth shut. "I was about to get to that. Yes, The Chancellor is currently imprisoned but he has not stopped progressing during his time of incarceration. In fact he has evolved much farther as result of his isolation. That is the reason we are now able to hide our thoughts and actions from the Administration. That pretty much sums up history. Are there any more questions?"

Robert's furrowed eyebrows revealed that he was thinking seriously. "Let me know if I've jumped to the wrong conclusion, but the way I see this, undergoing this training means that we are aligning ourselves with The Chancellor in some kind of cosmic battle. How will this help him succeed where he failed before? What happens if we fail?" asked Robert.

Samyaza pressed the tips of his long white fingers together in a prayer-like position. "Whew, you don't pull any punches do you, Robert? It is a cosmic battle. When you are trained you will have the first abilities of enlightenment. The laws of the eternal require a majority of Yehhovaw's offspring to be on the path to ascension before he can be overthrown. This is the third time in history when enough people have rejected Yehhovaw to enable this to happen. The first time Yehhovaw responded by flooding the whole Earth, killing all but those loyal to him. The second time was just before the Great Time of Trouble. He pulled his followers into a state of semi-enlightenment and devastated the planet to keep himself in power. Now we have another chance. The number of people alive now on Earth is far greater than those that are semi-enlightened."

Jim's math didn't add up. "Wait a minute. Aren't most people on Earth loyal to The Sovereign? The underground can't possibly have that big of a following."

Samyaza raised his eyebrows, making his face appear much longer and thinner. "Most people are obedient but not loyal. They are very much like Josu who keeps his nose clean but would do what he wants if there were no Enforcers. We believe that once the underground is trained, we will be able to release Robert's documentation and recruit enough people to restore your freedom."

Robert exhaled sharply. "Whew! That sure puts a lot of pressure on my work. But you haven't answered what happens if we fail."

Samyaza's eyes narrowed and his mouth turned down, becoming very sullen. "If we fail, then we will experience death in a sense, but instead of becoming semi-enlightened like the Enforcers, we will be imprisoned with The Chancellor. We will have to wait until there are again enough people on Earth to break free from the evil Yehhovaw and Yehowshuwa. There is no guarantee that we will ever achieve this balance again." His eyes lit up and he smiled. "However, I don't believe we will fail this time because of the advancements that The Chancellor has made."

Jim felt wide-eyed as he asked, "Are you saying that there is the possibility that we could end up in prison for eternity if we fail?"

Samyaza nodded solemnly. "Yes, that is a very slim possibility. That is a risk that you need to consider if you decide to go further. Are you still committed and ready to start training?"

Robert quickly answered, "Yes."

Jim looked at Robert. He wasn't 100% sure. Robert's smarter than me and he didn't hesitate. I guess I can commit too, based on that. Jim nodded agreement.

Samyaza rubbed his hands together and smiled with his thin lips. "My superiors were right about you. You are ready. Not many would have responded positively to what we've discussed in the past few minutes. I sense that you have both committed yourselves to working for the freedom of all mankind so let's get started with your training."

He turned to the coffee table and lit the candles at each point of the pentagram and at the center. "These candles represent points of light that are eternal. At each point is the name of one of the founders of the Council of Enlightened Beings. The center represents their agent here, Ben-Shaachar. We will call upon them to train our minds. Now focus on the center and repeat with me their names."

Samyaza led Robert and Jim in a rhythmic low chant, repeating each of the five names written on the chart by each candle. Jim quickly memorized the names and began to focus on the one candle in the center of the pentagram.

Jim felt a strange sensation coming over his body. At first he felt as if he were losing his balance and was falling forward but he realized that he was holding steady and the sensation slowly ceased.

Samyaza whispered, "Let your consciousness fall into the flame. Do not let your body hold you back. Fall into the flame."

Robert felt his body falling into the flame even though he knew he was not moving. The sensation increased as he continued to chant and look at the slight flickering of the candle. He tried to pay no attention to his body and it seemed as if he were being drawn into the flame. In an instance he was not aware of his body but was surrounded by darkness.

He felt as if he were just waking up and opening his eyes. He looked around and saw a great flat plane stretching as far as he could see in every direction. The plane appeared to be a highly polished floor that emanated a barely visible glow from five tiny points of light in the distance. He stood still and the lights began to revolve around him and come closer. He watched for several minutes as the lights took on shapes. Five names echoed louder and louder as the lights drew near.

The lights transformed into the shape of a person's face. The darkness beneath and around each diminished. Robert saw that they were human figures clothed in long floor-length black robes with hoods over their heads. They floated slightly over the plane, gliding smoothly toward him. He couldn't distinguish their features because the light coming from under the hoods was too bright. Somehow, he was able to adjust to the light and wasn't blinded. As they approached him within the last three meters, they brought their arms from under the folds of the robe exposing hands that radiated light. They joined hands and circled Robert, all the time repeating one name after another.

Robert felt no fear but a strong sense of curiosity as they stopped circling him, broke the circle and lined up before him. There was silence. Robert instinctively dropped to his knees as dread suddenly swept over him. "Who are you and what do you want of me?" he asked. He didn't know what he was supposed to do in the presence of these beings.

They spoke in unison, "We are they upon whom you have called. Arise, Robert, and choose who will be your guide."

In sequence from Robert's left they spoke. "I am Harum. I am Opparum. I am Mararum. I am Rorarum. I am Amorum. Choose well and you will receive the desires of your heart."

"I choose the one who is to the left of the one on the right. I choose Rorarum."

"You have chosen well, Robert, as we expected and as you should," spoke Rorarum with a thunderous voice that seemed to roll from the blackness above and resounded from the five corners of the plane.

He glided forward toward Robert. "Open yourself to me and I will teach you all you need to know," he said quietly and gently. He kept coming closer and closer until he was face to face with Robert. "Open yourself to me," he repeated. "You have studied well and accepted our teaching through Gustav. It is now time for you to take the next step. Open yourself to me. Invite me in."

"Come in," responded Robert.

Rorarum passed into Robert then came back out at his side facing the others. "It is done. Come, Robert, and I will show you what you need to know for this time."

Immediately Robert and Rorarum were standing in the inner court of a shopping mall full of people walking busily to and from the various shops. Rorarum turned to Robert and asked, "You see all these people? Look at them carefully and tell me what you see."

Robert glanced from side to side. "There are many people here. Men and women of all ages as well as children. Some appear to have some purpose in mind while others are leisurely strolling without anything in mind. There are a few people sitting on benches or just standing and watching. Wait a minute, there is a person standing by the fountain and he is an agent of the Administration." Robert turned to Rorarum and asked, "How did I know that?"

"You have been given many abilities that you will learn to use in time. The first is to identify those who belong to our realm and their allegiance. Look around you more."

Robert turned around looking at the different people. "I can see several Administration agents. It looks like some of them are actually invisible to other people, but I can see them. Oh! Over there by the fountain is one who is loyal to The Chancellor Ben-Shaachar."

"You are correct, I know him. His name is Argon. He was sent here many millenniums ago with The Chancellor. Watch him closely."

Argon glanced over toward Robert and Rorarum, nodded his head and walked across the mall to where an Administration agent was watching people. Argon said a few words to the agent who raised his arm and pointed down the mall. He made a few more gestures that made it apparent that he was giving directions to Argon. Argon nodded his head a few times, smiled and walked the way that the agent had directed.

Robert didn't know how but he understood what was happening. "I see, Rorarum, the agent didn't even recognize that Argon was one of you and treated him as if he were simply another person in the mall. Argon was able to completely mask his identity and his thoughts from the Administration's agent. Impressive." Robert turned to Rorarum. "I also understand that you will now teach me to be able to do the same as well as shelter those around me. It is as clear as if you had already told me exactly what you were going to do. You're communicating directly with me in my mind, aren't you? Telepath? No need to answer, you already have. Why am I even talking to you? Oh yeah, habit. Yes, I'm ready to return."

Again Robert found himself on the plane but this time he was alone with Rorarum. They stood face to face and looked at each other as Rorarum silently taught him what he needed to know.

Jim jerked and opened his eyes wide. For a second he didn't know where he was. He looked back and forth, seeing both Robert and Samyaza with their eyes closed. Samyaza was quietly repeating the names of the five eternal beings while slightly rocking back and forth. Robert quietly sat erect and stiff like a granite statue. Jim checked the time and discovered that he must have been asleep 45 minutes.

He leaned back in the pillow-chair. Not having slept much the night before, the low lights, and flickering candles made him drowsy. He napped and watched until the candles were almost ready to burn out. If they burned any lower they could start the chart on fire. Jim waited until the last moment and blew them out with one breath like the candles on a birthday cake.

As soon as the last candle went out Samyaza stopped chanting and opened his eyes. Slowly he looked at Jim then Robert. He whispered, "You blew out the candles." It wasn't a question or an accusation.

"Yeah, they were about to burn the chart."

"I see." Samyaza sat back in the chair. "How long have you been watching?"

"A few minutes."

"What do you remember about the session?"

"I heard you say something about letting us fall into the flame, I felt a bit of vertigo as if I lost my balance. From there I don't remember anything. I fell asleep. I woke up after 45 minutes and have been dozing on and off for a couple of hours."

Samyaza rolled his eyes and shook his head slightly. "You never made contact? No dreams, nothing? You just had a good nap?"

"Yup, I take it that wasn't the desired result?" Somehow, Jim wasn't disappointed.

"No." Samyaza said no more.

"So what's happening with Robert? Is he OK? He looks so stiff."

"Yes." Samyaza closed his eyes briefly. "He is in deep communion with Rorarum. We will wait for him to come back. We should be quiet and not disturb him."

"Fine, I'm going to slip into the kitchen and get a cup of coffee, would you like some?"

"No, I don't require any," snapped Samyaza quietly.

What a grump. Jim went into the kitchen and found his mug from earlier in the sink. It still looked fairly clean. He put it in the beverage dispenser and pressed the coffee button. He didn't turn on any lights or open the drapes to disturb Robert. He soon returned and sat down. He thought that Samyaza was a bit of a scary character as well as a grump and didn't want to irk him so he just sat there and wondered what was happening.

Suddenly Robert's eyes opened and he looked around the room. "I'm back!" he announced. "Samyaza, you didn't tell us you were one of The Chancellor's agents."

"I see that you have been properly trained to recognize agents of both sides. Are you able to protect yourself and those around you?" he asked.

Robert seemed extremely cheery, "No problem. Rorarum has provided everything I need for now. As I have time, he will continue to teach me more, but for now I'll be able to protect us. He has dispatched a team to secure the archeological site and has asked you to arranged for a vehicle to transport Jim and me along with our necessary equipment. Thank you, Samyaza, for the introduction. As soon as you have made the software upgrades to our ECDs and secured our transportation, you may go back to making sure Gustav keeps out of trouble." Robert handed their ECDs to him.

Samyaza bowed slightly but his tall frame made it appear to be quite a pronounced obeisance. "As you wish, sire." He disappeared.

Jim was shocked. "Holy cow! Where did he go? What is going on, Robert? Did I hear right? He is like an Enforcer but works for The Chancellor?"

Robert quickly and excitedly told Jim about his encounter with Rorarum. He explained that Rorarum was now his mentor.

Jim was amazed by everything he heard. "So you can just look at a person and tell if he's one of us or if he's an agent from the spiritual realm and who's side he's on?"

Robert nodded confidently. "Yup, that's about the size of it. I can tell if a person is an Enforcer, Messenger, or Encourager even before they make themselves visible. I can even tell if one is nearby before they are close enough to monitor us, then block their ability to hear us or our thoughts. I can tell when The Sovereign is tuning in on us and block that monitoring as well."

He leaned across the table and slapped Jim's knee. "We were right when we thought Yehowshuwa was limited in his power and this proves it. We are on our way to freeing our bothers and sisters."

Robert stood up and stretched. "We need to tell Samantha and Kevin that we are taking off soon. But I don't think it's wise to tell them exactly what has happened. Only that I've had the training and can protect our conversations. As soon as Samyaza returns we'll see if they can meet this afternoon. I think they both have a couple of finals this week and then it's winter break so we may not see them again for a while."

"Sounds good to me," said Jim trying to sound enthused but not feeling nearly as committed as he had before the séance. The whole thing had spooked him.

Robert began to pace the living room as he talked, "See if you can contact Josu and set up a meeting with him after your last final. While you're with him, I'll get our equipment lined up. Within a week we should be headed for the site."

Jim didn't know how to tell Robert about his own training but the week with Josu pushed the issue. "Uh, Robert, about the meeting with Josu? I thought that was going to wait until after I received my training. According to Samyaza, I flunked the first lesson."

Robert stopped pacing and stared at Jim. "What?"

"I didn't make contact like you did. I fell asleep."

He shook his head. "No."

"Yes."

Robert sighed deeply, "Don't worry about it. I'll make sure that the people working with Josu have already been trained so you'll be able to introduce them and they'll take care of any opposition surveillance. As a matter of fact, this would be a good opportunity to check in with my mentor and find out who was chosen to lead this front of the battle." Robert closed his eyes for a moment and looked like he was concentrating, trying to remember something that had slipped his mind.

After a few seconds he again opened his eyes. "Well, that was a lot simpler than I thought it might be. Once I get the hang of it, I think I'll be able to communicate with him without even concentrating. It appears that Rorarum has had some people protecting Josu for quite some time, which explains why he's been able to get away with some of the stuff he's said. Anyway, they remained hidden until an opportune time such as this. They will use Idakzeu to work with Josu. He was their prime protector before the Great Time of Trouble. He was incarcerated with The Chancellor but recently escaped. Oh, don't tell Josu that he is an agent from the spiritual realm. He will reveal that to Josu when he is ready."

Jim stared at Robert a few seconds then spoke, "Robert, you're starting to freak me out. You're taking this as if it were second nature to you and you've been doing it all your life. What really happened to you while you were in that trance?"

Robert sighed slightly, sat down facing Jim and answered, "My eyes have been opened to something greater than I ever imagined. All the times we met with Gustav and others, we were talking theory. The theory doesn't come close to the reality of the other dimension or realm. Along with my eyes being opened, I've been able to see how important our role is in a cosmic struggle that has been going on for thousands upon thousands of years. I would say that I'm much more focused, energized, and in control. Before I was unsure and felt as if big things were progressing and happening while I only knew a small part of a big picture. Does it bother you that I was given this insight and you weren't?"

"Yeah, it does. But I think you explained it pretty well. I'm still on the outside looking in through a dirty window while you have moved to the inside." Jim felt like he was left behind.

Robert stood again and patted him on shoulder. "Patience, my young friend. I'm sure you will soon share the same experience. As soon as I'm more comfortable, I believe I may even be able to train you. Until then I hope you can trust me."

"OK, Robert, I think that helps." I think I trust you but I'm not sure what we've gotten ourselves into.

While they were talking, Samyaza returned with their ECDs and placed them on the coffee table. Robert acknowledged his service with a nod of his head, then Samyaza left again.

Robert and Jim called Kevin and Samantha. They set up a time to meet at the student union.

Chapter 34

December 12, 998 ASR

The student union cafeteria was almost deserted on a Saturday afternoon but Kevin went to their usual table and waited for Samantha to arrive. He asked her to come a few minutes before the appointed time so he could prepare her for Robert's news about his training.

He watched as she entered the cafeteria's south entrance and took a quick glance around. Her perky walk brought her quickly to the table and she sat down. "So what do I need to know before Robert arrives?"

"I've been told that this news about his training is going to be beyond anything you've encountered before. Apparently things are advancing very fast and Robert has made contact with some of The Chancellor's agents that have been freed from prison," warned Kevin.

Her eyes widened, "Oh my, it has progressed that far? I had no idea that things were going that fast. So what can we expect?"

"Hopefully not much since The Sovereign is with us. However, I wanted to warn you so that you aren't caught off-guard. Remember that your goal is to be in on the ground floor of these discussions so that you can rescue the newly recruited. While we are certainly concerned about Robert and Jim's welfare, we can't let them know what we know. If Robert is in as deep as I understand, he could actually be a threat to us and wouldn't hesitate turning us in. Remember what Elder Gregapalous told you about the possibility of danger if the underground found out about us."

"Thanks for the heads up, Kevin. But I think I'll be OK. Oh, here they come now."

Kevin's back was toward Robert and Jim as they approached from the north entrance. He turned around. When he spotted Robert he felt the hair on the back of his neck stand on end. He knew his reaction was because of the presence of Robert's mentor, Rorarum, who was with him.

Robert immediately started talking as he sat down. "Hi guys, I'm glad you could meet us today. A lot has happened since last night and I'd like to share it with you. After we left, Samyaza filled us in how the underground will be able to help us. They have some amazing capabilities to camouflage the archeological site so that we don't have to worry about the stuff we were talking about yesterday. Jim and I will be able to come and go without detection. On top of that, Jim has already been set up with an underground contact in Josu's area that will be able to get him involved. Samyaza was really able to get things started."

"So what about this training to shield yourself from the Administration that he talked about? When will that happen?" asked Samantha.

"Samyaza came back this morning and gave us our first training session and I've actually learned how to protect myself and anyone within a few feet of me. So we can talk freely right now as long as no one physically hears us. I would say that it went well, wouldn't you, Jim?" Robert looked and sounded very confident.

Jim avoided eye contact and looked at the table top. "Yeah, it did for you but I totally flunked the first lesson."

"What happened, Jim, did you fall asleep in class?" asked Kevin knowing perfectly well what happened.

Jim looked a bit sheepish but replied, "As a matter of fact, that's exactly what happened. I guess we stayed up too late last night and I didn't sleep very well. Too much excitement."

"No, you didn't?" asked Samantha as she tried to suppress a laugh but didn't do a very good job.

"You think that's funny, Sam? I'm surprised at you," said Kevin as he caught her eye with a wink to let her know he was in complete agreement while making sure that Robert and Jim could only hear what appeared as a minor rebuke.

"It doesn't matter for now," said Robert. "He will have more opportunities to get trained and so will you. However, things are moving quickly and Jim and I will be leaving at the end of next week to examine Professor Robison's discovery. I'll be involved with getting our supplies together and Jim will introduce the underground to Josu. This may be our last get-together until we come back."

"We're certainly going to miss you guys. We've had some great discussions here. I'm not sure the cell meetings will be the same without you either. But tell me, how does this 'protection' work?" asked Kevin.

Robert's eye twitched when he started his explanation, "My training was only the basics so I don't really know how it works. Kind of like electricity. I know how to use it but right now it's more like turning on a light without knowing that there are wires in the walls. When you are trained you can to do the same. I'm promised I'll know more as I advance in the training."

He doesn't have the slightest idea of what's going on. Kevin nodded but mentally he was shaking his head.

"So you just turn on this protection shield whenever you want to talk about underground stuff?" asked Samantha.

"I could, but I can sense whenever there may be someone monitoring the conversation so that it's only necessary to flip the switch if it's dark." Robert sat straight and puffed out his chest as he answered.

"So, right now, can you sense any darkness?" probed Kevin.

"No, as a matter of fact, I can't. Why are you asking?" replied Robert with a bit of irritation in his voice.

"Just curious." Kevin looked around the near vacant cafeteria. "Since the place is nearly empty I was hoping you could point out someone who might monitor us. I would like to see if they look any different from anyone else. But maybe another time?"

Robert relaxed a bit. "Maybe by the time we get back you'll get your training and will be able to see for yourself. Sorry I can't satisfy your curiosity now."

Kevin was confident that Robert had no clue that he was an Enforcer. "That should be quite interesting, I can hardly wait. Since we can talk freely now, why don't you tell us what you'll be up to while we're going through the drudgery of the next quarter? Sorry about distracting you; I'm sure that's what you wanted tell us in the first place."

"Yeah, wow, we have a lot to do." The excitement returned to Robert's voice. "The first thing to do is line up all the equipment and provisions we'll need. We could be gone as long as three months and still not fully explore the caves. From Professor Robison's notes there was a clean spring very near so we will have plenty of water."

Robert gestured to Jim who was still looking rather glum in contrast to his usual animated self.

"While I'm here, Jim will meet with Josu and Idakzeu, the underground director in that area. We are quite confident that Josu will embrace and lend a hand to the cause. When he gets back we'll leave."

"You're not going home for The Sovereign's birthday?" asked Samantha. "It's only two weeks away."

Robert was stopped in his tracks. "Oh – I hadn't thought of it. I've been so excited about the find and other things that happened that it slipped my mind. My parents would be ticked but I've been away before during the holidays." He closed his eyes for a second. "Jim, would it be OK with you to continue with our plans, or would you like to go home for the break and start at the beginning of the year?"

Jim answered quickly. "The past few holidays haven't been very happy times. The idea of going home this year conjures up dread and repulsion. The thought of going with you is the opposite. If you're going, I'm going. I didn't have any plans other than going to the beach and that sounds like it would just be a two week waste of time when we've got something important to do."

Robert clapped his hands. "Great, then the plan is still on. When you get back from visiting Josu we're off. When we get back, we'll look you two up and fill you in on what we found."

"Good luck, guys." Kevin felt a bit odd wishing them good luck, but offering a blessing in The Sovereign's name probably wouldn't be wise. "It sounds like it'll be quite an adventure. Personally I don't think I'd like running around underground for three months not knowing exactly what I'm looking for."

The four of them continued to talk as in times past, joking and generally enjoying each other's company. Kevin saw a subtle change in Robert that was very unsettling.

December 19, 998 ASR

On Saturday Jim arrived at the North West Regional transit center. As he stepped out of the convy he was greeted by a tall broad-shouldered man with blond hair and fair skin.

"Greetings, Jim, I'm Idakzeu. I trust that your journey was pleasant."

"Hi, Idakzeu. Oh, the trip was pleasant enough, as much as you can expect for a marathon trip in these things. Actually I slept most of the time. Say, you can protect us, can't you? I mean, I haven't had the training, or better, I haven't completed it yet. Look at you, though, blond hair, blue eyes and fair skin. No wonder you need an introduction to the Quebash."

"Oh, don't worry Jim, our conversations will be quite safe," Idakzeu chuckled along with Jim. "Yes, your observation is correct. My appearance is not one that would endear me to them. This brings up the subject of my name, Idakzeu. That is my code name in the underground. It is a reference to their homeland and is translated 'Quebash Fatherland.' I used it because of my responsibilities helping them in the past with their struggle for freedom. They probably wouldn't take kindly to me using that as a name so why don't you just call me Sven. Beside, don't I look more like a Sven?"

Jim lead the way Josu's cafeteria.

"Yeah, I think Sven fits you much better. Well, there's Josu waiting for us. I gotta tell you though, as important as you getting this introduction is, the highlight of visiting with Josu is sampling his gastronomic delicacies. I've had the opportunity to sample some breakfast and lunch menus. Arriving later in the day, I'm anticipating an entrée that will round out my Quebash culinary experiences." Jim's mouth was already watering just talking about Josu's food.

They arrived at the cafeteria and Josu gave Jim a very fatherly and strong hug as Sven watched.

"Josu, I'd like you to meet the local underground director. This is Sven. Sven, this is my great, great, oh who knows how many greats, grandfather Josu."

"I'm very pleased to meet you, Mr. Taratoricakena." Idakzeu extended his hand. Jim was impressed that he pronounced Josu's name perfectly.

Josu looked Idakzeu up and down then shook his hand without expression. "I'm pleased to make your acquaintance, but if we are going to work together please just call me Josu as I'm sure we will soon become friends and colleagues. But first, I have prepared a special dinner for you. Please come in, sit and eat and we will talk business."

Josu led them to the back of the cafeteria where it became customary for him to talk privately with people. As they sat down Zuma brought out soup to start their dinner.

Josu smacked his lips. "We'll start tonight with adlasurrp, a very tasty soup made with leek, onion, potato, cod and garlic. A very delicious introduction to our main dish.

"The main course, gentlemen is Filet de Pork with Specialty Peppers. It is a pork filet mignon sliced in strips, marinated in a sauce of olive oil and one of our favorite specialty peppers."

Josu simulated stirring in a pan with his hands as he continued. "It is fried, then sweet peppers are added just before it is finished cooking. Served to you on a bed of tender young spinach. It is a simple dish and accompanied by our famous sheepherder's bread.

"For dessert you will be treated to our Gypsy's sleeve. A very delectable cake roll with a cinnamon filling sprinkled with powdered sugar." He touched his thumb and middle finger to his lips and pulled them away with a kissing sound.

"Josu, this is a fantastic meal. I will relish it with great pleasure. May our impending joint operations have the spice and care that you have shown in your food preparation." When the food was served Idakzeu ate with obvious delight, oohing and aawing over every bite.

He sure knows how to butter up Josu!

"Sven, Jim's good friend, Robert, was a bit hesitant when he first dined with us. It seems that some of our favorites were not on his list. How do you feel about, oh, squid cooked in its own ink?"

"Are you kidding? That sounds like it would be most intriguing. Do you have a recipe?" Idakzeu's interest appeared genuine.

"Ah, inside of that light exterior beats the heart of a Quebash. I think we are going to get along very well. Tell me, what did you have in mind for our alliance?"

"Robert and Jim already filled us in on your tenuous relationship with The Chancellor during the Great Time of Trouble and how you kept your traditions secret until now. I applaud your abilities to maintain your cultural heritage. We are in complete agreement with what you've been doing. We would like to do for the rest of mankind what you have accomplished and more. When I explain what more we can do, I think you'll be very interested. However, you must know that we are working very closely with The Chancellor. Do you think that'll be a problem?"

Josu shrugged his shoulders. "I'd have to find out just what he expects of us and what we can expect from him. According to all accounts his previous goal was to become total dictator of the world and have everyone serve him. While he seemed to have left my ancestors pretty much alone, we'd have to have some guarantees that we would be able to remain independent," answered Josu.

Idakzeu leaned back and spread his hands out shoulder wide and height. "I don't think that will be a problem because most of those accounts are all lies that The Sovereign has propagated. The Sovereign is so successful at hiding his own true motives and distorting The Chancellor's motives that I'm not surprised that you would be leery of working with him."

Idakzeu's speech and manner were so relaxed that Jim could see Josu's face softening. It was hard not to trust Idakzeu.

Still, Josu answered cautiously, "Well, why don't you tell me about these motives, what we can expect and what we can do for you? I'll take this information to our other elders and then we'll see what comes of it. If it's as good as I expect then we may be able to form an alliance."

"Excellent, let me give you a bit of a history lesson that most people have never heard."

Idakzeu repeated essentially the same story that Samyaza told Robert and Jim with a few more details. Clearly, Josu was intrigued with what he was hearing; especially when he learned that the future for him and mankind was much more than an eternity serving The Sovereign.

Josu interrupted, "Talk about independence! Our people have some kind of inborn desire to be independent but we've always identified it with our nation. This is much greater. It stirs such a desire in my heart that it is pounding." Josu place his hand over his heart.

Finally Idakzeu finished his monolog. "So what do you think, Josu? Any questions?"

"What you told me is very intriguing. The potential for mankind and us stirs within me a desire for more beyond this world. However, these stirrings will not keep me from asking for the third time what The Chancellor would expect from us in return for his help."

Idakzeu shook his head. "You don't believe that all The Chancellor wishes to do is to fulfill his vows to the Council of Enlightened Beings to free mankind from Yehhovaw and his son The Sovereign?"

Josu put his palm-up hand out in front of Idakzeu and pointed to it with his other. "I would like to know specifically what he expects us to do in the short term. However, most important, what will be our affiliation with him? Then finally, what will our affiliation be after this freedom has been won? I don't want to walk into something that gets us free from The Sovereign and then puts us in bondage to another tyrant."

Idakzeu chuckled. "I like your directness. Since your people have maintained their independence while giving the appearance of subservience to The Sovereign, we believe that you should be the first people in the general population to be brought into the underground and trained. Once you are fully trained you will then assist in recruiting and training others."

Josu interrupted, "Are you saying that we would be trained before people like Jim, who has been in the underground?"

"You would be receiving training at the same time as others like Jim and Robert who are currently participating in the discussion groups. They have already been introduced to concepts that have prepared them for training. To be quite blunt, there is a risk that people who have not been in the discussion groups may not be as receptive to the training. That is why we want you to be the first. We believe that you will be successful and that will be a strong testimony to others who have not had the opportunity to avail themselves of the discussion groups. This will greatly facilitate our ability to recruit the rest of the population who haven't terminally allied themselves with The Sovereign."

Josu nodded. "OK, that's the short term interaction. What will be our affiliation?"

Idakzeu continued using his charismatic smile and assuring voice. "Your affiliation with The Chancellor could be best described as partnering. I know you are concerned that this could simply substitute Ben-Shaachar as a ruler over you in place of The Sovereign. As partners, you will be trained and learn all the resources available to you that he can provide. When you use these resources you will have to use them in accordance with his directions only until The Sovereign is overthrown. I guarantee you that you will not be under his thumb."

Josu nodded thoughtfully. "And after that?"

Idakzeu looked up to the ceiling as if gazing into the heavens. "When this is over, the Council of Enlightened Beings will send guidance counselors who will then show you how to use what you learned to continue on your way to enlightenment and ascension. The Chancellor will be reassigned so that there will be no risk of anyone thinking that he is doing this simply to replace Yehhovaw and The Sovereign."

"Tell him the consequences if this doesn't work. What if Josu and our people can't recruit enough people or somehow The Sovereign still has enough power to resist this attempt at freedom?" Jim remembered Samyaza's answer. It still got on his nerves but he wanted Josu to know all sides of the issue.

Idakzeu shot Jim an evil glance but regained his charismatic composure and answered, "There is always that possibility but we believe it to be extremely remote. The Chancellor has progressed very rapidly during his time of confinement and we are currently operating at levels we never dreamed about before. However, if we are defeated then The Sovereign will probably imprison you along with The Chancellor."

Josu squinted his eyes. "That's it, we are imprisoned forever?"

Idakzeu shook his head. "Ben-Shaachar is patient. He will find within himself the right formula to overpower Yehhovaw and defeat The Sovereign. Then mankind will be freed, if not this time then the next. When The Chancellor is finally victorious he will free all those who have been imprisoned by The Sovereign."

"It sounds like we really only fail if we align ourselves with The Sovereign in this eternal battle," said Josu thoughtfully.

"That's right, Josu. Either now or maybe thousands of years from now, you will be on your way to enlightenment as long as you resist The Sovereign. Otherwise you will always be in subjection to him."

Josu nodded slowly "Our elders are suspicious of outsiders so I will tell them all you have told me. I'm sure that they will agree with me and we will be able to start training our people very soon."

"Excellent, Josu. This has been one of the most important meetings in the history of mankind. The next will be with your elders. I'm looking forward to meeting them after they've joined in the battle."

They stood and Josu shook hands with Idakzeu. Jim had mixed feelings. He felt important by being the one who brought about this possible alliance but he didn't feel good.

December 19, 998 ASR

Marilyn sat at the kitchen table pondering the recent changes in her life. She stirred her favorite herbal tea and took a sip.

Her relationship with Justin was continually improving as Justin demonstrated his love, even when she was trying to influence his decisions with the board. Only the week before she almost threatened to move out if he didn't do all he could to approve a new agency, one in which she intended to be a key player on its board.

My plan would have worked if it wasn't for that blasted Markus. Unfortunately for her, Markus, the Board's statistician, did in-depth research to determine if the community needed the new agency. With his usual monotonous recital of statistics he reported to the Board that there were already three duplicate agencies within the boundaries of their parish that were made up of twenty community boards. He had all the demographic details regarding who would possibly use the services of the agency and how far clients had to travel to receive services. He continued with information for the past ten years that showed there was very little change in the use of the services and polls indicated that there wouldn't be any changes in the foreseeable future. When he finished, the Board unanimously voted not to approve the new agency.

Marilyn made Justin pay for his vote. He weakly explained how he would have lost credibility with the other members of the Board if he had voted for the agency in light of the detailed documentation that Markus provided. He even had the audacity to say that it just wouldn't be right and Board members were selected based on their integrity. They were not supposed to let anything other than what was best for the community influence their votes. He said the other members would censure him for trying to establish an agency just so his wife would have a prestigious position on its board. How she burned with anger over that!

Still, she was enjoying the affection and confidence that Justin was expressing about her. On the other hand, she was also becoming uneasy because she was not able to control him the way she used to. In many of their daily routines Justin acquiesced to Marilyn's desires and whims but he was also letting her know his preference. On occasion, he would ask her to accept his inclination. Even though she felt more accepted and loved than any time before in their marriage, she felt she was losing control of her family.

Her thoughts turned to her children. She tried to stay very involved with her married children's families. And how did they react? They set "boundaries" that limited her ability to help direct them. Over the years, Marilyn felt less in control of their lives. It made her all the more determined not to lose her influence over Robert's and Justin's lives. Then Robert had to rebel and write his book. Now Justin was changing, too. She had mixed emotions about that. While she felt comforted and like she belonged, she detested feeling out of control.

Marilyn noticed that she had a message on her ECD. *That's funny, I didn't notice a message earlier and I've been available all morning.*

She opened her ECD and saw that it was a video message from Robert. When she looked at the message she was greeted by Robert's smiling face. *I know that look; he has some news that I'm not going to like.* "Hi, Mom, you won't believe what just happened," he said eagerly, "I've just received some incredibly important evidence that has been unearthed in a remote dig. This is very significant and ties in with the research for my book so I'm leaving immediately to check it out. I'm really sorry to have to break the news to you like this but I'm not going to be able to come home for the holidays as I had planned. Jim and I will be on our way by the time you get this message and will be out of touch for up to three months. I love you, Mom, and I'll see you when I get back. Tell Dad I love him too and will miss being with you for the holidays."

There is no way in this green Earth that he's going to get away with this. Marilyn was more that angry. She was determined to make sure that Robert came home for a least one day. *He owes me at least one day; after all, I'm his mother and I've done so much for him. It is his responsibility to obey me and...* Her thoughts trailed off as she entered his id into her ECD and waited for him to answer.

Roberts face popped up on her screen, "Hi..."

Before another word came from her ECD she stated talking, "Young man, you listen to me and listen good." She stopped when she realized that Robert was still talking.

"You've reached Robert Maskil and I'm not available right now. I'm away on a dig and unreachable for a long time. Leave a message and I'll get back to you eventually." Roberts face dimmed and a text message and computer voice said, "Record your message now."

Marilyn angrily closed the connection without leaving a message. *It's only ten in the morning so he must have queued this up to come now. That no account brat. I'll show him.* She knew that Justin was still at the hardware store and she didn't have anything to do that couldn't be put off so she left the house and headed for the store.

When Marilyn arrived, she barged in the front door and started directly to the back employee-only-section of the store where Justin's office was located. She was about to crash through the swinging doors when she noticed Justin off to her right helping a customer with some doohickeys. She yelled at him, "Justin, your office, now!" Then she continued into the back room and stomped into his office, marched to his desk, turned around, folded her arms and started tapping her foot while she waited for Justin to catch up.

Justin hurried in the door and closed it behind him. He spoke calmly, "Honey, what's wrong? You look like you've just learned about a horrible tragedy."

"You betcha! I've heard just about the worst news I've heard for a long time. First, Robert has interviews right in his home town and doesn't even stop to say hello. Now he says he can't come home for the holidays and has the nerve to tell me in a recorded message instead of face to face. Now, what are you going to do about it?"

Justin stammered, "Uh, well, OK. I'll give Robert a call and see what I can do to convince him---"

"That isn't going to work," interrupted Marilyn, "I've already tried to call and he isn't answering. He says he's already on his way to the dig and won't be available until who knows when. Since you can't seem to do anything right without direction, I'll tell you what you'll do. You will use your influence as a Board member to get the Administration to locate him, stop him, and send him back here for a decent holiday."

Justin put his hand over his mouth for a second then answered, "I can see that this has really upset you, Honey, but---"

"Don't give me any of that 'honey but' stuff. Right now I'm sick and tired of your lovey-dovey ways of manipulating me to try to get me to do whatever you want. I know where you are going with this 'but' so save it. Just do what I said and do it now." She stormed out of the office and went home, leaving five curt messages for Robert as she went.

December 21, 998 ASR

Robert looked at his messages Monday morning and deleted all from Mom without even watching them. He noted that Dad called but didn't leave a message.

What they don't know won't hurt them and I'll simply screen all my calls until we're gone.

While Jim was visiting with Josu, Robert lined up the equipment and supplies that he needed to explore the site. Fortunately Professor Robison's notes contained enough detail for him to get a good idea of what he would encounter in the caves as well as information on the supplies the professor left behind. This made his job a lot simpler.

As promised, Samyaza delivered a transport that couldn't be traced by the Administration. It was a lot better than he expected since all he anticipated was a vehicle capable of carrying the equipment in an enclosed area. What arrived was a combination truck and mobile home. Samyaza proudly gave him a tour of the living quarters and command center which featured two plush high-backed chairs facing the broad wrap-around windshield. Behind the control center was the living area with a very inviting but modest couch and upholstered chair opposite an eating nook. The nook consisted of a table that could be folded down, revealing a cushioned bench that doubled as additional seating. Next came the kitchen, fully equipped with range, instant heating device, refrigerator, sink, garbage disposal, and cupboards with all the essential dishes and utensils.

The bathroom was small but adequate with a shower but no tub. Samyaza showed him the control panel for the disposal unit. It took care of all wastes, including that from the garbage disposal, almost instantaneously converting all byproducts into odorless fertilizer that could be safely spread on front yard grass. The panel also monitored waste water from both the kitchen and bathroom that was recycled into the reactor. Any overflow was perfectly potable and channeled back into the holding tanks. The indicators showed all tanks were full.

There were three bedrooms designed for a family of six but Robert knew he would take the double bed in the larger bedroom and let Jim take a berth in one of the two smaller rooms. With overhead, under-bed, and berth storage there would be plenty of room for their clothes.

"Sir, will these accommodations be satisfactory?" asked Samyaza.

"Yes, these will be quite sufficient. You've done a good job." Robert gave him a slight pat on the back as they left the living quarters.

"I'm glad you're pleased. However, I hope that the cargo area will be even more impressive."

They walked around to the back and Samyaza opened the back double door. The cargo area exposed a large cavernous hold that was more than adequate to hold the large equipment Robert had on order. Along one side were various shelves and cabinets that were perfect for the smaller equipment. At the far end of the area was a huge cold storage unit. They wouldn't need to leave the site to replenish food. There was also a large water storage tank and a water purification system that would allow them to refill from any source of water, whether fresh or saltwater.

"Ah yes, Samyaza, I would say you've done an excellent job. This will do very nicely."

Samyaza face beamed with pride. "Thank you, Sir. Thank you very much."

As soon as Samyaza left, Robert started making his rounds picking up equipment and supplies. By the end of the day when Jim arrived he was fully stocked and ready to go. Since Jim arrived late on Monday night they decided to leave early the next morning.

December 22, 998 ASR

When they got up Jim put on his backpack to haul it out to the van. He was very impressed by the huge vehicle they were about to use to travel a third of the way around the world. "Wow, what an impressive rig! But why's it so big?"

"Come on and take a look in the back and you'll see." Robert led the way to the back, opening the door to expose the stockpile of equipment and supplies. The shelves were all neatly stacked and organized with smaller tools and containers for preserving and storing ancient artifacts.

"Now come on around to the front and take a look at our luxury mobile tent." He led Jim to the front side entrance.

The first thing that caught Jim's eye was the kitchen to his left. He walked in and opened the refrigerator door. "Hey, Robert, this is really cool. I think I could really get used to riding around the world in this thing. What's in here? What kinds of good stuff will we be eating? Looks like we only have a few days worth of fresh fruit. Do you think we'll be able to get more?"

"I'm sorry to disappoint you, but we could be out there a long time so most of our food is frozen and we'll be way too far from any stores. But there might be enough in the land to satisfy you. Since this is one of the least known areas on Earth I'm not sure what to expect. I didn't want to take chances of finding nothing but pine cones."

Jim took off his backpack and started down the narrow hallway to the larger back bedroom. "Well, let's get going. I'll just toss my stuff in the bedroom back here an---"

Robert cut him of quickly "Uh, toss your stuff in one of the other two rooms. I've got first call on that room."

Jim stopped short, thought a moment, *well, he is the boss,* then responded, "OK, but then I get to drive first."

"No, I don't think so. But I'm not going to drive either. This rig is just too big for either of us to handle it on manual. You can set the course but it's going to be driving itself. Here's the coordinates of our destination." Robert showed him the coordinates on his ECD.

Jim was disappointed but realized that he would probably have some difficulty navigating in the downtown streets anyway. He slipped into the right hand plush driver's seat, started working on the computer controls, and entered the destination. The console brought up a map and outlined the course. Jim spent a few minutes reviewing the proposed course. It showed a fairly direct route out of Midrib and onto the main highway leading through the neighboring farming communities. The road continued through undeveloped areas and directly to a port city on the ocean. From there the course went northwest straight across the ocean and then followed several kilometers away from the shore line. It continued up a gulf and went ashore at a small port. From there it went inland following smaller and smaller roads until it reached the wilderness area. It wound around mountains and through valleys until the final destination was shown blinking on the console.

"How long will it take us to get there?" asked Robert, hovering over Jim's shoulder.

Jim traced the route with his hand. "This thing creeps through cities and towns at sixty kilometers per hour, cruises at about a 150 kilometers an hour on the open roads, top speed is 300 over open waters but ---"

Robert interrupted, "Just tell me how long."

"Uh, OK, 54 hours and 37 minutes after we get started, barring any episodes like waiting for sheep and goats to cross the road out in the boonies."

"Time's a'wasting, man. Hit the button and let's be on our way." Robert pointed to the console and sat down in the left hand driver's seat.

Jim pushed the execute trip button. The huge machine slowly rose from the ground and pulled out into the street as it left the alley behind Robert's apartment building. It quickly took them to the nearest highway entrance where it merged with other traffic, primarily trucks and service vehicles along with an occasional personal transport. After leaving the vicinity of Midrib they picked up speed as the traffic diminished. They were on the way to the port of Hedland about 500 kilometers west of Midrib.

Robert stood up and walked back to the living area. "OK, Mr. Research Assistant, since this thing will drive itself, why don't we get back to some of those archived books that should be waiting for us? We have plenty of time to see if we can find anyone before the Great Time of Trouble who believed that things were getting better."

Jim didn't want to do research. Most of his long distance travels were by underground convy. This surface trip showed him country he had never seen. He swiveled the chair toward Robert. "Slave driver! Can't we just look awhile at this beautiful country? Can you believe that this area was once called the Great Sandy Desert? Who would have thought that these fertile farms, flowered plains and forests were once nothing but sand, rocks and parched ground? Do you ever wonder, Robert, that maybe what The Sovereign did was right?"

Robert's face started to get red as he answered, "Excuse me? What did you just say? Have you gone soft in the head? Can't you see that he has done this simply to lull people away from the truth? Had the Last Battle gone the way it should you would be on your way to enlightenment where this would look like a desert in contrast to what is in store for you. Now let's get to work. I'll start with books written by authors beginning with A and you can do B. We'll take every other letter." He flopped down on the couch and opened his ECD.

Robert's anger seemed out of character for what Jim thought was simply a thought-provoking comment. But he dutifully opened his ECD. He was pleased to see that all the books he requested were now available on line. Within a few minutes he forgot about Robert's outburst as he started looking up books and trying to quickly determine the author's perspective. He was glad that he had the books translated as well. It would have been impossible for him to read the ancestral languages. The current universal language developed primarily from what was English but it had changed significantly.

He methodically looked through the preface, table of contents, and the first chapter until he was certain the book parroted The Sovereign's position, then he discarded it. Books that were not obviously pro-Sovereign were listed and rated on a scale of one to ten with ten being openly hostile to The Sovereign.

After an hour and a half Jim was getting restless at the tedious task and got up from the driver's seat, noting that they still had about another hour and a half before they reached the ocean. "I've got to rest my eyes a while. How about a cup of coffee?"

Robert didn't look up. "Yeah, sounds good. You won't believe what I've found already. A guy by the name of Andersen in ancient Holland wrote a lot. It appeared that Holland was one of the countries that led the way in incorporating the freedoms and way of life that The Chancellor helped foster. He has glowing reports and descriptions proving that The Sovereign's oppressive rules had suppressed people and they were finally starting to live and grow as they should."

Robert looked up. "Huh? What'd you say?"

"How about a cup of coffee?"

"Oh yeah sure, that would be great." Robert went back to his ECD.

Jim went to the kitchen and got two cups of coffee from the beverage dispenser and brought one back to Robert. "How about a short break?" he asked.

"Thanks for the coffee. You go ahead. This is so fantastic I can't put it down. I had no idea that society had advanced this far before the Last Battle." Robert took the cup and continued to read.

Jim decide to just stare out the window a while and absorb the new surroundings as they continued to speed over some low mountain ranges. As he watched the trees fly by and occasional wild animals, he had the strangest feeling that the hills themselves were calling out to him. "Look at us. How do you think we got here? How were we transformed from a desert to the lush productive land that you now see? How does even one blade of grass exist and grow?"

He shook off the thoughts and ruminated how quickly his life had changed. Only a few months ago he was laying on the beach gazing at the clouds, getting upset that he was soon going to have to go to work. Now, he couldn't wait for the quarter to end but exploring musty old books wasn't what he'd expected. *Oh well, we'll soon be exploring caves and the ruins of an ancient city. That will be a lot better than page after page of philosophical garbage.* He thought it was funny how discussing philosophies with others, especially in secret places at night was so much more exciting than reading about them, yet there was Robert, completely absorbed in these books.

Jim had been staring out the window longer than he thought. He noticed more traffic on the road and he could see the port's tall buildings in the distance. The auto pilot showed him that they were two minutes ahead of the predicted schedule. After another ten minutes they slowed to urban speed and began making their way to the docks in the bay. Jim was amazed as the rig came to the public water front, glided down the ramp, and over the water. In another ten minutes they were outside the bay, traveling at 300 kilometers per hour.

In the distance Jim saw an object ten stories high moving along the horizon. It looked like a large warehouse coming directly toward them. They quickly drew closer and the sea-going transport glided by, a kilometer to their starboard.

"Robert." Jim said staring at the huge transport.

No response.

"Robert!" He yelled.

Robert jerked his head up from his studies. "Huh? What is it?"

"This thing is supposed to be untraceable by the Administration, right?" asked Jim.

"Yeah, so?" answered Robert with some irritation in his voice.

"So aren't these things supposed to register with the traffic control center so that they don't crash into other trucks, transports and the like? I mean we just passed a transport and if it didn't know we were here, couldn't we have just as easily run into it?"

"You worry too much, Jim. They all probably have sensors that detect other objects and avoid them. Otherwise we could just as easily run into a bear or a tree when we get into the wilderness," said Robert as he frowned. "Don't you have something better to do than stare out the window?"

Jim stood up. "Yeah, as a matter of fact I do. It's way past lunch time. How about I fix us a couple of sandwiches?"

Robert's frown disappeared. "Oh, I hadn't noticed the time. That's a good idea. I need to stretch my legs too."

They both went back to the kitchen. Jim fixed a couple of sandwiches while Robert prepared some peaches and strawberries. They both stood around and ate over the sink.

After lunch they both went back to their studies and continued until evening when Jim was eager to play around in the kitchen and fix something a bit more elaborate for dinner. After a while Robert was lured to the kitchen by the smell of chicken Alfredo and broccoli. This time they sat down at the table to eat.

After dinner Robert went back to the books but Jim just couldn't force himself to spend another hour in research. Instead he looked up some recent plays that had been recorded and watched one on his ECD. As time went on they both fell asleep, Jim on the couch with his ECD still playing. The last he remembered was seeing Robert in the right hand driver's chair turned to left hand chair and his feet on the seat.

A voice pulled Robert out of his sleep. "Hello, Robert. How are your studies going?"

He opened his eyes and saw himself standing before Rorarum on the same great plane where he first met him. "How did I get here?"

"That is not important. You are doing well but we need to spend more time together for your training is not complete. Come with me." Rorarum reached out his hand and took Robert's. They were immediately transported to a narrow valley between two very rugged mountains. The valley ended in a box canyon.

"Do you see the cliff at the end of the valley?"

"Yes."

"You will be arriving here soon and your vehicle will be stopped by this cliff but you will not be at your destination yet. What you see is our camouflage, securing an area within which you will be able to work. I will now show you how we have set this up and how you will be able to see through it and enter."

Communication between Robert and Rorarum became non-verbal as he showed Robert the secrets of their abilities. Robert could feel Rorarum taking control of his body and his mind. The experience and the revealed knowledge of ways known to man thousands of years ago were even more exhilarating than when he first encountered this being only a week ago. He felt as if the mysteries of the whole universe were quickly opening to him.

"Enough, this is too wonderful for me. I can't take it all in at once." Robert's head was spinning.

"You are quite right. You can't take it all in, but each day you will be able to progress farther. Tomorrow we will meet again and I will reveal more to you. Now look at the valley and tell me what you see." The glow under Rorarum's hood pulsated as he spoke.

Robert concentrated on the cliff. "With my eyes I can see the cliff but with my mind I can see beyond it. The valley doesn't end but continues. What appears to be a mountain above it is but a shadow without substance."

"Very good. You are learning to see with your mind's eye, the all Seeing Eye that illuminates each of us. When you reach this point, you will simply switch off the auto pilot and drive through the cliff. You will have to approach it so that it seems as if you were docking up against it. It will continue through when it doesn't meet resistance. After you are inside you can reengage the auto pilot for the remainder of your journey." Rorarum faded and Robert was left alone in darkness.

"Tomorrow I want you to call on me for more training." Robert was startled by the sharpness in Rorarum's voice.

He awoke with a jerk and dropped his ECD on the floor. He wondered if he only had a dream but it was just as real as when he first met Rorarum. As he pondered the encounter he realized that everything was clear in his mind, unlike dreams that quickly fade. *Well, I'll know for sure when we get near our destination.* He looked around but didn't see Jim. The time on the console let him know they still had eight hour before they reached the port. He decided to go to bed.

December 24, 998 ASR

Robert woke up to the smell of sausages and hash browns shortly before they arrived at the port of Shuwiyan. He stumbled into the kitchen still not quite awake. "You're up early, Jim, and you got breakfast already made. Are you feeling OK?" He scratched his day old beard and got a cup of coffee from the dispenser. "Ah, this sure tastes good this morning."

"Sure, I'm feeling fine. I just got to bed a lot earlier than you did. It looks like we'll hit land in a little while. We have been about ten kilometers from the shore since we entered the gulf and passed a couple of fairly large cities. There's a lot of marine traffic passing by and running parallel with us. It's amazing to see all the

different ships. I haven't seen this aspect of our world. It kind of makes me wonder
what other things I've overlooked."

"My, aren't we getting rather introspective? What brought this on?" asked
Robert as he noted that Jim's rambling was more coherent than normal.

"Oh, nothing in particular." Jim shrugged. "I guess it seems a bit strange not to
be in school and actually classified as working. Looking out the window makes me
realize that all I've ever known is purely theoretical. How are your eggs?"

"They're great. I'm always amazed at your cooking abilities. Maybe someday
you'll be a famous chef or run a restaurant like Josu. But talking like that assumes
everything will be just the way it is now. Who knows what the world will be like
once we bump The Sovereign out of the way. We'll have all this and more. He's
been holding us back and with him out of the way we will be able to accomplished
anything we want. I'm really beginning to look forward to it. How about you?"

"Yeah, sure, I'm looking forward to running my own little universe. Hey, look,
we're slowing to enter the port right now," Jim said in a monotone as he stood at
the sink and chewed on a sausage. His eyes were focused out the window.

Robert followed Jim's gaze. "Wow, we're going to be at the site soon. I'm
going to shower and shave. Thanks again for breakfast." Robert slapped Jim on the
back and went into the bathroom.

When he finished cleaning up, Robert joined Jim in front of the control console
to watch as the transport cruised up one of Shuwiyan's three public ramps and
started negotiating the larger truck route around the city. The city was quite old
and travel through the city would not be easy for the large vehicle. Even though
the truck route was longer it was much quicker and they were soon on a major
highway heading northwest toward the rugged mountains that were now visible.

"How much farther do we have?" asked Robert.

"We have about 250 kilometers of high speed highways then we start on the last
segment of the trip with 290 kilometers of side roads and boondocks. Estimated
time is about six and a half hours."

"What? I thought we were much closer than that."

"It would be an hour and half if this thing could travel as fast here as it can over
the water," replied Jim.

"I can fix that." Robert switched off the auto pilot and took over manual control.
He accelerated to 200 KPH. A warning light started to blink. At 250 KPH a
warning horn started blaring. Robert felt a thrill as he rapidly overtook and passed
other vehicles. He reached over to the console and switched off the horn. "So how
do you like this ride, Jim? Hold on to your seat; we're going even faster."

"I don't think you should be doing this, Robert." Jim's knuckles were turning
white as he gripped the arm rests of his chair.

Soon they were speeding along the bidirectional highway at 300 KPH and still
accelerating. Robert was enjoying the challenge but saw that Jim was petrified.
They were quickly closing on a farm transport that recently pulled onto the
highway. He barely had time to swing into the other lane and pass. He could see
the farm vehicle in the rear view panel shaking in their wake.

"Robert, please slow down. This is way too dangerous and the Administration
will surely find out. Those other people we're passing will report us even if this
thing can't be tracked."

"Don't worry, my young friend. I have everything under control. They can't even see us." Robert was using his newfound ability to cloak their vehicle.

Another vehicle approached in the opposite direction. They passed each other on a gentle bend in the highway. Robert couldn't hold the van in their lane but swung wide crossing the center of the road.

"I'm not too sure you can handle this speed. The back of the van narrowly missed the other vehicle. I don't want to end up splattered all over the highway."

Robert ignored Jim's whining. He was having too much fun. They continued to pick up speed. The road was straighter now. He could see a long way ahead where there was an unusually large farm harvester in the highway. As they approached it, Robert started to pass as before. As if from nowhere a passenger convy was coming from the opposite direction. He felt his adrenalin kick in as the two vehicles were about to meet at a combined speed of 500 KPH. He pulled up and the convy slipped underneath with only a couple of centimeters to spare.

He heard a horrific grating noise. The antigravity fields from the upper vehicle must have slammed the smaller convy onto the pavement. A glance at the rear view panel showed it emerge from the back of the van. It shot sixty meters in the air like a watermelon spit out of a kid's mouth on a hot summer day. Its automated system must have tried to adapt to the sudden removal of the force from above. The convy quickly stopped as Robert and Jim sped away.

"You've got to stop this, Robert, NOW!" shouted Jim.

Robert turned toward Jim. "This is what it's all about, Jim. Don't you feel the excitement, the freedom and challenge?"

Jim was staring straight ahead. His face was white as a sheet. "Look out!" he shouted then leaned forward and hit the emergency shut down switch.

The huge machine quickly came to a stop and automatically pulled to the side of the road.

"Now why did you do that?" Robert was angry. He wanted to punch Jim in the face. He stood up menacingly as he leaned over Jim.

Jim was sweating and apparently quite angry as well. "Look out the window, you fool. At the speed we were going we would have never negotiated that turn ahead. Even the obstacle protection system wouldn't have prevented a crash. Now would that thrill have been worth it? What's gotten into the level-headed Robert I signed up with at the end of the summer?"

Robert slowly turned and looked out the window. As he turned he saw the unusually sharp bend in the road and the cliff that he would have surely hit. He had paid too much attention to the convy that they had run over. He felt limp and flopped down in his chair. "I'm sorry, Jim, I don't know what came over me."

They both just sat there staring out the window for a while.

Robert was having a discussion that Jim couldn't hear while his eyes were open and he continued to stare out the window.

Rorarum, what have you done to me? I would have never done anything that crazy before.

A loud rolling laugh echoed through Robert's head.

We have given you the first taste of freedom, Robert. That is all. With freedom comes responsibility and unfortunately, while under the influence of The Sovereign, you haven't had the opportunity to develop the ability to determine when and how to use your freedom. It has taken us hundreds of years of training to mature so that we can understand and use these great powers with wisdom. You have lived a short while under the rule of one who would suppress these abilities as well as the wisdom that is needed to handle them properly. It isn't surprising that with only a few days of training you would act as you did. Remember this as a part of your training process. We would not have let you crash for your mission is far too important.

Robert didn't think it was all that funny.

Rorarum continued. Now be honest with me. You did experience the thrill, didn't you? Wasn't it worth the momentary scare, thinking you could have crashed? Think about it. When you have gained wisdom, these and greater ecstasies will await you.

Robert had inwardly calmed down and had to admit he really enjoyed most of the adventure. *Yes, it was exciting.*

Don't forget we will need to work on your training each day, said Rorarum.

I think that would be a good idea. Robert agreed. He was going to need a lot more training time with Rorarum to keep from killing himself.

Robert's mind returned to the more tangible things at hand.

"Robert?"

"Yes, Jim," he replied quietly

"Are you going to be OK?"

"I believe so. I learned something about myself that proved to be a very valuable lesson. Why don't you get us going again? I'm going to do some meditating." Robert stood up.

"Some what?"

"Meditating. You know, quiet thoughtful contemplation. I need to empty my mind, then concentrate on the task at hand so I can develop my spirit in readiness." Robert took a couple of steps toward the back.

"Since when have you started this?" asked Jim as he turned around in the console chair.

Robert turned back to Jim. "Since about five minutes from now. During my training with Samyaza I was told how to do it and that I should be doing it every day but I've been too busy. This episode has reminded me that I need to do this in order to keep what I learn under control."

Robert went back to his bedroom and closed the door. He felt their vehicle start moving again. *Jim must have already completed the restart protocol.*

Robert sat on his bed cross-legged and wondered what this posture had to do with contacting Rorarum, especially since he just talked with him. However, he dutifully unrolled the pentagram chart that Samyaza had given him. He lit a candle and placed it in the center of the pentagram, closed his eyes and began to chant Rorarum's name. Within a few seconds he was again transported to the plane where he and Rorarum first met.

He walked toward the figure that was seated on an ornate arm chair elevated from the plane on a platform with several steps leading up to it. He ascended the stairs and knelt before the chair, bowing his head. *I have come, Master, to learn from you.*

It is good that you came as you were told. I know you are wondering why. It is part of the discipline that you need to learn. As you grow in your knowledge and powers you will see why this form is important. Come and walk with me as I teach you, Robert. Rorarum got up out of the chair and took Robert by the hand.

Robert sensed Rorarum's thoughts. For the next hour and half Robert learned details about the beginning of the universe. He understood how Yehhovaw enslaved mankind. He saw as if his mind were a blank screen with images of history being projected upon it. He absorbed sights, sounds, smells, feelings, and even the tastes of the struggle between Ben-Shaachar and Yehowshuwa before Yehowshuwa became a man. He observed how The Chancellor trained people to use the powers within themselves to communicate with him and his associates, to heal physical infirmities caused by Yehhovaw, and even to tell the future. He saw how these abilities were distorted and used for harm by The Sovereign's followers, but who blamed The Chancellor instead.

Rorarum led Robert as he learned a few chants and mantras in an ancient tongue that he had never heard. Since they were quite repetitive he was able to pick them up quickly. They were already giving him a sense of inner peace and confidence that he hadn't felt before.

When Robert emerged from his room he was greeted by Jim's call, "Hey, good thing you're out now. I think we have trouble up ahead."

While he was meditating the vehicle had left the highway. They were slowly going up a narrow valley that was closed at the end by a sheer cliff extending about 1,250 meters straight up. It slowed as it approached the cliff, then stopped. The console blinked a warning on the screen, "Path obstructed. Unable to complete prescribed course."

Robert sat down in the unoccupied left hand driver's seat and started to switch the controls to his side. "No problem. We'll be able to continue in a jiffy."

Jim punched the lock-out button so that control couldn't be switched. "Oh no, you don't. The last time you drove this thing you just about killed us."

Robert's anger started to flare until he remembered his recent training. "Fine. I'll tell you what to do and you can get us going. I think you'll enjoy this when you see it. Switch off the auto pilot and nudge us up against the cliff as if you were going to park it."

Jim looked at Robert and cocked his head sideways, quietly muttering something Robert couldn't understand. He did as he was told. The large machine slowly came to the cliff and appeared to touch it but instead the streamlined nose disappeared into the mountain. Jim stopped the forward motion as his eyes got big.

"I told you that you'd like this. Keep going."

Jim again moved the vehicle forward and the windshield disappeared and then the console. Robert and Jim passed through to the other side where Jim stopped the coach and looked back. "Wow, this is like some kind of one way mirror. And look at what's ahead. The canyon really extends on into the mountains. I'll bet that from above it looks like we just went into a tunnel. So this is the camouflage Samyaza was talking about. I'm really impressed."

"I hope you will also be impressed by other things as well but for now you can restore the auto pilot and we should be at the site in a few minutes."

Chapter 35

Chuck, Demetrius, and Raymond met in the sensor array equipment room on the 25th story of the ship. It was at the northwest corner, as far away from any normally occupied spaces as they could find. It was late at night. Only a skeleton crew was on duty.

"Thanks for meeting with us, Raymond. I'll get right to the point. Since you were the only one that objected to us going to Eden and since you were the first person I lost contact with when my telepathic abilities diminished, we were wondering if you have any second thoughts about helping The Chancellor." Chuck didn't know how else to broach the subject.

Raymond looked first at Chuck then Demetrius before answering. "First, tell me, why are we meeting in such a remote location?"

"I don't know if it will do any good, but I wanted to be as far away from any listening ears or minds as I could get. I don't want our conversation overheard by anyone other that the three of us." Chuck sat down on the floor of the narrow room and leaned against the wall of equipment cabinets with their flashing lights. He was tired. He hadn't slept well since his first dream about Zophia. He motioned for the others to sit.

Demetrius and Raymond also sat. Demetrius said, "I'll give it to you straight, Raymond. We're scared. Chuck's having bad dreams about Zophia taking over the world and I've having dreams that all end up in blazing furnaces or the bottoms of volcanoes. However, in both our dreams The Sovereign Yehowshuwa appears and tells us to trust him and we'll be safe. Chuck seems to think you might have some insight but he doesn't want Zophia to get wind of our second thoughts."

Raymond let out a sigh. "Whew, I was beginning to wonder if I was the only one that thought Zophia and the rest of the crew had gone crazy. Give me some more details of your dreams."

Chuck related his first and last dream to Raymond in as much detail as he could remember. He was amazed that over time they hadn't completely faded.

Demetrius then told his dream stories. "How about you? Have you had any weird dreams like this?"

"No, I haven't," said Raymond matter-of-factly. "But I have had serious second thoughts."

"Why is that?" asked Chuck.

"I never liked the idea of going to Eden, but when I got there, I swear I was hypnotized by them. Everything I knew about The Sovereign to be true, I found myself rejecting. Everything they said, I simply accepted as fact. However, when we left, verses from The Sovereign's book that I learned as a kid started coming back to me. I decided to look them up and compare them to what we were told on Eden." Raymond leaned forward and lowered his voice.

"I started at the beginning of his book and read the whole thing. Suddenly things started to make sense." He shook his head. "From the moment they showed up, they started feeding us lies. They caused us to doubt that The Sovereign created everything. Look at this." Raymond took out his ECD and showed them a passage.

In the beginning was Logos, and Logos was with Yehhovaw, and Logos was Yehhovaw. The same was in the beginning with Yehhovaw. All things were made by him; and without him was not anything made that was made.

"Logos is Yehowshuwa. When we bought that first lie we were susceptible to every other lie about The Sovereign Yehowshuwa. The only truth they've told us is that they are working for Ben-Shaachar."

"I think I understand," said Chuck as he nodded in agreement.

Demetrius wrung his hands. Sweat was forming on his brow. "What about Eden, and all the abilities we were given? They sure seem real to me. Have you seen what Zophia and her first training group have been doing?"

Raymond's eyes got big, "Oh, yeah. I've seen what she's been doing. I can't explain Eden, those abilities, nor how Zophia is able to accomplish all those feats. I've also been watching our crewmates who are in training. They are becoming arrogant, boastful, and lustful. When I went by what's left of the hydroponic gardens on the way here I saw Elizabeth and Wilfred---"

Chuck put up his hand, "You don't need to explain. I've seen the nudity and what comes with it. So, what do you suggest? I don't like what I see but I have to admit that even as Captain of this ship, I don't know what to do."

"My gut is with Chuck. I've been so confused I'm not sure I can think straight. You seem to have an understanding of The Sovereign's book. What should we do?" Demetrius pulled out a handkerchief and wiped his forehead.

"My understanding isn't all that great either, but I think I figured out a few things. I renewed my loyalty to The Sovereign and that has given me peace about whatever happens. That would be the first step for you." Raymond looked intently at Chuck, then Demetrius.

Chuck shook his head. "We are who-knows-how-many light years from Earth. How do we do that?"

Raymond selected another passage on his ECD. "Look at this."

Am I only at hand, says Yehhovaw, and not also afar off? Can any hide himself in secret places that I can not see him? says Yehhovaw. Do not I fill heaven and earth? says Yehhovaw.

"You mean he is here with us right now?" asked Demetrius?

Raymond nodded, "Yup. And look at this one." He showed them another passage.

Repent therefore, and be converted, that your wicked deeds may be blotted out, then times of refreshing shall come from the presence of Yehowshuwa.

"Yeah, that's what I need. Some refreshing. But we've really screwed up. How do we know that he will forgive us?" asked Chuck.

Raymond said nothing. He showed them yet another passage.

If we confess our crimes, he is faithful and just and will forgive us and purify us from all unrighteousness.

"That's it? Just like that, he'll let us off the hook?" Demetrius asked softly. "That's hard to believe."

Raymond was already looking up another passage on his ECD. "Yeah I know what you mean, but look at what he says about believing."

That if you will confess with your mouth The Sovereign Yehowshuwa, and shall believe in your heart that Yehhovaw has raised him from the dead, you shall be saved.

"I think that's about it. That's the way to renew or establish your loyalty to him. Repent, confess, and believe. Of course believing he is Sovereign means we are going to act like it and obey him. What do you think? Are you ready to get into his good graces?" asked Raymond.

"Even with all of this, why did he send Rol-el to intercept us in the first place? And what about the armada that tried to prevent our return? Can I trust someone who did that?" asked Demetrius.

"What makes you think that The Sovereign was behind those attempts?" replied Raymond.

"Well, Berekiah assured us that…" Demetrius' voice trailed off as Raymond just nodded his head.

Chuck started to say something but stopped when Demetrius bowed his head and started crying. Instead, Chuck closed his eyes and silently asked Yehowshuwa to forgive him. He recalled all he had said and thought while on Eden and since. He spent several minutes asking for forgiveness. Peace flooded over him and he knew that something changed in his heart. The Sovereign was no longer a mighty ruler that was quick to punish wrong. Now he was a friend. *This is what Dave was talking about when he said he knew Yehowshuwa.*

He opened his eyes and saw Raymond with a big grin on his face. He looked at Demetrius who had stopped crying and appeared calm.

"So what's next, Captain?" asked Raymond.

A thought came to Chuck. "I think we need to share this with whoever will listen. Tomorrow, I'll arrange a meeting of all crewmembers who aren't in training. I'll ask for volunteers for the next training session. Anyone who holds back will be a candidate for our next meeting. Hopefully we'll need a bigger room than this."

Chuck, Demetrius and Raymond talked for a while. Raymond provided them with some encouraging passages before they left.

As Chuck returned to his quarters he started to think about how he might regain control of the crew that was in training or was eagerly seeking training. At this point it seemed quite hopeless, yet he still had an inner peace. He knew everything would turn out OK.

December 24, 998 ASR

Robert eagerly watched out the front window as their truck approached a clearing on the side of a mountain. Two people, a man and a woman, were standing beside a tent waving to them.

"Who are those guys?" asked Jim.

"I think they are our underground helpers that are maintaining our shield. Let's see."

The huge coach stopped five meters from the tent. Robert jumped out as soon as the door safety released. The woman greeted them, "Welcome, Robert, Jim. We've been expecting you. I'm Ingra and this is Hector. We are here to keep the area secure. Jacquelyn is inside the tent and you will meet her when her shift is over."

"Hi, pleased to meet you," said Jim. "What's Jacquelyn doing that she has a shift?"

"Each of us takes turns keeping up the shield. We have to extend a great amount of energy in concentration to make sure this area appears to be under a mountain so we each take a shift," explained Hector.

"You have to watch the equipment that closely? I'd think it would be automated," said Jim.

Ingra and Hector looked at each other quizzically then at Robert.

"Jim isn't trained yet so he isn't aware that all this is done through the powers you have found within yourselves. Thanks for taking care of the place. Is that the entrance over there?" Robert pointed to what appeared to be a depression in the ground with a huge tree trunk covering part of it.

"Yes. That's where Eric fell into the cave just as that tree crashed down and hit the rocks above him," answered Hector.

They all walked over for a closer look. There wasn't much room to get in and out of the hole leading to the caverns inside the mountain.

"What do you say we get right to work?" Robert turned to Hector and Ingra. "Would one of you guys mind moving that tree so we can get the equipment in to widen the entrance?"

"Right away, Sir." Ingra extended her hand toward the tree and it began to shake, then suddenly leaped up, crashing down about fifteen meters beyond the hole. The earth shook at the force of its landing.

"What in the world was--- how did you---, what, I mean, who???" stammered Jim.

"I said you'd be impressed by more things," chuckled Robert. "Thank you, Ingra."

"That was a demonstration of telekinetic abilities, Jim. Once you have completed advanced training, these and other wonders will be within your capabilities," explained Ingra.

Robert left Jim shaking his head in obvious disbelief as he walked back to the truck and opened the rear compartment. He went to what appeared to be a cabinet the size and shape of an antique roll top desk. He pulled up the cover to reveal several dials and computer controls. After switching the machine on, it raised up off the floor of the storage area. Robert pulled on its handle and it easily followed him out of the truck.

Jim helped Robert ease the machine into the depression. Robert quickly made a few adjustments and calibrations using its laser to mark out what looked like a doorway on the rock around the entrance. He put on a pair of goggles and tossed another pair to Jim. "Don't look directly at the rock without some protection. This thing will generate a lot of heat and light." He made some last second adjustments and turned away. "OK, let's get out of the way while it does its work."

Both of them climbed out of the hole and the machine proceeded to cut through the rock with its cutting lasers. The brilliant light reflecting off the molten rock would have blinded them without the goggles. They watched as it quickly opened a wider doorway. Ingra and Hector watched without wearing goggles.

"We're going to have to let that cool for a few minutes before we try to get through. In the meantime, get us a couple of hard hats with headlights on them. They should be on one of the shelves on the left." Robert opened his ECD to check the Professor's notes. "The first thing I want to do is find out what's in that vault they found. Meet me in the cabin and we'll pack some water and something to eat. It will probably take us a couple of hours to get to the vault."

Within a few minutes they were ready to go into the cave. Robert showed Jim how the controls on the laser cart worked so he could navigate up and down over the uneven terrain inside the caves. Jim pushed the laser equipment through the new opening while Robert led. It easily fit through the still warm entrance and into the larger chamber inside. Robert looked at his notes and pointed to a passageway to their right leading downward. He turned on inertial tracking on his ECD so they wouldn't get lost. He also set a small glow lamp at various intervals to providing an easier return path.

They turned and scraped their way along tunnels, stopping frequently to check the professor's notes in order to pick the right passage whenever they found the route branched. After twenty minutes they had to stop and use the laser to burn a larger opening for the cart. While they were waiting for the rock to cool they decided to explore a few of the other passages.

"Robert, I thought I caught a reflection down this tunnel, let's go see what it is," said Jim excitedly.

"Lead the way; I'm right behind you."

Robert followed Jim down the passage that narrowed considerably. He watched the beam of light from Jim's headlamp moving right and left as Jim moved his head. Robert thought he saw a reflection just to Jim's left when Jim suddenly stopped.

In an instant Jim screamed at the top of his lungs, turned around, and frantically started running back up the passageway. Jim bowled Robert over and scrambled past him.

Robert got up and ran back up the tunnel after Jim. He didn't know what he was running from but wasn't taking any chances. He caught up with Jim who was crouching behind the laser cart. It was now pointing toward the passage where Robert had just emerged. Jim's headlamp was scanning the ceiling and walls of the cavern. Robert heard Jim's whimpering between gasps of breath.

Robert jumped and rolled out of the way incase Jim decide to fire the laser at whatever was back in the cave. "Jim, what did you see? What are we up against?"

"R-r-r-obert, you didn't tell me about this."

"About what?"

"Spiders. You didn't tell me there were spiders down here. Big, huge, ugly spiders."

"How big, where?"

"Monster-sized." Jim was still hyperventilating. "I felt the web on my face then looked up. Right before my eyes. I hate spiders."

"Point that cart another way. I'm going back to have another look."

Robert warily made his way back down the passage, scanning back and forth, up and down. Soon he was back to where Jim panicked. He finally saw the spider trying to repair its web. Its body was about a half centimeter long and with its legs extended it appeared to be about one and a quarter centimeters long. It was white and probably blind. He reached up and gently took the spider in his hand. "So how did you get so far down here little guy? And what's more, what do you eat? Let me introduce you to Jim."

He returned a few minutes later to find Jim cowering on a rock. "How big did you say that spider was?"

"I don't know. It was huge and ugly too."

Robert opened his hand. "Is this the little guy that caused such terror?"

Jim jumped up and huddled against the wall. He turned his face back toward Robert and yelled, "Get that thing out of here. What are you tying to do? How can you touch it? Please get it away from me."

"Don't you know that these little critters don't hurt people anymore? The Sovereign has made sure of that."

"Yeah, so maybe The Sovereign's power doesn't work down here and below the shield. What if the monster is poisonous and bites you?" Jim had his back against the wall and his right forearm and elbow shielding his face.

"Hmm, good point." Robert clapped his hands together and wiped them on his pants. "Is that better?"

"Oh yuck. Why'd you have to do that in front of me? Yeah, it is better. Man, I'm getting out of here. Who knows how many more of the buggers there are down here."

"Hey, slow down, we've got work to do. You can't run out on me just because of a spider that has been smooshed. Think about it. Above ground there are about two hundred million spiders per square kilometer in an open pasture. Down here there's only one in a million and he's gone. Think about our camping trip last summer. I didn't hear any complaints about spiders then and they were all around us."

Jim appeared to calm down and relax.

"The rock has cooled down enough for us to get through so let's move on."

Jim hesitated but pushed the laser cart through the opening. Robert led the way again. Jim's headlamp beam kept flashing back and forth much more rapidly than Robert's. *Looking for more spiders, no doubt.*

After negotiating some sharp turns Robert stopped suddenly. Before him was a crevice that was about sixty meters deep and ten meters wide. He consulted his ECD and announced to Jim, "It looks like we're still on the right path. According to the Professor's notes, we'll have to go down there next."

"And just how are we going to do that? We don't have any climbing equipment. I can see where they hooked up and repelled down to the bottom," said Jim as he peered over the edge.

"Dang! I knew I forgot something. Maybe we can use the laser cart. There's room for both of us to sit on it and we can use the height control to drop us down to the floor below," answered Robert.

Robert hopped up on the cart and it bounced as it adjusted to his additional weight. Jim then hopped on and again it bounced. The back of the roll top side was away from the crevice so they both looked like they were sitting on a high bench facing the cave wall. Since the cart didn't have any directional control except up and down Robert pushed off the side of the cavern with one foot. The cart coasted toward the crevice then tilted back and suddenly dropped as it went over the edge. Robert and Jim both screamed and the cart responded with a series of loud warning beeps. Robert hung on for dear life.

Fortunately the cart righted itself and its inertial system adjusted the rate of descent so that it didn't smash into bits at the bottom. It slowed, reached the bottom, and stopped at the correct level above the floor of the crevice.

"Wow! That was quite a ride. Better than any amusement park I've been to. Let's do it again, Robert." Jim's voice dripped with sarcasm.

Robert caught his breath and let his heart slow down before he answered. "Now I'm more concerned about how we get back up than coming down again. If we adjust the height to get to the top then push it over the top, won't this thing think it needs to adjust and send it smashing into the roof of the cave?"

"Ouch! Make sure you let me off before you try that," said Jim as he got off the cart.

"Take a look at this, Jim." Robert jumped off and picked up a chunk of glass weighing about two and a half kilograms. It looked like it had once been part of some kind of electronic equipment that was melted by an intense heat. It had a few wires protruding from it and part of a sheet of metal with hundreds of tiny holes in it.

They both started looking around and could see all kinds of debris. In fact, it appeared that they were now walking on or in the ruins of an old building. As they started down the tunnel designated by the Professor they saw twisted girders protruding out of the dirt. Rock and crumbled cement formed the passageways. There was no sign of any wood, paper, plastic or any other combustible material. There were only pools of ash that settled in pockets and hadn't been washed away by underground streams when heavy rains saturated the mountains above.

Robert was in awe of the silence of what once was a thriving and noisy metropolis. Only their footsteps and the occasional drip of water disrupted the wonder he felt.

"If this is the ancient capital of The Chancellor, then it was destroyed in one hour. How sad that a city with such splendor is now sitting in such ruins. All the harpists, flute players, and trumpeters vaporized, never to make merry again. Merchants and tradesmen, bride and bridegroom all mercilessly killed. All they wanted was freedom to grow to their full potential. Jim, I feel like we are treading on hallowed ground," contemplated Robert aloud.

"It seems very eerie to me. I get the feeling that there are..." Jim paused. "...spirits all around."

"You're right, Jim. There are spirits here. I can sense them. Ah, here we are. This is the staircase that the professor mentioned. At the bottom we'll find the vault."

As usual Robert went ahead and Jim followed with the cart. As soon as he started to push the cart down the twisted steep staircase the cart started to beep.

"What's going on with that thing?" asked Robert.

"I'm not sure. It looks like there's some kind of warning on the console. It says that the incline is too steep for the current settings and it wants me to consult the instruction manual."

Robert returned to watch Jim punch some buttons on the console. The instruction manual popped up to the page with the current error.

"It looks like we should have read this before jumping off the cliff back there, Robert. This shows how to manually adjust the front and back of the cart for an incline greater than ten degrees. I guess with all the screaming I didn't hear it beep when we went over the edge."

Jim adjusted the settings and they continued slowly down the steps while the laser case maintained its level position. When they reached the bottom they entered a chamber, most of which was still intact because it was heavily reinforced. A few meters in front of them they saw in the gleam of their headlight the door to the stainless steel vault.

Robert had never seen such a secure device. He had read about them, though, and knew its combination lock was designed to thwart the cleverest of thieves. The massive stainless steel bolts inside the door and the door itself would resist the destructive force of the most powerful explosives that could be used without destroying the building around it. Heat, moisture and time seemed to have had no affect on it as it stood quietly shut.

"Let's cut this thing open and see what's inside. If my research is correct we can cut out the locking mechanism but probably can't pull all the bolts back out, especially if the vault was twisted even slightly during the earthquake. It will probably be easier to cut a new door."

Robert positioned the laser cart in front of the vault's door and set the controls to cut a rectangular opening one meter wide by two meters high. He set the depth to one hundred centimeters. They both put on their goggles and fired up the laser. The reflection of the blinding beam filled the chamber with daylight brightness, then dimmed as it punched deep into the outer layer of the door, spewing molten metal and sparks in every direction. After a minute the laser shut itself off. Robert examined the hole that was about one centimeter in diameter.

"That went through the front of the door then some empty space. It barely touched the back of the door. I'm going to set the depth for another fifty centimeters and see if that goes all the way through."

Again the beam shot across the chamber and through the same hole in the door. After it shut down Roberts's examination revealed that it penetrated all the way through the door. He then set the laser on automatic and switched it on. Immediately it shot out the beam which then slowly started tracing the outline of the specified door.

"Well, it took a minute and a half to penetrate the door so that means we've got a 24 hour wait before we can see what's in there. Let's have lunch and make sure it's working OK. Then we can go back out and come back tomorrow. We'll need a winch or something to pull that section out of the door and we can bring it back with us."

"That lunch thing is the best suggestion I've heard for a long time. I'm famished," replied Jim.

August 19, 998 ASR

Zophia approached Chuck's office door and paused before pressing the call button to announce her arrival. *So far Chuck has resisted my advances, Mararum. What do you suggest?*

Chuck really needs to be trained soon. It is vital to the rest of the crew for him to show his leadership. Since he has not succumbed to your womanly charms, perhaps it would be best if you eased back and appealed to his ego, using his position as head of the ship instead, answered Mararum.

Zophia wanted more from Chuck and for the first time realized it was because she wanted to conquer the Captain. Mararum was right, there was more than one way to get him where she wanted him. She pressed the button knowing that her name would be spoken to Chuck.

The door slid open and she walked purposefully to his desk and stood at attention.

"Have a seat, Zophia, what's on your mind today?" asked Chuck.

She sat down and adjusted her chair down as Chuck brought his up slightly. All these years of pumping our chairs up and down. I should have known I couldn't just come on strong with him. He looks more relaxed already. "Thank you, Captain. I've come to discuss our second training class. We, I mean, you, as Captain, need to determine who will be in the next class. In fact I was hoping you would lead the way."

"I'm glad you brought that up, Zophia. I've thought a lot about that. I know that you want me in the next class but I've seen how eager some of the crew is to get trained. I would hate to bump them just because I'm the Captain." Chuck leaned forward knitting his eyebrows together.

Oh – Zophia was having a hard time trying to pick the filthiest, most vulgar word of the many she now knew – *he isn't buying it.*

Chuck continued. "I've called a meeting for everyone who hasn't been trained yet. We'll meet in the mess hall at 4 PM." Chuck held up four charts labeled with the training dates and space for ten people to sign on each. "This is really old fashioned but I'll let people pick when they want to train and I'll take the earliest empty slot."

Zophia relaxed. That just might work. Mararum, do you think we can influence those people so that there will be room for Chuck in the next class?

Certainly! Unless someone is completely sold out to The Sovereign, we have our ways to guide people. Perhaps we will make it appear that there are only nine openings for the next session, replied Mararum.

Excellent! The more I see your powers, the more I know I chose the right path.

"Very good, Captain. I believe that's an excellent way to select the classes. Unless you have something else for me, I need to catch up on some of my duties." Zophia stood.

Chuck leaned back in his chair smiling and clasped his hands behind his head. "No, I didn't have anything else."

How I would like to walk around his desk and --- Zophia resisted the temptation but turned and walked out the door.

She only had two hours before the meeting and she wanted to work on some interface algorithms for the ship's computer system, Hal.

When Zophia arrived in the mess hall with only two minutes to spare, she quickly counted and discovered that all but two of the untrained crew had already arrived. Chuck had the charts on a table at the front and was standing between the table and the crewmembers who were seated at tables near him.

At exactly 4 PM, he began. "I'm going to make this quick and simple. Many of you have been bugging me about when you will have the opportunity to be trained. On this table I have the sign-up charts for each of the remaining classes. Ten people per class."

The last two people arrived and Chuck frowned. "As I was saying to those who arrived on time, I have sign-up charts for the remaining training classes. I'll let you pick the class you want. The first class is on your left, the last is on your right." Chuck stepped to the side of the table and motioned to the table with his hand. "Go for it."

Zophia was now standing near the front of the room. She laughed inside as 34 crewmembers rapidly stood up and rushed the front table. Chairs crashed to the floor and one table was overturned. Her amusement abated as people started pushing and shoving each other. Everyone was trying to get to the first sign up sheet. Elbows flew, feet tripped, and bodies hit the deck. Only Demetrius, Raymond, along with Eunice, and Ichiro, the latecomers had not rushed the table. They stood at the back with mouths wide open.

Chuck scooped up the chart and held it above is head yelling, "Stop. Stop it right now."

Zophia rolled her eyes and used her telekinetic power to freeze everyone in place.

Chuck's face was pale as he looked at Zophia. "Thank you. Can you just set them all on the floor?"

"My pleasure." Zophia sat the crew on the floor and released them.

"That didn't turn out exactly the way I thought it would. I had no idea you were so eager that you would actually bloody your fellow crewmembers." He paused and looked at his crew. A few were hanging their heads. "Is everyone OK?"

Heads nodded.

"We'll do it different this time. Ali, you got the closest so you get first choice." Chuck pointed along the front of those sitting closest. "You guys are next so form a single line and everyone fall in from your current position.

The line formed orderly and people started signing their names. Chuck walked to the back of the line and whispered something to Eunice and Ichiro before taking his place at the end.

Zophia stepped closer to the table and watched as the tenth person ignored the blank line for the first class. *Very good, Mararum. As you said, they are ignoring the position we have reserved for Chuck.*

Demetrius was fifth from the end. He stepped up and signed on the fourth chart. Raymond took the pen and signed on the blank line on the first chart.

"No," Zophia yelled. "You can't sign there."

Raymond turned with a puzzled look on his face. "Why not? No one else took it."

Zophia narrowed her eyes and scowled at Chuck. She spun on her heels and left the mess hall. As she walked briskly toward her quarters she contacted Mararum. *So Raymond has gone to the other side. How else could he have seen the open position?*

You are right, Zophia. If he didn't belong to The Sovereign he would not have known that the position was available. We need to watch him until he goes to the first training session where we practice telekinetic skills. At that time I think he will have an accident, replied Mararum.

Hal, I want you to track Raymond's every move and report to me where he is and who is with him. Zophia tried out her new telepathic command interface to the ship's computer. She looked at her ECD where Hal acknowledged her command. A small window opened up showing Raymond with Chuck, Eunice, Demetrius, and Ichiro. They were leaving the mess hall. *That worked now I just need to get Hal to talk back to me telepathically.*

She stopped in her tracks and watched as the five icons moved together toward the western side of the ship. Something isn't right. Why would the last people to sign up all be going to the same place with Raymond? Hal, give me audio. I want to hear what they're talking about.

She could only hear Demetrius' heavy breathing. She imagined his short pudgy legs working hard to keep up with the others. They were moving quickly.

Zophia continued to watch the icons weave through Aman's passageways, up lifts, and finally passed through an airlock to the hangar bay. They stopped behind Alpha Shuttle near the hangar bay door.

"OK, I don't think we were followed and even if we were, they couldn't hear us here," she heard Chuck break the silence.

"What's this all about, Chuck?" asked Eunice.

"I noticed how hesitant all of you were to sign up for Zophia's training. You two arrived late and none of you charged the signup table like the rest of the crew. I would like to know where you stand. Have you changed your mind about backing The Chancellor Ben-Shaachar against Yehowshuwa?" asked Chuck quite gruffly.

That's the way to go Chuck. Root out the turncoats.

There was a long silent gap before she heard Raymond sigh and respond, "I don't know about the other, Chuck, but I have no intention of taking the training or joining with anyone who is rebelling against The Sovereign. You said you were fair and would make allowances for anyone who changed their mind."

"Yes. I did say that but I can't have you running around the ship subverting those that are eager to join the battle against Yehowshuwa." Chuck's voice was not as gruff but still stern. Zophia's heart started beating faster as she wished she could be there united with Chuck in this examination.

She identified Ichiro's voice, "I'm with Raymond, Chuck. But to be very specific, Yehowshuwa is my Sovereign. I've rehashed everything that's happened on Eden and afterwards and don't buy any of the garbage we were fed by Tia-le, Mime, and all the rest. If you're going to back Ben-Shaachar then you are on the wrong side and will be sorry for eternity."

He is dangerous. With an attitude like that, he and Raymond will both need to have an accident. Now how do Demetrius and Eunice fit in?

"What about you, Demetrius? Where do you stand?" asked Chuck.

"I'm with these two. Chuck. I know that may disappoint you but I can't support you either," answered Demetrius.

Eunice spoke up, "I was really afraid to tell you that I, too, have pledged my loyalty to The Sovereign Yehowshuwa. I thought Ichiro and I were the only two sane people and didn't know what to do. Now, I'll stand with them and you can do whatever you want."

Zophia shook her head. *Now there are four. This may be too hard to cover up with an accident.*

Her thoughts were interrupted by Chuck. "Now that I know where you two stand I can tell you that I'm with you. Sorry about the little charade, but we needed to make sure you were loyal to The Sovereign. Now we need to figure out how we can stop Zophia and the rest before we get back to Earth."

"Nooooo!" shouted Zophia.

You know what you have to do Zophia. Don't hesitate or you may never have another chance.

Hal, override safety protocol. Open the hangar bay doors.

The icons for Chuck, Demetrius, Raymond, Eunice, and Ichiro moved toward the open door and disappeared.

Hal, erase and scrub all of my commands to follow Raymond, conversations transmitted, and commands to open the door. Replace them with logs showing the following details and that Captain Andrews overrode safety protocols and accidentally opened the door. Erase and scrub my commands to alter the logs. She relayed Mararum's account of the incident to Hal.

There was no response on Zophia's ECD. She reviewed the history on her ECD and found nothing, not even the response that she received when she instructed Hal to track Raymond.

She felt like a zombie as she returned to her quarters, stripped, and sat cross-legged in the middle of the floor. She sought comfort in Mararum. She was instantly on the grassy knoll with the barren tree. Mararum held her fast as she sobbed in his arms.

Chapter 36

Robert and Jim both took off their packs and enjoyed their meal in the glow from the laser. When they finished eating they started back up the stairs when Jim suddenly stopped. "Robert, how are we going to get back up that crevice without the cart?"

Robert smacked himself on the forehead and swore. "That's the only way down here as far as I know and that took us four hours. At least we don't have to take the cart all the way back and we don't have to cut through any more rock. What a waste of time, at the best we are going to lose another three hours. How stupid could I be not taking climbing equipment?"

Jim started to say something but Robert cut him off. "Don't even answer that!"

They shut down the laser. It turned out that going uphill with the heavy cart was not as bad as Robert expected. They adjusted the controls so that the rear of the cart rose higher than the front pushing it forward. It pulled them up the stairwell. Soon they were back at the cliff.

"So how are we going to work this?" asked Jim.

"I think we jump on and ride it to the top. We hop off and then slowly pull the cart to the edge. Once we get the front of it barely over the edge we can keep the rear setting on sixty meters and set the front to a couple of centimeters as we quickly jerk it past the edge."

"Sounds kind of risky to me. Why don't we just ride it to the top and leave it there in mid air while we go get the other stuff we need?"

Robert paused and looked at him, "I knew I brought you along for some reason. Hop on."

The rest of the return trip was uneventful. They didn't even need Robert's ECD with its inertial guidance. The glow lamps provided ample direction. Robert headed straight for the cargo hold. He got the equipment he wanted and emerged with two hard-shelled backpacks. He tossed one to Jim.

"Try this on for size."

"What is it?"

"It's an antigravity back pack. Strap it on and use the joystick to go wherever you want: up, down, left, right, forward and backward. It's one of the latest inventions with some super improvements in the power cells. These will beat scaling that chasm with ropes," explained Robert as he pulled on his backpack.

He pulled the joystick around in front of him. Up and down was controlled by depressing a plunger on top of the stick and the other directions were controlled by moving the stick in the direction he wanted to go. The only other control was an on/off button. He switched the button to "on." The joystick righted itself and the thumb plunger went to the neutral position. He pressed down on the plunger and felt the pack lifting him off his feet. He continued to press until all of his weight was being supported by the pack. A bit farther down and he started to rise off the ground. He quickly removed his thumb from the plunger and the pack gently set him down on the ground again.

Jim was also experimenting with his pack. "Pretty cool, Robert. As usual it looks like it has a safety device built into it so that I can't go up a kilometer, let go of the joystick and drop like a rock." Jim went up a couple of meters then started zooming around the camp area, swinging through the trees. "Hey, this is great; look at me!"

"OK, enough fooling around. Let's get back there and turn the laser back on so we don't have to wait another whole day to get into the vault." He felt he had already wasted enough time.

"Sure enough boss," called Jim as he practically dove for the cave entrance and disappeared.

Robert walked in but couldn't see Jim anywhere. He started down the passage way toward the next glow lamp in the distance. He saw another light coming rapidly toward him. It was Jim's headlamp. He was about ready to dive for shelter thinking that Jim had seen another spider when Jim reversed direction and came to a skidding stop in front of him.

"You aren't planning on walking all the way down there again are you? With all those lamps to guide me, I can go about fifteen KPH. That's more than three times faster than walking. This is what I call fun."

Robert turned on his pack and started following Jim. It took him longer to get the hang of it but he was soon keeping up with Jim. To his delight they quickly arrived back at the chasm where the laser cart was still waiting for them.

Their second trip down the stairs was much quicker than the first and they soon had the laser set up burning a new door in the vault.

As soon as he was sure that the laser was working properly, Robert announced that they should return to the van.

Jim rapidly headed for the stairs. "Race you to the surface," he called as he vanished up the stairway. Robert didn't waste time charging after him. He was going as fast as he could and they both banged against a few walls as they flew up the passageways. Fortunately, they didn't lose their hardhats which took a few lumps as well. When they arrived at the surface it was night and they flew out of the opening like a couple of bats, laughing and screaming.

"I knew that working with you was going to be a lot of fun," yelled Jim as he just about slammed into their vehicle.

Jacquelyn and Ingra shook their heads and muttered just loud enough for Robert to hear as he nearly collided with them, "Humans."

December 24, 998 ASR

Justin agreed to see if there was a way to contact Robert after a week of constant hounding by Marilyn. For the first five days she was simply angry but in the last couple of days she was acting more concerned and her anger abated. He sat down in his office and started by logging into the Administration's system as a Board member. Without that access he wouldn't be able to do much more than look up contact ids for people. Since Robert was still officially under his Board Justin was able to access his records. This was the first time he tried looking up data for someone so he fumbled through many screens before he stumbled upon Robert's ECD logs.

Well, this is interesting. It looks like Robert was still in Midrib for several days after he left his recorded announcement that he was gone and unavailable. That makes sense. He sent his message to Marilyn so he didn't have to explain to his mother why he wasn't going to be home for the holidays. After that he simply screened his calls.

Wow! Look at all the calls Marilyn made to him. Four an hour for three days straight until she quit. She must have used an auto dial option that would alert her if he actually answered and she didn't get the recording.

I don't understand this. The logs simply stop on the 22nd. No recording of incoming or outgoing messages. There aren't any global positioning logs either. It's as if he suddenly dropped off the face of the earth.

Justin picked up his ECD and called Robert. The screen flashed a system message "Connection Unavailable" and a recording announced that the connection was not available.

That's the first time I've ever seen anything like this. Justin looked back at Robert's log and his call had not registered. Well, I guess I now know why Marilyn became more concerned than angry. I feel better about hacking into these records. I wonder what's going on. Justin continued to look up procedures for Board members inquiring about people under their jurisdiction. Finally he found a request form to report anomalies. He filled out the required data and made sure that his request was entered not just as a Board member concerned about one of his flock but also as Robert's father.

Justin sent the request and sat back in his chair. I wonder how long it will take for the Administration to respond to this request. I have a feeling that it will be weeks before anything happens.

Justin started to look at his store inventory when a knock sounded on his office door.

"Come in," called out Justin.

The door opened, revealing a large black man whose shoulders seemed to be as wide as he was tall at about 190 centimeters. His afro hairdo was like a large halo surrounding his head and his soft brown eyes flashed with joy and life. He was wearing a light-weight short-sleeved white shirt open at the collar, his huge biceps pushing the sleeves until they looked like the seams would pop. His white walking shorts emphasized his muscular thighs. "Hello, Justin. I'm J'Bar and I understand you're having trouble contacting your son, Robert," he said as he entered the office and extended his hand.

Justin stood up and shook his hand but was speechless, partly because of the man's looming presence as well as the fact that he arrived so quickly after filing his request.

J'Bar laughed, "Kind of surprised, huh? May I have a chair and I'll see what I can do to clear up your concerns?"

"Oh, excuse me. I, ah, yes, I'm surprised. I thought that surely the Administration wouldn't act so quickly on my request. We don't usually get such prompt responses."

"It really depends on the request and how urgent The Sovereign categorizes it. We don't get many missing person requests. So why don't you fill me in on what happened?"

Justin told J'Bar about Robert's disappearance and his plan to do archeological research. "Do you have any idea where he is or what he's doing? Is he alright? How is it possible that his recorded message went away?"

J'Bar rubbed his chin thoughtfully, then spoke, "I can see how you would be concerned and you certainly have a lot of unanswered questions so I'll take them one at a time. First of all, he is OK and he is at the archeological site with Jim. The exact location of that site has not been revealed to me but The Sovereign has assured me that he knows and he is monitoring both of them. I can't comment on why Robert led you to believe that he left for the site but was still in Midrib, but your guess is probably correct."

Justin just nodded. That's a polite way of saying Robert was being a jerk.

"Finally, Robert reprogrammed his ECD so that he can completely disconnect it from the communications system whenever he wants. When he disconnects the system responds to any call with the disconnected message. Of course, we were aware that it happened and normally someone would check it out. The communication technicians were notified by The Sovereign that this was not a problem and that Robert would reestablish connection when he was ready."

Justin was perplexed by the last explanation. "Why would Robert do that? How would he do that? He isn't an electronics guru."

"No, he isn't, so he had someone help him. According to what I've been told and am allowed to tell you, the research he is doing is very sensitive and that apparently, 'dropping off the face of the earth' as you put it, is necessary and approved by The Sovereign. That is all I can tell you because that's all I know." J'Bar spread his open hands before him.

"Well, thanks, J'Bar. It helps to know he's OK and that The Sovereign is still in touch with him. What am I going to tell Marilyn? I don't know if she will accept this." Justin was not looking forward to explaining all this to his wife.

"You can tell her what I've told you but you must make it clear that she may not tell anyone else unless they ask where he is and why they can't contact him. Then she should tell them only that he is at a dig doing research in accordance with The Sovereign's will. Is that clear?" asked J'Bar. His huge smile had faded to reveal a very stern countenance.

"Yeah, that's clear but she probably won't like it. I don't understand this secrecy either." Justin fidgeted in his chair.

J'Bar's smile returned. "You know, neither do I. You may want to talk to Albert before you break the news to her. Unless you have some more questions, then I think it's time for me to go."

"No, that's all. I certainly appreciate your help."

"The Sovereign bless you."

"And you."

J'Bar disappeared in a poof of light and Justin sat pondering what he was going to say to Marilyn. He sent a message to Albert.

At Albert's advice Justin went home at noon rather than wait until the end of the day to tell her what he discovered . As he related his research and the visit from J'Bar, Marilyn sat stone-faced, saying nothing until Justin finished.

"So the Administration is totally behind Robert's actions, lying to us that he had already left and even letting him stay hidden so we can't contact him in any way and now they want us to cover up for him. Is that it?" asked Marilyn.

"Uh, no. I don't think that's quite the way it is. J'Bar admitted that Robert had lied but he didn't say they approved of it. I'm sure there are many other sensitive things that go on in the Administration that we're not allowed to know. We're simply to tell the truth but not all the details. Even J'Bar didn't know all the details," answered Justin.

Marilyn smiled pleasantly but spoke sarcastically, "You call it what you want but I don't like it one bit. I'll follow the party line but that young man has a lot of explaining to do when he comes home."

August 19, 998 ASR

Chuck heard the creak of metal behind him. He turned in time to see the hangar bay doors fly open. The vacuum of space loomed before him and the other four conspirators. Before he could utter a word, his breath was taken away as he was swept off his feet and launched into blackness. *You said I would be safe if I trusted you, Yehowshuwa.*

Chuck felt his lungs exploding and searing pain in his eyes as streaks of multicolored lightning flashed across what had been his vision. He knew his eyes were no longer functioning, probably not even in his head any longer. Blackness prevailed as he gratefully lost consciousness.

Suddenly, he jerked as he felt the solid seat of a chair beneath him. His eyes worked but he couldn't believe what he saw. Sitting across a dark, wooden, rustic table was Demetrius. His eyes were wide and his mouth hung open loosely. On his left at the head of the table was Raymond, grinning from ear to ear. Ichiro sat beside Demetrius frowning and looking around at what appeared to be the inside of an ancient log-cabin. It was a very familiar location.

Eunice sat beside Chuck and leaned forward whispering, "I didn't think heaven would look like this. What's going on? Why are we sitting at a table completely set for a meal in a cabin in the mountains?" She pointed to the window that filled the A frame wall behind Demetrius and Ichiro.

The two men turned to look at the fabulous view of a large meadow surrounded by towering fir trees in front of a lake reflecting the grandeur of snow capped mountains.

A familiar voice called from the adjoining room. "Hang on just a minute and I'll explain everything. You arrived just in time and dinner will be served shortly."

Pleasant odors wafted from the room. Smells of fresh meats and vegetables cooked to perfection, something they hadn't experience for nearly 25 years.

The Sovereign came into the room, expertly balancing two covered dishes on each arm and with a dish in each hand. Before anyone could move or say a word, he had placed the platters before each person and one at the empty chair across from Raymond. Chuck was stunned as apparently were the others. He didn't know what to do but started to get to his feet as Yehowshuwa sat down.

"No, no. Remain seated, my friends. You have known me such a short time, I don't expect you to know what to do. We are about to celebrate your arrival with a wonderful meal prepared especially for each of you. So, let's thank my father for this abundance."

The Sovereign reached out a hand to Ichiro and Eunice and bowed his head. In turn the rest took hold of hands around the table. "My dear father, Yehhovaw, thank you for these that you have given to me. They have followed your will and will now be with me forever. They will experience pleasures at my right hand and you will be with us forever. Thank you for this food that we can enjoy together. All comes from you and we give you thanks, glory, and honor in it all."

Chuck found the courage to speak, "So, we're all dead?"

Yehowshuwa laughed throwing his head back. "Yes and no. You died but you are now alive. Very shortly you will begin to really understand what real life is. So uncover your dishes and eat. I know your favorites so don't be surprised. As to why you are here, this is a perfect implementation of the imperfect getaway that Chuck enjoyed as a child. I wanted you all to be together when you arrived so I picked Chuck's favorite place."

Chuck knew before he lifted the cover to his plate that he would find roasted pheasant with mashed potatoes and gravy, green peas, and applesauce. He slid his chair back and bowed down to the floor before his king. He knew all was well and he was indeed safe as he heard the other chairs sliding out from the table.

The Sovereign spoke softly, "Thank you. Welcome to my kingdom, my good and faithful servants."

December 25, 998 ASR

The next day, Robert and Jim went back into the caverns to explore while the laser continued to cut through the massive door. With the antigravity packs they were unhindered whenever they found underground cliffs or cervices. Robert marveled that there was no end to the myriads of passages. Once they got deep enough, they continued to run into evidence of the once great city that had been destroyed. At one point they found a twisted street sign.

"What's it say, Robert?" asked Jim.

"I don't know. Let's see if we can straighten it out enough to scan it and get a translation. It should confirm whether or not this was the capital."

Jim pounded on the metal, jumped up and down on it and finally got it flat enough to scan.

Robert's ECD recognized the lettering after he told it to use ancient Arabic. "It appears to be the name of a street all right. It's Kadri Street. Now all I need to do is run that through the databases about The Chancellor's capital and see if it matches up. Bingo. Take a look at this map."

Robert showed the map of the capital to Jim with Kadri Street highlighted. "Now all we need to do is find a couple more landmarks and we might be able to map out the place. It's interesting that Professor Robison spent nearly three months running around down here and there isn't any mention in his notes about landmarks. Either we're incredibly lucky and he was incredibly unlucky or someone tampered with his notes before giving them to us. Oh, well, it's time to go back and see our hole in the vault. Later, let's see what else we can find to make sense of this place."

When they arrived at the vault the laser had already finished cutting through the top of the door and shut down. They attached their winch to the handle and anchored it to a girder that was protruding from the opposite wall. Once everything was hooked up they plugged the winch into a power outlet on the laser cart. Slowly the cutout section of the door screeched as metal ground against metal. Finally, it dropped to the floor and fell flat with a resounding thud.

"I'm sure glad you brought that winch, Robert. I have no idea how we would have gotten that big slab of steel out of the hole without it. It must weigh around five hundred kilograms."

Robert paid no attention. He was already stepping into the vault. Jim quickly followed him.

When they stepped in, Robert was surprised at how bright it was with only their two headlamps. Yet the light had a strange yellowish sheen.

"What is this?" asked Jim as he pointed at several rows of yellow bricks stacked two meters high and filling nearly a third of the vault.

"It looks like it must be gold bullion," answered Robert as he started to examine a series of small locked cabinets opposite the gold.

"I don't get it. Why would they stash all this gold down here?"

"Didn't you have any classes in history before the Last Battle? Gold was used to back up their money which was really worthless paper. At least that was the theory. Eventually it all became a sham but countries kept as much gold as possible. I would imagine this was part of The Chancellor's deposit needed to finance his war," answered Robert as he studied the cabinets.

"What's really of value to us would be documents stored in these drawers. Can you see if the handheld laser will reach this far? We'll need to cut each one of these locks to get them open."

Jim went out and brought back goggles and a handheld laser attached to a cord that powered it from the laser cart. Robert put on the goggles and started experimenting on the locks to see how to cut them open.

Robert was very excited when he looked in the first drawer he opened. "Wow! It looks like even paper survived the fire, dampness and everything else for the last thousand years. It's in remarkably good shape and we won't need to restore it before looking at it. Jim, start cutting these bolts at either side of the box while I start going through the contents."

Jim appeared to enjoy popping the boxes out of the wall then briefly looking at the contents. Robert had him sort the contents, putting jewelry in one stack, coins in another, paper money in a third, and documents in the last.

Robert ignored everything except the documents. He was able to read enough of the ones that were in ancient English to determine if they were of any importance. However, there were other languages and he scanned part of them into his ECD to find out if they were relevant to his research.

"That's the last of the boxes, Robert. Find anything useful yet?"

"No, nothing," he said disgustedly. "If we weren't on a mission to find documentation I'd like nothing better than to examine every last item. Maybe that can be done once we are free and have millennia to spare. Let's pack this stuff up and take it back. The university will certainly enjoy having this for their displays of ancient civilization. I can also get you set up to examine the documents in detail when we get out."

They put the contents of the boxes in bags that they brought and piled some on the laser cart along with the winch. The antigravity packs made it much easier for them as they were able to strap the remaining bags directly to the packs..

"What are we going to do with all that gold?" asked Jim as they left the vault.

Robert shrugged his shoulders. "I guess we'll leave it here. It isn't worth much anyway."

For the next two days Robert stayed almost exclusively in the van's small living quarters, translating documents and reading them, trying to find something that would be useful. He appreciated Jim's help but his attention span was pretty short. He let Jim take frequent breaks to hike in the woods or explore in the caves.

During lunch on the second day Jim picked up a book they found just inside the vault on the floor near an overturned chair and table. "What's in this book?"

"Oh, that. It's just the log of all the visitors who had a box. Apparently they made them sign in and out." Robert wasn't concerned with who had been in the vault. Beside, he was getting depressed since they hadn't found anything worthwhile in two days.

"What's this writing in the front of the book?" asked Jim as he opened it.

"I don't know; probably just procedures for checking people in and out. If you're really interested why don't you scan it in and translate it?" Robert answered sharply. Jim's questions about unimportant artifacts were beginning to get on his nerves.

"Sure, why not?" said Jim quietly. He finished his lunch and took the book with him to the left driver's seat.

Robert returned to the drudgery of examining more important documents from the locked drawers.

A few minutes later Jim interrupted again. "Hey Robert, you remember when we found that street sign?"

"Yeah," answered Robert not really wanting to listen to Jim.

"You said if we could find another landmark that we could map the whole city. How about if I gave you the address of the vault?"

"What? What did you say?" Jim had his full attention now.

"The address of the vault is on the first page of this book."

"Really? Wow! Let me see." Robert nearly leaped to the front of the vehicle.

Robert took Jim's ECD and started looking at the pages he scanned in. "Jim, this is a miracle. Not only do we have the address of this vault, but we have the address of two more vaults." As he continued to read he became more and more excited. "Look at this, this confirms that the vaults were all built for The Chancellor and the third one is listed as being in his office building. We've got to get to that one."

Robert handed the ECD back to Jim.

"Here, put these addresses into the map program and use the inertial measuring system to show where the vault is in relation to the street we found. Let me know when we have a layout of the city. I'm going to get some of the sounding equipment to see if we can map out some of the tunnels without having to walk down every dead end." Robert jumped out the door and headed for the back without looking back.

By the time Robert retrieved the sounding equipment Jim had a map of the city according to the records they found in the archives. However, it was soon obvious that the great earthquakes and destruction of the city by The Sovereign had significantly changed the layout. The elevation of the first vault was nearly 300 meters higher than the street sign and they should have both been within five meters of the same elevation. It wasn't as if the city had been buried and could now be unearthed. It had been turned upside down, shaken, and then tossed out.

Robert and Jim worked for the next few weeks trying to map the various caverns and passageways in the proximity of where they believed the third vault should be located. The rough mountains interfered with their sounding equipment and gave many faulty readings. Often, they had what looked like a path in the right direction but had to work their way through side tunnels, only to find hundreds of meters of rock between them and their destination. Occasionally they were able to cut through the rock and continue in the newly found passages. Painfully and slowly they were able to open passages into the heart of the mountains.

Chapter 37

Samantha walked alone past the campus library. The underground cell meeting was scheduled to meet in a vault used to store ancient manuscripts. She rounded the building but saw two men she didn't recognize loitering near the rear entrance. She was already late but couldn't take a chance being seen entering the library. She continued past them and stopped to consult her ECD.

It took her a few minutes but she located an entrance in an adjacent building with a tunnel that led to her destination. She sighed with relief but knew that Gustav would still berate her for being late. Better late than not showing up at all; she didn't want to jeopardize her ability to get the discussion topics. They proved very useful when rescuing new recruits from the underground.

Samantha grimaced as the door squeaked and she entered the vault. Every eye turned and looked at her.

"Sorry I'm late," she said and quickly sat in an available chair forming a circle for the discussion group.

Gustav stared at her until she felt very uncomfortable but she kept her eyes on him. She wasn't going to let him intimidate her.

"Sam," Gustav paused for what seemed like an eternity, "we were discussing an alarming trend that has occurred. Apparently someone with knowledge of our discussion topics has been neutralizing our recruitment efforts. We've had a higher than normal drop out rate this year."

He paused again. His eyes narrowed and seemed to consume her as they roamed up and down. *I know he's looking for some kind of reaction.*

"You wouldn't happen to know anything about that, would you?" he asked.

He was obviously in a foul mood. But then he had been ever since Samyaza sided with Robert.

Samantha caught a slight movement of Kevin's head three chairs to the left of Gustav. She knew Gustav was bluffing.

Samantha looked sideways and rolled her eyes. "Yeah, every time I get a discussion topic, I walk around the campus asking people if they are new recruits and what they think of the last topic. Then I tell them how stupid they are for getting sucked into believing them. What do you think I am – some kind of fool – or are you?"

Hillary snickered and Gustav shot her a mean glance before returning his attention to Samantha. "Just checking. So why are you late?"

"For one thing there were two guys hanging around near the entrance so I had to find an alternate route," said Samantha, thankful that she had an excuse.

"You weren't alone on that one," said Kevin. "We all had to do that."

Gustav smiled. "That was my idea. I posted them out there to see who would follow protocol and take a different entrance. I thought maybe a turncoat wouldn't be as careful. You all passed that little test. By the way, the problem with recruitment isn't limited to our campus."

Mike asked, "What do we know about the problem? Are these Enforcers or other Administration officials that are coercing recruits to bail out?"

Gustav shook his head. "We don't know much. Whoever is doing this is very effective. We've tried to talk to the ones who left but they aren't willing to talk to us."

Kevin waved for attention and Gustav looked his way. "Are you telling us that every new recruit that was contacted by the enemy turned back? Haven't any of us resisted and let our cell leaders know what's going on?"

Gustav put his hands up. "No, a few resisted and informed us. Unfortunately they can't say much about the incident. It is so frustrating. Our group lost Alicia. She won't talk. Erik resisted. Erick, tell us what happened to you."

Erik looked down at the floor and his face turned red. "Well, all I can say is that a guy came to my dorm room last week. He said he wanted to talk to me about the last discussion topic. He tried to convince me that it was all a bunch of hooey and that The Sovereign knew everything about the cell meetings I attended. I didn't believe him for an instant."

He looked up at Gustav and quickly looked back at the floor when Gustav stared unsmiling. Gustav spoke slowly enunciating each word. "Tell us all you know about this man, Erik"

"I don't remember much."

"Anything!" shot back Gustav.

"His name was Brad or Brent or something like that. I, I, can't even describe him," stammered Erik.

Gustav turned to the group. "That sums up what everyone who didn't desert said. It's almost like their minds were wiped. We have no idea who these people are but you can be assured we will find them and eliminate this threat. We are particularly interested in a woman who calls herself Amanda who seems to be very effective."

I'm sure glad I wear a disguise when I contact people! I better start using different names too. "Does this mean that the Administration knows what we are doing? What are we going to do?" asked Samantha. She hoped that this would mark the end of the underground but knew they wouldn't give up that easily.

"Ah!" said Gustav as he raised a hand pointing with one finger to the ceiling. "We are going to lay a trap. All recruits are being warned and we will provide each of you an alert program that will trip on your ECD when you ask, 'Are you really with the underground?' It will secretly notify our operatives who will then trail or capture the hapless enemy to discover who is behind all this."

Twila asked, "What will happen to these – enemies – guys?"

Gustav paused and smiled, "We will neutralize them."

Samantha spoke before she thought, "How can you do that? The Sovereign will know immediately if someone is killed."

Gustav smile turned to a sneer, "That's what you think! I've been told that even highly visible personages have 'disappeared.'"

Kevin raised his eyebrows, "Yeah, like our Professor Robison last quarter. He vanished and no one knows where he went."

"Yeah, like him," added Gustav quickly.

Did I miss something or did Kevin just bait Gustav? "But Robert said The Sovereign did that because he was part of the underground." Samantha cocked her head sideways quizzically.

Gustav turned red and stammered, "Yeah, well, maybe it wasn't him, but I'm informed we have our ways so just speak up if someone starts trying to talk you out of the movement."

Gustav started the evening's discussion topic. Samantha paid little attention. She was contemplating how she could continue to ease people out of the underground without being caught.

March 28, 999 ASR

Robert stood at the end of a tunnel deep inside the mountain staring at a huge twisted, rusting steel girder sticking out of the rock and cement debris. As he turned, its shadow formed a rough question mark from the glow of his headlamp. It seemed to mock him and his attempt to find the missing vault. He hated it. He kicked it.

The earth shook and Robert jumped under the protection of the hated beam. A few rocks dropped from the ceiling but nothing more occurred at the minor tremor. *The Sovereign must be causing these to scare us out of the search. Surely he knows we are somewhere around here but the shield is keeping us hidden. I'll bet he only wanted us to find the first vault and he's guessed we're digging deeper.* The increased frequency of the recent quakes wasn't improving his mood.

"Hey Jim, you OK?" Robert yelled down the tunnel.

Jim's eager response broke his dour mood, "Come and look at this! I think it's the vault!"

Robert hurried to the instrument console and looked at the soundings of a box-shaped cavern. "You're right Jim, this could be it. But why didn't we see this before?"

"The sensor array! It's pointing almost straight up. As we've gone from passage to passage, we've been scanning straight ahead and only a few degrees above or below us. It tipped over during that last quake. After it stopped I checked the console. 'Ta da,' there it is," answered Jim with one out-stretched arm extended toward the instrument panel.

"I'll bet The Sovereign didn't want that to happen during the quake," laughed Robert. "Wow, it's still thirty meters above us and as far as I can tell there isn't anything leading near it. It looks like we are in for a lot of cutting to get to it, not to mention cutting into it. Let's get to work."

They backtracked to some passages that were closer to the same level and started the arduous task of cutting through forty meters of rock, dirt, steel girders and concrete. They cut at different angles with the laser cart dropping small chunks that they moved down the passages where they deposited the debris. After several days they exposed the shining wall of the stainless steel vault.

Robert pondered aloud how he would get into the safe. "We have to be careful cutting through this wall so we don't damage the contents inside. Let's just cut the opening large enough to squeeze through rather than opening a door big enough for us to walk in like we did before. It'll also be a lot quicker." Robert set the laser to cut a circular hole through the wall.

A few hours later they were able to remove the outer wall revealing the back of the safety deposit boxes still intact. Robert carefully cut the back off the deposit box cabinet with the hand laser. He was surprised to find all the boxes empty. Finally they used the cart's laser to cut through the boxes and the front of the cabinet, pushing the mess of metal forward and onto the floor of the vault.

Robert crawled through the hole. Jim passed the hand held laser to Robert, then followed him into the vault.

In the center of the floor was another safe bolted to the door. "Do you notice anything weird about this vault, Jim?"

"Hmm, place looks like a perfectly empty vault except for that thing there in the middle of the floor," answered Jim with a shrug.

"That's just it. It's empty. Look at those other deposit boxes. The keys are still in each one of them. It's almost as if this whole vault was put here just to make sure that whatever is in this little safe would be protected." Robert bent over to examine it more closely. "This little box is built to sustain extremely high temperatures for long periods of time."

"That's great," sighed Jim, "That means it's going to take, like a hundred hours, to cut through that thing with the handheld laser."

"No, not at all. Look at this. See the way this door is built? There's no lock. It's meant to be opened without any problem once we got into the vault."

"Well, Robert, why don't you open it?"

"What if it's empty too?"

"Sometimes you are so weird, Robert." Jim spun the spoked wheel on the door, pulling the bolts into the door with a clank, and swung it open.

Robert peered inside the small opening which revealed one shelf with a mass of unidentified rubbish next to a flat metal box that was about one centimeter thick and twelve centimeters square. He cautiously removed a sample of the mass and looked at it closely. "Dang, this looks like it was a paper document but it's been wet and has almost completely decomposed. If this was so important you'd think they would have made sure the safe was water tight as well." His voice fell as he thought that whatever was in the small metal box might also be destroyed.

He carefully retrieved the small box and they both stood looking at it as Robert turned it over. It had a hinged lid and an indent on one end to open it. As he prepared to open it he said, "I sure hope they didn't go through all this trouble to just protect some lousy piece of jewelry." He slowly opened the lid to reveal a metal disc mounted in the case by a latch through a hole in the center. He pressed the latch, popping the disc free. He lifted it out and turned it over. The underside reflected rainbow colors from his head lamp. "It looks like there may have been some kind of label stuck to the dull side but it disintegrated just like the document in here. What do you suppose this is?"

"Beats me, I've never seen anything like this before, but I'll bet it's some kind of computer storage device," answered Jim.

"I sure hope so because it's obvious that there isn't anything else here. Let's take this out and see if we can find some more information about computer systems during the Great Time of Trouble. If this contains some kind of data it may be exactly what we've been looking for. We certainly haven't found anything else here that has helped us."

They squeezed themselves back out the hole in the vault and started the long trip back to their camp. When they finally arrived it was late at night and they were exhausted but not too tired to start looking up ancient computer systems.

"Hey, Robert, I think I found what we want. Look at these antiquated machines. Can you believe that the first computers were bigger than a house and had almost no memory?" Robert was glad Jim was his assistant. He always found information faster than Robert did.

Jim showed Robert a series of storage devices in historical order from something called floppy disks to plastic disks.

"I don't need a history lesson, did you find our metal disk?" asked Robert sternly.

"Hold on to your hat, this is where it starts getting interesting. The floppies gave way to hard plastic disks that used lasers to burn the data on the disk and retrieve it. Look at this picture and how the light reflects like a rainbow from it."

"Yeah, that does look a lot like our, but ours is definitely metal. What does it say came next?"

"According to this, metallic disks were developed later for long term storage of vast quantities of data. The new disks were not widely used for home use but were primarily used by businesses and governments where long term preservation of huge amounts of data was important. To read the data from the disk you have to use the multiple lasers with different colors and the same hues as the lasers used to burn the disk. This thing can store a million terabytes of data indefinitely. They thought this was the ultimate in storage devices."

Robert laughed, "You would think they would know better than that. In just a few years every storage system they invented became obsolete."

"One way or another, we're going to need someone with technical expertise in ancient technologies to be able to read this disk and then convert the data to something that our current systems will be able to decipher. Man, I hope they didn't try to encrypt it on top of it. I think this is exactly what we've been looking for. Let's head for home. There are a couple of guys at the university that will be able to help us." With that, Robert set the auto pilot for home and they both turned in for the night. He was too excited to sleep even though he was dead tired.

Chapter 38

S amantha stopped outside the Whitmore dormitory at 8:00 PM. She was nervous. Her last two attempts to dislodge new recruits from the underground were unsuccessful. At first, both were quite willing to discuss the topics but they eventually become quite belligerent. The last contact even threatened to make sure Samantha didn't approach anyone else if she ever returned. She was thankful they hadn't used the code words to trigger their ECD to alert the underground. She believed that it was only by The Sovereign's intervention she had been able to continue the last two months.

Samantha paused to pray that this contact would be more open and would not alert the underground operatives. She approached the main entrance door which opened for her. She caught a glimpse of the red-headed-short-black-leather-skirted woman she had become for this encounter. The short skirt made her feel uncomfortable but reasoned it was ok since it was not as revealing as a bathing suit.

She arrived on the 11th floor and knocked at her prospect's door.

The door opened just before Samantha was about to knock again. A short dark young woman stared at her from deep brown eyes surrounded by black eye shadow in the shape of upside-down stars. Her long black hair parted in the middle of her head and fell heavily on either side of her face.

"Who are you?" she growled from lips painted black.

Samantha tried to reply pleasantly, "I'm Adnama. I'm taking a survey and would hope you could answer a few quick questions for me." She varied the letters of her middle name ever since she learned that her middle name, Amanda, was known to the underground.

"If it doesn't take too long" she snapped as she shifted her weight and leaned against the door jam.

OK, this may not go too well but here goes. "First of all, could I have your first name?"

"Kalenjin," she answered flatly.

"Thanks, Kalenjin. The first question is 'Are you interested in spiritual things?'"

"Not if they involve The Sovereign." Kalenjin rolled her eyes showing obvious contempt.

"Good, that qualifies you for the next question. Do you feel that The Sovereign restricts our freedoms?" Samantha was pretty sure how she would answer.

Kalenjin stood straight. "Are you kidding? That dictator has run rough shod over us for too long."

"So, Kalenjin, would you like to receive some literature from others who think the same as you?" Samantha already knew her name and that she was receiving *The Question's* discussion topics.

Kalenjin finally broke into a smile. "Sweetie, I already get *The Question*."

"You do? Hey that's great. You know, if you have a couple of minutes, I'd like to talk to you about the last topic. Do you mind if I come in?" Samantha didn't want to be in the hall where someone could overhear their conversation.

Kalenjin stepped aside and gestured for Samantha to come in. "Sure, always have time for a sister."

Samantha walked in to the dimly lit room. The walls were painted black and heavy black curtains covered the window obliterating the evening's twilight. She sat down on the couch underneath a painting of a goat's head. She faced a pentagram painted on the opposite wall with candles mounted at each point. They were the only source of light. Upside-down stars, Teutonic runes and other symbols she couldn't identify were painted on the wall.

"Interesting décor. How did you come up with it?" asked Samantha. She never saw anything like it before outside of her studies. It sent a shiver down her spine.

"We've been fortunate to have our cell leader take some advanced training and he has helped us prepare for our training. Providing this ambiance helps us clear our minds and open ourselves to being enlightened about the true nature of The Sovereign." Kalenjin sat down beside Samantha. "So what's on your mind?"

"I'm still a bit confused by our last discussion topic. The one that was talking about Yehowshuwa's supposed death and resurrection. Anyway I was doing some research about it and came up with some documents that clearly opposed *The Question's* conclusion that his death was faked. Take a look at this." Samantha opened her ECD and showed it to Kalenjin.

"See, it says that when they came to Yehowshuwa and found he was already dead, they did not break his legs. Instead, one of the soldiers pierced Yehowshuwa's side with a spear, bringing a sudden flow of blood and water.

"So what does that have to do with anything?" asked Kalenjin.

"You've taken the basic biology course, haven't you?" asked Samantha.

"Yeah, so?"

"If you remember, when a person or animal dies the blood cells separate from the serum and settle to the bottom. When the soldier pierced The Sovereign's side he punctured the sack around his heart which had filled with blood. The blood had already separated giving the appearance of blood and water. It proves that Yehowshuwa was indeed dead. He couldn't have faked that." Samantha hoped that she could plant a seed of doubt in Kalenjin's mind. If she doubted *The Question's* conclusion of this topic she might be open to the truth about The Sovereign Yehowshuwa.

Kalenjin sat up straight. "Are you really with the underground?"

Samantha's ECD sounded a sharp chirp. *I'm sure glad Kevin programmed my ECD to only chirp when the key words were spoken.* She closed it quickly and stood up. "Hey, I gotta go. See you around." She quickly went to the door, hurried down the hallway and went into the stair well.

"Hey, come back, we need to talk," she heard Kalenjin's call just before the fire door closed behind her.

She ran up the stairs to the 12th floor. Her plan was to dump her disguise then calmly go back down the elevator. She peeked out the door seeing two men in black suits at the far end of the hallway. She jumped back quickly and went up another floor. *How did they get here that fast? I wonder if they knew I was coming here tonight or there was another alert that we didn't know about.* Samantha's heart was racing and she knew it wasn't just because she had run up two flights of stairs.

Samantha heard the door to the stairwell open below her. She didn't have a choice, she had to exit to the 13th floor. She didn't even look but burst through the door into the hallway. There was no one on the floor so she started running to the elevator. She reached the elevator, pressed the call button, and looked behind her. To her horror the two men in black were now coming toward her.

They were approaching too fast. There was no way she could outrun them to the other end of the building. *Please, please, Yehowshuwa let the elevator get here before they do.* She had hoped to slip on her long skirt and blouse, remove her wig and contacts before she was seen. *Maybe in the elevator.*

The elevator door chimed as the first of the men reached out and took her arm. She jerked away and fell backwards into the elevator only to be caught by strong hands behind her. She felt her feet lifted off the floor as she was picked up and placed inside the elevator facing the back wall.

"This is not the woman you are looking for. The one you are looking for went down the opposite stairs. You need to hurry to catch her."

Samantha turned quickly to see Kevin's back. She looked into the eyes of the two men who had almost caught her. They looked at her then at each other, shaking their heads.

"No, that isn't her. We must hurry," said the one on the right in a monotone. They both dashed away as the elevator door closed.

Kevin turned around. "Quick, change your disguise before we reach the first floor." He emphasized "first floor" and the elevator started down.

It took her only a few seconds to become a more proper young blond coed.

Samantha and Kevin casually walked out the front door past two more men in black standing just inside the entrance. They didn't speak but turned away as if they had something private to discuss.

Once outside Samantha asked, "How did you do that? They had me dead to rights but they acted like they'd been hypnotized."

"Maybe they were. I think we had some help from one more powerful than us," answered Kevin with a laugh.

"I'm also glad you got the alarm from my ECD when Kalenjin used the code words. You initiated our retraction procedures just in time." Samantha's legs were still shaky but she was starting to breath easier.

March 31, 999 ASR

When Robert and Jim returned to Midrib they wasted no time finding Dr. Jonathan Krebs who was the leading expert in ancient computer systems. Together they entered the Antiquities Auxiliary Building, found his office and knocked on the door.

"Come on in," answered a crusty old voice.

Robert opened the door and they entered Dr. Krebs' office. It looked more like a junk yard than an office. Odd metallic and plastic boxes, gadgets with wires dangling from them, and other unidentifiable objects were strewn all over the room. Some were on the floor in piles, others on his desk and some on shelves among books that were just as old as the parts. Some were only a couple of centimeters in size and others stood in the corner looming a couple of meters in height. Many had lights and buttons on them while others had slots and hole for inserting all kinds of things that Robert couldn't imagine.

"Good morning, Dr. Krebs. I hope we aren't disturbing you."

"Not at all, Robert, my boy. It's good to see you. Why, it's been at least five years since you've brought me some piece of equipment that you unearthed," answered Dr. Krebs. "I keep telling you to call me Jonathan. I don't need all that formality."

Dr. Krebs was an older man who had personally seen most of the changes in computers in the last five hundred years. He had white, frizzy, unkempt hair and long bushy eyebrows generally going upward but with several strays that were going in every direction. He extended his hand from the sleeve of a long white lab smock that should have been washed several weeks or months earlier. He smiled warmly as his sagging jowls disappeared with the upturn of his mouth. He shook Robert's hand. "You know, you should come around more often, not just when you have yourself an old computer gadget that you can't identify."

"Ah, you know me too well, Jonathan. But we're pretty sure what we have. This is my assistant, Jim, and he's identified it." Robert jerked his thumb toward Jim.

"Pleased to meet you, Dr. Krebs." Jim and Dr. Krebs shook hands. "I believe we identified this from some of your research. It's a metallic storage disk from the era of the Great Time of Trouble."

Dr. Krebs took the box that Jim handed him. His eyes were wide. "Whew! That would be quite a find. But why bring it to me if you've already identified it?"

"Jonathan," whispered Robert as he tapped on the case, "it's perfectly preserved. We want you to get the data off of it."

Dr. Krebs turned the case over in his hands as they started trembling. He opened it slowly, then pressed the center latch and carefully removed the disk, holding it by its edge, circling it with his thumb and fingers, being careful not to touch the gleaming surface.

"I've never seen one of this age that was intact." He held it up to the light. "Those that survived the Last Battle had their data transferred to more modern devices and then most were recycled before anyone decided that they should be saved for museums. Where did you find this?"

"It was at a site that Professor Robison was working at before he disappeared." Robert went on to describe finding the vault and the appearance that it was built specifically to save the single disk. He didn't mention that he believed it was The Chancellor's headquarters.

"So do you think you'll be able to find out what's on it?" asked Jim.

"Oh, yes, most definitely. But it may take a while. Our best bet is to see if I can find a functional reader in the basement. It would take a week or so to get it hooked up and to get the protocols loaded to decipher the data. As old as they are it is highly doubtful if they still work. Second best would be to find one that we can rebuild. If we can't find one then we'll have to build one from scratch. That would take months," Dr. Krebs answered almost mechanically as he placed the disk back in the box.

"This is really important. Do you think you could make this your top priority?" asked Robert, hoping his eyes portrayed the proper amount of begging.

"This is ancient history sitting right in our hands. I'll get right on it. Unless you have something else for me." Dr. Krebs started for the door.

"That's all, thanks," replied Robert, delighted that Dr. Krebs was quite eager to start work on the disk.

March 31, 999 ASR

Samantha crossed the commons area as she approached the student union building. The light breeze scented with spring fragrances whipped her short hair more than it would have when it was longer. She missed her longer blond locks but they proved to be a problem when she donned different wigs.

She had just received a message from Robert that he and Jim were back and wanted to meet as soon as possible. *I wonder what the urgency is.* She agreed to meet them even though it was just before the end of the quarter and she was studying for finals. She was looking forward to seeing them but she was also apprehensive about what they might have found to help the underground.

She entered the cafeteria and spotted them at their customary table with Kevin. "Wow, you guys look pasty white. Have you been hiding in a cave?" asked Samantha as she sat down.

Robert laughed, "Yes, as a matter of fact we have. We spent most of the time underground."

He told them about entering the shield around the site, finding the first vault and then the key to finding a second. Even though Samantha had a keen interest in history, Robert provided much more information than she wanted regarding archeological procedures for preserving specimens. She was very concerned when he shared that he meditated daily with Rorarum. The story was getting very long and she was relieved when he finally told about finding the computer disk and taking it to Dr. Krebs.

"So during this time you were taking more training directly from this Rorarum guy who contacts you telepathically? What have you learned?" asked Kevin.

"Strange as it seems one of the biggest things is patience. I also received visions of Earth's true history, not The Sovereign's lies. It's through the eyes of those who are opposed to The Sovereign and Yehhovaw. As we suspected from our discussion groups our current history books contain a very different story than what Rorarum revealed."

Samantha had to hold her tongue to keep from yelling, *It's just part of their big lie, Robert. Wake up!* Instead, she just nodded her head.

"Through this study I learned how events and their timing in the world and in the spirit realm have long reaching effects. The underground is much more that we ever imagined also. It has been operating almost since the beginning of the world, attempting to free mankind. This is where the patience comes in. I now can see that sometimes we have to wait patiently for many years, even thousands, to achieve our purposes," continued Robert as a serene look came across his face.

Samantha looked at Jim for his reaction but he looked away, not meeting her gaze.

Robert became more serious, leaning forward. "I also found that there are times when the good of the many is more important than the good of the one. We must be prepared to give all we have for the cause and that isn't something we can do until we are completely convinced that the cause is right and just. I'm sure that the data on that disk is going to be a blockbuster when it comes to revealing the truth and convincing the world that what we've previously thought was right is really a huge outrage."

Samantha spoke quietly, "I have a feeling that you will find the disk will line up perfectly with what you learned as well as what the underground teaches us." She had a level of awe in her voice that she was sure Robert mistook for reverence.

"I can't wait to see what's on it. Will you give us a sneak preview?" asked Kevin.

Samantha thought that Robert looked very self-assured as he settled back in his chair. "I think that would be quite appropriate, my friends."

Robert turned to Kevin. "You know that my training has given me a better sense of the spiritual realm than I had before I left. I sense in you a great strength. You, too, have grown since we last met, which brings me to a question I have for you."

"I have?" said Kevin as his eyebrows shot up. "I guess you are more attuned. What's your question?"

"As soon as we returned, we retrieved all our messages but the only messages were text messages from the Administration. They were the usual announcements except for an invitation. I think order is really a better word, to come to the annual feast in the capital." Robert sighed.

"It appears that since we both left the world of academia and now are classified as working we were selected to attend. I've never been there before and have only read about the whole shindig." He leaned forward, "To tell you the truth, I'm very uncomfortable with the prospect of appearing before The Sovereign, even though I'll just be one of millions attending. With what I now know, I feel that I won't be true to myself if I go. Besides it could be dangerous if I'm found out. What do you think?"

Samantha was taken aback about the invitation. She couldn't imagine Robert going through the rituals with Rorarum in control. She watched Kevin.

Kevin took a deep breath before answering, "I agree. With your current state of consciousness you would only be paying lip service to The Sovereign. However, if your mind-cloaking skills are good enough he will never know it. But you should be concerned about what will happen if you don't show up. Spurning the 'invitation,'" Kevin made quote signs with his fingers, "without a good excuse will immediately flag you for disciplinary action. I don't think you can afford that at this time."

Robert covered his mouth with his right hand and nodded.

"However, this is something that could be very eye-opening for you. Your perspective has changed dramatically over the last few months. Go to the feast and see for yourself what it's all about. It may confirm to you what you learned, adding fuel for your book."

Samantha stared at Kevin. She couldn't believe he said that. *You will need to explain that one to me later.*

Robert nodded again, "Ah, I see the wisdom in what you're saying. While I was sure I could cook up a good excuse I hadn't thought of the benefits of actually attending." He turned to Jim. "Well, Jim, it looks like we'll be out on the road again in a couple of days, though this time we can take public transportation."

"How about you, Jim? You've been uncharacteristically quiet. Have you been getting some training too?" asked Samantha.

Jim looked down at the table. "Nah, since I didn't connect with anyone during the first training I guess I'm still in a holding pattern for the right time. Besides, with Robert getting all this knowledge, I don't feel like I need to bother anyone to get it."

"What did you do while Robert was meditating? It seems like he spent quite a bit of time doing that," she quizzed.

"I hiked around in the mountains, read books, watched some videos, and thought a lot. I felt funny while we were there. I can't describe it but there was something unnerving about walking on top of an ancient city that was destroyed in an hour and not being able to see a trace of it. Then in a matter of minutes I was walking through the caverns and rubble. It caused me to think about the whole battle and the Great Time of Trouble."

"So you got some new perspectives as well?" she probed.

"Yeah, you might say that."

"And can you share that perspective?"

Jim paused glanced at Robert then answered, "It's hard to put into words and I'm still putting all the pieces together. I guess it takes me longer, especially without the help of someone like Rorarum."

Kevin interrupted and Jim seemed relieved. "I would like to hear more about that sometime, Jim. But now, I need to get back to studying for my finals. How about you, Sam?"

Samantha took the hint and stood up. "Me too. Thanks for sharing your adventure with us. I'll look forward to hearing about your trip to Yeruwshalayim."

After Samantha and Kevin left the building she asked him why he had encouraged Robert to go to the feast by implying it would help him write his book.

"First of all The Sovereign wants him at the feast. I'm sure he didn't get invited simply because this was his first non-academic job. Second, he will see a symbolic representation of what The Sovereign has done for us spiritually. It will either soften him toward Yehowshuwa or it will harden him. If the latter, he will twist the truth for his book."

She understood as a passage came to her mind, See, I lay in Zion a stone that causes men to stumble and a rock that makes them fall, and the one who trusts in him will never be put to shame. Zion, an ancient name for The Sovereign's capital.

December 13, 998 ASR

Zophia relaxed behind Chuck's old desk, leaning back in her chair as far as it would go without tipping over. She enjoyed the freedom that she and the rest of the crew had since they completed their training. Running the ship was much easier. Just as she used her telekinetic ability to adjust the chair down slightly, each crewmember could do his or her job in a fraction of the time it took before.

Remembering how Chuck always adjusted it up so he would be eyelevel with her brought back memories of his demise. She laughed aloud at how easily the crew dismissed his fate. Hal's recording of his plot to destroy the Aman and escape in the shuttle convinced the crew that his death was his own fault and very deserved.

Oh Chuck, if you only hadn't gone over to the dark side. What beautiful music we could have made together. Music that Alex and I now enjoy---and Buckly--- and Wilfred---and Elizabeth. Alex was her favorite.

Mararum interrupted her thoughts. You are now about to enter The Sovereign's jurisdiction. You need to enable your cloaking plan so that he will not detect you. Since this will be the first attempt for humans to maintain a cloak we should test it out.

Zophia directed her thoughts to the crew. May I have your attention? We are about to enter The Sovereign's domain and it is time for the first cloaking watch to report to the bridge.

She left her office and paused in the passageway, knowing that Alex was on his way to the bridge. He rounded the corner and she watched him come toward her. She enjoyed watching his gait ever since he shed his jumper and joined the rest of the crew in nudity. It still pleased her how everyone's inhibitions melted after completing training. She could see why The Sovereign would consider them dangerous.

Zophia and Alex stepped onto the bridge as the first watch assembled. In the center of the bridge the captain's chair was replaced by an intricately woven carpet. In the center was a golden pentagram surrounded by signs of the zodiac in scarlet. All were set against a deep blue background. Mararum gave Zophia the pattern. Different members of the crew took turns weaving it by hand. The five crewmembers of the first watch sat down cross legged on each side of the pentagram as they were taught on Eden.

"We are cloaked, Alex," said Zophia.

Alex responded, "Hal, launch the probe."

While she was confident that the cloaking worked against the Administration, Mararum still wanted to see evidence that it would also be effective against those in the physical realm. She turned her eyes to the forward view screen which displayed the probe's transmission. It slowly left Aman showing the wall of the giant box on the viewing screen. As it moved further and further away, the wall became more recognizable as the space ship. Just after Aman filled only half of the screen there was a slight waver on the screen as if the ship were being viewed through a heat wave, then it disappeared to be replaced by the blackness of space and a sprinkling of stars.

"Hal, are we still receiving a transmission from the probe? Can we see it?" asked Zophia.

"Yes, Captain, the probe is still functioning correctly." Hal displayed the tiny probe on the view screen.

Zophia was elated and she could feel Mararum's thrill as well. "Superb! Bring it back in, Hal."

Chapter 39

Robert and Jim got off the interregional convy near Yeruwshalayim the afternoon before the feast was to begin. They entered a sea of people moving toward convy booths for local connections.

"If I had know there would be this many people here I think I would have looked for a way out. This is ridiculous. Look at all these people. It's going to take us an hour just to get a convy to our hotel," grumbled Robert as he consulted his ECD to see where to find the convy.

"I'll bet that's the convy right over there," said Jim, pointing to a very long line of people.

Robert looked up to see where Jim was pointing, then back at his ECD and back again and sighed. "Yup, that's it. How did you know?"

"It's the longest line I could see," answered Jim flatly.

Robert and Jim picked up their bags and joined the queue waiting for their outbound convy.

When they got in line Jim asked, "Why are there so many people here?"

"It's The Sovereign's stupid requirements to worship him with delegations from all over the world. I'm glad the requirements have changed." Robert shook his head. His mood wasn't getting any better and he really didn't want to be there.

"What do you mean? What's changed?" asked Jim.

An older man ahead of them turned around. "You better be careful who you are calling stupid. And you, young man, where have you been that you don't know the history of this festival?"

Robert was glad that he was protecting his conversation from the prying Administration. He was alarmed at forgetting that anyone loyal to The Sovereign could report him. Jim responded before he had a chance to say anything.

"Ex---cuse me," drawled Jim. "Until recently I've been in university but they don't teach anything there about," he waved his hand at the mass of humanity, "this."

The stranger smiled but rolled his eyes slightly, "I understand. It was the same with me until I got my first invitation. For many years The Sovereign required the attendance of every adult male from every family to attend. Many family members also attended. As the population of Earth grew Yeruwshalayim simply couldn't hold all the people. The rules have changed over the years so that attendance at the feast is by invitation or lottery for available seating."

He looked around, then whispered, "Fresh out of university, huh? Is *The Question* still circulating?"

Robert relaxed, "You know it is, otherwise you wouldn't have asked. We can talk freely as long as others don't overhear us. I've been trained." He extended his hand.

The stranger took Robert's hand in both of his and said quietly, "I've heard of the training. What wonderful news to meet someone who has it. I've also heard that this may be the last festival. It's almost time."

The line was moving much more quickly than Robert realized. The man turned and boarded a convy without saying another word.

Robert and Jim stared at each other. Robert didn't know what to make of those parting comments. Jim voiced his lack of knowledge, "What was he talking about?"

Robert nudged Jim through the open door of the next convy and announced the name of their hotel. "I think that maybe The Sovereign won't be sovereign sooner than we think," he whispered quietly to Jim.

Check-in at their hotel was uneventful. All their accommodations were arranged when they responded to their invitations. Robert was pleased that they had the afternoon free for some sight-seeing.

"Do you have anything you'd like to see?" asked Robert.

"Yeah. Since we'll be at the temple tomorrow and every day for the next week I'd like to see what the countryside looks like. There's a tour bus leaving in about ten minutes that will take us north," answered Jim as he looked up from his ECD.

"Sounds good to me. Let's go."

They both returned to the hotel lobby where the excursion was assembling and boarded the bus. As soon as it was loaded it rose gently from the ground and started making its way through the crowded city while the tour guide started explaining some of the local points of interest.

"Good afternoon, ladies and gentlemen. My name is Ruth and I'll be your guide today. As you know, your hotel is just south of Yeruwshalayim in the Territory of Binyaamiyn. This tour will take us through the capital and around the sacred mount where you will be able to see the temple. We will cross over the Living River that flows from the temple and follow it to the Living Sea. We will then continue north about 200 kilometers along the Yardeen River which connects The Sovereign's Sea in the Territory of Eprayim. We'll circle the Sea then return via the coast. I'm sure you will enjoy the trip.

"If this is your first time to the feast, raise your hand," asked Ruth.

Nearly everyone on the bus raised his or her hand.

"Wonderful, I'm sure that you all will be very pleased and find this a very joyous occasion. We are currently passing through the area to the east of the Old City that once was designated as pasture land to sustain the inhabitants of the city other than the priests and temple workers. The Old City was five square kilometers and the city including the pastureland was 31.25 square kilometers. As you can see today with the high rise buildings in the Old City that the land around it would not be able support all the people who now live and work there. Much of the pastureland has been converted to business and residential areas along with abundant parks."

Robert only half paid attention as Ruth droned on, spouting facts about the original use of the land around the temple, where the temple workers and priests lived, and their shift schedules.

"The temple is still the original size, a square of 250 meters. The original open area around it was only 25 meters wide but has now expanded so that up to twenty million worshipers can participate in the sacrifices."

Robert had a hard time imagining how twenty million people could possibly be involved at one time.

"We are now approaching the temple as you can see if you look out the left front side of the bus. We'll turn around when we get to the tourist viewing area so that everyone will have a chance to see it without crawling over your neighbors."

The bus approached the temple from the east which is the front side. It went no further than the designated bus vantage point slightly south of the temple and about one and a half kilometers away. It slowly rotated so that both sides of the bus had ample time to look and take pictures. The temple was located on top of the hill. Locals called it a mountain but from Robert's perspective, having spent so much time in rugged mountains, it was only a hill. It was much smaller than Robert expected. It was only three stories high, each level wider than the one below.

Ruth began again, "In very ancient times the temple and its surrounding buildings were much more impressive because the ancient kings delighted in adding on to the prescribed temple area. The earliest temple that was destroyed over 3,500 years ago was adjoined by the king's royal palace. The replacement temple was much more modest than the first but later kings again enhanced it for their own glorification. The finished structure was a magnificent feat of architecture but was also destroyed some thirty years after The Sovereign, before his own death and resurrection, predicted it would happen."

His supposed death and resurrection, shouldn't you say? thought Robert.

"Another temple was built before the Great Time of Trouble but it was not authorized by The Sovereign or his father. It was conceived and built by the zeal of men who sought to honor Yehhovaw but would not acknowledge his son as their sovereign. The Chancellor capitalized on their zeal and eventually took it over as a means of directing worship to himself. Of course this false temple was destroyed during the Last Battle."

Now that might be something to investigate further. Did The Chancellor really want people to worship him or is that just more Administration propaganda?

"When The Sovereign returned to rule he had the temple rebuilt to the specifications he gave through one of his seers about 2,600 years before. Since he wanted all people to come and worship here he has not added any buildings around the temple. Tomorrow you will be here along with millions of others participating in the worship and festival."

Robert shook his head. I can hardly wait – not!

"You can see right now that there is a large assembly of people entering the temple area. The one leading the procession is our Prince. He is a direct descendent of our second king, Daawiyd. The Prince is a cousin, many generations removed, of The Sovereign. He is the head of our country's government, the senior elder on our National Board. In addition to that he is the senior elder on the World

Board. All the land extending from the city to the seas on the west and to the border of the land on the east belongs to him. From this land he brings the animals for the sacrifices."

Robert pondered that this one person actually owned land while the rest of the planet was only managed for The Sovereign. It didn't sound fair.

"When you enter the temple area tomorrow, you will enter either the south or north entrance. When you leave you must continue and leave by the opposite gate. This is the custom that The Sovereign established and we still abide by his will. The Prince, on the other hand, can enter from either direction but must exit the same way he came in."

More rules and more exceptions. Yehowshuwa is more inconsistent than I thought.

"Now we will follow the Living River that flows from the temple and down the mountain to the Living Sea. As you can see it starts as not much more than a trickle of water coming out from under the south side of the temple. If you were to wade through it there you would only get your feet wet. It miraculously gets deeper and deeper as it flows away from the temple to the east. Here, one and a half kilometers from its source it is already a deep river." The bus was now moving alongside the river and down the mountain. "The trees that you see along both sides of the river bear fruit all year long. They are representative of all the fruit-bearing trees in the world since The Sovereign restored the earth to its original design. All of our medications, what little we need, come from the leaves of these trees."

Jim nudged Robert and whispered, "The salve that healed my blister came from one of these trees?"

"So she says," answered Robert.

The bus quickly descended down the mountain following the river and came to the Living Sea which was about forty kilometers from Yeruwshalayim and about a thousand meters lower than the city. When Robert looked back up to where they were a few minutes before he understood why the locals called it a mountain and not a hill.

"This beautiful sea is a large source of marine food for the surrounding area, even though the sea is about 400 meters below the oceans of the world and has no outlet."

As the bus traveled north just off-shore, Jim looked out the window. "Look at that, Robert. White sand beaches, resorts, sailboats, multicolored sails, and even fishing vessels. When I see all this I get homesick for my own ocean beach hometown. With all that's going on, do you think I'll ever have a chance to spend a summer surfing again? I have a hard time understanding how this body of water can be kept alive by one river. According to Ruth, it was too salty to sustain life before The Sovereign's return and the beaches were more like mud baths," rambled Jim.

"You wonder too much, Jim. It's just The Sovereign's ruse to make people think he's something more than he is," whispered Robert.

"We are now leaving the Living Sea and will follow the Yardeen River to The Sovereign's Sea, the origin of the Yardeen River. The first point of interest will be where The Sovereign's people first came to inhabit this country. They crossed the

Yardeen River and took the city of Yerechow. This may seem unimpressive but the river was at flood stage and stopped flowing as they stepped into the water. In a little while we'll show you where the water piled up in heap upstream. Right now you can see the present city of Yerechow that was destroyed when we took over the land over 4,500 years ago at Yehhovaw's command."

Yeah, and slaughtered thousands of innocent people and their animals too, thought Robert.

Ruth continued to point out different places of interest along the trip from the Living Sea to The Sovereign's Sea. They passed various mountains or the location of where historic mountains had once been before the Last Battle. The history of The Sovereign's people as well as what he did after his return were always at the heart of her tour narrative. Rorarum's teachings were always at the center of Robert's thoughts as he contended with each narrative.

As they traveled around The Sovereign's Sea Ruth pointed out various locations where The Sovereign performed miracles and taught the people and his disciples. Robert felt uncomfortable when Ruth described how he cast out a legion of demons from a man on the shores of the sea.

"Robert, think about sitting over there in the grass and eating along with 5,000 other people from just a few loaves of bread and a couple of fish. Wouldn't that be amazing?" stated Jim.

Robert lightly slapped Jim on the arm with the back of his hand. "I think you're impressed only because you haven't eaten for a while."

After circling the sea, the bus traveled over the mountains near Mount Tabowr and through a broad valley. "We are now passing through the valley of Migrown where the armies assembled for the Last Battle," Ruth went on to explain how each of the armies came from different directions and assembled in the valley ready to march against the capital one hundred kilometers to the south. She gave a short but fairly accurate account of the battle. Robert was convinced that most of the facts about location and timing were OK but her comments about the motivation of the armies were nothing but The Sovereign's propaganda.

They crossed the country and arrived at the coast near Mount Karmel. "It was on this mountain that one of Yehhovaw's seers confronted the false priests who worshiped spirits. He challenged them to build an altar and call down fire by their spirits to burn up the sacrifice. Of course, nothing happened even though the priests tried all their incantations. Then Yehhovaw's soothsayer drenched his altar, wood and sacrifice with water until it would have been impossible to start a fire. He called upon Yehhovaw and immediately fire came down from the sky, burned up the sacrifice, the stone altar, the soil, and the water that had overflowed and was in a trench around the altar. The people then understood the true nature of Yehhovaw. They seized the false priests so that the seer could kill them all. It was a graphic lesson that we need to remember - allegiance to anyone but The Sovereign and his father can be fatal."

It is also symbolic of the Last Battle, yet to come.

Robert was startled. Was that in his mind or did Ruth say that aloud? He also wondered if she was looking directly at him when she said that. Jim slunk down in his seat.

"Did you hear what she said about that being symbolic?" whispered Robert.

Jim straightened up. "Huh? I only heard the word fatal and didn't like it."

They traveled from Mount Karmel to Yapho following the coast and turned inland to return to the capital. All the while Robert was thinking about how The Sovereign deceived people into thinking that what Ruth said about The Sovereign's beneficial nature and his supposed sacrifice for people's iniquities was the truth. He knew the real truth now that he had spent much time with Rorarum. For the remainder of the trip back to the capital he pretty much tuned out Ruth.

April 2, 999 ASR

Tsvar approached The Sovereign as he stood on the patio outside of his palace office overlooking the capital. "Greetings, my Lord," he said as he bowed.

Yehowshuwa paused a moment then turned to greet Tsvar. "Ah, Tsvar, I'm glad to see you. What brings you here?"

"You do, my friend. I haven't seen you this way before. You appear, what can I say, sad. This is not like you. Something is bothering you."

"You're right. I am sad because of what is about to happen. Come and see what I see."

The Sovereign opened Tsvar's mind so that he could see the space ship nearing the solar system. He saw five crewmembers sitting in the middle of the bridge on an intricately woven pentagram. Surrounding each of the crewmembers was an aura of light pulsating in rhythm with the person's breathing. Each aura touched the one beside it. Sparkles of light flickered in and around each figure.

Tsvar gasped at the vision, "This must mean that they are now firmly under The Chancellor's control."

"Yes, that's true. They have made their decisions, but unlike those who took Ben-Shaachar's mark during the Great Time of Trouble, they still have a chance to turn back. However, it's very disappointing that they had the truth with them for most of their lives and they rejected it and gave themselves over to The Chancellor's lies. Within four days they will arrive home."

"And then it will begin?"

"Yes."

"It is indeed a good reason to be sad."

"Yes, but this evening is the festival and that is reason to rejoice, even though it will be the last time we celebrate in this manner."

April 2, 999 ASR

When the tour ended Robert and Jim had a few minutes to freshen up before joining the rest of the guests in the hotel's banquet room for the Festival Meal. Robert insisted upon waiting until the last minute before leaving their room. They entered the huge banquet room at the first door and stopped.

"There must be 500 tables in here. Where are we supposed to sit?" asked Jim as he stepped beside Robert just inside the door.

Robert quickly looked at his ECD and noted the table number. "Great, table 478, and the one here is 350. It looks like we have to go to the opposite end of the room. At least it's in the back where we can hide."

Robert walked briskly along the back of the room. The head of the room faced the west and the rays of the setting sun cast shadows from the head table which was on a raised platform in front of the windows.

They passed many low tables with people reclining around each on pillows. There were twelve places at each table, ten along one side and one on each end. Robert spotted their table and quickly sat down where his name tag appeared on the left side of the table. Jim reclined beside him.

The man seated at the end leaned over and whispered, "We are just about to begin. I already explained to the others that guests are all seated at the long edge of the table. My name is Zekaryah. My wife, Miryam, and I are from the clan of Leviy, the people of Yisra'el. We are all one family here tonight. I function as a surrogate father and teacher, and my wife is the mother of our family at this table. Oh, excuse me, the sun has set and we will begin."

As soon as the sun disappeared, The Sovereign appeared at the head table and announced, "Welcome to this feast to celebrate your redemption from slavery. As you know, the first time this meal was celebrated was when my people were still in the land of Mitsrayim. They gathered in small groups, usually one or more families. After they were free and the first temple was constructed they would gather in the courts of the temple. For the years following the destruction of the temple they again met in houses. Tonight, we are meeting in the shadow of the temple as we have for nearly a thousand years. For many kilometers around the temple people like you are gathered in larger rooms or courts as I lead you in this time of remembrance. This is not only a time for my people, but all people, to remember. This is done so that you will understand and experience the tastes of slavery and freedom so that you can teach your children. In this way all generations may know and experience freedom from slavery. Let us begin."

Miryam, at the other end of the table, stood and prepared to light two candles at the center of the table. She knelt down before each candle. She started to sing and her voice blended with the other women in the room. "Blessed are you, Oh Sovereign our King. You are ruler over all things, the planets, stars, galaxies, and the whole universe. We are blessed to have you rule over us. You have made us pure by your sacrifice. We light these candles that we might be a light to the world."

Robert scoffed inwardly at the King of the universe title. The Council of Enlightened Beings must be very patient putting up with his self-acclaimed importance.

The Sovereign spoke without sign of amplification equipment, yet Robert was able to hear him plainly, "I have earnestly desired to eat this meal with all of you. I eat it with great joy because we do it in the kingdom of my father. This meal is divided into sections and each begins by drinking from a special cup of wine. The fruit of the vine is a symbol for joy that can only be achieved in holiness. We celebrate that my father set apart and purified those he chose."

Set apart must be a euphemism for putting them under his bondage.

Zekaryah stood and poured wine into each guest's cup, then raised his own and sang, his voice blending with those singing at other tables. "Blessed are you, Oh Sovereign our King. You are ruler over all things, the planets, stars, galaxies, and the whole universe. We are blessed to have you rule over us. Thank you for giving us your joy, freedom, and all your provision."

Robert watched the words of response and instructions appear on a small screen behind his plate near the far edge of the table. In unison with the others he held up his cup and read aloud, "Blessed are you, Oh Sovereign and our King. You are ruler over all things, the planets, stars, galaxies, and the whole universe." Robert stopped and mouthed the remaining words. He couldn't voice what he didn't believe. "We are blessed to have you rule over us. You chose us to be pure. You gave us this festival for rejoicing in you and all you have done for us. This feast is a day to celebrate our freedom from the evil that lurks within us. This is a sacred gathering to remember when you rescued your people from the ancient land of Mitsrayim and when you freed us from the bondage of our own evil nature by making us your pure people. You proved that we are free when you were raised from the dead." Robert sat his cup down without drinking from it.

Pure! Ha! All he did was set rules and restrictions on us so that we can't become who we were meant to be.

Zekaryah stood, taking a cup, basin and towel and announced to his table, "We wash our hands before the meal as a symbol of purity that is not from ourselves but from The Sovereign." He poured water over one hand then the other and then dried his hands and passed the implements to Robert.

Robert awkwardly poured water from the cup over first one hand then another, dried his hands and passed everything on to Jim.

After the washing ceremony, The Sovereign spoke again, "We eat bitter herbs dipped in saltwater to understand that life is not always easy. It reminds us to thank my father, Yehhovaw, even for the troubles we face in life."

What's bitter is realizing that he has subtly enslaved us and now he wants us to thank him for it? I wonder what's next.

Next, Zekaryah dipped a piece of bitter herb he called maror in a small dish by his plate and held it up, singing the same old stuff about the galaxies but changing the last phrase, "You provide for all of our needs from the earth." Then everyone dipped their maror and ate together. The small dish contained saltwater. It was indeed bitter.

Again The Sovereign spoke as he held up three flat round disks, "These three pieces of unleavened bread, matza, that are wrapped together in a cloth are a symbol of my father, me, and our spirit, we who are triune. The middle piece will be broken in half symbolizing my death. One half will be hidden representing the time while I was dead and buried."

Zekaryah held up the bread wrapped in a cloth, removed the middle piece, and broke it in two. He placed one half in a napkin and placed it under his pillow. He then replaced the other half back in the cloth. He lifted the wrapped matza and waited while the participants read from their screens.

"This is the food that our ancestors ate in the land of Mitsrayim. It represents the hardship that they faced. Let everyone who is hungry come and eat of the bread that gives life. Let all who are in need come and celebrate for all that we have comes from you, our Sovereign."

The Sovereign explained the next section of the meal, "We now come to our instruction for the evening. This is the cup of instruction. The youngest at each table will help us get started."

Robert followed the example of Zekaryah and filled his second cup with wine.

Robert's screen went blank but Jim's had something on it. Jim read in unison with the youngest at other tables. "Why is this night different? We usually eat whatever kind of bread or vegetables we want but this night there is only unleavened bread and bitter herbs. Why do we recline at low tables instead of sitting at the table? Why do we dip herbs in saltwater?"

The Sovereign answered, "This night is different from all other nights because we celebrate when Yehhovaw physically rescued my people, Yisra'el. That night was a foreshadowing of when I rescued my people and the Gowyim from slavery to their evil desires and into freedom and from death into blessing. Listen very carefully and your questions will be answered."

Jim leaned over to Robert and asked, "What's a Gowyim?"

Robert shrugged his shoulders but Zekaryah whispered, "It means anyone who is not a descendant of Yisra'el, The Sovereign's ancestor."

"When your children ask you what this tradition means you will answer them, explaining that this is a remembrance of the sacrifice to Yehhovaw when he spared the sons of Yisra'el in the land of Mitsrayim but struck the firstborn sons of Mitsrayim. In the same way, all of Yisra'el and all Gowyim have been freed from evil because I, the firstborn son of Yehhovaw, was struck down in your place."

The response screens lit up and the hall echoed with the words the participants recited together, "We were all slaves to the king of Mitsrayim and to the king of evil, The Chancellor Ben-Shaachar, but Yehhovaw rescued our ancestors from the king of Mitsrayim with a mighty hand and outstretched arm. He rescued all of us from the king of evil when The Sovereign stretched out his arms and died in our place. Otherwise we would all be slaves to this day."

Robert was taken aback. I didn't realize that The Sovereign's festival blatantly defamed The Chancellor.

The Sovereign continued his propaganda, "Many years ago in Mitsrayim the children of Yisra'el were enslaved by the king. They were forced to make bricks from mud and straw so that the king could build cities, palaces and pyramids for himself. They were beaten by the slave drivers until they cried out to Yehhovaw for help even though they didn't yet know his name. In the same way, all people were slaves to Ben-Shaachar and the evil that lived within them. My father sent Mosheh to the king and commanded him to let my people go. When the king refused, Yehhovaw sent ten horrible plagues against the Mitsrayimites."

"Blood," read Robert as he put his fingers in his cup and dropped a drip of wine on his plate. He didn't know how to escape the instructions without drawing attention to himself.

He did the same thing as each of the remaining plagues was read.

"Frogs. Gnats. Flies. Death of livestock. Boils. Hail. Locusts. Darkness. Death of firstborn."

The Sovereign continued, "The king relented and let my people go, but soon changed his mind and pursued them until he trapped them against the sea. The people were afraid and called to Yehhovaw. My father heard and parted the water so that Yisra'el escaped on dry ground. When the king's army tried to follow the waters returned and drowned them all. Mosheh and the children of Yisra'el escaped and were free to come to this land that my father had promised to them."

Again the screens on the tables came to life. A song was displayed, titled "He Has More" and all sang:

> Yehhovaw saved Yisra'el from slavery in Mitsrayim, and gave us the law to show our evil – but He Has More.
> Yehhovaw gave us the law to show our evil, and showed the hope of freedom in the sacrifice – but He Has More.
> Yehhovaw showed us the hope of freedom in the sacrifice, and sent Yehowshuwa to teach us – but He Has More.
> Yehowshuwa came to teach us to live, and to die in our place – and He Has More.
> Yehowshuwa died in our place, and if he were not raised from the grave – Well, then, our faith would have been in vain – but He Has More.
> Yehowshuwa did rise from the grave, and promised to come again – and He Has More.
> Yehowshuwa came back again, and defeated Ben-Shaachar – and He Has More.
> Yehowshuwa defeated Ben-Shaachar, and rules over us.
> Yehowshuwa rules over us – and that is enough!

When the song ended Robert could feel his face hot with the anger that he felt. The Sovereign continued the history of the festival. "The food we eat is symbolic and the three most important elements are the lamb, the matza and the bitter herbs. The story isn't complete if the meaning hasn't been passed on."

Robert was quite ready to leave. He didn't care if the meaning was passed on or not.

Zekaryah took the bone of a lamb from his plate and held it up as The Sovereign continued, "On the night before the children of Yisra'el were to leave, my father told Mosheh to instruct them to take a pet lamb for each household and kill it at twilight. They spread some of the blood on each doorpost and on the lintel above the door of the house in which they were to eat the lamb. The blood was spread in the form of a cross to signify the means of my own death. They ate the roasted lamb but didn't break any of its bones. This was also a symbol of my death when none of my bones was broken. They did not go outside because the messenger of death was going to kill the firstborn of all who were not inside a house covered by the blood of the lamb."

Yuk, Yehhovaw is so bloody and masochistic. I can see why the Council of Enlightened Beings wants him stopped.

"They obeyed and were saved but the Mitsrayimites did not and there was not a single household where the firstborn was spared."

Zekaryah passed the bone around the table for each to see. As it was passed he explained, "Yehowshuwa our Sovereign gave us this good news to share with others. Just as the blood of the lamb protected the children of Yisra'el that night, the blood of Yehowshuwa protects us from the judgment we all deserve, for there isn't one of us who hasn't violated at least one of Yehhovaw's laws. Is there anyone here who can say they have never lied? Yehowshuwa's earthly brother stated rightly that if we have failed to keep even one of his laws then we are just as guilty as if we had broken them all."

Robert glanced at the bone and passed it quickly to Jim. Jim gazed at it until Robert nudged him to pass it on.

"When Yehowshuwa was killed on the cross, he was completely innocent. He had not broken any commandment," said Zekaryah as he moved his right hand in the shape of a cross. "He was like the innocent pet lamb that had to die to keep the firstborn of each household from dying. It wasn't enough that he died; he had to be raised from the dead to prove that he is Yehhovaw's son and that he was innocent and that his death was an acceptable sacrifice in payment for our inability to live a perfect life."

Wait until the world finds out that he didn't really die. That will shatter this farce.

"The children of Yisra'el were required to put the blood of the lamb on the door, in the form of a cross," Zekaryah again gestured with his hand forming a cross. "We are required to apply the blood of Yehowshuwa to our souls by believing that he already paid the penalty for our transgressions. We must accept his death in our place to be saved from eternal judgment. If we are depending on some other way such as trying to be good enough, which we can never do *or by trusting someone who says we can become enlightened*, then we are trusting in ourselves and not him. We must let him be The Sovereign over our lives and yield to him."

The words about enlightenment echoed in Robert's head as if he were the only one who could hear them.

Just wait and see for yourself what I will become.

Zekaryah then held up a piece of chazeret, another bitter herb, and The Sovereign spoke, "My father told them to eat the roasted lamb, the matza, and bitter herbs. Tonight we eat herbs dipped in haroseth to remind us of the bitter slavery in Mitsrayim. The dip is to remind us of the mortar used laying the bricks and the saltwater is to remind us of the many tears."

Yehowshuwa's voice echoed throughout the large hall, "Life without me is bitter and will end in eternal death. I have taught you through my servants that all have gone astray and fallen short of the perfection my father requires. Without me you have no choice but to obey the evil that is within yourself. It is only I who can set you free from this slavery."

The only evil in us is that which you manufactured to keep us in slavery. When we are all free from you then we will no longer be bitter slaves.

When The Sovereign finished, Zekaryah lifted up a piece of matza and spoke in unison with the other teachers at each table, "When the children of Yisra'el left Mitsrayim they didn't have time to let their bread rise before Yehhovaw delivered them. We eat matza to remember their hasty departure from Mitsrayim."

Yehowshuwa replied, "The matza is made without leaven. Many times I used the symbol of leaven in association with evil that lies in every heart. Only a little is required to spread throughout the whole lump of dough and only one transgression is enough to ruin a life. When my father provided a way out of Mitsrayim the children of Yisra'el didn't hesitate but left quickly. I provided the way for everyone to remove that leaven of evil from their hearts and their lives when they place their trust in me. All who make haste to accept my offer will be saved. Those who wait too long will be left behind just as any of the children of Yisra'el who waited for their bread to rise would have been left behind in slavery."

Zekaryah spoke again, "Our children asked why we recline instead of sit. It is because we are no longer slaves and in bondage but are at ease. We have been delivered by the mighty hand of Yehhovaw. We are at ease to show that we no longer work for our freedom from evil because The Sovereign has already done the work for us."

Robert read silently as everyone recited, "Oh Sovereign, our Maker, Sustainer, and Redeemer, there is no one like you and we bow before you in worship, praise, adoration. We lift your name high and exalt you with great joy. We extol your virtues and honor you above all beings for you are Yehhovaw and our Sovereign Yehowshuwa. By your mighty hand performing wonders and miracles you rescued Yisra'el. By your sacrifice on our behalf you saved us from a life in bondage to evil. Instead of sorrow you give us joy and bring us into Yehhovaw's kingdom of The Sovereign where there is light instead of darkness."

How many thousands of years have they been fed this stuff? Don't they know that they have been taken from the path of true light and kept in darkness that prevents any progress beyond the limits of this so-called sovereign?

All the teachers raised their cup of wine and sang together as before, adding, "You have redeemed us and our forefathers so that we may come together here to eat the matza and bitter herbs."

Robert downed his cup of wine quickly. He needed something to get through the rest of the program. He finished the first cup that he hadn't touched earlier. He felt the buzz almost immediately and relaxed.

Everyone else drank together, then washed their hands. Robert ignored the overworked blessing of The Sovereign that they read from their scripts.

Zekaryah held up the matza wrapped in cloth and sang something about Yehowshuwa being the bread of life. He passed the matza and tore off a piece before passing it along.

Robert ate his piece while the others proclaimed the same old blessing. They then ate the piece of matza.

Robert dipped the bitter herbs in the haroseth and held them up eye level. He was supposed to recite the blessing, "You have made us pure by the bitter suffering of Yehowshuwa. We eat in memory of his suffering." Instead, he mumbled, "Here's to your suffering at the hands of Ben-Shaachar, Yehowshuwa." He ate the herbs.

Zekaryah then passed the bottom matza around, instructing everyone to take two small pieces. He then put some bitter herbs and haroseth between the two pieces and ate the sandwich. Robert added another glass of wine as Zekaryah frowned.

Someone announced that the beginning ceremonies were completed and it was actually time to eat the rest of the meal. Once they got past the bitter herbs and propaganda, Robert thought the food wasn't all that bad. He was quite hungry and the wine was helping him ignore commentaries from Zekaryah or The Sovereign.

When everyone finished eating, The Sovereign started what Zekaryah described as the final ceremonies. He said something about children searching for the hidden bread. Zekaryah held up the piece of matza that had been broken and hidden.

Yehowshuwa then stood and spoke to them while he also held up the broken piece. Robert smiled as he vaguely realized The Sovereign's speech was slurred, "Thish bread m body ... broken for you. ... was hidden, I dead three days. ... found ... is displayed, I ... resurrected ... showed myself to over five hundred people. ... proof that I am who I ... believes ... live forever ... you ... have new body. Take of the bread and eat. Remember ..." He broke a piece and handed the matza to the teacher closest to his platform. In turn each teacher broke and passed the matza to the next person at his table and to the teacher at the next table. Every one took a piece and ate it. When the piece came to Robert's table, it had not diminished in size. It must have been the wine.

Robert heard that it was time to pour a third cup of wine even though he had stealthily refilled his second cup and finished it.

Zekaryah sang something about thanking The Sovereign for grace, goodness, the food, and ruling over everyone with an iron rod and not utterly destroying us like he would like to do because he couldn't stand the sight of anyone who would oppose him. Anyway, that's what Robert thought of the song.

The room resounded with a loud, "Amen."

I can't wait for this to be over. His promise of eternal life pales in comparison to what we were meant to be. Has everyone here been duped? Duh, of course they have, but not for long.

The Sovereign continued with some dribble about redemption, blood of sheep, goats, and no forgiveness without shedding blood. He said something about these sacrifices had to be done over and over again because they didn't remove the guilt but covered it.

Oh boy, here comes the old blood and guts stuff again. Robert thought he was going to get sick.

His head cleared momentarily. He couldn't shut out The Sovereign, "It is my blood that gives you eternal life when you believe in me. Drink this cup with me now proclaiming your faith and trust in me for your eternal life."

Everyone raised their cup and spoke together that idiotic blessing and pledged their allegiance to The Sovereign.

Well, I for one pledge my allegiance to another, one who will be able to free me and those who haven't been mislead into your trap. Robert drained his cup with a gusto he hadn't felt before.

Even though his head was swimming, he heard The Sovereign, "My father said that Elijahu would come and announce my arrival. John did this when he came before me announcing I was the lamb of Yehhovaw who was to take away the evil of the world. Before I came back this last time Elijahu also spoke to the world as one of my two faithful witnesses. He was given great power to refute The Chancellor Ben-Shaachar and his evil deeds. Ben-Shaachar killed him but my father raised him from the dead and took him back into his spiritual realm while the world watched."

Zekaryah spoke in unison with the other teachers and Robert plugged his ears. He didn't want to hear that horrid phrase again but he couldn't block out the new ending, "In the past we drank this cup with the hope that Elijahu would come and announce Yehowshuwa's imminent arrival. It was the cup of hope. Now we drink this cup of promises fulfilled. Thank you, Yehowshuwa, for coming first to save our souls and then coming again to rule as our Sovereign."

The Sovereign raised his hands and pronounced some kind of blessing on the people gathered in the room. Robert had heard more than he wanted. As soon as it was over, Robert grabbed Jim, pulled him outside, and started back to their room. He wasn't too steady.

He noted with satisfaction that many other people were also leaving but he could hear others still singing praise to The Sovereign.

"I'm so glad that's finally over. I can't believe the garbage I heard. What a waste of time. I wonder what Kevin thought I might get out of that. What'd you think, Jim?" asked Robert as they entered their room and he flopped on the bed.

Jim lowered his eyes and looked at the floor, shuffled his feet, thought a second or two, then looked Robert in the eye as he answered, "It was very enlightening. I saw an aspect of The Sovereign that I hadn't seen before and I think I understand a lot more about the struggle we're engaged in. Didn't Kevin say something about this confirming to you what you've learned and that it would add fuel to your book?"

Robert wasn't thinking very well but he did remember something. "Hmm, that's right he did and he was right. If there was ever any doubt in my mind about the true nature of The Sovereign, it has been dispelled tonight. Before tonight I had no idea what went on during this festival and I'm sure most people don't either. I now realize that contrasting what he said to what I've learned will make a significant addition to the book. You're so smart, Jim, thanks."

Jim laughed lightly.

The wine and bitter herbs weren't mixing too well in Robert's stomach. "I don't know if I'll be able to handle going to the sacrifice tomorrow, not to mention the whole week. I think it's going to be too revolting for me."

"Aw, you'll do OK. Just remember who you serve and you'll get through it. Perhaps meditating with Rorarum will give you what you need. Me, I'm going to take a walk and clear my mind. I'll see you a bit later," said Jim.

"Good idea Jim, I'll see you later."

Jim left the room while Robert prepared to meditate. The room revolved around him and he laid back down on the bed. A second later he ran to the restroom and barely made it in time emptying his stomach in the commode.

Chapter 40

The next day Robert struggled to get up early. His head hurt. He groggily shook Jim and staggered into the bathroom. After a good hot shower, he felt better.

They barely got to their designated shuttle in time to go to the temple for the morning sacrifice. On the way the bus guide explained that they would be greeted by temple workers from the clan of Leviy. They would select ten people and provide instructions for the sacrifice. When they arrived they were near the back of the huge courtyard in front of the temple. It was not far from where the tour bus had given them the picturesque view the day before.

Robert's name was called by a different worker than Jim. He joined the others who gathered around the man.

"Welcome to the festival sacrifice. I am Salmon and will be your teacher this morning. I am here to instruct you as we go through the ceremony and answer any questions you may have. Yehhovaw long ago said there would be a day when ten people from different nations would take a child of Yisra'el by the robe and ask him to teach and lead them to the house of Yehhovaw. This prophecy is fulfilled for you this day. Without our presence to guide you in the proper way to approach the ceremony you would undoubtedly make a mistake and could very well incur Yehhovaw's wrath, which in the past has resulted in death or disease."

Oh great. If he really knew what I thought, I'd probably be killed right now.

"Before The Sovereign came, you Gowyim would not have been allowed to come any closer to the sanctuary than this first lower wall that surrounds the temple. However Yehowshuwa has made us all one family and we can all come before him. But in these ceremonies we must approach him in the proper manner with all due respect and honor."

Robert decided he should outwardly try to show the proper attitude.

"Today is the festival which celebrates The Sovereign's provision. If you were involved in agricultural pursuits you would come today with some of your first crops and first born animals. Since few have any crops or animals of your own, animals are provided here. The animal sacrifice must be a year old lamb without defect. This lamb will represent the first of your labors. In a few minutes we will go to the south side of the temple where the sacrificial livestock are held and you will select a lamb. You will take this lamb to the priests along with a grain offering and a drink offering. Are there any questions?"

Robert raised his hand and when Salmon nodded he asked, "What exactly is going to happen to this lamb that we select and turn over to the priest?"

"The lamb will be killed by the priests and some of the blood will be sprinkled on the altar. A portion of the lamb will be burned and part of it will be cooked and

eaten by the priests. In the past this all belonged to them, however today you will
be more involved with the sacrifice since you are also considered a priest. You will
be joining the priests eating their portion," explained Salmon. "This is a festival
and all that isn't burned is to be eaten with joy. There are many priests so you will
be spending the day with them feasting and giving thanks to Yehowshuwa for his
provision. It is a celebration and time of great joy."

*That is just plain disgusting. I certainly enjoy eating meat but why do they waste
any by burning it? And the only reason they do it is to worship The Sovereign? It
doesn't make sense to me.*

Robert's expression must have given him away. Salmon said, "Robert, if it
helps, think about it as a huge outdoor bar-b-queue with friends and family."

It was all Robert could do to pick out a lamb. He quickly pointed to the first one
he saw and the attendant grabbed it under the chin with one hand and the other on
its backend to maneuver it to the gate. The attendant showed Robert how to take
hold of it so he could take it the rest of the way to the priest. It unexpectedly shook
its head and Robert lost his grip on the wool under its chin. The sheep immediately
turned around and trotted back to the pen. Robert ran along behind, bent over, still
holding on to the wool on its backend. It stopped at the gate and he was able to get
his grip under the chin again. On his next attempt he got it about half way when it
suddenly stopped and wouldn't budge. Robert pulled and pushed but didn't have
enough animal skills to manage the sheep.

An attendant came over to help him. "I don't understand why this animal is
giving you so much trouble. It's acting like it doesn't want to go with you."

"Yeah, well, if I were going to get my throat slit I wouldn't want to go with me
either."

"You don't understand. These are sacrificial sheep. Before the Last Battle all
animals resisted death, but now The Sovereign has changed their nature. They are
willing to give their lives. Even at meat processing facilities animals walk in with
little or no prodding. These are especially docile and willing. It is their nature and
their desire."

The attendant had to go all the way with Robert until they arrived inside the
temple where a priest took over. Robert was revolted when the priest slit its throat
and drained its blood. He looked away. He was glad that he didn't actually have to
do any of the work. A team of priests quickly and efficiently dressed it out and
took the prescribed portions to the altar where they were consumed in the flames.
The other portions would be cooked and sent to a common area where he went to
wait.

Jim entered the pen after Robert's group and carefully looked over the sheep.
He petted a few and looked in their eyes. He wasn't sure why but he knew he
would know when he found the right one. He found a completely black sheep and
knew it was the one. He somehow felt that he could identify with this one that was
different from most of the others. He knelt down and looked at its face. "Are you
the one that will be a free will offering to The Sovereign for me?"

"Baaa."

"I think that's a yes," he said with a tear in his eye. "Come with me." He walked over to the gate and the attendant opened it for them. The sheep followed Jim up the hill. Jim passed Robert as he chased his sheep back to the pen. In the temple courtyard, Jim watched quietly as the priests did their work and then followed them to the altar. The priest handed him a portion of the meat from the front quarter and he waved it as did the priests and others who were presenting their sacrifices. He placed it on the altar, then withdrew to the back of the courtyard and watched for a while.

He watched Robert and others exit as soon as they delivered their lambs. Some followed their sacrifices as he had. Some waved a portion and others did not. Some lingered near the altar and others left quickly.

A man came up behind Jim and stood with him. "Do you understand what you have just done?"

Jim turned to look at him. He looked like so many of the other priests who were working in the temple area. He had a turban on his head and a linen robe. "I think so but this is all very new to me. My teacher explained that the lamb represented the first of my work as if it were the first of a crop or a first born animal. In this offering, I'm acknowledging that all I have comes from The Sovereign one way or another, even my ability to work and I'm thanking him for it. However, I feel as though that sheep cost me nothing. It was given to me and all I had to do was lead it up to the priests."

"Well said, my son. You have learned much. However, that lamb did cost you something. I saw the tear in your eye when you knew it was the right one. Let's go and join the others and continue in the feast," replied the priest as he put one hand on Jim's shoulder.

The two walked together to the common area and they joined Robert and the priests that were preparing the lamb and the rest of the meal. Some were still tending the cooking pots and others were bringing fresh baked bread along with a variety of vegetables and fruits that were brought as first fruits. Jim and the priest sat next to Robert at the round table. They were seated with two other people from Jim's original group of ten.

Robert looked intently at the priest as he and Jim sat down. "Don't I know you? You seem rather familiar but I can't place where I've seen you."

"Yes, we've met, but I don't think you could say that we know each other."

The priest then stood and spoke to the group, "Today we are celebrating a festival of thanksgiving. As with all our festivals we are here to enjoy ourselves in the presence of The Sovereign who reigns forever and is the one who enables us to have joy eternal. We eat, we drink, and we will dance together. The music and some of the dances also tell the stories of our past before Yehowshuwa reigned. Some are simply fun to do. This is also a time of teaching so that we all have a better understanding of how Yehowshuwa is not only The Sovereign, but also The Redeemer.

"You are all here for the first time. Last night you took part in the festival that for many ages was in anticipation of when Yehowshuwa would give himself up as a sacrifice for the evil of mankind. In addition to this festival all males were required to come to another festival in the fall which was a day of atonement. Each of you here today will also be required to take part in our modern day equivalent of that festival."

Robert rolled his eyes. *Not another festival. Isn't this one enough for Yehowshuwa?*

"In that ceremony one lamb was slain for all people. Its blood was sprinkled inside the innermost place in the temple where Yehhovaw's presence was made know to the people. However only one man, the high priest, was able to enter that area and only once a year with the blood of the sacrifice. To enter that area he had to pass through a veil that separated the innermost part of the temple from the outer area." The priest pointed to the temple's entrance.

"In addition to this annual reminder of man's shortcomings everyone who committed an infraction of the law was required to bring an offering to pay the penalty for his specific misconduct. Many of my people still follow this tradition, as do a few of you Gowyim."

Robert tried to tune out what was being said but couldn't. He tried to meditate with Rorarum but couldn't seem to connect. *I'm just too distracted.*

"This annual ceremony represented the time in the future when Yehowshuwa would die and his blood would be the sacrifice that covered all the evil done by mankind. When Yehowshuwa died the veil of the temple was torn from top to bottom showing that the separation between Yehhovaw and mankind was forever removed." The man raised his hands together above his head and pulled them apart as he spoke of the veil being torn.

"When a person brought an animal for his personal transgressions, it showed that even though the annual sacrifice covered the transgressions of all people, each individual was responsible to settle the matter personally with Yehhovaw." The priest paused and looked at Robert expectantly, "You have a question, Robert?"

"Yes, I do." *How did he know my name? I still can't remember where we met.* "Last night we were told that the blood of The Sovereign paid the price for all of mankind's wickedness and that was done once for all. Now you say that there needs to be this modern day sacrifice. Why are these sacrifices still being done if The Sovereign already paid the price?"

"That is a very good question, Robert. In fact, many people have asked it. In the past these sacrifices looked forward to the time when the perfect sacrifice, Yehowshuwa, was to come. So now these sacrifices look back in commemoration of that one perfect sacrifice. Instead of a solemn ceremony, it is another time of rejoicing. It is a time when we come together as one people to give honor to Yehowshuwa. In the same way, individuals bring sacrifices for their own transgressions not because they obtain forgiveness by the sacrifice, but in recognition that they have already received forgiveness based on the great price that Yehowshuwa paid and that they appropriated when they began a personal relationship with him."

"Since The Sovereign reigns with tight control and prevents his law from being transgressed, why are people doing this?" challenged Robert.

"When Yehowshuwa came the first time, did he not say that what you thought as well as what you did count as transgressions? You may have seen The Sovereign's agents preventing physical action that would have resulted in evil, but I don't think you've ever seen them stopping a person from having their own private thoughts, have you?"

"No, I haven't."

That means that right here in the heart of The Sovereign's capital and in front of his temple he can't do a thing about what I think about him. I am protected. That proves there is no way he's going to be able to stop us.

"So even though Yehowshuwa has control over the outward functioning of society to enforce law and order without exception, each of you has your own free will to submit to him or not. Submission comes from within and is not just outward conformity."

I believe he just confirmed that we don't have to submit to Yehowshuwa and we can get away with it!

"Before I leave you I want to let you know that in this temple, there is no veil. You were told that you are all priests if you have accepted Yehowshuwa's payment for the penalty of your transgressions and have submitted yourselves to him. That means you can go into the innermost part of the temple into the very presence of Yehowshuwa who is the radiance of Yehhovaw's glory and his exact representation. He desires to have a personal audience with you and to be your friend as well as your Sovereign. When you know The Sovereign you will also come to know his father, Yehhovaw. They both want you to get to know them." At that, the priest disappeared.

"Who was that? He wasn't one of the regular priests. Was he an Enforcer or Messenger?" asked Robert. *Why couldn't I detect him?*

"If you don't remember where you met him before I don't think I can tell you who it was," replied Jim.

The others at the table just looked at Robert with blank faces as if he were speaking a foreign language. They turned back to their meal and conversations with each other.

Robert leaned over and whispered to Jim, "I think we've met our obligations here. Let's get back to the hotel and get out of here. This whole place gives me the creeps and I can't wait to get back and see how Krebs is doing at reading that disk."

"Do you mind if I do a little sightseeing first? There are a couple of places I'd like to see and I want to check out the beaches down by the Living Sea. I know how anxious you are to get going on the book but Krebs said it would take a week or so to read the disk and I have a huge backlog of references waiting for your perusal. Unless you've got something more to work on, I'd like to take another day or so."

"Suit yourself," said Robert disgustedly. "Personally I don't want to be this close to the Administration's headquarters. Just be careful because I won't be around to protect your conversation. It would probably be best if you didn't discuss your occupation with anyone."

"Gottcha. I'll be careful," said Jim.

When the meal was finished the priests got up and started to demonstrate a dance. They went through the steps twice then invited everyone else to get up and join them. Robert took this opportunity to leave and go back to the hotel.

Jim stood up and a priest quickly grabbed his hand and the hand of the person on his left. Soon all were snaking around the tables doing a traditional dance. Once everyone learned the steps they started over again and the tempo increased with each verse until the novices couldn't keep up. The line disintegrated in laughter and clapping.

After several dances Jim figured that Robert was long gone so he went back out of the temple to the parking area where the busses were continually bring new festival participants. He found the location where unorganized groups were arriving and being greeted by priests. Some people continued on alone and others were accompanied by the worker that greeted them. He approached one of the priests wearing a turban and linen robe.

"Hi, I'm really new at all this and was wondering if there was someone here who could help me out." Jim was nervous.

"Greetings in the name of Our Sovereign, Yehowshuwa. My name is Helon and I think I'll be able to help you; after all, that is my job. How can I help you?" The large man's smile and tone of voice was very comforting.

"My name's Jim. Yesterday I went to the festival meal at my hotel and learned a whole lot more about The Sovereign than I'd ever known. I guess it never made sense to me before. Then today a priest, I'm sure it was The Sovereign himself, told us about the offering for our personal transgressions." Jim looked down and shuffled his feet. "He also said that we could go into the innermost part of the sanctuary and meet with him. I would like to do that, but first I think I need to bring that offering he was talking about."

"Do you understand that the personal offering for transgressions is only symbolic and you must first deal with this on a spiritual level?" asked the kindly priest as he placed one hand on Jim's shoulder.

"Well, I kind of guessed that but, like I said, this is all new to me and I need help. I don't know how to do that."

Helon nodded. "Walk with me toward the Living River and I'll go over the basics with you." As they walked and talked, Helon clarified that Jim understood everything from the evening before and this morning.

"To sum it up, we must agree with Yehhovaw about our own nature and our deserved punishment. We must also believe that Yehowshuwa has taken that punishment for us. We must have a desire to turn from our wicked ways and follow Yehowshuwa. Then he will cleanse us and we can have fellowship with him. When you do this you have accepted the free gift of eternal life that Yehowshuwa died to provide for you. Does this make sense?" asked Helon.

"Yes, but it seems like I still need to do something," replied Jim as they stopped about a hundred meters from the Living River.

"The only thing you can do is to tell Yehowshuwa you have failed to meet his perfect standard and ask for his forgiveness. Tell him you want to accept his free gift of eternal life and that you are willing for him to be your Sovereign. That means you're willing to do whatever he says. If you want, you can look over at the temple and tell him right now. He will hear you even if you were 10,000 kilometers away." Helon pointed to the temple to the west.

Jim turned to face the temple. "I don't even know how to address you, Yehowshuwa, but I guess I've got a lot to learn. Helon, here, says you can hear me and for some reason I know that you can, even though I've doubted your abilities in the past. I haven't just fallen short of your perfect standard. I've even desired to overthrow you. Forgive me for this and all the other horrible things I've wanted to do and have done. They all seem so disgusting to me now. I can't imagine why you would want to forgive me and give me eternal life but I would like to accept whatever you have for me and I'll be your servant and I won't fight you anymore. Thanks." He fell to his knees and wept as he felt a peace come over him.

Jim looked up at Helon, "I felt really dirty and like I didn't belong, but I was still drawn here. Now it's different. I feel clean and like this is where I belong."

Helon helped him stand and gave him a big hug. "Welcome to Yehowshuwa's family. We are brothers in him. I know you want to make that offering and you are ready now. But one of the things that Yehowshuwa asked us to do is to be dunked in water to demonstrate to the world that we have identified ourselves with his death and resurrection. People have been doing that for thousands of years when they come to faith and turn their lives over to him as you've done. What better place to do that than here in the Living River that flows from the temple? The living water represents his spirit that gives eternal life. When you turned your life over to him, his spirit gave you new life and is living in you."

"Really? He is living in me? That's awesome! And I know it's true. Yes, I'd like to be dunked but again, I don't know how to go about doing that." Jim felt like jumping up and down like a little kid.

"Come walk with me beside the river until it is deep enough and we'll wade out there and I'll dunk you. When you go under that water you will be identifying yourself with his death and burial for your misdeeds just as if you were dying to yourself. When you come up from the water you will be identifying yourself with his resurrection and living for him."

The two men walked about 750 meters from the source of the river to where it was flowing waist deep. As they walked down into the water a small group of people gathered on the shore and watched.

Helon turned to the people and called to them, "Come closer. Today we have a new brother in Yehowshuwa. This is Jim and he has just turned his life over to The Sovereign. In obedience to him Jim is going to be dunked." He turned to Jim. "Jim, do you believe that Yehowshuwa is Yehhovaw's son and that his death has given you eternal life?"

"Yes, I do."

"Have you pledged your allegiance to Yehowshuwa and acknowledge him as your Sovereign and Liberator?"

"Yes, I have."

"With your confession of faith, I dunk you in the name of our Father, Yehhovaw, Yehowshuwa his Son, and his spirit. You are buried just as was Yehowshuwa." Helon placed his hands on Jim's head and pushed him straight down under the water, then took him by the shoulders and lifted him up. "You are raised to walk in the new life that Yehowshuwa has given you."

Jim jumped up and splashed the water yelling, "Yes, thank you, Yehowshuwa," over and over. The crowd burst into applause. When he finally calmed down he climbed out of the river with Helon and they walked back to the temple dripping wet.

As they walked back to the temple Jim asked why they always entered or left the area by the north or south gates and not the east gate, which was closed.

"Many years before Yehowshuwa came the first time, Yehhovaw told us that this temple would be rebuilt as it is today. When he described it and the division of the land for each of our clans he also gave the seer a vision that he would come and dwell in this temple. After Yehowshuwa returned and the Last Battle was over the temple was finally rebuilt according to those plans. When the temple was dedicated, Yehhovaw's glory came and entered the temple area by the east gate. The gate was then closed and has not been reopened since, signifying that his glory will never leave."

"His glory entered the temple? What does that mean?" Jim was definitely confused.

Jim appreciated Helon's patience as he answered, "That's pretty hard to answer but you will see for yourself in a little while. His glory is a representation of his being. At different times he has given people visions of himself. When the soothsayer saw the vision he had a hard time describing what he saw. That was several thousand years ago. So people expected an other-worldly magnificent demonstration of his presence when he came through the east gate. But when it happened everyone was surprised, but also realized that they should have known better. They hadn't considered that Yehowshuwa is the exact representation of his glory so it was quite an epiphany for them when they saw The Sovereign Yehowshuwa walk through the east courtyard gate, through the inner gate, and into the temple. After he went in, smoke filled the sanctuary. No one has seen him come out."

Jim raised a hand to stop Helon and show his bewilderment. "How is that? I mean, he was at our hotel when we were having the festival meal last night. And I'm sure he was the priest that talked to us just a little while ago, though he appeared different."

"He exists because he is. Why can't he be in two or even more places at one time?" responded Helon.

"But he has a physical body that he took on when he became a man. I still don't understand. Doesn't a physical body require being at only one place at one time?"

"You need to remember that when Yehowshuwa was raised from the dead his body was changed to what we call a glorified or ascended body. It doesn't adhere to the limitations of time and space to which we're restricted. After we die these bodies that get old will be replaced and we will also receive a body like his and like the Enforcers. They can appear and disappear just as he does but they can only be in one place at one time because they are created beings. He can be at any number of places at the same time because he was never created. He has always been. He is the self-existing one."

When they arrived back at the temple, they went again to the holding pens where Jim again selected a sheep as before, except this time it was a ram. As he brought the ram, Helon explained that Jim would place his hands on it and confess his transgressions before the priests killed it.

"When you do this you will be looking back in time at the sacrifice that Yehowshuwa made of himself. This is a commemoration of that time. It reminds you that your wickedness has horrible consequences. Just as the innocent sheep will die, so innocent Yehowshuwa died. The sheep's death will be quick but his was slow and agonizing. It's a time to contemplate what your personal evil cost him. While he died for everyone it has been said that he loves you so much that if you were the only one with wickedness in your heart he would have died just for you."

Jim's emotions bounced around. He was sad that he had caused Yehowshuwa's death but also elated to know how much Yehowshuwa loved him. It was bittersweet.

"After you place the offering on the altar and it is burned, you will then go up the stairs to the entrance of the sanctuary to meet with Yehowshuwa. The offering isn't a requirement for you to visit with him. He is the one who has opened the way and many visit without bringing this offering. May Yehowshuwa give you joy as you meet with him."

"Thank you very much, Helon. You were here when I needed you." Jim and Helon embraced.

"Thank you, Jim. What a joy it is to be able to explain the good news to one with such a tender heart as yours. I've been doing this now for 452 years and Yehowshuwa has brought thousands of people just like you to me.

Jim took the ram and explained to the priests that this was an offering to cover his intentional transgressions as well as for those of which he was unaware. Jim placed his hands on the sheep's head, thought about as much of his bad behavior as he could, and confessed it. He took a long time. They prepared the animal appropriately when he finished.

Jim followed the priest and watched as he dipped his finger in a bowl of the blood and touched it to the horns of the altar, then poured the rest of the blood at the base of the altar. He then placed the fat portions on the fire. As Jim watched it looked like fire came down out of the sky and burned up his offering, but he wasn't sure because there was already a lot of flame and smoke from the many other offerings that were being made.

Jim then looked up at the main temple building and could see the doorway to the outer chamber with a rolling cloud of smoke just inside. *According to Helon, that comes from the glory of Yehowshuwa.* He took a deep breath and started up the stairs leading to the entry. When he came to the door he paused for a moment and wondered if stepping through the door into the smoke would be the last thing he ever did. As he paused several people walked past him. In fact, there was a steady stream of people walking in and coming out, yet he felt as if he were the only one standing there.

Jim glanced back to see Helon still watching as he stepped into the cloud and the outside world disappeared.

April 3, 999 ASR

Ben-Shaachar was getting tired of using emissaries to communicate with the outside world. He wanted to flex his muscles and break free now. However, he knew he must wait only a short time before he would be contacted from the outside and the final touches of his plan would fall together.

Oh Mighty One, may I interrupt your thoughts? Abathar's whinny mind pierced the darkness.

The Chancellor was actually pleased to hear from him. *Of course, my loyal servant. What do you need?*

I have the reports you requested about this year's recruitment failures.

This can't be good news. I can sense Abathar shaking in his cell. The Chancellor sighed, Go ahead, Abathar. Give it to me.

Gloria reports that they have only been able to capture two infiltrators---

What! There must be thousands of them. What is wrong with that woman? Maybe that's the problem. She's become too accustomed to her disguise and she's thinking like a human. I think I'll--- Ben-Shaachar remembered his new calmer approach and quieted down, I'll ask for the remainder of your report, Abathar, before I decide what to do with Gloria.

Thank you, Sir. Even though she has only neutralized two infiltrators, recruitment losses have dropped to 2.8%, which is only 0.7% higher than last year. Gloria reports that the new recruits have been trained to alert us quickly and the enemy agents have been scared off. In addition to that the rate of attempted conversions has decreased by 80%. It appears the enemy has lost the taste for battle. Abathar paused.

Ah, that's much better. Let Gloria know that she has again done a good job. Do you have a report on Robert?

Abathar's voice perked up, Oh, yes. Robert has found the disk we left behind and returned it to Midrib to get the data from it. His voice trailed off slightly as he added, Yehowshuwa required Robert to go to his abominable feast. Rorarum and Robert have gone to Yeruwshalayim.

You must be kidding me! What got into Rorarum that he would let Robert get anywhere near The Sovereign at this critical time? The Chancellor thought, Just when I think I can trust these flunkies one of them goes and pulls a stunt like this.

Rorarum said that it would solidify Robert's resolve as he would be able to introduce counterpoints to everything The Sovereign said. He also said that Robert would be revolted at the sacrifices and that would enhance his documentation when it is all put together.

Hmm, pondered Ben-Shaachar. We did plan on using the sacrifices as a means to sicken and turn people from The Sovereign. All I can say is that it had better work. We can't afford to lose Robert.

Abathar continued, Mararum reports that the C.B.R.S Aman's crew is still 100% possessed. They will be entering orbit around Earth in four days.

The Chancellor laughed loudly. The Chancellor Ben-Shaachar's Rescue Ship Aman. When we get out of here make sure I remember to give Ana a reward for planting that in Zophia's mind. I'm laughing so hard it makes me want to cry.

Abathar joined in the mental laughter.

Finally, Ben-Shaachar was able again to question Abathar without breaking into guffaws. *How is Berekiah doing? Is he ready?*

Yes, my Lord. Berekiah is standing by to coordinate documentation efforts.

Very good my friend. We are right on schedule. I can almost taste our freedom now. The Chancellor was very pleased.

Chapter 41

Jim waved his hands in front of his face, trying to clear away the smoke that wasn't smoke. It didn't choke him or smell like normal smoke. Instead, it smelled sweet and wonderful like a very precious perfume. He took several more steps and the smoke cleared so that he could see. He found himself alone in a room that was thirty meters high, ten meters wide and thirty meters deep. All the walls and floor were overlaid with gold which reflected the light from seven oil lamps, one on each branch of a large golden lamp stand. The flickering lamps caused the whole interior of the room to gleam and glisten in the yellow light.

On his right was a golden table with twelve long loaves of bread laid out side by side. The table was a meter long, a half meter wide and one and a half meters high.

Directly ahead of him and about twenty meters away stood a square golden altar one half meter on each side and one meter high. At each corner there was a horn curving up. Incense was burning on the altar mingling with the smoke from Yehowshuwa's glory as it ascended to the ceiling.

On either side of the golden altar were the two parts of a thick veil that would have separated the first two thirds of the room from the back third had it not been drawn back and fasten to the wall so it wouldn't close. The veil was made from finely twisted scarlet, purple and blue linen. It was woven with a pattern of Messengers worked into the fabric.

Beyond the veil and at the end of the room stood two large golden Messengers facing forward and with their wings extended from their sides. The outer wing of each touched the walls and the inner wing tips touched the other Messenger. Each was five meters high.

Beneath the wings was a throne with six steps leading up to it. On either side of the steps stood a golden lion positioned toward the throne but with its head turned toward anyone who would approach the throne. The throne was overlaid with gold and inlaid with ivory. Beside the two armrests two more lions stood parallel to the throne and facing forward.

Jims eyes were drawn to one sitting on the throne. Jim had never seen The Sovereign look like this. He was dressed in a robe that reached down to his feet and had a golden sash across his chest. His feet, though without shoes or sandals, were glowing like bronze in a furnace. His hair was like wool and white as snow and his face was like the sun shining at noon. His eyes were like blazing fires. He spoke and it was like the thunder of a mighty waterfall, "Welcome, Jim."

In an instance Jim fell on his face. The awe of the scene stunned him but the one who was on the throne overpowered him. He lost strength or will to stand in his presence. He fainted.

When he opened his eyes Yehowshuwa looked like an ordinary man but was still dressed in the robe and sash. Yehowshuwa was holding him upright, then threw his arms around him with a warm embrace. Jim had never felt this safe and truly at home. Even the warmth and tie to family that he had felt with Josu didn't compare to this. He now knew what love was.

"My Sovereign, I have plotted against you and I don't deserve to be welcomed like this."

"You're right Jim, you don't deserve to be forgiven but I've paid the price for all your wrongs, large or small. The best part is that I will not remember them. Your adoption by my father was registered before I created the earth, but it was not competed until the moment you called to me outside the temple. You have become my brother. That is called grace, which has been lavished on you by my father, Yehhovaw," said Yehowshuwa with tears of joy in his eyes. "So let's look to the future and not dwell on the past. I know that you have a lot on your mind. Why don't you tell me about it?"

"Yes, I do. But I'm not sure where to start. I want to thank you for accepting me and forgiving me. I hate to think about where I was headed, but now I have hope instead of fear." Jim looked around inside the temple. "But I think I need to get oriented a bit first. When I walked in here there were many other people coming in at the same time and many were walking out,. Where am I and where are they?"

Yehowshuwa laughed a warm, cheerful, and loud laugh. "You'd be surprised how many first time visitors want to know the same thing. It's simple and yet it's not. That smoke at the door you walked through is a gateway between the physical realm of Earth and the spiritual realm. Whenever Yehhovaw manifests himself on Earth, a portal is open and the only thing that your senses can comprehend is the swirling cloud or smoke as you see it. Since I am the exact representation of his being, because he is in me and I am in him, then this smoke is present with me when I want to manifest myself this way. As I visit different locations around the world, I'm not usually accompanied by the smoke, such as last night at the Festival Meal." He led Jim over to the steps to the throne where they sat down to talk.

"You are more -- this is -- more awesome than I can imagine. So, I'm like in the spiritual realm right now?"

"Yes, in fact, you are in the true sanctuary that is not on the physical but the spiritual earth. The one you saw outside is only a copy of this one. As far as the other people are concerned, they are all meeting with me in groups or individually as they have need. At this very moment in time, which doesn't really exist here but does if you were watching the door of the temple from outside, I am meeting with hundreds of people. I am also conducting business and governing the affairs of the earth. I am listening to and acting on all the petitions of people who are calling on my name in every part of the world. I am meeting, talking to, and having fun with those whom you call Enforcers, the ones who have been transformed and have bodies like mine. I am communing and feasting with those who know me and have died but have not yet received transformed bodies. I have no limitations and neither does this temple. Outside of these walls is a realm that you can't begin to imagine. Everything that you have seen on Earth is only a shadow and dim representation of what is here and waiting for you to enjoy someday in the future."

Jim blinked, trying to absorb all he heard. "Wow! Then I'll bet you know people's thoughts even when they aren't with you." Jim paused, "That means Robert can't really block your ability to know his thoughts or what we've been talking about."

Again Yehowshuwa laughed. "I knew that was on your mind. As a matter of fact, I even know what you are going to say before you say it."

Jim looked Yehowshuwa in the eye and answered, "I believe that there isn't any power great enough to prevent you from knowing anything."

The Sovereign nodded with a smile, "You are quite right, my son, but the answer to your next question is no. I don't want you to tell Robert what you know at this time. He is deeply involved with the underground and he isn't at a point where he will be receptive. I will let you know the right time if you are the one to tell him. In the meantime, you can tell your other friends, Samantha and Kevin, everything that happened to you here and what you learned.

"However, I want you to stay with Robert and assist him. Don't worry about the outcome of the book. Everything is under my control, whether it looks like it or not."

Jim wiped away imaginary sweat from his forehead, "Whew, that takes a load off my mind. But I'm concerned about Robert and don't really understand what's going on. When we went for training with Samyaza he met this Rorarum guy. Just who is he?"

"Samyaza is a low level Messenger in The Chancellor's army of evil spiritual beings that I created and rebelled against me before I created Earth. I know you thought he was a human because he disguised himself to appear that way. Rorarum is one of The Chancellor's higher level lieutenants. He and the other four names that Samyaza used in the chant are all at the same level in his hierarchy."

Jim scratched his head. "Why do they think you can't tell what's going on?"

"That's because I'm about to release The Chancellor from his prison. Of course, he thinks that he has somehow gained some power that he didn't have before and has taught his demonic forces to hide themselves from me. As they do that they are then able to pass by the guards of their dungeon and escape. They have started a program of deception that is being spread by the underground. At the proper time he also will escape and rally mankind to fight against me."

"So you are tricking him?" asked Jim.

"No, I'm not tricking him. His powers were always restricted, even from the day I created him. I removed some of those restrictions so that he now has some ability to hide himself from his brothers who remained loyal to me, the ones you call Messengers. He wants to believe that he is also capable of hiding things from me. I am simply letting him believe what he wants. This is part of free will. The same applies for Robert and has applied to many people, especially before and during the Great Time of Trouble. People gather those around them that will tell them what they want to hear to suit their own desires. The same thing can be said of The Chancellor along with all his cohorts. When he gets something in his mind and it seems right to him, regardless of the fact that he should know better, he believes it. If it were not so he would never think he could become the same or better than my father or me."

Jim stood and paced as he digested what he heard. He stopped and summarized, "So he wants to surpass you so badly that he believes he can. His rebellion is so fixed in his mind that he won't change and you let him believe what he wants because that's the way free will works."

"That's a pretty good summary Jim. You're a quick learner. What else would you like to know?" The Sovereign stood and joined Jim.

"What about Josu and my people? Is there any hope for them?"

"There is always hope. However, for the most part they will follow The Chancellor, as will most of the rest of mankind. As you have opportunity you can share with them but doing this and staying in the underground will be very dangerous for you. Right now you aren't ready. Therefore you will spend the next forty days here with me in an intensive study program."

Jim stared at Yehowshuwa. "Did I hear you right? You want me to stay here with you for forty days? How can I do that? It's not that I don't want to, but I don't know how that can happen. I mean, I don't even see a john."

The Sovereign laughed again. "Good old practical Jim. You have a lot to learn about what I can and can't do. I took care of Mosheh for forty days and nights on top of a mountain. I'm sure you won't be any problem for me. And don't worry about anyone else wondering where you are. Everything will be taken care of. What do you say?"

"How could I say no? You are my Sovereign and I want to do whatever you want me to do." Jim bowed his head before Yehowshuwa.

"Good, then we can get started. The first thing is to get you up to speed with what I've already told people and had them write down thousands of years ago. This will take the biggest part of your time here. Look here and you will be able to read it for your self. I've scheduled specific passages and after you finish each we will discuss it. We will start with the creation of all things. This is the way it happened. Pay careful attention."

The Sovereign pointed to the swirling clouds at the entrance to the tabernacle and a large scroll the size of the doorway appeared. Jim began to read the brief yet detailed account of how The Sovereign created everything, specifically how he established life on Earth. As Jim read, the scroll would unwind or rewind when he looked back up. When he finished the prescribed section, the scroll disappeared and was replaced by what appeared to be a three dimensional projection. He saw Earth appear along with the sun, moon and stars. He watched as the waters were separated and land appeared followed by plants, animals, and finally the first two people. He could see the rotation of the earth and the clear and unmistakable verification that all of creation was completed in six days.

The projection faded and was replaced by the scroll again. This time the scroll contained poetic prophecy and praise set to music. As he read the music played with lyre, harp, tambourines, and other various instruments. Somehow Jim was able to read at the right speed without previous knowledge of the tunes or the scriptures.

At the end of the selected songs, a selection of words of wisdom appeared, followed by a reading depicting the life of Yehowshuwa during his first appearance on Earth. When the history of Yehowshuwa was finished a projection of the events along with sound was played similar to the first one depicting creation.

"Do you have any questions about what you've read or seen?" asked Yehowshuwa.

Jim had questions and Yehowshuwa answered each one. Jim and The Sovereign discussed the section and then started the next section. As the day progressed, the same scenario of reading, viewing, and dialogue occurred. After a few days the only change occurred when the historical writing about Yehowshuwa and his followers ended and letters of instruction were started. With these the visions ceased until the eleventh day when the prophecies of the Great Time of Trouble, the Last Battle, and beyond were introduced. At this time the visions returned.

During the eleven days Jim took no breaks but continued from one session to another. He wasn't fully aware of time passing as he was completely absorbed in what he was learning. When he finished the last section he started over again. This time Yehowshuwa asked him questions at the end of each lesson. He taught Jim how to apply each lesson to his own life.

Yehowshuwa set up role playing situations to teach Jim. Once, he was a family member eating at a picnic. The interior of the temple disappeared and Jim was sitting on the ground in a grassy meadow surrounded by beautiful trees with a canopy of bright blue sky. A rain cloud came and completely drenched the family and him. He had no way to tell if the scene was real or a vision. His emotions were completely engaged, as well as his physical senses. The Sovereign explained that he had transported him outside the temple to interact with the people in the spiritual realm beyond Earth.

As The Sovereign tested Jim and they went over his writing, Jim found himself being transformed. First, he found the truth. Second, he found how that truth applied to real situations in his life. Third, he practiced applying those truths during the role plays.

"Jim, after forty days of study it is time for you to return. You are as prepared as you can be without having known me all your life. You may feel that you are completely prepared but you aren't. However, by relying on my spirit living in you and not on your own strength you will be able to persevere. Don't forget that I'll always be with you and that I love you."

"Thank you, my Sovereign, for the privilege of learning directly from you. I understand where we are in history and I know I'll be back here soon, one way or another. I love you too."

Yehowshuwa and Jim embraced, then Jim turned and walked through the smoke and back into the bright sunlight outside the temple. At the bottom of the stairs Helon stood looking up at him. He waited with a quizzical look on his face as Jim came down the steps.

"Well that was a might short stay. Why did you turn around so quickly?" asked Helon.

Jim looked at his ECD and noted that the date hadn't changed or the time since he entered the temple. He gave Helon a hug. "Thank you for introducing me to Yehowshuwa. I've just spent the best forty days of my life with him. What was it? Only about ten seconds from your perspective?"

"Praise to Yehowshuwa! It wasn't more that two seconds from the time you disappeared to the time you came out. Hardly enough time to turn around. Are you allowed to tell me what happened?"

"I've been to spiritual boot camp." Jim explained to Helon about his training as they walked across the court and out the opposite side from where they entered.

"This is amazing. I don't think I've ever heard of anything like this before, but it's been a while since I watched anyone new going into the temple. What are your plans now?" asked Helon.

"I'm going back to the university to talk to some friends of mine that are as entangled in rebellion as I was. Then I'll carry on with the work I've been assigned. It's the same as before I came here, only I'm working for a different person now. Before it was for The Chancellor and now it's for The Sovereign."

Jim went back to the hotel and found Robert taking a nap. His entrance woke him.

"What are you doing back here? I thought you were going sight seeing in this god-forsaken country," asked Robert as he rubbed his eyes.

"I saw what I needed to see and it didn't take as long as I thought so I decided to head home. Somehow the beaches on the Living Sea aren't as attractive without surf to ride. What about you? I thought you'd be long gone by now." Jim sat down in a plush chair.

"I went to the regional transit center and the place was so crowded that I could barely make my way in the door. There were lines backed up all over the place and an attendant said it would probably take two to three hours before I could get out. I thought I'd come back, take a nap then go back tonight. He said outgoing convys wouldn't be a problem then."

"Great, then it sounds like we'll be able to go back together. Let's go and get something to eat. I feel like I haven't eaten for forty days."

"You're always hungry Jim. There's no way you would last forty day without eating. I'm with you, let's go."

At dinner Jim eventually asked Robert, "What would you say if I found out that The Sovereign was somehow able to overhear our conversations and know our thoughts in spite of your training?"

"Excuse me? Did you say you found out that The Sovereign can penetrate my shield?" Robert stopped in the middle of a bite of a steak.

"No, I was speaking hypothetically. I was just wondering what you would say or do if I did find out that everything we've been planning was known to The Sovereign." Jim studied Robert's face for his reaction.

"Well, that's the stupidest thing I've ever heard of. I know for sure that he can't hear what we're talking about. And I'd wonder who was filling you with that kind of junk." Robert continued eating.

"That's kind of what I thought. I just wanted to make sure you were still in control. You know, being here in Yeruwshalayim and being in such close in proximity to The Sovereign, I thought maybe it might affect your ability or something. You're sure we're OK?" Jim looked directly at Robert's face.

Robert put his fork down and sat back in his chair. "You know, sometimes I think you are absolutely paranoid. Yes, Jim, I'm in control and can tell even now that he can't hear us. Satisfied?"

"Yeah, thanks. I appreciate your confidence." Jim smiled and cut a portion of mutton chop.

Jim and Robert finished dinner, then returned to their hotel room and packed up. They arrived at the transit center at 11:30 PM and were able to make a connection within a few minutes. They would arrive back at Midrib late Sunday afternoon.

Robert had received a message from Dr. Jonathan Krebs that they he would have the data from the disk available Tuesday morning so he gave Jim Monday off to relax. Jim was very thankful. He was exhausted.

April 4, 999 ASR

As soon as Jim got back to his dorm he contacted Kevin and Samantha with a conference call. He first called Samantha.

"Hey Jim, what's up?"

"I have something I'd like you and Kevin to know. I'd like to conference him in with us if it's OK with you."

"Sure, go ahead."

When Kevin answered Jim could see both Samantha and Kevin on his ECD. "Hi guys, what's happening? I didn't expect you to call us from Yeruwshalayim."

"Yeah, it turns out that the first festival meal and the sacrificial ceremony the next morning were required. After that it was voluntary if we wanted to stay longer. Robert couldn't wait to get back here so I'm actually back on campus. I found out some really important stuff and want to let you in on it. Can we meet together in a few minutes or later tonight?"

"I'm free. Do you want to meet over at the student union?" asked Samantha.

"Uh, no, I really don't want us to be seen or overheard for this conversation."

"Why don't you come over to my dorm? It's still early and it would be OK," offered Samantha.

"That would work for me, too," added Kevin.

"Okey doekey. I'll see you in fifteen minutes. Bye." Jim disconnected.

When Jim arrived at Samantha's dorm room, the door was open and Kevin was already seated on the couch across from Samantha. "Come on in," said Samantha as he stuck his head in the door.

Jim sat down beside Kevin, who made the first comment, "I assume since you didn't want anyone to see us that you haven't gone any further in training, like Robert."

Jim rolled his eyes. "You can say that again. But I didn't want Robert to accidentally happen along during this conversation either. You see, I'm concerned about his ability to hide conversations and such. How would it affect your involvement with the underground if I told you that while I was in Yeruwshalayim I discovered that The Sovereign has monitored every single conversation we've had, even while Robert was protecting us?" Jim made little quote marks in the air when he said, "protecting."

Kevin and Samantha looked at each other with wide eyes. Jim was sure he rattled them. After a long pause Kevin began, "What you are saying has several implications. First of course is that this protection stuff simply isn't working for Robert, and I would assume others, but they don't know it. The second is that you said every conversation has been monitored, which implies that The Sovereign hasn't lost any of his ability to know what's happening in spite of all our speculations about his limitations."

"If this is true then where else has the underground been wrong? I certainly would want to get some more facts and seriously rethink my involvement," added Samantha.

"Even before that, I'd want to know how you found out about this and why you haven't told Robert," finished Kevin.

Jim was really nervous. Kevin and Samantha could easily tell Gustav or Robert what he was about to say. *Man, this could be the end of everything for me.* "I approached Robert last night at dinner with the same question and his reaction demonstrated that he wasn't even open to the possibility that this could be true. From his viewpoint there isn't any question of his ability and the limitations of The Sovereign. Since he was so closed I thought I'd better not say anymore."

He paused and looked each of them in the eye before continuing.

"Since you seem open to questioning and finding out more about this, I'll tell you what happened." Jim swallowed hard. "While I was in Yeruwshalayim, I met The Sovereign and he told me."

Kevin and Samantha's mouths fell open at this revelation. Kevin recovered first; however, he appeared to be a bit cautious, "How do you know he wasn't just fabricating this to intimidate you?"

Jim shook his head but answered, "Because he was able to relate to me word for word conversations Robert and I had while we were protected." Jim again made the little quote marks in the air.

"OK, you certainly have my attention, but why would he suddenly tell you all this? I mean, if he knows what's going on, why hasn't he just packed us up and shipped us off to a retraining facility and quashed the whole underground? Is he giving us a second chance or what?" asked Samantha.

"Yeah, you might say he is giving us a second chance."

"Before we go too much farther why don't you tell us more about the circumstances of this meeting? I haven't heard of him just popping in on people very often," inquired Kevin.

"Let me start with what's happened over the last few months since Robert received his training. I've noticed that he's changed and it's not for the better." Jim related the incident on the way to the site of The Chancellor's old capital. "Robert almost got us killed. Even though he says he's learning about patience, he gets angry quite easily and is becoming very close-minded. These changes got me wondering if this happens to everyone who is trained.

"While we were at the dig I had a lot of time to think about things. Robert found everything to be a confirmation of what he wants to believe about The Sovereign. He isn't open to finding the truth and that isn't what he used to be like. I was finding more and more information that led me to believe The Sovereign is more honorable than I had suspected." Jim was quite somber as he related these events.

"Then we went to the festival meal. The Sovereign was there at our hotel in the banquet room with us. I couldn't believe it and thought it was a very well-done hologram. The more I watched the more certain I became that it was him. I later found out that he attends all the meals in the vicinity of the capital, all at the same time."

Jim paused again and checked Kevin and Samantha's expressions. So far so good. They are nodding and neither of them has panicked or threatened to expose me.

"When we went through the meal I was really impressed by what I heard. I've heard before what The Sovereign had done for us. Somehow that night it made sense to me like it never had before." As Jim related his story up to his dunking, his fear dissipated and he felt joyful. He stopped there to see if Kevin and Samantha were going to kick him out.

"So even before he told you about being able to listen to all our conversations, you asked him to forgive you?" asked Samantha as she leaned close.

"Yeah. And it was like a heavy weight had been lifted off me." Without any signs of negativity from them, Jim was encouraged and became excited.

Kevin grinned and asked Jim, "So you've gone over to the other side and you've spilled your guts to us. What do you expect us to do?"

Kevin's grin puzzled Jim but he answered, "Well, since we've been friends I was hoping you would reconsider your allegiance to him but you haven't heard it all yet."

Samantha became strangely stoic. She folder her arms as if to distance herself but the corners of her mouth kept twitching like she wanted to laugh.

Jim continued to explain his forty days with Yehowshuwa.

"Wait a minute. You haven't been gone forty days, only two or three. What are you talking about?" asked Samantha.

"It seemed like forty days to me except I didn't get hungry or thirsty or anything." He then explained that Helon observed it to be only a couple of seconds.

"So what do you guys think? Has what I've told you make you want to reconsider your allegiance to The Sovereign?"

Samantha and Kevin looked at each other then back to Jim and answered together, "No."

"What? Don't you understand that he knows exactly what we've been up to? Don't you understand the eternal consequences if you're on the wrong side?" asked Jim with exasperation.

"Yes," they said together.

"I don't get it. If you understand then how can you not change your allegiance?"

"Oh Jim, Yehowshuwa has been our Sovereign for years. For a long time we've been asking him to open your mind so that you would come to this decision. We're so happy that you are now a member of the family!" exclaimed Samantha as she jumped up.

Jim stood and Samantha gave him a surprisingly strong hug for a girl. Kevin waited in line, then embraced him also.

"So you've both known Yehowshuwa all the time and you've been slinking around in the underground masquerading as unrepentant rebels. Well, you certainly had me fooled." Jim clasped his hand over his mouth. "Oh my, and Robert with all of his training couldn't tell the difference either. That would be just too funny if it wasn't so sad."

"I know what you mean," said Samantha. "But what are you going to do now that you've changed sides?"

"The Sovereign make it quite clear that I'm to continue to assist Robert. Perhaps there will be a time when he is open and I'll be able to talk to him. Perhaps I can send some research information his way that will challenge him enough to rethink the direction of his book. But what have you two been up to?"

Samantha explained to Jim how the very first discussion topic had set her off and how she had talked to Kevin, who had then directed her back to her Board Elder. She filled him on how they were able to identify people who had received discussion topics.

"We've been stealing new recruits. We aren't the only ones but it is good to know that we've at least put a dent in the underground's juggernaut and have been noticed," replied Kevin. "I'm very glad that we'll be working on the same team now, even if in slightly different arenas."

"Me, too. I wonder why The Sovereign didn't tell me you guys were on the same team?"

"Maybe because he enjoys watching the thrill we get when we meet new believers and get to know them," said Samantha.

"Maybe because he was testing you to see if you'd go through with telling others about your conversion, even though it could cost you a lot," added Kevin.

"I learned that he only tells us as much as we need to know at the time, that's for sure. Well, Robert and I are going to meet with the wizard of ancient technology Tuesday morning to see if he has any data from that disk and I'm beat so I think I'll go home and crash for a day. Except for Yehowshuwa being with me, I was wondering if I was going to be all alone. Sure is good to know we're together in this."

April 5, 999 ASR

Marilyn and Justin were relaxing at home in the evening. She believed that their relationship was improving despite the setback when Robert disappeared. They were both reading when Marilyn's ECD spoke, "Robert is calling."

"Connect him to the home screen," she told her ECD.

Immediately Robert's smiling but pale face showed on the screen in their living room.

"Hi Mom, Dad. I'm back!"

"Yes, we know you've been back for a week and haven't even called until now," replied Mom. "What do you have to say for yourself?"

Robert started to roll his eyes then stopped. He must have realized that he was making a video call and not just audio. "Sorry, Mom, but give me a break. I've been really busy since I got back. The Sovereign made us go to the festival in the capital and I am absolutely beat."

Despite his pale face, he certainly doesn't look tired, but I can certainly sympathize with him having to go to the festival. "Oh, I'm sorry dear, you do look quite pale. Are you OK?" Marilyn's motherly instincts kicked in even if he did look well.

"Yeah, I'm doing OK. I'm so pale because Jim and I have been underground exploring the caves of a buried city. We've had very little sunlight for the last few months. I must look like a ghost to you."

"Well, your father and I are glad you finally called. You know we tried to contact you all during your mysterious dig, but we were always getting a disconnected message and we couldn't get much out of the Administration except that you were on their business."

Robert scowled, "You didn't get my automatic reply message while I was gone?" he asked.

"No, the first five days we got your message, then suddenly a disconnect message came back," replied Marilyn.

"Hmm, maybe when we went underground the ECD wouldn't connect anymore," said Robert thoughtfully. "So, what did the Administration say when you asked them where I was?"

Marilyn glanced at Justin. His eyebrows went up a little. He must have known that Robert was purposely misleading them since the disconnect occurred while he was still in Midrib.

"All they knew was that you were at the site but didn't know where and that the research you were doing was very sensitive," answered Justin. "When are you going to let us know what you found?"

So you're going to let him get away with that?

"Sorry, Dad, as they said it is sensitive and the powers that be have made it clear that I can't reveal anything until I get the OK." Robert looked relieved. *He knows he just got off the hook.* Marilyn wasn't happy but she decided not to make it an issue at this time.

"Enough of that talk for now, when are you coming home to see us?" asked Marilyn bringing up a better issue.

"Well, Mom, tomorrow morning we should get the result back from one of our finds. If it turns out to be what we expect, then I will be very busy for a while. I can't promise anything."

Marilyn set her jaw, knowing he could see her expression. "Robert, you need to come home and make up for missing the holidays and keeping us in suspense for the last few months," she demanded.

"Mom, I promise that as soon as I can get a break I'll be back. If all goes well I think you'll be proud of me and the wait will be worth it," replied Robert.

That took Marilyn off guard. She was expecting an argument and was going to dig her heels in. The one thing she wanted was for Robert to make an impact on the world that would make her proud. But she still felt that The Sovereign was keeping her son from her. "Then please keep in touch until you can come home."

"I sure will, Mom, Dad. But right now I have to go. It's been good seeing you."

"Bye, Son," said Justin.

"Bye, Robert," said Marilyn.

The screen went blank.

Justin pondered aloud, "I wonder what Robert is up to. It can't be good if he feels he needs to deceive us."

Marilyn pondered why The Sovereign wouldn't let her have details of what her son was doing. *He doesn't have any consideration for a mother.*

Chapter 42

Whack, whack, whack.
Whack, whack, whack.
"Jim, are you in there?" yelled Robert.

No answer. Whack, whack, whack. Robert hammered on Jim's dorm door again. A couple of heads popped out of nearby doors. "What's all the noise, man?"

"Just trying to wake Jim up," said Robert.

"Why don't you just open the door and try to rouse him inside and leave us with some quiet?" answered one of the dorm neighbors.

For a second Robert also wondered why he was hammering on the door. He turned the knob and walked it. Jim's bed was neatly made but there wasn't any sign of him.

"Hey, Robert, you ready to go?" called Jim as he walked in the open door.

Robert just about jumped out of his skin. "Hey, yourself. Don't scare me like that. What are you doing? Why aren't you sleeping like usual when I come over early?"

"Oh, I got up to do some reading and stuff and went outside into the garden. I'm ready to go; how about you? I've got some fresh coffee if you want to take a cup with you."

"Sounds good, but since I don't have to drag you out of bed there isn't any hurry. Time zone changes mess you up? They sure screw me up. I slept too much yesterday then couldn't sleep last night. When I did it seemed like it was only a few minutes before my alarm went off," said Robert as he went into the small kitchenette with Jim.

"Not this time. I slept like a baby last night." Jim poured coffee into two disposable cups. "When I got back I found a message on my ECD telling me that I have to move. I didn't even think about it but now that I'm not a student I can't stay on campus anymore. Do you know if there are any vacancies in your building?"

As they walked over to Dr. Krebs' office Robert had Jim call his building manager. There was a small apartment available but the manager said it was very small and no one seemed to want it. Jim snapped it up. It was still twice as large as his dorm room. The manager gave him the name of a mover. The mover promised to drop off some boxes at his dorm.

"Cool, all I've got to do is load up the boxes and the movers will take them to my new digs. This working for a living has its moments. My own place, people to help move, what a deal," said Jim.

"Just wait. If this makes you happy, you won't be able to contain yourself when we have a new government." They arrived at Dr. Krebs' office and knocked on the door.

"Come on in, Robert. I've been expecting you," called Dr. Krebs from the recesses of his office. As they entered he came from the back with a very serious look on his face.

"How's it going with the disk? What have you found?" asked Robert.

"It went well. I actually found a functional disk player in the basement. The tricky part was using its interface to download everything. Fortunately our computers were able to receive the data so I now have the whole thing on a data module. There were hundreds of thousands of file on it. It looked like it was almost the entire collection of books and newspapers from the whole world." He handed the module to Robert. "But I'm very concerned about what you have here."

"That sounds fantastic. So what's the concern?"

"The default opening video. I set it up on the module so that when you access it the same video will start. Go ahead and look at it."

Robert took out his ECD, put the data module up to it and the screen started showing a video. As the screen came to life the title "The True Story" faded in over a background of stars and swirling cosmos. Haunting, unearthly music increased in volume. Robert felt an overpowering sense of a divine presence. The title was replaced by swirling gasses and a bright light, resulting in the formation of Earth. The scene zoomed in rapidly upon Earth. He imagined that on a large screen it would have drawn him in as if he were falling from a great height. Clouds rapidly approached but became a mist which disappeared, yielding the great ocean beneath. The descent continued as the ocean came up and the scene plunged beneath without a splash. The water appeared to expand and then come under a microscope. With each passing second he looked deeper and deeper into the structure of the water, seeing molecules of dissolved minerals and chemicals.

A lightening bolt shot through the waters. Some of the minerals fused together to form a more complex structure. Several molecules joined together and the scene started to draw back. He watched jelly-like substances become cells that divided over and over again, filling the water.

Whoa! This sure dispels Dr. Ntari's version of creation. It really did happen the way the underground has supposed and Rorarum explained.

He continued to watch as small plants and animals evolved in the ocean, then invaded barren land. Trees grew and animals covered the plains and frolicked in the lush forests. Lions grazed peacefully among antelope.

People appeared without clothing and walked alongside the animals, all as tame as domesticated pets.

The scene changed to reveal a very handsome man standing in front of a large screen. The scene behind his image froze as he spoke. "Dear children, it saddens me deeply to realize that there can only be one reason you are watching this documentary. It is because I, Ben-Shaachar, failed in my efforts to restore Earth to its natural and beautiful beginning, which you have just seen. I humbly ask for your forgiveness. Yet because you are viewing this presentation, I am hopeful that, with your help, I still have one more chance to restore the true purpose of Earth and free mankind once and for all. To do this I will show you the true story of the history of your people, a history that has been hidden and repressed by one who posed as your friend. What you are about to see is shocking. It strikes at the very heart of everything you have been taught since you were born. There is no way I can completely prepare you for this, but I do ask you to keep an open mind."

Dr. Krebs interrupted, "Put that thing on hold. You know who that is on the video?"

"He said he was Ben-Shaachar, The Chancellor," said Jim.

"And what's the problem with that?" asked Robert.

"I looked through the whole video and some of the other reference material. This is the biggest fabrication I've ever heard and seen. It is pure fiction but it is being presented as the gospel truth. The other thing is there is stuff in here that is absolutely against The Sovereign's law."

"Really! Like what?" asked Jim.

"There are detailed instructions on occult practices that are intended to put a person in direct contact with The Chancellor or his rebellious forces. I don't know where you dug this up, but it appears to me that it should have stayed buried. It is obvious to me that somehow The Chancellor has some plan to get out of captivity and this was intended to play a part in it. He stashed this before the Last Battle as some kind of backup plan in case he lost. He believed that whoever found it would use it to free him. Well, it's good that you found it so we can turn it over to the Administration. I'd sure hate to have this fall into the wrong hands," explained Dr. Krebs.

"Yeah, if it's as bad as you say we'd better contact someone in the Administration that will know what to do with it. So is this the only data module or did you make another copy?" asked Robert.

"I made another copy as a backup before I looked at the first one in detail," he pointed back at his desk.

"I think I'd better take both modules and the original disk just to be safe," said Robert as he started toward the desk.

"That won't be necessary, Robert. I contacted the Administration myself just a few minutes ago and they're sending someone over to pick up all three." Dr. Krebs held up his hand to stop Robert.

"You what?" screamed Robert as he grabbed Dr. Krebs by his lab coat. "You can't turn that over without letting me finish my research on it."

Dr. Krebs shook himself free and took a couple of steps back. "What's wrong with you? Don't you realize that the only people who have the ability to really analyze that are in the Administration? Just the little I saw makes me feel like I've been wallowing in a filthy garbage pit or something. This is pure evil. Now give me that module and I'll keep it for the authorities." He put his open hand out toward Robert.

"No, you give me the other module and the disk or you'll wish you hadn't," said Robert with a menacing sneer. "And you'd better hurry."

Jim stepped between Robert and Dr. Krebs and spoke quietly to him, "Ah, Dr. Krebs, I think it would be best at this time just to give Robert the stuff. When the Administration guys arrive you can send them over to get it from Robert. It's not like he can hide it from them anyway." He turned to Robert, winked at him, and gently pushed him away. When Robert backed up Jim whispered to Dr. Krebs,

"He's been under a bit of stress lately and I think you should just humor him. The Sovereign already knows about this and knows he found the disk. It'll be OK."

Dr. Krebs squinted his eyes at Jim, causing his bushy eyebrows to merge together. He took another look at Robert who was seething near the door. "OK, but I'm going to tell them how he reacted and why I don't have everything," he said quietly as he slipped behind his desk and pulled the disk and another data module from a drawer in his desk.

Robert quickly stepped forward and snatched them from Dr. Krebs. "Come on, Jim, let's get going."

Rorarum, I trust you'll be taking care of the stupid Doctor.

Don't let it concern you, Robert. The mop-up crew is on the way.

Robert and Jim left Dr. Krebs's office and started down the hallway. As they turned the corner to the main entrance to the building they almost bumped into two men in black suits and white shirts.

"Excuse me, could you tell me where Dr. Krebs' office is located?" one asked.

Robert smiled and pointed down the hall, "Sixth door on your left."

Jim looked back at the Antiquities Auxiliary Building, wondering how long it would take for the Administration people to come after them. *I wonder how Robert will handle that.*

"That was quick thinking back there, Jim. Thanks. It was much easier than tearing the place apart looking for the disk and module. Oh, and that bit about not being able to hide it from the Administration was a real kick," said Robert.

"Yeah, no problem. So what are you going to do when the Administration shows up? Those two guys are probably following us right now."

"Those two?" laughed Robert, "they weren't from the Administration. Rorarum sent them to make sure Dr. Krebs doesn't tell the Administration about anything. I'd say that right about now, Dr. Krebs and Professor Robison are swapping stories about how they were spirited away."

"Oh." Jim's emotions plummeted. He had felt good that he prevented Robert from doing anything violent but now he felt icky about not recognizing the two men as evil, as well as being a part of Dr. Krebs' disappearance.

They arrived back at Robert's apartment where he had a larger screen and better speakers to view the data on the module. Robert put the module on the device and the starting video appeared.

"The True Story" faded in over a background of stars and swirling cosmos. Haunting unearthly music increased in volume until Robert fast forwarded to where they had been interrupted by Dr. Krebs.

Jim pondered the differences between The Chancellor's account of history and The Sovereign's. *So The Chancellor is sticking to his evolution story for the origins of man. I wonder why he just can't accept that Yehhovaw created everything from nothing and did it in six days, unless it means that he would have to admit that Yehhovaw made him too.*

The camera came back to a close up of The Chancellor's face. "In the non-physical realm there exist innumerable immortal beings."

Not only does he deny his own source of existence but he also claims that there are other beings that exist and have a council greater than Yehhovaw. Yet Yehhovaw has clearly stated that there is none like him; he doesn't know of any and he knows all.

The screen again came into view and showed angelic-like beings helping people dressed in animal skins make fires, then teaching them to read and write.

Wow, Ben-Shaachar was masquerading as a Messenger from the very beginning.

As The Chancellor continued to interpret history and the arrival of Yehowshuwa, Jim continued to evaluate the video. He was irritated particularly with Ben-Shaachar's distortion of Yehowshuwa's birth, purpose, temptation, death, and resurrection. Ben-Shaachar called Yehowshuwa a product of rape and accused him of wanting to set up his kingdom immediately.

The Chancellor's attempt to get Yehowshuwa to worship him was described as Ben-Shaachar's attempt to dissuade Yehowshuwa from trying to rule over Earth.

It's interesting that he didn't show the cross and Yehowshuwa's blood that was shed. The cross is still a sore point for him because it is the means by which we can have peace with Yehhovaw.

The video finished with The Chancellor speaking, "There is only one reason you are viewing this documentary. It is because we have lost the battle. We hid this disk and protected it in every way we knew how. Now that you have found it and are watching it, we know that The Sovereign is in power and that he has thoroughly brainwashed the entire population with his own version of history. We believe that you have been destined to carry on this battle and spread the truth to mankind. The battle for freedom and the truth will not be easily won but we are confident that you will be able to help us escape imprisonment. When our forces are freed we will be able to assist you in informing your brethren of the truth. Together we will overcome.

"We have included on this disk detailed documentation supporting the summary that you have viewed. Please review it carefully. We don't want you to be misinformed since we are now asking you to help free mankind. We can't free you alone and you will not be able to free yourselves without our help. Therefore, we also provided you the means to contact us. We trust you to make the right decision.

"May you become one with the universe and find your true enlightenment in eternal ascension with me."

The screen went blank for a moment, then was filled with an index of documents. Robert immediately started scrolling through the list.

"Whew! That was quite a powerful video. I've never heard of any of this before. What do you make of it, Robert?" *If I hadn't just read The Sovereign's account and history of the world I think I would have been sucked into believing this totally. There is something very captivating about The Chancellor and I could see in Robert's eyes that he completely believes everything Ben-Shaachar said.*

"Hmm?" Robert hesitated then looked away from the screen. "Oh, sorry, I just wanted to find the documents to contact The Chancellor. This all tracks with what

I learned from Rorarum. With these documents we'll be able to prove that The Sovereign and his dad have been setting us up for thousands of years."

"So who's going to believe this?"

"What do you mean? It's the truth. What's not to believe?" Robert was becoming agitated.

"Cool it, Robert. Stop and think for a minute. You get this disk from The Chancellor's private vault and release it to the world. Isn't The Sovereign going to say that it's all manufactured data? If what this says is true, then The Sovereign has the preponderance of the evidence on his side. You know that he has taught everyone to believe that evidence can't come from a single source. It must be corroborated by at least one other source." Jim explained calmly, hoping that Robert would listen to reason.

"Well, it does fit with everything we learned in the underground about him, doesn't it? People will recognize it for the truth when we publish it. If I can contact The Chancellor with this information won't that show that it's for real?" Robert pointed toward the screen.

"You're going to try to contact The Chancellor?" Jim couldn't believe his ears.

"Sure, why not? Isn't that what we want to do? Join forces and overthrow The Sovereign?"

"Yeah, sure, go ahead." I can't believe he wants direct contact with Ben-Shaachar.

Robert turned back to the screen and started looking through the documents. Jim interrupted him again. "Uh, excuse me, boss, let me try. I'll be able to find it faster than you with your computer skills."

Robert sat back and put his hands in the air. "Go ahead, whiz kid."

Jim took over control from his ECD and started entering some search commands, then let the ECD do the search. The screen went blank and then started filling with documents that matched Jim's search criteria. Within twenty seconds the screen stopped filling after searching through millions, if not billions, of documents.

"Take a look at the first one on the screen. According to the search criteria it has the highest probability of matching what you're looking for. The next one has a slightly lower probability and so on and so forth down the list."

Robert opened the document and started reading. "OK, how did you manage to figure out this search criteria? I mean, this is the one I'm looking for."

"Elementary, my dear Robert. How did Samyaza get you in contact with Rorarum? I looked for documents that had the pentagram, candles and chants in them. I figured that contacting The Chancellor would probably be somewhat like contacting Rorarum. I added Ben-Shaachar's name to the search also." Jim stood up. He felt too uneasy to stay seated.

"Yup. You were right. This is very similar to contacting Rorarum and I'm not going to waste any time." Robert got up and went into his bedroom. He returned quickly with his pentagram, and candles. He asked Jim, "You want to come along?"

"Thanks Robert, but you know how I seem to have a problem with that kind of stuff, like falling asleep as soon as the chanting begins. Why don't I go and get us a pizza and bring it back. You'll probably be hungry since it's getting close to lunch time anyway." Jim was already walking toward the door.

"Yeah, sure," said Robert as he became preoccupied setting up the candles. He had the mantra to contact The Chancellor on the screen.

Jim closed the door behind him. He didn't feel good at all. His stomach was churning.

April 6, 999 ASR

Robert lit the candles and closed the drapes. He sat down cross-legged in front of the pentagram placed in the middle of the floor and closed his eyes. He took a series of deep breaths and tried to calm himself. He was so anxious to do this that he took several minutes to reach the calm state required to start the process. Finally, he felt ready and started the chant. It was much more complicated than simply repeating names he used before. The words were unknown to him but had a meter and rhyme that helped him concentrate and he repeated it over and over.

Suddenly Robert was immersed in an oppressive darkness. It absorbed all sound. All he could hear was his own chanting. An eternity passed as he waited, straining to see or hear something outside of himself. He hoped that soon his eyes would adjust and he would find himself on a great plane as he had when he first contacted Rorarum.

Nothing.

He stopped chanting and the silence revealed the sound of his own pulse inside his head. He tried counting with it to see how long he had been waiting in the darkness. The longer he counted, the louder it became until it was the roar of a mighty river. He reached a thousand. *Fifteen minutes more or less.* Still there was no contact. He wasn't sure how long he was going to be able to listen to his heart pumping so loudly. It also felt like each beat was beginning to shake his whole body. *If I don't make contact in another five minutes I'm going to pull out of this.*

He counted to 350 and decided to break the trance. Nothing happened. He was still in the darkness with his pulse rate increasing. As hard as he tried, he couldn't open his eyes. He started to panic, then he thought he heard something. It was like a whisper in his mind.

Please wait.

What, what did you say?

Please wait. This time it was just a bit louder.

Slowly the darkness started to change ever so slightly. Robert waited for what seemed like another eternity but it was tolerable this time because the darkness kept turning to a lighter and lighter gray, even though he still couldn't see anything. He seemed to be in a fog under bright sunlight. He held his hand up in front of his face but couldn't see it.

I'm glad you waited, Robert.

Who are you? I can't see you. Where are you?

My name is Ben-Shaachar, The Chancellor. You can't see me because we are in my prison. The darkness and silence you experienced when you first arrived is where I've existed for nearly a thousand years. His voice was deep and strong with a musical quality that inspired immediate confidence, just as it had in the video.

How awful. It felt like I would go crazy after only a few minutes. How did you survive? asked Robert.

It is in my nature to survive and to grow stronger each day. It is in your nature, too, and that is why I came to help in the first place. As Ben-Shaachar spoke the gray mist that blinded Robert started to dissolve and he was able to perceive the end of his nose. I am working on clearing up our connection so that you can see me. With my own people I have not had a reason to give them the same visual representation of myself that I know you need.

As the mist thinned Robert was gradually able to make out the shape of a man standing about a meter away from him. His features began to sharpen and it quickly became apparent that he was facing the same ruggedly handsome man he had seen in the video a short time before.

Look around you, Robert. Ben-Shaachar waved his right hand to his right and it disappeared into the mist. This is the cell I've been held in for nearly a millennia. I know you can't see the walls because they aren't physical. I've been able to expand my abilities to remove the darkness and the veil that has enshrouded me so that you can see me.

How is it that I'm able to contact you? It seems to me that this prison would work both to keep you in and anyone else out, said Robert.

It should if it were a prefect prison. However perfect The Sovereign thinks he is, The Chancellor puffed out his chest, I've always found ways to get around his restrictions. You must have watched the opening video on the disk I left behind?

Yes, Sir, I did. At the end you said you left detailed instruction on how to contact you. My assistant found the document and I have come according to your instructions in it.

Since you saw the video you know that for thousands of years your people have contacted me and my people through prescribed procedures. The Sovereign blocked those channels when he imprisoned us. I reserved the channel you used for such a time as now. If The Sovereign were all knowing he would have seen me put it on the disk. Not too sharp for someone who thinks he is omniscient, is he?

No, but why haven't you escaped yet?

Ben-Shaachar cocked his head as his smile broadened. My, you are full of questions, aren't you? Stay with our plan and you will someday be the one to answer questions. I am able to communicate with my troops here and through them to ones who have escaped. However, if I were to take the same route out that they did, I would be detected. My personal energies are much greater than any of my subordinates and can't be hidden. However, I will escape when enough of you call me through this channel and it won't matter if I am detected or not. It will be too late for The Sovereign.

Robert imagined a radiant globe lighting dark tunnels when he thought of The Chancellor trying to escape. He was eager to help in any way. *What do I need to do?*

When you return, you will need to continue to work for some time to help rally the needed number of your people so that The Sovereign can be defeated. You have the information from the disk that will provide compelling arguments to convince people that they have been duped. But this will not be enough to sway most people. As we speak, a star ship has returned from an extended exploration of the galaxy. The crew has information that will support everything I've provided on the disk. Open your mind to me as you have to Rorarum and I'll provide you the way to contact them and give you the rest of the plan.

I bow before you and open my mind to you, Ben-Shaachar. Robert closed his eyes and knelt before The Chancellor.

He heard Ben-Shaachar chuckle under his breath and felt his hand on the top of his head.

Robert opened his eyes and was back in his living room with Jim sitting on the couch watching him. The candles were cold stubs, the drapes were open, allowing pale moonlight to dimly illuminate the room.

"Welcome back to the land of the living, Robert. I was beginning to wonder if you were coming back at all. I assume you made contact?" asked Jim.

"Yes, I did. Man, am I hungry and thirsty, too. Didn't you say something about going out for a pizza before I started the incantation?" Robert glanced around still trying to adjust to his return.

"Yeah, that was fourteen hours ago. I'll go warm it up and then you can tell me what happened."

"Fourteen hours? Waiting seemed like a long time, maybe an hour at the most, but I could have sworn I talked with The Chancellor for only a few minutes. Hey, just bring it in cold. It's better that way. I gotta go to the bathroom real bad, too. I'll see you in a minute."

When Robert came back he ravenously devoured pizza. After four slices he slowed down and told Jim all that had happened.

"I've heard about that star ship. Didn't it leave about twenty five years ago?" Jim pulled out his ECD and did some quick research. "Yeah, here it is, but they aren't scheduled to return for another five years. The Chancellor says that they have already returned? I can't see anything about them returning early."

"Hmm, well, I believe him so I'll bet they're back. If they have evidence as The Chancellor says, then I imagine they're staying hidden so The Sovereign doesn't know they're here."

"I can't wait to see what they have," said Jim.

"I'm beat, but first thing in the morning I'm going to contact them. You can be back here at eight, can't you?" asked Robert as he stretched and lay down on the couch.

"No problem. I'll see you in the morning." Jim picked up a slice of cold pizza and headed out the door.

The last thing Robert remembered was the sound of the door closing.

Chapter 43

Zophia was sure that if anyone were watching they would have seen a slight shimmering of the stars as the cloaked ship entered a very high, non-geosynchronous position above Earth. She was still being careful and kept Aman on the dark side of the earth to make sure that no one could observe its shadow against the sun. After a day she still hadn't received any word from Berekiah so the officers gathered in her office to discuss their situation.

"Alex, is there any evidence that anyone knows we're here?" asked Zophia.

"No, Captain. We've been monitoring all the broadcast channels and there isn't any news anywhere that we've returned. Of course, that wouldn't tell us if The Sovereign knew or not but we'd expect Aman would be swarming with Enforcers if he did," replied Alex.

"I wonder where Berekiah is," pondered Zophia aloud.

"Maybe the battle isn't going as well as we expected and he was recaptured," chimed in Marti.

Alex responded, "I guess that could be an explanation, but I really doubt it. Don't you think our guides would let us know if something like that happened?"

Zophia shook her head. "Mararum hasn't said a word to me and for some strange reason it didn't occur to me to ask. I just assumed Berekiah would see us and come aboard like he did before. Maybe we do need to let them know we're home. I'll ask Mararum to relay a message." Zophia closed her eyes for a few seconds and suddenly Berekiah appeared in all their minds.

So, just where are you guys? We were wondering if you had fallen out of space or got captured by The Sovereign. Just before you entered The Sovereign's territory you disappeared. He looked around at the officers and grinned. Whoa, I'm in your minds, not really on Aman. You have advanced, haven't you?

You mean to say the cloaking scheme Mararum gave us kept you from seeing us? Zophia was impressed that it worked so well.

Ah, I see, you have a cloaking system from the Council of Enlightened Beings. It must be even better than The Chancellor's. Welcome home. Welcome home. We are delighted that you chose to join forces with us. On behalf of The Chancellor I'll be working directly with you to help spread the word of freedom to all mankind. I'll let The Chancellor know you have returned. Robert, the one who has unearthed The Chancellor's documentation, should be contacting me shortly. We want to bring him back here, I mean, there. If you'll send your shuttle to these coordinates and keep it cloaked we will meet you about 12:30 PM using the time at these coordinates, instructed Berekiah. Oh, I don't think that Robert and his assistant are quite ready for all the advances you've made – so maybe the crew should get dressed before they arrive.

Zophia laughed. Nudity seems so natural now that we don't think about it. I suppose we will have to revert back for a while. We'll send the shuttle, Berekiah, and we'll see you shortly, fully dressed.

April 7, 999 ASR

Jim woke early the next morning to find the boxes the movers had left in the hall. He took a look at them and groaned. He wasn't read for packing. Getting up early to meditate and study was a good idea but his body wasn't used to it. He had wasted the previous day watching Robert's trance. He was thankful that he had used the time to study about the occult so that he would be prepared to understand what Robert was doing.

He threw the boxes in his dorm room and left for his scheduled appointment at Robert's apartment. When he arrived the door was open and he walked in.

"Hey, Robert, are you ready for another trip into the nether world?"

"Hey yourself, Jim," called Robert from the kitchen. "Have you had breakfast? I'm not taking any nether world trips today. Our contact will be coming to us."

"Yeah, I grabbed some takeout on the way over. I really like those sausage and egg biscuits at that stand in the corner of your building. Sure glad they don't clog people's arteries with cholesterol like they did before The Sovereign restored our genetics," said Jim to test Robert's reaction as he walked into the small kitchen.

Robert was seated at his breakfast bar with a piece of toast spread with peanut butter. He scoffed, "Yeah, don't get me started on The Sovereign. Just wait until he's toppled and all mankind is back on the right track. Things will be even better than the way they appear to be now."

Jim wasn't surprised by Robert's spin on The Sovereign's benefits. "OK, I'm ready to meet this contact. How are you going to do it?" He leaned up against the refrigerator.

"The Chancellor showed me how to establish contact with one of his associates who has been on the outside for quite a while. He is the primary contact for the star ship. For some reason he didn't tell me his name though." Robert took another bite of his toast.

Jim was wondering why The Chancellor was sending Robert through all the rigmarole.

"Here we go." Robert put his toast down and touched his index fingers to his temples, closed his eyes, and started to mumble something that Jim couldn't distinguish. He abruptly stopped and opened his eyes and looked around. "Hmm. Where is he? I thought he'd be here by now."

"Just like that? He pops in like an Enforcer or something?" Jim turned around to survey the kitchen.

"I don't know, but that's what I was expecting." Robert frowned.

"You sure you did it right?" Jim was beginning to think that the whole thing with The Chancellor was Robert's delusion when a short pudgy guy in a faded flowery shirt suddenly appeared, sitting on the stool beside Robert. He had a cup of coffee in a takeout container.

"Sorry for taking so long, gentlemen, but I was just getting a cup of coffee downstairs and …" he shrugged his shoulders as if to say, "What else could I do?"

"Berekiah! You're my contact?" asked a very surprised Robert.

"Yes, Robert. It's good to see you again."

"You already know this guy?" asked Jim.

"Jim, meet Berekiah. I never mentioned this to you before but he appeared to me during my Board review for employment. He encouraged me and gave me some directions that have helped direct my path since then."

"Good to meet you, Jim." He stood and reached out a hand to Jim.

"Glad to meet you, too." Jim shook his hand. He wasn't really glad to meet any of The Chancellor's henchmen. *So these guys have been manipulating Robert since last summer, if not longer.*

"Well, Robert, it appears that you have been quite successful. If you hadn't reached the goal of getting the disk with its data and then getting in contact with the boss, we wouldn't be sitting here together." Berekiah sat back down.

"Wait a minute. You knew about the disk? If you knew about it, why didn't you just tell Robert where it was instead of letting us traipse all through those caverns for months?" asked Jim.

"Jim, Jim," Berekiah spread his hands out, "don't you understand? If we just told you where to find it, then it would look like a setup. You wouldn't believe that it was documented before the Last Battle and neither would anyone else. Speaking of which, you did make a backup copy of the data module, didn't you?"

"No, we have the backup that Dr. Krebs gave us," answered Robert.

"You might want to check that backup."

Robert went into the living room and came back with the module and the disk. He placed it on his ECD. Nothing appeared. "How did this happen?"

"The good Dr. Krebs gave you a blank and kept the backup copy for himself. But don't worry; our guys got the copy when we picked him up." Berekiah winked.

Robert quickly made a copy of the good module using the blank one that he got from Dr. Krebs. "OK, now I've got a backup copy."

"Great. Now the stakes are getting higher so we need to make sure that the original disk and the backup copy are kept safe where the Administration can't find them. Oh, and you'll never want to let your copy out of your sight. As soon as we deposit the goodies we'll take you two for a ride to talk with the crew of the star ship." Berekiah clapped his hands and stood up. "Let's get cracking."

Robert stood up while Jim picked up the disk and started for the door but Robert stopped him. "Where are you going, Jim?"

"Uh, I don't know, I thought you did."

"I don't either. Berekiah?"

"Details, details. Let's go downstairs to the coffee shop. Samyaza is supposed to meet me there and we can give the stuff to him. Since he has been keeping your underground cell secure for several years I think we can trust him to keep the data hidden until we need it. Let's see, oh, yeah. Then we have an appointment to meet the shuttle to the star ship at 12:30. We'll take a convy out to the country. Even though the shuttle will be hidden from the Administration we can't exactly drive it downtown." Berekiah raised his eyebrows and grinned. "Is that enough detail for now?"

"Suits me. I could use a cup of coffee anyway," said Jim. *This guy's cavalier attitude is really annoying.*

The three went downstairs, met Samyaza, and got a cup of coffee and some sandwiches. Soon they were on a convy heading out to the trailhead that led into a wilderness area. After they arrived at the trailhead they started up the trail.

"The shuttle should be just over that next rise. There's an open area to the right that is large enough and out of the way so that we won't be noticed," said Berekiah.

When they reached the top of the rise Jim looked to his right and saw the shuttle sitting in front of some trees.

"Where's the shuttle? I thought you said it would be just over this rise," asked Robert.

Jim was about to speak when Berekiah answered, "See those trees to the right? We're using a shield just like you had around your archeological site. We'll be able to walk right through those trees and you'll see for yourself."

Jim looked closely again and he could just barely see a shimmering of light between him and the shuttle. "Berekiah, you guys do such a great job. I'm really impressed." *Not!* He laughed.

When they approached the shuttle Berekiah reached out as if touching a tree where the air shimmered. His hand passed through the shimmer. He turned and gave them his characteristic grin as he walked through the veil. Jim wasn't impressed. Just for kicks he put his hands together back to back and stretched out his arms so that his finger tips penetrated the light. He pulled his hands to either side as if he were drawing back a curtain. He took a big step as though he were stepping over a high threshold.

The pilot greeted them as they walked up the ramp and into the shuttle. "Welcome aboard, gentlemen. My name is Irene and I'll be your pilot today. We'll be taking off in just a minute if you'll have a seat." She sat down at the control console and started making some adjustments as they took their seats.

"Is Irene one of your people?" asked Robert quietly.

"No, she's one of yours, a member of the star ship crew," answered Berekiah. "Why? Are you interested in her? She is a good-looking lady."

"Since I couldn't see through this cloak with my mind like I could at the archeological site, I was wondering who was providing the shield for the shuttle."

Berekiah grinned widely, "Irene is doing that. You will find out when we get to Aman that the crew has been liberated from many of The Sovereign's restrictions. The crew has been trained more extensively than even our people."

"Really! I had no idea we were capable of advancing this far in such a short time," exclaimed Robert.

"The crew has had a lot of time to be trained and to meditate on their trip home. That and the fact they've been outside of The Sovereign's area of influence gave them a head start on their way to enlightenment," replied Berekiah as he sat down behind Irene.

The shuttle vibrated slightly as it started to ascend. It was the only indication Jim had that they were leaving. Jim sat beside Irene and watched her push full throttle. The speedometer registered maximum atmospheric speed in less than ten seconds. The view panel quickly went dark and stars appeared. He could tell that Irene had nosed the ship straight up, then leveled off when they exited the atmosphere. The guidance system registered a trip of 6,000 kilometers in less than ten minutes. She slowed abruptly and passed through what looked like a curtain of stars, then the huge star ship was visible in the view panel.

Since the view panel in the shuttle was only a representation of what the sensors could distinguish, even Jim could not see the star ship from a distance. Both he and Robert gasped at their first view of Aman when it appeared suddenly.

"Quite an impressive machine, isn't it?" said Irene.

"Yeah. Especially when it suddenly appears like that. I looked at some of the pictures Jim found last night but they just don't do it justice."

She flew the shuttle inside the open hangar door, then waited for it to close behind her. As soon as the instruments registered that the air pressure had been reestablished Irene flipped a switch, the shuttle door opened, and the ramp rolled out. "Here we are. Captain Assir will be coming through that door over there any second now."

On queue the door opened. A very tall dark lady dressed in a blue jump suit stepped through the door. Robert gasped and whispered to Jim. "She looks almost exactly like Dr. Ntari's wife. I think I'm in love."

Jim rolled his eyes. Robert was losing his grip on reality. He had never before expressed himself like this at his first meeting of a woman. *I wouldn't be surprised if that isn't Rorarum talking.*

Chapter 44

Zophia and Alex led the visitors to Aman's ready room where they sat down around the conference table.

Berekiah took charge of the meeting. "Zophia, could you briefly fill Robert and Jim in on what has happened with your adventure into space?"

Zophia proceeded to give a history of their travels, including The Sovereign's adamant insistence that there was no other life in the universe outside of Earth. "You can imagine how shocked we were when we were intercepted by beings from another planet."

Robert laughed, "Yeah! That alone blows away all his claims."

She continued, describing the attack on the H.S.S.S. Ramah by Rol-el, rescue by Tia-le, and enlightenment received on the planet Eden. Zophia explained they renamed the ship to B.S.R.S Aman because Ramah could mean deceived and Aman meant truth.

"I understand completely," said Robert, nodding his head. "When we bring out the truth, The Sovereign's deceit will be exposed and we'll be able to win our freedom."

Zophia knew at that point that Robert certainly was the right choice to disseminate their knowledge to the world. She continued to explain how closely the mission came to failure when the Aman was again attacked and she was killed, then resurrected.

She kept a close eye on Robert as she talked, pleased at his reactions – his disgust at The Sovereign's abuse of mankind, his enthusiasm when mankind's potential was explained. She was especially pleased that he let his eyes wander over every part of her body. *I can't wait to know him better.*

She glossed over Chuck's accidental death but Jim interrupted. There was something about Jim that she didn't like.

"Excuse me, but how could the safety protocols possibly be overridden on such a sophisticated ship like this?" asked Jim.

Zophia sighed, "Well, I really didn't want to go into any detail, but from what we could discern in our investigation, Chuck and the others were planning on destroying the Aman when we got back to Earth. They were simulating an escape plan but inadvertently activated the real sequence and opened the hangar bay door. I didn't want to smear his reputation since he had led us gallantly until we noticed he started distancing himself from those committed to the cause."

"You mean that after all the evidence and his commitment, he reversed himself?" Robert asked as his eyebrows shot up.

Berekiah answered, "We know that there are going to be many people who will reject the evidence, Robert. However, we are confident that nearly 90% of the population will believe your and Zophia's reports, just as 90% of the crew has fully embraced the cause."

Jim's face paled as he asked, "90% of the Earth will believe this? Wow, that's hard to imagine."

Robert ignored Jim's comment and leaned forward. "Can you show us some of the documentation you brought back? I can't wait to see it."

"Certainly, Robert," Zophia took a good long look at Robert. "If you would look at the view screen instead of me, we'll start the presentation. Hal, history overview on screen."

The title "Earth History" faded in over a background of stars and swirling cosmos. The familiar video and music still inspired her.

The presentation continued as it had before with narration and dates calculated in Eternal Time. Once Robert took his eyes off of Zophia, he sat transfixed to the screen . Jim sat back with his arms crossed and a deadpan expression. Berekiah maintained his usual ear to ear grin, clapping occasionally.

When the presentation finished Robert spoke up, "That is truly amazing. It fits perfectly with what I've learned." He explained how he was doing research for his book and how all the accounts of the Last Battle and what led up to it seemed to be a cover-up or scheme to keep The Sovereign in control. He told them how he and Jim searched the caverns and confirmed they were the ruins of The Chancellor's capital. He handed his data module to Zophia. "This is the data we found on a disk hidden in a vault and preserved for us. Would you show the starting video?"

"That shouldn't be a problem, as long as your data storage devices haven't changed too much in the last twenty five years." Zophia took the module, hesitated for a second then put it on Jim's ECD. "Hal, can you load the video from this module?"

"Yes, Zophia, I can."

Zophia closed her eyes and said through her teeth. "Show it now, Hal." Even with her best efforts to remove them, Hal still had some of the quirks David programmed.

"The True Story" faded in over a background of stars and swirling cosmos. Haunting unearthly music increased in volume as the title appeared. The scenes continued with much of the same detail as the program Zophia brought back from Eden's library. There were few differences, except for the narration by The Chancellor.

When it finished Berekiah asked, "What do you think? I'd like to hear what each of you has observed."

Zophia started, "I think they support each other without question. How could anyone doubt this documentation?"

Robert agreed, "Zophia is right. While the accounts are the same, the one I found is presented from The Chancellor's perspective. The one that you brought back is presented from an outsider's viewpoint. This provides a very strong argument for their validity."

"I'm not an historian but I'm persuaded that we have what it will take to convince others," added Alex. "We knew that without this substantiating evidence we wouldn't be able to sway enough people to be of any use."

Jim was quiet, then all eyes turned to him. "Just remember that I'm only the assistant here and no expert. The consistency between the two accounts is remarkable and can only be attributed to the fact that they are from the same source," said Jim.

"This is going so wonderfully! But Robert and Jim really need to know a bit more about the powers you developed. Zophia, would you explain how you got these abilities and give us a demonstration?" asked Berekiah.

"Certainly. When we first met with the inhabitants of Eden, they suggested we do some research in what was called the occult in old Earth history. We discovered that it had a lot to do with contacting others in the spiritual realm and that it was forbidden by Yehhovaw and The Sovereign. However we were already way out of his will and with the aid of the Edenians we found that the real reason he condemned the practice was that it was precisely these activities that put people in contact with The Chancellor and his forces. They also enable people to free themselves from The Sovereign and advance toward enlightenment. While we were on Eden we were trained in many of the occult practices. Because we were outside of The Sovereign's influence we were able to achieve skills rapidly that usually take many years to develop on Earth. Jim, would you like your ECD back now?"

"Uh, sure," answered Jim somewhat bewildered.

His ECD left its place sitting on the table beside Zophia and flew to him across the table. Jim's eyes got very large at the sight.

"We have already received the training that every person who unites with us will receive. All of us can teleport objects." Zophia raised her hand palm out and extended it toward an empty chair. A beam of energy instantly melted a ten centimeter hole through the back of the chair.

Robert and Jim quickly pushed their chairs back away from the smoldering chair. Robert turned and smiled. *He must know I have these powers, but Jim looks afraid.*

"In addition we have telepathic abilities and can contact each other and share our thoughts and visions."

Berekiah took over, "While these outward manifestations are quite impressive, you are probably wondering what practical use they have, other than protecting star ships. These are signs to prove to you and others that Zophia and the crew have powers beyond what you would expect. They signify advancement that is only the beginning of possibilities for them and for all mankind. They show that it is possible to connect with the spiritual realm beyond what The Sovereign allows and to evolve into beings that will equal or surpass him. They prove that The Sovereign has been lying and keeping the truth about your potential from you so that you would serve only him."

Robert responded, "I expect they also will be the means to overthrow The Sovereign. Hey, I'm ready to go. What's next?"

Berekiah reached over and slapped Robert on the back. "You're right! That's the attitude! The next part of the plan is to finish your documentation and get it ready for publication. Of course you will want to include what the star ship uncovered in its travels to verify your findings. While you are doing that we will issue a call to all who are in the underground to report to training camps. At the training camps the star ship's crew will work with people to develop the same abilities as they have. Selected underground members will plan the dissemination of the documentation. When the documentation is ready they will take control of Earth's communication systems. You will present your findings to the entire world. Zophia will announce the return of the star ship and expose how The Sovereign tried to prevent it from returning and revealing their findings."

Berekiah paused, looked at each in the room nodding their heads, then continued, "After the entire population has had a chance to review the information we will communicate an invitation to join with their brothers and sisters who are already committed to freeing all mankind."

Jim rather sheepishly raised his hand and Berekiah nodded to him. "Robert will testify that I'm kind of a fraidy cat but I just need to ask something."

"Go ahead; I'm sure we can alleviate your fears," said Berekiah.

"Thanks. I know that we've been able to hide a lot from The Sovereign, but when thousands of people suddenly disappear for the training camps, don't you think he'll notice that?"

Berekiah grinned and shrugged his shoulders. "Millions, not thousands, will be trained at one time. We've been operating for over seventy years now and kept everyone active even after they've left university. Over a year ago we scheduled people for training and had them request vacation times to correspond. The people who are now in position to take over the communications system will be the first trained but they will go back to their normal jobs and remain undercover so that we will be able to communicate to the rest of the world when we are ready."

"How did you know when to start training?" asked Jim.

"We have more powers that you realize, Jim. As Zophia mentioned in her summary, ascended beings have some ability to predict the future," said Berekiah as he leaned back in his chair.

"OK, but do you think Yehowshuwa will stand by after you take over the communications network and let you use it again to invite people to join the cause?" Jim shook his head.

Berekiah stroked his beard and pursed his lips as he paused. "Hmm, very perceptive of you, Jim. At that point it could possibly be all-out war. We aren't sure what the enemy will do to retaliate but we believe that he will again respond with forces of nature. With that in mind, I'd say that you are right. We may not be able to send out a second communication. I'll bring that to the attention of The Chancellor. I suspect he has already considered that possibility and will provide the details of how people can join us when the documentation is broadcast. Perhaps he even has a different plan."

"Anything else, Jim, or anyone else? Yes, Zophia?"

"When does training start? We've been aboard ship for a long time and are very eager to back to Earth and liberate our brothers and sisters."

"We must start as soon as we're finished here. We have multiple training camps set up. We'll divide the crew so that there will be one member per camp, except for the younger children. They will go along with one parent. Henry and Barbara's son, Michael, is old enough and skilled in the new ways so that he will also be a trainer."

Zophia thought for a second, "We need to leave at least two people aboard the ship to keep it cloaked until the announcements are made that it returned."

"Of course, we've planned for that." Berekiah gave the coordinates of the training camps to Zophia, then explained to Robert and Jim what they were going to do. "With our telepathic abilities, I've provided Zophia with the coordinates of the training centers. She is now having a virtual meeting with the crew and assigning them to camps. By the time I'm done explaining this to you it will be all arranged and the crew will be going to the hangar bay for deployment in five shifts. Irene will transport them on the shuttle. The first shuttle will be leaving in twenty minutes and you will take it to go back and start work on your portion of the plan. After you are ready to publish you will be taken to a training center where you will complete your training. You know how to contact me if you have any questions or run into any problems." He disappeared.

Zophia handed two data modules to Robert. "This has our ship's log since setting course for Eden and returning to Earth. You will be able to view our first encounters with the aliens, what we logged about our visit on Eden, and our return journey, including the battle. The second one has as much of the documentation from Eden's library as we could fit on it." Her fascination with Eden's technology had not ebbed. She explained how the data was captured by the Council of Enlightened Beings and recorded in the molecular structure of the crystals which made up the library building. "Since we couldn't bring back that much data with us, we downloaded a significant portion to Hal's memory. From his memory we extracted only that which corresponds with the data you found."

Robert took the modules and nodded soberly. "My job is to condense this down to something that people will be able to digest in a few hours and come away convinced that The Sovereign is not the beneficial leader he says he is. We better get moving."

"We'll take you back to the hangar bay. Your shuttle is just about ready to leave." Zophia took Robert's arm and led the way back to the hangar bay. She could sense his excitement at her touch. She saw them off along with the first crewmembers going to training camps.

After they left Zophia turned to Alex and asked, *What do you make of those two?*

They seemed like a couple of sharp and committed people to me. There is a lot riding on Robert's abilities to put this together. Why do you ask?

I was able to read Robert's thoughts and you're right about his commitment. However, I wasn't able to see anything in Jim's mind, replied Zophia.

Zophia, you know we aren't supposed to eavesdrop on another's thoughts without asking first.

I know, but I was prompted by Mararum to check them out because so much is riding on them. Robert was immediately aware of my presence and cooperated fully. He let me run around in his head wherever I wanted. I found that Jim's primary qualification as an assistant is that he is Robert's friend. Robert values his input and he has been quite helpful, especially when it comes to digging information out of computer systems. However, with Jim, I could only read random thoughts that didn't make any sense.

Alex frowned and replied, Didn't Berekiah mention something about Jim not having any training? Maybe he needs that even to let someone else in. I wouldn't be concerned. He was the one that noticed a possible flaw in the plan.

Yeah, you're right, Alex. If he weren't committed, why would he bring that up?

April 8, 999 ASR

Zophia watched the front view screen of the shuttle as Irene piloted the craft toward the surface of the earth. She was coming in very hot and the dark night side of the earth grew rapidly, filling the screen with twinkling city lights. Suddenly Irene changed course and only the rim of the earth appeared as she headed east. The brightness of the sunrise was quickly dampened by the view screen. Brightness and contrast were restored so Zophia recognized continental features on the bright crescent below. Again, the screen was abruptly filled with the earth and just as quickly billowing clouds appeared directly in front of them as the gravitational deflectors cut a path through the atmosphere for the small ship.

Zophia was glad that the internal gravitational generators kept the passengers from sensing anything more than a mild tug as Irene jerked the shuttle straight down toward the surface at full speed. The deflectors kept them from burning up as it entered the atmosphere. She slowed the shuttle as she approached the surface and pulled out of the steep dive. The forward deflectors were no longer needed as the speed dropped to 400 kilometers per hour and the mountains in front of them could be clearly seen.

Irene pulled up at what seemed to Zophia the very last second as she zoomed up and over one mountain peak and down into a narrow valley, weaving between mountains and hills. The mountains were lush with verdant green trees watered by the nightly rains and mists. All around there were abundant flowering vegetation and wild animals that paused briefly from their frolicking as the transport shot past. Without slowing, she dropped in altitude and headed straight for the side of a mountain. Zophia was pretty sure she knew what was coming but still couldn't watch as the craft plunged into the side of the mountain. It passed through the veil, exposing a high plateau that opened up before them. Inside the shield the trees were brown and parched, stream beds were littered with rocks once covered by bubbling water. There wasn't a trace of any living flora or fauna.

The shuttle approached a landing site just outside newly constructed buildings rising up from the floor of the plain. Irene wasted no time closing the distance and did a full back-thrust power landing.

Irene, why didn't you just come straight down here instead of flying over the mountains and through the valleys? And what's with all the sharp turns, dives and crazy flying? asked Zophia.

It's fun, Opparum likes it, and besides, after today I won't have the opportunity to fly much. I really don't know what's going to happen but I'm sure it'll all be very different. I might as well get as much of a kick out of it as possible. I don't even know if we'll be seeing each other again.

Can't you still communicate with everyone you've dropped off on previous trips? I can. Even though we'll be scattered over the whole planet we'll still be connected. Just think, as we add more and more people with this training, we'll be like one entity but still individuals. We will still be as close to each other as we've been the last few months and even more so as we continue to evolve.

Yeah, I guess I know that but give me a hug anyway. Zophia gave Irene a hug, said goodbye to the others, grabbed her bag, and went down the ramp where she was greeted by the blast of dry hot air from the arid plateau. A tall slim man wearing dark glasses, a black leather jacket with no shirt and tight leather pants welcomed her.

After they were a safe distance away, Zophia turned to watch the shuttle rise off the ground, then suddenly nose up and disappear. She just shook her head, then continued toward the administration building.

"We are certainly pleased to have you here to help in our training, Zophia. My name is Galva and I'm the leader of this camp. From what we understand you have developed your skills beyond that of other humans."

"If we are going to be successful, billions of humans will be where I am a few months from now. What is on the agenda for today, Galva?"

"If you don't mind, we would like you to meet with our spiritual advisors as soon as possible. I'll show you to your quarters, then we'll meet whenever you're ready."

"Good, I'll just drop my stuff off and we can get started right away. I've waited a long time to get going on this and I find that I need very little rest anymore." She stopped and wiped her brow. "I don't remember any place on Earth being this hot. It looks like this whole plateau hasn't had any rain for at least two years. Couldn't you have picked a better place for a training camp?" asked Zophia.

"When we first arrived this area was just as lush as the surrounding mountains and valleys. Not long after we raised the shields the rains stopped and haven't returned. We believe that the shields have something to do with changing the weather patterns and preventing the rain," answered Galva.

"You must be right since the parched area starts right at the edge of the shields."

They were whisked away from the landing site in an open transport. It stopped near the administration building which was close to the center of the complex. From there they walked to the nearest dormitory. The billet that Zophia was assigned was a small apartment with a bedroom, living room, kitchen, and bathroom. It was nearly three times the amount of space she'd had for the past twenty five years. She dropped her bag inside the door and took one look around. "This is more than adequate. I'm ready to meet with the advisors whenever you are."

"Good, we can meet now. The conference center is just on the other side of the administration building. I'll show you the way."

Galva explained that the conference center was a large covered stadium with five sides. It was built primarily underground with only the entrance level and the structure needed to support the roof visible above the ground. Revolving doors were spaced all around the building so that people can quickly enter and exit.

As they entered the nearest revolving door and pushed through, the opaque door effectively shut out the bright daylight so that they entered into a dimly lighted interior. The foyer extended in both directions. It was about twenty meters deep and revealed openings leading to the auditorium. Zophia stopped at the top after entering the massive auditorium. Each row was about one and a half meters wide with pillows fastened to the floor. Each row was about a meter lower than the one above it. She guessed that the building could accommodate at least one hundred thousand people at a time. Far below she could see an ornate tile pentagram on the floor. Each side had only enough room for a single person to sit in front of it. Five orange glowing bulbs were suspended in the air above the pentagram without any visible means of support. Below each bulb was a pyramid pointing upward to the globe. After her eyes adjusted to the low lighting, she could see that the walls were decorated with pyramids, octagons, and pentagrams separated by pictures of goat heads and unicorns. *Just like on Eden.*

"Are your spiritual advisors Harum, Opparum, Mararum, Rorarum, and Amorum?" asked Zophia.

"Why, yes they are. But how did you know that since we haven't told anyone?" replied Galva.

"Did you think that I wouldn't recognize the pattern of the conference center and not know the names of the founders of the Council of Enlightened Beings? Perhaps you underestimate the training we already have." Zophia was beginning to wonder if the preparations for training were really ready for her and the rest of the crew. "Shall we get on with it?"

Galva bit his lip and replied. "Yes Ma'am."

They walked down to the center and each sat down cross-legged on a pillow in the front row. Zophia concentrated on the center of the pentagram and started chanting the names of Harum, Opparum, Mararum, Rorarum, and Amorum along with Galva. In a flash they appeared, standing at the five corners of the pentagram and spoke in unison. *It's good to see you again Zophia, Galva.* Zophia hoped that it wasn't lost on Galva that they addressed her first and that they knew her. *Please alert all your crewmembers to meet in four more of your hours in the conference centers in each of the training camps. When you are assembled call upon us and we will provide you with what will be needed to start training.* They vanished.

Zophia stayed in her meditative posture. She immediately summoned everyone on the crew. Some were still on the star ship waiting to be transported to their training camps while others were on their way. A few were awakened from sleep since they had arrived at their camp in the middle of the night. It only took her a few seconds to notify each to be ready for the all-camps conference and to make sure that the camp leader was present along with the senior staff of each camp.

"It looks like we have about three hours and fifty nine minutes to kill before the big meeting. Why don't you show me around the camp?" said Zophia as she smiled with satisfaction. *I'm sure Galva knows I'm now in charge and he is nothing more than my administrative assistant.*

Galva lowered his eyes and replied, "Yes Ma'am. We have a vehicle outside that we can use to cover the entire camp in that time."

They went outside, walked back to the administration building, and got in a smaller transport. "All the complexes are built the same. The training center is the hub. We can train up to one hundred thousand people at each session. The administration building which we just left has a few offices to coordinate placement of trainees and all the logistics that goes with operating a small city. As you can see, the buildings are clustered with five larger buildings that are dorms and the smaller buildings near the center are the dining halls for each group of dorms. The training camp is laid out as one huge pentagram that radiates out from each side of the training center. The total capacity of the camp is one million."

The transport took them past the dorms on one side of the pentagram.

"We are headed to the advanced training fields at the north end of the camp. We were instructed to build it so that everyone in the camp could assemble there at one time."

As they approached the training area Zophia commented, "It looks like reviewing stands and parade grounds very similar to some I saw in Earth's earlier history. They were strictly for military use."

"I can't say exactly what will be happening here. All we were told is that it would be for advanced training. Do you know anything about the training, how long it will take or what the extent will be?" asked Galva.

"Oh, yes. Everyone on the Aman has been through the training. However, we didn't have such a large area to practice our skills. I suspect that we will both find out how long it takes when we have our meeting. Let's get something to eat before the meeting." Zophia enjoyed watching Galva squirm. *Ben-Shaachar's pawns really don't like to be under the authority of a human.*

Galva took Zophia back to her dorm cluster and they stopped at her dining hall. The dining room was huge but still not large enough to seat everyone in the dorms it served. "I can see that you will have a mammoth job on your hands when the camp is full. The logistics of getting people in and out of the training center, serving meals, and supplying everything needed is going to be quite a challenge. I'm glad you're doing that and not me," said Zophia to encourage Galva, not that she cared about him but because she needed him to do his job efficiently.

After eating they went back to the conference center where they entered into their trancelike meditation. When they started, the center suddenly appeared to be occupied with the crew from the star ship and the camp leaders. The founding members of the Council of Enlightened Beings again appeared positioned at the five sides of the pentagram facing the audience in the rows before them. It didn't matter where the people sat when they arrived; they now appeared to be evenly divided among the five enlightened beings. Zophia heard only Mararum who was standing before her.

Greetings and welcome to this conference of leaders. I, Mararum, will be your leader and focal point for the training as I was on the star ship. As you can see you have been divided into groups of five; however, the training for each group will be the same. In the next twenty four hours the first trainees will arrive at your camp. By the end of the day there will be one hundred thousand people in each camp and you will instruct them to assemble in this center for their first training session. Training will then start for the first group. This training will take eighteen hours. Each of us will channel our energies through Aman's crewmembers because at this time you are the only ones that we can work through.

When the first session is finished they will have guides, just as we guide you. Their new guides will complete their training. When their guides take over you will be free to supervise advanced outdoor training. Each day you will start the training for the next group. This will continue for the next ninety days without interruption. You will be working hard but it will all be worth it.

The day after each group receives its initial training in the center, they will report to the parade grounds north of the camp for nine more days. After their tenth day they will return to their homes and continue to function in their roles within society until we summon them.

Zophia felt the excitement in the room as everyone realized that within ninety days nearly 450 million people would have the same powers as she possessed.

Camp leaders, you can see from this schedule that after ten days the camps will be full and maintain a population of one million people until the training cycle has completed. Every person who has stayed true to the underground will have been trained by this time. You will be very busy making sure that everyone's physical needs are met during this time.

Once training is completed we will release the true story about The Sovereign's enslavement of the human race. Everyone on Earth will be given directions to a local training site along with the name of a person who has completed this training. They will be asked to join this person if they want to learn how to become free and find their own eternal destiny.

The following day we will work through each graduate to train the rest of mankind who is willing to join forces with us. Ten days later we will have finished the training and will join forces to fight in the very last battle. Are there any questions?

The room erupted into cheers and applause. Zophia stood clapping loudly. Tears of joy came to her eyes, knowing that the end was almost at hand.

Chapter 45

Zophia spent the next day talking with Mararum for encouragement, then she contacted each of the other crewmembers to encourage them. Finally, she spent some time meditating to prepare herself for the first session.

When the time arrived, she stripped, then donned her long brown hooded training robe. She left her apartment and walked to the conference center, through the revolving doors and down the aisle to the center of the pentagram. She looked from side to side as she walked down the aisle and saw row after row of trainees each dressed in the ceremonial robe and hood that was provided for them. In her mind she could also see Alex, Marti, Buckly, and all the other crewmembers walking to the center of the pentagram at 42 other sites around the world. Their minds were joined.

Each crewmember spoke in unison with Zophia, "You have all received instructions ahead of time about this training. Some of you have already received some training to protect your thoughts and conversation so this isn't new to you. However, many of you have not had any training so you will need to follow the instructions precisely. You will find this will be much more intense than any previous training you received. We will be here eighteen hours today with very few breaks. You will find that you will not need breaks as you gain power within yourselves. Since time is of the essence we are going to start immediately."

Zophia raised her hands above her head. A pillar of fire rose from her hands and ascended to the ceiling of the auditorium. The roar from the flames echoed in the immense stadium and the room became as light as noonday. Recruits all over the room immediately closed their eyes and put their hands over their ears. Just as quickly the flame disappeared and there was silence.

"In case there is any doubt in anyone's mind, you also have this power within you. You will learn how to tap into it as I have. First we will contact our enlightened leader. He will first work through me, then you will be shown how to get in touch with your own person assistant, an ascended being. When you finish today you will be able to speak to your guide at any time."

Zophia flipped her hood over her head.

"Put up your hoods, sit cross-legged, close your eyes, and concentrate on the center of the pentagram." Zophia looked around the auditorium and everyone that she could see complied with her command. "Very good. Now we will begin the mantra."

"Harum Opparum Mararum Rorarum Amorum." Zophia began extending Mararum's influence, as she did aboard the Aman. This was much more difficult and she felt perspiration on her brow as she expended her spiritual force. Slowly, his influence grew, extending from herself to the first row, then the second and on until it reached the top of the auditorium.

Mararum and Zophia jointly taught the huge throng for the next three hours. They taught the art of communicating telepathically with each other so that they could share thoughts, but more importantly so they would be receptive to their new guides. When they took their first break Zophia checked in with the rest of the crew and found that each had progressed at the same rate.

After the break Zophia announced, "You are now ready to be introduced to your personal assistants or guides as they are sometimes called. These are ascended beings who will work with each of you individually. You will receive the name of the assistant you are to contact. You will then use that name and the techniques we taught you to reach them. They will instruct you for the rest of your training."

Zophia stood by as Mararum contacted the 100,000 trainees in the auditorium and those in the other arenas where he was training at the same time. Each person was impressed with a different guide's name. It took him no more than five minutes to accomplish this feat. She marveled at his power.

Mararum and Zophia instructed the trainees, You now have the name of your assistants and the mantra to summon them. After you have called upon them you are to obey them as they instruct you and help you release the power that is within you. When you have fully developed your powers at the end of the ten days of training your assistants will remain with you. Call upon them daily. Now contact your assistants.

Zophia listened as 100,000 people began their chants, simultaneously calling on the name of their guide. She knew what was happening. As she had met Mararum on the prairie and Henry had met his guide on a vast plane, each person was meeting an enlightened being in a unique setting tailored to each individual's personality. Soon each trainee would invite a spirit to enter in and teach them great and wonderful things they had never even dreamed about.

Mararum turned to Zophia. This part of the session is finished. You have opened the portal to these minds and their assistants will guide them just as I have guided you. They will be together as I am with you. Today you have a 14 hour break, but tomorrow at this time you will help supervise the advanced training on the parade grounds.

I understand. It is marvelous to behold all these and to sense the power that is building within them. Since we are on Earth and still in The Sovereign's realm of influence, even though shielded, I thought that their training would take longer than ours, replied Zophia.

You and your crew are the reason that this is happening so quickly. You opened a huge crack in The Sovereign's vulnerability when you learned about your own power. The Chancellor has widened that crack into a chasm as you make yourself available to him through us, explained Mararum.

I'm glad to be of service. Zophia was elated.

She exited the building knowing that for the next 14 hours the students would learn telekinetic and pyrotechnic skills.

April 8, 999 ASR

Jim returned to Midrib with Robert. The next morning they met with Berekiah and started working on the documentation that would be released after all current underground members were trained.

"Of course a book is simply out of the question," said Robert. "No one will simply pick up a newly published book and read it right away even if The Sovereign commanded it. What we'll need is a video program."

"Guys, I'm kind of stumped on this. How are we going to get anyone to look at a video or anything else? How are we going to get people all over the world to take this seriously enough to stop what they are doing and look at it?" asked Jim.

Berekiah looked at Jim, then Robert and said, "You know, Jim, we really need to get you through some more training. If we could do this with telepathy it wouldn't take as long.

"As we mentioned on the Aman, we have people in the communications service that have already planned for a world wide announcement. We have engineered software that will enable us to control every communications device in the world. We will take over the communications systems and make it look like The Sovereign himself is requiring everyone to view the video at the same time."

Does Robert realize that they already have this planned out? This brainstorming session is nothing less than The Chancellor carrying out his plan and Robert is just a pawn they are manipulating.

"Ah, I see," said Jim. "So what we need to do now is figure out the format of the program so that it will have the most impact. We need to decide what to select from Aman's logs and The Chancellor's documentation and how to present it so that people will be swayed to join us."

"Well said, Jim. Even without your training, you express wisdom that is seldom demonstrated in many who are among our ranks," complemented Berekiah.

Jim was not impressed by the compliment.

They spent the next few hours discussing various ways that they could accomplish what Jim described. As he suspected, the course of the documentation and the format was directed by Berekiah, but Robert appeared to think that he was in control and was making the decisions.

Of course, when this appears they want it to look like all the conclusions were from humans who thoroughly analyzed the information they received instead of what it is, the direct manipulation of all involved by The Chancellor's forces.

After a few days it became apparent that Jim was not contributing to the ongoing development of the documentary. Berekiah had all the contacts in the underground already lined up to start filming. It seemed that as soon as Berekiah planted an idea, Robert made a suggestion, then Berekiah was immediately able to implement it.

May 6, 999 ASR

At the end of the fourth week Jim approached Robert. "Hey boss, it looks like things are really working out well now. You have all the documents I've dug up. You and Berekiah are putting it together without any problem. Do you think it would be OK if I took a couple of days off and went to visit Josu?"

"Hmm, you've had a lot of input to this, Jim. I'd hate to let you go right now."

"You overestimate my worth, Robert. But I think it might be important for me to see how things are going with Josu and the work he's doing with the underground."

Berekiah interrupted, "What Jim says has merit, Robert. I've heard that there are difficulties with some of the Quebash. He may be able to smooth things over with them."

"Hey, that's a great idea, Jim. How long do you think it'll take?" asked Robert.

Jim laughed to himself at how quickly Robert changed his mind. "I don't know. Four or five days maybe. It kind of depends on what's going on. Do you have any insight on this, Berekiah? I hadn't heard from Josu for quite a while and was unaware that there were any problems."

"Nothing specific. Those people are a very closed group and even though they pledged to support us, they don't like to reveal their internal conflicts. As far as we know they have some disagreements between some of their elders. If Jim can help out, we should let him stay as long as he is needed," replied Berekiah.

Wow! The Sovereign must be directing this. I can't believe that Berekiah would want me to "help" if he knew who I am and what I want to do when I get there. Even The Sovereign's enemies are unaware of his ability to accomplish his will.

"Hey, it's settled then. Jim, you can take off and come back when you are ready. But don't take too long. We don't want you to miss our training camp," said Robert.

"OK, boss. I'll be back as soon as I can."

That evening, Jim met with Samantha and Kevin, filling them in on his plan to visit Josu. They agreed to pray for his safety so that the underground would not discover his motive and that he would be able to persuade Josu to extricate himself and others from the underground. The next morning he left Midrib.

May 7, 999 ASR

On his way to the North West Coast regional center, Jim called Josu to make sure he would have time to meet with him. When they made the connection Josu appeared on Jim's ECD. Jim was astonished to see that he looked significantly older than the last time they talked.

"Jim, my son, it is good to see you. It has been quite a while since we talked. How are things going with you?" asked Josu, but without his usual enthusiasm.

"Hmm, now that I think about it, things couldn't be better. But you look quite tired. Are you feeling alright?" asked Jim as he tried to be cheerful and not let his concern for Josu's appearance alarm him.

"Oh, it is nothing." Josu waved his hand past his face. "Many things are happening very quickly and I'm having trouble trying to keep up. It makes me tired. So, tell me, how is it going with the documentation? Is everything going as planned?"

"Yes, I can say everything is going as planned. Robert and Berekiah, his underground contact for publication, have all they need so it's pretty much the two of them putting all the pieces together. Because it's going so well, I managed to get some time off to come and see you. I have some interesting developments that I'd like to share with you in person. Matter of fact, I'm on my way right now and should arrive in about ten hours. Do you think you'll have time for me to visit?" asked Jim.

Josu's eyes brightened considerably. "That is wonderful, my son. Why yes, I will meet you at the cafeteria. I would be delighted to see you in person. How long do you think you can stay?"

"I think I could stay a week or so. I feel kind of displaced by Berekiah. In fact, I think he wanted me out of the way so they let me take some time off."

"Ah, I see. Interesting developments, being displaced, and you can take a week off. Yes, we will talk more in person. We have room in our house so you will stay with us."

"Thanks, Josu, that will be perfect. See you in the morning."

Jim sat back in his seat and started studying Yehowshuwa's scriptures. He had a lot of time and figured he might as well use it productively. After a few hours of alternating study and prayer he drifted off to sleep. When he woke up he stretched his legs and walked around the convy for a while. The intercontinental convys were quite roomy and provided a snack bar where Jim settled in for a while. *This food is nothing compared to Josu's but it'll hold me until I get there. Hmm, I'll arrive about breakfast time. I hope Josu has something special. Oh my, I wonder what a whole week of Quebash cooking will be like.*

May 8, 999 ASR

When he arrived at the regional center, Jim quickly headed for Josu's cafeteria. Josu was waiting for him at the back table. He quickly got up and threw his arms around Jim. Jim was taken back because this hug wasn't the same fatherly hug he usually got. This was a thank-heaven-for-a-friendly-face hug.

"What is it, Josu? What's wrong?" asked Jim.

"You remember Zuma?"

"Yeah, I think so. Isn't she the one that made that wonderful omelet? She would be my cousin about twenty times removed," answered Jim.

"Yes, yes, that is right, she is my daughter. She went to the training center two weeks ago and when she came back she was so different. She quit work here but that wasn't the most upsetting thing. She was so rude and disrespectful to me that I couldn't believe it. Then it got worse. She told me about the horrible things she had done at that camp. Jim, we need to talk about this underground and what's going on. I'm afraid we're mixed up in something that is very terrible." Josu was talking faster than usual, hardly stopping to take a breath.

"I know that I've been down on The Sovereign's controlling ways. I know I've wanted freedom for our people so we could be independent. But this just doesn't seem right. I've been watching the kids coming back from the camp and I've seen the same detestation in their eyes. It wasn't until Zuma came back and dumped on me that I realized what was happening." Josu had tears in his eyes.

"What about the rest of the elders? What is their reaction to this?" asked Jim.

"We seem to be split evenly about it. About half of us are horrified. Some of the others don't seem to notice; others think the changes are positive because they give the youngsters the motivation to throw off The Sovereign. It baffles me how they could think that these attitudes could be beneficial for anything," replied Josu. "You must have seen the changes in your friends as well. What do you make of it?"

"To tell the truth, I haven't had much contact with our cell group since we got back from the archeological dig. We've been busy working on Robert's documentation. However, I'm not surprised that this is happening. Robert has changed a lot since his preliminary training," replied Jim as he frowned.

"Did you expect this to happen? Did you know that this underground was going to turn our people into rebellious, disrespectful, rude, bad-mannered bums?" Josu's dark leathery face was starting to get a red tinge. "How could you do this to us?"

Jim held up both hands. "Please, Josu, calm down and I'll explain. It has to do with the recent developments I've told you about. I didn't know when I introduced you to the underground that this would happen; I just recently found out about it myself."

Josu's agitation quickly subsided. "I'm sorry, my son, I should let you explain. It's just that this has me so upset that I feel I'm on the verge of either exploding or crying. What are these developments?"

Jim began to tell his story, "As I mentioned, Robert changed after his first training. He started to show some of the same symptoms that you have described, but not as intense." He then described the "thrill" ride that nearly ended in a high speed wreck on their way to The Chancellor's old capital. "When we arrived I had the weirdest feeling that we were treading on evil ground. I can't explain any more than that, but at the same time Robert seemed to feel the exact opposite. I did a lot of thinking when I had spare time. I thought about how much the world has changed since the days before the Great Time of Trouble. Deserts are now fertile fields, we lack nothing, and we don't have wars or murder. We live in safety. There was evidence in The Chancellor's capital that it wasn't always that way."

Josu nodded thoughtfully.

"Anyway after we got back we were required to go to The Sovereign's capital for the annual feast. When we arrived there I had feelings of good and peace. Again, Robert felt the opposite. He said he could feel the oppression of The Sovereign from the moment we arrived. He was concerned for the people who had to live under it. Have you ever been to the annual festival?" asked Jim.

"Ah, yes, I have. Several times as a matter of fact. As an elder of our people I've gone representing many families."

"Then you are familiar with The Sovereign actually being in each location and presenting the story of his people's rescue from slavery. And how it was not just an historical incident but was designed to be a prophetic picture of the future when he died to rescue us all from our evil ways?"

"Yes, yes, but I've always thought that it was just metaphorical since we are not all evil. Hmm, yet now I'm beginning to question that after seeing what is happening," said Josu more contemplatively than before.

"Josu, you've been like a father to me and I appreciate that and also greatly respect you for accepting me as your son. But before I go on it might be a good idea to establish a baseline of what is good and evil. Would that be OK?"

Josu frowned at Jim's request but agreed.

"Josu, would you consider yourself to be a good person?"

"Yes, especially after what I've seen happening to our people." He rolled his eyes.

"Would it be all right to test you to see how good you are?"

Again Josu frowned but agreed.

"Do you think the Ten Commandments would be a good test?" asked Jim.

"Sure. I haven't killed anyone or committed adultery; this should prove to be an OK test," replied Josu as he smiled.

"One of the commandments is 'Thou shalt not lie.' Josu, have you ever told a lie?" asked Jim.

"Well, sure, who hasn't? That just being human," replied Josu.

"I'm not asking about others but you. If you have lied, what does that make you?" persisted Jim.

Josu looked away. "OK, that makes me a liar."

Jim prayed silently and pushed on, asking Josu about stealing, anger, lust, and taking The Sovereign's name in vain. To his amazement, Josu didn't throw him out but was convicted that he wasn't a good person.

"So by your own admission you are a lying, thieving, blaspheming, murderous adulterer at heart. So do you still think that you're a good person?" asked Jim.

Josu's eyes got wide. "No, I see what you mean, Jim."

"You've already admitted to breaking five of the commandments. If The Sovereign were to judge you right now, what do you think would be the outcome? What do you think he would do to you?"

"I would be guilty, that's for sure. He would sentence me to eternal fire," said Josu very soberly.

"You're right. But you know that he has already paid the price for all that you've done wrong. If you admit your need for him to save you from that judgment and let him be your sovereign, just as he told you during the festival, if you ask his forgiveness, then you will not be condemned." Jim kept his eyes on Josu's.

"That's what I came to understand as I participated in the festival. It all made sense to me for the very first time. The next day I made my decision to surrender my life to The Sovereign and accept his forgiveness for my evil. I have done everything you have, Josu, and I was actively plotting treason against him."

Josu interrupted, "So you've become loyal to The Sovereign? Just like that?"

"Yes. But there's more. I then offered a sacrifice as a memorial to what he had already done and I was told that I could go into the temple and visit with Yehowshuwa."

Josu interrupted again, "I was told I could do that but I've never dared to do such a thing."

"I understand. I decided to go in and I wasn't the only one but when I got inside I was all alone with him. It was like I spent forty days learning from him and understanding the truth. He told me conversations that had occurred while Robert was supposedly blocking all his attempts to monitor us. He truly is omniscient and omnipotent. I discovered how good and loving The Sovereign is and that he has a glorious future planned for us when we trust him. I found out the truth about The Chancellor and that his is not omnipotent and this plot to overthrow The Sovereign will fail. I discovered how evil he is. His goal is simply to keep as many people as possible from trusting Yehowshuwa just to spite him. People who go through the training become evil because they submit themselves completely to Ben-Shaachar. This is the development that I came to tell you." Jim put his hands out in front of Josu as if handing him a plate.

Josu's jaw dropped then he spoke, "Now I understand."

"Robert thinks I'm here to turn around some of the problems that the underground is having with some of the elders. But the only reason I came was to warn you and see if you would like to place your trust in The Sovereign before it's too late. Would you like to do that?" asked Jim.

"After 860 some years of rebellion, do you really thing he will forgive me? I don't think so," answered Josu hanging his head shaking it.

"Yehowshuwa said that every offence would be forgiven. He said that whoever hears his words and believes in him who sent him will have eternal life. If you believe, you will cross over from death to life. Yehowshuwa already did his part in providing purification for you and me. All you need to do is tell him you are sorry and you are willing to turn your life over to him."

"How do I do that?"

"He is listening right now. Just talk to him and say it."

"That's pretty scary. If he's listening now then he has heard every word I've ever spoken against him. Are you sure he will forgive me?"

Jim wanted to shout and shake Josu, but he whispered emphatically. "Yes, he said so; now get on with it!"

Josu looked down at the table and started talking, "OK. Yehowshuwa, Jim says you're listening and I believe that. That means you know everything I've ever said or done and most likely thought too. Forgive me. I now know you are sovereign and I'm turning my life over to you. Thank you for dying on the cross all those years ago to rescue me." Josu looked up at Jim and asked, "Did I forget anything?" He was smiling and it looked like the weight of the world had just been lifted from his shoulders.

Before Jim had a chance to answer they were interrupted by a stranger who had just walked up to the table, "May I sit with you two? I just overheard your conversation." Both of them looked up and stared. "I'll take those astonished expressions as an invitation," said Yehowshuwa as he sat down beside Josu and placed his arm across his shoulders.

"Josu, I'm here to let you know that you are forgiven and you didn't miss anything. And to answer your question, no, I don't normally pop in and physically visit everyone who changes their allegiance. My spirit is now living in you just as he does in everyone who is loyal to me. He is enough to let you know that I am with you always. I just thought it would be fun to welcome you into the family since you were the oldest living holdout."

"I don't know what to say except thank you. Can I get you something to eat? This little cafeteria has some of the best Quebash recipes in the world," asked Josu.

"No, not today my friend. You have served me many times and didn't know it. This time I will serve you." Yehowshuwa waved his hand across the table and it was immediately filled with many of Josu's favorite dishes. The three of them talked, dined, laughed, and planned for over an hour until The Sovereign left them.

They quickly left for Josu's home to tell his wife about his change of heart. With Jim's help she, too, changed her allegiance and joined Yehowshuwa's family.

During the next week Jim and Josu met with individual Quebash leaders, attempting to turn them from the rebellion against The Sovereign that had persisted for untold generations. With only a few exceptions most decided that their best future was with The Sovereign instead of against him. Soon they spread the word among their people and kyboshed some of the efforts of the underground. Most of the young people continued in their plans but the majority of the older generations reversed directions.

May 13, 999 ASR

When Jim returned to Midrib, there were many unhappy people and one of them was Berekiah.

"What is it with those people, Jim? I thought you knew them and would be able to influence them to resolve their problems and get the whole community going in the right direction. Give me an explanation of what happened," demanded Berekiah.

"As soon as I arrived, I met with Josu and told him the truth as I know it. He certainly seemed eager to accept it and helped set up meetings with all the elders of his people. When I talked to them it seemed like there were only a few that took exception to what I said," explained Jim. "Why, what happened?"

"It seems like they must be a very two-faced people then. Apparently after you left they had a meeting with Sven in which they announced that they would no longer cooperate with him. They said they had pledged their allegiance to The Sovereign and kicked Sven out. Your Josu was the chief instigator."

"No!" said Jim in mocked disbelief. "They didn't! What's that going to do the cause?"

Berekiah snorted in disgust then remembered himself and turned on his trademark grin, "It is of no great consequence to the cause. It is only a few of the older ones that are lost. In all, we estimate that only about 100,000 will not be joining us. Fortunately Sven still had his contacts among the younger people and most of them are following through with the training.

"What we set out to prove in the first place, that people who haven't been involved in the underground are susceptible," Berekiah stopped mid sentence then continued, "I mean are still inclined to join us. Bottom line is that even though your efforts didn't bear fruit, we are still on target."

Didn't bear fruit, huh? I would think 100,000 souls would be considered quite a bit of fruit.

Chapter 46

Robert, Jim, Samantha, and Kevin were selected for the last round of training. Robert finished his documentation and along with Jim was finally free to attend. Samantha and Kevin, being first year underground members, were scheduled for the last round and Robert requested that they all attend together.

That night they met at the transportation center near the university and took a convy to the wilderness trail where Robert and Jim had met the shuttle to the space ship. As they walked over the rise they were met by a solitary person. In the dark they could see other groups of people on their way down the hill with flashlights to show their way. Behind them several other people were coming up the slope.

"Good evening, travelers. Where are you going?" asked the dark figure.

"We are looking for ways of expanding our horizons," answered Robert with the phrase that was provided when they received their instructions to attend training.

"Welcome, your shuttle will arrive in five minutes. You can see the others before you but they will disappear before you reach them. Proceed in the same direction and at the bottom of the hill you will find a large boulder. Walk through it and you will find them."

"Thanks, I think we'll be able to find them easily enough," Kevin answered with a smile.

A few minutes later they entered the cloaked area and the transport soon arrived. 150 people piled in and it took off at full speed. Three hours later they were approaching the training camp as the shuttle charged ahead up a river toward a waterfall. As they drew closer, the vehicle's operator announced that they were now going to plunge through the waterfall and not to be alarmed.

After they went through the "waterfall" they approached the camp. They could see the lights from hundreds of other shuttles all converging on the complex. Their shuttle took them to their assigned dormitory.

"Oh man, is it hot here," said Jim as he stepped out of the shuttle into the night's heat. "Why's it so hot?" he asked a guide.

"All we know is that after the shields went up, the rains stopped. We believe they interfere with the weather patterns," he answered.

Jim replied, "Whew! It feel more like The Sovereign made good on his threat to withhold rain from any land that turned to other spirits," as he wiped his brow.

"Where did that malarkey come from, Jim?" asked Robert. He was astounded that Jim would say such a thing.

Samantha just stared at Jim. She also must have wondered why Jim would make such a statement.

Jim just shrugged his shoulders and followed their guide to the dorm. They were assigned small rooms for their ten day stay. They also received instructions to report to the auditorium promptly at 8:00 AM immediately after breakfast.

June 28, 999 ASR

Samantha got up early, which was only two hours after their arrival, and headed down the empty hall to the common shower and toilet facilities. As she entered she was shocked to see both men and women already standing at the row of twenty sinks taking care of various personal grooming needs. She didn't know that it would be a co-ed facility. What was most distressing was that of the five people ahead of her, three were completely naked, two guys and a gal. She had no choice but to continue in because there were no other facilities and she needed to use them. Fortunately, the stools had stalls with doors that closed providing privacy, unlike the shower room. When she finished she quickly washed her hands and ran back to her room without making eye contact with anyone else in the restroom. *The shower can come later.*

When it was breakfast time the sun had only been up a couple of hours. Samantha checked the outdoor temperature. At 38.3 degrees, it was much hotter than any place she knew about on Earth. She put on a swim suit then the brown robe she was provided at check in time. She made a dash for the dining hall to meet Robert, Jim, and Kevin. As she hurried, it was apparent that she was one of the very few to actually wear her robe. Others were wearing very little if anything and carrying their robes.

Samantha breathed easier in the air conditioned dining room. She went through the cafeteria style food line, quickly taking some ham and eggs, pancakes with maple syrup, and a big glass of orange juice. She kept her eyes low but found Kevin and Jim sitting at a table in a corner with their backs toward her. She sat down and they shifted their chairs enough so she didn't have to look back at the nudity and obscene behavior exhibited by many of the people in the large room.

"Hi guys, what a marvelous place!" said Robert as he came up behind them and sat down opposite them. He looked out the window at the lawn between the dorms and the dining building. "Except for the heat anyway. The only green for kilometers is around the dorms."

He craned his neck for a better view. "Marvelous place! You guys see how free everyone is here? I've never seen anyone taking such liberties with each other before. I get a feeling that this is just the beginning of what we'll experience after we defeat The Sovereign. Isn't this great?"

"I don't think you have the slightest inkling of what it'll be like," answered Kevin. "It will be so much different than what you've ever seen that you will be blown away."

"Yeah, you're probably right. Wow, I can't wait," responded Robert. Samantha was sure he didn't have a clue of what Kevin really meant.

For the next twenty minutes Robert kept making comments about how much he liked the camp and the other three took turns trying to divert the conversation, especially when he wanted to detail his experiences of the morning taking a public shower with other people of both sexes. Finally it was time to leave and go to the auditorium.

Samantha was extremely apprehension about what they were going to do during the training, but it was also a relief to get away from Robert's growing lust.

The foursome walked into the auditorium and found their assigned space. Apparently, Robert arranged to have them seated together. When Zophia entered Robert whispered to Kevin and Samantha, "That's Zophia, the captain of the star ship."

"Is that the one you told us about, who saved the star ship?" asked Kevin.

"Yeah, from what I've heard she has advanced faster than anyone else, but when we finish up here this week, we'll almost be as powerful."

"So why is she leading the group today?" asked Samantha.

"I understand she has some sort of ability that helps us bridge the gap and connect with the people in the other realm. After we cross the bridge then we're on our own, so to speak, but we'll have a mentor to assist us," answered Robert quietly.

"If we all get an assistant from the other realm, why are you here? Don't you already have a connection with Rorarum?" asked Jim. "And isn't he supposed to be one of the big honchos?"

"I've been told that this is just to close the gap on some of the training so that I'll have experienced the process like everyone else and will be able to train others. I'll still have Rorarum as my mentor."

Any continued conversation was stopped as Zophia announced that the session was about to begin. Samantha jumped as Zophia presented an attention-getting pillar of fire.

Samantha followed Zophia's directions and sat down cross-legged, pulled her hood over her head, closed one eye and kept her head down so that Zophia couldn't see her open eye. When everyone started chanting the mantra, she didn't join in but began to ask The Sovereign for protection and to be able to bluff their way through the rest of the day. She asked that when everyone was supposed to be in telepathic communication with each other Robert wouldn't notice that he couldn't connect with any of his friends.

It was a long three hours but Samantha prayed earnestly all the time. During the break, she met with Kevin and Jim to ask The Sovereign for protection so that Mararum would not detect that he couldn't implant a name into their minds. They didn't want anyone in the spiritual realm to be aware that three of The Chancellor's henchmen didn't get released from prison when they should have.

When others were receiving their guides, Samantha, Kevin, and Jim slipped out when they saw Zophia leave the auditorium. They had learned from other classes that everyone would be in a trance for several hours and people finished at different times. There was no need for them to stay.

As they escaped from the auditorium several other people were also attempting to exit, furtively glancing about. It was pretty obvious to Samantha the neither group was where they should be if they were serious about the underground and defeating The Sovereign. They approached each other in the foyer.

Kevin spoke first, "Fancy meeting some people ducking out on the training. What's the matter; didn't you want some ascended being taking over your soul?"

"It didn't seem quite right for us since we already have a better spirit living in us," answered a young woman. "What are you doing here?"

"I was about to ask you the same thing. It seems that The Sovereign has led us here for some purpose but at this point it hasn't been revealed to us. How about you?" asked Samantha.

"Pretty much the same thing. We've been undercover in the underground, trying to dissuade as many as possible before they got too involved. When we got our notice to come we all felt that this was where we needed to be. We know several others from our campus that were called earlier but didn't go. They didn't believe it was the right time. We thought we were the only ones to attend training until we met you."

"That sounds like our situation as well. By the way, I'm Kevin, this is Sam, and Jim," said Kevin.

"I'm Gilda and this is Lex, Brad, Millie, Hamilton, and Sophie. We're pleased to make your acquaintance."

"Why don't we get out of here and find a place where we can find out what we're up against? We don't want to draw any attention," said Lex.

"Let me take a look outside and see what's going on. If we all leave at once it might not look good either," said Jim as he headed for the nearest door. He left through the revolving door and returned only a few minutes later.

"We can all leave at once but we will stand out like a sore thumb if we don't head in the same direction as everyone else. I asked a guy where everybody was going and he acted like I was a complete dufus until I explained I was on a quick break from the first class. He explained that it was time for everyone from the previous classes to report to the training grounds for the next round of training. It seems to me that we can all go there and talk on the way. When we get there, we'll see what we'll be up against for the next few days."

"Sounds good to me," said Hamilton and the others nodded in agreement.

Kevin hesitated as they started to follow Jim. "You guys go ahead. I'm going to sneak over to the administration building and see if I can find out anything there."

"Suit yourself but you better be careful. I think the people or whoever they are that work there aren't involved in any of the training so they may wonder why you aren't where you're supposed to be," said Samantha.

Kevin took off his training robe and stashed it behind the door. "I'll just go over there like I'm a new arrival or that I'm a quick learner. I don't think one person will draw as much attention as a whole gang. I'll meet you all back at the dorm tonight if not earlier."

Samantha along with Jim and her new friends exited the auditorium and found a shuttle heading to the parade grounds while Kevin walked toward the administration building.

Robert quickly absorbed the new information that he needed since he was already well acquainted with Rorarum. He came out of his trance and was surprised to see that his three friends were already gone. He left the auditorium but didn't see anyone in the vicinity. With his enhanced telepathic power he checked with others in the camp to see what was happening. He learned that everyone was at the training ground. He also found one person who recently talked to Jim and saw him arriving at the training ground with seven other people. He hopped on a shuttle and also headed for the training ground. *I wonder why I can't contact the others since they've already finished today's training.*

When Robert arrived at the parade grounds he immediately found the eight watching the ongoing training. They were huddled close together by a grandstand. He decided to sneak up behind them and eavesdrop before challenging them.

"I don't know about this. Look at the way they're using telekinetic powers to move rocks. And that other group is throwing globs of fire all over the place. I think we ought to find Kevin and get out of here before we're found out," said one of the strangers.

"I hate to say it but I think you're right. We better get moving," agreed Samantha.

As they were about to leave Robert stepped out from behind the grandstand and interrupted them, "Hey, guys, what's going on and who are your fiends?"

"Oh, hi, Robert, uh, these are some people we met when we finished training. It seems that we all finished about the same time so we thought we'd come up here and watch the fireworks. I suspect you finished so quickly because of your connection with Rorarum," responded Samantha.

"Yeah, you're right, Sam." Robert stopped and looked at Samantha, then reached out his hand to her cheek and ran his fingers through her hair. "Say, you know I've always admired you Sam. Not just your brilliance but your beauty as well. Since everything is changing, why don't you and I take advantage of our new freedoms while your friends watch the games? Or maybe one of your lady friends here would like to join us too?"

Samantha started to pull away from Robert but he grabbed her robe tearing it as she pulled back. "Let's not waste time, Sam," he said as he clutched her arm and started reaching for the top of her swim suit.

Jim quickly intervened, took hold of Robert's hand before he could do anymore, and pulled him around so that they were face to face. "What's wrong with you, Robert?"

"I should ask what's wrong with you, Jim, and your friends here. Why can't I communicate with any of you and why should Sam resist my advances? Perhaps you should be explaining yourselves."

Zophia approached the group. Telepathically, she halted all training and called for everyone to join her and Robert. Within a minute they were surrounded by thousands of people. Robert could tell, through Zophia, that training in the other camps was also halted and even those who just received their assistants were all linked together. *I want all of you to witness what is about to happen,* said Zophia.

"Robert, Jim, it's good to see that you've made it to the final training. I understand you've completed your documentation. Congratulations. However, I would like to know what's going on," asked Zophia.

"Thank you, Zophia, it's good to see you too. It seems that Jim and his friends here have a bit a problem with my behavior toward this luscious young beauty, Sam. But as you know, her resistance isn't what bothers me the most."

Jim and the others were now ashen as Zophia turned to Jim. His shoulders slumped. "Jim, when we first met I couldn't read your thoughts and I still can't, yet you've supposedly finished your initial training and have accepted an assistant. I demand that you open your mind to me. That goes for the rest of you also."

Jim straightened up and replied strongly, "I'm afraid that's not going to be possible, Zophia. You see, my mind belongs to The Sovereign and there is no way that you or any of your assistants or mentors can have it. He that is in me is more powerful than he that is in you."

"Then you and Sam are the two I've been warned about. We'll see where the power lies, Jim," said Zophia as she pointed her finger at him. Immediately, he was completely consumed in flames and within a millisecond all that was left were a few ashes on the ground.

A roar of applause erupted from all those who were surrounding them, including Robert.

Samantha screamed and fell to her knees, covering her face. The other six backed away.

"Is there now any doubt who is more powerful?" Zophia asked both aloud and telepathically. "Now as for the rest of you, you have a choice. You can either join us or keep your allegiance to the ineffective Sovereign who can't even save his own. If you don't join us we'll send you home so that you can warn others that resistance is futile. What will it be?"

Through tear stained face and clenched teeth Samantha looked up and yelled, "Even if you were to fry me on the spot, I would never forsake The Sovereign and become one of The Chancellor's slaves."

The other six affirmed Samantha's conviction.

"Very well, it will be as you asked." The three men burst into flames and left small piles of ashes.

"What! You said you would send us back if we didn't join you. What are you doing?" screamed one of the remaining women.

"You didn't really think we'd let you go and warn The Sovereign, did you? You will make it even easier to overcome our enemy with such childish thinking." Zophia turned to the crowd and asked, "What do you think we should do with them?"

A woman stepped forward from the crowd, "I think we ought to incinerate them all right after we mash them under a huge rock. Especially that one." She pointed to Samantha.

Samantha stood, still sobbing. She choked out, "I know you! Your name is Helga. You worked at the distribution center with my cousin Tom. What are you doing here?"

"Ha, I didn't work with Tom. I worked as a slave under that hypocritical Sovereignite. Your father also oppressed many of my friends out on that farm as slave labor. You are no better than him," responded Helga, shaking her fist at Samantha with a sneer on her face.

Zophia interrupted, "I admire your devotion, Helga. But your solution is too merciful. Robert, you and I will escort these ladies back to the administration building and lock them up. This evening you and the others can have your sport with them when training is over. The rest of you return to your training with fervor and tonight you will witness their punishment," announced Zophia.

The crowd roared its approval and dispersed back to the training grounds, leaving Robert and Zophia alone with the four captive women. A shuttle approached on its automated schedule and Zophia told them to get on it.

"Not on your life and you can't make me," said Samantha. "I'm not going anywhere with either of you."

Zophia just laughed. She used her telekinetic powers to lift all four off the ground and onto the shuttle before they knew what was happening. "You have a lot to learn, ladies, but unfortunately for you it won't help you at all." Robert and Zophia got on behind them and watched to make sure that they didn't try to get away.

Zophia, Kevin came here with me and I can't contact him either. Do you have any knowledge of where he might be? asked Robert.

No. Galva, have any of you seen a stranger wandering around the camp? Someone who doesn't respond telepathically? Zophia included Robert in her query.

Galva responded to both, No, we've been checking in new people all morning and have been making sure we can see their thoughts just as you instructed as soon as the infiltrators were detected. It is possible that he left with the departing class before we started looking.

Spread the word to everyone who just graduated. If there is anyone on one of the shuttles who doesn't respond, dispose of him on the spot.

As soon as Zophia's shuttle arrived at the administrative building they took the women to a locked basement room. They quickly opened the door, shoved them inside and relocked the door behind them. *Galva, keep a double guard at all times. Has the exiting class reported back yet?*

Yes, Ma'am. They didn't find anyone suspicious on any of the shuttles. We've scanned everywhere within the camp's shield and everyone is accounted for. We don't understand how he got away or how he's hiding if he's still here, replied Galva.

At this point I doubt it will make any difference if he got away but it would be more satisfying to know how this Kevin guy has evaded us. Robert, why don't you think of something special for your friend Sam and the others tonight? said Zophia.

Oh I think I can dream up a couple of things if you will link up everyone in the camp to view it all, replied Robert gleefully.

I'll do even better. I'll even have everyone experience whatever you experience.

Robert returned to his room for his usual time of meditation with Rorarum. When he entered he found Kevin sitting in his visitor's chair waiting for him.

"So there you are! I was wondering where you were hiding," said Robert to Kevin while he contacted Zophia to let her know that he'd found Kevin. *Zophia,*

Kevin has been hiding in my room. Send a couple of people over to take him into custody.

There was no answer from Zophia.

Zophia, where are you? Anyone, can you hear me?

Still there was no answer from anyone.

Rorarum, can you hear me?

"What's the matter, Robert, can't any of your friends talk to you?" asked Kevin.

"It doesn't matter, come with me and it will go well with you."

"Just like it went well with Lex, Brad, and Hamilton when they thought Zophia would let them go? I think not, Robert. Why don't you sit down and we'll have a little chat?"

Robert's anger flared and he pointed his finger at Kevin. "I don't need anyone else. I'll zap you myself if you don't come with me." Nothing happened and he poked his finger in Kevin's direction again. Still nothing happened.

"What are you waiting for? Go ahead and fry me just the way Zophia killed your old friend Jim. Didn't that make you the least bit sad that your closest friend of the past three and a half years is dead because you brought him here and led him into this underground movement?"

"Shut up! You don't know what you're talking about. He was my friend until he betrayed The Chancellor by going over to the other side. I suspect you've been on The Sovereign's side all along, haven't you?" Robert stammered.

"Yes, you're right, but doesn't that make you wonder about everything you've been taught? You said you could detect The Sovereign's agents and shield your thoughts and conversations from him, yet there I was all the time in front of your nose and you didn't have the slightest suspicion. Sam has always been loyal to The Sovereign and you didn't know. When Jim discovered the truth about The Sovereign you didn't know that and neither did any of your comrades. When you were on the space ship getting the lies that they had brought back, Zophia couldn't read his mind then either, but no one knew he was completely sold out to The Sovereign." Kevin stood and approached Robert.

"She certainly found out about it today, didn't she? And look where he is and where Samantha and the others are. It seems to me that you are the one that should be wondering, not me," sneered Robert as he backed up. He didn't want to get too near Kevin.

"Well, why don't you just contact your friends or kill me now? If what you've been told is the truth then you have found the power within yourself to do that, haven't you?" challenged Kevin as he backed Robert into the door.

"I don't know why I can't do either of those, though you know I'd like to smash you like a bug right now." Robert said but felt no power to back up his words.

"I'll tell you why you can't. It's because you've bought into one of the oldest lies known to mankind. You believe that you can become like Yehhovaw. You want that so strongly that you are ignoring all evidence that says Yehhovaw is unique and that you are nothing like him and never will be. The Sovereign has at this point completely blocked all your friends from deceiving you so that you can see that all these powers don't come from you but from them. Because he is capable of binding them you should believe Yehowshuwa and not your friends. This, Robert, may be your last chance to act on what you've been taught since you were a child and reject the lies that you've embraced in the last few years," warned Kevin.

Robert edged around Kevin and stood in the middle of the room. "Ha, what a joke. Do you really think I'll turn my back on The Chancellor just because you have somehow temporarily rendered me powerless? When we have all joined together along with billions of others, then we'll see if The Sovereign can block any of our powers."

"You are surrounded by about one million people who have your powers. They missed you as soon as you were cut off from them. They are attempting to contact you at this moment and they can't. What makes you think that billions will be able to do anything against The Sovereign Yehowshuwa? I'm going to leave you in a couple of minutes. Please take this time to think and change your ways. Follow The Sovereign. It is a decision that will give you eternal life instead of eternal death."

"Eternal life on The Sovereign's terms is eternal death and oblivion. Who in their right mind would want to be under his thumb for eternity when they could be enlightened and far surpass him? I think not, Kevin. Why don't you just admit that you and everyone like you are about to see that you could have had much more but chose subjection to a demented being instead. Leave while you have the chance. If you are found here then you will receive a thousand times worse treatment than The Chancellor has endured for the past thousand years," sneered Robert as he pointed his finger at Kevin. How he wanted fire to lash out as it had from Zophia.

"Is that your final answer?" asked Kevin sadly.

"Get out of here!" Robert lunged at Kevin and grabbed him by the throat. "I'll kill you with my bare hands if you don't."

Robert squeezed with every ounce of strength within him, but his hands passed through Kevin as if he were a hologram. Kevin took one of Robert's hands as he almost lost balance and straightened him up with a jerk. No, he hadn't been trying to kill a hologram.

"I'm going now. Until the day you die you will always be accepted if you turn to The Sovereign and ask him to forgive you." Kevin disappeared.

Robert, where have you been? asked Zophia and Rorarum at the same time.

It was Kevin. Somehow he was able to keep me from contacting you and using any powers against him. He must be an Enforcer. He just vanished, answered Robert.

June 28, 999 ASR

Chancellor, we've just received a report from Rorarum that an Enforcer from The Sovereign has penetrated one of our camps and temporarily severed his contact with Robert. Abathar's thoughts burst through the quiet like a buzz saw.

Abathar, I don't know why you get so excited about such trivial matters. I was quite aware of the matter as it happened. Don't fear and let our comrades know that I am completely aware of the channel through which the intrusion occurred. I am leaving it open as a trap but after it has been sprung it will be sealed and never available again. The Sovereign will not be able to use it to rescue his puny agent. He has shown his vulnerability by using it so soon. It was obviously an attempt to neutralize Robert and his witness to the rest of the world. I welcome his attempts because I become stronger with each one. Ben-Shaachar was scrambling to understand how Robert was rendered powerless. He wouldn't admit his bewilderment so that none of his subordinates to lose confidence in him.

I should have known you were aware of this, Excellency. Forgive me for doubting, replied Abathar

Soon, my brother, we will not have need of these foolish humans any more. Once The Sovereign is defeated we will enslave them or snuff them out if they resist. That will be the final feather in our cap. Yehhovaw's pride and joy will be completely enslaved or eliminated and that will forever bring him grief, misery, anguish, and sorrow. I can't wait to see him suffer.

Chapter 47

Samantha, Gilda, Sophie, and Millie fell to the floor as they were thrust into the small dark cell. The light was very dim and they couldn't see after coming out of the bright, cloudless day.

"Whatever are we going to do?" whimpered Millie. "Do you suppose they might be right about The Sovereign losing power? I mean how could all this happen? Why do they have this power and why did he let this happen to the guys and why is he letting this happen to us?" she cried.

Samantha groped toward Millie and put her arm around her. "We've been living in an environment where nothing like this would have ever been permitted but now it seems we've been cast back into the time before the Last Battle. I've read about some of the stuff that happened but I can't really appreciate what it was like. I just don't have any point of reference. I don't understand why The Sovereign has permitted this at this time but because I know him I know that he isn't out of control."

"I don't understand either. I agree that he is in control so I think we should pray," responded Gilda.

"Good idea. We're involved with something way beyond anything we can take care of in our own power," agreed Samantha.

A voice came out of a dark corner of the room. "Indeed, it would be a good idea to pray, but I wouldn't get my hopes up too high if I were you."

The ladies jumped back against the door and screamed.

"Easy, ladies, we've been here all along but in the darkness and your distress you simply didn't notice us. Let me introduce ourselves. I'm Dr. Jonathan Krebs and this is Professor Robison and his assistant Eric. The professor and Eric have been here for nearly a year and I've been here about three months. It's been hard to know exactly because we have had no distinct way to tell time."

"Professor Robison!" shouted Samantha. "I was supposed to be in one of your classes but you went missing. Because of that Robert got your notes and found that bunk about The Sovereign being a deceiver from the site you discovered. And Dr. Krebs, that name sounds familiar but I can't place it."

"Ah, I would be the person responsible for extracting the data on the disk Robert and his assistant found. If it weren't for the three of us, I believe none of us would be here today. We have lost hope that we will ever be rescued," said Dr. Krebs as he sat down on a bunk.

"I haven't lost hope. I still trust The Sovereign even if he doesn't get us out of this pickle and I think it would be good to pray before we get any more discouraged," replied Samantha.

The four women fell back to the floor on their knees and started to pray aloud one after another. Samantha took her turn, "Father, you know exactly where we are and our troubles. You and only you know why we were spared and the others were killed today. We mourn losing them but know that they are safe with you. We know that even now you can hear us behind the so-called shields that the enemy has set up. We know that the powers they boast of are nothing compared to your omnipotence. We pray for Kevin that you would protect him and keep him safe. And Lord, we also ask that we would be able to accomplish your will here. We are afraid for what they have threatened to do to us. We admit that this frightens us even though we know that nothing can separate us from your love. We have never had to face this kind of evil in our lives. Give us strength so that we won't do anything that would make you ashamed of us."

"I feel better now, but I'm still not looking forward to whatever they have planned for us tonight," added Millie. "Help us to face whatever will be happening tonight."

The men joined them in prayer and they continued for a few minutes, then sat down on the other bunks to wait. The men were completely unaware of where they were or what was happening outside of their cell. The ladies filled them in on everything they knew.

Just before midnight, the guard opened the door and with two other men, led the women outside to what had once been a grassy area near the building. The way was lined by men and women who hooted and hollered, taunting them with obscenities and blasphemies against The Sovereign. They cowered together and clung to each other as they entered a large opening in the crowd where they were met by Zophia, Galva, and Robert.

"Bring them to the center of our little arena," commanded Zophia. "Robert, why don't you tell them what you have planned?"

"I imagine that you aren't about to change your mind and join with us, are you?" asked Robert.

"Not on your life, Robert. You will see that The Sovereign will prevail no matter what despicable things you do here tonight," responded Samantha.

"I'm not about to join you either," said Gilda.

Millie bit her lip and trembled but managed to speak, "I'll stay true to The Sovereign no matter what you do."

"Me too," answered Sophie.

Robert smiled with excitement, "I was hoping you wouldn't change your mind so I can have it my way. As you found out on your way to your confinement, we can hold you so that you can't resist. You can either relax and enjoy this or fight and be forced, but I'm going to have my way with each of you while the world watches and participates in my pleasure. Zophia will be channeling everything so that every trainee and all who have been trained in the whole world will experience what I experience. When I am done you will be executed, or maybe we'll repeat this again tomorrow night," said Robert.

At that moment there was a commotion near the edge of the circle of people watching. Samantha saw Kevin shove aside several people and walked toward the center.

"Ah, if it isn't the hero Kevin come to save his ladies," scoffed Zophia. "We knew you were coming and have a little surprise for you. Everyone, hold him so he will have to watch with the rest of us."

With a wave of his hand, Zophia, Galva, and Robert were sent sailing in opposite directions into the crowd. Several people were bowled over as their sprawling bodies collided. By the time they got up Kevin had reached the women.

Fire! cried Zophia.

Samantha found herself along with Kevin, Gilda, Sophie, and Millie standing on the roof of the dining hall. She saw that the ground where they previously stood was now replaced by a vaporized hole in the earth five meters in diameter and six meters deep. A column of smoke gushed out and rose five hundred meters in the air. The people around the flame fled.

After the circle of people widened, Zophia announced to all, "As you can all see the interlopers have been vaporized, proving that none can defy us." The crowd cheered and rejoiced at their victory, even though it should have been obvious that their victims vanished before the ground under them was destroyed. She then dismissed the assembly.

Zophia turned to Robert as they were leaving. "The trap was a success. We have eliminated Kevin but we didn't get a chance to make an example of the ladies. If you come with me I can make up for it."

Samantha whispered to Kevin, "This place has turned Robert into a monster. Is there no hope for him?" She was glad the darkness hid her tears.

"There's always hope with Yehowshuwa, Sam. But we need to leave now. I'll take each of you to a place where you will be safe."

An instant later, Samantha was at home with her parents.

June 28, 999 ASR

Jim suddenly found himself standing on the white sand of a pristine beach. To his left he could see an endless stretch of beautiful turquoise water slowly growing darker as it extended to the horizon. To his right the beach was lined with tall palm trees shading clumps of deep grass. The sky above was deep blue with a few puffy clouds floating near the horizon. Looking behind, he could see four sets of footprints that stretched back around a curve of the beach. Lex, Brad, and Hamilton suddenly appeared in the other three set of footprints. In the distance ahead a lone figure walked toward them.

"Where are we?" asked Hamilton as he stopped and turned around, taking in the scene. "Didn't we just get scorched and yet here we are without so much as a singed hair."

Brad answered, "Beats me. We must be dreaming or something. Look at our footprints. How could we have made them? We were just at the training camp."

"Ha! I'll bet you guys are surfer beach bum wanabees, aren't you?" exclaimed Jim.

Lex shrugged his shoulders and answered, "Yeah, the three of us grew up together and practically lived on the beach but what does that have to do with," he paused and gestured to their surroundings, "this?"

"Look up ahead of us past that guy coming toward us. See how that point juts out into the ocean? Look at the trees and how they are swaying in the wind. Listen, can't you hear the surf on the other side? This is the most perfect surfing getaway in the universe!"

"I don't get it," said Hamilton as he shielded his eyes from the sun.

"Perfect surfing getaway! We're dead. Where do you think we would end up?" Jim pointed to the person waking toward them, "That's Yehowshuwa coming to welcome us."

The others turned and faced Yehowshuwa. All four of them ran to him, dropped to their knees and bowed down at his feet. He waited awhile then stood them up. "My friends, you have been faithful. Enter into your rest and enjoy yourselves here for a while. There are others here as well and of course, I'm always here. Oh, there's a lot more here than just surfing but you have earned this rest."

June 29, 999 ASR

The following day after lunch Robert and the rest of his class reported to the parade grounds. Per his instructions from Rorarum, he formed ranks with the others after picking up a small stone from one of the bins along the training field. Each person stood about five meters away from each other and dropped the stones on the ground.

His first task was to apply the telekinetic training he learned. He concentrated on the stone and within a few minutes was able to make the stone rise up in front of him. By the end of the day he was able to launch the pebble at 1,600 kilometers per hour, maintaining complete control over its trajectory even while it was out of sight as well as traveling too fast to observe. Robert felt as if that small rock had become an extension of his being.

June 30, 999 ASR

In the following two days he learned how to team up with others and put massive boulders through the same maneuvers directly over their heads as well at a distance. He joined with a thousand to lift a five metric ton boulder, then pitch it ten kilometers away to hit a target dead center. When they progressed to this point the different teams began projecting their ballistic boulders in sequence with other teams, pulverizing the targeting area and making the ground shake like a sustained earthquake.

July 2, 999 ASR

During the next three days of training he applied what he learned about generating fireballs, laser beams and lightening bolts. As with the telekinetic training he again started small and progressed to much greater feats. For his final test he again joined a team to remove all the boulders from the target area and put a huge rock the size of a house on the target grounds. The entire class of one hundred thousand vaporized the boulder in an instant.

July 5, 999 ASR

The final three days were devoted to defensive training. By this time the ability to cloak himself was like child's play. Robert used cloaks that looked like trees, buildings, open meadows, and whatever else he and his teammates could dream up.

Robert learned more serious defensive measures on the last two days as they again started with individual shields and worked up to team protection. Two people started out throwing fire balls at each other and either repelling them back at the sender or absorbing them without harm.

July 7, 999 ASR

On the final afternoon the class divided into two groups ten kilometers apart and staged an all out battle with each other. Robert's team was assigned to be the initial defender. The aggressor team started the action by sending a boulder flying at Robert and his squad. The defenders failed to stop the boulder so they used its inertia to deflect it beyond the group. His stomach shook as it crashed into the ground.

You realize that if we hadn't changed our strategy at the last minute we would all be dead, said Robert to his team. The only thing that saved us was our own powers and our ability to act as a group. Robert was shocked. The training exercise suddenly became a life or death struggle.

In angry retaliation, Robert's team sent a volley of 50,000 golf ball-sized stones speeding back at 1,600 kilometers per hour. The enemy would only have 4.44 seconds to communicate among themselves and form a defense. Robert was amazed to see a dome of fire appear just above them, vaporizing the rocks as they hit the shield.

After the last projectile disintegrated, the dome rose from above the first team, forming a super heated globe that sped toward Robert. *Deflection!* Popped into his mind and he joined with the group but the sphere only momentarily bounced away. It turned on them as Robert's team received a vision of how to absorb the energy without harm.

The five metric ton boulder that had originally been tossed at Robert's team was now launched back at the first team. It was counteracted by a laser blast but the huge rock became remarkably maneuverable and eluded the deadly beam. While the first team was busy with the boulder, Robert announced a plan to fire another torrent of small rocks toward the first team with bolts of lightening and laser beams intermixed.

A shiny hemisphere suddenly covered the first team. The pebbles bounced off and the other energy beams were absorbed by the shield. When the boulder came crashing down on the dome, it broke in half and bounced harmlessly away. *I didn't see anything like that in our training. How did they do that?*

However, Robert's team wasn't finished with their retaliation. The earth opened beneath the first team, dropping their shimmering dome and the entire group into an abyss. As the ground started closing in over them the dome changed to a sphere and shot back up from the crevasse before it was crushed.

The sphere advanced quickly toward Robert and his team while it started shooting lightening bolts at them. The first couple of lightening bolts were successfully absorbed but Robert could feel himself weaken. The team quickly consulted with each other and formulated another plan just as another fire ball followed the lightening. Robert was very encouraged that their combined experience led them to a solution that was not in their training either. They waited until it would appear as if the fire ball were about to destroy them. Robert transported himself just before the intense heat melted the gravel where he and his team was standing.

Robert's team was now scattered across the battle grounds. Still linked together, they pushed the sphere containing their enemy skyward two kilometers above the training area. They caused the sphere to dissolve, spilling the enemy into the air. Fireballs, lightening bolts, laser beams and rocks were quickly speeding towards the falling bodies from fifty thousand different locations across the plain. As soon as the huge sphere dissolved it was replaced by fifty thousand individual bubbles. Again, Robert was astounded as they descended rapidly through the onslaught of offensive fire, dodging as they approached the sources of the last attack.

As they reached the ground Robert's team put up their own defensive shields. A bubble approached Robert and he threw everything he and his team could imagine against his aggressor. The sun had set but the glow from the battle lit up the valley. Thunder from the campaign echoed from the mountain walls. Robert had little time to ponder the events but realized they were in a stalemate.

Zophia called a cease fire. Darkness and quiet prevailed.

Congratulations to all of you. You have completed your training. As you now know and as could only be demonstrated in a free-for-all battle, you are quite capable of changing attack and defensive strategies in an instant. You can act as individuals or in unison but always as a team that is intimately integrated with each other. In this short amount of time you have surpassed your training with innovative new offensive and defensive maneuvers. We will succeed. Down with The Sovereign, said Zophia.

Down with The Sovereign! the class responded.

Robert met Zophia after the class was over and enjoyed his last night with her. He would leave for home in the morning.

July 8, 999 ASR

The dim light inside the tiny cell below the administration building blinked out. Professor Robison heard the lock on the door click open. No one entered. The hum of the air conditioner stopped.

"So what do you suppose happened?" asked Eric.

"I don't know, but I'm going to find out," said Robison as he groped for the door and pushed it open. He cautiously ascended the dark stairs followed by Eric and Dr. Krebs. When they reached the top there was still no one in sight.

"According to what the ladies told us, this was supposed to be the last ten days of training for the underground. Maybe they all left. I wonder what happened to the women. I can still hear the shouts and cheering after they were taken away," whispered Robison as they reached the building's front door.

"I'm surprised that they let us live and fed us while we were here. From what the women said, there wasn't any reason for them to do so. They certainly cremated their friends without hesitating," said Dr. Krebs.

"I imagine that The Sovereign has control of our safety even in this forsaken place. Why he let the ladies and their friends die is beyond me. But now what are we supposed to do? It looks like this place is hundreds of kilometers from the nearest civilization," said Eric.

"Let's explore a bit. Maybe we can get the power back on and find some communication devices. There's no telling how long we may be here and I don't want to stay a minute longer that I have to," said Professor Robison.

As they stepped out a light drizzle started to fall, settling the dust that was prevalent all over the camp.

The three quickly found the power generator and started it up again. They located the nearest mess hall and found that there was enough food for them to survive as long as there was power to keep the refrigeration units running. However, they couldn't find any communication devices or vehicles of any kind.

July 8, 999 ASR

Robert returned alone from training. The shuttle was packed with people who had also just finished. They were all ecstatically talking about the future. In only one week the big announcement would be made and they would become the conduits for the rest of the world's training.

He returned to his apartment, walked in and closed the door. As excited as he had been on the bus, he now felt a huge letdown. For the first time since he had seen his friends vaporized, he missed them.

His work was completely turned over to the underground leaders and now there was nothing to do but wait. Being alone emphasized his longing for Zophia. His evenings with her had left him aching for more. He was sure that she was the only one for him until he learned that in each class she found someone different to be with every night. That didn't do a lot to make him feel that she had any special feeling for him. *It's strange that this new freedom is so breathtaking and so infuriating at the same time.*

In anger and hunger he contacted Hillary from his cell group who had finished the training earlier. She was willing and available to welcome him back from training and to practice what she had learned in her extracurricular activities at camp.

July 12, 999 ASR

People who had been trained first had first choice where they would be when his documentation was broadcast but the last few trainees were assigned locations to ensure that no one in the world would be without a mentor. However Robert was considered part of the higher echelon he was able to choose his home town.

Robert waited until Monday to return home. There was no way he wanted to be hauled off to worship services on Sunday. He wanted to be home soon enough to be in a position to help his parents make their decisions to join him when the great announcement would be made.

Right after The Sovereign is bound I'm going to start developing my powers to disappear and reappear wherever I want. No more of these tedious convy rides for me. I can't wait to see what this world will be like without his shackles. The images of Eden that Zophia showed me will come true here as well, I'm sure of that. It seems that we have even progressed beyond them already. I don't know why it takes the Edenians so long to develop the powers that we learned in only ten days. Maybe humans are just a lot more powerful. Yeah, that's probably it and that's why The Sovereign was so intent on stopping us. He knew we could advance even more quickly than his father did. Even though he mused about the future all the way home, the journey seemed much longer than before.

July 13, 999 ASR

Robert arrived home later than he planned. The convy schedules were slowed because many of the system's supervisors, without notice or reason, hadn't reported to work. At the regional center lines of people waiting for food at cafeterias clogged the corridors. Fewer workers and an interrupted food supply left travelers hungry and irritable. *These people will soon be receptive to a new regime.*

As he walked the last block to his parent's house he noticed that some of the yards didn't look as neat and trimmed as usual and the street hadn't been swept either.

He opened the front door and called out, "Hi, I'm home. Anyone here?"

Mom answered from the kitchen, "We're in here, Robert."

He dropped his bag by the stairs, went into the kitchen, and greeted his solemn parents.

"Hi, Mom, Dad, what's with the long faces? I thought you'd be a bit more excited to see me."

"It is good to see you, Robert." Mom got up and gave him a hug and Dad followed suit. "We were just talking about what's happening and we don't understand it."

"Huh, what's happening? Did I miss something?"

Dad explained as they sat down around the kitchen table, "It started slowly but we noticed it a few weeks ago. Many people aren't reporting for work and it's starting to show. For the first time in my life, I've run out of some products in the hardware store. I usually fill out requests for what I need and it's delivered within a couple of days. Now it's taking over a week. That's just an example."

"Oh, so the transportation slow down and un-swept street aren't just my imagination?"

"No, that's just more of the symptoms. We've been talking and wondering why people would suddenly stop working and why The Sovereign isn't doing anything about it. Aren't Enforcers supposed to intervene when people shirk their responsibilities?" asked Mom.

"Maybe there are more people goofing off than there are Enforcers," said Robert, knowing quite well that there weren't enough Enforcers to keep the Administration's agenda running.

"I don't know, Son, there's no real way of knowing how many there are but I don't think it has anything to do with how many Enforcers there are," responded Dad.

"Well, the only other conclusion is that The Sovereign doesn't have as much power as he says and there isn't anything he can do to get people back to work. It's either that or he simply doesn't care."

"Robert! That's blasphemy. How can you say that?" retorted Dad.

"No, Justin, he was just saying what we were both thinking but afraid to say," said Mom.

Dad turned quickly toward Mom and spoke sharply, "I wasn't thinking that at all. There has to be another answer. I'm surprised that you would think that, Marilyn."

Mom propped her head up with both elbows on the table. She didn't even look at him but just raised her hand as if to block his words. "Oh, don't be such a fuddy duddy, Justin. There are a lot of things that just don't add up about The Sovereign. It isn't treason to wonder why things don't always make sense."

Robert interrupted, "Hey, guys, why don't we talk about something else? This doesn't seem like it's very profitable." *Wow, Mom sounds like she may be very receptive to joining, but not Dad. It would be better to talk to them separately.*

"That sounds good to me. Besides it's all too depressing. So, Robert, you said you were coming home, but you didn't tell us the occasion. How long has it been since you visited or even called us?" asked Mom

Oh man, I'm home less than ten minutes and Mom's back at the nagging. I wonder how this will work out after The Sovereign's out of the picture. Maybe when she's out from under his influence she'll be able to free herself up. "Sorry about not keeping up with you but I've been very busy wrapping up my documentation on the Last Battle."

"Oh, so it's still about that book, is it? When are you going to publish that thing and get on with your life?" snipped Mom.

"I was trying to tell you, Mom. It really isn't going to be a book but a video and it's finished. It will be published this Friday. I came home so that when it comes out I could be here with you guys to talk to you about it after you've looked at it."

"What makes you think that I will look at it?" sniffed Mom.

Robert shook his head. He couldn't believe Mom still hadn't warmed to his work.

"Marilyn, he's done a lot of work on it. Of course we'll look at it, but why do we have to wait until Friday? Can't we see it now?" asked Dad.

"The Administration doesn't want anyone to get a sneak preview. Only those who have been authorized will be able to see it before then." *They don't need to know that it's the underground administration that doesn't want anyone seeing it too soon and alerting The Sovereign. Something a Board Elder might do.*

Mom sat up straight. "Oh, wow, I am impressed. I would have thought this was just another documentary that would be filed away along with the thousands of others that have been produced. But to have the Administration be this tight about its release means that it must be something else. I guess we'll just have to wait," said Mom.

Robert wasn't sure if she was being sarcastic or not.

"So what are you going to do after it's released? Are you going to write another book or are you going to get a job?" she asked.

Sarcastic! Robert smiled but didn't take the bait. He waited a few seconds, appearing to ponder his future. "Right after the publication I've been assigned to do some follow-up work with people who want to look deeper into the insights I've received while doing the research. That will take a few days, then I've been invited to take what I've learned directly to The Sovereign along with some of my colleagues. After that I understand that I'll be taking up a position in the Administration."

Mom's jaw dropped. "Oh my goodness, this is all because of the documentation that you put together? And I've been putting you down and trying to get you out of it. Oh my goodness. I'm so sorry. But, oh, this is exciting. What will you do for The Sovereign?"

"I'm sorry, Mom, I'm not at liberty to tell anyone until it's announced. But I can tell you that it will be a very high level position."

Dad raised his eyebrows and sat back. "This sounds like it's a lot bigger than I ever thought it would be too. If it's going to be released Friday, why haven't I heard anything about it?" asked Dad.

"Have you been talking to Henry much lately? What's the biggest thing on his mind?" asked Robert.

"He's been running all over the place talking to just about everyone in the community about their loyalty to The Sovereign. But what's that have to do with this?"

"Why is he so concerned about people's loyalty to The Sovereign? That's the key to why you haven't heard anything about this," prompted Robert.

"He thinks that there is a majority of people who aren't loyal to The Sovereign and that he only has a short time to help people change that. The rest of us on the Board find it hard to believe that such a large number of people aren't loyal to The Sovereign. Do you know of anyone that isn't loyal to him?" asked Dad.

"Absolutely! One of the reasons I was allowed to continue with my book was that I had the respect of many people who are younger and are actively subversive. They accepted me as part of their underground movement. The Sovereign suspected that he was losing the allegiance of a huge portion of society and he is hoping that this documentary will reverse that affect."

"Did I hear you right? Did you say that you were a part of a subversive underground movement?" asked Dad, his voice raising.

"Yes, that's right. When I made my motion for occupation I showed the Board some of the underground's publications and explained what the younger generation was thinking. I pointed out how I was in a unique position to gain their confidence and that this book would be instrumental in helping them make good decisions."

"Why didn't you tell us about this?" asked Mom.

"Sorry, Mom, this had to be kept so secret that only the Board members could know and of course even Dad couldn't be told because he wasn't at the confidential portion of the hearing. But now that it's about to be released I can tell you this much. You can't say anything about this until after Friday, though."

"I had no idea that any of this was going on. But why has Henry been on such a campaign? He hasn't just been talking to the younger people in the community but everyone," said Dad.

"I can't answer that one. Maybe he's just being over zealous," replied Robert.

"Maybe. Well, since you can't tell us anymore about this I was wondering if you could give me a hand at the store tomorrow. Then we'll only have one day left until your document is released and you'll have to get back to work. How long has it been since you've even been to the store? Ten or fifteen years?" asked Dad.

"I think it's been more like twenty years, Dad. Yeah, that might be a very interesting little break." After the document is released and we have overcome The Sovereign I have a feeling that it will never happen again.

"Good. It's getting late so I think I'll turn in. I'll see you at breakfast then. Good night, Son. Are you coming to bed soon, Marilyn?"

"I think I'll stay up a while and chat with Robert if it's OK with you," replied Mom.

"Good night, Dad."

"That's fine." Dad left and went upstairs.

After he was out of earshot Mom turned to Robert, "I sense something different about you, Robert. It seems to me that you're hiding something from us and your father doesn't have a clue. As a matter of fact, he never really had a clue about a lot of things. He's been so stubbornly loyal to The Sovereign that he can't even see how the Administration has had us under its thumb for ages. I suspect that your little documentary isn't exactly going to please The Sovereign, is it?"

"What are you saying, Mom. Aren't you loyal to The Sovereign?"

"Now I wouldn't say that, Robert. You know how faithfully I've stood beside your father, especially as a Board member. I worship every Sunday and do all I'm supposed to and maybe even a bit more. All I'm saying is that I feel miffed that I've had to do all this." Mom looked away as she spoke.

"So you might say that you feel oppressed by the Administration?" pressed Robert.

"You might say that. Now tell me about your video, documentary or whatever you're calling it. Does The Sovereign really know what's in it and what your goals are?"

"Mom, you have spent all your life concerned that The Sovereign is going to send one of his Enforcers to come and straighten you out if you didn't make the mark, haven't you?" Robert wanted to lead the direction of the conversation.

"Yes, that's fairly accurate, but you're avoiding my question."

Yes I am. "Not really. I'm just trying to help you answer your own question. The reason you've lived in fear is that you believe that The Sovereign knows all and that's why he'd send an Enforcer if you screwed up. If he knows everything you've done then what makes you think that he might not know about my video and my goals?"

Mom's eyes narrowed, shifting them back and forth across Robert's face. She spoke slowly, as if choosing her words carefully, speaking in almost a whisper, "Because – I – don't – believe – you're – telling – the – truth."

Robert smiled as he looked his mother straight in the eyes, "If I'm not telling the truth then what part of what I've said isn't the truth? I've said The Sovereign knows all things so he must know about what's in my documentation."

Mom hesitated for what seemed like an eternity. She first looked down at the kitchen table, then out the window that was dark against the night, then at the kitchen sink. She pursed her lips, gritted her teeth, then took a deep breath and said, "How can you be sure that he doesn't know everything?"

"That's a long story, Mom. Are you sure you want to hear it?"

"No! This is too wrong. We shouldn't be talking about these things or we'll both be shipped off for retraining or worse, killed for treason." Mom put her hands over her ears, put her elbows on the table, and closed her eyes. After a minute she opened her eyes, looked around, and took her hands away. "No one has come to get you?"

"No one."

"Then tell me."

Robert and his mother talked late into the night as he explained how he first started to wonder about the precise consistency of all the accounts of the Last Battle and ended with the training he had just received. He conveniently left out a few details like his friends being killed and some of his extracurricular activities.

"So this malarkey that you were giving your father and me earlier tonight about a future job in the Administration was really in a new administration?"

"That's right. In just a few days from now there will be a new administration and if you join with us you will advance beyond anything that you've ever dreamed about. You will never have to fear The Sovereign Yehowshuwa again."

Mom shook her head. "All I've ever dreamed about is an eternity serving The Sovereign, whatever that means, in a realm totally devoid of all the pleasures, as limited as they've been, on Earth. I can't imagine how boring it would be to spend eternity worshiping him in the clouds or around some huge throne in space. What you've told me about being able to continue to advance beyond this life and never ceasing to grow even after enlightenment all sounds too good to be true. How do I join?"

"Just wait until Friday and you'll have your chance right after the publication. I'm really glad you've decided to take this route with me. I feel that for the first time in my life we're on the same page." Robert was delighted.

"I'm sorry, Robert. If I had only known this years ago I wouldn't have kept trying to mold you into someone that would become a big wheel in the Administration. Thanks for putting up with me but more so, thank you for telling me everything tonight. I suspect that we shouldn't tell any of this to your father. I don't think he's open to any of it." she laughed quietly.

"I think that would be a good idea. I think he will need to see the complete documentary before he will be convinced. Hopefully he'll realize that broadcasting it should prove that The Sovereign isn't all powerful or all knowing or he would be able to stop it before we even start it. Oh man, look at the time. I'm going to need a bit of rest if I'm going to the store with Dad in the morning."

"Oh, I forgot about that. Will you be OK?"

"Sure, I don't need nearly as much sleep as I used to. I have been able to tap into power that you'll soon learn about, too. But I do need to check with my mentor for a while so I'll turn in now. Good night, Mom."

"OK, I'll see you in the morning. Good night."

Chapter 48

The Sovereign Yehowshuwa sat on his ornate throne with the twenty four members of the High Council seated on their thrones before him.

"I've summoned you here because it is about to begin. At exactly 3:00 PM Sovereign Mean Time the underground will start their offensive. Watch with me and pray that few will believe them."

Immediately, he transported his friends in a vision so that they could see the events taking place in the GCCC, Global Communication Control Center, in Yeruwshalayim.

Horace Beckler keyed the code for the world wide emergency broadcast into the communications system. The Sovereign explained how Horace and other clever technicians working for the underground had inserted the code into the Administration's communication system months earlier. It would signal every personal ECD, private and public display screen to power up if needed and sound an alarm.

"Horace, along with his colleagues, were the first trained at The Chancellor's camps. They have carefully planned work schedules so they are the only ones on duty today," explained The Sovereign.

Horace checked his ECD when it sounded the piercing pulsating tone. The tone was followed by a video of The Sovereign who spoke forcefully, "This is a mandatory world wide public announcement. Please be prepared to give your full attention in five minutes."

Tsvar, viewing the vision with The Sovereign, blurted out, "You even allowed them to make it look like you are commanding the world to watch their lies?"

"Yes. It wasn't difficult for them and it fits into my plans," answered The Sovereign. "It was allowed but it doesn't bring any joy."

For the next five minutes the notification and alarm were repeated. The Sovereign showed his council people all around the world in all time zones roused from sleep or stopping work to assemble in work areas, homes, or the nearest community center. Some who were isolated from others used their ECD to watch the announcement.

"Most people are curious to find out what I have in mind since this is the first time that a world wide announcement has ever been made, much less a mandatory one as the underground has claimed. If people were to think about it, they would realize that I've always passed important announcements down from the top and eventually through the local board." The Sovereign knew how each individual reacted to the announcement.

The vision shifted to Joyce Chin, the director of the communications industry, in her afternoon staff meeting. Every ECD in the room shrieked with the alarm.

She quickly started issuing commands, "The Sovereign would never do this without letting us know. Jim, find out who did this and where they are. Maja, find out if this is localized or if it really is a global announcement. John, check GCCC and see what's going on there."

"Joyce, I can't get through to our security office. My ECD is jammed on this announcement and I can't get it to do anything else," said Jim.

"Me neither," said Maja.

"Same here," came a chorus around the conference table from all of her subordinates.

"Then let's go downstairs and find out what's happening."

The entire team got up and went into the hall where Joyce pressed the down button on the lift. They waited and nothing happened. The call light was on but the lift wasn't responding. Joyce headed for the stairs.

"Uh, Joyce, its 210 flights down to the GCCC. Are you going to walk all the way down there?" asked John.

She turned and answered, "No, I'm going to run and you better be right behind me." In an instant she was gone and her team followed behind.

The High Council watched Joyce fly down the stairs holding the hand rail, skipping several steps and then jumping to the next landing. It would take her over ten minutes if she could keep up the pace and not break a leg. The illegal broadcast was going to start in just one minute.

The vision shifted to Walter Fishbein, the GCCC security staff supervisor who had just finished his shift and was leaving the building when his ECD sounded the alarm. He silenced the alarm tone as he stared at it and mumbled, "This isn't right. There isn't any such code as a world wide emergency announcement and even if there was, I would have known if this were about to happen," as he tried to contact his security office. His ECD was locked.

Walter turned around and hurried back into the building. The lifts didn't respond so he took the stairs down two floors to the security office. It was vacant. He looked at the monitors and found part of the crew standing in the hallway outside the GCCC, just one more level below the security office. The rest of them were in the hallway outside of the equipment room on the lowest level of the building. He hurried out the door, down one more flight of stairs, and emerged at the end of the hall opposite the guards.

Jason, who worked for Walter, casually saluted. "Hey Walter, what are you doing here? I thought you were off-duty."

"What's going on? Why is everyone here and on the equipment floor? Even more important, what's this phony world wide emergency announcement nonsense?"

"All I can say is that we've been ordered here to make sure no one enters the communications center until the announcement has been completed." Jason shrugged.

"Well, I'm going in to find out who is doing what. I'm pretty sure that this isn't from The Sovereign."

Jason held up his hands chest high. "I'm afraid the order applies to you too, Walter. When they said no one is to go in, that includes you."

Walter glared at Jason. "You report to me, now step aside because I'm going in."

Jason sneered back, "I used to report to you but now I have new leaders and new orders. So just go back upstairs and watch the announcement like a good old boy."

Walter outweighed Jason by at least fifty kilograms and was head and shoulders taller. He repeated in a slow quiet voice, "Step aside because I'm going in."

Before he could take a step forward, the High Council saw Walter fly through the air backwards as Jason laughed. He hit the door to the stairs with such a force that the metal door broke off its hinges and flew into the stairwell. Walter crumpled on top of it, a motionless mass, as blood oozed from his ears and nose.

July 16, 999 ASR

Robert and his parents were having breakfast when they were interrupted by the irritating alarm on their ECDs and their home communications center.

"What's that?" asked Dad.

"I believe that means that my documentary is about to start," answered Robert. He opened his ECD and said, "Yup, we have five minutes. Let's finish breakfast, then go in and watch on the big screen. It'll look a lot better."

"I don't believe this. The Sovereign is asking the whole world to watch this? I've never heard of anything like this happening before. Well, I guess this was much bigger than anything I ever thought it would turn out to be. Congratulations, Son," said Dad.

They quickly finished eating and left the dishes for later. Dad led the way into the living room and settled in his favorite chair while Mom and Robert sat on the couch. They arrived just before the countdown ended.

The five minute countdown finished and the picture of The Sovereign was replaced by the opening scene from Robert's documentary. A very attractive couple appeared walking hand in hand in a beautiful garden. They turned and faced the camera.

"Thank you for taking this time to listen and watch the following special program. This program is of such earth shattering importance that we felt it necessary to have everyone in the world see it at the same time. We know that this is quite inconvenient for some of you but we are sure that you will agree that it is worth it when you see the information that we bring to you," stated the man. His smile, tone of voice and mannerisms were very charismatic. Every fiber of his being shouted, "You can trust me."

In like manner, the woman continued the introduction, "As many of you recall, about twenty five years ago, with the Administration's authority, we sent a star ship to explore the deep reaches of outer space. The Sovereign assured us that we would not find any life in the universe other than what has originated here on Earth. However, deep down in our hearts each one of us was hoping that we would find some kind of life. That space ship has returned earlier than expected because they indeed found life. For the next few minutes we will show you a brief summary of their voyage and beings they encountered. Much of what you will see has been taken directly from the ship's logs."

Dad interrupted, "I can't believe it. Why wasn't the news that they'd returned released?"

"Shhhush, Justin. I want to hear what they have to say," said Mom.

"Just listen, Dad. You'll get answers to everything as it continues," said Robert. The screen showed billowing clouds over the top of the star ship as it launched.

The two hosts of the program next appeared in a studio setting with two four plush chairs seated around a coffee table. There, they interviewed Zophia as she explained how they came about setting course for the planet they called Eden. She included that she believed the information they received came from someone in the Administration.

The High Council's vision changed back to Joyce and her team as they reached the security office. They followed the same path as Walter but stopped short when they found his body in the stairwell. Three of the team members raced back up the stairs trying to find a place where they could relieve their stomachs.

Cautiously, John walked around Walter and peeked down the hall. A tongue of flame blazed in front of his face, singed off his eyebrows and blistered his nose. He retreated quickly.

"Back off and do not try to enter the communications center until the broadcast is over or you will receive a worse fate than Walter," shouted Jason. "I suggest you watch the documentation as you have been commanded."

"What are we going to do?" asked Maja.

"I don't know," replied Joyce. "In all my 600 and some years, I've never faced a situation like this. I've only read about them in history. Let's go back up to the lobby and watch what's going on. At least we will know what we'll have to deal with when this hijacking is finished."

Robert enjoyed his finished work as he watched scenes surrounding the star ship's interception by Rol-el, instructions to turn around, the attack and death of Dave, and their rescue by Tia-le were all vividly displayed. This was followed by more interviews of the star ship's top officers. They carefully explained how they made their decision to continue on to Eden.

"Robert, what is all this about? This is absolutely blasphemy and treason! How could you possibly pass this trash off as the truth? Can't you see that you've bought into a huge lie? I'm turning this thing off and we are not going to watch a single moment more of it in this house." Dad tried to use his ECD to switch off the living room console but it wouldn't respond. He went up to the unit and tried to use the power switch but it continued to show the documentary. He went behind the system and unplugged the unit but the internal backup power source kicked in.

Dad turned to Mom. "Come on Marilyn, we're not staying to watch this."

"Calm down Justin. Don't you think you better watch and see what's being said? As a Board member, I'm sure people will ask you questions, especially since your son put the documentary together. How will you answer them if you don't know what was said?" asked Mom.

Dad was very agitated but sat down. He took a shot at Robert, "You've got a lot of explaining to do, young man."

The broadcast continued, showing scenes from Aman's logs and from the logs of the crewmembers that they had made while they were on Eden. The pattern continued as segments of Aman's journey were followed by interviews of crewmembers. The longest uninterrupted sequence from the logs was the history of Earth that they retrieved from Eden's library. The battle on the way home was also graphically displayed, including Zophia's ability to save the ship from certain disaster.

"While Aman was returning to Earth with this amazing information, one of our archeologist-historians and his assistant were diligently looking for clues to the true nature of The Sovereign. He interviewed many of the oldest people in the world seeking to find someone who knew survivors of the Last Battle. Let's talk now with Dr. Robert Maskil," said the charming woman.

During the interview Robert was able to relate why he first started looking into the stories of the Last Battle and how the consistency of the stories bothered him as a historian. The hostess also asked questions that drew on his involvement with the underground. He revealed that the discussion groups started him questioning The Sovereign's abilities and motivation.

"So, Robert you decided to write a book about the Last Battle. You were determined to find out if there were any other versions of the Last Battle that had been suppressed by the Administration. Weren't you afraid that The Sovereign would find out about this and try to interfere with your efforts?"

"Yes, I was. However, something unusual happened that gave me confidence that I would be able to do this without hindrance. My local Board decided to pull my student status and that would mean I wouldn't have the time to work on the book. I made a motion for employment specifically to work on the book. During the motion I had to reveal that there were a lot of people who were skeptical about The Sovereign and that this book would help them make up their minds."

"Did your Board realize that you intended to show that The Sovereign had purposefully repressed information and distorted historical records for his own purposes?" asked the charming male host.

"At the time I made the motion to my Board, I was simply looking for the truth. I didn't intend to bring any dishonor to The Sovereign. However, as my research continued I came to the conclusion that he has rewritten history to cover up his father's evil and his own complicity."

Dad gasped loudly when he heard Robert's accusation but he didn't interrupt.

During his interview Robert detailed his research. He used excerpts from the interviews he conducted with various people to show how they conspired to show

The Sovereign in a good light. Then he used his interview with Josu to show that not everyone had the same view of The Sovereign before the Last Battle.

He also discussed the books that he was able to access from the archives only because he had been given the special access card. "I don't think The Sovereign ever expected me to find these books. I believe he thought they were safely buried and inaccessible. What The Sovereign touted as the best for us has not always been regarded by many people as the best for mankind."

"Robert, all this is interesting and appears to cast dispersion on The Sovereign in the same way that the aliens on Eden and the crew of the star ship have claimed, but do you have any proof that he has been deceptive and controlling?"

Robert continued to describe how he was led to research the archeological site that Eric discovered and that Professor Robison started working before he mysteriously disappeared. He explained how he verified the authenticity of the location and the disk he found with The Chancellor's documentary. They then displayed the introductory video.

After the video directed by The Chancellor was finished, the interviewers joined Robert again. The charismatic host asked, "Robert, the evidence that the star ship has provided and this documentary that you found appear be in agreement. Could you sum this up so that it's clear for anyone who might be confused?"

"I'd be glad to. There are five basic points that we have discovered and proved through this documentary. These will be displayed on the screen as I explain each one."

"The first point is that The Sovereign is a liar and can't be trusted. He and his father have deceived mankind as soon as he became jealous of our potential."

"The second point is that mankind was destined for much greater things than we ever believed. Because The Sovereign is jealous, he kept this from us and kept us in bondage to himself for ages."

"The third point is that The Chancellor is our true savior and came to free us. He is not evil as The Sovereign has claimed."

"The fourth point is that this documentation is irrefutably true. The fact that we are using The Sovereign's own communication system to present this proves that he is not all powerful as he claims."

"The fifth point is that some of us have already defied The Sovereign and have gained powers that he has prohibited."

At this point Dad was so agitated that he got up and paced behind the sofa, shaking his head but keeping quiet. Mom sat quietly.

The charming hostess asked, "What then is the purpose of our presentation today? You've obviously proved these points. What is next?"

"First we need to let you know that there are over four hundred million people who have been trained with the aid of the star ship crew. We have done this without any instances of interference from The Sovereign. We did this without his detection for the last ninety days since the star ship returned. Just a week ago one of my colleagues finished training and would like to show you what can be accomplished in a short time. This is Hillary and she will give you a demonstration."

Hillary entered and sat down in the chair next to Robert and the interviewing team. The coffee table in front of them had a glass of water for each. Hillary motioned toward the glass in front of her and it rose from the table to her eye level. The water started to bubble and steam as it got hotter and hotter. The water quickly boiled and disappeared while the glass started to glow red hot. The glass then started to melt and formed into a spherical glob while it grew even hotter. She then twisted her hand upward and closed her fist as if she were snatching the glass out of mid air. The remains of the glass was then surrounded in flame and disappeared.

"Thank you, Hillary," said Robert as he nodded to her. He faced the camera again and continued, "Our power grows exponentially with each person as millions of us link together. The purpose of all of this is to let everyone know we can all be free from The Sovereign's oppression if we join together. We will have the power to defeat him when we are all united. We have power now to resist him as has been shown, but with everyone cooperating together we will end his oppression and be on our way to enlightenment and our true destiny"

"And how will we join together?" asked Miss Charming.

"Each of you received this entire documentary on your ECD. Along with it are the directions about how to join with a trainer in your area who will guide you to receive the same powers as the rest of us. When that is completed we will gather together and receive our final instructions to overthrow The Sovereign. When he has been imprisoned, we will finally be free and will be able to establish a society even better than the one on Eden. We will be able to continue to enlightenment, ascend, and become even greater than The Sovereign or his father.

"If you ever wondered about The Sovereign, if there is more to life, and if there is more after death than serving The Sovereign, if you've ever just wanted to do something that The Sovereign says is wrong and you've wondered why he prohibits it, then please follow these directions and learn more. You won't be sorry."

Mr. Charismatic closed the documentary by reiterating what Robert summarized and explained how the underground operated undetected for many years preparing people for this time.

Dad came around in front of the sofa, already pointing his finger and shaking it at Robert before he even started to speak. He started to say something when The Sovereign started to speak from the display console. Dad turned to the screen, then stepped aside.

"My dear children. You have just seen The Chancellor's version of history and you have heard the accusations made against my father and me. It is now time for you to decide who you want to believe and serve."

"How's he doing that?" asked Robert as he jumped up. "The documentary was supposed to repeat again."

The Sovereign continued, "You have seen for yourself how I restored the earth to a near perfect environment. You have not had to suffer the diseases that plagued your ancestors before the Last Battle. The earth has produced abundance for you at my command. Your work has been a pleasure for you and you have lacked nothing. There are no poor among you and everyone has abundant opportunities for education.

Robert started to make a comment but Dad shushed him, "It's your turn to listen, even if you don't like what you hear."

"You have known my rule here on Earth for a thousand years. Until this uprising I have suppressed evil so that you would know what it is to live without fear and reap the benefits of living without the temptations of The Chancellor and his minions."

"I started with one man and one woman. My father walked with them and talked with them. They lived in a perfect environment and only had to obey one simple commandment. Ben-Shaachar came to them, not to save them, but to tempt them to disobey me just as he himself had disobeyed and tried to declare himself sovereign, even though he was created by me. They chose to listen to Ben-Shaachar and as a result of their disobedience I altered their perfect environment as their punishment. Given a perfect environment and the presence of Yehhovaw, mankind did what was evil. They forfeited the right to rule over the earth and passed along to their descendants the capacity to do evil. At that time I told them that I would eventually provide a way for mankind to escape the consequences of their disobedience and would also provide a way for their descendants to be restored to the position that they were originally created to enjoy, and even more."

Robert tried to turn off the console but it would not respond.

"From that time I let mankind rule themselves by building cities and governments that should have suppressed evil but did not. Though I talked with many and they knew what I required of them, they became corrupt with evil in their hearts. The Chancellor claimed to help them find their freedom from me but instead he led them into ever increasing wickedness. At that time I did destroy all of mankind except for one man and his family. Ben-Shaachar is prepared to train you in that same evil if you follow his directions in the previous broadcast.."

Robert stopped trying to shut off the broadcast and pointed to the screen. "What kind of loving father would kill almost every one on Earth?"

"Even the descendants of this one man were again lured into evil, so I selected another man and through his family I created a nation. I tested them, strengthen them, and I purged them. I gave them my word that they might teach other nations to follow me and I gave them good laws to live by. Not laws made up from their own imagination. It was impossible for them to obey all the laws, not because I was cruel, but to show them that it was impossible for anyone to be perfect and live by my perfect standards in their own power. I let them know what was necessary to be reconciled to me when they did not meet the requirements of my law. This was through the sacrifice of innocent animals in place of their own death. Sacrifices were pictures of my death that I would endure to pay the penalty for all disobedience. Through all this, people continued to be disobedient."

Robert wanted to leave the room but for some strange reason he sat down and listened. Each point of his several hour documentary was being countered by Yehowshuwa.

"I then came and became human. I gave up my position with my father to do this. I lived in perfect obedience to the laws so that when I was unjustly killed it would be a payment for the disobedience of all mankind. I was raised from the dead and returned to my father. I sent my spirit to live in people who believed in me and trusted in my death as payment for their disobedience, knowing that they deserved death instead. By my spirit they had the power within to live obedient lives in loyalty to me. Yet people rejected my offer of forgiveness and evil continued until the Last Battle was over."

"For the past thousand years, I have been available to each of you so that you would know what it is like to live with me among you. My spirit has been available just as he was when I was not physically present. Ben- Shaachar has been imprisoned so that you could not blame him for your own evil desires."

It was now Robert's turn to pace while Dad and Mom sat and watched. "Mom, you aren't getting sucked into this, are you?" She simply held up her hand and kept her eyes on the screen.

"Now he has been released and you have to decide if you will fulfill all your wishes to become greater than me as The Chancellor has promised or if you will believe me when I tell you that there is no such thing as enlightened beings and you cannot become one, much less a sovereign."

Robert quickly interjected "Don't forget about the Council of Enlightened Beings that I told you about. We can become like them." Dad glared at him but Mom paid no attention.

"The Chancellor said that when he has overthrown me his job here is done. He said that he will return to his previous path of enlightenment and become a sovereign. I tell you the truth. He has no plan to return because he has no place to go. He intends to enslave you and if you resist, he will destroy you. He is not interested in your welfare but hates you because you remind him of me."

"He will also lie to you if you ask him what will happen if you should fail to overthrow me. He will tell you that he will again have another chance and that at the worst you will be imprisoned until he is successful. However, I tell you the truth. I have predicted this time and the outcome. When you fail you will enter into eternal punishment where the flame is not quenched. If you decide to believe me you will live forever with me."

Robert tried to destroy the screen with a plasma burst but he couldn't even get as much as a spark to appear. *Just like when Kevin threatened me at the camp. What if he's right?*

The Sovereign concluded, "If you believe me, then I want you to continue to do your normal jobs and keep the world's infrastructure running. Many people will be abandoning good sense in order to follow after The Chancellor's training so many of you will undoubtedly have much more work to do. I'm asking others who are not involved in essential work to lend a hand. In a few days I will make arrangements for you to come to Yeruwshalayim to be with me before Ben- Shaachar mounts his final attack on us. Don't take time to pack any belonging because everything you need will be here. The time is very near."

The screen went blank for a moment then start replaying The Sovereign's speech. Robert walked to the console and turned it off. The screen went blank. *Just as I suspected. Only a temporary setback. The Chancellor is back in control.*

"I take it that you are firmly behind this treason and that no amount of reasoning will be able to dissuade you from your course of action." Dad stood slowly. His face was long and sad. He showed no signs of the anger Robert saw earlier.

"That's right, Dad. I've seen the evidence first hand and I'm absolutely sure that The Sovereign is malicious and has to be taken down. I'm prepared to do whatever is needed to do that."

"I'm sorry, Son, that you have chosen this path. I fear I will never see you again and your eternity will be in torture and agony. Please reconsider," begged Dad.

"I'm sorry too, Dad, because it hurts to be at odds with you. But I know that after The Sovereign is subdued you will see the error of following him. The Chancellor will free you along with all who are in bondage to Yehowshuwa. We will grow together into enlightenment and ascend to fulfill our destinies."

Robert turned to his mother. ""I have to go. Mom? Are you ready?"

"Yes, dear. Let's go," answered Mom.

"No, you can't do this, Marilyn. Why would you want to do this? I won't let you." Dad jumped up and started to grab Mom by the arm but Robert used his powers to throw him back in his chair and keep him from moving.

"That's the reason I'm going, Justin." She shook her finger in his face. "I've lived in your shadow nearly my whole life. Your little lovey-dovey ploy these past months was an attempt to control me as well. And if it wasn't you it was The Sovereign and all his rules. I want to be free to become anyone I want to be. I don't want who I am to be defined by you or The Sovereign," spat out Mom.

"Mmfplhf dtosld fffmsfs ssffrddht," mumbled Dad. Robert kept his mouth shut so he couldn't answer Mom. "Mffffetis! Rrrfffofffft!" he continued to try to speak until Robert started to constrict his throat.

"Leave her be, Dad. I won't let you harm her any more."

Mom and Robert left together while Dad squirmed in his chair. Robert didn't release him until they were on the convy and on their way to meet the rest of Robert's prodigies.

Chapter 49

As Henry watched the broadcast he kept praying that there would be time to rescue a few more people from The Chancellor's evil scheme. Tears were dripping down his cheeks as he and his wife, Wanda, knelt before his view screen and asked The Sovereign to intervene in the hearts of people in his community so that he would have another chance to talk to them and convince them to trust in The Sovereign.

When The Sovereign finished they bowed in worship and sang praises to him. After a few minutes he left and went to the community center. *Perhaps some people will be going there to look for guidance.* As he left his house to walk the short distance to the center he noted that there were many more people on the street than usual. Most seemed to be younger but there was also a good percentage of middle aged folks. They were all heading toward convy stations. Henry's walk took him past three stations before he would arrive at the community center.

At the first station there was a large group of people waiting for a cab. He recognized most of them as being under his jurisdiction so he asked, "Friends, where are you going?"

"Shut up, old man," replied a younger woman with two small children. "Didn't you see the broadcast? You don't have any say over what we do or say so just keep walking if you know what's good for you."

"Yeah, don't try to stop us, as if you could," replied another while others joined in with various taunts and abusive comments. The older ones kept their mouths shut or turned away so that Henry couldn't look them in the eye.

"Please, Alicia, leave your children with me. I'll take good care of them," said Henry.

"Are you kidding? Why would I want them to be trapped in your world when they can become free too? Go on, get moving. We don't want any help from you," she yelled and clenched her teeth.

He was about to say something more when a young man came up to the station and requested a cab for the city center. The second loudmouth in the group shoved him away and toward Henry, "Hey, no one is going into the city today. We're all heading out of town. All of our mentors are outside the city. Why don't you go along with sanctimonious old Henry here?"

"But I need to get to work today," he protested.

More people were gathering and the crowd was getting larger. The sign above the convy station showed that all the request for cabs were outbound from the city. A cab arrived and was immediately filled and left, still leaving a large crowd at the station.

Henry put his arm on the young man's shoulder, "Come along with me, Glen. It'll be OK if you're a bit late today. I imagine that if they let you call a cab it would be a long time before any were free to take you to the city."

The two arrived at the community center a few minutes later to be greeted by a small group of people who were obviously distraught. Questions and comments came from various people almost at the same time, "Henry, we're so glad you're here. We're so confused about what we need to do. How could this awful thing be happening? Oh and that young Robert Maskil, he seemed like such a nice young man. How did he get involved? He said you approved the work that lead up to this. Why didn't you stop him?"

Henry raised his hands and brought them down slowly several times until people quieted. "Now just calm yourselves down. Things are going according to plan except it isn't the plan we would choose. Come on inside and we'll chat about it." When everyone got inside and seated Henry continued, "Now the first thing I need to know is if any of you are here because you're debating whether or not to go out to meet your mentor?"

Two people, a young woman and an older man raised their hands.

"Tony and Felicia, I'm going put this as simply as I can. I'm kind of a simple guy so that's all I can do. You just heard The Chancellor's story and The Sovereign's story. What The Sovereign said is true and what The Chancellor said is a bunch of hooey."

Henry quickly explained how everyone has disobeyed Yehowshuwa's commands at one time or another. They seemed to understand their need to be forgiven. So he told them how to pledge their allegiance to The Sovereign and receive his pardon. They would know him personally, become part of his family, and have eternal live to be with Yehowshuwa forever.

"So what was said on the broadcast about being in slavery to The Sovereign is true. You're asking us to put ourselves in slavery to The Sovereign so that we can know him and be part of his family instead of what?" asked Felicia.

"Instead of burning forever," answered Henry.

Toney's eyes got big at that, "You're telling me if I don't trust The Sovereign to cover for all the wrong things I've done that I'll burn forever? The choice is being forever tortured or being The Sovereign's slave, but being his slave lets me live as part of his family as well?"

"Yup. That pretty much sums it up."

"The Chancellor said that this whole eternal fire thing was made up just to keep us in line and in submission to The Sovereign. You know, I think he's right. I'm outta here." Felicia abruptly turned on her heels and left.

"What do you say, Tony, you want take a hike too?"

"The way I look at it, I've got a choice to trust The Sovereign and be a child of Yehhovaw or to believe The Chancellor and run the risk of eternal torment if he's wrong. Well, I've always believed The Sovereign but never trusted him and nobody's ever quite made the connection to being punished forever so plain. I think I'll go with The Sovereign if he'll have me."

"Oh, make no mistake about it. He will take you. Let's ask him right now. Simply close your eyes and talk to him. He'll hear you. Tell him something like this. Yehowshuwa, I know that I've offended you and I need you to forgive me.

You died to take my punishment and I thank you for that. I trust you and want to live for you so you'll be my sovereign."

Tony repeated aloud what Henry said. Henry was about to say something when there erupted a loud clapping from the back of the hall. Everyone turned around to see The Sovereign standing there with a big grin on his face clapping his hands louder than anyone could imagine a person could clap. It filled the room like thunder as everyone watched his nail scared hands come together over and over. When he stopped he came forward and wrapped his arms around Tony, pulling him close. After a minute or so he stood back and held Tony with one hand on each shoulder.

"Tony, you are my son and you will be with me always. I love you and will never leave you. I'll be living in you just as I am in Henry and all the rest of the people here. Welcome to my family."

He then turned and addressed everyone in the hall, "At the end of ten days I will send for you and bring you to be with me in Yeruwshalayim as I said I would after The Chancellor's broadcast. So don't fear and continue to do your work until then. I'll see you when you arrive." The Sovereign then disappeared in a flash of light.

July 16, 999 ASR.

Robert and his mother arrived at their designated rendezvous in the country. His camp was in a heavily wooded area on the shore of a small lake. Those that prepared the area for the camp cleared an acre for tents and two other areas about a kilometer away where the new trainees could sharpen their skills. He found tents and provisions stashed for a hundred people for ten days just where his instructions had indicated.

As soon as he arrived Robert introduced himself to those who were waiting. He brought the supplies out of hiding and assigned people to erect a large canopy that would allow all of his disciples to gather together without being drenched by evening rains. Under the canopy they assembled a low platform in the shape of a pentagram. At each corner an oil lamp was mounted on a pole. Around the platform pillows were placed on the ground for all who were in attendance.

As others arrived he talked with them for a while and explained that they would begin training as soon as it got dark. All day people continued trickling into the camp. Some came alone and others in small groups or families as people made choices to meet their mentor. Twelve hours after the broadcast finished, Robert received news that about three quarters of Earth's population had relocated to the myriads of camps located outside the cities and suburban areas around world.

By the time the sun started to go down Robert's camp was completely set up and he was ready to start training his new recruits.

In the darkness Robert waited until everyone was seated and then walked down an aisle, up onto the pentagram shaped platform, and addressed the audience, "Welcome to your training. We'll start in just a minute but first, we need to light the lamps." Robert raised his hands over his head and clapped them together. As he did five tongues of fire emanated from them, shot toward the lamps and started them burning. A dim warm glow filled the area under the canopy, giving just enough light to illuminate Robert in his robe.

"First we are going to contact our enlightened leader. He will be working through me during the initial phase of the contact, then you will be placed in contact with a personal assistant. When you finish tomorrow morning you will be able to contact your spiritual guide at any time," announced Robert as Zophia had done before him.

Robert told everyone to put their hoods over their heads and went through the same introduction Zophia used, including the chant calling on the five founding members of the Council of Enlightened Beings. Within a few minutes everyone was deep in a trance. They were later introduced to their personal guides. Robert watched their minds as they all invited their mentors to come in to them and lead them in their training.

Robert's work was done but he remained with the group as they went through the night learning the basics of occult powers. After a few hours rest, they assembled outside of the camp to start practicing what they had learned the previous evening.

After the first day of training, extracurricular activities followed the same licentious pattern as Robert had enjoyed at his camp. By the end of the second day of training the whole camp decided that they would imitate the Edenians and become nudists, except when their training required them to wear their ceremonial robes.

July 25, 999 ASR

On the final day of training the group broke into two to learn how to aggressively use their new abilities against each other. The surrounding environment didn't afford the huge boulders that were available at the larger camps so they improvised by uprooting trees. Falling debris, deflected fireballs, and errant lightning bolts devastated the area between two companies. A small hill was leveled before the conflict came to an end.

At the conclusion Robert summoned them back to the pavilion, "It is my pleasure to tell you that we are now ready to join with our brothers and sisters around the world to completely and finally remove The Sovereign and his father from power."

The camp yelled and screamed their approval and began to chant, "Down with The Sovereign, down with The Sovereign."

After a few minutes Robert raised his hands to silence them and continued, "By this time tomorrow everyone will have finished their training and we will join with them." Again the camp erupted into applause and Robert had to silence them. "But right now we are going to celebrate. We have over two hundred liters of wine and while you were trying to kill each other I secured for us four of the biggest pigs you've ever seen. In open defiance to The Sovereign we are going to sacrifice these swine, drink their blood, and roast their meat with our own powers. We will be doing this in honor of The Chancellor and invite him to free himself and lead us to victory." Robert yelled at the top of his lungs, "Let the party begin."

As they rose up in revelry and drunkenness they used their skills to dig deep into the ground until they found enough rocks to fuse together and form into a glassy statue of an angelic being. Before the image cooled it glowed with the super heat that they used to form it.

This is Ben-Shaachar, the one who is leading us in victory. Let us bow down before him and worship him, for he and his companions are worthy of our adoration. He has sacrificed thousands of years which he could have devoted entirely to his own advancement to come and free us, explained a voice in Robert's mind. Show him your gratitude by indulging in your freedom now.

The orgy continued and intensified. It continued for several hours until the participants fell asleep from exhaustion or passed out from the wine.

Chapter 50

The Sovereign summoned his High Council as soon as the combative training finished at the first camp.

"Brothers and sisters, friends, the time has come. The Chancellor will be released in a few minutes. Bring my people to me. Some of you have easier assignments than others."

"As you wish," they answered as they bowed before him then left in flashes.

The Sovereign watched as each of the High Council members immediately relayed the message to their subordinates and they in turn passed the command on. Within a few seconds the High Council members and everyone underneath them, including Enforcers, Encouragers, Board representatives, and Messengers were dispatched throughout the world. He followed each one of them, knowing the thoughts and dispositions of those who remained loyal.

Justin was at his hardware store wondering why he even came in to work. No one had been in for three days and he was starting to get depressed. He missed Marilyn and Robert but every time he thought about them he asked The Sovereign to bring them back. It was the only way he knew to keep the sorrow from being overpowering. He was strengthened but he also knew that he would probably never see either of them again.

Suddenly he was startled out of his musing by a voice, "Justin, why are you looking so down in the dumps? It's time to go."

Justin looked up to see a large black man with a serious but friendly face standing before him. He was dressed in white jeans and a white open-collared shirt. "Who are you?"

"My name is Bartholomew Washington. I'm a member of the High Council and I came to pick you up for the trip of your life. You have remained faithful to The Sovereign and have remained at your post to the end. Now, he wants you and everyone else to come for a banquet that he's giving. Are you ready to go?"

Justin stood there for a few seconds with his mouth open in disbelief. "Why would someone as important as you come for me?"

Bartholomew rolled his eyes up slightly, "Now I know why he said some of us had easier assignments than others," he mumbled to himself. "Justin, I don't really have time to explain to you that we are all servants and we do The Sovereign's bidding and all that. At this point we've got a hurry-up job to do so every available person in the Administration has many assignments. You just happen to be mine. So shall we get on with it?"

"Uh, yeah, is there anything I should take with me?"

"Are you serious, man? Think about it for a minute. The Sovereign has invited you to his banquet and you think you can bring anything to add to that? He has provided everything, just as he has for your salvation. All you need to do is come along. Now let's get going because time is running out. Take my hand."

Bartholomew reached out his hand toward Justin who also extended his hand forward. As soon as their fingers touched they both disappeared from the store.

At the same time Henry was at the community hall comforting a couple whose daughter went to the training camps. As they were talking, Maria and two other people appeared in the room with them.

She interrupted, "Good morning, Henry. I hate to interrupt your work but it is time to go."

She turned to the couple and reassured them, "These two gentlemen, Johan and Chin, will escort you while I take Henry. I know that you are concerned for your daughter but The Sovereign has requested your presence now."

Henry responded, "Oh, it's so good to see you, Maria. I was hoping you'd be the one to come and get me. Let's go." Maria touched Henry's elbow and they both disappeared.

The other two people talked briefly with Johan and Chin, then they followed Maria and Henry.

Three people in gleaming white robes appeared at Zophia's abandoned training camp before Eric, Professor Robison, and Dr. Krebs, much to their relief. "I should have known you wouldn't dress in black suits," said Professor Robison as they were escorted away.

All around the globe the same scenario occurred within a few seconds of The Sovereign's command. It didn't matter whether people were alone, in groups or sleeping. Each was transported in an instant to Yeruwshalayim.

Meanwhile, Robert struggled to consciousness and watched through blurry eyes as small babies and young children suddenly vanished. He saw a few older children who hadn't participated in the training start talking to themselves. Most then disappeared but a few remained. Robert fell back asleep.

The Sovereign prepared Yeruwshalayim for everyone's arrival. The temple remained but the city in front of it was transformed into a huge open air banquet area. He set up rows upon rows of tables with chairs facing the temple. Each table was set with plates, utensils, and goblets of pure gold alongside the finest linen napkins sitting on intricately woven lace tablecloths. He filled each table with the finest foods anyone had ever seen, smelled, or tasted.

When people appeared, they were seated at prearranged places. Before each person were some of their favorite foods. Roast pheasant, steak and lobsters, fresh barbequed salmon, potato salad, baked beans, Caesar salad, Waldorf salad, yellow Jell-o with shredded carrots and walnuts, lasagna, peanut butter and jelly sandwiches, barbequed ribs, shrimp cocktail, spinach soufflé, escargot, and Peking duck were all available along with dishes from every nationality. When Josu arrived he was impressed that his favorite dishes were also included, but they looked and tasted better than anything he or his best chefs had ever prepared.

It took only fifteen minutes from the time that The Sovereign gave the order until the vast area in front of the temple was filled with billions of people. Samantha and Kevin were seated together near Josu and his wife. Henry, his wife Wanda, Maria, and the rest of his Board along with Justin and Bartholomew were at the table next to them. Tazi Ntari and his wife were at the same table with

Thelma Thornton and their escorts. As soon as the last person arrived The Sovereign came out of the temple and down the steps to the head table. Those that he chose to sit with him were already present.

The huge congregation stood to their feet as he approached and broke into applause that continued until he raised his hands to quiet them. "My brothers and sisters, I am so pleased to see you all here. I've been waiting for this day since the beginning of time. After we have finished this feast there will no longer be any death or mourning or crying or pain because I will make everything new. I am the beginning and the end and I am about to give you all living water so that you will never thirst again. You will all see my new kingdom with a new Earth. You will see my new city that I have prepared for you and you will inherit the city, the earth, and the whole universe. But for now we will dine together and have sweet fellowship until you see our enemies forever vanquished."

He paused and surveyed the crowd. He was thankful and joyful that so many were with him. Yet he yearned for more to be with him. It was bitter-sweet feeling.

"After the last of you arrived, I released The Chancellor and he is now about to assemble the greatest army ever amassed to come here and destroy us while we feast. Do not fear, because I am greater than him and you will see your deliverance. But enough of that, let's eat."

The Sovereign raised his hands to the sky.

"Father, thank you that you have always told the truth. Thank you that we can trust you in every situation. Thank you for these that you have given to me. Thank you for the provision of the wonderful feast prepared for us."

Following The Sovereign's prayer there was a resounding "Amen" that echoed from every mouth at every table. Then everyone sat down to enjoy the meal and the perfect weather. One of the tables started to sing a song of praise to The Sovereign. Each table picked up the tune and instruments suddenly appeared on the tables. Those who could play joined in as well. Each musician had his or her favorite instrument.

As the time passed the sun did not move and the temperature didn't change.

July 26, 999 ASR

The Chancellor felt stronger than he had ever felt before. Just ten day prior, he had said good-bye to Abathar. Abathar went to become the mentor of some sorry human being. The dungeon was now empty except for him.

As soon as the camps formed his image and worshiped it, he knew he would be able to break free. He experienced more and more elation as he could hear and feel the incantation of billions of people who summoned him to join them. He didn't need Abathar to relay any more messages or information as he felt The Sovereign's control over him weaken and finally disappear. He burst from his dungeon. *My power has never been stronger and I have more followers than ever before, even if they don't realize who they are serving. Surely The Sovereign will not be willing to destroy so many and as he hesitates I will vanquish him once and for all.*

Ben-Shaachar's presences in the heavens caused the night skies around the world suddenly to became as light as day. Where the sun was shining it appeared only as bright as the moon during the day. Ben-Shaachar roused everyone in every training camp from sleep. He could hear and sense all his worshipers as he linked their minds together with his.

With every mind connected together Ben-Shaachar tuned in to Robert as he stared up at what had been an evening sky to see the manifestation of the most beautiful person he had ever seen. The Chancellor's glowing figure was immeasurable as it filled the heavens around the earth. *I had no idea that he was so beautiful,* Robert said to Marilyn who came out from her tent and stood beside him.

He is indeed all he has claimed all these years. He is the most exalted ascended being. If he is this majestic and glorious, how awesome and great those of the Council of Enlightened Beings must be. Looking at him I can imagine how we will grow and become as great and even greater. What a thrill, she added as she and everyone knelt and bowed before The Chancellor.

Stand, my fellow warriors and see your deliverance. You have done well and as promised I am here to lead you to victory over the so-called Sovereign. We will now go to his capital and we will simultaneously hurl mountains upon him after we scorch his precious city with heat ten times hotter than the sun. He and his patsies are there partaking in their last meal. The scum doesn't even have the courage to let them know that their end is about to come. Ben-Shaachar showed them in their minds exactly how he was going to transport them to Yeruwshalayim and how they would join with him to do as he had said.

In an instant Robert found himself a few kilometers from Yeruwshalayim. He was surrounded by billions of other as they encircled the city and The Sovereign's temple. He glanced behind him and it looked as if the people with him numbered more than the sand on the seashore. He could see in the distance ahead of him a much smaller crowd seated at tables before the temple. They appeared insignificant compared to those with him. There was no hint that they even knew the city was surrounded. If any of them knew, they didn't let on. Then he saw them all stand, push back their chairs and kneel before The Sovereign. As Yehowshuwa raised his hands Ben-Shaachar gave the command to sear everything in sight.

Robert closed his eyes and concentrated harder than he had ever concentrated in his life, even harder than during the final contest when he was sure his life depended on it. He visualized an intense flame directly above the temple just as he was instructed. Mom was still by his side and he knew she was doing the same along with Zophia, every member of the star ship crew, Gustav, and Robert's old cell group. They were like- minded, along with all the rest who were standing around Yeruwshalayim. In the sky above them The Chancellor hovered, guiding their thoughts and adding every ounce of his power to theirs.

Robert saw in his mind a small black cloud slowly start to appear very high in the sky above the temple, far above the vision of The Chancellor who appeared to be at least ten kilometers in height. The cloud kept getting bigger and bigger as Robert continued to concentrate on bringing a flame of such magnitude upon the city that it would be vaporized in the blink of an eye. Soon the cloud filled the sky and blotted out the sun, leaving the only illumination coming from The Chancellor below the cloud and from The Sovereign still standing before the temple with his hands in the air.

"Stand and watch your deliverance," commanded The Sovereign.

Everyone in the banquet stood and turned to see the hoard that surrounded them. Beyond the city limits darkness hid the details of the enemy. Yehowshuwa's people were like actors on a stage illuminated by the light of The Sovereign while the enemy was like the audience veiled in murkiness and obscurity. In spite of the fact that they were clearly outnumbered there was no panic, only peace. As a single body they all dropped to their knees and pleaded with The Sovereign, "Open their eyes and let them see the truth. Let there still be time to save them."

The Sovereign responded to his people and time stood still.

Yehowshuwa watched as on his cue, Encouragers, Board advisors, Enforcers, and all levels of the Administration immediately left the banquet and stood among those in the enemy ranks.

"Robert, I have come to you as an ambassador from The Sovereign. He has a message for you," said Maria as she stood before Robert.

All around him motion had ceased. No one was breathing, twitching a muscle or blinking yet this beautiful woman was standing before him talking to him. She was radiant in the gloom from the dark sky overhead.

"How did you get here?" he asked.

"That is not important except that it proves that there is no hope for you to succeed. In a few short seconds it will be all over and The Chancellor will be defeated forever. Yehowshuwa wants to extend his grace to you and forgive your rebellion. All you need to do is admit you are wrong, ask his forgiveness, and surrender to him. He will then bring you into his family and you can join the banquet and feast with him and the rest of us."

Rorarum wrapped himself tightly around Robert's mind.

"All that you have done will be completely blotted out. It will be as if you have always been his beloved son. He loves you so much that he suffered and died so that even now you will be able to live with him forever. Just turn to him," she pleaded.

Rorarum threw his wings around Robert so that he could no longer see Maria.

"In the mighty name of Yehowshuwa I command you, Rorarum, to release Robert so that he can make his own decision," said Maria with authority in her voice that sounded as if The Sovereign himself had spoken.

Rorarum crumpled to the ground and lay there like a huge bat that had been flattened under a ten-story sea-going transport.

Robert's eyes cleared and he could again see the scene around him. The black cloud poised in the sky with The Chancellor below. Billions of stationary people were standing around him while he could see The Sovereign and his followers in the distance beckoning to him to come and join them. Maria asked once again, "Won't you come? The invitation is still open."

"No, I think not," said Robert. Immediately Rorarum resumed his grip on Robert's mind. Maria disappeared. Robert froze in time as well as all who surrounded him while Maria went to her next charge to offer reconciliation.

At the banquet cheers and applause erupted when the first Administrator returned with a repentant rebel. One after another appeared and were reunited with loved ones. The Administrators immediately left so that every soul would have an opportunity to know The Sovereign's love and forgiveness.

People prayed, cheered, and praised Yehowshuwa. Justin was on his knees when Marilyn appeared beside him. With a shout he leaped to his feet and wrapped his arms around her. They stood there holding each other and crying. They both kneeled down to join others in prayer.

Kevin stood before Zophia and disabled Mararum in the name of Yehowshuwa. Her jaw dropped as she saw her mentor, no longer a handsome, virile lover but a shadow of scum on the ground. She looked at The Sovereign with his hand raised, then at Kevin. "You were in our camp!" she exclaimed to Kevin.

"Yes. You can see that you have been deceived. You have only this moment to decide if all you really know about The Sovereign is right or believe what this helpless scum has told you." Kevin motioned to the still form of Mararum.

"In the midst of us calling down fire, The Sovereign is able to do this?" she stated, then fell to her knees. "Oh Lord Yehowshuwa, forgive me." She and Kevin disappeared and reappeared at a table before The Sovereign.

The Sovereign kept the sun shining without moving for what could have been hours or a second when the last administrator returned. Millions were added to the joyous celebration before him but billions remained outside.

The cloud then began to turn from black to a deep purple, then red as it slowly became brighter and brighter. Quickly the red turned to orange then yellow and finally a white so bright that Robert and the billions with him could see it even through their tightly closed eyes. They felt the intense heat as the cloud was now a pure flame hotter than the center of the sun. It dropped like a rock upon Yeruwshalayim. The heat became so intense that Robert thought for a moment that he was going to burn up. He and the rest of the people reacted just as they had in training and threw up their defensive shields to protect themselves from the dreadful heat that was descending.

The cloud turned into a huge ring of fire that came down around the capital. The temple, Yeruwshalayim, the mountain it was standing on, and all the land around it including everything that could be seen shimmered and disappeared. The sun and the moon along with all the stars in the sky streaked away in every direction and blinked out.

Epilogue

Eternity

Suddenly Robert was all alone and it was dark, oppressively so. He looked about but couldn't distinguish anything. It was also very silent and it reminded him of when he first met The Chancellor in his dungeon. He started to panic, thinking that they had failed and that he was now in the same dungeon with The Chancellor. He spoke out loud, "No. I will that this darkness be removed and that there will be light."

Slowly his perception changed so that it was no longer dark but he still could not see. He felt like he was floating in space as he felt no weight but could still feel his arms and legs as he moved them. Yet he couldn't see his hand in front of his face. "I will that this fog dissipate so that I can see."

The mist in front of Robert started to clear and he was able to faintly make out the form of a gigantic throne with what looked like a hundred marble steps leading up to it. The throne was pure white and a bright light was shining forth, cutting through the fog that surrounded Robert. He then felt solid ground underneath his feet but he still couldn't see them. He looked around but all he could see was fog and the throne directly ahead of him. His legs disappeared beneath him as they were lost in a swirling mist.

How strange this state that I'm in. Is this what it is to be finally free from The Sovereign? Is this the first stage of enlightenment? I wonder who's on this throne; perhaps it is The Chancellor or Rorarum.

Rorarum, is that you up there?

There was no answer.

Zophia, can you hear me?

There was no answer.

Ben-Shaachar, is that you?

Again there was no answer.

That's strange. I can't seem to contact anyone. Perhaps this is a test to see if I'm capable of achieving true enlightenment. I need to draw upon my training to find the power within me to reconnect with others.

"Robert, come up here," boomed the voice of the one sitting on the throne.

Robert cringed at the volume and the authority of the voice. "Who are you? Are you Ben-Shaachar?" asked Robert without trying telepathy.

"I am the beginning and the end, the alpha and the omega. I am who I am and there is none other like me. Come! Now!" The voice was so strong and issued with so much authority that it was impossible for Robert to resist. He started up the stairs, shielding his eyes from the intense light.

"What do you want from me?" he asked as he struggled up the last few steps. Each step was harder and harder for him to negotiate as the brightness of the being on the throne sapped his energy and he was now on his knees before him.

"Don't you recognize me?" he asked.

The brightness subsided and Robert looked up to see The Sovereign seated on the throne. His eyes were blazing fire and at the same time deeply saddened.

"But how can you be there?" Robert was shocked at the realization that he, The Chancellor, and billions of people had failed to destroy him. "I mean, how did you survive? We had so many people all aligned together with Ben-Shaachar to disintegrate you and all that were with you."

"Robert, you should know you can't destroy me. All things exist because of me. If I did not exist then there would be nothing. You would not be. Now, that is enough of your questions; it is time for you to give account of your life and to be judged to see if you are worthy to enter into eternal life with me or to spend eternity being punished for your transgressions."

Two huge sets of books appeared in the air before The Sovereign. "Let the books be opened!" commanded his mighty voice.

Yehowshuwa opened the first book. "Robert, this book contains everything that you ever said or did during your life. Every detail is here. You understand that in order to be deemed worthy of eternal life you must have lived a perfect life of spotlessness, for my father can not and will not tolerate any evil or the slightest impurity. As I read through the details of your life I will continue until I reach a point in your life where you have done something wrong. Are you ready to begin?"

Robert swallowed hard knowing that it wouldn't take him long to find a time when he had messed up. "Yes," he said.

The Sovereign started reading. "The book contains the time and date when you were conceived. I watched over you while you were being formed in your mother's womb and saw that you were growing just as I had designed you and planned for your birth before the world was even made. You were born on the day and at the time I prescribed. From there you grew to be a fine child, blessed with parents that I had chosen for you. They began to teach you to talk and to know right from wrong. You did many foolish things but didn't know any better. Your parents were consistent to keep you away from things that could harm you and they continued to teach you. Then when you were just a little over two years old, when you had just been told not to hit your cousin in the face, in defiance to your mother, you hit your cousin. You knew better but you did it anyway. I will stop at this offence and overlook earlier ones because of your ignorance. What do you have to say for yourself, Robert?"

Robert was flabbergasted, "How can you condemn me for something I did when I was only two years old? I don't even remember that."

"Oh, you think I'm being unfair because of your age? Well, then why don't you tell me what age you should be before you are held accountable for your behavior?"

Robert blurted out, "Fifteen."

"Fifteen it is." The Sovereign rustled through several pages in the book and stopped. "Here it is, your fifteenth birthday. Your mother prepared a special chocolate cake for you. She told you not to touch it because it was being saved for your party later in the evening. When she left the kitchen you sneaked in, cut a thin slice for yourself, carefully pushed the cake together, and covered the areas you messed up with leftover frosting. You disobeyed your mother and thought that you would never be caught and you weren't, at least not by your mother. Now what do you have to say for yourself? Surely you remember that occasion."

"OK, you got me there but just how big of a deal is taking a piece of cake that I was going to eat in a little while anyway? Surely this can't be worthy of eternal punishment," argued Robert. "Besides, haven't I done enough good things to make up for that?"

"Yes it is a big deal. One of my commandments, as you know, is to honor your father and your mother. In your disobedience to your mother you revealed the nature of your soul and that is to do evil. Rebellion is the same as divination and you certainly know about that, don't you? I could go on and on and list every single offense you have committed during your life time. But just to demonstrate how far you've gone wrong, let's say you did only three minor little things wrong each day of your life, like little fibs, or bad thoughts. Do you think that would be pretty good?"

"Well, yeah, that wouldn't be too bad."

"OK, so you just turned seventy and I'll only start counting at fifteen. Do the math, Robert. Three times 365 days in a year times 55 years adds up to 60,225 'little' baddies. We haven't even talked about the 'biggies' yet. Now how pure do you really think you are? Do you think you are pure enough to live forever in the presence of one hundred percent purity?"

"Now just a minute here. What gives you the right to judge me?" Robert thought that maybe a diversionary tactic would take the heat off him.

Suddenly, lightening flashed with great bolts flying past Robert which then turned and circled him. The following thunder boomed and rocked him, bowling him over and throwing him down to the bottom of the stairs.

The Sovereign's voice was the thunder and it made Robert cower at the foot of the stairs. "You know good and well that I am your creator and because of that you are accountable to me. I know you know this because I have put in every man a conscience so that no matter how much he tries to deny it, he knows that some things are truly right and others are wrong. Now get back up here and I will look in this other book to see if your name is written in it."

Robert felt he had no strength left but found just enough to comply with The Sovereign and crawled back up the stairs. The Sovereign waited for him to reach the top and stand before him again.

"Remember that the penalty for any wrongdoing, no matter how small or great, is death. You can't make up for any wrong by doing good because you could never be good enough to make up for even the smallest offense. The second book is what I call the book of life because it contains all the names of the people to whom I have given the right to live forever with me. These people understood that they deserved eternal death for the evil that they committed but that I paid the penalty that they deserved when I was wrongfully killed. Since I have never done anything wrong, my death pays the penalty for any who will come to me. But they did more than just understand, they came to me and admitted that they were wrong and that my ways were right. They thanked me and asked me to forgive them for offending me by their evil, no matter how small or great it was. They then asked me to take control of their lives and free them from their evil ways. When they did that I sent my spirit to live in them and changed them so that they no longer had the desire to do evil."

The Sovereign opened the second book.

"If your name is in this book you will live with me forever in paradise, but if it isn't then you will be punished according to your actions written in the first book."

He started thumbing through the pages. He sadly shook his head then stopped and looked down at Robert. "I'm sorry for you, Robert. Your name isn't here. Depart from me, you who are cursed, into the eternal fire prepared for Ben-Shaachar and his minions."

The throne vanished and Robert found himself still alone and in darkness in spite of the tremendous fire that surrounded him. Every fiber of his being screamed in pain and agony. His scream echoed into nothingness, a never-ending cry that would never be heard by any other being. All he wanted to do was to stop existing, yet he lived on.

The Sovereign called Joseph, Adolph, Jezebel, Benito, Mao, Judas, Madalyn, and Athaliah. They all woke up along with billions of other who had been dead, some for thousands of years. It didn't matter how they died or whether they were buried, cremated, or eaten by wild animals. They woke up after what seemed to them to have been only an instant after their death. They woke to the darkness surrounding them. It was terrible and hideous for them. If anyone could have heard them, their combined screams would have deafened anyone within a few kilometers. Soon their fear abated as the darkness started to dissolve and finally, they too, were standing before the great white throne totally amazed that they were alive – but still alone.

"Madalyn, come up here."

"No. I refuse. I know I'm dead and I shouldn't be able to hear or see or even be aware of anything. Since I can see you that means I was totally wrong and you do exist. But I still don't believe in you which means you have no power over me. So you can just go to hell." The words were no sooner out of her mouth than she found herself at the top of the stairs kneeling before The Sovereign.

"Wrong again, Madayln. Just because you choose not to believe in me doesn't change the facts that I am and that you are accountable to me. So now you, like everyone else, will be judged by the things you have done."

"You go right ahead and do what you want but don't expect me to cooperate."

The Sovereign opened the book of Madayln's life and quickly found that she, like the others, had early in her life done things to offend The Sovereign by breaking many of his basic commandments. He looked in the book of life and didn't find her name there. His voice was sad but still contained authority and conviction as he told her to depart and she also left his presence to be alone in the lake of fire for eternity.

Out of the mist they came up one by one as they were called. Some were defiant. Others tried to make last minute amends. They were told that they already made their choice while alive. After they died it was too late. Now, they were to face judgment. Some offered excuses blaming their parents, environment, lack of education, or even Yehhovaw himself. When The Sovereign confronted them and explained that each person was accountable for their own actions they couldn't refute the facts.

Some said that if Yehhovaw had made himself known to them personally they would have been OK. The Sovereign explained that Adam and Eve had known him but still rebelled. Some wanted to argue that if they had been left alone their conscience would have led them correctly but The Sovereign explained that after the first two people were banished from the garden people followed their conscience and it was one of the worst times of evil in history. Some said that if Yehhovaw had simply told them how to live they would have turned out OK. The Sovereign explained that even with his laws clearly known, his own people had rebelled repeatedly. He explained to others that even when his spirit was freely available, they rejected him. They couldn't say that they would have believed if the environment was perfect because it had been for a thousand years and billions still refused to believe. They were all told to depart forever from the presence of The Sovereign.

The Chancellor, Abathar, Mine, Rol-el, Tia-le, Ana, Berekiah, and the rest of The Chancellor's minions including the Council of Enlightened Beings were already in the lake of fire. This time there was no dungeon and there was no escape. Each was alone and never again would they communicate with one another or any of mankind. All that remained was the unending heat and despair.

In the place where Earth had been just a few seconds before, The Sovereign sat on the great throne now towering above Jim, Dave, Chuck, and all the others who had died loyal to him after the Last Battle. Unlike Robert and other rebels, they were in bright light and could see and talk with each other. Behind them stood everyone who had been with The Sovereign at the temple only moments before. As soon as they realized where they were, they bowed before the throne, then rose and cheered when The Sovereign Yehowshuwa stood and motioned for them to stand.

The Sovereign had all the time in eternity. He wasn't in a hurry. He started calling names.

There were two worlds being judged at the same time, those who could see only themselves and were alone and those who gathered together in the brightness of The Sovereign.

"Jim, come up here."

Jim scrambled up the stairs as fast as he could go and fell on his face before The Sovereign.

"Stand up, Jim. It is time for your judgment. You know about the books, the one with all you've done and the one that has the names of all to whom I've given eternal life. Hmm, this is interesting. As I look through the first book I see that there are a lot of places where portions have been blotted out. Do you know anything about this, Jim?"

"You know, Yehowshuwa," responded Jim.

"Yes I do. When you turned to me just a few months ago and asked me to forgive you, I applied the blood I shed on the cross to cover and blot out every one of these offenses. So based on what I read here, you have lived a perfect life."

"Oh Sovereign, you know that I haven't been perfect." Jim hung his head.

"If you say so, but all I choose to remember is shown in this book. So I'll just look in the second book and see if you name is written here." The Sovereign opened the second book and started thumbing through it. He stopped in the middle of a page and the light shining from his face became even more intense as he smiled and looked down at Jim. "Here is your name, just as when I recorded it. Come, Jim, you are blessed by my father so now take your inheritance, which is the kingdom that was prepared for you before the creation of the world."

The Sovereign stood and touched Jim on the shoulder as he bowed before him. Jim stood and Yehowshuwa embraced him. Jim walked back down the stairs to the cheers of the huge congregation. Yehowshuwa knew the cheers were not for Jim but for his own mercy and grace.

He then called the name of Dr. Ntari's mother, Haile. The crowd continued to cheer as the tall dark African bounded up the stairs and bowed before Yehowshuwa. In like manner one after another name was called of those who had been loyal to The Sovereign and had died after the Last Battle and before the end of his millennium reign.

"Henry, it is now time for you to come up," called out The Sovereign. Like the others, Henry eagerly climbed the stairs and bowed before The Sovereign. "Henry, you are like those whom I transformed before the time of Great Time of Trouble. You have never experienced death and you never will. But you and all who have lived to the end of this millennium will now be judged." The Sovereign opened the books and also welcomed him into his kingdom.

Some said it took months and others said it was only from one Sabbath to another while others thought it was only a few hours or a few minutes. But eventually all of mankind came and bowed before The Sovereign. He was merciful to those who were humble and loyal to him. He presented them all before his throne without fault and great joy. Nothing they had done wrong or failed to do was brought up before the rest of mankind. He also didn't let them see those who had rebelled being judged and thrown in the lake of fire since many were friends and family. Instead they were occupied rejoicing with each person that went up the stairs and received his or her inheritance.

Zophia was the last person called and given entrance into his eternal kingdom. The Sovereign pointed beyond the throng and proclaimed, "Now my father and I will live with you. You are my people; we will be with you forever. We will wipe away every tear. Death, crying, mourning, and pain will never be known again. I have made all things new! Behold!"

Yehowshuwa presented to them a new Earth and universe. Yehowshuwa carried them all to a high mountain to watch the new Yeruwshalayim coming down from among the sparkling stars of the heavens. The city was more than any could fathom. It was 2,200 hundred kilometer square and 2,200 kilometers high. When it finally descended and rested on the earth, its highest buildings were beyond the atmosphere of the previous Earth. The brilliance and radiant presence of

Yehhovaw and Yehowshuwa lit the city.

"This is your inheritance, the new Yeruwshalayim, the new Earth, and the whole new universe. Let us enter into everlasting joy together."

Other Books by Ray Ruppert

Inspiration
Reflections on First and Second Peter

Peter's teachings written to the early Church come alive and become relevant to Christian life in the present world. Mr. Ruppert doesn't shy away from tough theological issues such as election and assurance of salvation. He brings a biblical view of actual persecution and suffering while offering insight into the hope of the Christian faith. Salvation and living holy lives in this present age are frequent topics.

This is only a summary of the first chapter! Laced with Scripture, Mr. Ruppert relates many passages to the topics he explores by examining both First and Second Peter verse by verse. He writes primarily in the first person as he examines how the Bible applies to himself. His insights will be a blessing to anyone who desires a closer walk with the Lord. Study questions are provided in the appendix for those would like to use this book for a small group study.

Education
Battling Satan with the Armor of God

Our worst enemy is Satan and it is no joke that he is seeking to devour us (1 Peter 5:8). We need to know our enemy or we will always be on the defensive and we will suffer defeat. We can't live a victorious Christian life if we underestimate Satan's power and abilities. We are told to take our stand against the devil's schemes (Ephesians 6:11).

This booklet will help us understand Satan's abilities and the spiritual realm in which he operates. It looks at the cosmic battle that has been waging since the beginning of time, Satan's origins, his fall, powers of heavenly beings, and more.

Knowing these things will help us understand Satan's capabilities so that we can use the armor of God to overcome his schemes and live a victorious Christian life.

Novel
The Voice of Con

Con artists Darryl Smith and his girlfriend Renee Cleve have the perfect scam helping Vietnam era draftees escape military service by enabling them to fail their physical and get a 4-F status. Darryl is aided by a voice that speaks to him, providing guidance and the power to manipulate others.

Their newest "client" is very wealthy and provides the temptation to get more than their usual pay for their draft dodging services. Instead of being on easy street they find themselves in over their heads as they come up against the mob.

Books for Kids
Cows for Kids Cow Fun and Facts

Written by Malinda Mitchell, Photography by Ray Ruppert - Cows for Kids, Cow Fun and Facts, is a fun filled learning experience about cattle. It's chock-full of beautiful photos of various breeds, colors, sizes, and ages of cattle. It's fun because you can tell what the cows are thinking! They have quite a sense of humor. It's educational as facts are interspersed with the fun.

Dairy cows are featured with actual photos of cows lining up to get milked and the actual milking operation. It is udderly fascinating and educational!

Since calves are so cute, there is an abundance of pictures of calves ranging from newborn to several weeks old. You'll learn what it takes for a newborn calf to be healthy.

You will also get to see young people grooming and preparing their animals for show. These 4-H and FFA youngsters are learning what it takes to care for and even breed cattle. When show time comes you can see the results.

The last section of this book shows how Werkoven Dairy and Qualco Energy have teamed up to provide an environmentally friendly farm that uses the manure to benefit farmers, fishermen, and families. "This book is a great learning tool." — Qualco Energy Board of directors

For added enjoyment, a fun quiz is at the end of the book. Be careful, there may be some trick questions.

Malinda is an accomplished author of many children's books. She lives in Mississippi. Ray Ruppert lives in western Washington where most of these pictures were taken. This is the second book that Malinda Mitchell and Ray Ruppert have produced together.

Respect and Enjoy God's Creation

Written by Malinda Mitchell, Photography by Ray Ruppert - God's creation is all around us. Malinda Mitchell provides great tips for children to learn how to respect His creation. Whether on vacation, visiting a farm, zoo, or just in their own back yard, children will be able to appreciate and learn more about the way we have been blessed with God's creation.

Each page is accompanied by photographs which will inspire children and adults alike.

You will want to get this book and read it to your younger children or have your older ones read it to you. You can discuss how God has provided for us through His creation and how we should take good care of what He has provided.

Malinda Mitchell resides in Mississippi with her husband, Alton. She has four grown children, a seventeen-year-old son, and eight grandchildren. Malinda has been writing fiction for all ages for more than forty years. Malinda's favorite interests are spending time with family and friends, writing, and still-life oil painting. Malinda also had articles published in the 2008 summer and 2009 spring issues of Once Upon A Time Magazine before they closed their doors. She also writes for a card company.

Ray Ruppert is an amateur photographer, and author. He lives in Washington State with his wife, Terri, where many of the pictures in this book were taken. The cover photo is of the Skykomish valley as seen from Wallace Falls.

See www.rayruppert.com for more information.

Made in the USA
Monee, IL
11 August 2020